English Dramatic Interludes 1300–1580

Darryll Grantley has created a comprehensive guide to the interlude: the extant non-cycle drama in English from the late fourteenth century up to the period in which the London commercial theatre began. As precursors of seventeenth-century drama, not only do these interludes shed important light on the technical and literary development of Shakespearean theatre, but many are also works of considerable theatrical or cultural interest in themselves. This accessible reference guide provides an entry for each of the (approximately 100) interludes and fragments, typically containing an account of early editions or manuscripts; authorship and sources; modern editions; plot summary and dramatis personae; list of social issues present in the plays; verbal and dramaturgical features; songs and music; allusions and place names; stage directions and comments on staging; and modern productions, among other valuable and informative details. The book has an up-to-date bibliography for each play, along with a general bibliography, indexes of characters and songs, and appendices.

DARRYLL GRANTLEY is Director of Graduate Studies in the School of Drama, Film and Visual Arts and is a founder member of the Centre for Medieval and Tudor Studies, both at the University of Kent. He has published widely in Medieval and Renaissance drama; with Peter Roberts he co-edited *Christopher Marlowe and English Renaissance Culture* (1996/1999); and with Nina Taunton, *The Body in Late Medieval and Early Modern Culture* (2000). He is author of *Wit's Pilgrimage: Drama and the Social Impact of Education in Early Modern England* (2000).

English Dramatic Interludes
1300–1580

A Reference Guide

DARRYLL GRANTLEY

CAMBRIDGE
UNIVERSITY PRESS

PUBLISHED BY THE PRESS SYNDICATE OF THE UNIVERSITY OF CAMBRIDGE
The Pitt Building, Trumpington Street, Cambridge, United Kingdom

CAMBRIDGE UNIVERSITY PRESS
The Edinburgh Building, Cambridge, CB2 2RU, UK
40 West 20th Street, New York, NY 10011–4211, USA
477 Williamstown Road, Port Melbourne, VIC 3207, Australia
Ruiz de Alarcón 13, 28014 Madrid, Spain
Dock House, The Waterfront, Cape Town 8001, South Africa
http://www.cambridge.org

First published 2004

Printed in the United Kingdom at the University Press, Cambridge

Typeface Photina 10/12.5 pt.   *System* LaTeX 2$_\varepsilon$ [TB]

A catalogue record for this book is available from the British Library

Library of Congress Cataloguing in Publication data
Grantley, Darryll.
English dramatic interludes, 1300–1580: a reference guide / Darryll Grantley.
    p.   cm.
Includes bibliographical references and index.
ISBN 0 521 82078 2
1. Interludes English – Bibliography.   2. English Drama – To 1500 – Bibliography.
3. English Drama – Early modern and Elizabethan, 1500–1600 – Bibliography.   I. Title.
Z2014.D7 G73
[PR643.157]   C, 1
016.822'041 – dc21   2003053210

ISBN 0 521 82078 2 hardback

For my mother and father

Contents

List of plays and fragments

Acknowledgements

I gratefully acknowledge the help and advice of Dieter Aichele, Christopher Baugh, Alan Beck, Peter Brown, John Court, Janet Cowen, Clifford Davidson, Teresa Hankey, Sydney Higgins, John McKinnell, Kathleen McLuskie, Mary McNulty, Sonia Massai, Peter Meredith, Peter Moore, Marion O'Connor, Michael Preston, Yoshiki Suematsu, Meg Twycross and Greg Walker, though none of these is responsible for any errors. I have also benefited over a long period from the expertise of several colleagues in the Centre for Medieval and Tudor Studies at the University of Kent and from the input of my students on the centre's MA degree, who have helped me to define what was needed in a work of this nature. A project such as this inevitably makes call on the assistance and expertise of librarians, and my thanks are due to the staff of the Templeman Library, University of Kent, Senate House Library, University of London and the British Library. I have also had useful help from Kate Sexton and Neil Boness of Sydney University Library, Christopher Bloss and Teresa Gibson of South Dakota University Library, Fenghua Wang of Pennsylvania University Library, Georgianna Ziegler of the Folger Shakespeare Library and David Blacow of Lancaster University Television. The assiduous scrutiny of an early draft by the two anonymous readers for Cambridge University Press produced criticisms and suggestions that resulted in a greatly improved product and the eradication of several errors. I should also acknowledge my debt to Peter Houle's 1972 book, *The English Morality and Related Drama: A Bibliographical Survey*, from which I have borrowed the ideas for several features of this volume. Finally, I would like to make special mention of the late Paula Neuss, a strong guiding spirit in the early years of my engagement with early drama and the person who inspired my interest in the topic in the first place.

Abbreviations

Add.	Additional
a.l.	line numbering restarts each act
AV	Authorized Version of the Bible
bib.	biblical
chor.	chorus
CHD	Chadwyck-Healey Database (online editions of plays)
dir.	director
d.s.	dumbshow
E	English
ep.	Epilogue
e.s.	extra series
fo.	folio
frag.	fragment, fragmentary copy
Greg	Greg, *Bibliography of the English Printed Drama to the Restoration*
imp.	imperfect copy
JL	Joculatores Lancastrienses
L	Latin
l.l.	left-margin or left-side line numbering
MS	Manuscript
n.l.	no line numbering
n.p.	no publisher identified
NS	new (modernized) spelling edition
n.s.	new series
op. *sd*	opening stage direction
o.s.	original series
pl.	planet (Allusions sub-sections)
PLS	Poculi Ludique Societas
pr.	prologue
pref.	preface
q.a.	quotation adapted/altered (Allusions sub-sections)
q.n.t.	quotation not traced (Allusions sub-sections)
sc.	scene

sd	stage direction
s.l.	line numbering restarts each scene
SR	*Stationer's Register*
STC	Pollard and Redgrave, *Short Title Catalogue*
t. p.	title page
V	Vulgate
w. ref.	with refrain (Songs and music sub-sections)
w.n.s.	words not supplied (Songs and music sub-sections)
w.s.	words supplied (Songs and music sub-sections)

See the introduction under the 'Stage directions and significant actions' sub-section for further abbreviations used in noting stage directions.

LIBRARIES AND COLLECTIONS

BL	British Library
BN	Bibliothèque Nationale, Paris
Bodleian	Bodleian Library of Oxford University
Cambridge	Cambridge University Library
Chapin	Chapin Library of Williams College
Dartmouth	Dartmouth College Library
Dulwich	Dulwich College Library
Dyce	Dyce Collection at the Victoria and Albert Museum
Eliz. Club	Elizabethan Club of Yale University Library
Emmanuel	Emmanuel College Library
Eton	Eton College Library
Folger	Folger Shakespeare Library
Glasgow	University of Glasgow Library
Harvard	Harvard University Library
Illinois	Illinois University Library
Indiana	Indiana University Library
Lambeth	Lambeth Palace Library
Lichfield	Lichfield Cathedral Library
Newberry	Newberry Library, Chicago
NLS	National Library of Scotland
NYPL	New York Public Library
Pepys	Pepys Library of Magdalene College
Peterborough	Peterborough Cathedral Library
Pforzheimer	Pforzheimer Library
PML	Pierpont Morgan Library
Rosenbach	Rosenbach Museum and Library, Philadelphia
Rylands	John Rylands Library, Manchester
St John's	St John's College Library, Oxford
Trinity	Trinity College Library, Cambridge

Trinity (D)   Trinity College Library, Dublin
Westminster   Westminster School Library
Worcester   Worcester College Library
Yale   Yale University Library

EDAM   Early Drama, Art and Music (monograph series), Kalamazoo, MI,
                  Medieval Institute Publications
EEDS   Early English Drama Society (editions), London, Gibbings & Co.
EETS   Early English Text Society (editions), London, Oxford University
                  Press
HFR   Huntington Facsimile Reprints, New York, G. D. Smith
LSE   Leeds Studies in English
Materialien   W. Bang (gen. ed.) *Materialien zur Kunde des älteren englischen
                  Dramas*, Louvain, A. Uistspryst (1902–14)
MSR   Malone Society Reprints, Oxford
REED   Records of Early English Drama, Toronto, University of Toronto
                  Press (see individual volumes in bibliography below)
Revels I   A. C. Cawley (ed.) *The Revels History of Drama in English, Volume I:
                  Medieval Drama*, London, Methuen, 1975
Revels II   R. Southern, T. W. Craik and L. Potter (eds.) *The Revels History of
                  Drama in English*, volume II, : 1500–1576, London, Methuen, 1980
TFT   J. S. Farmer (gen. ed.) Tudor Facsimile Texts, London, T. C. & E. C.
                  Jack

AJP   *American Journal of Philology*
AM   *Annuale Medievale*
ANQ   *American Notes and Queries*
Archiv   *Archiv für das Studium der neueren Sprachen und Literaturen*
AULLA   *Journal of the Australian Universities Language and Literature
                  Association*
BFE   *Bulletin of the Faculty of Education* (Mie University, Japan)
BHS   *Bulletin of Hispanic Studies*
BSUF   *Ball State University Forum*
C&M   *Classica et Mediaevalia*
CD   *Comparative Drama*
CE   *Cahiers Elisabethains*
CL   *College Literature* (Westchester State College)
CR   *Chaucer Review*
DR   *Dalhousie Review*
EA   *Etudes Anglaises: Grande Bretagne, Etats Unis*
EaT   *Early Theatre*

E&S	Essays and Studies
EJ	English Journal
ELN	English Language Notes
ELR (Kyoto)	English Literature Review (Kyoto Women's University)
EngS	Englische Studien
EnterText	EnterText: An Interactive Interdisciplinary E-Journal (online journal)
ES	English Studies
ESC	English Studies in Canada
ET	Essays in Theatre
FCS	Fifteenth-Century Studies
Greyfriar	Greyfriar: Siena Studies in Literature
HLQ	Huntington Library Quarterly
HSNPL	Harvard Studies and Notes in Philology and Literature
JDSG	Jahrbuch der deutschen Shakespeare-Gesellschaft (Shakespeare Jahrbuch)
JEGP	Journal of English and Germanic Philology
JMEMS	Journal of Medieval and Early Modern Studies
L&C	Language and Culture
LNQ	Literature in North Queensland
MÆ	Medium Ævum
M&H	Mediaevalia et Humanistica
M&L	Music and Letters
METh	Medieval English Theatre
MFLAE	Memoirs of the Faculty of Liberal Arts and Education (Yamanashi University)
MLN	Modern Language Notes
MLQ	Modern Language Quarterly
MLR	Modern Language Review
MLS	Modern Language Studies
MP	Modern Philology
MQ	Mystics Quarterly
MRDE	Medieval and Renaissance Drama in England
MS	Mediaeval Studies
N&Q	Notes and Queries
NM	Neophilologische Mitteilungen
PBSA	Papers of the Bibliographical Society of America
PMLA	Proceedings of the Modern Languages Association
PQ	Philological Quarterly
QQ	Queens Quarterly
RAA	Recherches Anglaises et Américanes
RAEI	Revista Alicantina de Estudios Ingleses (Alicante University)
R&R	Renaissance and Reformation/Renaissance et Réforme
REEDN	Records of Early English Drama Newsletter
RES	Review of English Studies

RenD	*Renaissance Drama*
RenFor	*Renaissance Forum* (online journal)
RenQ	*Renaissance Quarterly*
RenP	*Renaissance Papers*
RLC	*Revue de la Littérature Comparée*
RLMC	*Rivista di Letterature Moderne e Comparte*
RLV	*Revue des Langues Vivantes*
RMS	*Renaissance and Modern Studies*
RORD	*Research Opportunities in Renaissance Drama*
SAJMRS	*Southern African Journal of Medieval and Renaissance Studies/Suider Afrikaanse Tydskrif vir Middeleeuse en Renaissance-Studies*
SB	*Studies in Bibliography*
SCJ	*Sixteenth Century Journal*
SCL	*Studies in Canadian Literature*
SCR	*South Central Review*
SEL	*Studies in English Literature 1500–1900*
SELL	*Studies in English Literature and Language* (Kyushu University)
ShakS	*Shakespeare Survey*
ShS	*Shakespeare Studies*
ShS(J)	*Shakespeare Studies, Shakespeare Society of Japan*
SLI	*Studies in the Literary Imagination*
SLJ	*Scottish Literary Journal*
SM	*Studia Mystica* (Texas A&M University)
SMC	*Studies in Medieval Culture*
SN	*Studia Neophilologica*
SP	*Studies in Philology*
SQ	*Shakespeare Quarterly*
SSL	*Studies in Scottish Literature*
STP:	*Studies in Theatre Practice*
TJ	*Theatre Journal*
TLS	*Times Literary Supplement*
TN	*Theatre Notebook*
TS	*Theatre Survey*
TSL	*Tennessee Studies in Literature*
TSLL	*Texas Studies in Language and Literature*
UDR	*University of Dayton Review*
USFLQ	*University of San Francisco Language Quarterly*
UTSE	*University of Texas Studies in English*
Viator	*Viator: Medieval and Renaissance Studies*
WSCRS	*Washington State College Research Studies*
YES	*Yearbook in English Studies*
ZAA	*Zeitschrift für Anglistik und Amerikanistik*
ZPD	*Zeitschrift für deutsche Philologie*

Introduction

The term 'dramatic interludes' in the title of this guide is used to encompass the whole range of non-cycle drama in English in the period covered by the book. It therefore includes not only the plays normally designated as interludes, but also such genres as saint plays, farces, early history plays and neoclassical drama. The description 'English' may equally be a little misleading, since it refers to the language in which the plays were written rather than to their geographical provenance. Thus a few Scottish and Irish plays in English are covered, while those emanating from England but written in Cornish, Latin or French have been omitted. A partial exception to this is *The Cambridge Prologue*, an Anglo-Norman fragment with a contemporary roughly parallel text in English, which has been included despite the fact that it may fall just outside the period remit of this guide.

The book covers the extant non-cycle drama in English up to 1580, the terminal date being around five or so years after the building of the first major permanent theatres in London, which signalled the emergence of a new commercial theatre culture. Liturgical drama, stray single plays that might be considered to have belonged to large urban cycles, and closet plays have been excluded (though a list of the last has been provided), but otherwise the whole diverse range of the non-cycle drama has been covered. This includes fragments, with the exception of some unnamed pieces dating from the fifteenth and sixteenth centuries that are too limited to exhibit anything of interest from a dramatic perspective. The late thirteenth-century fabliau *Dame Sirith* has not been included though the *Interludium de Clerico et Puella*, to which it bears some relation, has been because of its much clearer dramatic identity. Omitted too (and perhaps unjustifiably so) is John Lydgate's *Mumming at Hertford*, dating from the early fifteenth century. Though mummings do not normally involve performed dialogue, this one unusually does, but it does not stand alone, complete in itself as a dramatic piece, and is part of a larger programme of festivity.

Though much of the drama from this period has been lost, what remains gives a clear sense of the great diversity of forms of playwriting and production that existed. Such a range and variety of drama was partly the result of the different traditions, classical and native, that informed theatrical writing. It was also partly to do with the considerably varying contexts of production (though this is not evenly represented in the extant drama): itinerant companies playing to noble households or more socially diverse urban audiences; religious drama, sometimes with an institutional connection; school and university drama, sometimes offered for court entertainment; and folk plays incorporated into village festive culture.

The beginnings of English drama are to a large extent obscured by the paucity of material, the problem being that play texts did not enjoy the status of literary, chronicle or devotional writing and were thus relatively unprotected from the depredations of time. We might at least be grateful that some plays began to be printed in the early years of the sixteenth century, helping to ensure their survival. As a result of the loss of so much we can only arrive at a tentative picture of the range of drama produced in England before the mid to late sixteenth century. Some things are apparent, however. The two early fragments from the fourteenth century, the *Interlude of the Student and the Girl* (*Interludium de Clerico et Puella*) and *The Pride of Life*, indicate that secular and religious, allegorical and non-allegorical drama were present alongside one another at an early stage. The pieces surviving from the fifteenth century, whole texts and fragments, allow a somewhat more detailed picture to emerge. The religious drama shows a variety of forms and approaches in both dramaturgical and thematic terms. *The Castle of Perseverance* dating from early in the century demands elaborate place-and-scaffold staging, the mid-century play of *Mankind* enlists scatological comedy into the dramatization of a religious theme, and *Wisdom, Who is Christ* begins to reflect on social issues alongside its spiritual concerns. A non-allegorical religious drama with challenging staging requirements is the miracle play, *The Croxton Play of the Sacrament*. Secular drama from this period includes the Robin Hood plays and, late in the century, the earliest extant author-identified interludes in Henry Medwall's humanistic pieces *Nature* and *Fulgens and Lucres*.

The sixteenth century not only fills out the picture, but broadens it considerably. The elaborate place-and-scaffold Digby *Mary Magdalen* and the possibly processionally staged *Conversion of St Paul* date from the early years and are the only two full examples of surviving saint plays in English. *Everyman*, also from early in the century, is among the last allegorical plays to be entirely religiously didactic in orientation, as most interludes in the period with this basis begin to orientate themselves towards social or political problems or concerns. These range from the early *World and the Child*, *Hick Scorner*, and *Youth* to the 'proverb' plays from the mid to late century, including *Enough is as Good as a Feast* and *Like Will to Like*, and the 'wit' plays that moralize the growing interest in education. Where the drama does continue to concern itself directly with religion, this is usually in the form of religious polemic, mostly Protestant in orientation, and exemplified strikingly by John Bale's plays. There are also, however, some non-allegorical interludes based on scriptural narrative, such as *Jacob and Esau*, *Godly Queen Hester* and *Virtuous and Godly Susanna*. From early in the century there is a strong representation of secular drama, both comic and tragic. The comic ranges from farcical pieces, like John Heywood's plays or *Gammer Gurton's Needle*, to serious dramas that avoided tragic action, such as John Phillip's *Patient and Meek Grissell*. Tragic drama included plays like *Cambises* that incorporated native elements such as the

Vice, to works structured more uniformly on classical dramatic formulae, like *Gismond of Salerne*.

The non-cycle drama in the period has a variety of auspices, which are likely to have had some determining influence on the nature of that drama. These include religious institutions, such as monasteries and confraternities dedicated to saints, the secular folk festivities of rural communities, the itinerant troupes serving the court and noble households and, secondarily, provincial urban communities, the educational institutions of various sorts – schools, universities and the Inns of Court, and finally particular individual promoters such as John Rastell and John Bale. The auspices of many if not most of the interlude plays are unknown, and so it is difficult to draw categorical conclusions about the relationship of the interludes to their contexts, though it is possible to make some general observations. Much of the early religious drama is associated with East Anglia, less for specifically religious reasons than the early prosperity of that region. With the decline of the dramatic production of religious institutions, the primary patronage of most non-cycle plays of the period up to the establishment of the London playhouses became predominantly the noble household, though this drama found wider audiences in provincial urban centres as well. There is less geographical specificity here, and the drama also develops a strongly social focus. It is probably true to say that the plays coming from these contexts are produced less with an eye to formal innovation – though this certainly occurs – than to the subject matter, which ranges over a variety of issues that concerned the elite. In the other major and increasingly important auspices of vernacular drama – the educational institutions: schools, the universities and the Inns of Court – one finds more evidence of interest in formal genres. The vernacular plays in these institutions emerged alongside traditions of classical drama and it is therefore unsurprising that classical forms are most strongly present in this drama. Adaptations of classical plays include *The Bugbears* and *Terence in English*, a version of Terence's *Andria*. Others are plays more loosely structured along the lines of classical drama, such as *Ralph Roister Doister* and *Gammer Gurton's Needle*. Particularly notable is the mid-sixteenth-century flowering of Inns of Court drama that produced a clutch of neoclassical plays in English, such as *Gorboduc, Jocasta, Supposes* and *Gismond of Salerne*.

Though classical forms find a place in the interlude drama, both within and without the academy right up to and beyond the coming into existence of the London playhouses, this drama also retains elements of native traditions. Many of the characters remain allegorical and most have discursive elements in their construction. The Vice may take a diverse range of forms, but remains prominently present as an animating force in many plays, and an element of *psychomachia* persists in the dramatic narratives surrounding several central protagonists. The moral orientation and didacticism of the drama, which have inspired the terms 'morality play' or 'moral play', came increasingly to centre around secular concerns, though continuing through the period to be nominally cast in theological terms. There is a strong political dimension to some of the drama, much of it embodying positions on religious conflict and doctrine, but many plays also reflect on issues such as marriage, social mobility, rank and social behaviour, economic competition and aspiration, the upbringing of youth and the transference of wealth across generations, servants, companions, judicial and other corruption, wealth and poverty, the management of money, trade, economic oppression and enclosures, and foreign immigration. The importation of narratives other than scriptural into the English drama, particularly from foreign or classical sources (seen as early as Medwall's *Fulgens and Lucres* at the end of the fifteenth century) becomes more commonplace, exemplified by plays such as *Jack Juggler*, *Apius and Virginia*, John Pickering's *Horestes* and George Whetstone's *Promos and Cassandra*. It was the remarkable range and variety of this drama, particularly in the sixteenth century, that helped make it the bedrock – technical and otherwise – for the sophistication of the early modern commercial theatre when it became established in London. However, it is far from this alone that makes it a rewarding area of study. The drama also derived its thematic diversity from the fact that it responded to the social and philosophical concerns of the society by which and for which it was produced.

Though many of the plays produced prior to the emergence of the London commercial theatre might appear to be simple and unsophisticated, the range of dramaturgical principles they embody also provides an insight into the depth of theatrical understanding and appreciation of which at least some of their audiences were capable. Though there would inevitably have been some element of discreteness in the types of plays presented to particular sorts of audiences, there was less capacity for self-selection of audiences than exists at present. Thus, the same or similar audiences could, for example, be faced with a raucous farce, a classical tragedy, a religious morality replete with abstract figures, or a secular play engaging a range of contemporary issues. Such audiences would necessary have been able to apprehend dramatic characters in different modes and on different levels, as conceptual figures and as psychological entities, or perhaps simultaneously in both capacities as combinations of the two modes. The development from dramatic character as abstraction to a more historical or psychological concept of representation was never a simple one, and the degree to which one mode impinged upon the other is an enduring feature of interest in early modern drama and beyond.

What is also striking in the fairly limited body of extant dramatic literature is the degree of formal and technical change and innovation occurring over a relatively brief stretch of time. However, what also becomes apparent when these plays are considered together is that in certain respects technical development was not simply a progression from early simplicity to later sophistication. Earlier drama possessed of the sort of resources that institutions – religious or educational – could provide, often yields evidence of considerable technical complexity in its staging, whereas plays of a much later date are largely devoid of dependence on either complex stage arrangements or sophisticated technology. The advanced stage technology evident in certain early religious dramas is later found in the court masque, inflected with developments imported from abroad, whereas the simple staging arrangements of Shakespeare's theatre seem clearly a legacy of the limitations placed upon itinerant companies in the sixteenth century.

Since the interest of early non-cycle English plays resides in the ways in which they engage historical and social developments of the period, and also in the range of representational modes they exemplify, the approach in this reference guide has been to try to incorporate these and other aspects in providing essential information about each in as economical a way as possible. Whether from a dramaturgical, technical, historical, textual or thematic perspective, it is intended to facilitate access to the drama, allowing quick reference to the main features and substance of the plays. The entries have been kept brief enough to allow a ready overview, but an attempt has been made to give a reasonably comprehensive introduction to the plays, and to give as full a bibliography for each as possible. The decision to include fragmentary interludes has been made on the basis that there is frequently enough evidence of their formal and thematic features to make them useful in any broad consideration of the drama.

What follows is an explanation of the various subsections of this guide, both within the play entries section and within the end matter.

Plays and fragments

The Plays section is compiled alphabetically by title, using the first significant words of the titles in English. Where titles include the words 'Play of', these words are bracketed and do not determine alphabetical order. A separate entry has been made for the Cupar Banns to the *Satire of the Three Estates* as this is, in terms of narrative substance, an entirely separate play. By contrast, *Promos and Cassandra*, a two-part play, has one entry split into two parts, since these share a continuous narrative.

Dates, authorship and auspices

Under this subheading the dates for each play are given, approximate where no precise dating is possible, the Stationer's Register dates (*SR*) where available, authorship where known, auspices where known and the entry number in Greg's *Bibliography of the English Printed Drama to the Restoration* (see bibliography) for those plays with early printings.

Texts and editions

Early printings or manuscripts are listed for each item, together with current locations and *Short Title Catalogue* numbers (see Pollard and Redgrave in bibliography). Modern editions are comprehensively listed for each play (including nineteenth-century editions after *circa* 1840, with a selected few prior to this date as well). Only published editions are included, not unpublished theses. It will become clear from the listings that several of the plays have yet to receive full editorial treatment, while some others (most notably *Everyman* and *Mankind*) have enjoyed considerable editorial and critical attention. The fact that plays are often buried in anthologies can make them difficult to track down, especially in the case of the more obscure ones, and so all modern collections containing this drama have been listed. So too have the Dodsley collections, as they are generally to be found in university libraries and may afford the readiest access to certain of the plays. John Farmer's collections and the Malone Society volumes also provide access to some plays that may prove otherwise difficult to come by. However, Dodsley, Farmer and many of the Malone Society's editions lack lineation and have only the most basic of editorial apparatus. Editions that make substantial cuts to plays, or present only extracts, have been excluded, as have adaptations.

Editions are listed with the most recent first, though this does not imply an order of preference in terms of quality of the edition. The editions I have used to extract data, and to which line references pertain, are marked with an asterisk. Where there are other editions with the same lineation, these are asterisked as well. As editions rarely differ markedly in line numbering, it should be relatively easy to locate allusions and other features from the line references given, even when this guide is used alongside non-asterisked editions. The selection of editions for reference here also does not necessarily designate any preference in terms of quality, since what has governed the choice has been both the probable availability in libraries and the forms of line numbering used. I have used lineated editions, where available, since these make it easier to locate stage directions, allusions and other features in the texts, and for the sake of simplicity editions with continuous lineation have been preferred over those that start numbering afresh in sections of the play. In some cases there are no editions with line numbering available, and in these cases page numbers are used to locate references, along with act and scene divisions where these are present. Editions that do not have line numbering are marked (n.l.) and in cases where the line numbering starts afresh each scene (s.l.) or each act (a.l.). Editions are marked to indicate whether they use original or modernized spelling.

Characters

The lists of dramatic characters follow the first occurrence of speeches (rather than first appearances) by characters in the plays, and are not necessarily as they are listed in the early versions or in modern editions. Where it has been considered useful, descriptive details that occur in the original character lists or in modern editions have been included. Throughout the word 'Vice', when referring to a category of dramatic character, is capitalized to distinguish it from the abstract concept. Mute figures or grouped figures are listed separately below the main lists.

Plot summaries

Though there has been an attempt to make these concise, they are designed not only to give an account of the narratives of plays, but also some idea of their shape as well. In these synopses, characters' names are italicized for the sake of clarity (since many of them are abstract). Occasionally, the names of characters that do not actually appear are also italicized, when it is clear that they are implicitly part of the story.

Brief commentaries

The commentaries are necessarily brief but attempt to give some idea of what is distinctive or interesting about the play being discussed, in terms of its conventions of representation, its place in the history of drama in the period, any important thematic or topical points of reference, or any elements of formal distinctiveness.

Below the commentaries on several of the plays and fragments are lists of those entries in the guide which deal with plays that have similar thematic or dramaturgical features. As this has been done fairly conservatively, exploration in entries not listed here could potentially yield further instances of correspondence between plays, albeit of a more limited extent.

Significant topics and narrative elements

The lists of topics in plays refer only to those subjects or narrative strands which are overtly present in the plays. In many cases there might be reason to argue for political or religious subtexts, and this has frequently been done in the critical literature, but these are not usually included here. The lists include topics and social referents that are present not only as part of the central themes or narratives, but also those that occur incidentally in the action of the plays. The lists are intended as a guide for readers seeking instances of specific narrative patterns or topics in the early drama.

Dramaturgical and rhetorical features

VERBAL AND GENERAL

The general dramaturgical features of each play or fragment are listed, such as changes of name on the part of characters (especially Vices), instances of dialect speech and specific rhetorical features. As these vary widely from play to play, no particular format is possible for their categorization, and they are listed broadly in the order in which they occur in the plays, except that the similar features are listed together and in the case where features recur in plays, they are listed only once. The dramaturgical notes are simply there as pointers to the potential of plays as objects of study, rather than as comprehensive descriptions of them.

COSTUME AND DRESS

Where there is designation of costume and dress and either indications for change of costume or clear indications in the texts that such changes occur, these are noted. However, where items of dress (for example, armour) are used as props in the action, they are listed as stage properties rather than as apparel.

STAGE DIRECTIONS AND SIGNIFICANT ACTIONS

All directions denoting actions are cited fully in the main list, as are those directions for speech, entry or exit where a particular manner is indicated, when characters are carrying objects, when they are performing some other activity at the same time (such as singing), or when speech is particularly juxtaposed with exit or entry. Modern editorial additions to stage directions are not included. In some editions it is not clear which directions are editorial or original and in these cases I have had to go back to the early printed texts. Directions which do not form part of the line numbering in the editions used are denoted *sd*, while those that do are marked as (*sd*). Some editions contain a mixture of these, certain directions being marginal in early printings. Actions cited without either of these are not directions but are inferred from the text, the relevant lines being noted. In the interests of economy of space, all directions that are simply for entry, exit, position or speech are separately listed (after 'simple entry', 'simple exit' and 'simple speech') with just the characters and locations, except in the case of plays with very few such directions where they are included in the main list. The naming of characters at the beginning of scenes is not usually taken as a direction for entry and is not normally included here. Where directions do not name the characters but just state, for instance 'exit' or 'exeunt', the characters' names are bracketed, except where they are designated by 'he' or 'she' directly after speaking, as in 'He goes out'. Also, for the sake of economy of space, names of characters are abbreviated (though only in stage directions and not elsewhere), and some other abbreviations are routinely used: att., attendant; k. or ki. (depending on whether a name or further element of the name is present), king; kn., knight; lac., lackey; ld., lord; ly., lady; ma., maid; mess., messenger; mus., musician; qu., queen; ret., retinue; ser., servant; sol., soldier. Plural forms are not abbreviated.

Where there is a mixture of English and Latin directions in a play, the language of each noted direction is signalled. Notes are included under 'Verbal and general' subsections pointing to whether directions are in English, Latin or both. However, these do not generally include the directions for exit, 'exit' and 'exeunt', which are conventional in plays whether other directions are in Latin or English.

The function of square brackets and round brackets in this section should be noted: square brackets signal a complementary interpolation where the text of the stage direction has gaps, while round brackets indicate an explanatory gloss, usually in the form of the name of a character who is clearly implied but not named in the direction.

SONGS AND MUSIC

All instances of songs, directions for music, or indications in the texts that songs or music are to be performed are recorded, including instruments where these are designated. Either titles or the first few words of songs (where present) are used to identify them. Where words of songs are provided in the text (or elsewhere), this is indicated.

SET AND STAGING

This includes all information yielded by the plays about the staging arrangements, such as space requirements, doubling arrangements, sets, machinery and pyrotechnics.

STAGE PROPERTIES

The listing of stage properties is based on directions for the use of these, or instances where it is clear from the texts that specific properties are used, though this does not preclude the possible use of further unrecorded properties for which there is no direction or indication. Play texts vary greatly in the information they provide about the use of such objects. Fixtures that are part of sets are not included, such as tombs, bowers or arbours. The listings include animals where there are either directions or clear indications in the texts for their use.

Place names and allusions

PLACE NAMES

All place names are recorded, even when these form part of noble or ecclesiastical titles. A few place names, which refer to ideas rather than real locations, are recorded under 'Allusions', the best example being 'Parnassus'. Where the places have not been identified, the citation is given in inverted commas. Names are given in modern form, with the form occurring in the text being given in brackets alongside where this differs significantly.

In several plays, references to places form part of formulaic rhetorical lists in which the alliterative potential of place names is often the only reason for their presence in the texts. The occurrence of these is indicated below the lists of place names, and the relevant entries marked with superscript numbers. These numbers are attached to the place names except where there are several citations, some of which may not form part of lists, and in these instances the numbers are attached to relevant line references.

ALLUSIONS

All references to classical, literary or scriptural texts are noted if they occur overtly in the texts. So too are references to mythological, biblical, hagiographical or historical figures when such figures are neither characters in the plays nor feature in the narratives of the plays.

References to Bible and other texts are only recorded when these are actual quotations, or where it is signalled in the text that the Scriptures or specific texts are being cited (as when the author is named). References in plays are generally to the Vulgate, and in most instances this is identical to the Authorized Version. In the case of the Psalms, however, there are differences, and modern editors vary in their practice, some recording reference as to the Vulgate and some as to the Authorized Version. I have included both, particularly since the numbering differences between the Vulgate and Authorized Versions are not consistent across the whole run of psalms. Page or section references to works alluded to are given in italics to distinguish them from line references in the plays, and books of the Bible are italicized in the same way as titles of literary works, to distinguish them from eponymous biblical figures who may also be recorded.

Where a narrative alluded to is populated by more than one figure (for example, Diana and Actaeon) both may be cited together, but one or other might also have another entry if they appear separately. In cases where two figures are cited together, the reference is placed alphabetically according to the name of the first. Where a writer is cited with a work, or a work is quoted from, and elsewhere the name of the same writer is cited without direct reference to his works, separate entries are made. References to God, Christ and the Virgin Mary are generally omitted because of their frequency, as are references to classical names for the sun and moon, such as Phoebus or Luna, where the usage is merely formulaic. Similarly, personified ideas with a semi-mythic status, such as Fortune or Mors, are excluded. Names of saints or divinities are not recorded when they are simply part of oaths.

As in the case of place names, note indicators show where the allusions are part of lists, often alliterative, suggesting that they are likely to be present purely because of their sound. These are attached to the names except where there are several citations, some of which may not form part of lists. In these instances they are attached to relevant line references.

Modern productions

Evidence for early stage histories is usually very limited but, where possible, indications as to first and other early performances are given under 'Auspices'. Material on modern productions is also patchy for the reason that while some plays have been the focus of considerable attention, most have had little or no performance, a fact that has frequently to do with factors other than the intrinsic qualities of the plays themselves, dramaturgical or otherwise. Another problem has been the documentation of performances when they do occur. This drama is usually produced in academic or festival contexts, rather than in the commercial theatre, and notice of the productions rarely percolates through to the critical press. Only performances that have the benefit of written accounts have been included. This may give a distorted picture of the present-day early drama scene, but the idea has been to refer to sources of usable material on the performances of these plays. Most references are to the useful production reports in the journals, *Medieval English Theatre* and *Research Opportunities in Renaissance Drama*, though some accounts and reviews from other publications are also cited. The entries give the place of performance, the company name and the director in brackets (where available), the date of the production and the location of the performance report. Under a separate heading, recorded performances, videotape, film or sound are also noted, with dates, directors and publication details where available. No claim is made for the comprehensiveness of the information in this section.

Bibliographies within play entries

A bibliography of critical reading is provided for each play. While I have attempted to make these as comprehensive as possible, some selection has been necessary in the case of a few plays on which a great deal has been written. Unpublished theses are excluded. Limitations of space have necessitated a little selectiveness with critical items that are simply brief notes, but many have been included where it appeared justified. Much useful critical material is to be found in the introductions to several of the editions, especially the modern ones, but these are not usually included in the critical bibliographies. Only critical articles that contain substantial material on individual plays are listed, so that those which deal with a large range of plays are only exceptionally included in the individual entry bibliographies (but may in some cases be listed in the bibliography at the end of the volume). The bibliographies also include references to books that contain substantial critical sections on individual plays. Publication details of all book-length studies are given in full in the general bibliography, with a brief citation by author and date in the entries. *Festschrifts* are referenced as other collections, alphabetically by the editors' names where these are known, and otherwise publication details are cited in full in the entries.

Publication details for journal articles are to be found in the bibliographies within individual play entries, but in the case of those that relate to more than one play, they are only briefly referenced in the individual entries, with details cited in full in the bibliography at the end of the volume.

End matter: indexes and bibliography

INDEX OF SONGS

Songs are listed alphabetically by title, with the entry number of the play or fragment in which they occur.

INDEX OF CHARACTER NAMES

This lists all the characters, both speaking and mute, together with groups of characters, which appear in the plays and fragments, with entry numbers. The list does not include characters who are named but who do not appear.

BIOGRAPHICAL ENTRIES ON WRITERS

The section on writers contains brief biographies of known authors of interludes, together with select bibliographical lists. This material has largely been drawn from the *Dictionary of National Biography*, with some supplementation from other sources.

BIBLIOGRAPHY

Here publication details are provided of the editions listed for each play, and also the critical items cited in short form in the bibliographies of individual entries. These include not only book length studies but also articles which relate to two or more plays.

FURTHER READING

This final section includes a number of works not listed in the main bibliography, with sections on specific genres of early drama and their auspices, and on particular aspects of the drama: stages, staging, performers and performance, speech and language, music, art and iconography. Included here also are works on the records of early drama as well as bibliographies and catalogues.

Plays

I   Albion Knight (fragment)

DATE, AUTHORSHIP AND AUSPICES

1537–66 (*SR* 1565 *c*. Aug.); anonymous; auspices unknown; Greg 38

TEXT AND EDITIONS

Extant originals

1566? printing by Thomas Colwell: Huntington (fragment: six leaves); *STC* 275

Editions

1994   CHD (CD-Rom and online transcription of Colwell printing, l.l., OS)
1907   Greg (1907b) (OS)*
1906   Farmer (4) (n.l., NS)
1844   Collier (n.l., OS)

SOURCES

No sources have been identified.

CHARACTERS

Injury   Justice Albion   Division
The following are also mentioned but do not appear in the fragment of the play
that is extant:

Principality   Peace   Maintenance   Rest   Old Debate   Double Device   Dame Plenty

PLOT SUMMARY

The fragment begins (not the start of the play) with *Injury* (as *Manhood*) arguing that
one cannot judge a person by appearance, whereas *Justice* says that frivolous apparel betokens want of discretion. *Albion Knight*, representing England, intervenes

to reconcile them. *Injury* then argues that the law favours the monarchy rather than the subjects, and the temporal lords rather than the lords spiritual. *Albion* is alarmed by this and *Justice* agrees that if this is the case, it should be reformed. Once *Albion* and *Justice* have departed, however, *Injury* in a 'boasting' speech reveals his true identity as a Vice. He declares that his intention is not peace in the kingdom, but rather discord, and that he intends to enlist the help of his friend *Division*. He goes off in search of *Division*, who duly arrives with a vaunting speech and heavily armed. *Injury* tells him what has happened and *Division* vows to make sure that there will be no peace between monarch and commons, or between the lords spiritual and temporal. With the aid of the spies *Double Device* and *Old Debate* he will put the monarch and the people out of sympathy with one another over issues such as taxation, the defence of the realm, and the administration of the law. Similarly he will set the lords spiritual and temporal in conflict over their political power. To prevent a marriage between *Albion* and *Dame Plenty*, the daughter of *Peace*, the two plan to send false messages to *Albion* about conflicts between *Principality* (the monarchy) and *Justice*, afterwards encouraging *Albion* to a life of prodigality. The fragment ends at this point.

PLAY LENGTH

408 lines extant

COMMENTARY

This is a play with a strongly political focus, referring to the dissension between the 'new' or rising men who had become prominent in Henry VIII's administration, and the established aristocracy. It also voices concern over the relationship between crown and parliament.

Other political comment and 'state of the realm' plays: **14, 37, 38, 59, 71, 76.**

SIGNIFICANT TOPICS AND NARRATIVE ELEMENTS

apparel; the administration of the law; nobility by birth versus nobility conferred; corruption in the state; the monarchy; the estates of the realm; taxation; the defence of the kingdom

DRAMATURGICAL AND RHETORICAL FEATURES

Verbal and general the Vices adopt aliases: *Injury–Manhood* 127–9, *Division–Policy* 377; *Division*'s vaunting entry speech in a different metre 168–97; extant stage directions in English
Costume and dress *Injury* is dressed in 'light (undignified) apparel' 14

Actions and stage directions 64 (*sd*): 'And then he (*Alb.*) takes both their (*Just.*'s, *Man.*'s) hands together, saying'; 166–7 (*sd*): 'Here *Inj.* goes out, and then *Div*, comes in with a bill, a buckler and a dagger'
Songs and music *Division* 'Have in the ruske' 168–97 (probably sung)
Staging and set the action is unlocalized and there are no indications as to set
Stage properties *Division*'s bill, buckler and dagger 166–7 (*sd*)

PLACENAMES

Westminster Hall 139

ALLUSIONS

John 7:24, 24; *Matthew* 7:16, 36

BIBLIOGRAPHY

Dodds, M. 'The Date of *Albion Knight*', *Library*, 3rd series 4 (1913) pp. 157–70
Jones, G. A. 'The Political Significance of the Play of *Albion Knight*', *JEGP* 17:2 (1918) pp. 267–80

2   All for Money

DATE, AUTHORSHIP AND AUSPICES

1559–77 (*SR* 25 Nov. 1577); Thomas Lupton; auspices unknown; Greg 72

TEXT AND EDITIONS

Extant originals

1578 printing by Roger Ward and Richard Mundee: BL; Bodleian (no t.p.); *STC* 16949

Editions

1994 CHD (CD-Rom and online transcription of Ward and Mundee printing, l.l., OS)
1985 Concolato (NS)*
1969 Schell and Schuchter (NS)
1910 TFT (facsimile, n.l.)
1904 Vogel (OS)
1851 Halliwell (n.l., OS)

SOURCES

No specific sources have been identified, but Lupton may have drawn on contemporary pamphlets; see the introduction to Concolato's edition, pp. 19–22.

CHARACTERS

Prologue
Science
Art
Money
Adulation
Mischievous Help
Pleasure
Pressed for Pleasure
Sin the Vice
Swift to Sin
Damnation
Satan
Gluttony
Pride
Learning with Money
Learning without Money

Money without Learning
Neither Money nor Learning
All for Money
Gregory Graceless
Moneyless and Friendless
William with the two Wives
Nichol Never out of Law
Sir Laurence Livingless
Mother Croote
Judas
Dives
Godly Admonition
Virtue
Humility
Charity

PLOT SUMMARY

The *Prologue* discourses on the value and misuse of both learning and wealth. The play then commences with the successive entries of *Theology*, *Science* and *Art*, who talk of their value to humanity and their potential misuse in being employed in the gaining of money. When they leave, *Money* appears boasting of how men of all estates covet him. He suddenly becomes ill and, though attended by *Adulation* and *Mischievous Help*, who have both made an entry, vomits and brings forth *Pleasure*. When *Money* departs, *Pleasure* explains that *Money* is his father while he in turn is father to *Sin*. He then also becomes ill and vomits, upon which *Sin* appears. After welcoming *Sin*, *Pleasure* goes off with *Adulation* and *Sin* too begins to feel ill. Attended by *Pressed for Pleasure* and *Swift to Sin*, he sits down and soon vomits, bringing forth *Damnation*. *Pressed for Pleasure* and *Swift to Sin* take *Damnation* off and *Sin* expresses satisfaction in his ubiquitous presence and powers. *Satan* then comes in and hails *Sin*, who, however, rejects and quarrels with him. *Satan* roars and summons *Gluttony* and *Pride* to persuade *Sin* to a reconciliation. They do this and to the joy of *Satan* the Vices plan to bring humanity to hell with the help of *Money*. After more banter *Satan*, *Gluttony* and *Pride* depart, soon followed by *Sin*, who sets off to find *Money*. Now *Learning with Money* and *Learning without Money* enter, the first rejoicing in both his assets while the other expresses his contentment with learning alone and warns about the corrupting dangers of wealth. *Money without Learning* next appears, seeking the help of *Learning with Money* in some law cases. When *Learning without Money* praises the merits of pure learning, the other two are rather scornful of him. The three debate the relative value of money and learning at length, *Money with Learning* initially favouring wealth but latterly coming to prefer learning, while the other two remain fixed in their positions. A beggar, *Neither Money nor Learning* then appears and *Learning without Money* undertakes to prove him richer than *Money without Learning*. *Neither Money nor Learning* details both his piety and his poverty and begs for money, which he is given by *Money with Learning*, but *Money without Learning* makes his excuses and leaves. *Learning without Money* deems *Neither Money nor Learning* to be endowed with riches and wisdom through his piety, which will earn him eternal joy. *Learning with Money* then undertakes never to be governed by his wealth, and he invites *Learning without Money* to become part of his household. They go off together and *Money* re-enters, complaining of how busy he has been in the business of corrupting justice. *Sin* then appears, having been equally busy. When they enquire about each other, they discover that *Money* is the grandfather of *Sin*, who goes on to report that his father, *Pleasure*, has a widespread following in the world. *Sin* now introduces a friend of his, a magistrate called *All for Money*, who has been well served by *Money*. They pledge friendship and *Money* departs, after which *All for Money* tells *Sin* to make a proclamation setting up a court in which judgements can be bought. The first client is *Gregory Graceless*, a thief and murderer who gains an acquittal with the payment of half his booty. Next is a young woman who has killed her illegitimate child, and she is given the same verdict for £100. *Moneyless and Friendless* then appears, to beg protection from the threats of a rich neighbour, but being without means or influence he is dismissed as guilty. *William with the two Wives* is next, seeking permission to divorce his old wife whom he had married for her money, and to marry a young one. On payment of a bribe he is duly given it. He is followed by *Nichol Never out of the Law*, who is granted land unjustly in a dispute with a poor neighbour. Then appears *Sir Laurence Livingless*, an ignorant and sinful Catholic priest in search of a living who, after payment, is engaged as chaplain to *All for Money*. Finally an ugly but lustful old woman, *Mother Croote*, is allowed to hire two witnesses to testify to her betrothal to an unwilling young man. After the proceedings, *All for Money* departs and *Sin* cites him as an example of someone destined for *Damnation*. *Sin* himself then leaves and *Judas* comes in as a damned soul bewailing his deeds on earth, to be followed by *Dives*, who does the same. At length *Damnation* arrives to drive them back to Hell, and *Godly Admonition* enters, drawing attention to their example and exhorting his audience to virtue. In this he is supported by *Virtue, Humility* and *Charity*, who make successive appearances, and they end the play with a prayer for the Queen, Council and estates.

PLAYLENGTH

1,571 lines, including prologue of 98 lines

COMMENTARY

Though the play throughout deals with the issue of the corrupting potential of money, particularly in relation to knowledge and learning, the principal thematic strands of the genealogy of sin and the debate over money and learning do not cohere well. The playwright makes profligate use of characters, most of whom appear once and only briefly, rendering extensive doubling likely. The structure is very episodic, and the piece may be viewed as comprising four relatively discrete playlets, each with a specific concern or focus:

(1) the allegory of the genealogy of sin;
(2) the debate about money;
(3) a display of judicial corruption and
(4) the exhortations of *Admonition* and the Virtues.

Other social ills plays: **15, 24, 38, 40, 52, 53, 71, 72** (frag.), **76, 94, 96, 98, 100**.

SIGNIFICANT TOPICS AND NARRATIVE ELEMENTS

learning, the sciences and their uses; wealth and its uses; the moral danger of money; the oppression of the poor; judicial corruption; bribery; land litigation; the marriage of old women and young men; divorce

DRAMATURGICAL AND RHETORICAL FEATURES

Verbal and general the play is described on the title page as 'Plainly representing the manners of men and fashion in the world now-a-days'; a rhetorical passage of questions in the prologue 50–68; a courtroom scene (scene 4); *Sin* has to declaim the proclamation after *All for Money* and asks whether he should use his man's voice or boy's voice 4.100; the Vice's reading of a proclamation, with a simultaneous undermining of its meaning 4.102–7; rustic speech: *Mother Croote* 4.408 *sd* ff.; *All for Money* repeatedly corrects *Mother Croote*'s English 4.427 ff.; stage directions in English

Costume and dress *Theology* wears 'a long ancient garment, like a prophet' 1 op. *sd; Science* is 'clothed like a philosopher' 1.28 *sd; Money* has 'the one half of his gown yellow, and the other white, having the coin of silver and gold painted upon it' 2 op. *sd; Pleasure* has 'fine apparel' 2.98; *Damnation* has 'a terrible vizard on his face, and his garment shall be painted with flames of fire' 2.186 *sd; Satan* enters 'as deformedly dressed as may be' 2.243 *sd; Gluttony* and *Pride* are dressed 'in devil's apparel' 2.282 *sd; Learning with Money* is 'richly apparelled' 3 op. *sd; Learning without Money* is 'apparelled like a scholar' 3.12 *sd; Money without Learning* is 'apparelled like a rich churl, with bags of money by his sides'; *Neither Money nor Learning* is clothed 'like a beggar' 3.205 *sd; All for Money* is apparelled 'like a ruler, or magistrate' 4.77 *sd; Gregory Graceless* is dressed 'like a ruffian' 4.123 *sd; William with the two Wives* enters 'dressed like a country man' 4.229 sd; Nichol Never out of the Law comes in 'like a rich franklin' 4.275 sd; Sir Laurence Livingless enters dressed 'like a foolish priest' 4.322; Mother Croote is 'dressed, ill favoured like an old woman. She shall be muffled' 4.407 sd; Judas enters 'like a damned soul, in black, painted with flames of fire, and with a fearful vizard' 5 op. sd; Dives has the same dress as Judas 5.22 sd **Actions and stage directions** 1 op. sd: 'Theo. comes in a long ancient garment, like a prophet, and speaks as follows'; 1.28 sd: 'Here comes in Sci. clothed like a philosopher'; 1.54 sd: 'Art comes in with certain tools about him of divers occupation'; 2 op. sd: 'These three (Theo., Sci., Art) going out, Mon. comes in, having the one half of his gown yellow, and the other white, having the coin of silver and gold painted upon it, and there must be a chair for him to sit in, and under it or near the same there must be some hollow place for one to come up in'; 2.28 sd: 'Here Mon. sits down in a chair, and Adul. comes in and speaks'; 2.46 sd: 'Here Mon. feigns himself to be sick'; 2.54 sd: 'Mis. He. comes in'; 2.76 sd: 'Here Mon. shall make as though he would vomit: and with some fine conveyance, Plea. shall appear from beneath, and lie there apparelled'; 2.103 sd: 'Plea. feigns himself sick, and speaks, sitting in a chair'; 2.121 sd: 'Here comes in Pr. f. Plea.'; 2.127 sd: 'Here he (Plea.) shall make as though he would vomit, and Sin, being the Vice, shall be conveyed finely from beneath, as Plea. was before'; 2.186 sd: 'Here shall Dam. be finely conveyed as the other was before, who shall have a terrible vizard on his face and his garment shall be painted with flames of fire'; 2.210 sd: 'Here they three (Sw. to Sin, Pre. f. P., Dam.) go forth'; 2.243 sd: 'Here comes in Sat., the great devil, as deformedly dressed as may be'; 2.267 sd: 'Here Sat. shall roar and cry'; 2.276 sd: 'Here he (Sat.) roars and cries'; 2.282 sd: 'Here comes in Glut. and Pri. dressed in devil's apparel, and stay Sin, that is going forth'; 2.318: Sat. dances; 2.382 sd: 'Here all the devils depart'; 3 op. sd: 'Here Sin goes out and Lea. w. M. comes in richly apparelled'; 3.10 sd: 'Here comes Lea. w/out M. apparelled like as scholar'; 3.52 sd: 'Here comes in Mon. w/out L. apparelled like a rich churl, with bags of money by his sides, and speaks'; 3.205 sd: 'Here he (Mon. w/out L.) shall clap his hands on his bags. Here comes in Nei. M. n. L., clothed like a beggar and speaks'; 3.251 sd: 'Here he (Lea. w. M.) shall give him (Nei. M. n. L.) something'; 3.253 sd: 'Here he (Nei. M. n. L.) shall ask his alms of Mon. w/out L.'; 3.272 sd: 'Here Mon. w/out L. goes out'; 3.284 sd: 'Here he (Nei. L. n. M.) goes out'; 4 op. sd: 'Here he (Lea. w/out M.) goes forth and Mon. comes in puffing'; 4.22 sd: 'Here comes in Sin, the Vice'; 4.77 sd: 'Here comes in All. f. M. in haste, apparelled like a ruler or magistrate'; 4.93 sd: 'Here Mon. goes out and All. f. M., sitting in a chair, speaks'; 4.101 sd: 'Here the Vice shall turn the proclamation to some contrary sense at every time All. f. M. has read it, and here follows the proclamation'; 4.115 sd: 'Here shall one knock at the door'; 4.123 sd: 'Here comes in Gre. Gr. like a ruffian and speaks'; 4.136 sd: 'Here he (All. f. M.) shall deliver him (Gre. Gr.) a paper and Sin and he go forth'; 4.168 sd: 'Here M/less a. F/less knocks at the door'; 4.205 sd: 'Here he (M/less a. F/less) goes forth'; 4.229 sd: 'Here comes in Wm w. t. t. W. dressed like a countryman, and speaks'; 4.233 sd: 'Here he (Wm.) shall reach him (All. f. M.) a purse'; 4.267 sd:

'Here he (*Wm*) goes forth'; 4. 271 *sd*: '*Nic. n. o. of* t. L. knocks at the door'; 4.275 *sd*: 'Here comes in *Nic. n. o. of* t. L., like a rich franklin, with a long bag of books by his side'; 4.279 *sd*: 'Here he (*Nic.*) reaches him (*All. f. M.*) something in a bag'; 4.315 *sd*: 'Here he (*Nic.*) goes out'; 4.319 *sd*: 'Here another knocks'; 4:323 *sd*: 'Here comes in *S. Lau. L/ess* like a foolish priest and speaks'; 4.331 *sd*: 'Here he (*Lau.*) reaches him (*All. f. M.*) something'; 4.395 *sd*: 'Here the priest and the Vice go out'; 4.401 *sd*: '*Sin* comes in and speaks'; 4.403 *sd*: 'Here one other does knock'; 4.407 *sd*: 'Here comes in *M. Cro.* dressed evil-favoured like an old woman; she shall be muffled and have a staff in her hand and go stooping, and she speaks'; 4.421 *sd*: 'Here she (*Cro.*) gives him (*All. f. M.*) money'; 4.488 *sd*: 'Here *M. Cro.* goes forth'; 4.505 *sd*: 'Here *All. f. M.* goes out'; 4.532 *sd*: 'Here the Vice goes out'; 5 *op. sd*: '*Jud.* comes in like a damned soul in black painted with flames of fire, and with a fearful vizard and speaks as follows'; 5.22 *sd*: 'Here comes in *Div.* with such like apparel and vizard as *Jud.* has, who speaks as follows'; 5.57 *sd*: 'Here comes in *Dam.*'; 5.62 *sd*: 'Here he (*Dam.*) speaks to *Jud.*'; 5.66 *sd*: 'Here he (*Dam.*) speaks to *Jud.*'; 5.67 *sd*: 'Here he (*Dam.*) speaks to *Div.*'; 5.86 *sd*: 'Here *Dam.* drives them (*Jud., Div.*) out before him and they shall make a pitiful noise'; 6 *op. sd*: 'Here comes in *God. Ad.*'

Staging and set the action is unlocalized except for the court scene (4) and no directions for set other than a door that is knocked at (4.115 *sd*) and the stage trick of characters being introduced by being 'vomited' (2.76 *sd*, 2.127 *sd*, 2.186 *sd*), which requires the use of a chair with a concealed compartment 2 *op. sd*; the action being very episodic and only three of the characters appearing more than once, the play affords a considerable potential for doubling

Stage properties *Art*'s tools 1.54 *sd*; *Money without Learning*'s bags of money 3.51 *sd*; alms for *Neither Money nor Learning* 3.251 *sd*; a proclamation 4.101 *sd*; a paper acquitting *Gregory Graceless* 4.136 *sd*; *William with the Two Wives*'s purse 4.233; *Nichol*'s long bag of books 4.275 *sd*; *Nichol*'s bag of coins 4.279 *sd*; *Mother Croote*'s staff 4.407 *sd*; *Mother Croote*'s coins 4.421 *sd*

PLACENAMES

Banbury 4.32; Westminster Hall 3.205

ALLUSIONS

Abraham 5.38; Balaam pr. 67; Cato 3.153; Cicero *Ad Herennium* II.21.34 3.262, IV.17.24 3.181; Cicero *Cato Maior de Senectute* XIII.44 (q.a.) 3.154, XII.39 (q.a.), 3.158; Cicero *De Finibus* II.17.58 1.87–9, II.34.114 3.289–90; Cicero *De Officiis* II.20.71 (q.a.) 3.74; Cicero *Paradoxon I.6* 3.185–6, VI.iii.50 3.176, VI.iii.51, 3.193–4; Cicero *Tusculanes* III.14.30 (q.a.) 3.106–7; Cicero *Verrem* I.24 3.65, II.20.71 (q.a.) 3.74, III.67.155 pr. 95; Daniel 1.13; Diogenes pr. 71; Dives[1] pr. 48, 3.226; Epicurus pr. 36; Horace 3.224; Horace *Odes III.16.17* 3.191–2; Judas[1] pr. 68, 1.80, 1.100; Juvenal *Satirae XIV.139* 3.169–70; Lazarus 3.227, 5.27, 5.31, 5.45; St Matthew 4.370;

St Paul 4.378; St Peter 5.16; Pliny the Elder *Naturalis Historia XII.17.40* (q.a.) 3.164–5; Publilius Syrus I.7, 3.224; Sallust 3.161–2; Seneca *Epistolae 82* (q.a.) 1.42; Seneca *Oedipus 528* 3.9–10; Terence *Adelphoe 98–9* 1.51–3; Themistocles 3.70

1 Included in allusions despite being characters in the play as they only make a brief appearance in the final section.

BIBLIOGRAPHY

Bevington, 1962, pp. 165–9
Craik, T. W. 'Some Notes on Thomas Lupton's *All for Money*', *N&Q* 199 (1954) pp. 233–5
Mackenzie, 1914, pp. 195–201

3   Apius and Virginia

DATE, AUTHORSHIP AND AUSPICES

1559–67 (*SR* 1567 *c*. Oct.); by 'R.B.' (Richard Bower?); performed by (possibly Westminster) boys at court; Greg 65

TEXT AND EDITIONS

Extant originals

1575 printing by William How for Richard Jones: BL; Eliz. Club; Huntington (imp.); *STC* 1059

Editions

1994	CHD (CD-Rom and online transcription of How printing, l.l., OS)
1972	Happé (OS)*
1911	Greg and McKerrow (facsimile)
1908	Farmer (10) (n.l., NS)
1908	TFT (facsimile, n.l.)
1874–6	Dodsley, vol. IV (n.l., NS)

SOURCES

Narrative sources are Chaucer's *Physician's Tale* and Livy's *History*, Book III.

CHARACTERS

Virginius	Mansipulus	Conscience	Comfort	Memory
Mater	Mansipula	Justice	Reward	
Virginia	Subservus	Claudius	Fame	
Haphazard	Apius	Rumour	Doctrina	

PLOT SUMMARY

The prologue starts with a passage in Latin and then moves into English, declaring the play's address to both virgins and married 'dames'. The play opens with a speech by *Virginius* extolling the virtues of his wife and chaste daughter, *Virginia*. Mother and daughter then enter and the idealized picture of the family is further elaborated, ending in a song in which each takes a part and all sing the refrain. The second scene opens with the Vice, *Haphazard*, introducing himself, after which he is joined by *Mansipulus* and *Mansipula*, a coarse couple who engage in a farcical quarrel and a physical fight. Another servant figure, *Subservus*, arrives and all four take part in a song. *Haphazard* ends the scene declaring his role in men's fortunes and emphasizing the uncertainty of life. The next scene introduces *Apius*, the corrupt judge/ruler, who expresses his desire for *Virginia*. *Haphazard* offers to help him to procure her, advising him to accuse *Virginius* of her abduction and to claim that she is not his daughter. *Apius* is tormented by *Conscience* and *Justice* but *Haphazard* takes charge of him and guides him out, leaving *Conscience* and *Justice* to lament. *Apius* next sends his messenger, *Claudius*, to summon *Virginius*. Outside *Virginius*'s house, *Haphazard* meets *Subservus*, *Mansipulus* and *Mansipula* who enter with a song, and they recount some of their mischief to him. The following scene has *Virginius* in *Apius*'s court where he is ordered to deliver up his daughter. When all leave, the figure of *Rumour* enters to call up the spirit of revenge. On learning of her fate, *Virginia* asks her father to strike off her head, which he does and later, prompted by *Comfort*, offers the head to *Apius*. *Apius* summons *Justice* and *Reward* to punish *Virginius*, but they turn on the judge instead and condemn him to prison for his deeds, while *Claudius* is sentenced to be hanged. *Apius* later commits suicide. *Virginius* pleads for *Claudius*'s life as he acted under duress, and his sentence is commuted to banishment, while *Haphazard* is taken off to be hanged. *Fame*, *Memory* and *Doctrina* then enter to honour *Virginia*'s name by inscribing her tombstone after, which the play ends with a song and an epilogue.

PLAY LENGTH

1,032 lines, including prologue and epilogue

COMMENTARY

This is a one of a small number of extant interludes about exemplary sexual virtue and one of relatively few in which women feature to any great extent. In the play women are seen entirely in terms of their roles within the family structure, something that is evident from their names. The mother is only given the name *Mater*, while *Virginia*'s name signifies not only her chastity but also refers to her (male) parentage. The status and functioning of the allegorical figures in the play is of some interest. *Apius*'s crisis of conscience is signalled by his ceremonial entry with the two allegorical figures, *Conscience* and *Justice*, whom *Haphazard*, however, dismisses as 'but thoughts'. Later *Conscience* apparently speaks off stage, thus suggesting the presentation of the quality as disembodied.

Other female virtue plays: **6, 34, 63, 70, 87, 97**.

Other plays featuring prominent women characters: **6, 30, 32, 43, 46, 51, 63, 70, 75, 87, 95, 97**.

SIGNIFICANT TOPICS AND NARRATIVE ELEMENTS

family life; chastity and virginity; lechery; judicial corruption and abuse of power; conscience; imprisonment and execution; the fickleness of fortune; retribution

DRAMATURGICAL AND RHETORICAL FEATURES

Verbal and general a (garbled) Latin passage commencing the prologue (subsequently translated) 1–10; *Virginia's* rhetorical eulogy on her parents 127–38; *Haphazard's* alliterative list detailing the facets of his identity 180–204 (the Vice is given generally to alliterative speech in this play); *Virginius's* alliterative lament 764–70; an elementary subplot, partially comic, involving *Mansipulus*, *Mansipula* and *Subservus* 211 ff.; stage directions in English

Costume and dress *Haphazard's* 'long side gown' 180

Actions and stage directions 140 *sd*: '(*Virginius, Mat., Virginia*) Sing here. All sing this'; 148 *sd*, 154 *sd*, 164 *sd*, 171 *sd*: 'All (*Virginius, Mat., Virginia*) sing this'; 251 *sd*: 'Here let him (*Mansipulus*) fight (with *Mansipula*)'; 284 *sd*: 'Sing here all (*Hap., Subs., Mansipulus, Mansipula*)'; 318 *sd*: 'All (*Mansipulus, Mansipula, Subs.*) speak this'; 428 *sd*: 'Here let him (*Ap.*) make as though he went out and let *Cons.* and *Just.* come out of him, and let *Cons.* hold in his hand a lamp burning, and let *Just.* have a sword and hold it before *Ap.*'s breast'; 559 *sd*: 'Here let *Cons.* speak within (offstage)'; 589 *sd*: 'Here (*Mansipulus, Mansipula, Subs.*) enter in with a song'; 600 *sd*, 606 *sd*, 612 *sd*: 'All (*Mansipulus, Mansipula, Subs.*) sing this'; 723 *sd*: '*Ap.* And *Cla.* go forth, but *Hap.* speaks this'; 729 *sd*: 'Here let *Virginius* go about the scaffold'; 815 *sd*: '*Virginia* here kneels'; 830 *sd*: 'Here let him (*Virginius*) proffer a blow'; 834 *sd*: 'Here tie a handkerchief about her (*Virginia's*) eyes, and then strike off her head'; 911 *sd*: 'Here enter *Jus.* and *Rew.* and they both speak this'; 979 *sd*: '(*Hap.*) Press to go forth'; 1010 *sd*: '*Doct.* and *Mem.* and *Virginius* bring a tomb'; 1014 *sd*: 'Here let *Mem.* write on the tomb'; **Simple entry:** *Mat., Virginia* 60; *Hap.* 174; *Mansipulus, Mansipula* 210; *Subs.* 278; *Ap.* 344; *Hap.* 383; *Hap.* 478; *Ap., Cla.* 498; *Hap.* 581; *Virginius* 671; *Ap., Cla.* 699; *Rum.* 735; *Virginia* 770; *Com.* 839; *Ap.* 855; *Virginius* 882; *Virginius* 982; **Simple exit:** (*Subs., Mansipulus, Mansipula*) 319; (*Hap.*) 344; (*Hap.*) 457; (*Con., Jus.*) 478; *Cla., Hap.* 553; (*Cla.*) 556; (*Ap., Con.*) 581; (*Hap.*) 671; (*Com., Virginius*) 855; **Simple speech:** 'All' (*Mansipulus, Mansipula, Subs.*) 318; *Hap.* 614; 'All' (*Mansipulus, Mansipula, Subs.*) 666, 669

Songs and music (w.s. to all except final song, all w. ref.) 1. *Virginius, Virginia, Mater*: 'The trustiest treasure in earth we see' 141–74; 2. *Subservus, Mansipulus, Mansipula, Haphazard*: 'Hope so and hap so, in hazard of threatening' 285–318; 3. *Mansipulus, Mansipula, Haphazard*: 'When men will seem misdoubtfully' 590–614; 4. *Fame, Reward, Justice* (and others?): song around *Virginia*'s tomb (w.n.s.) 1020

Staging and set the localities in the play are only designated by presence of the principal characters, and a tombstone is carried on stage to mark *Virginia*'s grave (1010 *sd*); that some sort of stage was erected is indicated by the direction for *Virginius* to 'go about the scaffold' (729 *sd*); an execution by beheading is performed on stage (834 *sd*)

Stage properties *Conscience*'s lamp, 428 *sd*; *Justice*'s sword 428 *sd*; a handkerchief for *Virginia*'s execution 834 *sd*; *Virginius*'s bloody knife 836; *Virginia*'s false head 896; a tombstone 1010 *sd*

PLACENAMES

'Benol's Lease' 628; 'Bridgemeadow' 628; Calicut 862; Crete 157; 'Gaffer Miller's Stile' 623; Greece 354; Hackney 863; 'Hodge's Half Acre' 623; Jericho 671; Sandwich 442; Seville 941; 'Simkin's Side Ridge' 625

ALLUSIONS

Adrice (?) 692; Aeolus 737; Alexander the Great 145; Apelles 353; Atropos 838; Charon 906; Cupid 25; Diana 891, Diana and Actaeon 81–5; the Fates ('Parcae') 8; the Furies 499, 533, 905; Icarus and Dedalus 157–64; Inach 375–6; Iphis 373; Juno 396; Jupiter and Io 374–6; 'Laceface' (?) 693; Limbo Lake 499, 533, 905; Mars 690; Mercury 380; Minotaur 693; Minerva 5 *passim*; Morpheus 520; Nisos and Scylla 151–4; Orpheus 378; Parnassus 86; Phoebus 380; Pluto 535–6, 755; Pygmalion 357; Salmacis and Hermaphroditus 360–2; Scylla and Charybdis 691–2; Sisyphus 511; Tantalus 509; Tarquin and Lucretia 558, 563; Venus 26, 889

REPORT ON MODERN PRODUCTION

Queen's College, Cambridge, 4–5 June 1991 [*METh* 13 (1991) pp. 112–13]

RECORDED PRODUCTION

Videotape: JL, dir. M. Twycross (Lancaster University Television, 1991)

BIBLIOGRAPHY

Ekeblad, I.-S. 'Storm Imagery in *Apius and Virginia*', *N&Q* 3 (1956) pp. 5–7
Farnham, 1936, pp. 251–9

Greene, 1974, pp. 357–65
Happé, 1965, pp. 207–27
Happé, 1998, pp. 27–44
Mullini, R. 'How Dramatic is a Story: Narrative *vs* Dramatic Structures in *Apius and Virginia*' in Lascombes, 1995, pp. 79–93
Southern, R. 'Methods of Presentation in Pre-Shakespearean Theatre' in Hibbard, 1975, pp. 45–53
Southern, 1973, pp. 462–6
Woolf, 1973, pp. 90–3

4   The Ashmole Fragment

DATE, AUTHORSHIP AND AUSPICES

c. 1500, anonymous, auspices unknown

TEXT AND EDITIONS

Extant originals

Manuscript: Bodleian MS Ashmole 750, fo. 168r

Editions

1994   CHD (CD-Rom and online copy of Davis, 1970, n.l., OS)*
1979   Davis (n.l., facsimile)*
1970   Davis (OS)*
1954   Robbins (OS)*

CHARACTERS

Emperor (addressed, but no speech)
Secundus Miles
High Priest (addressed, but no speech)

PLOT SUMMARY

The extract is a speech of a soldier first reassuring his emperor that he will defend him, and then turning to address a High Priest and make an offering of a dagger to 'Mahound'.

PLAY LENGTH

12 lines extant

COMMENTARY

The speaking figure is one that is commonly found in the early scriptural drama, particularly cycle and saint plays, a boasting soldier carrying out the commands of his tyrant master and forming part of a chain of command to enforce pagan law.

SIGNIFICANT TOPICS AND NARRATIVE ELEMENTS

a violent 'boast'; a pagan offering; 'Mahound' (Mohammed/a pagan god)

BIBLIOGRAPHY

Robbins, R. H. (essay) 'A Dramatic Fragment from a Caesar Augustus Play', *Anglia* 72 (1954) pp. 31–4
Wright, S. K. 'Is the Ashmole Fragment a Remnant of a Middle English Saint Play?', *Neophilologus* 75:1 (1991) pp. 139–49

5   The Bugbears

DATE, AUTHORSHIP AND AUSPICES

1563–6; John Jefferes (?); possibly performed at Gray's Inn, or by boys

TEXT AND EDITIONS

Extant originals

Manuscript: British Library MS Lansdowne 807, fo. 57 seq.

Editions

1994   CHD (CD-Rom and online copy of Bond, 1911, l.l., s.l.)
1979   Clark (s.l., NS)*
1911   Bond (s.l., OS)*
1897   Grabau (s.l, OS)

SOURCES

Narrative sources include Antonfrancesco Grazzini, *La Spiritata* (1561), Terence, *Andria*, and *Gl'Ingannati* (anon., *c.* 1531). For the magical elements the author appears to have drawn on Johannes Weier's *De praestigiis daemonum* (Basel, 1563); see the introduction to Clark's edition, pp. 55–60.

CHARACTERS

Amedeus, father to Formosus	Manutius, lover of Iphigenia
Biondello, his servant	Carolino, his servant
Trappola, friend of Biondello	Iphigenia, daughter to Cantalupo
Cantalupo, father to Iphigenia	Catella, her maid
Squartacantino, his servant	Brancatius, father to Rosimunda
Piccinino, servant to Camillus	Donatus, brother to Brancatius
Tomasine, nurse to Rosimunda	Phillida, maid to Rosimunda
Formosus, son to Amedeus	

Rosimunda and Camillus form part of the action, but do not appear. Singers (boys) for the final song.

PLOT SUMMARY

The play opens with *Amedeus* castigating *Biondello* for not getting up in the night to check on strange noises in the house, and *Biondello* undertakes to fetch an astronomer to investigate the phenomenon. In the next scene he gets his friend *Trappola* to pretend to be an astronomer, and relates to him the story of how *Amedeus*'s son *Formosus* has secretly married and made pregnant his lover, *Rosimunda*. Her father *Brancatius* is, however, unable to pay the large dowry demanded by *Amedeus* and so the match cannot be recognized. Furthermore, *Amedeus*'s elderly neighbour, *Cantalupo*, is intent on marrying *Rosimunda* and has not only offered his own daughter *Iphigenia* as a bride for *Formosus*, despite her being in love with another man, but also the desired dowry of three thousand crowns. *Formosus* cannot, however, reveal his secret marriage for fear of being dispossessed by his father. To solve the problem, *Biondello* proposes to steal the money for *Rosimunda*'s dowry from *Amedeus*, and pretend that the money has been put up by her uncle. The plot is to make *Amedeus* think that the money has been stolen by spirits, and to this end *Formosus* has led his father to believe that the house is haunted, supporting his contention by making strange noises in the house at night. *Trappola*'s role would be to help in this endeavour by feigned necromancy. The scene then switches to *Cantalupo*, who is being derided by his servant *Squartacantino* for attempting an amorous pursuit at his advanced age, but *Cantalupo* goes off to preen and prepare himself for his wooing. There is a lacuna in the text, after which *Formosus* appears with his friend *Camillus* preparing for the haunting and the theft. *Formosus* also asks *Thomasine* after his *Rosimunda*, who is feigning illness to conceal her pregnancy. *Camillus*'s servant *Piccinino* now brings in some devilish masks for the haunting. In the next scene *Manutius*, *Iphigenia*'s lover, hears the news that *Formosus* is to be betrothed to *Iphigenia* and when she comes in they mutually express their sorrows over their impending enforced parting. However, *Manutius* then encounters *Formosus* who makes it clear that he has no intention of taking *Iphigenia* from him. *Squartacantino* appears once more to describe with ridicule his master's passion and when he exits *Amadeus* comes in, soon joined by *Brancatius* and *Cantalupo*. The old men talk about *Rosimunda*'s illness and the haunting of *Amedeus*'s house, until *Biondello* comes along with *Trappolo*, whom he introduces as an astronomer able to banish the spirits. *Trappolo* talks at length about the various types of spirits and his intended exorcism of them, giving a demonstration of the ritual. He claims to be Nostradamus and he warns the old men not to come near the place until his work is done. In the following scene, *Iphigenia* discusses her hopes and fears with her maid, and sings a song. When *Biondello* meets *Thomasine* he relates the trick to her and, after *Amedeus* and his friends arrive, ventures into the house only to come running out talking of the horrible spirits he has seen there. The old men then go in warily to have a look, but themselves retreat in fear and go off. *Formosus* now appears and describes how they frightened the old men with fireworks and took money from *Amadeus*'s chest. *Squartacantino*, while pretending himself to doubt the news, reveals to *Cantalupo* that *Rosimunda* is pregnant, which his master then goes off anxiously to try and verify. *Trappolo* reports to *Amedeus* that the spirit problem arose because he was trying to take *Iphigenia* away from *Manutio*, that if they persisted in this action *Cantalupo*'s house would be similarly plagued, and that the spirits have taken from his chest a sum equal to that which he is being offered as *Iphigenia*'s dowry. *Trappolo* next approaches *Cantalupo* to persuade him of the undesirability of his pursuit of *Rosimunda*, and he goes off to undo the bargain with *Amedeus*. *Donatus* now arrives to play the bountiful uncle and, after *Biondello* has repeated more of the progress of the plot, offers to pay *Rosimunda*'s dowry. *Amedeus*, not realizing that it is his own money which is being used, is overjoyed and now gives his blessing to the match between her and his son. *Thomasine* reveals that *Rosimunda* has been cured of her malady, and *Manutius* comes in to say that he has been given *Iphigenia*'s hand in marriage. *Biondello* closes the play with some remarks to the audience, including an invitation to the wedding, and there is a final song.

PLAY LENGTH

1,800 lines extant

COMMENTARY

The play is one of a handful of early Italian comedies in English, but is unusual in being adapted from a number of sources rather than being a translation of a single play. The well-developed servant intrigue is an important Roman comedy element in the play, as is the absent (and pregnant) heroine, and the play is more complex in plot and structure than its principal source.

Other plays based on classical or Italian models: **7, 32, 37, 41, 43, 88, 91, 92**.

Other secular comedies: **30, 41, 46, 47, 75, 88, 91, 92, 95.**
Other plays with foreign (non-biblical, non-classical) settings: **6, 7, 12, 13, 32, 33, 47, 70, 74, 83, 88.**

SIGNIFICANT TOPICS AND NARRATIVE ELEMENTS

masters and servants; miserliness; superstition; ghosts and haunting; (feigned) necromancy; servant intrigue; a frustrated lovers plot; a superannuated lover; feigned illness; a concealed pregnancy; apothecaries and medicines; exorcism

NOTE: line numbering is by scene; references are therefore to act/scene/line

DRAMATURGICAL AND RHETORICAL FEATURES

Verbal and general Act 2, scene 2 and part of scene 3 is missing; *Trappola*'s exorcism rituals (with a circle) 3.3.78–126; *Trappola* takes the name Nostradamus 3.3.133; *Trappola*'s lists of spirits 3.3.55–73, 114–20; several cuts by a reviser are evident, especially to the fifth act; a five-act play with scene divisions; the play is set in Florence; characters in each scene are named at the head of the scene

Costume and dress *Cantalupo*'s clothing is 'stale of fashion' and he is 'lapped in fur' 1.3.41–3

Actions (no stage directions) 3.2.28–9, 32: *Amedeus* knocks on *Trappola*'s door; 3.3.118: *Trappola* draws a circle

Songs and music (w.s. to all, all w. ref.) 1. *Cantalupo* 'O love I die' 1.3.67–82; 2. *Piccino* 'A–spriting, a–spriting, a–spriting go we' 2.4.1–14; 3. *Squartacantino* 'I fear mine old master shall sing this new note' 3.1.1–18; 4. *Iphigenia* 'Lend me you lovers all your pleasant lovely lays' 3.4.45–63; 5. Singers 'Sith all our grief is turned to bliss' 5.9.76–82; **Instrumental:** music for the last two songs appears on fo. 76 of the manuscript

Staging and set the single setting is a street in Florence, before the houses of *Amedeus, Brancatius* and *Camillus*, possibly each with a door on to the playing area; a door is knocked at in 3.3 and one is possibly shut and locked in 4.2; locations are clearly indicated in the dialogue; there is little action on stage, much of it being narrated

Stage properties *Biondello*'s counterfeit key 1.1.75; *Cantalupo*'s coin 'crusado' 1.3.59; devil masks 2.4.17; *Trappola*'s paper 3.3.99

PLACENAMES

Arno 2.4.16; Cornwall 3.1.29; Italy 3.3.139; Orleans 3.3.24; Paris 3.3.25; Venice 4.1.17

ALLUSIONS

Acheron 3.3.103; Alecto¹ 3.3.70; Briareus¹ 3.3.70; Cerberus¹ 3.3.69; Charon 3.1.54; Cocytus 3.3.103; St Cornelius 1.3.12; Grandgosier 3.1.44; Hecate¹ 3.3.73; Hercules 1.1.3; *John 16:20* 3.2.1; Limbo lake 3.3.102; Megæra¹ 3.3.70; Giorgius Nepos (?) 3.3.135; Nostradamus 3.3.133; *Orlando Furioso* 5.2.66; St Paul 3.3.138; Phlegethon 3.3.103; Pluto¹ 3.3.69; Proserpine¹ 3.3.69; River Styx 3.3.103; Tisiphone¹ 3.3.70; Venus 1.3.10, 1.3. 86, 3.1.24, 47

1 Part of *Trappola*'s lists of spirits.

BIBLIOGRAPHY

Bond, 1911, pp. xiii–cxviii
Guinle, F. 'The Songs in a Sixteenth-Century Manuscript Play: *The Bugbears*, by John Jeffere', *CE* 21 (1982) pp. 13–26
Schücking, 1901, pp. 36–55

6   Calisto and Melebea (The Beauty and Good Properties of Women, as also their Vices and Evil Conditions)

DATE, AUTHORSHIP AND AUSPICES

1527–30; anonymous; possibly written for Rastell's stage; Greg 10

TEXT AND EDITIONS

Extant originals

c. 1525 printing by John Rastell: Bodleian; BL Bagford Collection (fragments: Harl. 5989/188, 192, 195, 197, 199, 201); *STC* 20721

Editions

1994   CHD (CD-Rom and online transcription of Rastell printing, l.l., OS)
1979   Axton (OS)*
1914 (?) Farmer (n.l., OS)
1909   TFT (facsimile, n.l.)
1908   Greg and Sidgwick (facsimile)
1908   Warner Allan (OS)
1905   Farmer (3) (n.l., NS)
1874–6 Dodsley, vol. 1 (n.l., NS)

SOURCE

This is based on a Spanish novel by Fernando de Rojas, *La Celestina*, or its later edition, *La tragicomedia de Calisto y Melibea*.

CHARACTERS

Melebea	Sempronio, Calisto's servant	Parmeno, Calisto's servant
Calisto	Celestina, the bawd	Dario, Melebea's father

PLOT SUMMARY

Melebea opens the play complaining of *Calisto's* suit to her, which, despite his high estate, she is determined to refuse and in fact does so when he makes his appearance. He complains to his servant *Sempronio*, who, despite his jaundiced view of women, agrees to help *Calisto* win her. To this end he approaches *Celestina*, a bawd who has previously done him service, and she promises her aid. *Calisto* then enters with another servant, *Parmeno*, despite whose misgivings he places his trust in *Celestina*. She seeks to ingratiate herself with *Parmeno* and insists they sing a song together. He nonetheless quarrels with her but she lectures him on the delights of the flesh. He departs and *Calisto* comes in with *Sempronio*, bringing *Celestina* money. *Parmeno* re-enters to warn his master that *Celestina* and *Sempronio* will be harmful to him, but he is sharply brushed off. The scene changes to *Melebea*, who is quickly approached by *Celestina* seeking to persuade her to enjoy the pleasures of youth before the onset of old age, and she presses *Calisto's* suit. Despite initial politeness, *Melebea* rejects her arguments with scorn and they quarrel. *Celestina* then changes strategy and says that she meant that, with all the holy relics which *Melebea's* belt has touched, the suffering knight thought that *Melebea* might be able to relieve his illness. At this *Melebea* relents and gives her belt for *Celestina* to take to *Calisto*. They go off and *Melebea's* father enters, soon followed by *Melebea* herself, to whom he relates a dream he had about her in which she was being fawned on by a bitch and nearly fell into a pit of foul water. *Melebea* then realizes the import of the dream, tells her father about *Celestina*, and begs his forgiveness for nearly falling prey to the old woman's wiles. *Dario* then concludes the play issuing a warning to all virgins, bemoaning negligence in the upbringing of youth, and offering a prayer for the governors of the realm.

PLAY LENGTH

1,087 lines

COMMENTARY

This is one of a number of plays about female virtue and the dangers it faces. It is heavily satirical of false piety, which is its main target, but it also satirizes the literary conventions of romantic love. The most noteworthy narrative features are the use of a pandar, and the contrasting roles of the servants, a form of *psychomachia*. This is not, however, developed very far.

Other female virtue plays: **3, 34, 63, 70, 87, 97.**

Other wooing plays: **57** (frag.), **75, 84, 87.**

Other plays featuring prominent women characters: **3, 30, 32, 43, 46, 51, 63, 70, 75, 87, 95, 97.**

Other plays with foreign (non-biblical, non-classical) settings: **5, 7, 12, 13, 32, 33, 47, 70, 74, 83, 88.**

SIGNIFICANT TOPICS AND NARRATIVE ELEMENTS

the nature of women; wooing; 'virtuous' bawds; youth and age; female chastity; dreams and prophecy; the upbringing of youth; good and bad servants; relics; witchcraft and charms; false piety; chivalric motif of a suffering lover; parental guidance

DRAMATURGICAL AND RHETORICAL FEATURES

Verbal and general the play is described on the title page as 'a new comedy in English in manner of an interlude, right elegant and full of craft of rhetoric, wherein is showed and described as well the beauty and good properties of women, as their vices and evil conditions, with a moral conclusion and exhortation to virtue'; three apparent divisions to the play, each beginning with a solo entry at lines 1, 311 and 633; *Calisto*'s formal eulogistic description of *Melebea* 220–47; *Sempronio* is a servant-intriguer; stage directions in Latin

Actions and stage directions 273: *Cal.* gives *Semp.* a gold chain; 457: *Cal.* gives *Cel.* his cloak; 485 *sd*: 'And they (*Par., Cel.*) sing'; 876: *Mel.* gives *Cel.* her girdle; 970 *sd*: 'Here *Mel.* shall not speak for a certain amount of time, but will stare with a sorrowful face'; 983 *sd*: 'And she (*Mel.*) kneels'; **Simple entry:** *Semp.* 373; *Cal., Par.* 392; *Cal.* 583; *Mel.* 632; *Cel.* 639; *Dan.* 919; **Simple exit:** (*Mel.*) 72, *Cal.* 611; *Par.* 632; *Mel.* 905

Songs and music 1. *Parmeno, Celestina* (w.n.s.) 485 *sd*; 2. *Parmeno* calls for the minstrel to 'strike up' and 'sing sweet songs' 574–5; **Instrumental:** lute music from *Calisto* (? see 107)

Staging and set the action is localized by the presence and dialogue of characters, and there are no indications as to set

Stage properties *Calisto*'s lute and chair 107; a gold chain for *Sempronio* 273; *Calisto*'s cloak (as payment) 457; gold (a purse?) for *Celestina* 585; *Melebea*'s belt 836

PLACENAMES

Arabia 229; Bethlehem 298; Rome 120

ALLUSIONS

Adam 174, 176–7; Alexander the Great 165, 851; St Appollonia 834; Elijah 175; Gabriel and the Virgin Mary 887; St George 855; Hector 852; Heraclitus 4; St John midsummer epistle 171–4; Narcissus 858; Nero and Poppeia 119–21; Nimrod 164; Paris and Venus 247; Petrarch 1; Phoebe 91; Phoebus 91; the Three Kings 298

REPORT ON MODERN PRODUCTION

Leeds (Durham Medieval Theatre Company, dir. J. McKinnell), 10 July 1996 [*RORD* 36 (1997) pp. 187–8]

RECORDED PRODUCTIONS

LP Record: BBC, *The First Stage*, dir. J. Barton (1970)
Videotape: Durham Medieval Theatre Company, dir. J. McKinnell, University of Durham (1996)

BIBLIOGRAPHY

Brault, G. J. 'English Translations of the *Celestina* in the Sixteenth Century', *Hispanic Review* 28 (1960) pp. 301–12

Geritz, A. J. '*Calisto and Melebea* (ca. 1530)', *Celestinesca* 4 (1980) pp. 17–29

Grossman, R. *Spanien und das elisabethanische Drama*, Abhandlungen aus dem Gebiet der Auslandkunde, Hamburgische Universität, 4, Hamburg, L. Friederichsen, 1920, pp. 48–57

Hogrefe, 1959, pp. 338–44

Hunter, 1965, pp. 43–52

Norland, 1995, pp. 244–54

Purcell, H. D. 'The *Celestina* and the *Interlude of Calisto and Melibea*', *BHS* 44 (1967) pp. 1–15

Reed, 1919, pp. 1–17

Rosenbach, A. S. 'The Influence of *The Celestina* in the Early English Drama', *JDSG* 39 (1903) pp. 43–61

Ruiz Moneva, M. A. 'Interpersonal Communication and Context Acessibility in the Interpretation of Ironic Utterances. A Case Study: Rastell's Version of *La Celestina*', *RAEI* 11 (1998) pp. 193–216

Southern, 1973, pp. 220–8

Ugualde, L. 'The *Celestina* of 1502', *Boston Public Library Quarterly* 6 (1954) pp. 206–22

7   Cambises

DATE, AUTHORSHIP AND AUSPICES

1558–69 (*SR* 1569 *c*. Sept./Oct.); Thomas Preston; possibly played at court, and offered for acting; Greg 56

TEXT AND EDITIONS

Extant originals

1570 (?) printing by John Allde: BL; Huntington; *STC* 20287

Editions

1994	CHD (CD-Rom and online transcription of Allde printing, l.l., OS)*
1976	Fraser and Rabkin, vol. I (s.l., NS)
1975	Johnson (OS)*
1974	Craik (NS)*
1966	Creeth (OS)
1934	Baskervill, Heltzel and Nethercot (NS)
1924	Adams (OS)
1910	TFT (facsimile, n.l.)
1897	Manly, vol. II (OS)
1874–6	Dodsley, vol. IV (n.l., NS)

SOURCES

Richard Taverner's *The Second Booke of the Garden of Wysedome* (1593) is the probable source. The first extant version of the story of Cambises is in Herodotus, however.

CHARACTERS

Prologue	Meretrix	Young Child	Cupid
Cambises	Small Hability	Mother	Lady
Counsel	Shame	Smerdis	Maid
Lord	Praxaspes	Attendance	Preparation
Knight	Commons Cry	Murder	Queen
Sisamnes	Commons Complaint	Cruelty	1st Lord
Ambidexter	Proof	Hob	2nd Lord
Huf	Trial	Lob	3rd Lord
Ruf	Otian	Marian	Epilogue
Snuf	Execution	Venus	

PLOT SUMMARY

The *Prologue* warns that rulers should not abuse their power or they will suffer ignominy, and introduces the example of *Cambises*, king of Persia. *Cambises* then commences the action by installing, on the advice of *Counsel*, the wise judge *Sisamnes* as regent before going off to make war on the Egyptians. As soon as the king leaves, however, *Sisamnes* declares his intention to enrich himself through corruption. The scene then switches to *Ambidexter*, the Vice, who provokes a quarrel among three swaggerers, *Huf*, *Ruf* and *Snuf*, and a whore, before slipping away to meet *Sisamnes*. He encourages the corrupt judge, who pursues his evil ways, which include bribery and oppression, until *Cambises* returns and *Sisamnes* is brought to justice. He is executed with a sword and flayed before his young son, *Otian*, who is to succeed him as judge. As the king takes up his rule again he is warned by his counsellor, *Praxaspes*, about his excessive drinking. In response, *Cambises* orders *Praxaspes*'s young son to be brought so that he can prove his hand by shooting the heart of the child with an arrow. To the horror of the boy's father and mother, he does this and orders the heart to be cut out. The scene switches to the king's brother, *Smerdis*, who expresses disgust at *Cambises*'s deeds and looks forward to the day when he will succeed and rule more justly. While initially feigning friendship with *Smerdis*, *Ambidexter* tells *Cambises* that his brother has been plotting his death. *Cambises* sends murderers to kill *Smerdis*, a deed which causes great distress at court, as *Ambidexter* gloatingly relates to the audience. The Vice then terrifies two peasants, *Hob* and *Lob*, by threatening to report their comments about the king's cruelty, and he proceeds to foment strife between them. *Hob*'s wife, *Marian*, puts a stop to their fighting and herself fights with *Ambidexter* until he eventually makes off. *Venus* and *Cupid* are now introduced to make the king fall in love with his cousin, whom he spies walking with a lord and playing music. Against her will he commands her to become his wife, and *Ambidexter* then reports the celebration at court of the king's marriage. He goes on to provoke a fight with *Preparation*, the steward who is preparing the banquet, and engages in further mischief by dropping a bowl of nuts. At the banquet *Cambises* tells his new queen a story of two lion whelps that fight, one killing the other, and she sorrowfully draws a parallel with his own killing of his brother. At this he becomes enraged and orders her death too, rejecting pleas from his courtiers to spare her. *Ambidexter* now enters weeping for the death of the queen, along with the king's other misdeeds. *Cambises* then comes in wounded in a hunting accident and dies, observing that his death is a punishment for his crimes. *Ambidexter* takes off for fear of being accused of murdering the king, while courtiers enter to bury their master. An epilogue craves the patience of the audience and prays for the queen and council.

PLAY LENGTH

1,192 lines, in addition to a prologue of 36 lines and an epilogue of 21 lines

COMMENTARY

This play, famous for its title-page description of 'a lamentable tragedy mixed full of pleasant mirth', has a plot complicated by a central figure of a king who is at first a corrector of corruption, but who then becomes corrupt himself. The ambivalence suggested by this is present also in *Sisamnes*, the regent, who is at the start a wise judge before he becomes tyrannical, and especially in *Ambidexter* the Vice, who takes delight in his mischief but who later shows himself capable of sorrow for evil. His moral role is modified by the fact that he performs classically the function of the Vice as engine of plot development and source of dramatic action, particularly in the subplot sequences. The play may contain resonances of tyrannical practices in the period, especially in respect of official repression of religious dissidence.

Other secular tragedies: **32, 37, 43.**

Other plays with foreign (non-biblical, non-classical) settings: **5, 6, 12, 13, 32, 33, 47, 70, 74, 83, 88.**

SIGNIFICANT TOPICS AND NARRATIVE ELEMENTS

a corrupt regent; a prostitute; bribery; an execution and flaying; a drunken ruler; a child murder and mother's lament; royal tyranny; a wedding feast; the king's murder of his wife; Bishop Bonner

DRAMATURGICAL AND RHETORICAL FEATURES

Verbal and general elements of comic subplot with plebeian figures: *Huf, Ruf, Snuf* and the prostitute 160–292, *Hob, Lob* and *Marian* 754–842; rustic speech: *Hob* and *Lob* 754 ff.; the lower class figures (especially *Hob* and *Lob*) are unmistakably English; stage directions in English

Costume and dress the king enters 'without a gown' 1152 *sd*

Actions and stage directions 36 *sd*: 'First enter *Cam.* the *Ki., Kn.,* and *Coun.*'; 125 *sd*: 'Enter the Vice with an old capcase on his head, an old pail about his hips for harness, a scummer and a potlid by his side, and a rake over his shoulder; 159 *sd*.: 'Enter three ruffians, *Huf, Ruf* and *Snuf,* singing'; 188 *sd*: 'Here let him (*Amb.*) swing them (*Huf, Snuf, Ruf*) about'; 201 *sd*: '(*Amb., Huf, Snuf, Ruf*) Fight again'; 202 *sd*: '(*Huf, Snuf, Ruf*) Draw their swords'; 209: The Vice and ruffians shake hands; 220 *sd*: 'Enter *Mer.* with a staff on her shoulder'; 237 *sd*: '(*Mer.*) Kiss'; 241 *sd*: '(*Mer.*) Kiss, kiss, kiss'; 265 *sd*: 'Here (*Snuf, Ruf, Mer.*) draw and fight. She must lay on and coil them both; the Vice must run his way for fear; *Snuf* fling down his sword and buckler and run his way'; 272 *sd*: 'He (*Ruf*) falls down; she falls upon him, and beats him, and takes away his weapon'; 340 *sd*: 'Enter *Sha.* with a trumpet black'; 356 *sd*: 'Enter *Co. Cry* running in; speak this verse; and go out again hastily'; 364 *sd*: '(*Co. Cry*) Run away crying'; 417 *sd*: '(*Pra.*) Step aside and fetch him (*Sis.*)'; 460 *sd*: '(*Exec.*) Smite him (*Sis.*) in the neck to signify his death'; 464 *sd*: '(*Exec.*) Flay him

(*Sis.*) with a false skin'; 474 *sd*: 'They (*Oti., Exec.*) take him (body of *Sis.*) away'; 488 *sd*: 'Enter *Ld.* and *Kn.* to meet the *Ki.*'; 530 *sd*, 531 *sd*: '(*Cam.*) Drink'; 553 *sd*: '(*Cam.*) Shoot'; 709 *sd*: 'Enter *Cru.* and *Mur.* with bloody hands'; 722 *sd*: '(*Cru, Mur.*) strike him (*Smer.*) in divers places'; 726 *sd*: 'A little bladder of vinegar pricked'; 739 *sd*: '(*Amb.*) Weep'; 812 *sd*: 'Here let them (*Hob, Lob*) fight with their staves, not come near [one] another by three or four yards; the Vice set them on as hard as he can; one of their wives come out, and all to-beat the Vice; he run away. Enter *Mari.*, *Hob*'s wife, running in with a broom, and part them'; 822 *sd*: '(*Hob, Lob*) Shake hands and laugh heartily one at another'; 833 *sd*: 'Here let her (*Mari.*) swing him (*Amb.*) in her broom; she gets him down, and he her down, thus one on top of another make pastime'; 838 *sd*: '(*Amb.*) Run his way out while she (*Mari.*) is down'; 842 *sd*: 'Enter *Ven.* leading out her son, *Cup.*, blind; he must have a bow and two shafts, one headed with gold and th'other headed with lead'; 870 *sd*: 'Here (*Ld., Ly.*) trace up and down playing (music)'; 880 *sd*: '(*Cup.*) Shoot there, and go out *Ven.* and *Cup.*'; 979 *sd*: '(*Amb., Prep.*) Fight'; 982 *sd*: '(*Amb., Prep.*) Fight'; 987 *sd*: '(*Prep.*) Set the fruit on the board'; 989 *sd*: 'Here let the Vice fetch a dish of nuts, and let them fall in the bringing of them in'; 1013 *sd*: '(*Ki.*, ret.) Sit at the banquet'; 1015 *sd*: '(musicians) Play at the banquet'; 1029 *sd*: 'At this tale told, let the *Qu.* weep'; 1126 *sd*: '(*Qu.*) Sing and (banquet party) exeunt'; 1126 *sd* (2): 'Enter *Amb.* weeping'; 1152 *sd*: 'Enter the *Ki.*, without a gown, a sword thrust up into his side, bleeding'; 1165 *sd*: 'Here let him (*Ki.*) quake and stir'; **Simple entry:** *Pro.* op. *sd*; *Amb.* 292; *Sis.* 306; *Ki., Ld., Prax., Sis.* 352; *C. Comp., Pro., Tri.* 372; *Exe.* 434; *Moth.* 572; *Amb.* 601; *Smer., Att., Dil.* 621; *Ki., Ld.* 653; *Smer.* 705; *Amb.* 731; *Hob, Lob* 753; *Ld., Ly., Ma.* 860; *Ki., Ld., Kn.* 872; *Amb.* 937; *Prep.* 964; *Ki., Qu.*, train 1009; *Cru., Mur.* 1100; three lords 1180; **Simple exit:** (*Kn.*) 60; *Ki., Ld., Coun.* 112; (*Sis.*) 125; *Huf* 248; (*Ruf, Mer.*) 292; (*Sis., Amb.*) 338; (*Sm. Hab.*) 340; (*Sha.*) 352; 'They three' (*Sis., Tri., Pro.*) 412; (*Prax., Moth.*) 601; *Smer., Att., Dil.* 668; (*Ki.*) 692; (*Amb.*) 705; (*Cru., Mur.*) 731; *Hob, Lob* 826; (*Ki., Ld., Ly., Ma.*) 937; *Prep.* 993; *Amb.*1057; *Ki.*, lords 1112; *Amb.* 1180; 'All' 1192

Songs and music (w.n.s. for either song) 1. *Huf, Ruf, Snuf* 159 *sd*; 2. the queen 'a psalm' 1126 *sd*; **Instrumental:** drums 111; *Shame* sounds a trumpet 340 *sd*; the *Lord* and *Lady* play on a lute and cittern 871 *sd*; fiddle music at the banquet 1016 *sd*

Staging and set an exceptionally large number of characters with a doubling scheme for eight players given on the title page as follows: 1. *Counsel, Huf, Praxaspes, Murder, Lob, 3rd Lord*; 2. *Lord, Ruf, Commons Cry, Commons Complaint, Smerdis, Venus*; 3. *Knight, Snuf, Small Hability, Proof, Execution, Attendance, 2nd Lord*; 4. *Cambises, Epilogue*; 5. *Prologue, Sisamnes, Diligence, Cruelty, Hob, Preparation, 1st Lord*; 6. *Ambidexter, Trial*; 7. *Meretrix, Shame, Otian, Mother, Lady, Queen*; 8. *Young Child, Cupid* (the list omits *Marian* and the *Maid*). materials (false skin, bladder, sword in king's side) for visual effects; the action is mostly either unlocalized or designated by the speeches of protagonists, but the *Lord* and *Lady* describe the garden in which they find themselves, possibly visually represented (861–70); a banquet, with appropriate stage properties, is held on stage at the end (1013 *sd* ff.)

Stage properties *Ambidexter*'s capcase (bag or wallet), old pail, skimming spoon ('scummer'), potlid and rake 125 *sd*; *Huf*'s, *Snuf*'s and *Ruf*'s swords and bucklers 202 *sd*; *Meretrix*'s staff 220 *sd*; *Shame*'s black trumpet 340 *sd*; *Execution*'s sword 460 *sd*; *Sisamnes*'s false skin for flaying 464 *sd*; a bow and arrow for *Cambises* 533; a bladder of vinegar (as blood) 726 *sd*; *Hob*'s and *Lob*'s staves 812 *sd*; *Marian*'s broom 833 *sd*; *Cupid*'s bow, lead and gold arrows 842 *sd*; the *Lord* and *Lady*'s lute and cittern 867; the banquet 967; fruit and a table 987 *sd*; *Ambidexter*'s dish of nuts 989 *sd*; the musician's stick and fiddle 1016; the sword stuck into the king's side 1152 *sd*

PLACENAMES

Egypt 95, 110; Persia pr. 15 *passim*; York 761

ALLUSIONS

Agathon pr. 1–10; Bacchus 485; Cicero ('Tully') pr. 7; Croesus 501, 505; Diana 846; Icarus pr. 22, 24; Jove/Jupiter pr. 31 *passim*; Mars 10 *passim*; Seneca pr. 11; the Three Sisters (the Fates) pr. 17; Titan 902

RECORDED PRODUCTION

Videotape: Durham Medieval Theatre Company, dir. J. McKinnell and D. Crane, University of Durham (1992)

BIBLIOGRAPHY

Allen, D. C. 'A Source for *Cambises*'. *MLN* 49:6 (1934) pp. 384–7
Armstrong, W. A. 'The Background and Sources of Preston's *Cambises*'. *ES* 31:3 (1950) pp. 129–35
Armstrong, W. A. 'The Authorship and Political Meaning of *Cambises*'. *ES* 36:4 (1955) pp. 289–99
Bevington, 1962, pp. 81–9, 183–9, 211–16
Brooke, 1996, pp. 99–107
Bushnell, 1990, pp. 95–103
Cartwright, 1999, pp. 102–8
Farnham, 1936, pp. 263–70
Feldman, A. 'King Cambises' Vein'. *N&Q* 196 (1951) pp. 98–100
Fishman, B. J. 'Pride and Ire: Theatrical Iconography in Preston's *Cambises*'. *SEL* 16:2 (1976) pp. 201–11
Happé, 1965, pp. 207–227
Hill, E. D. 'The First Elizabethan Tragedy: A Contextual Reading of *Cambises*'. *SP* 89:4 (1992) pp. 404–33
Kaplan, J. H. 'Reopening King Cambises' Vein'. *ET* 5 (1987) pp. 103–14
Knapp, R. S. 'Resistance, Religion and the Aesthetic: Power and Drama in the Towneley "Magnus Herodes", *Cambises* and *Richard III*'. *RORD* 33 (1994) pp. 143–52
Linthicum, M. C. 'The Date of *Cambyses*'. *PMLA* 49:3 (1934) pp. 959–64
Myers, J. P. 'The Heart of King Cambises'. *SP* 70:4 (1973) pp. 367–76
Norland, H. B. '"Lamentable tragedy mixed ful of pleasant mirth": The Enigma of *Cambises*'. *CD* 26:4 (1992/3) pp. 330–43
Ribner, 1965, pp. 53–60
Southern, 1973, pp. 510–19

Starnes, D. T. 'Richard Taverner's *The Garden of Wisdom*, Carion's *Chronicles*, and the Cambyses Legend', *UTSE* 35 (1956) pp. 22–31

Strozier, R. M. 'Politics, Stoicism, and the Development of Elizabethan Tragedy', *Costerus* 8 (1973) pp. 193–218

Wentersdorf, K. P. 'The Allegorical Role of the Vice in Preston's *Cambises*', *MLS* 11:2 (1981) pp. 54–69

Woolf, 1973, pp. 93–105

8   The Cambridge Prologue

DATE, AUTHORSHIP AND AUSPICES

possibly late thirteenth century; anonymous; auspices unknown

TEXT AND EDITIONS

Extant originals

Manuscript: Cambridge University Library MS I. 18, fo. 62r

Editions

1994   CHD (CD-Rom and online copy of Davis, 1970, l.l., OS)
1979   Davis (facsimile)
1970   Davis (OS)*
1950   Robbins (OS)*

PLOT SUMMARY

The lines consist of warnings to an audience, in both French and English, to be quiet and pay attention, on pain of punishment by an emperor.

PLAY LENGTH

22 lines extant (in each language)

COMMENTARY

The speaker of the prologue is evidently a messenger figure who is representative of a tyrant, the emperor. The nature of the speaker and his master is emphasized by not only his threatening tone, but also by his references to 'Mahun'. The bilingualism of the passage is an interesting feature, and French and English passages say much the same things, though neither is a direct translation of the other. Aside from the complete plays, the *Mystère d'Adam* and *La Seinte Resurrection*, this and the Rickinghall fragment are the only known remains of Anglo-Norman drama.

SIGNIFICANT TOPICS AND NARRATIVE ELEMENTS

a 'boasting' speech; a tyrannical emperor; 'Mahun' (Mohammed/a pagan god)

BIBLIOGRAPHY

Legge, 1963, pp. 328–31
Robbins, R. H. (essay) 'An English Mystery Play Fragment ante 1300', *MLN* 65:1 (1950) pp. 30–5

9   The Castle of Perseverance

DATE, AUTHORSHIP AND AUSPICES

1382–1425; anonymous; possibly from Lincolnshire, and certainly East Anglia; auspices unknown

TEXT AND EDITIONS

Extant originals

Manuscript: Folger MS. V.a.354 (formerly MS 5031), fos. 119–36

Editions

1994   CHD (CD-Rom and online copy of Eccles, 1969, l.l., s.l., OS)
1979   Happé (OS)
1975   Bevington (OS)*
1972   Bevington (facsimile with transcription)*
1969   Eccles (OS)*
1969   Schell and Schuchter (NS)
1908   TFT (facsimile, n.l.)
1904 (repr. 1924)   Furnivall and Pollard (OS)

SOURCES

No direct sources have been identified, but the play shares ideas that occur in poems such as the *Psychomachia* by Prudentius and the *Chasteau d'Amour* of Robert Grosseteste, Bishop of Lincoln.

CHARACTERS

Primus Vexillator (1st Standardbearer)
Secundus Vexillator (2nd Standardbearer)
Mundus (the World)
Belyal (the Devil)
Caro (the Flesh)
Humanum Genus (Mankind)
Bonus Angelus (Good Angel)
Malus Angelus (Bad Angel)
Voluptas (Lust)
Stulticia (Folly)
Detraccio (Detraction/Backbiter)
Avaricia/Cupiditas (Avarice/Covetise)
Superbia (Pride)
Ira (Wrath)
Invidia (Envy)
Gula (Gluttony)
Luxuria (Lechery)
Accidia (Sloth)

Confessio (Shrift/Confession)
Penitencia (Penitence)
Caritas (Charity)
Abstinencia (Abstinence)
Castitas (Chastity)
Solicitudo (Industry)
Largitas (Generosity)
Humilitas (Humility)
Paciencia (Patience)
Mors (Death)
Garcio (Boy)
Anima (Soul)
Misericordia (Mercy)
Justicia (Justice)
Veritas (Truth)
Pax (Peace)
Pater (God the Father)

PLOT SUMMARY

The Vexillatores or Standardbearers lay out the plot of the play and pronounce a blessing on the audience. The *World*, the *Devil* and the *Flesh* introduce themselves with 'boasts' on their respective scaffolds, before *Mankind* enters, helpless and weak. The *Good Angel* and *Bad Angel* immediately begin a verbal tussle for him and *Mankind* is in indecision as to which of their paths to choose. When the *Bad Angel* tempts him with wealth however, he chooses a worldly path despite the warnings of the *Good Angel*. The *World* then summons his knights, *Lust* and *Folly*, and sends them to recruit followers for him. They are presented with *Mankind* by the *Bad Angel* as a gift for the *World*, to whom they conduct him, and he welcomes *Mankind* with promises of riches. *Detraction* or *Backbiter*, the *World*'s messenger, then begins a 'boast' saying he will lead *Mankind* to the Seven Deadly Sins. After *Mankind* is endowed with wealth, *Backbiter* leads him to *Avarice* while the *Bad Angel* exults in his triumph over the sorrowing *Good Angel*. *Avarice* teaches *Mankind* corrupt ways, and summons forth the other Deadly Sins, *Pride*, *Wrath* and *Envy*, from *Belial*'s scaffold, and *Gluttony*, *Lechery* and *Sloth* from the *Flesh*'s. They all give *Mankind* instruction appropriate to their natures, which he receives readily, and he luxuriates in his worldly prosperity. At this point the *Good Angel* enters lamenting the loss of *Mankind*, while being mocked by the *Bad Angel*. He enlists the help of *Confession*, who attempts to convert *Mankind*, but he resists until pierced by *Penitence*'s lance. He then confesses his sins and receives absolution. To keep him safe from sin, *Confession* conveys him to the Castle of Perseverance, where he is instructed by the Virtues *Charity, Abstinence, Chastity, Industry, Generosity* and *Humility*. The *Bad Angel* now arrives to mount an attack on the Castle and he sends *Backbiter* to summon the *World*, the *Flesh* and the *Devil*. The *Devil* berates *Pride, Envy* and *Wrath* for letting *Mankind* go and he gives them a beating. *Backbiter* next visits in turn the scaffolds of the *Flesh* and the *World* to relate the news, and they punish their Vices in a similar way. The *World*, the *Devil* and the *Flesh*, accompanied by their Vice attendants, all go to the Castle and raise their standards. The Infernal Trinity and Vices are marshalled in their attack on the Castle by the *Bad Angel*, while *Mankind* is defended by the *Good Angel* and the Virtues. The Virtues pelt the attackers with roses, the symbol of the Passion, driving them back. The attack is repeated and again roses are used to repulse the assailants. The *World* then changes strategy and sends *Avarice* to seduce *Mankind*. He as an ageing man falls prey to the temptation and, to the dismay of the Virtues, goes off to join *Avarice*. *Mankind* is rewarded with a thousand marks but soon, however, *Death* comes to claim him. He pleads desperately but vainly with the *World* and, while his goods and properties are given to a young boy, he dies calling on *God*'s mercy. He then re-enters as the *Soul* and the *Good Angel* fears he will not be able to save him, while the *Bad Angel* with relish describes his forthcoming punishment. His dying call for mercy has, however, summoned *Mercy*, one of the Four Daughters of God. She and *Peace* proceed to argue for *Mankind*'s salvation against their sisters *Truth* and *Justice*, who urge his damnation. Finally, *God*, sitting enthroned, makes the decision that *Mankind* will be saved, and the daughters are detailed to fetch him from the *Bad Angel*. *God* delivers a speech reminding the audience of the inevitability of death, and the play ends with the singing of the *Te Deum*.

PLAY LENGTH

3,649 lines extant, including Banns of 156 lines (two leaves containing around 200 lines lost)

COMMENTARY

This is both an important example of a place and scaffold play, and also the most substantial early morality in English, with many of the conventional elements that are characteristic of the genre. Most notable among these is the *psychomachia* or struggle for man's soul between the divine and infernal forces; others include the presence of the Seven Deadly Sins and the coming of death. *Mankind* enters as a *tabula rasa* in the play, his weakness and vulnerability being emphasized. The play has elements of the 'ages of man' topos about it, especially in its presentation of avarice as a sin of old age. It also contains the fullest extant example of the debate of the 'Daughters of God' in English drama, a motif found in other literary genres as well.

Other plays with probable place and scaffold staging: **23**, **48**, **63**, **72** (frag.), **83**, **85**

SIGNIFICANT TOPICS AND NARRATIVE ELEMENTS

a psychomachia; fall and redemption; the Infernal Trinity: the World, Flesh and Devil; the Seven Deadly Sins; confession and absolution; the 'remedia': virtues ranged against and combating specific vices; a siege of a Castle; avarice and old age; the dance of death/death the leveller; a debate between the body and the soul; a debate of the Four Daughters of God

DRAMATURGICAL AND RHETORICAL FEATURES

Verbal and general the *World*'s alliterative geographical list of places over which he claims domination 170–80; the *World*, *Devil*, *Flesh* and *Backbiter* enter with strongly alliterative 'boasts' at 157, 196, 235 and 647 respectively; most stage directions within the body of the play in Latin (English ones marked below)

Costume and dress 'the 4 daughters shall be clad in mantles, *Mercy* in white, *Righteousness* in red altogether, *Truth* in sad green, and *Peace* all in black' frontispiece diagram *sd*; the *Flesh* is 'flourished in flowers' 237; *Mankind* enters 'naked of limb and loin' 279; *Mankind* is dressed in bright jewellery 701; *Avarice* has 'rich array' 831

Actions and stage directions (several detailed directions on frontispiece diagram for staging – see 'Staging and set' below); frontispiece diagram *sd*: 'and they (D. of God) shall play in the place altogether till they bring up the soul' (E); 455 *sd*: 'Pipe up music' (E); 457–8: the *Wo.* trots, trembles and hops for joy; 490 *sd*: 'Then they (*Wo.*, *Lu.*) descend to the place together'; 574 *sd*: 'Trumpet up' (E). 'Then *Lu.*, *Fo.*, the *B. Ang.* and *Man.* [go] to the *Wo.* and let him (*Lu.*) say'; 614 *sd*: 'Then *Man.* ascends to the *Wo.*'; 646 *sd*: 'Trumpet up' (E); 1009 *sd*: 'Then *Pri.*, *Wra.*, *En.*, *Glut.*, *Lech.* and *Slo.* will go to *Av.* and let *Pri.* say'; 1336 *sd*: 'Then they (Virtues) will go to *Man.* and let him (*Conf.*) say'; 1377: *Pen.* pierces *Man.* with his lance; 1445 *sd*: 'Then he (*Man.*) descends to *Conf.*'; 1490: *Man.* kneels in penitence; 1507–32: *Conf.* absolves *Man.*; 1697 *sd*: 'Then he (*Man.*) will enter (Castle)'; 1705 *sd*: 'Then they (Virtues, *Man.*) will sing "Eterne Rex Altissime" and let him (*Man.*) say'; 1745 *sd*: 'Then he (*Back.*) will go to *Bel.*'; 1766 *sd*: 'Then he (*Back.*) will summon *Pri.*, *En.* and *Wra.*'; 1777 *sd*: 'And he (*Bel.*) will beat them (*Pri.*, *En.*, *Wra.*) on the ground'; 1790 *sd*: '(*Back.* calls) To the *Fle.*'; 1811 *sd*: 'Then the *Fle.* will call to *Glut.*, *Slo.* and *Lu.*'; 1822 *sd*: 'Then he (*Fle.*) will beat them (*Glut.*, *Slo.*, *Lu.*) in the place'; 1835 *sd*: '(*Back.* calls) To the *Wo.*'; 1852 *sd*: 'Then he (*Back.*) will sound the horn to [summon] *Av.*'; 1863 *sd*: 'Then he (*Wo.*) will beat him (*Av.*)'; 1898 *sd*: 'Then the *Wo.*, *Cov.* and

Fol. will go to the Castle with a banner and let the *Dev.* say'; 1968 *sd*: 'Then they (*Fle.*, *Glut.*) descend to the place'; 1968 *sd* (2): 'The *B. Ang.* must say to *Bel.*'; 1981 *sd*: (*B. Ang.* says) To the *Fle.*'; 1990 *sd*: '(*B. Ang.* says) To the *Wo.*'; 2145: the Virtues pelt the Vices with roses; 2198 *sd*: 'Then they (Virtues, Vices) will fight a long time'; 2377 *sd*: 'Then they (Virtues, Vices) will fight a long time'; 2409 *sd*: '(*B. Ang.* says) To the *Wo.*'; 2556 *sd*: 'Then he (*Man.*) descends to *Av.*'; 2841–2: *Dea.* stabs *Man.* through the heart; 2920 *sd*: 'Then let him (*Boy*) go to *Man.*'; 3228 *sd*: 'Then they (*D.* of *God*) ascend to the *Fath.* all together, and let *Tru.* say'; 3560 *sd*: 'The *Fath.* sitting on the throne [says]'; 3574 *sd*: 'He (*God*) should say to (his) daughters'; 3385 *sd*: 'Then they (*D.* of *God*) ascend to the *B. Ang.* all together and (*Pe.*) says'; 3593 *sd*: 'Then they (*D.* of *God*) ascend to the throne (of *God*)'

Songs and music (w.n.s.) 1. Virtues 'Eterne Rex Altissime' 1705 *sd*; 2. Various 'Te Deum Laudamus' (?) 3649; **Instrumental**: the *Primus Vexillator* calls for trumpet blasts 156; *Belial* blows on a bugle 228; pipe music 455 *sd*; a trumpet 574 *sd*, 646 *sd*; *Backbiter* blows a horn 1852 *sd*; *Belial* hears trumpets sounding 1898; *Belial* calls for 'clarions' 2197 and bagpipes 2198; The *Flesh* calls for trumpet blasts 2376–7

Staging and set the frontispiece to the manuscript contains several detailed directions as to staging and a stage plan with the scaffolds arranged as follows: south – *Flesh*, west – *World*, north – *Belial*, north-east – *Avarice/Covetise*, east – *God*; there is provision for a ditch or barrier to be made around the *platea*"; the Castle is in the middle with a bed for *Mankind* underneath it, and *Avarice*'s cupboard at the foot of the bed; it also contains the direction: 'and he that shall play *Belial* look that he has gunpowder burning in pipes in his hands and in his ears and in his arse when he goes to battle'; *God* is described as 'sitting on the throne' ('sedens in trono') in the character list; a blank for the place name is left in the Banns addressed by the Vexillatores to the audience, possibly suggesting a travelling play (134, 145); the character list claims 36 characters, though only 35 are named, the missing character possibly being *Conscience*, who is named in the Banns but who does not appear in the play

Stage properties *Mankind*'s bed – frontispiece diagram; *Covetise*'s cupboard – frontispiece diagram; *Belial*'s pipes with gunpowder – frontispiece diagram; *Pride*'s bugle 228; *Penitence*'s lance 1379; banners for *Belial* and the Vices 1936 *passim*; *Gluttony*'s faggot and lance 1961, 1963; roses for the battle 2145; *Covetise*'s thousand marks 2726; *Death*'s lance 2807

PLACENAMES

Achaia[1] 170; Aegean ('Gryckysch') Sea[1] 173; Assyria[1] 170; Babylon[1] 172; Brabant[1] 172; Brittany[1] 172; Burgundy[1] 172; Calvados[1] 171; Calvary 2087; Canaan[1] 171; Canwick (gallows of) 2421; Cappadocia[1] 171; Carlisle 201; England 1744; Flanders[1] 175, 224; France 175,[1] 1553; Friesland[1] 175, 224; Galicia 173[1] 1742; Germany ('Almayne')[1] 170; Greece[1] 173; Kent 201; Macedonia[1] 174; Normandy[1] 175;

Pyncecras[1] (land of the Pincenarii in Thrace) 176; Paris[1] 176; Pigmy Land[1] ('Pygmayne') 176; Rhodes[1] 178; Rome[1] 178; Thrace (? 'Trage')[1] 177; Wales 1744

1 Part of an alliterative list of places over which the *World* claims domination.

ALLUSIONS[1]

Acts 8:32 3552; Adam 1622, 3339a, 3340; Athanasian Creed 3636a; Cato 866; *1 Corinthians 13:1–3* 1612; *2 Corinthians 1:3–4* 3313a; King David 2984, 3468, 3471; *Deuteronomy 32:18* (q.a.) 3391a, 3404, *32:39* (q.a.) 3610a; the Dry Tree in Eden 177; *Ecclesiastes 5:9* (q.a.) 2638a; *Ecclesiasticus 7:40* (V) (q.a.) 410a; *Ezekiel 34:10* (q.a.) 3623a; *Galatians 6:5* 3163a; Goliath 1929; *James 1:2* (q.a.) 2007a, *1:20* 2124a; *Jeremiah 29:11* (q.a.) 3560a; *John 5:14, 8:11* 1528, *2:17* 2599a, *19:28* 3352, *19:30* 3356; *Luke 1:50* 3469a, *1:52* 2094a, *14:11, 18:14* 2107a; *Matthew 4:2* (q.a.) 2277a, *7:21* (q.a.) 3167a, *10:22* 1705a, *18:7* 2163a, *25:41–6* 3472–7; St Michael 3617; Alexander Nequam *De Naturis Rerum* ('the boke of kendys') 2513; St Paul 1496, 1611; St Peter 1496; Pontius Pilate 3348; *Psalm 10:8* (V)/*11:7* (AV) (q.a.) 3382a; *17:26* (V)/*18:26* (AV) 1696a, *32:5* (V)/*33:5* (AV) 3573a, *36:4* (V)/*37:5* (AV) 2020a, *38:7* (V)/*39:6* (AV) 2985a, *48:11* (V)/*49:10* (AV) (q.a.) 2612a, *48:18* (V)/*49:17* (AV) 2625a, *50:8* (V)/*51:6* (AV) 3252a, *57:11* (V)/*58:10* (AV) 3443a, *84:11* (V)/*85:10* (AV) 3521a, *88:2* (V)/*89:1* (AV) 3378, *88:29* (V)/*89:28* (AV) (q.a.) 3374, *116:2* (V)/*117:2* (AV) (q.a.) 3284, *144:9* (V)/*145:9* (AV) (q.a.) 3456a; *Romans 8: 8* (q.a.) 1631a

1 References marked 'a' occur outside numbered lines.

CONCORDANCE

Preston, 1975

REPORTS ON MODERN PRODUCTIONS

1. St Bartholomew the Great Church, Smithfield, London, dir. H. Davies, 23–7 May (and tour, 3–24 June) 1978 [*RORD* 21 (1978) pp. 100–2]
2. University of Toronto (PLS, dir. D. Parry) 4–6 August 1979 [*RORD* 22 (1979) pp. 142–5]
3. Manchester, dir. P. Cook, 29 April–2 May 1981 [*METh* 3:1 (1981) pp. 55–6]
4. 'The Four Daughters of God' (from *The Castle of Perseverance*) Pittsburgh (Duquesne University Medieval and Renaissance Players, dir. W. Racicot and N. Andel) 7–9 and 13 April 1999 [*RORD* 39 (2000) pp. 244–7]
5. University of California, Irvine, dir. R. Cohen 1–10 June 2000 [*RORD* 40 (2001) pp. 197–202]

RECORDED PRODUCTIONS

LP Record: BBC, *The First Stage*, dir. J. Barton (1970)
Videotape: PLS, Scotiabank Information Commons (1980)
Videotape: Insight Media, produced by M. Edmunds, text ed. David Parry (1982)

BIBLIOGRAPHY

Belsey, C. 'The Stage Plan of *The Castle of Perseverance*', *TN* 28:3 (1974) pp. 124–32
Bennett, J. '*The Castle of Perseverance*: Redactions, Place and Date', *MS* 24 (1962) pp. 141–52
Bevington, 1962, pp. 117–23
Bevington, D. '"Man, Thinke on Thine Endinge Day": Stage Pictures of Just Judgment in *The Castle of Perseverance*' in Bevington, 1985, pp. 147–77
Butterworth, P. 'Gunnepowder, fyre and thondyr', *METh* 7:2 (1985) pp. 68–76
Cornelius, 1930
Davenport, 1982, pp. 106–29
Davidson, 1989, pp. 47–82
Emmerson, R. K. 'The Morality Character as Sign: A Semiotic Approach to the *Castle of Perseverance*', *Mediaevalia* 18 (1995 for 1992) pp. 191–220
Fifield, M. 'The Arena Theatres in Vienna Codices 2535 and 2536', *CD* 2:4 (1968–9) pp. 259–82
Fifield, M. 'The Assault on the *Castle of Perseverance*: the Tradition and the Figure', *BSUF* 16:4 (1975) pp. 16–26
Fifield, M. '"The Castle of Perseverance": A Moral Trilogy' in Selz, 1969, pp. 55–62
Fletcher, A. '"Covetyse Copbord schal be at þe Ende of the Castel be þe Beddys Feet": Staging the Death of Mankind in *The Castle of Perserverance*', *ES* 68:4 (1987) pp. 305–12
Forstater, A. and J. L. Baird, '"Walking and Wending": Mankind's Opening Speech', *TN* 26:1 (1971–2) pp. 60–4
Haller, 1916, 87–96
Happé, P. 'Staging *L'Omme Pecheur* and *The Castle of Perseverance*', *CD* 30:3 (1996) pp. 377–94
Hayes, D. W. 'Backbiter and the Rhetoric of Destruction', *CD* 34:1 (2000) pp. 53–78
Henry, A. 'Dramatic Function of Rhyme and Stanza Patterns in *The Castle of Perseverance*' in *Individuality and Achievement in Middle English Poetry*, ed. O. Pickering, Cambridge, D. S. Brewer, 1996, pp. 147–83
Hildahl, F. E. 'Penitence and Parody in *The Castle of Perseverance*', *Acta* 13 (1987) pp. 129–41
Holbrook, S. E. 'Covetousness, Contrition and the Town in the *Castle of Perseverance*', *FCS* 13 (1988) pp. 275–89
Kelley, M. R. 'Fifteenth-Century Flamboyant Style and *The Castle of Perseverance*', *CD* 6:1 (1972) pp. 14–27
Kelley, 1979, pp. 29–63
Keppel, 2000, pp. 73–5, 82–4, 86–102
Lascombes, J. 'De la fonction théatrale des personages du Mal', *METh* 11 (1980), pp. 11–25
Levey, D. 'The Structure of *The Castle of Perseverance*', *Literator* 7:1 (1986) pp. 48–57
Lombardo, 1953, pp. 267–83
McCutchan, J. W. 'Covetousness in *The Castle of Perseverance*', *University of Virginia Studies* 4 (1951) pp. 175–91
Miyajima, 1977, pp. 33–67
Nelson, A. '*Of the Seuen Ages*: An Unknown Analogue of *Castle of Perseverance*', *CD* 8:1 (1974) pp. 125–38
Parry, D. 'A Margin of Error: the Problems of Marginalia in *Castle of Perseverance*', in Johnston, 1987, pp. 33–64
Pederson, S. I. 'The Staging of *The Castle of Perseverance*: A Re-Analysis', *TN* 39:2 (1985) pp. 51–62

Pederson, S. I. 'The Staging of *The Castle of Perseverance*: Testing the List Theory', *TN* 39:2 (1985) pp. 104–13

Pederson, 1987

Pickering, O. S. 'Poetic Style and Poetic Affiliation in *The Castle of Perseverance*', *LSE* 29 (1998) pp. 275–91

Proudfoot, R. 'The Virtue of Perseverance', in Neuss, 1983, pp. 92–109

Ralston, M. E. 'The Four Daughters of God in *The Castle of Perseverance*', *Comitatus* 15 (1984) pp. 35–44

Rendall, 1981, pp. 255–69

Richardson and Johnston, 1991, pp. 111–26

Riggio, M. C. 'The Allegory of Feudal Acquisition in *The Castle of Perseverance*' in Bloomfield, 1981, pp. 187–208

Schell, E. T. 'On the Imitation of Life's Pilgrimage in *The Castle of Perseverance*', *JEGP* 67:2 (1968) pp. 235–48, and in Taylor and Nelson, 1972, pp. 279–91

Schell, 1983, pp. 27–51

Scherb, V. L. 'The Parable of the Talents in *The Castle of Perseverance*', *ELN* 28:1 (1988) pp. 20–5

Scherb, 2001, pp. 148–63

Schmitt, N. C. 'Was there a Medieval Theatre in the Round? A Re-examination of the Evidence', *TN* 23:4 (1969) pp. 130–42, 24:1 (1969) pp. 18–25, and in Taylor and Nelson, 1972, pp. 292–315

Smart, W. K. '*The Castle of Perseverance*: Place, Date and a Source' in *Manly Anniversary Studies in Language and Literature*, Chicago, University of Chicago Press, 1923, pp. 42–53

Southern, 1957

Taylor, B. S. *Selections from the Castle of Perseverance*, Sydney, University of Sydney Press, English Texts 3

Towne, 1950, pp. 175–80

Tydeman, 1986, pp. 78–103

Ward, P. H. 'The Significance of Roses as Weapons in *The Castle of Perseverance*', *SM* 14:2/3 (1991) pp. 84–92

Wenzel, 1967, pp. 47–66

Willis, J. 'Stage Directions in *The Castle of Perseverance*', *MLR* 51:3 (1956) pp. 404–5

10   Christ's Burial

DATE, AUTHORSHIP AND AUSPICES

c. 1520; anonymous; probably of northern origin; possibly for monastic production

TEXT AND EDITIONS

Extant originals

Manuscript: Bodleian MS E Museo 160 (formerly MS 226)

Editions

1994   CHD (CD-Rom and online copy of Baker, Murphy and Hall, 1982, l.l., OS)
1982   Baker, Murphy and Hall (OS)*
1976   Baker, Murphy and Hall (facsimile, n.l.)
1896   Furnivall (OS)* (different line numbering for *Christ's Resurrection* below)

1843   Wright and Halliwell, vol. ii (n.l., OS)

SOURCES

The two plays (this and *Christ's Resurrection*, **ii**) are likely to have been based on Carthusian meditational material; see the introduction to the edition by Baker, Murphy and Hall.

CHARACTERS

Joseph of Arimathea   Mary Salome   John the Evangelist
Mary Magdalene   Nicodemus
Mary Jacobe   Virgin Mary
                       Mute: Christ crucified

PLOT SUMMARY

The play is preceded by a prologue, stipulated as not to be spoken if the piece is played, offering it as a devotional text to readers. This is followed by a plaint by *Joseph of Arimathea* about the death of Christ, which possibly constitutes the spoken prologue. He hears sounds of weeping off stage and the three Marys, together with *Mary Magdalene*, enter lamenting, first together and then alternately, the cruelty of Christ's death. *Mary Magdalene* describes to *Joseph* the sorrows of the Virgin at the Crucifixion and, weeping, she goes on to describe the Passion itself, being consoled by two of the other Marys (the Virgin not apparently being present at this point). *Joseph* delivers a sermon on the redemptive power of Christ's death, until *Mary Magdalene* again takes up her plaint. *Joseph* urges her to stop, pointing out the purposes of Christ's death, but she emphasizes Christ's mercy and the pity of the deed. Another *Mary* also tells her to cease mourning and suggests instead that they take the body and bury it. *Joseph* reports that he has permission from Pilate to take the body, but that he is awaiting the arrival of *Nicodemus*. When he does arrive he is lamenting, but is stopped by *Joseph*, who fears his weeping will rekindle that of the women. They take *Christ's* body, during which the sorrowing *Virgin Mary* arrives with *John the Evangelist* and falls into a swoon. She is revived and comforted by the others, but when again overcome with sorrow, she once more swoons and is again comforted. On her request she is given the body to hold in her arms, which she does while she reflects on Christ's birth and death, and also on his broken body. She is then persuaded by *Nicodemus*, *John* and *Joseph* to relinquish the body and they bury it, while *Mary Cleophas* and *Mary Salome* attend on the *Virgin Mary* and *Mary Magdalene* goes off to buy ointments to anoint the body.

PLAY LENGTH

862 lines

COMMENTARY

This play and *Christ's Resurrection* (**11**) are effectively one play, designed to be played on Good Friday and Easter Sunday respectively. It is possible that they were not originally intended for performance but may have been adapted for this purpose after their original composition. The play contains a prologue addressed to the reader, with the instruction that this be omitted if it is played.

Other biblical plays: **11, 16, 34, 42, 44, 48, 63, 77, 90, 93.**

SIGNIFICANT TOPICS AND NARRATIVE ELEMENTS

a providential perspective on the death of Christ; Joseph of Arimathea as a character; Mary Magdalene as a woman of sorrows; the sorrows of the Virgin

DRAMATURGICAL AND RHETORICAL FEATURES

Verbal and general the formal planctus of the Marys 56–79; planctus of the *Virgin Mary* 612–791; a pietà 799–809; several directions cancelled in the MS; stage directions in either Latin or English

Actions and stage directions 55 *sd*: 'Off [stage] the weeping of the three Marys' (E); 55 *sd* (2): 'Three Marys say all together in a voice' (E); 55 *sd* (3): 'The three Marys must go' (L); 391 *sd*: '*Nic.* comes' (L); 434 *sd*: '*Jos.*, ready to take *Chr.* down, says' (E); 449 *sd*: '*Mary*, Virgin and Mother come then saying' (E); 455 *sd*: '*Mary Virg.*, says, [and] falls in [a] swoon' (E); 507 *sd*: 'And she (*Virg. Mary*) falls into a swoon' (L); 832 *sd*: '(two Marys) Depart' (L); 833 *sd*: 'He (*Chr.*) is buried' (L)

Staging and set the prologue title calls the play a 'treatise or meditation of the burial of Christ', but a direction at the end of the prologue indicates that it is designated for performance on Good Friday afternoon (56 ff.); the play may have been altered to prepare it for performance; directions indicate a cross from which *Christ* is taken down, and a place for burial

Stage properties *Christ*'s cross 128

PLACENAMES

Mount Calvary 28, 29; Egypt 633; 777; Judea 35

ALLUSIONS

Angel Gabriel 490; Herod 632; *Isaiah 44:22* (?) 245–7, *53:2* 645; *John 3:13* 434, *19:20* 210; *Luke 23:21* 53; Simeon 500, 503

CONCORDANCE

Preston, 1977

BIBLIOGRAPHY

Baker and Murphy, 1968, pp. 290–3
Schmidt, 1885, pp. 393–404
Taylor, G. C. 'The English "Planctus Mariae"', *MP* 4:4 (1907) pp. 605–33

11   Christ's Resurrection

DATE, AUTHORSHIP AND AUSPICES

c. 1520; anonymous; probably of northern origin; possibly for monastic production

TEXT AND EDITIONS

Extant originals

Manuscript: Bodleian Library MS E Museo 160 (formerly MS 226)

Editions

See **10**

SOURCES

See **10**

CHARACTERS

Mary Magdalene	Angel	John the Evangelist
2nd Mary (Cleophas)	Peter	Christ
3rd Mary (Salome)	Andrew	

PLOT SUMMARY

Mary Magdalene opens the play with a lament on Christ's death and the cruelty of the Jews, and she is joined by *Mary Cleophas*. They resolve to go and anoint the body, at which point *Mary Salome* joins them. When they come to the sepulchre, however, the angel tells them that *Christ* has risen. *Mary* falls into a bitter lament for his sufferings, especially when she sees the blood-stained winding sheet, and when the other Marys try to comfort her she declares that she has failed in her duty by leaving the sepulchre and not being present at the rising of *Christ*. The three women then exit and *Peter* enters with a lengthy plaint expressing similar regret for his lack of faithfulness to *Christ*. At the end of this he falls to the ground and weeps bitterly until he is comforted by *Andrew* and *John the Evangelist*, who remind him of the purpose of *Christ*'s death and the fact that *Christ* has entrusted the keys of heaven and hell to him. *John* delivers a sermon on the death of *Christ* and its redemptive power, and they all go off after *Peter*'s peace of mind is restored. A sorrowing *Mary Magdalene* now re-enters looking for *Christ*, and when she is addressed by a man she takes to be the gardener, she pours out her grief to him. He reveals himself to her as *Christ* and, after the 'noli me tangere', takes his leave. She is then joined by the other Marys, to whom she expresses her joy, and *Christ* himself briefly reappears to greet them. The women sing the *Victime Paschali* and are joined in this by *Peter*, *Andrew* and *John*, who enter at this point. After the singing, *Mary* gives the apostles the news of the Resurrection. *Peter* and *John* run to the tomb to verify this, and general rejoicing ensues, culminating in all singing *Scimus Christi* before *John* concludes the play with a farewell to the audience.

PLAY LENGTH

766 lines

COMMENTARY

This play is a companion piece to or part of the same work as *Christ's Burial* (see **10**). It dramatizes scriptural material which features prominently in liturgical drama, and despite some narrative expansion, the formal elements of especially the plaints from that drama are to be found here. There is an emphasis on the guilt felt by those closest to Christ and in this respect Mary and Peter are parallelled, both expressing bitter grief and being consoled by the two other Marys and two apostles respectively.

Other biblical plays: **10, 16, 34, 42, 44, 48, 63, 77, 90, 93.**

SIGNIFICANT TOPICS AND NARRATIVE ELEMENTS

the cruelty of the Jews; Mary Magdalene as a woman of sorrows; Mary Magdalene's self-accusation; St Peter's self-accusation; divine accommodation of human frailty; the Crucifixion; the Resurrection and redemption

DRAMATURGICAL AND RHETORICAL FEATURES

Verbal and general a non-spoken prologue (see **10**); *Mary Magdalene*'s *planctus* 1–60; a *Quem Quaeritis* sequence 134–266; *Peter*'s *planctus* 267–398; a *Hortulanus*

sequence with a 'noli me tangere' 601–28; *Peter* and *John*'s race to the tomb 721 *sd*; most stage directions in Latin

Costume and dress *Christ* enters dressed as a gardener 601 *sd*

Actions and stage directions op. *sd*: '*Mag.* begins, saying' (E); 60 *sd*: '*Sec. Mary* comes in and says' (E); 105 *sd*: '*Thd. Mary* comes in' (E); 133 *sd*: 'The *Ang.* speaks' (E); 134 *sd*: 'Three Marys together say' (E); 266 *sd*: 'Then the three Marys go out. *Pet.* enters, weeping bitterly' (L); 398 *sd*: 'And thus he (*Pet.*) falls to the earth, weeping bitterly. And., brother of *Pet.*, says' (L); 557 *sd*: 'Then *Jo.* departs and *Pet.* says' (L); 569 *sd*: '*Mary Mag.* enters' (L); 601 *sd*: '*Jes.* enters, in the guise of a gardener, and says' (L); 618 *sd*: '*Jes.* says, "Mary", *Mag.* answers "Raboni"' (E/L); 628 *sd*: '*Jes.* departs' (L); 637 *sd*: '*Sec. Mary* enters with *Thd.*' (L); 665 *sd*: 'Then *Jes.* enters and greets the three women. However, the women say nothing to him, but fall at his feet' (L); 691 *sd*: 'Then these three sing the same, that is "Victime Paschali" – up to "Di[c nobis]" singing it in separate phrases or at least by alternate lines. Then the apostles run to them, namely *Pet., And.,* and *Jo.,* singing this, as follows: "Dic nobis, Maria, quid vidisti in vi[a]?" The women respond, singing, "Sepulcrum Christi viven[tis]" et cetera, up to "Credendum est". The apostles, responding, sing: "Credendum est magis soli Marie veraci quam Judeorum turbe fallaci". The women again sing: "Scim[us] Christum surrexisse vere". The apostles and women together sing as though with conviction: "Tu nobis Christe rex misere[re]. Amen". After the song *Pet.* says. <It is sufficient if they sing the same notes and chants as in the aforesaid sequence>. *Pet.* says after the song' (L); 721 *sd*: 'Then they (*Pet., Jo.*) will go. Running ahead, *Jo.* says' (L); 755 *sd*: 'Then all together sing "Scimus Christum" or another sequence or hymn of the Resurrection. After the song *Jo.* says, making an end (to the play)' (L)

Songs and music 1. three Marys, *Peter, John, Andrew* 'Victime Paschali' (words partially supplied) 691, 691 *sd*; 2. three Marys, *Peter, John, Andrew* (*Scimus Christum* 'or another Resurrection sequence or hymn', w.n.s.) 755 *sd*

Staging and set the play is designated for performance on Easter Sunday; there are no clear indications as to set, but *Christ*'s sepulchre is specified (160)

Stage properties *Mary Magdalene*'s ointment 49; a blood-stained winding sheet 162

PLACENAMES

Canaa 132; Egypt 86; Galilee 132, 139, 166, 716; Israel 31; Jerusalem 594, 597

ALLUSIONS

Abraham 85; Cain and Abel 15–16, 37; King David 352; Herod 28; Jacob 22; *John 20:13* 140, *20:15* 602, *20:16–17* 618 *sd*–619; Joseph (son of Jacob) 23, 37; Judas 345, 357; Lazarus 129; *Matthew 16:19* 458, *26:31* 431, *28:9* (q.a.) 665 *sd*; *Psalm*

40:10 (V)/*41:9* (AV) (q.a.) 353–4; Simon the Pharisee 232; *Song of Solomon 2:14* (q.a.) 566, *3:1–2* (q.a.) 579–80, *5:8* (q.a.) 594–6; *Use of York* ('Victime Paschali') 690 *sd*

CONCORDANCE

Preston, 1977

BIBLIOGRAPHY

Abel, P. 'Grimald's *Christus Redivivus* and the Digby Resurrection Play', *MLN* 70:5 (1955), pp. 328–30
Baker and Murphy, 1968, pp. 290–3
Brawer, R. A. 'The Middle English Resurrection Play and its Dramatic Antecedents', *CD* 8:1 (1974) pp. 77–100
Schmidt, 1855, pp. 393–404

12   Clyomon and Clamydes

DATE, AUTHORSHIP AND AUSPICES

1570–83; anonymous (attributed to George Peele by Dyce and Kellner, but see Greg's edition and the essays by Larsen and Ashley, listed below); original auspices unknown, but revived by the Queen's Men in the 1590s; Greg 157

TEXT AND EDITIONS

Extant originals

1599 printing by Thomas Creede: BL; Folger; Harvard; Huntington; Newberry; Pforzheimer; (further copies extant); *STC* 5450a

Editions

1994	CHD (CD-Rom and online transcription of Creede printing, l.l., OS)
1968	Littlejohn (OS)*
1913a	Greg (OS)*
1913	TFT (facsimile, n.l.)
1888	Bullen, vol. II (s.l., NS)
1829–39	Dyce, vol. III (n.l., OS)

SOURCES

The principal source is *Perceforest*, a fourteenth-century French prose romance (second and third volumes); see the introduction to Littlejohn's edition, pp. 38–49.

CHARACTERS

Prologue
Clamydes, son to the King of Swavia
Juliana, daughter to the King and
    Queen of Denmark
Clyomon, son to the King of Denmark
Subtle Shift, the Vice
The King of Swavia
1st Lord
2nd Lord
Alexander the Great
Bryan Sans Foy, an enchanter
Boatswain

Neronis, daughter to the Queen of the strange
    Marshes
Thrasellus, King of Norway
Rumour
Corin, a shepherd
The Queen of Denmark
Providence
Page
Mustantius, brother to the King of the Strange
    Marshes
The Queen of the Strange Marshes
The King of Denmark

Mute: Heralds, Soldiers, Servants, Ladies, Knights

PLOT SUMMARY

The prologue introduces the main ideas of the play in very general terms. The action is opened by *Clamydes*, Prince of Swavia, who has landed in Denmark, where, in order to win the hand of *Juliana*, the king's daughter, he promises to slay a fierce dragon that has been consuming maidens. *Juliana* gives him a silver shield and tells him that if he wins her he will also become heir to her father's throne, as her only brother, *Clyomon*, has disappeared while on his travels. The scene then switches to Swavia, where *Clyomon*, carrying a golden shield, meets the Vice *Shift* (calling himself *Knowledge*) and engages him as a servant. *Shift* tells his new master that the king's son, *Clamydes*, is about to be knighted. *Clyomon*, using a trick, usurps *Clamydes*'s place in the ceremony and makes off accompanied by *Shift*, who is subsequently caught but professes not to know the name of his new master. *Clamydes* vows, however, to pursue the ursurper to avenge his honour and before he departs he is dubbed a knight by his father. There follows a brief episode in Macedonia, where *Alexander the Great* is returning from battle, which is followed by a confrontation between *Clamydes* and *Clyomon*, whom he has now tracked down. They agree to meet and fight before *Alexander*'s court in fifteen days, and *Clamydes* goes off to fight the dragon. He is warned by *Shift* of a dangerous enchanter in the Forest of Marvels, where the dragon lives, *Bryan Sans Foy*, himself also enamoured of *Juliana*. In return for a charm against enchantment, *Shift* then alerts *Bryan* to *Clamydes*'s coming. *Clamydes* manages to kill the dragon, but is put to sleep and imprisoned by *Bryan* with magic. For his part, *Clyomon* has, forced by adverse weather, landed in an unknown country, where he has met and fallen under the protection of *Neronis*, daughter of the *King of the Strange Marshes*, and begins to despair of meeting his commitment. *Clamydes*, after being freed by *Shift* with the help of a charm stolen from *Bryan*, makes his way to *Alexander*'s court, *Bryan* nonetheless retaining his shield and sword with the dragon's head. The scene then switches back to *Neronis*, by now in love with *Clyomon*, who, however, departs to meet *Clamydes*. There follows brief episode in which *Thrasellus*, King of Norway, is seen on his way to capture *Neronis*, with whom he is unrequitedly in love. When *Clyomon* arrives in Macedonia he learns that *Clamydes* has not turned up, but on then resolving to return to *Neronis*, he is informed by *Rumour* that she has been captured. When she next appears however, she is in a forest dressed as a man, soon becoming the servant of an old shepherd, *Corin*, *Clyomon* arrives and meets *Thrasellus*, kills him and then meets *Corin*, who helps him to nurse his wounds and to bury the dead king. *Clyomon* leaves his shield and sword on the grave to show who killed *Thrasellus*. There is a brief appearance by *Shift* to relate that *Neronis*'s father has died of grief at losing her and that his kingdom is now contentiously divided between his wife, who is pregnant, and his brother *Mustantius*. *Neronis* is then seen coming upon *Thrasellus*'s grave and seeing *Clyomon*'s shield, supposing that he is buried there. She is about to kill herself with grief when *Providence* intervenes to tell her the truth. *Clyomon*, disguised, meets *Neronis* while on his way to defending her mother and, neither recognizing the other, he engages her as a page. On his arrival he finds that *Clamydes* is his opponent *Mustantius*'s champion. Before they can fight, however, *Alexander* demands they reveal who they are and when *Clyomon* is disclosed as the King of Denmark's son, *Clamydes* embraces him as a friend. The conflict being at an end, they go off to Denmark, where *Clyomon* is reunited with his father. *Bryan Sans Foy* is still posing as *Clamydes*, but when challenged by the real one, he lacks the courage to fight, is exposed and imprisoned. The play ends with the uniting of the lovers, *Clyomon* with *Neronis* and *Clamydes* with *Juliana*, who prepare for a double wedding.

PLAY LENGTH

2,219 lines, excluding prologue of 18 lines

COMMENTARY

This play has strong similarities to *Common Conditions* (see following entry): the ambivalent role of the Vice, the convoluted and sometimes clumsily constructed plot, the use of a (poorly specified) trick, and the tendency to break the narrative with inserted episodes of different strands of narrative in order to signal the passage of time. These may, however, as easily be ascribed to the conventions of this sort of sentimental romance as to supposed common authorship.

Other plays with foreign (non-biblical, non-classical) settings: **5, 6, 7, 13, 32, 33, 47, 70, 74, 83, 88.**

SIGNIFICANT TOPICS AND NARRATIVE ELEMENTS

chivalry; magic; disguise and imposture; a disguised heroine; concealed royalty and nobility; a dragon-slaying; sorcery; a divided kingdom

DRAMATURGICAL AND RHETORICAL FEATURES

Verbal and general Vice's alias: *Shift–Knowledge* 327; rustic speech: *Corin* 1287 ff.; *Corin*'s neighbours all have English names; *Neronis* adopts the name *Cur Daceer* (Cœur D'Acier) 1639; the play is divided into scenes, but with no act division; stage directions in English

Costume and dress *Clyomon* and *Shift* are 'booted' (dressed in gear for travel) 105–6 (*sd*); *Alexander* is 'valiantly set forth' 358–9 (*sd*); *Bryan* wears *Clamydes*'s clothing 825–6 (*sd*); *Neronis* has 'man's apparel' 1254 (*sd*); *Shift* is in a courtly gown 1477 (*sd*)–1478; *Neronis* is dressed as a shepherd boy 1513 (*sd*), then as a page 1596 (*sd*); *Clyomon* (or his shield) is 'strangely disguised' 1623 (*sd*); *Shift* is clothed as a whiffler (ceremonial steward) 1676 (*sd*); *Clamydes* is clothed dressed 'like a champion' 1694–5 (*sd*); *Clyomon* is dressed for combat 1774 (*sd*); *Neronis* is decked up 'gallant and gay' 2140

Actions and stage directions 37 (*sd*): 'Enter *Jul.* with a white shield'; 104–5 (*sd*): 'Enter *Sir Cly.*, *Kn.* of the Golden Shield, son to the *K.* of *Den.*, with *S. Shi.*, the Vice, booted'; 118–20 (*sd*): 'Here let him (*Shi.*) slip on to the stage backwards, as though he had pulled his leg out of the mire, one boot off, and rise up to run in again'; 196 (*sd*): 'Enter *S. Shi.*, running'; 220–1 (*sd*): 'Enter the *K. of Swa.*, with the *Her.* before him, *Cla.*, three lords'; 261–3 (*sd*): 'Here let him (*Cla.*) kneel down, *Cly.* with *S. Shi.* watching in place, and as the *Ki.* doth go about to lay the mace of his head, let *Cly.* take the blow, and so pass away presently'; 273 (*sd*): '(lords) Pursue him (*Cly.*) and bring in *Shi.*'; 282 (*sd*): 'Enter *Shi.* brought in by the two lords, who pursued *Cly.*'; 358–9 (*sd*): 'Enter *K. Alex.*, as valiantly as set forth as may be, and as many soldiers as can'; 637 (*sd*): 'Enter *Cla.*, with the head upon his sword'; 661 (*sd*): 'Here let him (*Cla.*) sit down and rest himself'; 698 or 701 (*sd*): '(servants) Carry him (*Cla.*) out'; 718–20 (*sd*): 'Here let them make a noise as though they were mariners. And after *Cly.* *Kn.* of *G. S.* come in with one'; 739–40 (*sd*): 'Enter *Ner.* daughter to Patranius, *K.* of the Strange Marshes, two lords, two ladies'; 825–6 (*sd*): 'Enter *Bry. s. foy* having *Cla.* his apparel on, his shield, and the serpent's head'; 850 (*sd*): 'Enter *Shi.* with sword and target'; 914 (*sd*): '(*Shi., Cla.*) Enter out' (not departing stage); 940 (*sd*): 'Enter after a little fight within, *Cla.*, three knights'; 967 *sd*: '[Enter] *Shi.* with a bag as it were full of gold on his back'; 1163–4 (*sd*): 'Enter *Cly.* with a kn., signifying one of those that *Cla.* had delivered'; 1196 (*sd*): 'Enter *Rum.* running'; 1225 (*sd*): 'Enter *Cla.* and *Shi.*, with his bag of money still'; 1254 (*sd*): 'Enter *Ner.* in the forest, in man's apparel'; 1225 (*sd*): 'Enter *Cla.* and *Shi.*, with his bag of money still'; 1376 (*sd*): 'Here let them (*Cly., Thra.*) fight, the *Ki.* fall down dead'; 1391 (*sd*): 'Enter father *Cor.* the shepherd and his dog'; 1449 (*sd*): 'Enter *Cor.* with a hearse'; 1477 (*sd*): 'Enter *Shi.* very brave'; 1513 (*sd*): 'Enter *Ner.* like a shepherd's boy'; 1546 (*sd*): '(*Ner.*) Sing here'; 1549 (*sd*): 'Descend *Prov.*'; 1565 (*sd*): '(*Prov.*) Ascend'; 1596 (*sd*): 'Enter *Ner.* like the page'; 1623 (*sd*): 'Enter *Cly.* with his shield covered, strangely disguised'; 1650 (*sd*): 'Enter *Bry. s. foy* with the (serpent's) head'; 1676 (*sd*): 'Enter *Shi.* like a whiffler'; 1694–5 (*sd*): 'Enter *K. Alex.*, the *Qu., Must.*, two lords and *Cla.*, like a champion'; 1734 (*sd*): '(Trumpets) Sound here once'; 1737 (*sd*): '(Trumpets) Sound second time'; 1774 (*sd*): 'Enter *Cly.*, as to combat'; 1903 (*sd*): 'Enter *Bry. s. foy* with the head on his sword'; **Simple entry:** *Cla.* 1; *Cly.* 417; *Cla., Shi.* 438; *Bry* 548; *Shi.* 583; *Bry., Shi.* 662; *Bry.*, two servants 696; *Cly. Boa.* 725; *Ner.*, two lords, two ladies 786; *Ner.* 991; *Cly.* 1030; *Thras.,* two lords 1121; *Cor.* 1287; *Thras.*, two lords 1336; *Cly.* 1359, *Cly.* 1574; *K. of Den., Qu., Jul.*, two lords 1882; *Ner.* 1933; *Jul.* 2027; **Simple exit:** (*Jul.*) 91; (*Cla.*) 104; (*Shi.*) 165; (*Cly.*) 205; (*Shi.*) 219; (*Cly., Shi.*) 270; (*Ki.*, ret.) 337; (*Cla.*) 346b; (*Shi*) 357b; (*Alex.*, ret.) 416; (*Cly.*) 499; (*Cla.*) 530; (*Shi.*) 547b; (*Bry.*) 624, 681, 708; (*Shi.*) 717; (*Boa.*) 738; (*Ner.*, ret.) 759; (*Cly., Ner.*, ret.) 824; (*Bry.*) 849; (*Cla.*) 932b; (*Shi.*) 939b; (*Cla.*, knights) 960; (*Cla.*) 982b; (*Shi.*) 990; (*Ner.*) 1109b; (*Cly.*) 1120b; (*Thras.*, two lords) 1162; (*Kn.*) 1179; (*Rum.*) 1210b; (*Cly.*) 1224b; (*Cla.*) 1241; (*Shi.*) 1253; (*Ner., Cor.*) 1335; (lords) 1350b; (*Cor.*) 1442; (*Cly.*) 1476b; (*Shi.*) 1512; (*Ner.*) 1573b; (*Cly.*) 1595, 1644; (*Ner.*) 1649; (*Bry.*) 1675; (*Alex.*, ret.) 1857; (*Cly.*) 1869b; (*Ner.*) 1881b; (*Jul., Bry.*) 1924; (*Ner.*) 1950b; (lord) 2016b

Songs and music 1. *Neronis* 'How can that tree but withered be' 992–1001 (probably sung); 2. *Neronis* (w.n.s.) 1546 (*sd*); **Instrumental:** trumpets sound for the tournament 1734 (*sd*), 1737 (*sd*)

Staging and set The ascent and descent of *Providence* suggests the use of stage machinery that would indicate that the play was written or adapted for the professional theatre.

Stage properties *Clamydes's* silver shield 37 (*sd*); *Clyomon's* golden shield 189; the mace of knighthood 261–3 (*sd*); *Clamydes's* sword with the dragon's head impaled on it 637 (*sd*); *Shift's* sword and target 850 (*sd*); *Shift's* bag of gold 967 *sd*; *Corin's* dog 1391 (*sd*); the hearse (coffin) for *Thrasellus* 1449 (*sd*); *Neronis's* crook 1520

PLACENAMES

Denmark 9 *passim*; Macedonia 362 *passim*; Norway 1201 *passim*; Swabia (Swavia) 8 *passim*

ALLUSIONS

Apollo pr. 6, 134; Atropos 652; Bellona 366; Cerberus 62; Diana 1991; Hector 1588; Hercules 61, 1700; Hydra 99; Jove 1553, 1562, 1636, 1856; Lachis 1541; Mars 85, 364, 551; Martha 1992; Minotaur 100; Muses 1993; Neptune 755; Pallas Athene 365, 409; Queen of Sheba 1992; Somnus 1658; Susanna 1991; Venus 553–5, 559, 1990, Vesper 1656

BIBLIOGRAPHY

Ashley, 1968, pp. 25–9
Cartwright, 1999, pp. 156–64
Cope, 1961, pp. 501–19
Cope, 1984, pp. 36–49
Fischer, R. 'Zur Frage nach der Autorschaft von *Sir Clyomon and Sir Clamydes*'. *EngS* 14 (1890) pp. 344–65
Kellner, L. '*Sir Clyomon and Sir Clamydes*: Ein Romantisches Schauspiel des 16. Jahrhunderts'. *EngS* 13 (1889) pp. 187–229
Kittredge, G. L. 'Notes on Elizabethan Plays: *Sir Clyomon and Sir Clamydes*'. *JEGP* 2:1 (1898) pp. 8–9

13   Common Conditions

DATE, AUTHORSHIP AND AUSPICES

printed 1576 (*SR* 26 July 1576); anonymous; offered for acting; Greg 69

TEXT AND EDITIONS

Extant originals

1576 printing by William How: Eliz. Club; *STC* 5592
Later printing: Huntington (imp.); *STC* 5592a

Editions

1994   CHD (CD-Rom and online copy of Tucker Brooke, 1915, l.l., OS)
1915   Tucker Brooke (OS)*
1908   Farmer (10) (fragmentary text, l.l., NS)
1898   Brandl (OS)

SOURCES

The title page announces that the play is 'drawn out of the most famous historie of *Galiarbus*, Duke of *Arabia*' – clearly a lost romance.

CHARACTERS

The Prologue
Galiarbus, the old Duke of Arabia
Clarisia, his daughter (afterwards
  Metrea, a maid)
Sedmond, his son (afterwards 'Nomides,
  a knight that loves Metrea')
Common Conditions, the Vice
Shift ⎫
Drift ⎬ tinkers
Unthrift ⎭
Lamphedon, a knight that loves Clarisia
  and fights for her

Sabia, daughter of Mountagos
Master of the ship ⎫
Master's mate   ⎪
Boatswain   ⎬ pirates
Ship's boy   ⎭
Mountagos, a Spaniard
Cardolus, a knight that fights with Lamphedon
Lomia, a natural fool
Leostines, a knight that loves Metrea
Two lords

PLOT SUMMARY

The prologue is a conventional disclaimer of any writing skill on the part of the writer and an entreaty for audience patience. *Galiarbus* then enters, sorrowfully telling his children that he has been exiled from Arabia by the king. They express the desire to join him, but he insists they remain behind. On his departure, *Common Conditions* arrives to warn the children, *Sedmond* and *Clarisia*, that they too are in danger from the king. When they go off, he reveals to the audience his real identity as the Vice, his real name *Mediocrity*, and the fact that it was he who falsely accused *Galiarbus* of treachery, thus occasioning his exile. He further reveals that, since he was leaving the court for fear of being found out, he has only encouraged *Galiarbus*'s children to flee for the sake of having company. He quits the stage and three tinkers enter, *Shift*, *Drift* and *Unthrift*, singing about their trade; they then attempt to rob the party on their journey. *Common Conditions* manages, however, to trick them and they leave. He then takes *Clarisia* off to Phrygia, promising to find both *Galiarbus* and *Sedmond*, who has also disappeared. When they go off *Sedmond* enters briefly to bewail the loss of his sister and father, before the scene switches to Phrygia, where *Galiarbus* has been made a lord, though is still grieving at his separation from his children. Having arrived at their destination, *Common Conditions* encounters *Lamphedon*, the Duke of Phrygia's son, who has seen and fallen in love with *Clarisia* and, now calling himself *Affection*, offers to help *Lamphedon* in his love quest, since he is in fact aware that *Clarisia* reciprocates his feelings. The lovers meet, exchange love tokens and plight their troth. When they leave there is a brief episode in which *Sabia* comes in and declares her love to *Nomides*, a knight who is actually *Sedmond* in disguise and now arrived in Phrygia, but he rejects her suit. After this, *Common Conditions* enters once more to relate how *Lamphedon*'s mother, the duchess, has become jealous of *Clarisia* since the Vice put about that she had become more popular with the people than the duchess herself. The lovers then appear on their way to escaping the duchess's wrath, encouraged by *Common Conditions*, by going to stay with King Mountaynio of Thrace, *Clarisia*'s uncle. *Common Conditions* changes role again, becomes the leader of a pirate band, and organizes the robbery of *Lamphedon* and *Clarisia*. What follows is an episode in which *Doctor Mountagos* gets his daughter *Sabia* to reveal the name of the man she loves, after which he goes off to devise a love potion for her to use. *Lamphedon* then enters lamenting the fact that the pirates in their attack threw *Clarisia* overboard, and when they enter singing a song he attacks them physically. To save themselves they reveal to him that she is not dead but is being held by one *Cardolus*, on the isle of Marofus, at which he pardons them and goes off to rescue her. Meanwhile *Common Conditions* informs *Clarisia* that *Lamphedon* is still alive and promises to help her find him. She must, however, become a maidservant to a local knight, *Leostines*, taking the name *Metrea*. *Lamphedon* comes upon *Cardolus* and threatens him until he agrees not only to set his prisoners free but also to pay a yearly tribute of 500 crowns. They go off to find *Clarisia* and *Nomides* enters declaring his love for *Metrea*, despite her demeaned status as a servant, and unaware that she is his sister. He is joined by a fool, *Lomia*, with whom he exchanges banter until *Metrea* herself enters, only to reject his suit. The scene switches to *Lamphedon*, who, despairing of finding *Clarisia*, is preparing to kill himself but who is stopped from doing so by *Common Conditions*, who takes him at first for *Cardolus*. He tells the supposed *Cardolus* that *Lamphedon* is after *Clarisia* and when *Lamphedon* angrily reveals himself, *Common Conditions* claims he knew this all the time and has only come to lead him to his lover. They go off and *Leostines* enters with *Metrea*. He announces that he is adopting her as his daughter, and she declares that she intends never to marry but always to remain a virgin. *Leostines* leaves and *Common Conditions* brings in *Lamphedon*, reuniting the lovers. The fool, *Lomia*, reveals the meeting to *Leostines* and *Common Conditions* (under the new alias of *Gravity*) confirms this to save his own skin, elaborating that they also intended *Leostines*'s downfall. *Leostines* sentences the lovers to death by poisoning. *Lamphedon* drinks the poison but before *Clarisia/Metrea* can drink hers, *Leostines* calls out suddenly to her not to drink it. She however replies that he is too late if he means by this to win her as a wife. At this point the play ends, the epilogue apologizing for the fact that the writer has been unable to finish the play through lack of time, and offering a prayer for Queen Elizabeth and the realm.

PLAY LENGTH

1,904 lines, including prologue of 20 lines and epilogue of 16 lines

COMMENTARY

This is a rambling play, clumsily constructed in many ways and containing a surprising admission by the writer that he has been unable to complete the narrative in the time permitted for a play. However, there is some attempt at signalling the passage of time by making breaks in the narrative through the insertion of short episodes of different strands of narrative. The lack of a conclusion to the play, and the drift of the story, would suggest that the playwright had in mind a happy ending, despite the point at which he has left it. The Vice is an interesting hybrid of the native specimen and the scheming servant of classical comedy, and though he often plots evil, his actions are far from consistently malevolent. He also repeatedly draws attention to his own cowardice. At times, especially in the pirate episode, he appears to be used as a general-purpose character to animate the narrative.

Other plays with foreign (non-biblical, non-classical) settings: **5, 6, 7, 12, 32, 33, 47, 70, 74, 83, 88**.

SIGNIFICANT TOPICS AND NARRATIVE ELEMENTS

chivalry; exile; criminal tinkers; romantic love; a love potion; the nature of women; highway robbery and piracy; the wheel of fortune; poisoning

DRAMATURGICAL AND RHETORICAL FEATURES

Verbal and general *Common Conditions* echoes *Sedmond*'s speech 98–107; several passages of stichomythia, most notably 98–106, 549–61, 696–704, 1731–40; the Vice *Common Conditions* adopts several aliases: *Mediocrity* 165, *Affection* 589, *Gravity* 1790; disguised identities: *Sedmond–Nomides* 771, *Clarisia–Metrea* 1235; the Spanish-accented English of *Doctor Mountagos* 1049 ff.; stage directions in English **Actions and stage directions** 72 *sd*: 'Both (*Cla., Sed.*) speak (together)'; 98 *sd*: '(*Con.* speaks) Within'; 210 *sd*: 'Here enter three tinkers, *Sh., Dr.* and *Un.*, singing'; 294 *sd*: 'Here enter *Sed.* with *Cla.* and *Con.* out of the wood'; 407–23: *Con.* climbs a tree; 423 *sd*: '(*Con.*) hollows (howls) in the tree'; 449 *sd*: 'Here enters *Sed.* wailing'; 477 *sd*: 'Here enters *Gal.* out of Phrygia'; 509 *sd*: 'Here enters *Lam.* out of Phrygia'; 548 *sd*: 'Here enter *Con.* standing privily'; 643 *sd*: 'Here enter *Lam.* suddenly'; 672–81: *Cla.* and *Lam.* exchange love tokens; 693 *sd*: 'Here enter *Con.* suddenly'; 933 *sd*: 'Here enters *Con.* suddenly'; 982 *sd*: 'The mariners (call) within'; 994 *sd*: 'Here enter the pirates with a song'; 1100: 'Here enters *Lam.* lamenting'; 1124 *sd*: 'Here enter the mariners with a song'; 1171 *sd*: 'They (*Lam.* pirates) fig[ht]'; 1673 *sd*: 'Here enters *Lam.* embracing his lady'; 1697 *sd*: 'Here enters *Lo.* [searching] for her mistress and the Vice jostling her'; 1750 *sd*: 'Here enters *Leo.* with a lord or two more'; 1810 *sd*: 'Here enters *Leo.*, two lords, leading *Lam.*, and *Cla.*'; 1858 *sd*: 'Here enters *Con.* alone, with a covered goblet'; **Simple entry:** *Gal., Sed., Cla.* 20; *Con.* 116; *Cla.* 623; *Nom.* 759; *Sa.* 731; *Con.* 893; *Lam., Cla.* 909; *Mo., Sa.* 1048; *Cla., Con.* 1208; *Lam.* 1274; *Car.* 1292; *Nom.* 1350; *Lo.* 1378; *Met.* 1422; *Lam.* 1501; *Con.* 1523; *Leo., Met.* 1584; *Con.* 1654; **Simple exit:** (*Gal.*) 70; (*Sed., Cla.*) 155; (*Con.*) 210; 'All' (*Sh., Dr., Un.*) 294; (*Sh., Dr., Un.*) 427; (*Con., Cla.*) 449; (*Sed.*) 477; (*Lam.*) 609; (*Con.*) 623; (*Lam., Cla.*) 693; (*Lam.*) 722; (*Nom.*) 884; (*Sa.*) 893; (*Con.*, pirates) 1048;

(*Mas.*) 1194; (*Cla., Con.*) 1274; (*Met.*) 1490; (*Lo.*) 1493; (*Lam.*) 1576; (*Lam., Met.*) 1726; (*Leo., Lo.* lords) 1796; **Simultaneous speech:** *Sed., Cla.* 72; *Sh., Dr., Un.* 427; pirates 1001, 1030, 1036, 1039; lords 1796, 1828
Songs and music 1. Tinkers 'Come merrily forth' (w.s., w. ref.) 211–42; 2. Pirates (w.n.s.) 994 *sd*; 3. Mariners 'Lustily, lustily let us sail forth' (w.s., w. ref.) 1125–46; 4. *Lomia* 'Hey delading, delading' (a catch, two lines only) 1379–80
Staging and set the title page states 'Six may play this comedy'; the action is mostly localized by references in the dialogue rather than the set, though there may be a wood represented from which characters emerge (294 *sd*) and there is tree on stage which is climbed by *Conditions* (423 *sd*)
Stage properties the tinkers' kettles and tools 218, 264, 270; a tree 387; the tinkers' halter 401; *Conditions*'s knife 418; a gem given by *Lamphedon* to *Clarisia* 672; a gold bracelet given by *Clarisia* to *Lamphedon* 676; a goblet of poison 1858 *sd*

PLACENAMES

Arabia 23 *passim*; Banbury 267; Crete 57; Phrygia 441 *passim*; Thrace 904, 919, 920, 981, 1042

ALLUSIONS

Aetes of Colchis 817; Alecto 1097; Apelles 544; Apollo 1605; Boreas 761; Cerberus 1205; Cicero ('Tully') 13; Cressida 801; Cupid 526 *passim*; Daedalus 55; Diana 518, 1632; Dido and Aeneas 814; Diomedes 820; Flora 309, 325; the Furies 669, 1512; Helen of Troy 800; Hercules 1204; Homer 13; Icarus 57; Juno 1619; Limbo lake 1158, 1512; Lucina (alternative name for Juno) 464; Mars 1208, 1288; Medea and Jason 804, 816–17; King Minos 55; Momus 14, 16; Muses 1518; Neptune 1106, 1116; Ovid 12; Penelope 683; Phaedra, Theseus and Hippolytus 802–3; Pluto 657, 668; King Priam 146; Seneca 12; Sisyphus 1511; Tantalus 1510; Tellus 307, 326; Theseus and Ariadne 818–19; Troilus 1281; Troilus and Cressida 821–3; Ulysses 1283; Venus 519, 876; Zephyrus 1117

BIBLIOGRAPHY

Bevington, 1962, pp. 191–4
Cope, 1961, pp. 501–19
Cope, 1984, pp. 36–9
Southern, 1973, pp. 535–9
Thompson, R. A. 'The Irony of Chaucer's *Legends of Good Women* perceived in 1576', *Archiv* 213:2 (1976) pp. 342–3
Tucker Brooke, C. 'On the Source of *Common Conditions*', *MLN* 31:8 (1916) pp. 474–8

14   The Conflict of Conscience

DATE, AUTHORSHIP AND AUSPICES

1570–81; Nathaniel Woodes; offered for acting; Greg 78

TEXT AND EDITIONS

Extant originals

1581 printing by Richard Bradocke in two issues.
Issue 1: Bodleian; Pforzheimer; *STC* 25966
Issue 2: BL (two copies, both imp.); Bodleian (imp.); Chapin; Eliz. Club; Folger; Harvard (imp.); Huntington; *STC* 25966.5

Editions

1994	CHD (CD-Rom and online transcription of Bradocke printing, l.l., s.l., OS)
1969	Schell and Schuchter (NS)*
1952	Davis and Wilson (facsimile)
1913	Farmer (facsimile, n.l.)
1911	TFT (facsimile, n.l.)
1874–6	Dodsley vol. VI (n.l., NS)
1851	Collier (n.l., OS)

SOURCES

The source is the story of Francis Spera by Matteo Garibaldi, translated in 1550 by Edward Aglionby; see Wine's 1935 essay below. The story is also found in Sleidan, *Vingt-neuf Livres d'Histoire* (1563).

CHARACTERS

Prologue	Hypocrisy	Cardinal	Gisbertus	Theologus
Satan	Tyranny	Suggestion	Paphinitius	Nuntius
Mathetes	Avarice	Spirit	Horror	
Philologus	Caconus	Conscience	Eusebius	

PLOT SUMMARY

The prologue (to the first issue of the play) relates that it is based on the history of Francis Spera, his name being changed to Philologus in the 'comedy' (the prologue to the second issue omits reference to him). The first scene is a monologue by *Satan* trumpeting his deeds on earth, claiming the Pope as his son, and naming the Pope's two champions as *Avarice* and *Tyrannical Practice*. In the following scene,

Mathetes and *Philologus* discuss the Old and New Testaments in Protestant terms, and *Philologus* asserts that God often afflicts the elect to test and strengthen their faith. Another single character scene follows in which *Hypocrisy* delivers a sermon that quickly becomes an astrological discussion, and he boasts about his closeness to the Pope. *Tyranny* and *Avarice* are then seen quarrelling over who will take the lead in corrupting men, *Tyranny* being somewhat scornful of *Avarice*'s cowardice. When *Hypocrisy* arrives apparently preaching against the Pope, *Tyranny* threatens him but *Hypocrisy* explains that he was only trying to embolden him. They fail to recognize *Hypocrisy* until he reveals his identity, but then they all fall to squabbling over the right to be leader. At length they agree to co-operate and plot to promote the cause of the Catholic clergy in duping the laity. To do this they decide to change both their names and apparel. This is followed by a scene in which *Philologus* bewails the return of corrupt Catholic ways to the land, and reaffirms his religious allegiance. *Hypocrisy, Tyranny* and *Avarice* exult in their success and *Tyranny* is confident enough to throw off his alias, *Zeal*. They discuss the reinstatement of Catholic religious practice and are joined by a priest, *Caconus*, who gives a further account of this. They are next joined by a *Cardinal*, to whom *Tyranny* brings *Philologus* as a prisoner. When he is examined, *Philologus* learnedly refutes first the inheritance of papal authority from St Peter and then the doctrine of transubstantiation. The *Cardinal* now sends *Tyranny* off to procure an undendurable torture for *Philologus*, prior to his being sent to prison, and *Avarice* to seize his goods. *Philologus*'s resistance begins to crumble and he declares his desire to embrace the Catholic faith, but asserts that his conscience stands in the way. To overcome this, *Sensual Suggestion* is sent to persuade him and, after a debate and a promise from the *Cardinal* of worldly wealth, *Philologus* is finally converted. In the following scene *Spirit* and *Sensual Suggestion* contend to draw *Philologus* in the opposite directions respectively of spiritual rectitude and worldly indulgence, and a similar struggle then takes place between *Conscience* and *Sensual Suggestion*. In both cases *Sensual Suggestion* triumphs and *Philologus* then begins a period of material well-being. He rejoices in this and extends it to his two sons, until he is suddenly visited by *Horror*, who reminds him of the damnation to come, and to the consternation of his sons *Philologus* falls into despair. He is visited by two theologians, *Theologus* and *Eusebius*, who attempt to persuade him of the mercy of God, but *Philologus* regards himself as too wretched to repent. They eventually depart, placing him in the keeping of his sons, and in a final scene a messenger gives an account of *Philologus*'s last despairing days and his suicide by self-starvation. In the second issue of the play, however, the messenger relates the alternative ending of *Philologus*'s eventual reconversion after a period of despairing self-starvation.

PLAY LENGTH

2,090 lines, excluding a prologue of 70 lines

COMMENTARY

One of the most notable features of this play is that it exists in two slightly different versions, the second omitting direct reference to the subject of the source story, Francis Spera, and changing the ending to one of salvation through reconversion rather than a final damnation. This Protestant piece is probably the clearest treatment of apostasy in the interlude drama, and in articulating an anxiety about counter-Reformation it presents a picture of vigorous religious persuasion and co-ercion. It also includes the most powerful extant representation of religious despair before *Doctor Faustus*. This is, however, a relatively undramatic play with little of theatrical interest.

Other political comment and 'state of the realm' plays: **1** (frag.), **37, 38, 59, 71, 76**.

Other Protestant and anti-Catholic plays: **24, 44, 45, 49, 50, 53, 58, 66, 85, 86** (frag.), **90, 93**.

SIGNIFICANT TOPICS AND NARRATIVE ELEMENTS

astrology; conflict between Vices; Catholic tyranny; the re-establishment of the Catholic faith; the veneration of saints and Catholic idolatry; the apostolic succession; transubstantiation; apostasy; religious despair; the doctrine of election; a *psychomachia*; suicide by starvation

DRAMATURGICAL AND RHETORICAL FEATURES

Verbal and general *Hypocrisy*'s speech on astrology 274–336; *Hypocrisy* has several asides printed in the margin 346, 353, 362, 369, 374, 379, 785, 398, 408, 413, 417, 419, 463, 487, 596, 622, 632, 754, 758, 766, 777, 785; Vices' aliases: *Tyranny–Zeal* 676, *Avarice–Careful Provision* 684–5; Scottish accent: *Caconus* 824 ff.; *Caconus*'s list of healing saints 893–907; *Tyranny* brings in the prisoner (*Philologus*) through the audience 975–6; *Philogonus*'s rhetorical passages of apostrophe 1397–403, 1726–32; a *psychomachia* conflict for *Philogonus* 1460–662; *Philologus* utters the Lord's Prayer 1838–44; a six-act play with scene divisions; minimal stage directions, in English

Costume and dress *Tyranny* dons 'grave apparel' (as disguise) 672, 680; *Caconus* wears a 'gown, cap and tippet, made of a list (with a border)' 823

Actions and stage directions 336 *sd*: '(*Hyp.*) Step aside'; 337 *sd*: '(*Tyr.*) Push *Av.* backward'; 531 *sd*: '(*Hyp.*) Fights (with *Av.*)'; 752 *sd*: '(*Hyp.*) Step aside'; 2038–40: *Philol.* kneels with *Theo.* to pray; **Simple exit:** (*Av., Tyr., Hyp.*) 696; (*Philol.*) 731; *Tyr., Av., Cac.* 954; *Tyr.* 1137; *Av.* 1215; *Tyr.* 1450; *Card., Hyp.* 1452; *Philol., Sug.* 1655; *Cons.* 1662; *Hyp.* 1676; *Philol., Gis., Paph.* 2055; *Theo., Eus.* 2076

Songs and music 1. *Tyranny, Avarice, Hypocrisy* (w.n.s., and not clear whether a song is sung) 693; 2. *Hypocrisy* 'Hey, derry, derry' (a catch, w.s.) 956–9

Staging and set the title page has a doubling scheme: 'The Actors names divided into six parts, most convenient for such as be disposed, either to show this comedy in private houses, or otherwise': 1. *Prologue, Mathetes, Conscience, Paphinitius*; 2. *Hypocrisy, Theologus*; 3. *Satan, Tyranny, Spirit, Horror, Eusebius*; 4. *Cardinal, Caconus*; 5. *Avarice, Suggestion, Gisbertus, Nuntius*; 6. *Philologus*. the action is unlocalized and there are no indications as to set

Stage properties *Philologus*'s looking-glass 1493

PLACENAMES

Antioch 1579; Babylon 1016, 1021, 1024; Cologne 882, 954; Egypt 56, 76; Horeb 162, 1581; London 952; Rabbah 585; Rome 704, 1012, 1017, 1021, 1023, 1025

ALLUSIONS

Abraham 218, 1536; St Ambrose 918, 1019; St Anthony the swineherd[1] 907; St Appollonia[1] (? 'Appollyne') 902; Aristides the Just 1958; St Augustine 918,[1] 1019; Babel 50; Bar-Jesu 2003; Bathsheba 586; Cain 1746, 2002; Cain and Abel 154; Cancer[2] 277; St Carp(?)[1] 899; Cato 1957; St John Chrysostom 153; Circe 1504; St Cornelius[1] 896; Daniel 166; King David 583, 586, 1536, 1582, 1611, 1811, 1995, 1997; King David and Absolom 159–60; Domitian 178; Elijah 1581; Elijah the Tishbite and Jezebel 161–2; Eve 42; *Genesis* 157; St George[1] 900; St Germaine[1] 901; Ham 2002; Herod 170, 175; Isaac and Ishmael 156; Isaiah 166; St James 175, 1934, 1979; Jeremiah 165, 1019; Joab and David 583–7; Job 211, 901,[1] 1536; *John 7:9* 1121, *9:1–3* 219–23, *12:25* 1633–4; St John the Evangelist 179, 219, 1032; St Joseph 213; Judas 575, 1746, 2003; Julian the Apostate 2004; Jupiter (pl.)[2] 279, 284; St Katharine[1] 906; *Legenda Aurea* (Jacob de Voragine) 910; Libra[2] 281; St Louis (?'Loy')[1] 907; *Luke 23:43* 1795; Luna[2] 277, 287, 330; Mary Magdalene[1] 905; Mammon 1622; Mars (pl.)[2] 281, 313; *Matthew 4:7* (q.a.) 1365–6, *4:8–10* 77–83, *5:13* (q.a.) 1096–7, 1104, *10:28* 1332–3, *19:24* 1542–3; Mercury (pl.)[2] 280, 295, 331; Micah and Baal's priests 163–4; Moses 70; St Nicholas[1] 904; Nimrod 49; St Paul 199, 1211, 1341, 1567, 1574, 1579, 1590, 1910, 1953; St Paul and Nero 177; St Paul *Philippians 1:23* 1569–70; St Paul *Romans 8:18* 1342–7, *9:32* 1954–5; St Peter 1000, 1012–3, 1025, 1037, 1043, 1635, 1782, 1786, 1826, 1978; *I Peter* 1934; Phoebe[2] 287; Primasius 1019; *Psalm 117:8* (V)/*118:8* (AV) 1614–15; *Revelation* 1024, *12:3, 13:1, 17:3, 7* 932–3; St Ruke (? 'Rocco')[1] 898; Saturn (pl.) 275, 309; Saul 1582, 2002; Socrates 1957; Sol[2] 283, 323; Solomon 1539; Francis Spera pr. 30, pr. 36, pr. 41–2; Susanna 1202; St Sylvester[1] 893; Taurus 276; Venus (pl.)[2] 285, 330; Whore of Babylon 1024

1 Part of *Caconus*'s list of healing saints.
2 Part of *Hypocrisy*'s speech on astrology.

BIBLIOGRAPHY

Bryant, 1984, pp. 96–114
Campbell, L. B. 'Doctor Faustus: A Case of Conscience', *PMLA* 67:2 (1952) pp. 219–39
Hunter, 1976, pp. 20–38
Mackenzie, 1914, pp. 137–43
Oliver, L. 'John Foxe and *The Conflict of Conscience*', *RES* 25:97 (1949) pp. 1–9
Wilks, 1990, pp. 59–65
Wine, C. 'Nathaniel Wood's *Conflict of Conscience*', *PMLA* 50:3 (1935) pp. 661–78
Wine, 1939, pp. 458–63

15   The Contention between Liberality and Prodigality

DATE, AUTHORSHIP AND AUSPICES

1567–8; anonymous; the play in its present form is likely to have been performed at court by the Children of the Chapel Royal in 1601, but is probably a revision of a play called *Prodigality*, for which there is a warrant of payment in 1567–8; Greg 190

TEXT AND EDITIONS

Extant originals

1602 printing by Simon Stafford for George Vincent: BL; Harvard; Huntington; Westminster; *STC* 5593

Editions

1994   CHD (CD-Rom and online transcription of Stafford printing, l.l., s.l., OS)
1913   Farmer (facsimile, n.l.)
1913   Greg (1913b) (OS)*
1912   TFT (facsimile, n.l.)
1874–6   Dodsley, vol. VIII (n.l., NS)

CHARACTERS

The Prologue
Vanity, Fortune's chief servant
Prodigality, suitor for Money
Postilion, his servant
Host
Virtue
Equity

Dandaline, the Hostess
Tom Toss
Dick Dicer
Captain Weldon (1st suitor)
Courtier (2nd suitor)
Constables
Sheriff

Tenacity, suitor for Money	Lame Soldier (3rd suitor)
Ostler	Tipstaffs
Money, Fortune's son	Judge
Fortune	Clerks
Liberality, chief steward to Virtue	Crier

Mute: kings to draw Fortune's chariot, Virtue's attendants

PLOT SUMMARY

The *Prologue* comments on the varied tastes of audiences and begs the play's audience to forgive its faults. A feather-bedecked *Vanity* then announces the imminent arrival of his mistress, *Fortune*, an enemy to *Dame Virtue*. The action proper, however, starts with the arrival of *Prodigality* and *Postilion* at an inn late at night, where they persuade the host to give them lodging. After a brief intervening scene in which *Virtue* rails against man's enslavement to fortune, the scene switches back to the inn, where *Tenacity*, seeking *Fortune* and accompanied by *Vanity*, now arrives to take lodging. *Vanity* is next seen with *Money*, *Fortune*'s son, and *Fortune* herself soon after arrives to pursue her rivalry with *Virtue*. *Liberality*, *Virtue*'s steward, comes in to promote his mistress's cause, but quickly makes way for *Tenacity*, who asserts his desire for wealth and favour at *Fortune*'s hand. He, however, has a rival in *Prodigality*, to whom *Fortune* desires to commit her son, *Money*. *Vanity* consoles *Tenacity* by suggesting that his time may yet come, and he goes off. The inn's hostess, *Dandaline*, then talks of catering to *Prodigality*'s wishes, including providing women for him, while reprobate companions in the form of *Tom Toss* and *Dick Dicer* arrive looking for him. They exit and *Liberality* enters to rail against the instability of *Fortune*'s gifts. He is solicited for aid by an old soldier, *Captain Weldon*, and tells him that the queen has commanded that reward should be given for his services. A courtier then approaches *Liberality* asking for preferment at court, and is informed that this will depend on his own virtues. Finally *Money* seeks his help as he is being ill-treated by *Prodigality* and his roistering friends. *Money* next repeats his complaints to *Vanity*, and when *Tenacity* reappears, *Vanity* reassigns *Money* to him. This provokes general dismay among *Money*'s erstwhile companions, and *Prodigality* attempts to scale the walls of *Fortune*'s house. She reacts by placing a halter around his neck and when he falls off his ladder he is nearly hanged, but for the breaking of the rope. *Fortune* now triumphs in her power, but *Prodigality* soon attacks *Tenacity* and steals *Money*, who has become very fat through lack of employment. They are pursued by constables who raise a hue and cry, and find that *Tenacity* has in fact been murdered by *Prodigality*. *Virtue* enters, attended by *Equity* and others, and after preaching moderation she complains to the *Sheriff* about *Prodigality*. When *Money* is recovered, *Liberality* takes charge of him and *Captain Weldon* is rewarded, along with other worthy suitors. *Prodigality* is apprehended, brought to court and sentenced to death, though there is some promise of mercy when he expresses repentance. The short prologue, spoken by *Virtue*, is an expression of reverence to the queen.

PLAY LENGTH

1,322 lines, including epilogue but excluding prologue of 30 lines

COMMENTARY

This is a secular interlude concerned with the issue of the management of wealth, arguing for a middle path between frugality and excess. There are no strong moral oppositions, the enemy of *Virtue* being *Fortune* rather than vice, and *Prodigality* is an essentially secular character who indicates a capacity for reform.
Other social ills plays: **2, 38, 40, 52, 53, 71, 72** (frag.), **76, 94, 96, 98, 100.**

SIGNIFICANT TOPICS AND NARRATIVE ELEMENTS

audience taste in the theatre; the vicissitudes and blindness of Fortune; the management of wealth; military service and remuneration; preferment at court; innkeepers; the golden mean; justice and punishment

DRAMATURGICAL AND RHETORICAL FEATURES

Verbal and general a passage on diverse audience tastes in the theatre pr. 7–13; rustic speech: *Tenacity* 137 ff.; a hue and cry 1042 (*sd*); a five-act play with scene divisions; stage directions in English
Costume and dress *Vanity* is 'all in feathers' op. (*sd*); *Fortune* has 'vestures wrought with gold' 263; *Money* complains that his clothes 'be but thin' 770
Actions and stage directions op. (*sd*): 'Enter *Van*. solus, all in feathers'; 59–60 (*sd*): '(*Post.*) rip, rap, rip, rap (knocking on inn door)'; 65–6 (*sd*): '(*Prod.*) rip, rap, rap, rap, rip, rap, rap (knocking on inn door)'; 243–4 (*sd*): 'Enter *For*. in her chariot drawn with kings'; 615 (*sd*): 'Fly goldknops' (to signify money being thrown about while *Prod*. sings); 843–4 (*sd*): 'Here *Ten*. goes to the inn for his ass.'; 903–5 (*sd*): 'Here *Prod*. scales. *Fort*. claps a halter about his neck, he breaks the halter and falls'; 954 *sd*: '(*Fort.*) Come down'; 982–3 (*sd*): 'He (*Mon.*) falls down upon his elbow'; 1042 (*sd*): 'The constables make hue and cry'; 1245–6 (*sd*): 'The *Ju*. placed, and the clerks. under him'; 1314–15 (*sd*): '*Virt., Equ., Lib., Ju*. and all come down before the Queen, and after reverence made, *Virt*. speaks'; **Simple entry:** *Prod., Post., Host* 45; *Virt., Equ.* 107; *Ten., Van*. 136; *Mon., Van*. 212; *Lib*. 293; *Ten*. 323; *Van., Ten*. 341; *Prod., Van., Ten., Host., Fort., Mon*. 368–9; *Dand*. 509; *Toss., Dic., Dand*. 541–2; *Prod., Mon., Toss., Dic*. 585–6; *Lib*. 617; *Lib. Wel*. 641; *Lib., Cour*. 682; *Mon*. 724; *Van., Mon*. 748; *Ten., Van., Fort., Mon*. 789; *Prod., Dic., Van., Toss* 847–8; *Van., Fort*. 928; *Prod., Mon., Toss., Dic*. 973; *Virt. Equ.*, attendants. 1075–6; *Virt., Equ., Lib., Mon., Sher*. 1136–7; *Wel*. 1201; tipstaffs, *Lib., Equ., Sher.*, clerks., *Cry., Prod., Ju*. 1230–1; **Simple exit:** (*Prol.*) 43; (*Virt., Equ.*) 134; (*Van*). 192; (*Lib.*) 321; (*Ten.*) 482; (*Van.?*) 493; (*Prod., Fort., Mon.*) 507; *Dand*. 568; (*Prod., Mon., Toss., Dic.*) 615; *Wel*. 680; (*Cour.?, Lib.*)

722; (*Mon.*) 772; (*Mon.?*) 845; (*Van.*) 879; *Van.* 953; *Const.* 1073; (*Equ., Sher.*) 1178; (*Mon.*) 1200

Songs and music (w.s. to all songs) 1. *Money* 'As light as a fly' (w. ref.) 214–25; 2. the kings drawing *Fortune's* chariot 'Reverence, due reverence' (w. ref.) 246–56, 291, 971; 3. *Prodigality* and *Tenacity* 'The princely heart, that freely spends' (w. ref.) 437–56; 4. *Prodigality* 'Thou that dost guide the world' (verses addressed to *Fortune* and *Money* respectively) 494–506; 5. *Prodigality, Tom Toss, Dick Dicer* (two lines only, addressed to *Money*) 'Sweet money the minion' 612–13; 6. *Tenacity* the scales (one line only) 843; 7. *Equity* (and others?) 'If pleasure be the only thing' (w. ref.) 1114–34

Staging and set the action is initially set in an inn with an opening door (59–60) signalled in the dialogue, and a later stage direction (843–5) suggests that it is marked as a location on the stage; much of the later action is not clearly localized; *Fortune* appears to have a house (330) with an opening upper window (897) and a throne from which she can 'come down' (954 *sd*); the play requires a stage trick involving *Prodigality's* near hanging, but being saved by the breaking of the rope (903–5 *sd*); there is a courtroom scene with a formal ordering of the officials (1244–313), and the judge evidently enters through the audience (1244)

Stage properties *Fortune's* chariot 243 (*sd*); gold thrown about by *Prodigality* 615 (*sd*); a ladder and halter for *Prodigality's* attack on *Fortune* 904–5 (*sd*)

PLACENAMES

England 1263; Flanders 1223; France 1223, 1263; Highgate 1265; Ireland 1223, 1263; Middlesex 1250, 1265; St Pancras (parish) 1266

ALLUSIONS

Jeremiah 51:58 820

BIBLIOGRAPHY

Craik, 1962, pp. 110–18
Hillebrand, H. N. 'Sebastian Westcote: Dramatist and Master of the Children of Paul's', *JEGP* 14:4 (1915) pp. 568–84
Scattergood, J. '*The Contention between Liberality and Prodigality* – A Late Morality Play', *Acta* 13 (1987) pp. 153–67
Smith, J. 'The Authorship of *The Contention between Liberality and Prodigality*', *NQ* 34:2 (1987) pp. 188–9

16   The Conversion of St Paul

DATE, AUTHORSHIP AND AUSPICES

first quarter of the sixteenth century; anonymous; possibly a travelling play and also a town play of probable East Midlands origin

TEXT AND EDITIONS

Extant originals

Manuscript: Bodleian MS Digby 133, fos. 37–50

Editions

1994   CHD (CD-Rom and online copy of Baker, Murphy and Hall, 1982, l.l., OS)*
1993   Coldewey (OS)*
1982   Baker, Murphy and Hall (OS, includes cancelled passage in MS, separate
         line numbering)*
1976   Wickham (NS)*
1976   Baker, Murphy and Hall (facsimiles, n.l.)
1975   Bevington (OS)
1933   Ayliff (n.l., NS)
1926   Tickner (n.l., NS)
1924   Adams (OS)
1897   Manly, vol. 1 (OS)
1896   Furnivall (OS)
1835   Sharp (OS)

SOURCES

Sources include the *Acts of the Apostles* (*9:1–27*) and the offices for the feast of the conversion of St Paul and the feast in commemoration of St Paul the Apostle; see the introduction to the edition by Baker, Murphy and Hall, pp. xxii–iv.

CHARACTERS

Poet (Prologue)	Annas	Servant	Ananias	Angel
Saul/Paul	1st Knight	Ostler	Belial	
Caiaphas	2nd Knight	God	Mercury	

PLOT SUMMARY

The prologue, spoken by the *Poet*, is a prayer followed by a brief introduction to the biblical story of the conversion of St Paul. *Saul* then enters as a knight and he is invested by the priests *Caiaphas* and *Annas* with the authority to pursue heretics. He collects his knights and, after a comic sequence involving an *Ostler*, a horse is brought to him. He rides off to Damascus and the *Poet* ('if he wishes') completes the action of the first station. *Saul* is then seen on the road to Damascus vowing violence towards Christians when he is struck off his horse by a sudden storm and falls blinded by lightning. He is led by his knights to the house of *Ananias* in Damascus. *Ananias* is at first afraid of the tyrant, but on *God*'s instructions he approaches him and later cures *Saul* of his blindness with the help of the Holy Spirit. *Saul* is instantly converted and the *Poet* concludes the next section. The third sequence opens with *Saul*'s knight telling *Caiaphas* and *Annas* of the conversion of their master, but they express scepticism about it and reiterate their determination to uphold Old Testament law. What follows is a sequence with devils who relate how they inspire *Caiaphas* and *Annas* and they lament the loss of *Saul* before disappearing with a flash of fire (this sequence is contained on three interpolated leaves in a different hand). In the final 'station' *Paul*, as he now is, appears as a disciple and proceeds to deliver a sermon to the audience. He is spied in this by a servant of *Caiaphas* and *Annas*, who carries the news back to them, upon which they give orders for *Paul* to be put to death. He is, however, warned of this by an angel and resolves to escape with the help of the disciples. The *Poet* concludes the play with an account of *Paul*'s escape and an apology for his own and the players' lack of sophistication.

PLAY LENGTH

662 lines

COMMENTARY

This is one of the few extant saint plays in England and characteristically gives an important place to staged miracle, which is done with technical sophistication. The play appears in the same manuscript (Digby) as another important saint play, *Mary Magdalen*. The action includes a comic sequence, a feature commonly found in plays of the period. The devil scene involving *Belial* and *Mercury* was interpolated in a different hand in the mid-sixteenth century.

Other biblical plays: **10, 11, 34, 42, 44, 48, 63, 77, 90, 93**.
Other conversion plays: **51, 63, 66, 83**.

SIGNIFICANT TOPICS AND NARRATIVE ELEMENTS

a spying servant; miracles and conversion; tyranny and the administration of justice; Mosaic law versus Christianity

DRAMATURGICAL AND RHETORICAL FEATURES

Verbal and general the prologue spoken by the author, who also acts as an explicator throughout; *Saul* introduces himself with a threatening 'boasting' speech 14–42; some comic stage business between the ostler and the servant 85–119; the poet is given a speech concluding the first station 'if he pleases' 154 *sd*; *Paul*'s sermon is addressed to the audience 502–71; the directions for dancing are inserted in a later hand; stage directions mostly in English with a few in Latin (Latin ones marked) **Costume and dress** *Saul* is dressed 'in best wise, like an adventurous knight' 14 *sd*; the *Ostler* wears a hood lined with silk and camlet 113–14; *Paul* appears in a 'disciple's weed' 501 *sd*

Actions and stage directions 13 *sd*: 'Dance' (performers not specified); 13 *sd* (2): 'Here enters *Sa.*, goodly beseen in the best wise, like an adventurous knight, thus saying'; 35 *sd*: 'Here comes *Sa.* to *Cai.* and *Ann.*, priests of the temple'; 56 *sd*: 'Here *Sa.* receives their (*Cai.*, *Ann.*) letters'; 84 *sd*: 'Here goes *Sa.* forth a little aside for to make him[self] ready to ride, the ser. thus saying'; 119 *sd*: 'Here comes the *First Kn.* to the stablegroom, saying'; 126 *sd*: 'Here the *Kn.* comes to *Sa.* with a horse'; 140 *sd*: 'Here *Sa.* rides forth with his servants about the place, out of the pl[ace]'; 154 *sd*: 'The *Poet*, if he pleases (to speak as follows)' (L); 154 *sd* (2): 'Dance' (performers not specified); 154 *sd* (3): 'Conclusion'; 161 *sd*: 'The end of that station and the second follows' (L); 168 *sd*: 'Here comes *Sa.*, riding in with his servants'; 182 *sd*: 'Here comes a fervent, with a great tempest, and *Sa.* falls down off his horse; that done, *Godh.* speaks in heaven'; 210 *sd*: 'Here the knights lead forth *Sa.* into a place and *Chr.* appears to *Anan.*, saying'; 244 *sd*: 'And *God* should go out' (L); 247 *sd*: 'Here *Anan.* goes towards *Sa.*'; 261 *sd*: 'Here *Sa.* is in contemplation'; 268 *sd*: 'Here comes *Anan.* to *Sa.*, saying'; 291 *sd*: 'Here will appear the Holy Spirit above him (*Pa.*)' (L); 345 *sd*: 'Dance' (performers not specified); 345 *sd* (2): 'Conclusion' (L); 359 *sd*: 'The end of that second station, and the third follows'(L); 411 *sd*: 'Here to enter a devil with thunder and fire, and to advance himself, saying as follows, and his speech spoken, to sit down in a chair'; 432 *sd*: 'Here shall enter another devil called *Mer.*, with a firing, coming in haste, crying and roaring, and shall say as follows'; 470 *sd*: 'Here they shall roar and cry, and then *Bel.* shall say'; 501 *sd*: 'Here they shall vanish away with a fiery flame, and a tempest'; 501 *sd* (2): 'Here appears *Sa.* in his disciple's weed, saying'; 599 *sd*: 'He (*Pa.*) withdraws for a short while' (L); 648 *sd*: 'Conclusion' (L)

   sd opening cancelled passage: 'Here appears *Sa.* in a disciple's weed, saying'

Songs and music music likely for the dances, but not specified

Staging and set this is a play for outdoor production: there are three 'stations', possibly pageant wagons or fixed scaffolds with the possibility that the audience moved between them, and a *platea*; there is likely to have been a raised level for heaven (182 *sd*); live horses were possibly used; the play makes considerable use of pyrotechnic effects (182 *sd*, 411 *sd*, 432 *sd*, 501 *sd*, the first of these being an effect integral to the narrative); the action is localized in Jerusalem, Damascus and the route between them, with *Caiphas* and *Annas* being specified as being in a temple (366 *sd*); a comment 'si placet' before the *Poet*'s first speech may suggest optional and varying modes of production; there has been some critical debate about the play's staging (see bibliography below)

Stage properties letters 56 *sd*; a horse 126 *sd*; the Holy Spirit (probably a dove) 291 *sd*; fireworks 411 *sd*, 432 *sd*, 501 *sd*; a chair for *Belial* 411 *sd*

PLACENAMES

Damascus 32 *passim*; Israel 263; Jerusalem 34 *passim*; Libya 32, 421

ALLUSIONS

Acts 9:25 652; *Ecclesiastes 10:13* (q.a.) 514; *Ephesians 5:5* 556; *Luke 14:11* 520; *Matthew 11:29* 542–3, *12:34* 560; *Romans 11:20* 528

CONCORDANCE

Preston, 1977

REPORTS ON MODERN PRODUCTION

Winchester Cathedral (King Alfred's College, Drama Department, dir. J. Marshall) 27–9 May 1982 [*METh* 4:1 (1982) pp. 71–2; *RORD* 25 (1982) pp. 145–6]

BIBLIOGRAPHY

Baker and Murphy, 1967, pp. 153–66
Davidson, C. 'The Middle English Saint Play and its Iconography' in Davidson, 1986, pp. 98–105
Del Villar, M. 'The Staging of *The Conversion of St Paul*', *TN* 25:2 (1970–1) pp. 64–8
Del Villar, M. 'The Medieval Theatre in the Streets: A Rejoinder', *TS* 14:2 (1973) pp. 76–81
Jeffrey, 1973, pp. 68–89
Marshall, 1994, pp. 111–48
Pentzell, R. J. 'The Medieval Theatre in the Street', *TS* 14:1 (1973) pp. 1–21
Pentzell, R. J. 'A Reply to Mary del Villar', *TS* 14:2 (1973) pp. 82–90
Scherb, V. I. 'Frame Structure in *The Conversion of St Paul*', *CD* 26:2 (1992) pp. 124–39
Scherb, 2001, pp. 94–105
Schmidt, 1884
Velz, 1981–2, pp. 311–26
Wickham, 1972, pp. 99–119

17   Courage, Kindness, Cleanness (fragment)

DATE, AUTHORSHIP AND AUSPICES

1531–47; anonymous; possibly Paul's boys

TEXT AND EDITIONS

Extant originals

Manuscript: British Library Add. MS 15233

Editions

1951   Brown, Wilson, Greg and Sisson (attached to *Play of Wit and Science*, **101**; OS)*

SOURCES

No sources have been identified.

CHARACTERS

Courage Kindness Cleanness Concupiscence (mute)

PLOT SUMMARY

Courage rallies his friends *Kindness* and *Cleanness*, but *Concupiscence* steals away, *Cleanness* explaining that where s/he is present, *Concupiscence* disappears.

PLAY LENGTH

14 fragments of lines extant

SIGNIFICANT TOPICS AND NARRATIVE ELEMENTS

'remedia': the countering of vice by the opposite quality of virtue

DRAMATURGICAL AND RHETORICAL FEATURES

Actions and stage directions 2 (*sd*): '*Kind.* comes in / a woman'; 8–10 (*sd*): '*Clea.* comes in and *Con.* stealeth away'
Staging and set no indications as to set

18   The Cruel Debtor (fragments)

DATE, AUTHORSHIP AND AUSPICES

1560–5 (*SR* 1565/6 *c.* Mar.); 'Wager' (Lewis or William?); auspices unknown; Greg 43

TEXT AND EDITIONS

Extant originals

1566 printing by Thomas Colwell: BL (fragment, three leaves); *STC* 24934

Editions

1911 and 1923   Greg (OS)*

SOURCES

The parable of the debtors in *Matthew 18:22–35* is a likely point of reference.

CHARACTERS

Flattery   Rigour   Simulation   Ophiletis   King Basileus   Proniticus

PLOT SUMMARY

Flattery opens the fragment by remarking that, though he is popular among courtiers, he has not found it possible to gain entry to *Basileus*'s court. His companion *Rigour* asks him about their friend *Simulation*, who skilfully combines a face of piety with covert cruelty. Because of *Simulation*'s skill at deception, *Rigour* thinks it would be a good idea to attempt to deceive him, and they agree to pretend to fight when he arrives, which they then proceed to do. When *Simulation* tries to stop them they turn on him and beat him, but he discovers the trick and swears vengeance, not being content with just their penitence. They then spy a gentleman coming, and pretend to be men of quality themselves, in order to find out his business. He is *Ophiletis*, who complains that he faces ruin because he has spent freely money borrowed from *King Basileus* and is now unable to repay his debt. The *King* is then seen talking to his bookkeeper, *Proniticus*, about debts repaid and the unpaid debt of *Ophiletis*. *Ophiletis* is summoned and *Basileus* is beginning to reprimand him when the fragment ends. The smaller fragment represents *Simulation*'s effort to stop the fight between *Rigour* and *Flattery*, and their turning on him.

PLAY LENGTH

two leaves amounting to 199 lines and a further fragment of 66 lines extant

COMMENTARY

The smaller fragment of the play was discovered separately and does not connect sequentially with the main fragment, which is in three sections separated by breaks. The narrative sequences involving *Flattery* and *Rigour* (in both fragments 1 and 2) bear little relation to the *Ophiletis* story, although possibly the general idea of forgiveness unites them. *Basileus* is presented positively and it is clear that the play involves a reworking of the biblical parable of the debtors.

SIGNIFICANT TOPICS AND NARRATIVE ELEMENTS

flattery and court life; conflict between Vices; deceit and trickery; debt and forgiveness

DRAMATURGICAL AND RHETORICAL FEATURES

(The initial numbers in the line references below refer to the printings of the fragments in the *MSC* volumes, rather than denoting any distinction between the fragments.)

Actions and stage directions 1.64 (*sd*): 'Here enter *Sim.*'; 1.75 (*sd*): 'Here enters *Oph.*'; 1.112 (*sd*): '(*Fla.*; *Rig.*?) Speak among yourselves a good way off'; 2.16 (*sd*): '(*Rig.*, *Fla.*) beat *Sim.*'; 2.27 (*sd*): 'Here *Fla.* must hold *Rig.*'

Staging and set there are no indications as to set, and the action is unlocalized

PLACENAMES

The Clink (prison) 1:130; London 1.131

ALLUSIONS

Alexander the Great 1.45; *John* 1:1 65; Seneca (q.n.t.) 1.133; Seneca *Hercules Furens 326–7* (q.a.) 1.67; Seneca *Phaedra 982* 1.11; Virgil 2.36; Virgil, *Aeneid 2.316–17* 2.35

BIBLIOGRAPHY

Blackburn, 1971, pp. 128–31

Furnivall, F. J. 'Three Leaves of the Interlude of *The Cruell Debtter* by W. Wager, 1566', *New Shakspere Society's Transactions* 5:1, appendix 1 (1877–9) pp. 2–10

19   Damon and Pithias

DATE, AUTHORSHIP AND AUSPICES

1564–8 (*SR* 1567 *c.* 22 July); Richard Edwards, Master of the Chapel; Merton College, Oxford; Greg 58

TEXT AND EDITIONS

Extant originals

1571 printing by William Williamson for Richard Jones: BL; Folger; Huntington; *STC* 7514

1582 printing by Richard Jones: BL; *STC* 7515

Editions

1994	CHD (CD-Rom and online transcription of Williamson printing, l.l., OS)
1980	White (OS)*
1957	Brown and Wilson (facsimile)
1924	Adams (OS)*
1914	Farmer (1914a) (facsimile, n.l.)
1908	TFT (facsimile, n.l.)
1906	Farmer (6) (n.l., NS)
1874–6	Dodsley, vol. IV (n.l., NS)

SOURCES

Sources are likely to include Plutarch's *Life of Dion*, Diogenes Laertes's *Lives of the Philosophers*, and possibly Thomas Elyot's *The Governour* (Book 2, ch. 11); see also Newlin's and Armstrong's essays below.

CHARACTERS

Aristippus, a Pleasant Gentleman	Jack, Carisophus's Lackey
Carisophus, a Parasite	Dionisius, the King
Damon, a Gentleman of Greece	Eubulus, the King's Counsellor
Pithias, a Gentleman of Greece	Gronno, the Hangman
Stephano, Servant to Damon and Pithias	Snap, the Porter
Will, Aristippus's Lackey	Grimme, the Collier

Nine Muses sing but do not speak

PLOT SUMMARY

The play is set in ancient Syracuse, which is ruled over by a bloodthirsty tyrant, *Dionisius*. It opens with a court philosopher, *Aristippus*, and a corrupt courtier, *Carisophus*, debating their views about philosophy and court life, and eventually swearing a friendship that turns out a little later to be fraught with suspicion and deceit. This forms the backdrop for the entry of *Damon* and *Pithias*, young Greeks visiting the city. They are devoted friends and share a servant, *Stephano*, who testifies to their closeness by his contentedness at working for two masters. He warns his masters that *Dionisius*, the king of Syracuse, is a cruel tyrant who only that morning has condemned a man to death for having a dream in which he killed the king. *Carisophus* meets *Damon* and, after failing to trick him into uttering treachery, for the sake of a reward nevertheless accuses him of being a spy and has him arrested. *Stephano* reports to a dismayed *Pithias* that *Damon* has been sentenced to death and *Pithias* pleads with *Aristippus* to intercede on his behalf. *Aristippus* is sympathetic but feels there is little hope except that the king's counsellor, *Eubulus*, might help. *Damon* is brought before the king, and when *Eubulus*'s plea for mercy fails, he asks for leave to go home to sort out his affairs, which is only granted when *Pithias* agrees to stand as a pledge. After a fond farewell from his friend, *Damon* departs and the interval is filled with two comic episodes. In the first, *Stephano* encounters and beats up the cowardly *Carisophus*, giving his own name in reverse to avoid detection. In the other, the servants of *Carisophus* and *Aristippus* at first quarrel and then co-operate to trick a collier, *Grimme*, by robbing him while making him drunk and giving him a shave. *Carisophus* then appears complaining to *Aristippus* that he has lost favour at court, having been accused by *Eubulus* of being a flatterer. They fall to arguing about the nature of friendship, and part on bad terms. On the day appointed for the execution *Damon* has not returned and, to the sorrow of *Eubulus*, preparations are made to execute *Pithias*, who declares himself happy to die for his friend. Just before the blow is dealt *Damon* turns up, having been held up, and the two friends argue for the right to die for each other. Overcome by this show of love, the king pardons *Damon* and reforms his own tyrannical ways, ending his rule of fear and resolving instead to command the love of his subjects. He invites the two friends to stay and share his wealth and his realm. *Carisophus* is driven from the court by the virtuous counsellor, *Eubulus*, who then goes on to deliver the concluding speech of the play.

PLAY LENGTH

1,774 lines

COMMENTARY

This is one of the most important expressions of the humanist attitude to friendship in sixteenth-century drama, and draws on a story which is referred to elsewhere in humanist literature. It also has implications for the developing contemporary definitions of social class and appropriate behaviour. *Grimme* at one point (1205–22) acts as a plebeian mouthpiece for satire on court life and folly, and the play is also concerned with courtier ethics.

Other plays with classical settings: **29, 39, 43, 57** (frag.), **91, 92**.

SIGNIFICANT TOPICS AND NARRATIVE ELEMENTS

philosophy and court life; court sycophancy; true and false friendship; manners and social identity; education; kingship and tyranny; a voluntary hostage; melancholy; drunkenness; hangman's booty

PRINCIPAL POINTS OF DRAMATURGICAL INTEREST

Verbal and general *Stephano* disguises his name by reversing it (*Onaphets*) 969; a comic subplot sequence involving the gulling of *Grimme* is used largely to denote the passage of time 1049–374 (the figures in which are clearly English despite the play's classical setting); rustic speech: *Grimme* the Collier 1093 ff.; *Grimme* speaks French learned as a soldier 1167; *Snap* probably ushers *Pithias* in as a prisoner through the audience 1539; *Eubulus* acts as choric commentator at the end delivering a form of epilogue 1735–60; the servants are used extensively as agents and spies; stage directions in English

Costume and dress *Damon* and *Pithias* are dressed 'like mariners' 138 *sd*; *Damon* is in 'mariner's apparel' 885 *sd*; new garments for *Damon* and *Pithias* 1711 *sd*

Actions and stage directions 138 *sd*: 'Here enter *Da.* and *Pi.* like mariners'; 587 *sd*: 'Here *Pi.* sings and regals play'; 619 *sd*: 'He (*Pi.*) speaks this after the song'; 786 *sd*: 'Here *Gro.* brings in *Da.*, and *Pi.* meets him by the way'; 885 *sd*: 'Here the regals play a mourning song, and *Da.* comes in in mariner's apparel, and *Ste.* with him'; 922–4: *Stephano* beats *Carisophus*; 1092 *sd*: 'Here enters *Gri.* the Collier whistling'; 1156 *sd*: 'Enter *Ja.* with a pot of wine and a cup to drink on'; 1268 *sd*: 'Here *Wi.* fetches a barber's basin, a pot with water, a razor and clothes and a pair of spectacles'; 1272–350: *Ja.* and *Wi.* shave *Gri*; 1275: *Ja.* steals *Gri.*'s money pouch; 1316 *sd*: '*Gri.* sings bass'; 1318 *sd*: '*Ja.* sings'; 1319 *sd*: '*Wi.* sings'; 1473 *sd*: 'Then the Muses sing'; 1582 *sd*: 'Here enters *Da.* running and stays the sword'; 1711 *sd*: 'Here enters *Eub.* with new garments'; 1724 *sd*: 'Here enters *Eub.* beating *Car.*'; **Simple entry:** *Ari.* op. *sd*; *Car.* 30; *Ste.* 150; *Car.* 158; *Wi.*, *Ja.* 179; *Ste.* 210; *Ari.*, *Wi.* 258; *Da.*, *Pi.*, *Ste.* 277; *Car.* 367; *Da.*, *Ste.* 379; *Car.*, *Sn.* 458; *Ari.* 465; *Car.* 494; *Pi.*, *Ste.* 559; *Ste.* 625; *Ari.* 645; *Dio.*, *Eub.*, *Gro.* 711; *Ari.* 1007; *Ja.*, *Wi.* 1048; *Sn.* 1082; *Gri.* 1354; *Sn.* 1358; *Car.*, *Ari.* 1374; *Dio.*, *Eub.* 1528; *Sn.* 1538; **Simple exit:** (*Pr.*) pr. 46; (*Car.*) 97; (*Ari.*) 138; (*Da.*, *Pi.*, *Ste.*) 158; (*Car.*) 179; (*Wi.*, *Ja.*) 210; (*Ste.*) 258; (*Ari.*, *Wi.*) 277; (*Da.*, *Pi.*, *Ste.*) 367; (*Car.*) 453; 'All' (*Da.*, *Car.*, *Sn.*) 465; (*Ari.*) 536; (*Ste.*) 644; (*Dio.*, *Eub.*) 858; (*Gro.*, *Pi.*) 885; (*Ste.*) 979; (*Car.*, *Ja.*) 1007; (*Ari.*) 1048; (*Sn.*) 1084; (*Ja.*) 1353; (*Gri.*, *Sn.*) 1374; (*Ari.*) 1441; (*Car.*) 1453; (*Gro.*) 1711; *Dio.*, *Da.*, *Pi.* 1716; (*Ste.*) 1724; (*Eub.*) 1734

Songs and music (w.s. to all songs) 1. *Pithias* 'Awake ye woeful wights' 588–619; 2. *Jack, Will* 'Too nidden' (three lines only) 1317–19; 3. *Jack, Will, Grimme* 'Such barbers God send you at all times of need' ('The song at the shaving of the Collier' w. ref., *Grimme* singing bass) 1325–49; 4. Muses, *Eubulus* 'Alas, what hap hast thou, poor Pithias, now to die' (Muses sing the refrain) 1474–5, 1480–1500; 5. Whole cast 'The strongest guard that king can have' 1761–74; **Instrumental:** regals 587 *sd*, 885 *sd*; a trumpet blows (off stage) 708

Staging and set apart from generally being set in the city of Syracuse, and partly in the royal court, much of the action is not clearly localized; there is little indication as to set; the extensive shaving scene with *Grimme*, and the climactic near-execution scene require only portable stage properties

Stage properties a chest 907; a pot of wine and cup 1156 *sd*; a barber's basin, pot of water, razor, clothes and pair of spectacles 1268 *sd*; a barber's chair 1270; a money pouch 1275; 'ointment' 1287–8; a sword 1511; *Pithias*'s old garments 1579

PLACENAMES

Athens 758; Croydon 1285; Greece 140, *passim*; London 1333; Palermo 1298; Sicily 245 *passim*; Sparta ('Lacedamon') 758; Syracuse prologue 35 *passim*; York 1333

ALLUSIONS

Diogenes 24; Furies 608; Horace pr. 24; Horace *Ars Poetica 11.141–2* 440–1; Horace *Epistles 1.2.27* 774, *1.10.24* 405, *1.17.23* (q.a.) 1027; Jupiter 566; Neptune 139, 146; Ovid *Heroides xvi[xvii].166* 432; *Psalm 7:16* (V)/*7:15* (AV) (q.a.) 1451; Pythagoras 231, 348

REPORTS ON MODERN PRODUCTION

Shakespeare's Globe, London, 7 September 1996 [*MeTh* 18 (1996), pp. 161–3, *Around the Globe* (Shakespeare's Globe Centre magazine), winter 1996, p. 8]

BIBLIOGRAPHY

Armstrong, W. 'The Sources of *Damon and Pithias*', *N&Q* n.s. 3 (1956) pp. 146–7

Armstrong, W. '*Damon and Pithias* and Renaissance Theories of Tragedy', *ES* 39 (1958) pp. 200–7

Cartwright, 1999, pp. 121–34

Cope, 1961, pp. 501–19

Cope, 1984, pp. 44–9

Durand, W. Y. 'Notes on Richard Edwards', *JEGP* 4:3 (1902) pp. 348–69

Durand, W. Y. 'A "Local Hit" in Edwards's *Damon and Pithias*', *MLN* 22:8 (1907) pp. 237–8

Grantley, 2000, pp. 62–5

Greene, 1974, pp. 357–65

Guinle, F. 'Concerning a Source of Richard Edwards' *Damon and Pithias*', *CE* 30 (1986) pp. 71–2

Hartley, A. J. 'The Color of "Honesty": Ethics and Courtly Pragmatism in *Damon and Pithias*', *MRDE* 11 (1999) pp. 88–113

Holaday, A. 'Shakespeare, Richard Edwards, and the Virtues Reconciled', *JEGP* 66:2 (1967), pp. 200–6

Jackson, J. L. 'Three Notes on Richard Edwards' *Damon and Pithias*', *PQ* 29:2 (1950) pp. 209–13

Kramer, J. E. '*Damon and Pithias*: An Apology for Art', *ELH* 35 (1968) pp. 475–90

Long, J. H. 'Music for a Song in "Damon and Pithias"', *M&L* 48 (1967) pp. 247–50

Mills, L. J. 'Some aspects of Richard Edwards's *Damon and Pithias*', *Indiana University Studies* 14/75 (1927) pp. 3–11

Mills, 1937, pp. 134–46

Newlin, C. M. 'Some sources of Richard Edwards's *Damon and Pithias*', *MLN* 47:3 (1932) pp. 145–7

Raschen, J. F. 'Earlier and Latin Versions of the Friendship Theme: I. "Damon and Pithias"', *MP* 17:2 (1919) pp. 105–9

Waldo, T. R. 'Music and Musical Terms in Richard Edwards's *Damon and Pithias*', *M&L* 49 (1968) pp. 29–35

20   D, G, T (fragment)

DATE, AUTHORSHIP AND AUSPICES

1531–47; anonymous; possibly Paul's boys

TEXT AND EDITIONS

Extant originals

Manuscript: British Library Add. MS 15233

Editions

1951   Brown, Wilson, Greg and Sisson (attached to *Play of Wit and Science*, **101**; OS)*

SOURCES

These have not been identified.

CHARACTERS

'D' 'G' 'T' (Tom)

PLOT SUMMARY

T (*Tom*) expresses his grievance at the apparent mockery of him by his two companions, *D* and *G*. They persuade him to put an end to their quarrel, however, and all go off singing a song.

PLAY LENGTH

13 lines extant

COMMENTARY

The only feature of any note in this tiny fragment is the song which ends the sequence.

SIGNIFICANT TOPICS AND NARRATIVE ELEMENTS

dispute and reconciliation between friends

DRAMATURGICAL AND RHETORICAL FEATURES

Actions and stage directions 12–13 (*sd*): 'Here they (*D, G, Tom*) sing 'Hey nony, nony, and so go forth singing'
Songs and music (w.n.s.) *D, G, Tom* 'Hey nony, nony' 12–13 (*sd*)

21   The Disobedient Child

DATE, AUTHORSHIP AND AUSPICES

1559–70 (*SR* 1569 *c.* Aug.); Thomas Inglelend; Christmas performance by boys at court and offered for acting; Greg 54

TEXT AND EDITIONS

Extant originals

1570 (?) printing by Thomas Colwell; BL; Bodleian (two copies); Dyce; Eliz. Club; Harvard; Huntington; Illinois; Pforzheimer; *STC* 14085

Editions

1994	CHD (CD-Rom and online transcription of Colwell printing, l.l., OS)
1908	TFT (facsimile, n.l.)
1905	Farmer (2) (n.l., NS)*
1874–6	Dodsley, vol. II (n.l., OS)
1848	Halliwell (1848a), vol. XII (n.l., OS)

SOURCES

No sources have been identified.

CHARACTERS

Prologue Speaker	Man Cook	Servant
Son (Young Man, Husband)	Maid Cook	Devil
Rich Man (Father)	Young Woman (Wife)	Perorator
	Priest	

PLOT SUMMARY

The *Prologue* tells the play's story of a wealthy Londoner's spoiling of his son, who becomes wayward, has a disastrous marriage, and is plunged into misery. *Father* and *Son* then enter and have a debate about the value of education, something which the *Son* rejects because of the rigours and harsh discipline of schooling. The boy wishes to marry and is opposed in this by his parent, who threatens to disinherit him, and when the *Son* departs the *Father* laments his earlier parental leniency. The scene switches to two cooks, who engage in banter while preparing the *Son*'s wedding feast. They relate that the boy has become alienated from his friends by persisting in wishing to marry a shrewish woman. The *Woman Cook* regrets her kitchen drudgery, and recalls when she learned Latin at school, but she is mocked by the *Man Cook*. They leave to get supplies and the young man (*Son*) and his lover enter, pledging their love, planning their wedding and finally singing a song. They go out and a *Priest* comes in telling of the prospective marriage and complaining about his unreliable parish clerk. He is followed by the *Father*, who laments his son's spendthrift ways and forthcoming marriage. On his exit the *Son* and his new *Wife* enter rejoicing in marital bliss, until they are interrupted by a *Servant* coming to report the arrival of a visitor. They go off and he is left on stage to describe their riotous wedding. He then exits and they re-enter, this time talking about the economic practicalities of their life. They fall to quarrelling and she beats him, eventually making him go out and sell faggots for a living. On their departure, the *Devil* appears boasting that it was he who moved the couple to strife, and earlier the *Son* to reject learning, and he warns the audience of his temptations which are designed to bring them to misery. When he leaves the *Son* re-enters making connections between his erstwhile recalcitrance and present misery, and he is joined by his *Father*, who confirms this and talks also of the horrors of a bad marriage. They finally go out and the *Perorator* ends the play with a sermon on the theme of 'spare the rod and spoil the child.' He is then joined by the other players and they offer a prayer for the queen, bishops and nobility before concluding with a song.

PLAY LENGTH

1,495 lines, including peroration, prayer for the queen and song

COMMENTARY

This is an 'upbringing of youth' play, characteristically with only one parent present. It both laments parental leniency and gives full expression to the horrors of school discipline. It makes connections between material welfare and the issue of education, but the play also focuses on marriage and its perils. It is an almost completely secular piece with no redemption at the end. The play is relatively lacking in dramatic action, apart from the marriage strife near the end, and characters normally enter either singly or in pairs, to state or debate their positions or to recount narrative. A curious feature is that none of the characters is given a name, but rather defined by their position in the family, possibly because of the narrative's emphasis on family relationships and the dangers of them.

Other youth and education plays: **33, 53, 56, 58, 61, 62, 64, 67, 68, 73** (frag.), **101, 103, 104.**

SIGNIFICANT TOPICS AND NARRATIVE ELEMENTS

education and the upbringing of youth; school discipline; bad marriage; a shrewish woman; inheritance; poverty and social decline; parish clerks

NOTE: no line-numbered edition; all location references are pages rather than line numbers

DRAMATURGICAL AND RHETORICAL FEATURES

Verbal and general the *Man Cook*'s misconstruction of the *Woman Cook*'s Latin 59; the *Son*'s and *Wife*'s Skeltonic list of marital pursuits, repeating 'Sometimes' 70–71; an 'ubi sunt' passage in the final song 92; a minor subplot element (the cooks); stage directions in English

Costume and dress having previously been 'clothed in costly array' the *Son* later wears 'a coat that is rent' 84

Actions and stage directions 55 *sd*: 'Here the *Son* goes out and the *R. Man* tarries behind alone'; 56 *sd*: 'Here the *R. Man* goes out, and the two cooks come in, first the one then the other'; 60 *sd*: 'Here the two cooks run out, and in comes the *Y. Man* And *Y. Wo.* his lover'; 70 *sd*: 'Here the *R. Man* goes out, and in comes the *Y. Man* his son with the *Y. Wo.*, being both married'; 72 *sd*: 'Here the *Ser.* of the *R. Man*'s *Son* comes in, with an errand to his master'; 73 *sd*: 'Here they (*Son, Wife*) go out, and their *Ser.* doth tarry behind alone'; 74 *sd*: 'Here the *Ser.* goes out, and in comes first the *Wife*, and shortly after the *Hus.*'; 76 *sd*: 'Here the *Wife* must strike her *Hus.* handsomely about the shoulders with something'; 77 *sd*: 'Here the *Wife* must lay one load upon her *Hus.*'; 77: the *Son* threatens his *Wife* with a knife; 78 *sd*: 'Here she must knock her *Hus.*'; 79 *sd*: 'Here her *Hus.* must lie along on the ground, as though he were sore beaten and wounded'; 79 *sd*: 'Here the *Wife* goes out, and the *Hus.* tarries behind alone'; 84 *sd*: 'Here he (*Son*) confesses his naughtiness, uttering the same with a pitiful voice'; 85 *sd*: 'Here the *R. Man* must be as it were coming in'; 85: the *Son* kneels before his *Fa.*; 91 *sd*: 'Here the rest of the players come in, and kneel all down together, each of them saying one of these verses'; **Simple entry:** *R. Man, Son* 46; *Pri.* 65; *R. Man* 67; *Dev.* 80; *Son* 83; *Per.* 88; **Simple exit:** *Prol.* 46; (*Y. Man, Y. Wo.*) 65; *Pri.* 67; *Son* 80; *Dev.* 83; *R. Man, Son* 88

Songs and music (w.s. to both) 1. *Son* 'Spite of his spite, which that in vain' (54 lines, w. ref.) 63–4; 2. Whole cast (?) 'Why doth the world study vain glory to attain?' (final song, 40 lines) 91–2

Staging and set the action is only vaguely localized, mostly in the family home, and there are no indications as to set

Stage properties a basket 60; the *Wife*'s weapon 76 *sd*; faggots 76, 77 *sd*; the *Son*'s earnings 76; the *Son*'s knife 77; clothes (washed by the *Husband*) 78

PLACENAMES

St Albans 58; London 45, 58

ALLUSIONS

Absalom 92; Aristotle 92; Aristotle, *Ethics* 71; Caesar 92; Cicero ('Tully') 50, 92; Crates of Thebes 72; Demosthenes 50; Dives 92; Eupolis 69; Heracles (? 'H'Erocles')

72; Hipponax 69; Jonathan 92; Ovid *Ibis 527–8* 69; *Proverbs 13:24* 89; Pythagoras 72; Samson 92; Socrates 72; Socrates and Xantippe 87; Solomon 89, 92

BIBLIOGRAPHY

Grantley, 2000, pp. 148–66
Holthausen, F. 'Studien zum älteren englischen Drama: II Thom. Ingelend's *Disobedient Child*, *EngS* 31 (1902) pp. 90–103
Young, 1979, pp. 103–17

22   The Durham Prologue

DATE, AUTHORSHIP AND AUSPICES

late fourteenth or early fifteenth century; anonymous; auspices unknown

TEXT AND EDITIONS

Extant originals

Manucript (Durham Cathedral Library): Durham Dean and Chapter MS 1.2. Archidiac. Dunelm 60, dorse

Editions

1994   CHD (CD-Rom and online copy of Davis, 1970, l.l., OS)*
1993   Coldewey (OS)*
1979   Davis (facsimile, n.l.)
1970   Davis (OS)*
1959   Cooling (OS)*

PLOT SUMMARY

The extract consists solely of a prologue calling for the audience's attention and telling of a rich and handsome knight who loses everything through mischance, is tempted by Satan, but resists with the help of the Virgin Mary.

PLAY LENGTH

36 lines extant

COMMENTARY

The play to which this is part of a prologue may possibly have been a dramatized version of a popular strand of devotional literature on the miracles of the Virgin.

SIGNIFICANT TOPICS AND NARRATIVE ELEMENTS

worldly loss and poverty; the temptations of Satan; the intercession of the Virgin Mary

23   Dux Moraud (fragments)

DATE, AUTHORSHIP AND AUSPICES

early to mid fifteenth century; anonymous; East Anglia; possibly for place and scaffold production, but auspices unknown

TEXT AND EDITIONS

Extant originals

Manuscript: Bodleian Library MS Eng. Poet, fo. 2 (R)

Editions

1994   CHD (CD-Rom and online copy of Davis, 1970, l.l., OS)*
1993   Coldewey (OS)*
1970   Davis (OS)*
1979   Davis (facsimile, n.l.)
1924   Adams (OS)*
1907   Heuser (OS)*

SOURCES

The play is likely to have some relation to poems printed in Heuser's edition and also by Carl Horstmann in *Altenglische Legenden, Neue Folge* (Heilbronn, 1881), pp. 334–8.

CHARACTERS

Dux Moraud
Implicitly present (but with no speaking parts): Wife, Daughter, Child, Priest

PLOT SUMMARY

(Sections in brackets follow Davis's reconstruction of the missing elements of the narrative). *Dux Moraud* introduces himself with a conventional alliterative 'boast', claiming both universal sovereignty and worldly well-being. (His wife tells him she is going on a journey.) He gives his approval, asks her to return soon, promises to avoid sin with Christ's help during her absence, and bids her farewell. He then turns to his daughter and declares his love for her, praising her beauty. (When she accepts his advances) he asks her to kiss him and suggests they go to her room. He then expresses fear (after the affair has apparently been discovered by his wife) that the 'traitor' will betray them, unless she is killed. He asks his daughter whether she has killed her mother and expresses satisfaction (after evidently learning that she has). He is then again gripped with fear of exposure (when his daughter gives birth to a child) and after requesting to see it, asks her to kill it. (Having been told that she has done so) he is restored to joy. He decides to go to the country, and a segment follows that is largely illegible. He utters another expression of worldly comfort and decides to go to church when he hears the bells ring. He is then moved to contrition for his sins and desires to see a priest. He confesses the incest, and the murder of his wife and child, undertaking to do penance. He then greets his daughter, telling her of his conversion to virtue. (She responds by giving him a fatal blow) and as death approaches he asks forgiveness for both himself and his daughter.

PLAY LENGTH

268 lines extant, some partially obliterated

COMMENTARY

This appears to be the speeches of one play character which Davis, largely following Heuser, has numbered into 22 segments. There are no stage directions, though the implied action is extremely dramatic and even sensational. The final repentance of the duke, prepared for by earlier expressions of piety, makes this a type of conversion play.

Other plays with probable place and scaffold staging: **9, 48, 63, 72** (frag.), **83, 85**.

SIGNIFICANT TOPICS AND NARRATIVE ELEMENTS

incest; marital infidelity; matricide; infanticide; conversion and penitence; parricide

DRAMATURGICAL AND RHETORICAL FEATURES

Verbal and general *Dux Moraud*'s alliterative opening 'boast'; no stage directions and all actions are implicit

Staging and set no indications for these; the action is relatively unlocalized, but a church bell is likely to have been used

BIBLIOGRAPHY

Craig, 1955, pp. 327–9
Heiatt, C. B. 'A Case for *Duk Moraud* as a Play of the Miracles of the Virgin'. *MS* 32 (1970) pp. 345–51
Heuser, 1907b, pp. 189–208
Homan, 1991, pp. 199–209

24   Enough is as Good as a Feast

DATE, AUTHORSHIP AND AUSPICES

1559–70; William Wager; offered for acting; Greg 57

TEXT AND EDITIONS

Extant originals

c. 1570 (?) printing by John Allde: Huntington; *STC* 24933

Editions

1994   CHD (CD-Rom and online transcription of Allde printing, l.l., OS)
1969   Schell and Schuchter (NS)*
1967   Benbow (NS)*
1920   S. De Ricci (1920a) (facsimile, n.l.)

SOURCES

Possible sources are the 'Matthew' Bible prepared by John Rogers (1537) and the *Exposition upon the Fifth, Sixth and Seventh Chapters of Matthew* (1532) as well as other homiletic material, and Wager also draws on *The Trial of Treasure* (**96**); see the introduction to Benbow's edition, pp. x–xi.

CHARACTERS

Prologue	Temerity	Enough	Prophet	Satan
Worldly Man	Inconsideration	Tenant	God's Plague	Rest
Heavenly Man	Precipitation	Servant	Ignorance	
Contentation	Covetous, the Vice	Hireling	Physician	

PLOT SUMMARY

The *Prologue* prays for eloquence such as that possessed by the classical writers, but affirms that, lacking the grace of those writers, he will only introduce the title of the play and not its argument or contents at the outset. The action commences with a debate between *Worldly Man* and *Heavenly Man*, with some contribution from *Contentation*, concluding in the conversion of *Worldly Man* to virtue. They depart and, after coming in singing a song, *Temerity*, *Inconsideration* and *Precipitation* meet the Vice *Covetous* and plot the downfall of the convert. A somewhat drunken *Covetous* dons official dress and gives himself and his companions new names to prepare for the assault on *Worldly Man*. They set off and encounter him in the company of *Enough*, his mentor who preaches against excess. *Covetous* feigns to weep for what he describes as *Worldly Man*'s social descent from earlier wealth, since he now lives simply like a 'churl'. *Covetous* and his friends quickly worm their way into *Worldly Man*'s friendship by promising him material prosperity and, despite *Enough*'s exhortations, *Worldly Man* abandons him to leave with his new friends. *Heavenly Man* enters briefly to bewail *Worldly Man*'s fall, and he is followed by *Tenant*, who complains bitterly of the racked rents he is having to pay because of unscrupulous landlords and an influx of foreigners that has made houses scarce. *Servant* then arrives with similar complaints of hardship and they are joined by *Hireling*, who also curses *Worldly Man* for his avarice. *Covetous*, now *Worldly Man*'s steward, appears and *Tenant* begs him for respite, but he is rejected. *Hireling* makes a similar plea with the same result. When *Worldly Man* himself appears, he is equally dismissive of their appeals, and he revels in his material wealth. However, he is cut short in this by the appearance of *Prophet*, who reminds him of the brevity of life and the judgement of God. *Worldly Man* suddenly becomes weak and lies down, whereupon *God's Plague* appears and delivers a sermon on the punishment ordained by God for the covetous. He goes to one side while *Covetous* returns, accompanied by *Ignorance*, to find *Worldly Man* having a troubled sleep from which they wake him to hear that he has been having a nightmare about damnation. They fetch a *Physician*, but it is too late to help *Worldly Man*. He decides to make a will but falls down in the making of it and *Satan* comes to carry him off to hell, thanking *Covetous* for his work. *Contentation*, *Heavenly Man* and *Enough* then enter to reflect on the effects of bad company and sin, soon joined by *Rest* who underlines the message of predestined grace for the elect. *Enough* reiterates the message of the play's title and *Contentation* concludes with a prayer for Queen Elizabeth.

PLAY LENGTH

1,547 lines

COMMENTARY

This is a Protestant morality with a Calvinist message about predestination, which is clearly stated towards the end of the play. It has, however, strong social and economic dimensions and refers to several abuses in the realm that were also the subject of contemporary pamphleteers. The interlude is one of the few not to represent a final redemption for the central character.

Other Protestant and anti-Catholic plays: **14, 44, 45, 49, 50, 53, 58, 66, 85, 86** (frag.), **90, 93**.

Other proverb plays: **52, 53, 94**.

Other social ills plays: **2, 15, 38, 40, 52, 53, 71, 72** (frag.), **76, 94, 96, 98, 100**.

SIGNIFICANT TOPICS AND NARRATIVE ELEMENTS

worldly ambition; drink and drunkenness; flattery; good and bad companions; extorting landlords and rack-renting; exploitative employers; foreigners in the realm; avarice; a dream about damnation; the making of a will; physical medicine and its limitations; predestination

DRAMATURGICAL AND RHETORICAL FEATURES

Verbal and general *Covetous* makes reference to a female member of the audience 482; *Covetous*'s nonsense speech 305–52; Vices' aliases: *Covetous–Policy* 503, 541, *Inconsideration–Reason* 492, *Temerity–Agility* 493–4, *Precipitation–Ready Wit* 496, *Ignorance–Devotion* 561 (also *Sir Nicholas* 1251); rustic speech: *Tenant* (Cotswold speech) 970 ff., *Ignorance* 1252 ff.; *Ignorance* speaks mock-Latin 1265–8; *Worldly Man* speaks in his sleep 1277–82; the *Physician* is called 'Master Flebeshiten' by his servant in 1358; *Satan*'s triumphal speech 1429–71

Costume and dress *Covetous*'s gown, cap and chain 409; *Worldly Man* is 'in a strange attire' 627 *sd*; *Enough* is 'poorly arrayed' 636 *sd*; the servant enters 'poorly' (dressed) 992 *sd*; *Worldly Man* is 'all brave' (finely dressed?) 1112 *sd*

Actions and stage directions 92 *sd*: 'Enter *Wo. M.* stout and frolic'; 280 *sd*: 'Enter *Tem., Inc.* and *Pre.* singing this song'; 304 *sd*: 'Enter *Cov.* the Vice alone'; 426 *sd*: '(*Cov.*) Be going out'; 428 *sd*: '(*Tem.*) Hold him (*Cov.*)'; 430 *sd*: '(*Cov.*) Come in again'; 440 *sd*: 'He (*Cov.*) fights them (*Tem., Inc.*) with a dagger'; 444 *sd*: '(*Inc.*) Lay hold on him (*Cov.*)'; 470: *Tem., Pre., Inc.* salute (and bow to?) *Cov.*; 476 *sd*, 479 *sd*, 482 *sd*: '(*Cov.*) Study'; 489 *sd*: '(*Cov.*) Speak to *Inc.*'; 577 *sd*: '(*Tem., Inc.*) Be going out'; 627 *sd*: 'Enter the *Wo. M.* and *En.* . Let the *Wo. M.* stand afar off in a strange attire'; 636 *sd*: '*En.* (enters) poorly arrayed'; 700 *sd*, 701 *sd*: '(*Cov.*) Weep'; 706 *sd*: 'Let the Vice weep and howl and make great lamentation to the *Wo. M.*'; 741 *sd*: '(*Wo. M.*) Go towards him (*En.*)'; 741 *sd* (2): '(*Cov.*) Pluck him (*Wo. M.*) back'; 948 *sd*: 'Go all three together (*Cov., Wo. M., Pre.*) and make you ready straight ways (for doubling)'; 992 *sd*: 'Enter poorly *Ser.*'; 969 *sd*: 'Enter an old man *Ten.* and speak Cotswold speech'; 1056 *sd*: '(*Ser.*) Run out'; 1087 *sd*: '*Hir.* make much curtsey'; 1112 *sd*: '(Enter) *Wo. M.* all brave'; 1184 *sd*: '(*Prop.* speaks) without' (offstage); 1186 *sd*: 'Let *Wo. M.* look suddenly about him' (when *Prop.* speaks); 1222 *sd*: 'Enter *Go. Pl.* and stand behind him (*Wo. M.*) awhile before he speak'; 1250 *sd*: '(*Go. Pl.*) Go out and stand at the door'; 1348 *sd*: '(*Phy.*) Be busy and daw (revive) him (*Wo. M.*) as though he were dying'; 1403 *sd*: '(*Wo. M.*) Fall down'; 1471 *sd*: '(*Sat.*) Bear him (*Wo. M.*) out upon his back'; **Simple entry:** (*Tem., Inc.*) 378; (*Tem., Inc.*) 578; *He. M.* 948; *Hir.* 1010; *Cov.* 1056; *Ign.* 1332; *Sat.* 1427; **Simple exit:** (*He. M., Wo. M., Con.*) 280; 'Both' (*Cov., Inc.*) 598; (*En.*) 866; (*He. M.*) 969; (*Hir. Ten.*) 1156; *Prop.* 1208; (*Ign.*) 1318; (*Phy.*) 1380

Songs and music *Temerity, Inconsideration, Precipitation* 'When *Covetous* is busy' (w.s.) 281–304

Staging and set a doubling scheme for seven players is provided on the title page: 1. *Worldly Man*; 2. *Prologue, Heavenly Man*; 3. *Contentation, Temerity, Ignorance, Satan*; 4. *Enough, Hireling*; 5. *Inconsideration, Servant, Rest, Prophet*; 6. *Precipitation, Tenant, God's Plague, Physician*; 7. *Covetous.* there is reference to a door (1250 *sd*), but no other indications as to set, and the action is unlocalized

Stage properties *Covetous*'s dagger 440 *sd*; a drink and a pillow 1346–7; paper and ink for the will 1400

PLACENAMES

Barnard-in-the-Field[1] 322; Blackheath[1] 305; Canaan[1] 308; Counters (prison) 361; Easilwood (?)[1] 311; England 570, 986; St Katherine's (hospital in London) 366; King's Bench (prison) 360; Kingston[1] 333; Marshalsea (prison) 360; Newgate (prison) 361; St Paul's Steeple[1] 330; Peterborough[1] 309; Spain[1] 307; St Thomas-a-Watering 365; Tyburn[1] 307; Walshingham 1332; Wapping 366; Warwick[1] 307, 313; Westminster Hall 936

1 Part of *Covetous*'s nonsense speech.

ALLUSIONS

Alexander the Great 232; St Anthony 343,[1] 1331; Aristotle 781; the Belides 27; St Bernard (of Clairvaux) 637; Caesar 232; Cicero 769 ('Tully'), 797, 937 ('Tully'); Circe 201; Croesus 188; King David 121, 181, 833, 1239; Dionysius 231; *Ezekiel 33:11* (?) 659; St Francis[1] 330; Goliath[1] 305; Sir Guy of Warwick and Colbron[1] 313; Heliogabalus 234; Robin Hood[1] 312; Ixion 25; *Jeremiah 22:29* (q.a.) 1191–2; St Mary Magdalene 733; Mercury 37, 44, 51; Muses 9; Orpheus 17; Parnassus 6; St Paul 224, 671; St Peter[1] 319; *Psalm 36:25* (V)/*37:25* (AV) 181–3; Pythagoras 1507; Seneca 759, 968; Sisyphus 24; King Solomon 239, 629, 795; Solon 188, 192; St Stephen[1] 318, 326, 329; Tantalus 23; Tarquinius Superbus 233; St Uncumber 339[1], 1331; Our Lady of Walshingham 1332

1 Part of *Covetous*'s nonsense speech.

BIBLIOGRAPHY

Adams, 1943, pp. 59–63
Bevington, 1962, pp. 81–3, 158–61

Craik, 1962, pp. 99–110
Eccles, 1981, pp. 258–62
Farnham, 1936, pp. 237–42
Kutrieh, A. R. 'The Doubling of Parts in *Enough is as Good as a Feast*', *ELN* 12:2 (1974) pp. 79–84
Neuss, 1984, pp. 1–18
Spinrad, 1987, pp. 98–102

25   Everyman

DATE, AUTHORSHIP AND AUSPICES

c. 1519; anonymous; auspices unknown; Greg 4

TEXT AND EDITIONS

Extant originals

c. 1515 printing by Richard Pynson: Bodleian (frag.); *STC* 10604
c. 1526–8 (?) printing by Richard Pynson: BL (imp.); *STC* 10604.5
c. 1528–9 (?) printing by John Skot: Huntington; *STC* 10606
c. 1530–35 (?) printing by John Skot: BL; *STC* 10606.5

Editions

(Note that, owing to the very large number of editions of this play, the following list is selective. For further early editions, see Stratman, 1972, pp. 554–64.)

2000   Walker (OS)*
1996   Trussler (NS)*
1994   CHD (CD-Rom and online transcription of Skot *c.* 1528–9 printing, l.l., OS)*
1993   Coldewey (OS)*
1985   Gray (OS)*
1984   Garbáty (OS)*
1981   Lester (NS)*
1980   Astington (NS)*
1980   Cooper and Wortham (OS)*
1975   Bevington (OS)*
1973   J. B. Trapp in Kermode and Hollander, vol. 1 (NS)*
1970   Robertson (OS)*
1969   Schell and Schuchter (NS)*
1963   Gassner (NS)*
1962   Hopper and Lahey (n.l., NS)
1961   Goodman (NS)*

1961   Cawley (OS)*
1956   Cawley (NS)*
1955   Heilman (NS)*
1953   Allen (n.l., NS)
1935   Parks and Beatty (NS)
1931   Hampden (n.l., NS)
1928   Schweikert (NS)
1926   Tickner (n.l., NS)
1924   Adams (OS)
1912   TFT (facsimile of first Skot printing, and Pynson fragment, n.l.)
1910   Greg (Pynson fragments in Bodleian and British Library; OS)
1909   Rhys (n.l., NS)
1909   Greg (1909a) (first Skot printing; OS)*
1906   Farmer (3) (n.l., NS)
1906   Farmer (1906c) (n.l., NS)
1904   Greg (1904a) (Skot edition 'at Britwell Court' now Huntington; OS)*
1874–6   Dodsley, vol. 1 (n.l., NS)

SOURCES

Though there has been some debate about which came first, this is considered to be a translation of the late fifteenth-century Dutch play, *Elckerlijc*, one of the plays of the Dutch rhetoricians or 'Rederijkers'.

CHARACTERS

Messenger	Fellowship	Good Deeds	Strength	Doctor
God	Kindred	Knowledge	Discretion	
Death	Cousin	Confession	Five Wits	
Everyman	Goods	Beauty	Angel	

PLOT SUMMARY

The *Messenger* calls for the audience's attention, gives a brief account of the play's narrative and introduces *God*, who complains that humanity is too mindful of material well-being and too little of the afterlife. He calls for his messenger, *Death*, and sends him to summon *Everyman* to a pilgrimage which he cannot escape. *Death* accosts *Everyman*, who begs for respite, but is told he must die that very day. *Everyman* immediately sets about seeking company for his journey. He goes first to *Fellowship* who, though he is happy to join *Everyman* in mirth and entertainment, declines to go with him now. *Everyman* next seeks out *Kindred* and *Cousin*, who respond similarly, *Cousin* complaining of a cramp in the toe and admitting that he too has an unclean reckoning. *Everyman* then looks for help from his worldly wealth in the form of *Goods*, who is trussed up in a corner, but *Goods* points out that it is actually *Everyman*'s love of him that compromises his chances of eternal life. Lamenting his past life, *Everyman* resolves at length to go to his *Good Deeds*. She, however, lies cold and bound up in the ground – the effect of his sins – and cannot stand up, but she sends him to her sister, *Knowledge*. *Knowledge* does agree to guide *Everyman* and takes him to a holy man, *Confession*, whom she describes as a 'cleansing river'. He prescribes penance and, after a long prayer, *Everyman* beats himself with a scourge. At this, *Good Deeds* arises from the ground and *Knowledge* gives *Everyman* a new garment, the garment of sorrow. *Good Deeds* reminds him of further friends, *Discretion*, *Strength* and *Beauty*, while *Knowledge* recommends his *Five Wits* as counsellors. *Strength*, *Five Wits* and *Discretion* offer to help *Everyman* while he is on earth, but declare that they cannot accompany him beyond the grave. *Knowledge* and *Five Wits* advise him to seek the final sacrament from the priesthood and he goes off. On his return he carries a cross, having received the sacrament, and is then brought to his grave. *Beauty*, *Strength* and *Discretion* now successively take their leave, followed by *Five Wits*. *Knowledge*, however, remains a while and *Good Deeds* continues to stand by him. When *Everyman* goes to his grave, accompanied by *Good Deeds*, *Knowledge* hears the singing of angels and an *Angel* comes to lead *Everyman*'s soul to heaven. A *Doctor* concludes the play with a warning against pride and a reliance on earthly things.

PLAY LENGTH

921 lines

COMMENTARY

This is one of the best known of the early moral plays and contains, in its central character, an important example of a generalized humanity figure. However, there are no Vices, as the play is concerned with the final point of man's life and is of the 'dance of death' trope rather than a *psychomachia*. Aside from representing aspects of the central character's moral psyche (and physical attributes), the allegory extends to figures that are synecdochic representations of social categories and material objects. The dance of death motif is worked through to emphasize both the inevitability of death and the aloneness of the human being in the experience, and the grave of *Everyman* – which is arguably visible throughout – represents a powerful visual *memento mori* that is central to the play's argument. The play presents a carefully structured progress from the external aspects of *Everyman*'s life to his own internal resources, and it also represents the penitential process in some detail.

SIGNIFICANT TOPICS AND NARRATIVE ELEMENTS

the impermanence of life; the dance of death and death as a leveller; death as a pilgrimage; the art of holy dying; material wealth and its disposal; bodily weakness and decline; physical penance; penitence and redemption; the sacraments; the throes of death

DRAMATURGICAL AND RHETORICAL FEATURES

Verbal and general the play is described at the outset as a 'treatise . . . in the manner of a moral play'; *Everyman* makes his will 697–705; only two stage directions, both for speech and in English

Costume and dress *Everyman* receives the 'garment of sorrow' 638

Actions and stage directions 605–7: *Ev.* scourges himself; 619: *G. De.* arises from the ground; 628: *Ev.* scourges himself again; 778: *Stre.*, *Disc.* and *Kno.* touch *Ev.*'s cross; 788–9: *Ev.* staggers; 880–7: *Ev.* sinks into his grave with *G. De.* (or exits stage); **Simple speech**: *God* 21; *Fell.* 205

Songs and music *Knowledge* hears angels singing 891

Staging and set the grave into which *Everyman* sinks may suggest a raised stage with a trapdoor (possibly from which *Good Deeds* speaks while 'cold in the ground') 486; there are otherwise no indications as to set

Stage properties *Everyman*'s book of accounts 503; a scourge for *Everyman* 561; *Everyman*'s cross 778

ALLUSIONS

Jupiter 407; Judas Maccabeus 787; Mary (Virgin) 597, 875; *Matthew 25:41* (part quotation) 915; Moses 596; St Peter 755

REPORTS ON MODERN PRODUCTIONS

1. New York (Classical Theatre Ensemble), dir. J. Keeler, 29 January–20 February 1982 [*New York Times*, 29 Jan. 1982, p. C14]
2. Edinburgh (Dublin University Players), dir. L. Parker, 25 August–4 September 1982 [*RORD* 25 (1982) pp. 149–50]
3. St Martin's College, Olympia, WA, dir. D. Hlavsa, 16–18, 23–5 April 1992 [see Greenfield's essay below]
4. University of Toronto PLS Festival (University of Western Ontario), dir. J. Lingard, 23–24 May 1992 [*RORD* 32 (1993) pp. 170–1]
5. Huntingdon College, Montgomery, AL, dir. M. Howley, October 1993 [*RORD* 34 (1995) pp. 186–9]
6. Chicago (Steppenwolf Theatre Company), dir. F. Galati, 22 November 1995–14 January 1996 [*RORD* 36 (1997) pp. 192–4]

7. San Francisco (Brown Bag Theatre Company), dir. L. Owen, 12–16 February 1996 [*RORD* 36 (1997) pp. 191–2]
8. University of Dundee (Medieval Theatre Group), dir. J.-A. George, March 1996 [*RORD* 36 (1997) pp. 189–91]
9. The Other Place, Stratford upon Avon (RSC), dir. K. Mitchell, 1996–7 season [*CE* 51 (April 1997) pp. 77–9, and see O'Connor's essay below]
10. University of Leeds (Workshop Theatre), dir. P. Meredith, 16 July 1997 [*RORD* 37 (1998) pp. 127–9]
11. Odense, Denmark (Medieval Drama Group, University of Dundee), dir. J-A George, A. Spackman and K. Nelson, 7 August 1998 [*RORD* 38 (1999) p. 149]

RECORDED PRODUCTIONS

LP Record: BBC, *The First Stage*, dir. J. Barton (1970)
Videotape: Insight Media, dir. B. Morris in association with H. Schless (1991)
Videotape: Durham Medieval Theatre Company, dir. J. McKinnell, University of Durham (1999)

CONCORDANCE

Preston, 1975

BIBLIOGRAPHY

Anderson, 1963, pp. 72–84
Bacquet, P. 'Everyman et l'orthodoxie catholique médiévale', EA 35:3 (1982) pp. 296–310
Brooks and Heilman, 1961, pp. 100–11
Conley, J. 'The Doctrine of Friendship in Everyman', Speculum 44 (1969) pp. 374–82
Cooper and Wortham, 1980, pp. ix–xlx
Cowling, D. 'The Angels' Song in Everyman', N&Q 233 (1988) pp. 301–3
Cunningham, J. 'Comedic and Liturgical Restoration in Everyman' in Davidson and Stroupe, 1991, pp. 368–79
Davenport, 1982, pp. 32–6
De Vocht, 1947
Duclow, D. F. 'Everyman and the Ars Moriendi: Fifteenth-Century Ceremonies of Dying', FCS 6 (1983) pp. 93–113
Fifield, 1967, pp. 37–45
Fletcher, A. 'Everyman: An Unrecorded Sermon Analogue', ES 66:4 (1985) pp. 296–9
Frost, C. 'Everyman in Performance', LNQ 6:1 (1978) pp. 39–48
Garner, 1987, pp. 272–85
Garner, 1989, pp. 59–70
Godfrey, R. 'Everyman (Re)considered' in Higgins and Paino, 2000, pp. 113–30
Goldhamer, A. D. 'Everyman: A Dramatisation of Death', C&M 30 (1966) pp. 596–616
Goodman, 1961, pp. 61–96
Greenfield, P. 'A Processional Everyman at St Martin's College (Olympia, WA, April 16–18, 23–25, 1992)', RORD 32 (1993) pp. 151–60
Haller, 1916, pp. 112–15
Harkness, J. 'Departure and Irony in Everyman' in Matthews and Schmole-Rostosky, 1988, pp. 59–67

Hillman, R. 'Everyman and the Energies of Stasis', Florilegium 7 (1985) pp. 206–26

Isano, M, T. Tadanobu and Y. Koshi 'A Comprehensive Study of Everyman', BFE 31:2 (1980) pp. 15–59, 32.2 (1981) pp. 13–44, 33.2 (1982) pp. 43–66 (in three parts)

Jack, 1989, pp. 131–9, 154–9

Jambeck, T. J. 'Everyman and the Implications of Bernardine Humanism in the Character "Knowledge"', M&H n.s. 8 (1977) pp. 103–23

Keppel, 2000, pp. 78–9, 82–4, 111–21

Kolve, V. A. 'Everyman and the Parable of the Talents' in Sticca, 1972, pp. 69–98, and in Taylor and Nelson, 1972, pp. 316–40

Lombardo, 1953, pp. 267–83

McRae, M. W. 'Everyman's Last Rites and the Digression on Priesthood', CL 13:3 (1986) pp. 305–9

Maguin, J.-M. 'Everyman ou la mesure du concept de héros' in Le Mythe du Héros: Actes du colloque interdisciplinaire, Centre Aixois de Récherches Anglaises 12–13–14 mars 1982, Aix-en-Provence, University of Provence, 1982, pp. 7–21

Manly, J. M. 'Elckerlijc–Everyman: the Question of Priority', MP 8:2 (1910) pp. 269–77

Mateer, M. 'The Woman in Everyman' in Higgins and Paino, 1998, pp. 223–35

Meier, H. H. 'Middle English Styles in Translation: A Note on Everyman and Caxton's Reynard' in Alblas and Todd, 1979, pp. 12–30

Mills, D. 'The Theaters of Everyman' in Alford, 1995, pp. 127–49

Mills, D. 'Anglo-Dutch Theatres: Problems and Possibilities', METh 18 (1996) pp. 85–98

Miyajima, 1977, pp. 87–95

Moran, D. V. 'The Life of Everyman', Neophilologus 56:3 (1972) pp. 324–30

Munson, W. F. 'Knowing and Doing in Everyman', CR 19:3 (1985) pp. 252–71

O'Connor, M. F. 'Everyman, The Creation and The Passion: The Royal Shakespeare Company Medieval Season 1996–1997', MRDE 11 (1999) pp. 19–33

Potter, 1975, pp. 221–32

Potter, R. 'Divine and Human Justice' in Neuss, 1983, pp. 129–41

Rastall, R. 'Music and Liturgy in Everyman: Some Aspects of Production', LSE 29 (1998) pp. 305–14

Rendall, 1981, pp. 255–69

Richardson and Johnston, 1991, pp. 97–107

Ryan, D. '"If ye had parfytely chered me": The Nurturing of Good Deeds in Everyman', N&Q 42 (1995) pp. 165–8

Ryan, L. V. 'Doctrine and Dramatic Structure in Everyman', Speculum 32 (1957) pp. 722–35

Sellin, P. R. 'The Hidden God: Reformation Awe in Renaissance Literature' in Kinsman, 1974, pp. 147–96

Spinrad, P. S. 'The Last Temptation of Everyman', PQ 64:2 (1985) pp. 185–94

Spinrad, 1987, pp. 68–85

Strietman, E. 'The Middle Dutch Elckerlijc and the English Everyman', MÆ 52 (1983) pp. 111–14

Takahashi, 1953

Tanner, R. 'Humor in Everyman and the Middle English Morality Play', PQ 70:2 (1991) pp. 149–61

Thomas, H. S. 'The Meaning of the Character Knowledge in Everyman', MQ 14 (1961) pp. 3–13

Thomas, H. S. 'Some Analogues of Everyman', MQ 16 (1963) pp. 97–103

Thundy, Z. P. 'Good Deeds Rediviva: Everyman and the Doctrine of Reviviscence', FCS 17 (1990) pp. 421–37

Tigg, E. R. 'Is Elckerlijc Prior to Everyman?', JEGP 38:4 (1939) pp. 568–96

Van Dyke. 'The Intangible and its Image: Allegorical Discourse and the last of Everyman' in Carruthers and Kirk, 1982, pp. 311–24

Van Laan, T. 'Everyman. A Structural Analysis', PMLA 78:5 (1963) pp. 465–75

Van Mierlo, J. De prioriteit van Elckerlyck over Everyman gehandhaafd, Antwerp, Standaard-Boekhandeln, 1948

Warren, M. J. 'Everyman, Knowledge Once More', DR 54:1 (1974) pp. 136–46

Wasson, J. M. 'Interpolation in the Text of Everyman', TN 27:1 (1973) pp. 14–20

Webster, J. 'The Allegory of Contradiction in Everyman and The Faerie Queene' in Richardson, 1976, pp. 357–86

Wood, F. A. 'Elckerlijc–Everyman: The Question of Priority', MP 8:2 (1910) pp. 279–302

Wortham, C. J. 'Everyman and the Reformation', Parergon 29 (1981) pp. 23–31

Wortham, C. J. 'An Existentialist Approach to Everyman', AULLA 19 (1978) pp. 333–40

Zandvoort, R. W. 'Elckerlijc–Everyman', ES 23:1 (1941) pp. 1–9

Zettersten, A. 'Everyman and the Computer' in Caie and Norgaard, 1988, pp. 87–94

26   The Four Cardinal Virtues (fragment)

DATE, AUTHORSHIP AND AUSPICES

dated by Greg between 12 October 1537 and 28 January 1547; anonymous; auspices unknown; Greg 21.5

TEXT AND EDITIONS

Extant originals

c. 1541–7 printing by William Middleton: BL (frag.); STC 14109.7

Editions

1994   CHD (CD-Rom and online copy of Greg, 1956, l.l., OS)
1956   Greg (OS)*

SOURCES

No sources have been identified.

CHARACTERS

Justice   Temperance   Wilfulness   Prudence   Fortitude/Poorly

PLOT SUMMARY

The fragment opens with *Temperance* and *Justice* waiting for the arrival of *Prudence*. *Wilfulness*, who is being held prisoner, curses *Prudence* and he continues his aggressive behaviour towards him when he does arrive. On the urging of *Temperance*, *Justice* orders *Wilfulness* to be taken out (of his cell) for punishment. He is brought before them and *Justice* asks *Prudence* what should be done with him. When *Prudence* expresses the wish that *Fortitude* were present, *Wilfulness* himself offers to act as a messenger and go to fetch him. They express their doubts about whether he would return if let go, but finally they bind him with an obligation of £20. With a combination of assurances and curses (presumably in asides) he departs, while the others discuss the damage he has done. *Fortitude* (now called *Poorly*) then arrives and tells of his fall from his erstwhile prosperity which, along with other woes in the realm, he and the others ascribe to *Wilfulness*. *Fortitude* tells of how he was led astray by *Wilfulness*, something he now repents. He is then restored to his former power and given a new garment, whereupon he offers up a prayer of thanks, confession and supplication for the protection of the realm. *Temperance, Prudence, Justice* and *Fortitude* pray for King Henry and Prince Edward and offer themselves as virtuous opposites to vice.

PLAY LENGTH

245 lines extant

COMMENTARY

The fragment consists of the final four leaves of an interlude, including the colophon and a woodcut. As in the case of many interludes, the moral concerns of this play are quickly invested with economic and political dimensions.

SIGNIFICANT TOPICS AND NARRATIVE ELEMENTS

corruption in the realm; wealth and poverty; the 'remedia' or cardinal virtues as counters against vice

DRAMATURGICAL AND RHETORICAL FEATURES

Verbal and general *Poorly* is restored to his former name of *Fortitude* 174–5; the player playing *Wilfulness* doubles as *Fortitude* (and since *Fortitude* later refers to his release from prison 182, he blends somewhat with *Wilfulness* as a character); one of the extant stage directions in English, the other in Latin
Costume and dress *Fortitude* is given a 'crown royal' and a new 'robe and garment gay' on his restoration 178–9
Actions and stage directions 62 (*sd*): 'Here they take him (*Wil.*) out (of prison)' (E); 78: *Wil.* seals the obligation with wax; 96 (*sd*): 'And he (*Wil.*) goes out [to play] *Po*.' (L)
Staging and set this is a court scene and the cell from which *Wilfulness* is brought is likely to be visible, as he speaks before he is led out of it
Stage properties a document of obligation 75; a wax seal 78

BIBLIOGRAPHY

Boas, F. S. 'The Four Cardinal Virtues', QQ 58 (1951) pp. 85–91
Boas, F. S. 'The Four Cardynal Vertues: A Fragmentary Morality', TN 5:1 (1950) pp. 5–10
Harris, 1965, pp. 157–68
Southern, 1973, pp. 349–51

27   The (Nature of the) Four Elements

DATE, AUTHORSHIP AND AUSPICES

1517–18; John Rastell; auspices unknown, but probably for performance on Rastell's stage; Greg 6

TEXT AND EDITIONS

Extant originals

1520 printing by John Rastell: BL (imp.); *STC* 20722

Editions

1994	CHD (CD-Rom and online transcription of Rastell printing, l.l., OS)
1979	Axton (OS)*
1971	Coleman (n.l., NS)
1908	TFT (facsimile, n.l.)
1906	Farmer (3) (n.l., NS)
1903	Fischer (OS)
1874–6	Dodsley, vol. I (n.l., NS)
1848	Halliwell, vol. XII (n.l., OS)

SOURCES

It is probable that Rastell used medieval scientific encyclopaedias; see the introduction to Axton's edition as well as Nugent's and Parr's essays below.

CHARACTERS

The Messenger	Studious Desire	Experience
Nature	Sensual Appetite	Ignorance
Humanity	Taverner	
	Dancers who sing	

PLOT SUMMARY

This didactic interlude opens with a long speech from the *Messenger*, who advocates both the use of the English language and scholarly study for the good of the commonwealth, instead of merely for the acquisition of wealth. For the proper knowledge of God it helps to understand the operation of the material world and the interlude will treat of this, serious matter being interspersed with mirth. *Nature* enters to explain, with the aid of a model, the nature of the four elements, the earth and the stars to *Humanity*, who is attended by *Studious Desire*. When *Humanity*'s understanding proves unsteady, *Studious Desire* promises to introduce him to

Experience, who will help him comprehend more fully. However, *Sensual Appetite* breaks into their company. He is a gallant who claims to appeal to the five wits, the pleasures of which he proceeds to explain to *Humanity*. *Studious Desire* is reluctant to relinquish *Humanity* to *Sensual Delight*'s company, but when *Humanity* says that he only wishes for temporary recreation, he relents and departs. *Sensual Appetite* then takes *Humanity* off to a tavern, where the *Taverner* lists the wines and food he has on offer. They order and *Sensual Appetite* describes the women who will join them. They follow the *Taverner*, who goes off to prepare the festivity, and *Studious Desire* enters with *Experience*, who describes his wide travels, effectively delivering a geography lesson in the process, including a description of the new lands in America. They leave and *Humanity* enters with *Sensual Appetite*, closely followed by the *Taverner*, talking of the entertainments enjoyed and to come. On the *Taverner*'s departure *Studious Desire* and *Experience* return, to the displeasure of *Sensual Appetite*, who takes his leave. *Experience* then tries to instruct *Humanity* in the art of navigating by the stars, but his pupil finds his teaching difficult. There is a gap of eight leaves in the copy (about 360 lines), in which *Humanity* apparently rejoins *Sensual Appetite*, accompanied by a new character, *Ignorance*. The resumed text has *Sensual Desire* telling how he has put to flight some enemies (probably *Studious Desire* and *Experience*) and he and *Ignorance* come across *Humanity*, who has been in hiding from the skirmish. They resolve on more revelry and *Sensual Appetite* exits to fetch dancers, who enter with him singing and dancing. When they leave, *Ignorance* leads *Humanity* in another song, before *Nature* comes in to reprimand *Humanity*. The rest of the play is lost from this point.

PLAY LENGTH

1,443 lines extant

COMMENTARY

This is a strongly humanistic play that seeks to provide instruction through the medium of drama and to promote the value of education for both social progress and moral improvement. The teaching is very specifically natural and geographical and there is a marked absence of classical allusion. There is a conscious effort to make this project more palatable to the audience, some of whom may be little disposed to serious matter, by introducing light diversions. These, however, also serve to provide one side of the implicit *psychomachia*, which draws obliquely on the tradition of the debates between the soul and the body, and there is a modified fall and redemption scheme. These are the only principles shaping the narrative, which is made up of alternating the serious lectures with the revelry.

SIGNIFICANT TOPICS AND NARRATIVE ELEMENTS

the four elements; wealth and poverty; scholarship and its uses; education and the commonwealth; popular science the geography of the earth; the nature of minerals and plants; the weather; cosmography; exploration and empire building; the new-found lands (America); astronomy and navigation; recreation; the five wits; gallants; the English language; taverns, alcohol and drinking; prostitutes and sexual dalliance

DRAMATURGICAL AND RHETORICAL FEATURES

Verbal and general *Sensual Appetite* enters as a 'huffing' gallant 405–9; the *Taverner*'s list of wines 561–5; *Experience*'s cosmography lesson 708–876; *Sensual Appetite*'s 'spelling lesson' 1000–5; lectures are incorporated in the text; there is much aureate speech; the virtuous figures generally use a rhyme royal verse scheme; briefer stage directions in Latin and longer ones in English

Actions and stage directions 147 *sd*: 'Here enter *Nat.*, *Hum.* and *Stu. D.* carrying a model' (L); 878 *sd*: 'And suddenly *Stu. D.* should say' (L); 1180–3: *Hum.* lies hiding and is discovered; 1312 *sd*: 'Then the dancers without the hall sing this wise and they within answer, or else they may say it for need' (E); 1334 *sd*: 'Then he (*Sen. A.*) sings this song and dances with all and evermore makes countenance according to the matter and all other answer like wise' (E); 1368 *sd*: 'And they (*Sen. A.*, dancers) go out singing' (L); **Simple entry:** *Exp.*, *Stu. D.* 658; **Simple exit:** *Sen. A.*, *Hum.* 658; *Tav.* 970

Songs and music (w.s. to all songs) 1. *Sensual Appetite* 'With huffa, gallant, sing tirl on the berry' 417–21' (probably sung); 2. Dancers, *Sensual Appetite* 'Time to pass with goodly sport' 1319–24; 3. *Sensual Appetite*, Dancers, *Ignorance* 'Dance we, dance we' (w. ref.) 1334–45; 4. *Sensual Appetite*, Dancers 'Now we will here begin to sing' 1365–9; 5. *Humanity* 'Down, down, down, down etc.' (a burden, one line) 1395; 6. *Ignorance* 'Robin Hood in Barnsdale stood' 1396–419; **Instrumental**: sheet music is supplied for the second song; music for the dances but not specified

Staging and set the title page notes that the play may be peformed in an hour and a half, but if desired several specified sections of 'sad' (weighty) matter might be omitted, reducing the play to three-quarters of an hour; where action is localized, this is done by the presence of characters and dialogue and there is no indication as to set other than the portable model, and the fact that *Ignorance* hides 'in some corner' (1180); after the list of characters is the statement: 'Also if ye list ye may bring in a disguising'

Stage properties an orrery or model (of the earth and heavens) 147 *sd*

PLACENAMES

Africa 671, 836; America 839; Asia ('Ynde') 671, 837; Asia ('India') Major 845; Asia ('India') Minor 844; Atlantic ('Great') Ocean 733; Barnsdale 1396; Boulogne 716; Britain 705; Calais 716; China ('Catowe') 852, 860; Denmark 728; Egypt ('the Soudans country') 832; England 704, 708, 863, 1143, 1147; Europe 671, 835; Flanders 717; France 718, 1143; Germany ('Almayne') 727; Gulf of Venice

725; Iceland 730; Ireland 714; Italy 721; Jerusalem 680, 841; Mediterranean 830; Naples 723; Norway 728; Portugal 720; Red Sea 842; Rome 722; Scotland 709; Spain 719; Turkey 833; Venice 726

ALLUSIONS

The Khan of Cathay 852, 860; Robin Hood 1389, 1396; Prester John 846; Moses 843; Amerigo Vespucci ('Americus') 840

BIBLIOGRAPHY

Axton and Williams, 1977, pp. 8–11
Borish, M. E. 'Source and Intention of *The Four Elements*', *SP* 35:2 (1938) pp. 149–63
Devereux, E. J. 'John Rastell's Utopian Voyage', *Moreana* 13:51 (1976) pp. 119–23
Djwa, S. 'Early Explorations: New Founde Landys (1496–1729)', *SCL* 4:2 (1979) pp. 7–21
Greg, W. W. 'Notes on Some Early Plays: Rastell's *Nature of the Four Elements*, Printer and Date', *Library* 4th series, 11 (1930) pp. 46–50
Hogrefe, 1959, pp. 262–74
Hyatt King, A. 'The Significance of John Rastell in Early Music Printing', *Library*, 5th series, 26:3 (1971) pp. 197–214
Nugent, E. 'Sources of Rastell's *Four Elements*', *PMLA* 57:1 (1942) pp. 74–88
Ozawa, 1984, pp. 1–23
Parks, G. B. 'The Geography of the *Interlude of the Four Elements*', *PQ* 17:3 (1938) pp. 251–62
Parks, G. B. 'Rastell and Waldseemüller's Map', *PMLA* 58:2 (1943) pp. 572–4
Parr, J. 'More Sources of Rastell's *Interlude of the Four Elements*', *PMLA* 60:1 (1945) pp. 48–58
Parr, J. 'Rastell's Geographical Knowledge of America', *PQ* 27:3 (1948) pp. 229–40
Reed, 1919, pp. 1–17
Southern, 1973, pp. 204–15
West, W. N. 'The Idea of a Theater: Humanist Ideology and the Imaginary Stage in Early Modern Europe', *RenD* 28 [1997] (1999) pp. 245–87

28   The Four PP

DATE, AUTHORSHIP AND AUSPICES

1520–8 (first printed *c.* 1533); John Heywood; auspices unknown, but probably for household or possibly court performance; Greg 21

TEXT AND EDITIONS

Extant originals

1544 (?) printing by William Middleton: BL; *STC* 13300
1560 (?) printing by William Copland: Bodleian; Eliz. Club; *STC* 13301
1569 printing by John Allde: BL; Pepys; Rylands; *STC* 13302

Editions

2000	Walker (OS)
1994	CHD (CD-Rom and online transcription of Middleton printing, l.l., OS)
1991	Axton and Happé (OS)*
1984	Clopper (facsimile)
1976	Fraser and Rabkin, vol. 1 (NS)
1963	Gassner (NS)*
1962	Hopper and Lahey (n.l., NS)
1937	De la Bère (n.l., OS)
1934	Boas (NS)
1924	Adams (OS)
1914	Farmer (1914a) (facsimile, n.l.)
1908	TFT (facsimile, n.l.)
1906	Farmer, EEDS (n.l., NS)
1905	Farmer (1) (n.l., NS)
1897	Manly, vol. 1 (OS)
1874–6	Dodsley, vol. 1 (n.l., NS)

SOURCES

La Farce d'un pardonneur, d'un triacleur et d'un taverneur appears to be the principal source, but there are other possible sources: see the introduction to the edition by Axton and Happé, pp. 38 and 42–5, and also Maxwell, 1946 listed below.

CHARACTERS

A Palmer   A Pardoner   A'Pothecary   A Pedlar

PLOT SUMMARY

The *Palmer* commences the play with a description of his extensive pilgrimages, both at home and abroad. He is challenged by a *Pardoner* about the value of pilgrimage and when he asserts that its purpose is to seek forgiveness of sins, the *Pardoner* argues that this could be gained with much less effort. However, when he reveals himself as a pardoner, the *Palmer* expresses scepticism about his views, but the *Pardoner* goes on to claim potency for his pardons. They are joined by the '*Pothecary*, who argues that, through his remedies, he has helped far more people to heaven than the *Pardoner*. A *Pedlar* then arrives and proceeds to describe his trade and wares. He expresses his pleasure in joining the company and, discussing with the '*Pothecary* how they might entertain themselves, they talk briefly about drinking before deciding to sing a song. The *Pardoner* rejects the dalliance and insists on a return to the former argument, appointing the *Pedlar* as judge of which of the three is most effective in helping men to achieve eternal salvation. The *Pedlar* declines to make a judgement, saying that they would work best in co-operation with one another by helping men to come to contrition, to gain remission of penance, and then despatching them to their graves. However, the three fail to agree on who should be the leader in this endeavour. To determine the leader, the *Pedlar* then devises a contest in a skill in which he believes them all to be expert: lying. First, however, the *Pardoner* displays his relics and describes their beneficial qualities, and the '*Pothecary* does the same with his remedies. After some wrangling, the *Pedlar* decides they should each tell a tale, the teller of the most unlikely one to be deemed the winner. The '*Pothecary* relates the story of his bizarre cure of a young woman and the *Pardoner* of a visit to hell to rescue a woman. When the *Palmer*, criticizing the *Pardoner*'s tale, says he has never seen a woman out of patience, they all accuse him of telling a great lie. On the basis of this the *Pedlar* judges him the winner, much to the annoyance of the other two, who refuse to follow him. Though the *Palmer* and *Pedlar* shrug this off, the *Pardoner* and '*Pothecary* are finally won over by the virtuous arguments of the *Palmer*, who ends the play with a blessing on the audience.

PLAY LENGTH

1,234 lines

COMMENTARY

This comic interlude consists of a rather meandering strand of conversation, and there is little action, though there is rudimentary characterization. The *Pedlar* is resolutely genial and interested in companionship, while the *Pardoner* has a far more businesslike orientation. The *Pardoner* is similar to the character in Heywood's *The Pardoner and the Friar*, and some of his relics are the same.

Other debate plays: **29, 31, 54, 69, 99, 102.**

SIGNIFICANT TOPICS AND NARRATIVE ELEMENTS

pilgrimage; pardons and pardoners; medicine; peddling; women's dress; drinking; a lying contest or storytelling game; relics; Corpus Christi plays; a visit to hell; the nature of women

DRAMATURGICAL AND RHETORICAL FEATURES

Verbal and general the *Pedlar*'s list of commodities 235–42; the *Pardoner*'s list of relics 496–558; the '*Pothecary*'s list of remedies 606–30; stories told within the play: '*Pothecary*'s 704–68, *Pardoner*'s 771–976; the *Pedlar*'s formulaic list of women in threes 1070–80; only two stage directions, both in English

Actions and stage directions 321 *sd*: 'Here they (*Ped., Pal., Par., 'Pot.*) sing'; 467 *sd*: 'Here the '*Pot.* hops'; 499–500: the '*Pot.* kisses the jawbone
Songs and music Pedlar, Palmer, Pardoner, '*Pothecary* (w.n.s.) 321 *sd*
Staging and set the action is unlocalized and there are no indications as to set
Stage properties the *Pardoner*'s relics: a jawbone 497, a toe 508–9, a buttock bone 521, a slipper 525, a tooth 538, a box 546, a glass 556; the '*Pothecary*'s remedies: a box (of rhubarb) 592, an ointment 606, several bottles of medicine 612–28

PLACENAMES

Amiens[1] 30; St Anne's of Buxton[1] 32; Armenia[1] 33; Our Lady of Boston[1] (Boston, Lincs) 39; St Botulph's (Boston)[1] 32; Bury St Edmunds[1] 39; Mt Calvary[1] 15; Canterbury[1] 45; Catway Bridge (Essex)[1] 46; St Cornelius (Rome)[1] 37; Coventry 832; Crome Hill (Greenwich)[1] 48; Dagenham[1] 36; St David's (Pembrokeshire)[1] 43; St Denis (Paris)[1] 43; St George's, Southwark[1] 34; Hailes[1] 41; King Henry's Tomb (Chertsey, Surrey)[1] 46; St James of Galicia (Santiago de Compostela)[1] 37; Jericho 100; Jerusalem[1] 13; Joshophat[1] 17; St Mark's, Venice[1] 44; San Matteo (Palermo)[1] 44; Muswell Hill[1] 48; Newmarket Heath 974; Mount of Olives 17; Our Lady's Shrine (Hampstead Heath)[1] 50; St Patrick's Purgatory (Donegal)[1] 40; St Paul's Churchyard 1013; St Peter's (Rome)[1] 23; Redbourn (St Albans)[1] 41; Rhodes[1] 29; St Richard's Shrine (Chichester)[1] 49; St Rocco's Shrine (Arles or Venice)[1] 49; Rome 21,[1] 102; 'St Ronyon's'[1] 31; St Saviour's (Bermondsey)[1] 47; Shrine of John Shorne[1] 45; Our Lady of Southwell (Notts)[1] 47; Surrey (? 'Sothery') 879; 'St Uncumber's'(?)[1] 31; Walsingham[1] 35; Waltham Cross[1] 35; Our Lady of Willesden (Middx)[1] 48; St Winifred's Well (Wales)[1] 38

1 Part of the list of places the *Palmer* claims to have visited on pilgrimage.

ALLUSIONS

Corpus Christi plays 831; Job 34; Noah 33; Seven Sleepers 526; Great Turk (poss. Tamburlaine) 538

REPORT ON MODERN PRODUCTION

University of Toronto, PLS Festival, 23–24 May 1992 (City College, New York), dir. S. Urkowitz [*RORD* 32 (1993) pp.164–5]

BIBLIOGRAPHY

Blamires, A. 'John Heywood and *The Four PP*', *Trivium* 14 (1979) pp. 47–69
Bolwell, 1921, pp. 101–5
Boocker, D. 'Heywood's Indulgent Pardoner', *ELN* 29:2 (1991) pp. 21–9
Cartwright, K. 'The Humanism of Acting: John Heywood's *The Foure PP*', *SLI* 26:1 (1993) pp. 21–46

Cartwright, 1999, pp. 24–48
De la Bère, 1937, pp. 74–82
Finkelstein, R. 'Formation of the Christian Self in *The Four PP*', *Acta* 13 (1987) pp. 143–52
Hogrefe, 1959, pp. 289–94
Johnson, 1970, pp. 89–96, 112–15
Lines, 2000, pp. 413–20
Maxwell, 1946, pp. 70–86
Miller, E. S. 'Guilt and Penalty in Heywood's Pardoner's Lie', *MLQ* 10 (1949) pp. 58–60
Symonds, 1900, 151–62
Walker, 1998, pp. 91–100
Whiting, B. J. 'A Dramatic Clyster', *Bulletin of the History of Medicine* 16 (1944) pp. 511–13

29   Fulgens and Lucres

DATE, AUTHORSHIP AND AUSPICES

c. 1497; Henry Medwall; probably for performance in the Great Hall, Lambeth Palace (under the patronage of John Morton); Greg 1

TEXT AND EDITIONS

Extant originals

c. 1512–16 printing by John Rastell: BL (frag.); Huntington; *STC* 17778

Editions

2000   Walker (OS)
1994   CHD (CD-Rom and online copy of Nelson, 1980, l.l., OS)
1981   Meredith (NS)
1981   Moeslein (OS)
1980   Nelson (OS)*
1976   Wickham (NS)
1966   Creeth (OS)*
1934   Boas (NS)*
1926   Boas and Reed (OS)*
1920   De Ricci (1920b) (facsimile, n.l.)

SOURCES

The play is based principally on Buonaccorso da Montemagno's *De Vera Nobilitate* (*c.* 1428), translated by John Tiptoft and printed by Caxton in 1481, but there are also native elements. See the introduction to Nelson's edition, pp. 20–3, and the essays by Reed and Fletcher listed below.

CHARACTERS

A   Fulgens   Lucres   Gaius Flaminius
B   Publius Cornelius   Ancilla (Joan)

PLOT SUMMARY

The players A and B open the action with a form of induction in which they engage in banter with each other and tell the story of the play. *Fulgens* then enters with a long speech describing his own socially elevated status and his beautiful daughter, *Lucres*, for whom he wishes to find a husband. He first engages in conversation with a noble suitor, *Publius Cornelius*, and then raises the issue with *Lucres* herself, giving her the right to choose a husband for herself. He asks her to hear the suits of both *Cornelius* and a humbly born suitor, *Gaius Flaminius*. She is approached by *Flaminius* but says she will consult her father. When she leaves, *A* attaches himself to *Flaminius* as his servant, and undertakes to press his suit to *Lucres*. *A* and *B* then pursue a discussion about fashions in dress, and *B* announces that he has become a servant to *Cornelius*. What follows next is a sequence in which the main plot is parodied by the competition of *A* and *B* for the favours of *Lucres*'s maid, *Joan*, all three engaging in vulgar banter. The suitors compete first by singing, then wrestling, and finally in a mock-joust in the form of a game – 'fart prick in cule' – using brooms and other kitchen implements. Finally *Joan* loses patience, beats them both and retires. *Flaminius* enters to ask about the progress of his suit and *A* tells him that he will have to take part in a debate with *Cornelius* in order to resolve the matter. It will take place before *Lucres* and she will choose the victor as husband. This news closes the first part of the play, and *A* and *B* open the second half with another induction reflecting on the matter and substance of the interlude. *Cornelius* enters and gives *B* a token to take to *Lucres*, which he then does, in the process scandalizing her with his lewd speech. They are joined by *A*, who commends his master to her before they leave and *Cornelius* approaches her himself, accompanied by *B*. *B* fetches some mummers, who perform a dance until the debate between the suitors commences. *Cornelius* presents an argument for the value of noble birth, while *Flaminius* argues for the importance of personal worth and ability. Finally, *Lucres* chooses *Flaminius* as victor and the play is concluded with a direct address to the audience by *A* and *B* on the matter of marriage and the social debate at the heart of the narrative.

PLAY LENGTH

2,353 lines; Part I, 1432; Part II, 921

COMMENTARY

This is a two-part, entirely secular interlude about what constitutes the basis of true nobility, with an outcome appropriate to the household of Medwall's patron, the 'new man' Cardinal Morton, Archbishop of Canterbury. The representation of the woman at the centre of the conflict is almost entirely in terms of her role as a passive prize, though the narrative requires she be given the choice of suitor. The coarse play of the servants provides a social and rhetorical contrast to the debate of the more elevated suitors, and the role of the servants in shaping much of the narrative is noteworthy. While the elite protagonists are classical, and so named, the servant figures are clearly English, as indicated by Joan's name and the several place-name references in their speech. There is close attention to the balancing of light with serious matter in the play, as in the mummers' dance preceding the debate.

Other marriage quest plays: **47, 57** (frag.), **61, 62, 101**.
Other debate plays: **28, 31, 54, 69, 99, 102**.
Other 'estates' plays: **31, 85, 94, 98**.
Other plays with classical settings: **19, 39, 43, 57** (frag.), **91, 92**.

SIGNIFICANT TOPICS AND NARRATIVE ELEMENTS

players and their status; the nature of nobility; social mobility; marriage; servants and lower-class behaviour; apparel

DRAMATURGICAL AND RHETORICAL FEATURES

Verbal and general A's and B's inductions to both parts of the play I.1–201 and II.1–133; *Fulgens*'s 'boasting' speech of self-introduction I.202–91; a comic subplot sequence I.861–1243; the wrestling match of A and B I.1146 *sd*; the jousting game 'fart prick in cule' I.1183–212; B uses a Dutch expression to one of the minstrels II.389; a formal debate by *Flaminius* and *Cornelius* II.441–705; the element of servant intrigue is structurally significant in the action; several slang terms used by A and B; the elite figures generally use a rhyme royal verse scheme; stage directions in Latin, with two exceptions

Costume and dress B is dressed richly, like a 'player' I.49–50; B gives notice that *Cornelius* will enter as a 'rutter' or gallant and describes his expensive clothing I.717–50; B says he is wearing an old garment, having newly come to *Cornelius*'s service I.762–4

Actions and stage directions I.op. *sd*: 'A enters saying'; I.201 *sd*: '*Ful.* enters saying'; I.291 *sd*: 'Enter *Pub. C.* saying'; I.359 *sd*: 'And (*Pub.*) goes out. Then *B.* says'; 409 *sd*: 'Enter *Ful., Luc.* and *Anc.* and (*Ful.*) says'; I.471 *sd*: 'Then after some pause, let *Luc.* say'; I.574 *sd*: 'And *Luc.* should go out. Then *A* going to *Gai. F.* should say thus to him'; I.685 *sd*: 'And *Gai. F.* should go out, and *B.* says'; I.833 *sd*: 'Avoid (depart) the place *A*' (E); I.853 *sd*: 'Come in the maiden' (E); I.994 *sd*: 'And he (*B*) will try to kiss her (*Jo.*)'; I.1004 *sd*: 'And he (*B*) will kiss her (*Jo.*). Enter *A*'; I.1125 sd: 'And then they (*A, B, Jo.*) will sing'; I.1146 *sd*: 'And then they (*A, B*) will wrestle'; I.1156 *sd*: 'Then he (*B*) throws down a glove'; I.1206 *sd*: 'And let *A*, having been thrown

down, say'; I.1237 *sd*: 'And both (*A*, *B*) having been beaten, the maid withdraws';
II.op. *sd*: '*A* enters saying'; II.72–3: *B* knocks on a door, then lets himself in; II.349
sd: 'And, scratching his head, let him (*A*) say after a small interval'; II.389 *sd*: 'And
then they (mummers) will dance'; **Simple entry**: *B* I.27; *Gai*. I.483; *Gai*. I.1243; *B*
I.1324; *Luc*. II.230; **Simple exit**: (*B*) I.393; (*Ful*). I.470; *Gai*., *A* I.1324; *Pub*. II.216;
(*B*) II.307; *A* II.355; (*B*) II.404; *Pub*., *Gai*. II.751; **Simple speech**: *B* I.359; *Luc*. II.404
Songs and music *Joan*, *A* and *B* (w.n.s.) I.1125 *sd*; **Instrumental**: minstrel music
for the dance II.389 *sd*

Staging and set A direction at the start of the play notes that it is 'divided into two
parts to be played at two times'; this is clearly a hall play performed in conjunction
with a banquet; the stage is called the 'place' (I.833 *sd*); the action is unlocalized,
except that the subplot takes place in a kitchen; there are no indications as to set
apart from the door at which *B* knocks (I.72–3)

Stage properties a gauntlet thrown by *B* I.1156 *sd*; *A* and *B*'s staffs and spears
(kitchen implements) and rope used in the mock joust I.1185–7, I.1189; *Gaius's*
letter for *Lucres* II.324

PLACENAMES

Africa II.477; Calais I.1084; Carthage II.476; Court of Common Pleas (Westminster)
I.805; England II.393; Italy II.525; Kent I.1110; Rome I.70, I.125, I.180, I.233, II.519;
Scotland II.811; Spain II.381; Wales II.393; York I.846

ALLUSIONS

Adam and Eve II.665; Alexander the Great II.474; King Arthur II.474; *Psalm 18:4*
(V)/*19:3* (AV) I.18; Scipio Africanus II.477

REPORTS ON MODERN PRODUCTIONS

1. Lancaster University, 27–29 March 1984, Christ's College Cambridge, 30
   March 1984 (JL), dir. M. Twycross [*METh* 6:1 (1984) pp. 44–8; *RORD* 27 (1984)
   pp. 185–6]
2. University of Cork, dir. A. Corbett, 9–11 January 1997 [*RORD* 37 (1998) p. 131]

RECORDED PRODUCTION

Videotape: JL, dir. M. Twycross (Lancaster University Television, 1985)

BIBLIOGRAPHY

Altman, 1978, pp. 18–30
Baskervill, C. R. 'Conventional Features of Medwall's *Fulgens and Lucres*', MP 24:4 (1927) pp. 419–22

Bevington, 1968, pp. 42–52
Colley, J. S. 'Fulgens and Lucres: Politics and Aesthetics', ZAA 23:4 (1975) pp. 322–30
Cope, 1973, pp. 101–7
Davison, 1982, pp. 20–33
Debax, 1994, pp. 15–36
Fifield, M. 'Medwell's [sic] Play and Non-Play', SMC 6 (1974) pp. 532–6
Fletcher, A. '"Farte Prycke in Cule": A Late-Elizabethan Analogue from Ireland', METh 8:2 (1986) pp. 132–9
Glage, L. 'Wer lacht über wen?: Henry Medwalls Interlude von Fulgens und Lucres', ZAA 25:3 (1977) pp. 254–63
Godfrey, R. 'Nervous Laughter in Henry Medwall's Fulgens and Lucres' in Lascombes, 1996, pp. 81–97
Grantley, 2000, pp. 59–62
Hecht, H. 'Henry Medwalls Fulgens and Lucres: Eine Studie zu den Anfängen des weltlichen Dramas in England' in Brandl, 1925, pp. 83–111
Hogrefe, 1959, pp. 278–83
Horner, O. 'Fulgens and Lucres: An Historical Perspective', METh 15 (1993) pp. 49–86
Jones, C. E. 'Notes on Fulgens and Lucres', MLN 50:8 (1935) pp. 508–9
Jones, R. C. 'The Stage World and the "Real" World in Medwall's Fulgens and Lucres', MLQ 32:2 (1971) pp. 131–42
Lascombes, 1995, pp. 66–80
Lowers, J. K. 'High Comedy Elements in Medwall's Fulgens and Lucres', ELH 8 (1941) pp. 103–6
Meredith, P. '"Farte Pryke in Cule" and Cock-fighting', METh 6:1 (1984) pp. 30–39
Merrix, R. P. 'The Function of the Comic Plot in Fulgens and Lucrece', MLS 7:1 (1977) pp. 16–26
Mullally, R. 'The Source of the Fulgens Woodcut', TN 30:2 (1976) pp. 61–5
Mullini, R. 'Fulgens and Lucres: A Mirror Held up to Stage and Society' in Higgins, 1997, pp. 203–18
Norland, 1995, pp. 233–43
Ozawa, 1984, pp. 1–23
Reed, A. W. 'Sixt Birck and Henry Medwall, De Vera Nobilitate', RES 2:8 (1926) pp. 411–15
Richardson and Johnston, 1991, pp. 141–4
Siemens, R. G. '"As Strayght as Ony Pole": Publius Cornelius, Edmund de la Pole, and Contemporary Court Satire in Henry Medwall's Fulgens and Lucres', RenFor 1:2
Twycross, M. (with M. Jones and A. Fletcher) '"Farte Pryke in Cule": The Pictures', METh 23 (2001) pp. 100–21
Tydeman, 1986, pp. 137–59
Waith, E. M. 'Controversia in the English Drama: Medwall and Massinger', PMLA 68:1 (1953) pp. 286–303
Whall, 1988, pp. 6–33
Willson, 1975, pp. 9–12
Wright, L. B. 'Notes on Fulgens and Lucres: New Light on the Interlude', MLN 41:2 (1926) pp. 97–100
Yamakawa, T. 'The Ideal Woman in Henry Medwall's Fulgens and Lucres', ELR (Kyoto) 14 (1970) pp. 45–59 (in Japanese)

30   Gammer Gurton's Needle

DATE, AUTHORSHIP AND AUSPICES

1552–63 (SR as 'Dyccon of Bedlam' 1562/3 c. Jan.); William Stevenson (?); played at Christ's College, Cambridge; Greg 67

TEXT AND EDITIONS

Extant originals

1575 printing by Thomas Colwell: BL (two copies); Bodleian; Dyce; Folger; Huntington; Indiana; NYPL; Yale; (further copies extant); *STC* 23263

Editions

1994   CHD (CD-Rom and online transcription of Colwell printing, l.l., s.l., OS)
1984   Tydeman (OS)*
1984   Whitworth (s.l., NS)
1976   Fraser and Rabkin, vol. I (s.l., NS)
1966   Creeth (s.l., OS)
1963   Gassner (s.l., NS)
1955   Heilman (s.l., NS)
1934   Baskervill, Heltzel and Nethercot (s.l., NS)
1934   Boas (s.l., NS)
1933   Ayliff (n.l., NS)
1924   Adams (s.l., OS)
1920   Brett-Smith (s.l., OS)
1910   TFT (facsimile, n.l.)
1906   Farmer (5) (n.l., NS)
1906   Farmer (1906a) (n.l., NS)
1903   H. Bradley in Gayley, vol. I (s.l., OS)
1897   Manly, vol. II (s.l., OS)
1874–6   Dodsley, vol. III (n.l., NS)

SOURCES

The main source is possibly *La Farce du raporteur*; see Whiting's essay below.

CHARACTERS

Prologue
Diccon, the Bedlam
Hodge, Gammer Gurton's servant
Tib, Gammer Gurton's maid
Gammer Gurton

Cocke, Gammer Gurton's boy
Dame Chat
Doctor Rat, the Curate
Master Bailey

Mute parts: Doll, Dame Chat's maid; Scapethrift, Master Bailey's servant

PLOT SUMMARY

The *Prologue* summarizes the story of the play and *Diccon* commences the action by telling of general consternation at *Gammer Gurton*'s house, which has enabled him to steal some bacon unnoticed. He meets *Hodge*, who, when he hears about the commotion, goes in and learns from the maid *Tib* that it is because *Gammer Gurton* has lost her needle. She can therefore not repair *Hodge*'s breeches, which he has torn again after she had recently mended them. *Tib, Hodge* and the boy *Cocke* are despatched to look for the needle, but none is able to locate it, and they eventually retire because of fading light. Singers from the ale-house conclude the first act with a song. *Diccon* then meets *Hodge* again, who is carrying some bread and complaining of the loss of the bacon, which he thinks the cat has eaten. They talk again about the missing needle that *Hodge* wants found, as he is to meet again a maid who has given him some encouragement and so he desperately needs his breeches mended. Promising to help, *Diccon* makes *Hodge* swear an oath to do what he says. When *Diccon* then starts uttering a charm to recover the needle, *Hodge* becomes terrified, fouls himself and rushes off. *Diccon* shouts after him and *Dame Chat, Gammer Gurton's* neighbour, approaches to ask what is going on. *Diccon* tells her that *Gammer Gurton*'s cock has been stolen and that *Tib* has suggested to her mistress that it was *Chat* who stole it, making her promise not to reveal that he told her this. When she goes off, *Hodge* and *Gammer Gurton* arrive successively to complain to *Diccon* that the needle is still missing, and *Diccon* tells *Gammer Gurton* that *Dame Chat* is the one who has stolen it, also making her promise not to reveal him as the source of the information. *Hodge* then enters with an awl and thong to mend his breeches, encounters *Gammer Gurton*, and they go off to confront *Chat*. *Chat* thinks they are talking about the cock, a fight ensues but with no conclusion, and *Gammer Gurton* decides to call in the curate, *Dr Rat*. *Hodge* in the meantime suspects the cat of having swallowed the needle, but *Gammer Gurton* will not let him kill it to find out. A complaining *Dr Rat* arrives, and *Hodge* tells him the story of the lost needle. *Diccon* enters and refuses to reassert his allegation before *Dame Chat*, but says he will go and talk to her privately. Once there, he tells her that *Hodge* is intending to break into her house and kill her hens. He then returns to *Dr Rat* to say he saw *Chat* using the needle and, supposedly to allow him to spy on her, he leads the curate to the hole in *Chat*'s house, through which he had previously warned her that *Hodge* would enter. Off-stage, sounds then indicate that *Chat* is beating and drenching the intruder, and *Dr Rat* appears bedraggled and hurt. He summons the *Bailey* who, however, has little sympathy with him as he was the intruder against whom *Chat* was defending her home. They nonetheless confront her, and she relates to them the warning she has received. They go to accuse *Hodge* but find that he cannot have been a culprit as his head is unharmed. *Gammer Gurton* again accuses *Chat* of stealing her needle and she indignantly retorts that only a few days earlier she had been wrongly accused of stealing *Gammer Gurton*'s cock. The confusion is slowly resolved and it emerges that *Diccon* is behind all the reports. He is fetched and when the *Bailey* accuses him he confesses. He is made to take an oath on *Hodge*'s breeches to reform his behaviour towards the people he has offended. In laying his hand on the breeches, he brings it down hard, which causes *Hodge* to feel a sharp prick. The needle is then discovered still stuck in the breeches from the earlier mending, harmony is restored and *Diccon* requests applause from the audience.

PLAY LENGTH

1,280 lines

COMMENTARY

This is an accomplished farce with something of the shape and form of a classical comedy, although firmly rooted in English Tudor village life. *Diccon* has all the characteristics of the Vice in his direct rapport with the audience, his ingenuity and his taste for gratuitous mischief. However, his appellation 'the Bedlam' suggests disorder rather than anything more morally serious, and he is not punished at the end. He in fact shows no signs of mental disturbance and is clearly a farcical device more than anything else.

Other secular comedies: **5, 41, 46, 47, 75, 88, 91, 92, 95.**

Other plays featuring prominent women characters: **3, 6, 32, 43, 46, 51, 63, 70, 75, 87, 95, 97.**

SIGNIFICANT TOPICS AND NARRATIVE ELEMENTS

a comic representation of village life; female scolding and neighbour conflict; an ale-house; food and hunger; magic and conjuring; scatology; a comic representation of a rustic cleric; servants play a significant role in the action; a bailiff in a policing role

DRAMATURGICAL AND RHETORICAL FEATURES

Verbal and general rustic speech: *Hodge* 45 ff., *Tib* 93 ff., *Gammer Gurton* 131 ff.; *Hodge*'s formulaic list of actions 334–8; *Hodge*'s oath 350–5; a scolding sequence between *Gammer Gurton* and *Chat* 603–29 (followed by fight); *Hodge*'s formulaic account to *Dr Rat* of the loss of the needle, repeating 'see now' 753–76; a five-act play with scene divisions; stage directions in English
Costume and dress *Hodge* enters with dirty clothes 45
Actions and stage directions 49: *Ho.* tears his breeches; 219: *Ga., Tib* and *Co.* kneel to search for the needle; 339 *sd*: '(*Ho.*) Pointing behind to his torn breeches'; 355 *sd*: 'Here he (*Ho.*) kisses *Di.*'s breeches'; 384–9: *Ho.* farts; 500 *sd*: '(*Ho.*) Pointing behind to his torn breeches'; 630–51: a physical fight between *Ga.* and *Ch.*; 930 *sd*, 969 *sd*: '(*Dr R.*) Showing his broken head'; 974 *sd*: '(*Dr R.*) Showing his head'; 1028 *sd*: '(*Ch.*) Thinking that *Ho.*'s head was broken, and that *Ga.* would not let him come before them'; 1237 *sd*: 'And (*Di.*) gave him (*Ho.*) a good blow on the buttock'

Songs and music Various cast 'Back and side go bare' (w. ref., w.s.; the song is sung off stage) 237–79; *Instrumental*: musicians play pipes and fiddles 561–2
Staging and set *Hodge* calls from above, as from an upstairs window, suggesting an upper level (213); there is likely to have been an opening door for *Chat*'s house (601), and another for *Gammer Gurton*'s house (754); the ale house and interiors are suggested by off-stage dialogue, but there may have been another door for the ale-house; the hole in *Chat*'s house features in the action and needs to be represented; *Gammer Gurton* at one point enters through the audience 507
Stage properties *Diccon*'s piece of bacon 42; *Hodge*'s piece of barley bread 293; a cup of ale for *Diccon* 471; a thong 565; an awl 568; *Gammer Gurton*'s needle 1246–7

PLACENAMES

Boulogne[1] 424; Cologne[1] 425; Thames 693; Tyne 693

1 Part of saints' names (see Allusions section below)

ALLUSIONS

St Anne 221; Beelzebub 831; Our Lady of Boulogne[1] 424; the Three Kings of Cologne[1] 425; St Dominic[1] 425; St Dunstan[1] 425; Hobgoblin 1199; Judas 540; Friar Rush (Rausch – a devil) 590

1 Part of the list of saints on which *Diccon* makes *Chat* swear

REPORTS ON MODERN PRODUCTIONS

1. Cardiff (Open Cast Theatre), 17 January 1975 [*RORD* 18 (1975) p. 64]
2. Winchester Great Hall (Medieval Players), dir. C. Heap, 11 June 1982 [*RORD* 25 (1982) pp. 146–7]

RECORDED PRODUCTION

LP Record: BBC, *The First Stage*, dir. J. Barton (1970)

BIBLIOGRAPHY

Altman, 1978, pp. 152–7
Bradley, H. 'Critical Essay (on *Gammer Gurton's Needle*)' in Gayley, 1903, pp. 197–204
Cartwright, K. '*Gammer Gurton's Needle*: Toward a Dramaturgy of Empathy', *RenP* 1993 (1994) pp. 117–40
Cartwright, 1999, pp. 75–99
Duncan, D. '*Gammer Gurton's Needle* and the Concept of Human Parody', *SEL* 27:2 (1987) pp. 177–96
Graham-White, A. 'Elizabethan Punctuation and the Actor: *Gammer Gurton's Nedle* as a Case Study', *TJ* 34:1 (1982) pp. 96–106

Humphrey, G. 'Gammer Gurton's Needle', EJ 7 (1919) pp. 24–8

Ingram, R. W. 'Gammer Gurton's Nedle: Comedy not Quite of the Lowest Order?', SEL 7:2 (1968) pp. 257–68

Kozikowski, S. J. 'Comedy Ecclesiastical and Otherwise in Gammer Gurton's Needle', Greyfriar 18 (1975) pp. 5–18

Kozikowski, S. J. 'Stevenson's Gammer Gurton's Needle', Explicator 38 (1980) pp. 37–9

McFadyen, N. L. 'What Was Really Lost in Gammer Gurton's Needle?', RenP [1982] (1983) pp. 9–13

Norland, 1995, pp. 280–91

Paster, 1993, pp. 116–25

Perry, C. 'Commodity and Commonwealth in Gammer Gurton's Nedle', SEL 42:2 (2002) pp. 217–34

Roberts, C. W. 'The Authorship of Gammer Gurton's Needle', PQ 19:2 (1940) pp. 97–113

Robinson, J. W. 'The Art and Meaning of Gammer Gurton's Nedle', RenD n.s. 14 (1983) pp. 45–77

Ross, C. H. 'The Authorship of Gammer Gurton's Needle', MLN 7:6 (1892) pp. 161–7

Southern, 1973, pp. 401–22

Spivack 1958, pp. 322–7

Toole, W. B. 'The Aesthetics of Scatology in Gammer Gurton's Nedle', ELN 10:4 (1973) pp. 252–8

Velz, J. W. 'Scatology and Moral Meaning in Two English Renaissance Plays', SCR 1:1 (1984) pp. 4–21

Wall, W. '"Household Stuff": The Sexual Politics of Domesticity and the Advent of English Comedy', ELH 65 (1998) pp. 1–45

Watt, H. A. 'The Staging of Gammer Gurton's Nedle' in Elizabethan Studies in Honor of G. F. Reynolds, Boulder, University of Colorado, 1945, pp. 85–92

Whall, 1988, pp. 137–65

Whiting, B. J. 'Diccon's French Cousin', SP 42:1 (1945) pp. 31–40

31   Gentleness and Nobility

DATE, AUTHORSHIP AND AUSPICES

1527–30; attributed to John Heywood, but see Dunn's essay below; possibly for Rastell's stage; Greg 8

TEXT AND EDITIONS

Extant originals

c. 1525 printing by John Rastell: BL (imp.); Bodleian (imp.); Cambridge; Pepys; STC 20723

1535 printing ('J. rastell me fieri fecit'): BL (frags.); STC 20723

Editions

1994   CHD (CD-Rom and online transcription of Rastell c. 1525 printing, l.l. OS)
1979   Axton (OS, edition based on Pepys copy)*
1950   Partridge and Wilson (facsimile)
1941   Cameron (1941a) (OS, edition based on BL copy)
1914   Farmer (n.l., OS)
1908   Farmer (12) (n.l., NS)
1908   TFT (facsimile, n.l.)

SOURCES

No principal source has been established, but there are several analogues: see Cameron's and Tucker Brooke's essays below.

CHARACTERS

The Merchant   The Knight   The Ploughman   The Philosopher

PLOT SUMMARY

The play is a three-sided debate 'in the manner of an interlude' involving a *Merchant*, a *Knight* and a *Ploughman*. The *Merchant* and *Knight* start the dispute, which is about the right to be called noble, and the issue of social rank as legitimized through birth or through personal achievement. The *Knight* argues for his class's role in war and the protection of the realm, while the *Merchant* emphasizes the skills of his class and its enrichment of the commonwealth. They are aggressively interrupted by the *Ploughman*, who claims ascendancy over both and attacks them with his whip. When pacified by the *Merchant*, he joins the debate. The *Knight* and the *Merchant* reiterate their arguments, while the *Ploughman* advances his claim to nobility on the basis of the self-sufficiency of his class. The *Merchant* replies that the beasts are also self-sufficient but the *Ploughman* retorts that man needs his intellect to provide for himself, which makes him noble. He also goes on to point out that it is on him and his class that the other two depend for their sustenance. At the end of Part I, the *Ploughman* departs on market business and the three agree to meet again. In Part II the *Ploughman* engages with the *Knight* on the importance of individual qualities over the glory of ancestry. When the *Knight* claims that his ancestors had the intelligence to organize society, the *Ploughman* attacks what he sees as their oppression and tyranny, and also he rounds on the *Merchant* for economic rapacity. Once again he beats the other two when they disagree with him, and he goes on to represent his own impoverished manner of life in terms of ascetic Christian values. The *Knight* and *Merchant* call his arguments idle chatter, at which the *Ploughman* withdraws, saying that argument does not make any difference anyway. The *Knight* and *Merchant* reach a form of agreement that wealth is necessary for governance and that nobility comes from using it with generosity and gentleness. The play is concluded by a *Philosopher*, who broadly concurs with the elite protagonists and exhorts the ruling classes to virtue.

PLAY LENGTH

1,176 lines

COMMENTARY

This is an almost completely secular 'estates' play, which replaces the clergy with the merchant class. It is a dialogue or debate play with little action, but has a comic thrust rather than seeking to arrive at social or political prescriptions. In the way in which it dramatizes the three men, the play becomes a good example of the role of dramatic convention and the representation of rank. The *Ploughman* ultimately undermines his own philosophical position with his unruly and violent behaviour but is nevertheless made the mouthpiece of satirical perspectives on several abuses of power by the ruling classes.

Other debate plays: **28, 29, 54, 69, 99, 102**.

Other 'estates' plays: **29, 85, 94, 98**.

SIGNIFICANT TOPICS AND NARRATIVE ELEMENTS

hierarchy and the constitution of the state; social estates; trade and manufacture; social conflict; economic change; extortion and oppression of the poor; the virtue of poverty and the imitation of Christ; the administration of the realm; education; social decorum; the question of what constitutes gentility; manners and social identity; authority and obedience

DRAMATURGICAL AND RHETORICAL FEATURES

Verbal and general the play is advertised as 'Of Gentleness and Nobility a dialogue between the Merchant, the Knight and the Ploughman, disputing who is a very gentleman and who is a noble man and how men should come to authority, compiled in the manner of an interlude with diverse toys and gests added thereto to make merry pastime and disport'; a two-part structure, but no further act and scene division; the physical attack by the *Ploughman* is the only dramatic action; a choric commentator at the end; one stage direction in English, the rest in Latin

Costume and dress the *Ploughman* refers to the extravagant dress of the *Knight* 894–8

Actions and stage directions 174 *sd*: 'Here the *Plo.* comes in with a short whip in his hand and speaks as follows' (E); 192 *sd*: 'And he (*Plo.*) beats them (*Mer., Kn.*)'; 714 *sd*: 'And here he (*Plo.*) beats them (*Mer., Kn.*)'; 982 *sd*: 'And they (*Mer., Kn.*) must go out'; 1013 *sd*: 'Here the *Kn.* and *Mer.* enter again'

Staging and set this is likely to have been a hall play; the action is unlocalized, and there are no indications as to set

Stage properties the *Ploughman*'s whip 174 *sd*

PLACENAMES

Newgate (prison) 463

ALLUSIONS

Abraham 819, 824; Adam 518; Cato *Distycha 1.10* 974–5; Eve 518; *Genesis 12:7* 819–20; Jack Herring (folklore figure) 185; *John 1:1* (q.a.) 841–2

BIBLIOGRAPHY

'P. B.' 'Of Gentylnes and Nobylyte' in Brydges and Haslewood, 1814, pp. 270–5
Bevington, 1968, pp. 76–82
Bolwell, 1921, pp. 90–5
Cameron, 1941a, pp. 9–92
Dunn, E. C. 'John Rastell and *Gentleness and Nobility*', MLR 12 (1917) pp. 266–78
Grantley, 2000, pp. 59–62
Hogrefe, 1959, pp. 283–7, 301–4
Johnson, 1970, pp. 120–7
Reed, 1919, pp. 1–17
Reed, 1969, pp. 106–12
Tucker Brooke, C. T. '*Gentleness and Nobility*: the Authorship and Source', MLR 6 (1911) pp. 458–61
Yamakawa, T. 'The Ploughman in *Of Gentylnes and Nobylyte*', ELR (Kyoto) 19 (1975) pp. 31–4, 21 (1977), pp. 1–15 (in Japanese)

32   Gismond of Salerne

DATE, AUTHORSHIP AND AUSPICES

1567–8; the 1591 version (*Tancred and Gismund*) ascribes the authorship as follows: Act 1, Rodney Stafford; Act 2, Henry Noel; Act 3, G. Al.(?); Act 4, Christopher Hatton; Act 5, Robert Wilmot. an Inner Temple play

TEXT AND EDITIONS

Extant originals

Manuscripts: British Library Lansdowne MS 786, Hargrave MS 205; Folger Shakespeare Library MS V.a.198 (frag.)

Editions

1912   Cunliffe (s.l., OS, based on Lansdowne MS)*
1912   TFT (facsimile, n.l.)
1898   Brandl (s.l., OS)*

SOURCES

The sources are Boccaccio's first novel of the fourth day of *The Decameron*, and (for a part) Dolce's *Didone*; see the introduction to Cunliffe's edition, pp. lxxxvi–xc.

CHARACTERS

Cupid, god of love
Gismond, King Tancred's daughter
Tancred, King of Naples, Prince of Salern
Chorus, four gentlemen
Lucrece, King Tancred's sister

Claudia, a woman of Gimond's privy chamber
Guisharde, the Count Palurine
Megæra, fury of hell
Renuchio, a gentleman of the privy chamber
Julio, captain of the guard

PLOT SUMMARY

Cupid opens the play trumpeting his might and his past conquests, and declaring his intention to make an assault on *Princess Gismond*. She is then seen lamenting the recent death of her husband, and wishing for her own death. Her father tries to console her but she remains distraught and the chorus ends the act with a reflection on the fragility of life. In the next act, *Gismond* expresses her sorrows to her aunt *Lucrece*, whose help she seeks in getting the king's decision on the question of her remarriage. *Tancred* declares his unwillingness to see his daughter married again, and wishes instead to keep her by him until his death, a decision which she accepts but with sorrow. The chorus closes the act by discoursing on worthy women in history as examples to *Gismond* and to other women. *Cupid* opens the third act revealing that he has infected *Gismond* with love for *Count Palurine*, and him for her, before returning to heaven. In the following scenes *Claudia*, a woman of *Gismond's* bedchamber, describes her mistress's agonized restlessness, and *Guisharde*, the *Count Palurine*, expresses his own passion for the princess. He receives a letter from her, concealed in a cane, confessing her love for him and telling him how he might steal into her bedchamber through a secret passage. The chorus closes the act with an affirmation of the irresistibility of love, and musing on its dangers. *Megæra* opens the fourth act with a resolution to implant wrath in both *Tancred's* and *Gismond's* hearts, to their mutual destruction, and *Tancred* then discloses that he has witnessed the intimacy between his daughter and *Count Palurine*. To punish them, he orders that *Palurine* be killed, his heart ripped out and presented to *Gismond*, and he tells his servant to set a watch by the secret passage. He then summons his daughter and confronts her with what he has discovered, but she remains defiant. When she goes off, *Palurine* is brought in a captive, and *Tancred* sentences him to be cast into a dungeon with further and direr punishment to follow. The chorus closes the act by contrasting the cruel ends of lovers governed by lust with the happier fate of virtuous ones. In the final act, *Renuchio* informs the chorus of the imprisonment and subsequent strangling of *Palurine*, the tearing apart of his body and the ripping out of his heart, which he carries in a cup. The cup is then delivered to *Gismond*, who immediately decides to join her lover in death and takes poison. *Tancred* is summoned and the dying *Gismond* requests that her body be buried with that of her lover. The grief-stricken king resolves to grant her request and, too afflicted with sorrow to live without her, to creep into the tomb himself and pierce his own heart. The epilogue closes the play with a favourable contrast between the horror of the play's story and the situation in England.

PLAY LENGTH

1,490 lines, including epilogue but excluding preliminary 'argument' of 39 lines

COMMENTARY

This Inner Temple play is strongly neoclassical in format, with much of the action occurring off stage and narrated. It bears some comparison to other Inns of Court plays, though it does not make use of dumbshows. Being an Inns play, there is a strong possibility that it may have had some political implications relating to the question of the Queen's marriage, in being an oblique affirmation of the desirability of marriage. The play was later revised and published as *Tancred and Gismunda* in 1591 by Robert Wilmot.

Other secular tragedies: **7, 37, 43.**

Other plays featuring prominent women characters: **3, 6, 30, 43, 46, 51, 63, 70, 75, 87, 95, 97.**

Other plays based on classical or Italian models: **5, 37, 41, 43, 88, 91, 92.**

Other plays with foreign (non-biblical, non-classical) settings: **5, 6, 7, 12, 13, 33, 47, 70, 74, 83, 88.**

SIGNIFICANT TOPICS AND NARRATIVE ELEMENTS

marriage and widowhood; the fragility of life; idealized women; lovesickness; illicit love; parental tyranny; suicide

DRAMATURGICAL AND RHETORICAL FEATURES

Verbal and general five acts with scene divisions, each of the first four acts ending with a chorus; the Chorus probably speaks the epilogue as well; the Chorus also takes a substantial part in the fifth act; stage directions in English

Actions and stage directions 1.1.op. *sd*: '*Cu.* comes down from heaven'; 1.1.68 *sd*: '*Cu.* enters into K. *Ta.*'s palace'; 1.2.op. *sd*: '*Gi.* comes out of her chamber'; 1.3.op. *sd*: '*Ta.* comes out of his palace'; 1.3.72 *sd*: '*Ta.* and *Gi.* depart into the palace'; 2.1.op. *sd*: '*Gi.* and *Lu.* coming out of *Gi.*'s chamber'; 2.1.76 *sd*: '*Gi.* departs into her chamber, *Lu.* abiding on stage'; 2.2.op. *sd*: '*Ta.* comes out of his palace'; 2.2.68 *sd*: '*Ta.* and *Lu.* depart into the palace'; 2.3.op. *sd*: '*Gi.* comes out of her chamber'; 2.3.4 *sd*: '*Lu.* returns from the palace'; 2.3.46 *sd*: '*Gi.* and *Lu.* depart into *Gi.*'s chamber'; 3.1.op. *sd*: '*Cu.* returns out of the palace'; 3.1.32 *sd*: '*Cu.* remounts to heaven'; 3.2.op. *sd*: '*Cla.* comes out of *Gi.*'s chamber; 3.2.50 *sd*: '*Cla.* departs to *Gi.*'s chamber'; 3.3.op. *sd*: '*Gui.* comes out of the palace'; 3.3.48 *sd*: 'He (*Gui.*) breaks the cane and finds a letter enclosed'; 3.3.56 *sd*: 'He (*Gui.*) reads the letter'; 3.3.88 *sd*: '*Gui.* departs into the palace'; 4.1.op. *sd*: '*Meg.* arises out of hell'; 4.1.44 *sd*: '*Meg.* enters the palace'; 4.2.op. *sd*: '*Ta*. comes out of *Gi*.'s chamber'; 4.2.88 *sd*: '*Ren*. goes to call *Gi*. but comes not in with her'; 4.2.170 *sd*: '*Jul*. departs into the palace'; 4.3 op. *sd*: '*Gi*. comes out of her chamber, called by *Ren*.'; 4.3.82 *sd*: '*Gi*. departs to her chamber'; 4.4.op. *sd*: '*Jul*. brings the earl prisoner'; 4.4.69 *sd*: '*Ta*. hastily departs into the palace'; 4.4.81 *sd*: '*Gui*. is led to prison'; 5.1.op. *sd*: '*Ren*. comes out of the palace'; 5.2.op. *sd*: '*Ren*. delivers the cup to *Gi*. in her chamber'; 5.2.24 *sd*: '*Ren*. departs'; 5.2.60 *sd*: 'She (*Gi*.) takes a glass of poison our of her pocket'; 5.2.79 (approx.) *sd*: '*Cla*. runs into the palace to tell the *Ki*. of *Gi*.'; 5.3.op. *sd*: '*Ta*. comes out of the palace'; 5.3.4 *sd*: '*Ta*. enters into *Gi*.'s chamber'; 5.3.48 *sd*: '*Gi*. dies'; 5.4.op. *sd*: '*Ta*. comes out of *Gi*.'s chamber'

Staging and set directions for entry and departure are routinely to two locations: the palace and *Gismond*'s chamber (probably at opposite ends of the central playing area), but the prison to which *Guisharde* is taken is likely to be off stage, as no stage action occurs there. There appear to be three levels as *Cupid* descends from heaven, and *Megæra* ascends from hell; the descents and ascents also suggest the possible use of stage machinery

Stage properties a cane and letter 3.3.48 *sd*; a 'bloody cup' 5.2.1 *sd*; a glass 'of poison' 5.2.60 *sd*

PLACENAMES

Asia 1.1.31; Britain ep. 19; Greece 1.1.43, 3.chor. 30; Macedon 1.1.38; Phrygia 3.chor. 31; Rome 1.chor.25; Salerno 4.1.18, 5.1.45, ep.15; Sestos 1.1.35; Troy 1.1.31, 1.chor.21, 3.chor.30, 3.chor.31 ('Ilium'), 4.chor. 4

ALLUSIONS

Aeacus 4.1.32; Aeolus 4.1.9; Artemis 3.chor.9–11; Artemisia and Mausolus 2.chor.17–24; Atlas 4.1.16; Avernus 1.1.14; Cato 2.chor.29; Diana 3.chor.21; Diana and Hippolytus 4.chor.38–41; Dido ('Elisa') 4.chor.9; Furies 1.chor.29; Hades ep.27; Helen of Troy 1.1.43, 3.chor.16, 4.chor.2; Hercules ('Alcides') 1.1.37; Hero and Leander 1.1.33–5, 4.chor.10; Io 1.1.18; Ixion 4.1.12–13; Jason 1.1.42; Jove 1.1.17 *passim*; Juno 1.1.20, 3.1.11; Lethe 2.chor.35; Mars 1.1.25, 1.2.26; Medea 1.1.42, 4.chor.9; Mercury 4.1.15; King Minos 4.1.32; the Myrrh tree 1.1.47; Paris 1.1.44, 3.chor.26, 4.chor.1; Penelope and Ulysses 2.chor.25–8; Petrarch and Laura 4.chor.45–6; Phaedra and Hippolytus 3.chor.15–16; Phoebus 2.1.5; Phyllis 4.chor.11; Pluto ep.22, 27; Pluto and Proserpine 4.1.26–31; Portia and Brutus 2.chor.29–36; (House of) Priam 4.chor.4; Rhadamanthus 4.1.32; Scipio 1.1.39; Sisyphus 4.1.9–10; the Stygian ferry 4.1.18; Tantalus and Pelops 4.1.4–8; Tarquin and Lucretia 2.chor.11–16; Tartarus 4.1.4, 4.1.29; Theseus 3.chor.16; Tityus 4.1.10–11, 4.2.76; Venus and Adonis 4.chor.37; Vulcan 1.1.28

BIBLIOGRAPHY

Clemen, 1961, pp. 76–84
Corti, C. 'Tancred and Gismund': Le fonti italiane di una tragedia "romantica" elisabettiana', RLMC 28
(1975) pp. 252–70
Cunliffe, J. W. 'Gismond of Salerne', PMLA 21:2 (1906) pp. 435–61
Griffin, E. G. 'Gismond of Salerne: A Critical Appreciation', RES 4 (1963) pp. 94–107
Habicht, W. 'Die Nutrix-Szenen in Gismond of Salern und Tancred and Gismund: Zur akademischen
Seneca-Nachahmung in England', Anglia 81:3–4 (1963) pp. 394–411
Iriye, K. 'A Stylistic Comparison of Gismond of Salerne and Tancred and Gismund', ShS(J) 4 (1965–6)
pp. 1–35
Kiefer, F. 'Love and Fortune in Boccaccio's Tancredi and Ghismonda Story and in Wilmot's Gismond of
Salerne', R&R 13:1 (1977) pp. 36–45
Klein, D. '"According to the Decorum of these Daies"', PMLA 33:2 (1918) pp. 244–68
Murray, J. 'Tancred and Gismond', RES 14 (1938) pp. 385–95
Ribner, I. '"Then I Denie You Starres": A Reading of Romeo and Juliet' in Bennett, Cargill and Hall, 1959,
pp. 269–86
Southern, 1973, pp. 486–94
Stilling, 1976, pp. 11–25
Wright, 1957, pp. 173–84

33   The Glass of Government

DATE, AUTHORSHIP AND AUSPICES

printed in 1575; George Gascoigne; probably a closet play; Greg 68

TEXT AND EDITIONS

Extant originals

1575 printing by Henry Middleton for Christopher Barker
Issue 1: BL (three copies); Bodleian; Dyce (two copies, one imp.); Eliz. Club; Folger;
Huntington; Illinois; Pepys (imp.); PML, Worcester; further copies extant; STC
11643
Issue 2: BL; NLS; Huntington; Harvard (imp.); STC 11643a

EDITIONS

1994   CHD (CD-Rom and online transcription of Middleton printing, s.l., OS)
1914   TFT (facsimile, n.l.)
1907   Cunliffe, vol. II (1910) (n.l., OS)*

SOURCES

No specific source has been identified, but the play is in the Christian Terence
tradition; see Spengler, 1888 for an account of this tradition.

CHARACTERS

Prologue
Phylopaes
Phylocalus
Fidus, servant to Phylopaes
Gnomaticus, a Schoolmaster
Onaticus, servant to the Schoolmaster
Phylautus, elder son to Phylopaes
Phylosarchus, elder son to Phylocalus
Phylotimus, younger son to Phylopaes
Phylomusus, younger son to Phylocalus

Lamia, the Harlot
Eccho, the Parasite
Pandarina, Aunt to Lamia
Dick Droom, the Roister
Chorus, four grave Burghers
Ambidexter, servant to Phylocalus
Severus the Markgrave
Nuntii, two messengers
Epilogue

PLOT SUMMARY

The *Prologue* promises a play, not in the Italian or Roman mould, but with 're-formed speech' and lists a series of moral sentences on which the work is based. The play begins with two neighbours, *Phylopaes* and *Phylocalus*, resolving to find a good schoolmaster for their four sons, each of them having two. A good servant, *Fidus*, recommends a virtuous master called *Gnomaticus*, who is duly engaged to prepare the boys for university, and they begin their studies with him. These start with a long lecture from the teacher before they all retire to dinner. The scene then changes to a harlot, *Lamia*, and her companions, who have noticed the boys and plot to ensnare them. The first act ends with a chorus reflecting on the problems of child-rearing and education. The studies continue but the two elder boys, *Phylosarchus* and *Phylautus*, show a quick understanding and soon become impatient with *Gnomaticus*'s teaching. They scorn their less quick-witted younger brothers, who doggedly persist in their studies, and they long instead for the greater intellectual challenge of the university. Soon, however, they turn their minds to other diversions and are found in the company of *Lamia* and her friends. *Eccho*, her parasite, obtains leave from *Gnomaticus* for them to be absent from their studies by bringing a message purporting to come from the markgrave summoning the boys as his kinsmen. *Lamia* pretends to be a gentlewoman in distress, in need of comfort and help from the young gentlemen, and the second act ends with a chorus bewailing the snares that lie in wait for the young. *Dick Droom*, a roisterer and companion of *Lamia*, begins the third act rejoicing at the entrapment of the young men, while in the next scene the two younger brothers express concern for their older siblings. When they return the two elder brothers claim that *Eccho*'s message was a mistake and the teaching recommences, but *Phylosarchus* is informed by his servant *Ambidexter* that reports have reached his father of his doings and that he is now resolved to send him to the university. The two fathers consult *Gnomaticus*, who recommends they be sent to the University of Douai, as Douai is a small town with less scope for vice. The two younger boys persist earnestly with their studies and the act ends with a chorus pointing to the differences between the virtuous and the vicious. After *Gnomaticus* reports to the two fathers that their elder sons have now become neglectful of their studies, the four young men depart for Douai, to the sorrow of the erstwhile companions of the elder two. The markgrave gives orders for the arrest of *Lamia* and her band, and *Gnomaticus* is brought news of the arrests. The fourth act ends with a chorus reflecting on the dangers that threaten virtue. *Dick Droom*, who has escaped arrest, opens the final act with a declaration that he intends to pursue his two former companions to Douai. In the next scene the fathers receive letters from their younger sons reporting that their elder brothers, accompanied by *Ambidexter*, are leading dissolute lives and are preparing to leave the university. However, one of the younger brothers, *Phylotimus*, has been recommended for the post of secretary to the Palsgrave, while the other, *Phylomusus*, has entered the ministry and is about to depart for Geneva. *Fidus* is despatched to bring *Ambidexter* and the older boys home and *Gnomaticus*, having arrived to enquire about their progress, is told the news about the boys. *Gnomaticus* himself soon receives letters with similar news. *Severus*, the markgrave, then appears and at first announces that there is too little evidence to convict *Lamia* and her friends. However, when *Gnomaticus* tells him of *Eccho*'s false message purporting to be a summons to the boys from the markgrave himself, he declares that fit punishment will be devised. *Fidus* enters with the news that, while *Phylomusus* has now become secretary to the palsgrave, and *Phylotimus* has become a reputed preacher in Geneva (Gascoigne having inadvertently swapped them around here), their elder brothers have come to grief. *Phylautus* has been executed for robbery at the palsgrave's court, an execution witnessed by his brother, and *Phylosarchus* has been whipped in Geneva for fornication and banished from the city. The play ends with sentences pronounced on the malefactors who perverted the boys: *Ambidexter* to be executed, *Eccho* whipped and banished, and *Lamia* and her aunt set on the cucking stool and then banished. The epilogue summarizes the principal points of the story and warns of the dangers of quick intelligence.

PLAY LENGTH

3,200 lines (approximately)

COMMENTARY

Though this is possibly a closet play, it is written very much along the lines of a piece for performance apart from the long speeches, most notably those of *Gnomaticus*, and it exhibits the humanist concerns found in much interlude drama. The play is in the tradition of 'youth' plays, which concern themselves primarily with education, social mobility and the threats posed to these by bad companions and other worldly factors.

Other youth and education plays: **21, 53, 56, 58, 61, 62, 64, 67, 68, 73** (frag.), **101, 103, 104**.

Other plays with foreign (non-biblical, non-classical) settings: **5, 6, 7, 12, 13, 32, 47, 70, 74, 83, 88.**

SIGNIFICANT TOPICS AND NARRATIVE ELEMENTS

friendship; social mobility and aspiration; education and the upbringing of youth; obedience to rulers; prostitution and sexual dalliance; high intelligence and its perils; bad companions; good and bad servants; crime and punishment
NOTE: As lines are not numbered, references are to page numbers

DRAMATURGICAL AND RHETORICAL FEATURES

Verbal and general the play is preceded by a prologue and eight 'sentences' laying down the moral precepts upon which it is based; the play is described as a 'comedy' despite its ending; it is set in Antwerp; *Gnomaticus* delivers a long lecture to his pupils referring to many texts in contemporary educational use 27–34; *Gnomaticus*'s list of moral precepts 33; *Phylotimus*'s verses on *Gnomaticus*'s precepts 55–6; *Phylomusus*'s verses on Gnomaticus's precepts 56–8; Gascoigne inadvertently switches the career destination of *Phylomusus* and *Phylotimus* later in the play (cf. 77 and 85); five acts with scene divisions; the first four acts end with a chorus, each probably spoken by one of the 'four grave burghers'; stage directions in English
Actions and stage directions op. *sd*: 'They (*Phylop., Phyloc., Fid.*) come in talking'; 12 *sd*: 'They (*Phylop., Phyloc.*) address their talk to the schoolmaster'; 15 *sd*: 'The fathers address their talk to their children'; 17 *sd*: 'He (*Phylos.*) speaks to his servant'; 25 *sd*: 'They (*La.*, companions) depart to their houses'; 35 *sd*: 'They (*Phylot., Phylom.*) go apart'; 36 *sd*: 'The ladies pass by, with reverence to the gentlemen'; 40 *sd*: '*Phylos.* beckons *Ec., Phylom.* and *Phylot.* go together'; 42 *sd*: 'She (*La.*) whines'; 42 *sd*: '*Phylos.* takes her (*La.*) by the hand to comfort her'; 42 *sd*: 'She (*La.*) begins to tell a tale'; 42 *sd*: '*Pan.* interrupts her (*La.*)'; 42 *sd*: 'They (*Phylos., Philaut.*) follow the ladies'; 56 *sd*: 'Finis quoth *Phylot.*'; 65 *sd*: 'The young men (four brothers) kneel down'; 67 *sd*: 'They (*Di., Ec.*) run aside'; 68 *sd*: 'He (*Sev.*) departs as the schoolmaster comes in'; 74 *sd*: '*Phylop.* goes aside with it (the roll)'; 74 *sd*: 'He (*Phyloc.*) reads also'; 76 *sd*: 'He (*Phyloc.*) delivers him (*Gno.*) the letter'; 77 *sd*: 'He (*Phylop.*) swoons'; **Simple entry:** *Fid., Gno.,* ser. 11; *Ona.* 35; *Ec.* 38; *Di.* 61; *Gno.* 68; **Simple exit:** *Fid.* 11; (*Gno., Phylaut., Phylos., Phylom., Phylot., Ona.*) 23; *Gno.* 34; *Gno.* 39; *Ec.* 41; *Gno.* 48; *Amb.* 50; *Phylaut., Phylom., Phylos., Phylot. Fid.* 65; (*Phyloc., Phylop.*) 65; *Sev.* 68; (*Gno.*) 70; *Nun.* 75; *Fid.* 76
Staging and set as a likely closet drama, this has no indications as to set, though there are several locations for the action, including the schoolroom, *Lamia*'s house and the markgrave's palace
Stage properties the messenger's roll of names and the letters for *Phylopaes* and *Phylocalus* 74

PLACENAMES

St Antlines 10; Antwerp 44, 50, 65, 66, 72, 74; Arabia 49; Brabant 62; Brussels 86; Chester 39; Delphi 31; Douai 11, *passim*; Egypt 21; Epirus 30; Europe 66; France 86; Geneva 75, 77, 87; Germany 86; Hungary 25; Israel 20, 22; Miletus 30; Olynthus 30; Samos 30; Thebes 31; Valencia 24

ALLUSIONS

Aaron 22; Abraham and Sara 21; Aeneas 30; Amadis of Gaul 42; Anaxagoras 69; Antenor 30; Apollo 31, 70; Aristo the Stoic 18; Cicero ('Tully') 27, 30; Cicero *De Divinatione* 32; Cicero *De Legibus* 20; Cicero *De Officiis* 16, 17, 21, 29; Cicero *De Roscio Amerino* 19; Cicero *Epistles* 17; Cicero *Tusculanae Disputationes* 30; Cillicon 30; Creon and Menecius 31; Curtius 31; Diogenes Laërtius 28; Duns Scotus 45; Erasmus *Apothegmes* 28; Erasmus *Colloquia* 16; Euripides 30; Euripides *Phoenissae* 32; *Exodus* 20:5 19, 20–1; Hippodamus 28; Ismael 21; Lasthenes 30; Linus 19; Lycurgus 30; *Matthew* 13 43; Moses 21, 22; Nilo 30; Noah 20; St Paul 29, 32, 70; St Paul and Silas 22; St Paul *Colossians* 3 32; St Paul *Ephesians* 6 32; St Paul *Romans* 8 29; St Peter and Cornelius 22; *I Peter* 2 29; Pherecydes 69; Philip the Apostle 22; Plato 18, 30, 31; Protagoras 69; Pythagoras 28, 69; Simonides of Ceos 18; Socrates 27; Solomon 28; Sophocles 29; Terence 6, 17, 26, 34; Virgil 17, 48; Xenophon 18, 27; Zopirus 30

BIBLIOGRAPHY

Feldman, A. B. 'Dutch Humanism and the Tudor Dramatic Tradition', *N&Q* 197 (1952) pp. 357–60
Helgerson, 1976, pp. 44–57
Herford, C. H. 'Gascoigne's *Glasse of Government*', *EngS* 9 (1886) pp. 201–9
Johnson, 1972, pp. 147–55
Salamon, L. B. 'A Face in *The Glasse*: Gascoigne's *Glasse of Government* Re-examined', *SP* 71:1 (1974) pp. 47–71
Schelling, 1892, pp. 259–66
Young, 1979, pp. 128–40

34   Godly Queen Hester

DATE, AUTHORSHIP AND AUSPICES

1525–9 (*SR* 1560/61 *c.* Jan./Feb.); anonymous; auspices unknown but possibly performed by boys at court; Greg 33

TEXT AND EDITIONS

Extant originals

1561 printing by William Pickering and Thomas Hacket: Huntington; *STC* 13251

Editions

1994   CHD (CD-Rom and online copy of Greg, 1904, l.l., OS)
2000   Walker (OS)*
1906   Farmer (4) (n.l., NS)
1904   Greg (1904b) (OS)
1870–2 Grosart, vol. IV (n.l., OS)
1863   Collier, vol. I (n.l., OS)

SOURCES

The play is based on the scriptural *Book of Esther*.

CHARACTERS

Prologue	Mardocheus	Pride	Arbona
King Assuerus	Hester	Adulation	Scribe
Three gentlemen	Pursuivant	Ambition	
Aman	Three Jews	Hardy Dardy	
	Choristers		
	Mute: waiting men, maidens		

PLOT SUMMARY

After a brief prologue introducing the topic, *King Assuerus* sets up a discussion on the relative merits of personal virtue as opposed to high birth. His three gentlemen agree on the value of personal virtue and proceed to extrapolate on its aspects, emphasizing justice. He then makes one of them, *Aman*, his chancellor and expresses his desire to choose a wife. He directs *Aman* to make a selection of the best maidens in the realm from whom one can be chosen. A Jew, *Mardocheus*, introduces his niece *Hester* to the king's pursuivant and she is taken to join the other maidens, who are presented by *Aman* to the king. On the basis of her great virtue, *Hester* is chosen and is taken off to be dressed for marriage. A sequence then follows in which three Vices discuss the king's chancellor. *Pride* (poorly dressed) says *Aman* has taken all the best clothes, *Adulation* that he has collected all the flatterers, and *Ambition* that his rapacity has caused poverty in the kingdom. They concede defeat, bequeath all their skills and vicious qualities to *Aman* and go off to a tavern, singing. The scene then switches to *Aman*, who exchanges a few words with *Hardy Dardy* (one of his yeomen, here in the role of jester or fool) before going to the king to persuade him to oppress the Jews. The king agrees and sends his pursuivants through the realm with orders to this effect. *Hardy Dardy* appears again to warn *Aman* that he will lose his head, but *Aman* ignores this and goes off. Three Jews and *Mardocheus* then approach *Hester* to request her help in saving the Jews, who are about to be killed. At a banquet which follows, she makes an impassioned plea to the king, after which *Aman* is apprehended and ordered to be hanged on the same gallows as he has prepared for *Mardocheus*, an irony that draws some comment from *Hardy Dardy*. *Aman*'s property is ceded to *Hester*, and *Mardocheus* is raised to public office. A letter is despatched throughout the land to announce *Aman*'s downfall and ordering that no harm be done to the Jews.

PLAY LENGTH

1,180 lines

COMMENTARY

This is a scriptural interlude that is noteworthy for its focus on the Jews as an oppressed minority, though it is likely they represent victims of more contemporary forms of oppression. It is also one of several in which 'female' virtues, particularly of submissiveness and chastity, are idealized. The role of the Vices is interestingly confined in such a way that there is no direct interaction between them and any of the historical characters. The discussion of the true nature of nobility is a recurrent preoccupation in the period, and the political abuses aired in the play are likely to have had satirical resonances. Despite the story's biblical setting the society of the play is identifiably English.

Other biblical plays: **10, 11, 16, 42, 44, 48, 63, 77, 90, 93.**
Other female virtue plays: **3, 6, 63, 70, 87, 97.**

SIGNIFICANT TOPICS AND NARRATIVE ELEMENTS

nobility of birth versus personal virtue; pride, dress and the sumptuary laws ('statute of apparel'); idealized female virtue; the scriptural history of the Jews; the role of queens; flatterers and the state; the poor; corruption; the oppression of aliens

DRAMATURGICAL AND RHETORICAL FEATURES

Verbal and general the Vices make a 'testament' 508–74 (leaving their vicious qualities to *Aman*) in a scene narratively discrete from the rest of the play; *Hardy Dardy* performs the role of fool or jester; all stage directions except one in English
Costume and dress *Hester* and her ladies are dressed in 'rich apparel of gold and pall (rich material) 332–3; *Pride* enters 'poorly arrayed' 337 *sd*; the king gives *Aman* robes of state 628
Actions and stage directions 14 *sd*: 'The ki. sitting in a chair, speaks to his counsel'; 103 *sd*: 'One of the gentlemen must answer, which you will'; 130 *sd*: 'Here enters *Am*. with many men waiting on him'; 140 *sd*: 'Here the ki. enters the traverse and *Am*. goes out. Here enters *Mar*. and a maiden with him'; 201 *sd*: 'Here *Am*.

meets them (*Hester*, train) in the place'; 210 *sd*: 'Then they (maidens) go to the ki.';
337 *sd*: 'Here departs the qu. and *Am*. and all the maidens. Here enters *Pr*. singing,
poorly arrayed'; 449 *sd*: 'Here enters *Amb*.'; 580 *sd*: 'They (*Pr*., *Amb*., *Ad*.) depart
singing and *Am*. enters'; 635 *sd*: 'Here the ki. enters the traverse and *Har*. enters
the place'; 810 *sd*: 'And he (*Am*.) must depart (L). Here enters a Jew and speaks';
854 *sd*: 'Then the Chapel do sing'; 868 *sd*: 'Here they (*Ass*., *He*.) kiss'; 878 *sd*: 'Here
must be prepared a banquet in the place'; 1102 *sd*: 'Here the *Scri*. doth read the
ki.'s letter'

Songs and music 1. *Pride* 'To men that be heavy and would fain be merry' (w.s.)
338–89; 2. *Pride, Adulation, Ambition* 580 *sd* (w.n.s.); 3. Chapel (choristers) 854 *sd*
(w.n.s.)

Staging and set the opening action is set in the royal palace, with the king
enthroned but, apart from returns to this location, the rest is unlocalized; a traverse
is referred to twice, probably a screen at the back of the stage (140 *sd*, 635 *sd*); the
king's chair may initially be behind the traverse; the term 'place' used several times
probably refers simply to the stage, rather than a *platea*; a banquet is held on stage
(878 *sd*)

Stage properties *Assuerus*'s chair 14 *sd*; *Aman*'s golden wand 629; *Assuerus*'s
wand 867; accoutrements and provisions for the banquet 878 *sd*; *Assuerus*'s letter
1102 *sd*

PLACENAMES

Babylon 147; Ethiopia 1104; France 479; India 1104; Jerusalem 141, 909; Scotland
479; Sheba 259; Shushan/Susa 1135, 1145; St Thomas-a-Watering 542, 803

ALLUSIONS

Abraham 950; Benjamin 142, 1065; King David 1092; Diocletian 37; Isaac 954;
Jacob 954; Jair 142; Jehoiachin 144; Maxentius 37; Moses 1088; Nebuchadnezzar
36, 143; Nero 37; Ovid 1019; Perillus and Phalaris 1022–37; *Proverbs* 11:14 (q.a.)
93; *Psalms* 1092; Salmanazar 36; Sennacherib 36; Queen of Sheba 259; Solomon
64; Statute of Apparel (sumptuary laws) 378; Tutivillus (a devil) 1023; Valerius
Maximus 1021; Virgil 834

BIBLIOGRAPHY

Bevington, 1968, pp. 87–93
Blackburn, 1971, pp. 70–6
Fox, 1989, pp. 240–5
Hogrefe, 1959, pp. 334–7
Southern, 1973, pp. 257–90
Walker, 1991, pp. 102–32

35   God's Promises (or God's Chief Promises)

DATE, AUTHORSHIP AND AUSPICES

1538; John Bale; St Stephen's, Canterbury, possibly to be performed in sequence with *John Baptist's Preaching* and *The Temptation of Our Lord*: see the introduction to Happé's edition (*Complete Plays of John Bale*, vol. 1) pp. 12–14; Bale relates in the 'Vocacyon of John Bale' that the plays were played in sequence in Kilkenny on the day of Queen Mary's coronation; Greg 22

TEXT AND EDITIONS

Extant originals

1547 (?) printing by Dirik van der Straten, Wesel: BL (imp.), Eliz. Club; *STC* 1305
1577 printing by John Charlewood for Stephen Peele: Huntington; *STC* 1306

Editions

1994	CHD (CD-Rom and online copy of Happé, 1985/6, l.l., a.l., OS)
1985/6	Happé, vol. II (OS)*
1909	Rhys (n.l., NS)
1909	Jones (OS)
1908	TFT (facsimile, n.l.)
1907	Farmer (8) (n.l., NS)
1874–6	Dodsley, vol. 1 (n.l., NS)
1838	Marriott (n.l., OS)

SOURCES

Bale drew on the *Book of Genesis*, but he may also have used prophet plays from the Corpus Christi cycles as models: see the introduction to Happé's 1985/6 edition, vol. 1, p. 12.

CHARACTERS

Bale as Prologue	Noah the Just	King David the Pious
The Father of Heaven	Abraham the Faithful	Isaiah the Prophet
Adam the First Man	Moses the Holy	John the Baptist
	A Chorus	

PLOT SUMMARY

Bale as the *Prologue* exhorts the audience to a contemplation of Christ's redemptive sacrifice and declares the subject of the play to be God's providence in the form of his promises to successive generations of humanity. The first act has *Adam* beseeching *God*'s mercy for his transgression and *God* replying that his salvation lies in hating eternally the serpent who wrought his downfall. *God* cites as the seal of this promise the creeping of the serpent and painful propagation for women, and *Adam* rejoices at *God*'s mercy while recognizing his own culpability. Speaking to *Noah* in the next act, *God* complains that *Adam*'s issue has not kept the covenant he made with mankind, and have followed sinful ways. He declares his intention to drown humanity, saving *Noah* and his issue and renewing the covenant with them, betokened by a rainbow. The third act has *God* continuing to detail the sins of man and *Abraham* negotiating to try to save Sodom and Gomorrah from his destructive wrath. *God* finally agrees to spare the small band of righteous people and gives *Abraham* the promise that his seed will be blessed, the token of which will be the practice of circumcision. *Moses* in the fourth act hears *God*'s description of the sins of his people, but reminds *God* that he appointed him to lead them out of slavery in Egypt, and prays that they may be saved. While reiterating his determination to punish sin, *God* says he will raise a prophet from among the Jews, the token of whom will be the Passover lamb. In the fifth act, *King David* acknowledges the continuing sinfulness of his people, particularly their idolatry, and his own transgression in numbering the people. For his contrition *God* promises that from his seed a redeemer will arise, in token of whom there will be a temple to be started by *David* and completed by his son Solomon, as Christ is to complete *God*'s work. The sixth act has *Isaiah* complaining of the sins of the Jews, but saying that their king, Ezechias, has taught them better ways, and begging *God* for a consolation for them. *God* promises a righteous lord, the sign of whom shall be that he will be conceived of a virgin of Israel. In the final act *God* continues to bewail the idolatry of the Jews but says he has decided to set aside rigour and instead win mankind by kindness. He confirms *John the Baptist* as both prophet and baptizer of Christ, and *John* then preaches a sermon before closing the play with a final anthem. *Bale* the prolocutor delivers an epilogue confirming the importance of faith and challenging the notion of free will.

PLAY LENGTH

982 lines, including prologue and epilogue

COMMENTARY

The play is highly structured, all the acts being formally almost identical. The division into seven reflects the division of the history of the world into seven ages (see Blatt, 1968, pp. 87–8), but before the backdrop of human history is a series of individual encounters that serve to emphasize the Protestant notion of the personal relationship between man and God. The use of prefiguration and typology recalls the representational conventions of the Corpus Christi plays, but the series of tokens which signify God's promises and the working out of the providential scheme of history presents a firmly Protestant slant on the material that forms the narrative substance of the great dramatic cycles. The play ends with an attack on the notion of free will, a concept strongly emphasized in Catholic doctrine.

SIGNIFICANT TOPICS AND NARRATIVE ELEMENTS

providence; Adam's fall; Noah and the flood; the destruction of Sodom and Gomorrah; circumcision; the plagues of Egypt; Moses and the deliverance of the Jews from Egypt; Old Testament history of the Jews; the temple of Solomon; the idolatry of the Jews; Isaiah as a prophet of the advent of Christ; John the Baptist as prophet of Christ; the concept of free will

DRAMATURGICAL AND RHETORICAL FEATURES

Verbal and general the colophon describes the play as a 'tragedy or interlude'; the play is divided into seven acts, each a two-character dialogue and each ending in an Advent antiphon, and very limited dramatic action; names of characters and stage directions in Latin

Actions and stage directions 70 *sd*: 'Here *Ad*. falls headlong to the ground, and after the fourth line he gets up again'; 178 *sd*: 'Then on bended knee he (*Ad.*) begins in a loud voice the antiphon "O Sapientia", which the chor. takes up, with an organ accompaniment, as he goes out. Or, with the same accompaniment, it could be sung in English, thus'; 296 *sd*: 'Then with a loud voice he (*No.*) begins the antiphon "O oriens splendor", dropping to his knees. The chor. follow this with organ accompaniment as before. Or in English with organ accompaniment'; 423 *sd*: 'Then with a high voice he (*Ab.*) sings the antiphon "O rex gentium", the chor. following with organ accompaniment, as previously. Or in English in this fashion'; 551 *sd*: 'Then in a clear voice he (*Mo.*) begins with the antiphon "O Emanuel" which the chor. follows, as before, with organ. Or let him sing in English'; 677 *sd*: 'Then in a melodious voice he (*Dav.*) begins the antiphon "O Adonai" which as before the chor. follows with organ. Or thus in English'; 798 *sd*: 'Then he (*Is.*) starts in a pleasingly harmonious voice the antiphon "O radix Jesse" which the chor. follows with organ. Or let him sing in English in this manner'; 879 *sd*: 'Here the *Lord*, extending his hand, touches *Jo.*'s lips with his finger, and he gives to him a tongue of gold'; 942 *sd*: 'Then in a resounding voice he (*Jo.*) begins the antiphon "O clavis David" which the chor. follows with organ, as before. Or in the English language thus'

Songs and music (all titles of the Advent antiphons given in Latin, with the option to sing in English, with English w.s.; all individual singers followed by a chorus accompanied by organs) 1. *Adam* 'O eternal sapience' 179–82; 2. *Noah* 'O most orient clearness' 297–300; 3. *Abraham* 'O most mighty governor' 424–8; 4. *Moses* 'O high king Emmanuel' 552–5; 5. *David* 'O lord God Adonai' 678–81; 6. *Isaiah* 'O fruitful root of Jesse' 799–802; 7. *John the Baptist* 'O perfect key of David' 943–7

Staging and set the action is unlocalized and there are no indications as to set; the seven stages of the action may have been accompanied by illustrations of the various 'signs' that are appropriate to them, delivered by God

Stage properties a tongue of gold for *John* 879 *sd*

PLACENAMES

Babylon 824; Egypt 440, 740; Israel 609 *passim*; Jerusalem 717, 718, 768, 792, 826, 888; Jordan 888, 890; Judea 718, 724; Mesopotamia 593; Red Sea 470; Samaria 717, 719, 733; Mount Sinai 680; Zion 767

ALLUSIONS

Aaron 503, 565; Abijam 726; Abimelech 842; Ahab 727; Ahaz 729, 742, 818; Ahazia 728; Amalech 482; Amon 818; Amos 834; Anath and Shamgar 569; Antiochus IV 823; Asa 786; Asteroth and Baal 587; Athalia 728; Baasha 727; Balaam 487; Baruch 837; Bathsheba 606, 618; Bel's priests 821; Cain and Abel 190, 280–6; Caleb 501, 568; Daniel 833; Dathan and Abiron 504; Dinah and Shechem 442; Eglon 595; Elah 727; Eleazar 849; Eleazar and Phinehas 565; Eli 578; Elijah 788, 881; Elisha 789; Enoch 284; Enos 282; Esau 438; Esdras 845; Esther 847; Eve 231, 279; Ezechiel 831; *Genesis 3:16* 140–1; Gideon 570; Goliath 662; Habbakuk 836; Haggai 835; Ham and Noah 310–2; Hezekiah 751, 786; Joannes Hircanus 849; Hosea 833; Huldah 837; Isaac 539; Jabin 596; Jacob 439, 540, 944; Jechonias 819; Jehoash 728; Jehoshaphat 786; Jehu 789; Jephthah 571; Jeremiah 832; *Jeremiah 1:6* 871; Jeroboam 725; Jeshua ('Jesus') 844; Jesse 771, 799; Jethro 565; Job 542; Joel 833; *John 1:33* 895–6; Jonah 834; Joseph 541; Joshua 501, 567, 586; Josiah 838; Jotham 729; Jozadek 844; Judah 444; Judith 847; Laban 441; Judas Maccabeus 848; Malachi 836; Manasseh 817; Mathathias 848; Melchisedech 542; Methuselah 283; Micah 789, 835; Mordecai 846; Naaman 790; Nadab 726; Nahum 835; Nathan 574; Nebuchadnezzar 822; Nehemiah 845; Nimrod 313; Obadiah 789, 834; Omri ('Joram') 727; Onan 446; Othniel 568; St Paul *1 Corinthians 10:1–4* 955–7; Phassur 822; Rachel 543; Raguel 544; Rebecca 543; Rechab 840; Rehoboam 724; Reuben 443; Samson 573; Samuel 574, 578; Sarah 543; Saul 579, 610; Seth 281; Shem 386; Shemeiaiah 822; Shimei and Ahithophel 580; Shishak 739; Sodom and Gomorrah 342, 355, 689, 691; Solomon 654, 785; Tobias 846; Tola and Jair 570–1; Tryphon 823; Uriah the Hittite 607; Zachariah 835; Zephanaiah 834; Zimri 727; Zipporah 544; Zorobabel 843

BIBLIOGRAPHY

Blatt, 1968, pp. 86–95
Blackburn, 1971, pp. 49–58
Happé, 1996, pp. 108–24

Harris, 1940, pp. 75–81
McCusker, 1942, pp. 73–85
Miller, E. S. 'The Antiphons in Bale's Cycle of Christ', *SP* 48:3 (1951) pp. 629–38
Miller, E. S. 'Antitypes in Bale's Cycle of Christ', *Annali dell'Istituto universitario orientale, Napoli, sezione germanica* 3 (1960) pp. 251–62
Roston, 1968, pp. 60–6
Sperk, 1973, pp. 41–6

36   Good Order or Old Christmas (fragment)

DATE, AUTHORSHIP AND AUSPICES

printed 1533, Rastell's colophon survives; anonymous though ascribed by Bale to Skelton; auspices unknown but possibly for Rastell's stage; Greg 14.5

TEXT AND EDITIONS

Extant originals

1533 printing by William Rastell: BL (frag.); *STC* 18793.5

Editions

1994   CHD (CD-Rom and online transcription of Rastell printing, l.l., OS)
1956   Greg (OS)*
1944   Frost and Nash (n.l., OS)

SOURCE

No source has been identified.

CHARACTERS

Old Christmas   Good Order   Riot   Gluttony   Prayer

PLOT SUMMARY

Riot and *Gluttony* are brought before the recently returned ruler, *Old Christmas*, to be punished for their reprobate ways. When asked for his advice about what to do with them, *Good Order* advises against perpetual imprisonment, saying that they could then spread subversion through those who visit them, and recommends banishment instead. The miscreants resolve to go to the 'new found land' and request spending money, but are told they will have to resort to begging. After an unnamed speaker condemns gluttony and praises abstinence, the fragment ends with a description of the nature of prayer and its benefits by a character called *Prayer*.

PLAY LENGTH

132 lines extant

COMMENTARY

The bulk of the play, now lost, clearly involves the rebellion for which *Riot* and *Gluttony* are being exiled. The reference to exile in America is one of the few references to the New World in early drama, and the idea of the spreading of sedition through prison visits may possibly be the expression of a contemporary anxiety.

SIGNIFICANT TOPICS AND NARRATIVE ELEMENTS

rebellion; the upbringing of youth; imprisonment; banishment; America; gluttony; prayer

DRAMATURGICAL AND RHETORICAL FEATURES

Verbal and general the extant sequence is essentially a courtroom scene
Staging and set the extant scene is set in a ruler's court, but there are no indications as to set

PLACENAMES

America ('the new found land') 76; England 77, 80

37   Gorboduc (or Ferrex and Porrex)

DATE, AUTHORSHIP AND AUSPICES

1562 (*SR* 1565 c. Sept.); Thomas Norton and Thomas Sackville; Inner Temple; Greg 39

TEXT AND EDITIONS

Extant originals

1565 printing by William Griffith: Bodleian (frag: title page); Huntington; *STC* 18684
   c. 1570 (?) printing by John Day: BL; BN; Bodleian; Dyce; Folger; Harvard (imp.); Huntington; Indiana; NYPL (further copies extant); *STC* 18685

1590 printing by Edward Allde for John Perrin: BL: Bodleian; Dulwich; Folger (part two only); Harvard (part two only, imp.); Huntington; Pepys; Petworth House; PML (part two only); Yale; (further copies extant); *STC* 18685 and 17029

Editions

1994	CHD (CD-Rom and online transcription of Griffith printing, l.l., s.l., OS)
1992	Tydeman (NS)
1976	Fraser and Rabkin, vol. 1 (s.l., NS)
1974	Craik (s.l., NS)
1970	Cauthen (s.l., NS)
1968	Scolar Press (facsimile n.l.)
1966	Creeth (s.l., OS)
1963	Gassner (a.l., NS)
1958	Thorndike, vol. 1, (s.l., NS)
1938	McIlwraith (s.l., NS)*
1934	Baskervill, Heltzel and Nethercot (s.l., NS)
1928	Schweikert (NS)
1924	Adams (s.l., OS)*
1912	Cunliffe (notes by H. A. Watt, s.l., OS)
1908	TFT (facsimile, n.l.)
1906	Farmer (6) (n.l., NS)
1897	Manly, vol. 11 (s.l., OS)*
1883	Toulmin Smith (OS)
1859	Sackville-West (n.l., NS)
1847	Cooper (n.l., OS)

SOURCES

The story is found in Geoffrey of Monmouth's *Histories of the Kings of Britain* (Gorbodugo), but Norton and Sackville were possibly using Grafton's *Chronicle* of 1556, which follows Geoffrey.

CHARACTERS

Videna, Wife of Gorboduc
Ferrex, elder son of Gorboduc
Gorboduc, King of Britain
Arostus, Counsellor to Gorboduc
Philander, Counsellor to Gorboduc (later to Porrex)
Eubulus, Secretary to Gorboduc
Chorus (four ancient and sage men)
Hermon, Parasite of Ferrex
Dordan, Counsellor to Ferrex

Porrex, younger son of Gorboduc
Tyndar, Parasite of Porrex
1st Nuntius
Marcella, the Queen's lady
Clotyn, Duke of Cornwall
Mandud, Duke of Logris (Britain)
Gwenard, Duke of Cumberland
Fergus, Duke of Albany
2nd Nuntius

Various mute figures in the five dumbshows: a king, mourners, kings, queens, soldiers.

PLOT SUMMARY

The play opens with the first dumbshow illustrating, with the use of a faggot of sticks, the strength of a realm in unity and its weakness in disunity. *Videna* then commences the main action, complaining to her son *Ferrex* that *King Gorboduc* is intending to do him the injustice of leaving half the kingdom to *Porrex*, *Ferrex*'s younger brother. In the following scene *Gorboduc* is seen discussing the question of the succession with his courtiers. *Arostus* supports the king's plan to divide the realm, arguing that the burden of rule would be more easily managed if shared, and urges him to put his sons on the throne before his death. *Philander* agrees with the division of the kingdom, but advises against the king's abdication in favour of his sons, arguing that *Gorboduc* in his life and rule provides a model from which his sons can learn. A third counsellor, *Eubulus*, argues against the division of the kingdom and in favour of the maintenance of primogeniture, warning that civil strife will ensue from the king's plan. *Gorboduc* thanks them and resolves to follow the advice of *Arostus*. The second dumbshow illustrates good and bad counsel by showing a king refusing wine in a glass, but accepting poison in a golden goblet, and falling down dead. The second act opens with *Ferrex* complaining to his courtiers of his father's division of the kingdom. *Hermon* agrees and encourages *Ferrex* to go to war with his brother, while *Dordan* opposes this, pointing out that *Ferrex* has received the richer part of the realm. *Ferrex* resolves not to attack his brother, but rather to prepare for a possible attack by him, and *Dordan* expresses his fears of impending strife. The next scene has *Porrex* discussing his brother's martial preparations with his counsellors. *Tyndar* describes the military build-up while *Philander* counsels communication with *Ferrex*. *Porrex*, however, has decided on a pre-emptive invasion and *Philander* bewails the conflict to come. The act is concluded by the *Chorus*, which comments on the evils of bad advice to rulers. The third act is preceded by a dumbshow of mourners to illustrate the sorrow at the murder of *Porrex* by his younger brother, the subject of the next act. *Gorboduc* enters, accompanied by counsellors, troubled by the turn of events and asking for vengeance to light on himself and not his sons. *Eubulus* then reads a letter from *Dordan* reporting *Ferrex*'s gathering of troops and urges *Gorboduc* to call his sons together for discussion. However, *Philander* now brings news of *Porrex*'s preparations for war, and soon afterwards a messenger announces *Porrex*'s invasion of *Ferrex*'s land, and killing of his brother. The *Chorus* concludes the act with a reflection on the cruelty and horror that has occurred. The next dumbshow has the Furies driving before them kings and queens who had murdered their own children, to illustrate *Porrex*'s prospective murder by his own mother. *Videna* enters lamenting the death of *Ferrex* and vows revenge. When she exits, *Gorboduc* comes in and *Porrex* is brought before him grieving over his actions. After laying out the events that led to the murder, he departs and shortly afterwards *Marcella* brings the news that he has been slain by his mother. She delivers a long lament and the *Chorus* reflects on the horrors of revenge. The final dumbshow portrays armed men marching about the stage in token of rebellion and war in the realm. The nobility of the country then appear and pledge vengeance for the murder of *Porrex*. *Eubulus* counsels obedience to the king, but when the others go off, *Fergus, Duke of Albany* is left on stage and reveals his intention to use the instability to attempt to gain the crown. He exits and *Eubulus* returns with the nobles, discussing the disorder in the realm. A messenger arrives to announce that the *Duke of Albany* is approaching to seize the throne, and the other lords resolve to resist him. *Arostus* urges the setting up of a parliament, but *Eubulus* reflects on the dangers to the realm caused by the absence of a clear line of succession, and expresses doubts about the value of a parliament. The play ends with his hope for the restoration of the crown to a lawful heir.

PLAY LENGTH

1,800 lines

COMMENTARY

This play is highly significant in the history of drama in English, being the first to use blank verse. It is also variously regarded as the first classical tragedy and history play in English. It uses the chronicle history of Britain to present a political lesson on the succession and to argue for the benefits of strong kingship. Its use of dumbshows to underscore the lesson inherent in each act is a noteworthy feature of the play; these are possibly drawn either from the native pageant tradition found particularly in civic and royal public occasions, or from the Italian *intermedii*. As an Inns of Court play, it is unsurprising that it is firmly in the same 'advice to princes' tradition as the *Mirror for Magistrates*, or that it involves a strong element of structured debate throughout.

Other secular tragedies: **7, 32, 43**.

Other political comment and state of the realm plays: **1** (frag.), **14, 38, 59, 71, 76**.

Other plays based on classical or Italian models: **5, 7, 32, 41, 43, 88, 91, 92**.

SIGNIFICANT TOPICS AND NARRATIVE ELEMENTS

royal succession and primogeniture; civil strife; history as a mirror; good and bad counsel to rulers; fraternal enmity and fratricide; revenge; foreign threats to the realm; insurrection

NOTE: editions have line numbering by scene and reference is to act/scene/line

DRAMATURGICAL AND RHETORICAL FEATURES

Verbal and general a dumbshow precedes every act, each with its actions interpreted for their allegorical signification; five acts with a formal act and scene division; there is little on-stage action outside the dumbshows, actions normally being reported, and there is only one stage direction outside the dumbshows; substantial classical reference; a formal debate pattern occurs throughout

Costume and dress wild men clothed in leaves d.s. 1; mourners clad in black d.s. 3; the Furies in black garments 'sprinkled with blood and flames, their bodies girt with snakes, with serpents instead of hair' d.s. 4; men in military dress d.s. 5

Actions and stage directions (the dumbshows have detailed stage directions not recorded here) d.s. 1: the breaking of the sticks; d.s. 2: the poisoning of the king; d.s. 3: mourners pass thrice over the stage; 3.1.28 sd: 'Eub. reads the letter'; d.s. 4: the driving of the kings and queens; d.s. 5: the marching of the soldiers and discharging of weapons

Songs and music music of violins d.s. 1; music of cornets d.s. 2; flute music d.s. 3; music of hautboys d.s. 4; drums and flutes d.s. 5

Staging and set the main visual elements of the play are contained in the dumbshows, where there is extensive use of stage properties; action within the main play is off stage and there are no indications as to set

Stage properties a faggot of sticks d.s. 1; a chair of state, glass of wine and golden goblet d.s. 2; *Dordan*'s letter 3.1.28 *sd*; a snake, whip and firebrand d.s. 4; arms, including firearms d.s. 5

PLACENAMES

Albany 5.1.167; Britain 4.1.80 *passim*; 'Camberland' 1.2.163; River Humber 1.2.345; River Simois 3.1.2; Troy 2.2.76 ('Ilion'), 3.1.10

ALLUSIONS

Althea d.s. 4; Apollo 1.2.chor.16; Athamas d.s. 4; Brutus (legendary founder of Britain) 1.2.165, 1.2.270, 2.1.196, 5.2.180; Cambises d.s. 4; Furies (Alecto, Megæra, Tisiphone) d.s. 4, 4.2.chor.11; Hecuba 3.1.14; Ino d.s. 4; Ixion 2.1.17; Jove 2.1.197 *passim*; Medea d.s. 4; Morgan 1.2.162, 3.1.chor.12; Phaeton 1.2.chor.16–18, 2.1.204–6; Phoebus 2.1.204; Priam 3.1.6, 3.1.16; Tantalus 2.1.17, d.s. 4

RECORDED PRODUCTION

LP Record: BBC, *The First Stage*, dir. J. Barton (1970)

BIBLIOGRAPHY

Babula, W. 'Gorboduc as Apology and Critique', TSL 17 (1972) pp. 37–43

Bacquet, P. 'L'Imitation de Sénèque dans Gorboduc de Sackville et Norton' in Jacquot, 1964, pp. 153–74

Bacquet, P. 'Structure et valeur dramatiques de Gorboduc', Filoloski Pregled (Belgrade) 1–2 (1964) pp. 247–59

Bacquet, 1966, pp. 217–89

Baker, 1939, pp. 9–47

Berg, J. E. 'Gorboduc as a Tragic Discovery of "Feudalism"', SEL 40:2 (2000), pp. 199–226

Berlin, 1974, pp. 80–127

Breitenberg, M. 'Reading Elizabethan Iconicity: Gorboduc and the Semiotics of Reform', ELR 18:2 (1988) pp. 194–217

Cartwright, 1999, pp. 108–21

Cauthen, I. B. 'Gorboduc, Ferrex and Porrex: The First Two Quartos' SB 15 (1962) pp. 231–3

Clemen, 1961, pp. 56–74, 253–7

De Mendonca, B. H. 'The Influence of Gorboduc on King Lear', ShakS 13 (1960) pp. 41–8

Dust, P. 'The Theme of "Kinde" in Gorboduc' in Salzburg Studies in English Literature: Elizabethan Studies, Salzburg, Institut für englische Sprache und Literatur, Universität Salzburg, 1973, pp. 43–81

Graves, 1994, pp. 92–104, 115–18

Griffin, 2001, pp. 80–4

Grosse, 1935, pp. 39–45

Hardison, 1989, pp. 171–82

Herrick, M. T. 'Senecan Influence in Gorboduc' in Bryant, Hewitt, Wallace and Wichelns, 1944, pp. 78–104

Ishida, H. 'The World of Gorboduc: A Milestone to Shakespeare's Histories', Studies in Language and Literature (Osaka University) 9 (1983) pp. 187–201

Johnson, 1959, pp. 157–71

Jones, N. and P. W. White, 'Gorboduc and Royal Marriage Politics: An Elizabethan Playgoer's Report of the Premiere Performance', ELR 26:1 (1996) pp. 3–16

Koch, F. 'Ferrex and Porrex: Eine literarhistorische Untersuchung' in Jahres-Bericht der Realschule zu Altona über das Schuljahr Ostern 1880 bis Ostern 1881, Altona, Peter Meyer, 1881, pp. i–xvii

Lascombes, 1995, pp. 66–80

McDonnell, 1958, pp. 70–86

Mehl, 1965, pp. 27–41

Moretti, F. ' "A huge Eclipse": Tragic Form and the Deconsecration of Sovereignty' in Greenblatt, 1982, pp. 7–40

Reese, G. C. 'The Question of the Succession in Elizabethan Drama', UTSE 22 (1942) pp. 59–85

Ribner, 1965, pp. 41–52

Schmidt, H. 'Seneca's Influence upon Gorboduc', MLN 2:2 (1887) pp. 56–70

Small, S. A. 'The Political Import of the Norton Half of Gorboduc', PMLA 46:3 (1931) pp. 641–6

Swart, 1949, pp. 64–80

Symonds, 1900, pp. 182–90

Talbert, E. W. 'The Political Import and the First Two Audiences of Gorboduc' in Harrison, Hill, Mossner and Sledd, 1967, pp. 89–115

Trousdale, 1982, pp. 118–24

Turner, R. Y. 'Pathos and the Gorboduc Tradition 1560–1590', HLQ 25:2 (1962) pp. 97–120

Vanhoutte, J. 'Community, Authority and the Motherland in Gorboduc', SEL 40:2 (2000) pp. 227–39

Wagner, M. 'The English Dramatic Blank-Verse before Marlowe (Part 1: Gorboduc)' in Städtische höhere Bürgerschule zu Osterode in Ostpreussen, Program-Abhandlung, Osterode, F. Albrecht, 1881, pp. 1–16

Walker, 1998, pp. 196–221

Watson, S. R. 'Gorboduc and the Theory of Tyrannicide', MLR 34:3 (1939) pp. 355–66

Whall, 1988, pp. 97–136

38   Hick Scorner

DATE, AUTHORSHIP AND AUSPICES

1513–16; anonymous; auspices unknown, but clearly written for private indoor performance and probably in or near London; Greg 3

TEXT AND EDITIONS

Extant originals

1515 (?) printing by Wynkyn de Worde: BL; *STC* 14039
1530 (?) printing by Peter Treveris: BL (frag.: two leaves); *STC* 14039.5
1550 (?) printing by William Copland/John Waley: Bodleian; *STC* 14040

Editions

1994	CHD (CD-Rom and online transcription of de Worde printing, l.l., OS)
1980	Lancashire (NS)*
1908	TFT (facsimile, n.l.)
1905	Farmer (3) (n.l., NS)
1897	Manly, vol. 1 (OS)
1874–6	Dodsley, vol. 1 (n.l., NS)

SOURCES

Ian Lancashire argues that the play draws on *Youth* and also cites the fifteenth-century *The Assemble of Goddes* and Chaucer's *Pardoner's Tale*; see the introduction to his edition, pp. 41–8.

CHARACTERS

Pity   Contemplation   Perseverance   Free Will   Imagination   Hick Scorner

PLOT SUMMARY

Pity and *Contemplation* enter successively and meditate on the Crucifixion, and they are joined soon afterwards by *Perseverance*. The three go on to discuss current social evils before departing on their way. *Free Will* then makes an appearance, joined by *Imagination* who boasts of his reprobate ways and his brushes with the law. *Imagination*'s kinsman, *Hick Scorner*, next arrives and tells them of his travels, also relating the departure of the virtues and the arrival of the vices in England. They decide to go wenching but when *Free Will* impugns the virtue of *Imagination*'s mother, they fall to fighting. *Pity* arrives to intervene and *Imagination* makes up his quarrel with *Free Will* in order to turn his aggression against *Pity*. He hurls false accusations at him and the companions bind *Pity* up and leave him fettered while they go off to enjoy more sport. *Pity* utters a long complaint about the many abuses in the realm, until he is finally discovered by *Contemplation* and *Perseverance*. He tells them what has happened to him, they release him and all set off to find the malefactors. *Free Will* returns with a vaunting speech about his riotous escapades, having been imprisoned but delivered by *Imagination* by means of a bribe with stolen money. He is accosted and castigated by *Perseverance* and *Contemplation*, whom he threatens with violence. He continues his defiance until he is threatened with the prospect of damnation and reminded of God's mercy. He then suddenly capitulates and is given a new garment in token of his reformation. *Imagination* arrives swaggering and is also preached at by *Contemplation* and *Perseverance*, until he too converts. He is also given new clothing and is renamed 'Remembrance'. *Perseverance* then concludes the play with a prayer for the spiritual health of the audience.

PLAY LENGTH

1,028 lines

COMMENTARY

This is a good example of a play structured along the lines of a basic religious fall and redemption scheme, but with reflections on a wide range of social ills and allusions to contemporary historical events and personalities. In his edition, Ian Lancashire has identified the Yorkist pretender to the throne, Richard de la Pole, and the adventurer John Baptist de Grimaldi as objects of satirical allusion. The play parallels the three-way conversation of the Virtues at the start of the play with that of the reprobate companions who succeed them on stage. There is some parallel too between the fettering and release of *Pity* on stage, and that of *Free Will* by *Imagination* (narrated).

Other political comment and state of the realm plays: **1** (frag.), **14, 37, 59, 71, 76**.
Other social ills plays: **2, 15, 24, 40, 53, 71, 72** (frag.), **76, 94, 96, 98, 100**.

SIGNIFICANT TOPICS AND NARRATIVE ELEMENTS

the Crucifixion; the oppression of the poor; the remarriage of rich widows; the corruption of clergy; sexual dalliance; judicial corruption; crime, imprisonment and hanging; benefit of clergy; ships and travel; prostitution; cuckoldry; highway robbery; bribery; bad companions; Tudor politics and contemporary history (allusions)

DRAMATURGICAL AND RHETORICAL FEATURES

Verbal and general *Free Will* pushes his way in (through standing servants) calling for room to move 156; *Imagination* enters as a 'huffing' gallant ('how, how') 192; *Hick Scorner*'s list of place names 309–22; *Hick Scorner*'s list of ships 332–7; *Hick Scorner*'s list of the virtues departing from England 340–52; *Hick Scorner*'s list of the vices arriving in England 368–79; *Imagination* is renamed 'Remembrance' on conversion 1016; there are no stage directions

Costume and dress *Free Will* receives a new garment 876; *Imagination* receives a new garment 1002

Actions 301: *Hi. S.* calls from off stage before entering; 423, 435: *Im.* threatens *Fr. W.* with a dagger; 440–55: *Fr. W.* and *Im.* fight; 514–28: *Fr. W., Im.* and *Hi. S.* tie up *Pi.*; 610–11: *Con.* and *Per.* release *Pi.*

Staging and set this is a hall play, likely to have been staged at a banquet; the action is unlocalized and there are no indications as to set, but at least two entrances appear to be necessary; *Free Will* and *Imagination*'s fight may spill over into the audience space (455); *Free Will* re-enters through the audience, which he greets in French (646–7)

Stage properties *Imagination*'s dagger 435; fetters 510–13, 515; a halter 518

PLACENAMES

Apulia ('Pouille')[1] 312, Aragon[1] 312; Babylon[1] 319; 'The Bell' (brothel, Bankside) 901; Biscay[1] 313; Bordeaux 752; Bridport 243; Brittany[1] 313; Burgundy[1] 311; Calabria[1] 312; Calais 730; Calvary 37; Canterbury 752; Cape St Vincent[1] 315; Chaldea[1] 322; Constantinople[1] 319; Cornwall[1] 320; Cowes[1] 316; England 329, 380, 565, 624; Flanders[1] 311; France[1] 309; Friesland[1] 311; Gascony[1] 313; Genoa[1] 316; Germany ('Almain')[1] 310; St Giles-in-the-Field 665; Greece[1] 314; 'Hart's Horn' (in Southwark) 901; Holborn 663; India[1] 322; Ireland 309,[1] 327; Kent 832, 941; King's Bench (prison) 512; London 383, 444; Ludgate 668; Naples[1] 314; Newfoundland (? 'the new found island')[1] 315; Newgate (prison) 236, 422, 508, 681, 684, 801, 949; Northumberland[1] 320; Portugal[1] 310; the Race of Ireland 362; Rhodes[1] 319; Rome 445; Salisbury 745; Scotland[1] 314; Seville[1] 310; Shooter's Hill 388, 543, 822; Spain[1] 309; 'The Swan Inn' (near Newgate) 681; Tartary[1] 322; Thames 418; St Thomas-a-Watering 838; Tyburn 244, 264, 829, 831, 897, 941; Westminster 842; Westminster Hall 217

1 Part of *Hick Scorner*'s formulaic list of places he claims to have visited.

ALLUSIONS

St Anthony 44; St Jerome 44; Job 788; John the Baptist 44; *Office of the Dead* (q.a.) 787

RECORDED PRODUCTION

LP Record: BBC, *The First Stage*, dir. J. Barton (1970)

BIBLIOGRAPHY

Greg. W. W. 'Notes on Some Early Plays: *Hycke Scorner*: Reconstruction of a Treveris Edition Known Only from Two Leaves', *Library* 4th series 11 (1930) pp. 44–6
Lancashire, I. 'The Sources of *Hyckescorner*', *RES*, n.s. 22:87 (1971) pp. 257–73
Schell, 1966, pp. 468–74
Southern, 1973, pp. 168–80
Walker, 1991, pp. 37–59

39   Horestes

DATE, AUTHORSHIP AND AUSPICES

printed 1567; John Pickering; offered for acting, probably for private theatre performance by an adult company (Rich's?), but possibly performed by boys at court; Greg 48

TEXT AND EDITIONS

Extant originals

1567 printing by William Griffith: BL; *STC* 19917

Editions

1994   CHD (CD-Rom and online transcription of Griffith printing, l.l., OS)*
1982   Axton (OS)*
1962   Seltzer, Brown and Bentley (facsimile)
1910   TFT (privately printed facsimile, n.l.)
1898   Brandl (OS)*
1866   Collier, vol. II (n.l., OS)

SOURCES

Probable sources include Lydgate's *Troy Book* and William Baldwin's *Treatise of Moral Philosophy*; see Merritt's essay below. Marie Axton has identified Baldwin's work as the source of Horestes's maxims; see the introduction to her edition, p. 26.

CHARACTERS

The Vice	Haltersick	Nature	Duty
Rusticus	Hempstring	Provision	Messenger
Hodge	Nestor	Herald	Egistus
Horestes	Menelaus	2nd Soldier	Commons
Idumeus	A Woman	Truth	
Counsel	1st Soldier	Fame	
Clytemnestra	Nobles	Hermione	

PLOT SUMMARY

The *Vice* enters followed by two countrymen, *Rusticus* and *Hodge*, who discuss the ills of warfare caused by the conflict within the royal family as a result of *Clytemnestra*'s murder of *Agamemnon*. The *Vice* foments a quarrel between the two, which they make up after he leaves. *Horestes* comes in pondering on his dilemma, of whether he should obey *Dame Nature* and forgive his mother for his father's death or exercise his duty to avenge him. Posing as a messenger of the gods, the *Vice* appears and encourages him to revenge. When *King Idumeus* enters with *Counsel*, *Horestes* begs him for the means to pursue the revenge and, with the support of *Counsel*, *Idumeus* grants him an army. The scene then switches briefly to a comic episode involving two soldiers in *Horestes*'s army, *Haltersick* and *Hempstring*, who fall to quarrelling and physically fighting. When *Horestes* re-enters he is lectured by *Nature* on the horrors of matricide, but he resists her arguments and is supported in his position by *Idumeus* and *Counsel*, who have returned. The scene changes to *Egistus* and *Clytemnestra*, whose amatory bliss, expressed through a song, is interrupted by a messenger, who reports the imminent invasion by *Horestes*. They go off to prepare their defences and there is a brief episode of conflict between a woman and a soldier, followed by the *Vice* singing about revenge and conflict. *Horestes* then comes in with his troops to besiege *Clytemnestra*, who, after a battle, is captured and taken off by the soldiers. When *Egistus* enters with his army, another battle ensues, which he loses and is apprehended and hanged on stage, *Clytemnestra* also being taken off shortly afterwards to execution. *Fame* then comes in to take on the role of spreading the news of *Horestes*'s deed. Now *Clytemnestra*'s brother, *Menelaus*, arrives seeking revenge for his sister's death and also accuses *Horestes* of causing hardship to his subjects by waging war, but he is pacified when *Idumeus* and *Nestor* persuade him of the necessity of *Horestes*'s actions. They are reconciled and *Horestes* is betrothed to *Menelaus*'s daughter, *Hermione*. The *Vice* enters briefly as a beggar, having lost his role in the new state of harmony that has come about. *Duty* and *Truth* crown *Horestes*, who is accompanied by *Hermione*, and there is acclamation by *Nobles* and *Commons*. Finally *Truth* and *Duty* deliver a joint sermon on the qualities they represent and to offer a prayer for the queen, council, nobility, clergy, judiciary, city councillors and the commonality.

PLAY LENGTH

1,205 lines

COMMENTARY

This is one of the earliest English plays to draw on the material of classical tragedy, though the ending of this play is not tragic. It is also the first extant English revenge play, though not in the Senecan tradition. Strife is a dominant motif, and the several subplot elements all contribute to the general impression of turmoil and conflict, even when handled in a comic way. The detail and complexity of the stage directions in the play are striking. The Vice in the play is never given a name, though he does at one point briefly adopt an alias. Though in some respects he fulfils the traditional function of a Vice, for much of the time he provides narrative infill and choric comment on the action. He also, however, embodies strife, as his redundancy at the end of the play confirms.

   Other plays with classical settings: **19, 29, 43, 57** (frag.), **91, 92**.

SIGNIFICANT TOPICS AND NARRATIVE ELEMENTS

revenge; civil strife; the visicissitudes of Fortune; matricide; honour and reputation; Nature as a motivating force; the horrors of war; the Oresteian legend reworked (with likely reference to Mary Queen of Scot's marriage to Bothwell)

DRAMATURGICAL AND RHETORICAL FEATURES

Verbal and general the play is advertised as 'a new interlude of Vice'; rustic speech: *Rusticus* and *Hodge* 22 ff.; *Vice*'s alias: *Patience* 92; *Hodge* interprets the *Vice*'s purported name as *Past Shame* 93; stage directions in the play (all in English) are extensive and detailed

Costume and dress *Hodge* has a new hat 55; the *Woman* is dressed 'like a beggar' 625 *sd*; the *Vice* puts off his beggar's coat and accoutrements 1058 *sd*

Actions and stage directions 54 *sd*: '(*Vi.*) Fight (with *Hod.*)'; 154 *sd*: '(*Ru.*) Up with thy staff and be ready to smite, but *Hod.* smite first'; 157 *sd*: 'And let the *Vi.* thwack them both (*Ru.* and *Hod.*) and run out'; 243 *sd*: '(*Hor.*) Kneel down'; 305 *sd*: '(*Hor., Vi., Id., Cou.*) Go out. [*Hal.*] enters and sings this song to the tune of "Have over the water to Floride" or "Sellenger's Round"'; 329 *sd*: '*Hem.* comes in and speaks'; 375 *sd*: '(*Hal.*) Flort (flick) him (*Hem.*)'; 379 *sd*: '(*Hal.*) Flort him (*Hem.*) on the lips'; 382 *sd*: '(*Hem.*) Give him (*Hal.*) a box on the ear'; 389 *sd*: '(*Hal., Hem.*) Fight at buffets with fists'; 397 *sd*: '(*Hal.*) Give him (*Hem.*) a box on the ear and go out'; 399 *sd*: '(*Hem.*) Go out. Let the drum play and *Hor.* enter with his men and then let him kneel down and speak'; 407 *sd*: '(*Hor.*) Stand up'; 451 *sd*: 'Let the drum play'; 453 *sd*: 'Let the drum play and enter *Hor.* with his band; march about the stage'; 499 *sd*: '(*Id.*) Embrace him (*Hor.*)'; 501 *sd*: '(*Id.*) Kiss him (*Hor.*)'; 505 *sd*: '(Soldiers) March about and go out'; 537 *sd*: '(*Id.*) Go out. Enter *Eg.* and *Cly.* singing this song to the tune of "King Solomon"'; 604 *sd*: 'Let the trumpet blow within'; 625 *sd*: 'Enter a *Wo.* like a beggar running before [the] *Sol.*, but let the *Sol.* speak first, but let the *Wo.* cry first pitifully'; 633 *sd*: '(*Sol.*) Go afore her (*Wo.*) and let her fall down upon the *Sol.* and all to bebeat (thoroughly beat) him'; 643 *sd*: '(*Sol.*) Take his weapons and let him rise up and then go out both'; 647 *sd*: 'Enter the *Vi.* singing this song to the tune of "The Painter"'; 679 *sd*: '(*Vi.*) Go out. *Hor.* enters with his band and marches about the stage'; 693 *sd*: 'Let the trumpet go towards the city and blow'; 695 *sd*: 'Let the trumpet leave sounding and let *Hera.* speak, and *Cly.* speak over the wall'; 725 *sd*: 'Go make your lively battle and let it be long ere you can win the city, and when you have won it, let *Hor.* bring out his mother by the arm and let the drum cease playing and the trumpet also. When she is taken, let her kneel down and speak'; 745 *sd*: 'Let *Hor.* sigh hard'; 748 *sd*: '(*Vi.*) Weep, but let *Hor.* rise and bid him peace'; 754 *sd*: 'Let *Eg.* enter and set his men in array, and let the drum play till *Hor.* speaks'; 768 *sd*: 'Strike up your drum, and fight a good while and then let some of *Eg.* men fly, and then take him and let *Hor.* drag him violently, and let the drums cease'; 790 *sd*: 'Fling him (*Eg.*) off the ladder, and then let one bring in his mother *Cly.*, but let her look where *Eg.* hangs'; 804 *sd*: 'Take down *Eg.* and bear him out'; 824 *sd*: '(*Cly.*) Kneel down'; 834 *sd*: 'Let *Cly.* weep and go out, *Rev.* also'; 838 *sd*: '(*Hor.*) [Go out], and let all the soldiers follow him in array. Enter in *Fa.*'; 848 *sd*: 'Enter this *Vi.* singing this song'; 943 *sd*: '(*Pro.*) Go out. (*Hor.*) Pause a while till he (*Pro.*) be gone out, and then speak treatably (moderately)'; 947 *sd*: 'Enter *Id.*, and *Pro.* coming with his cap in his hand afore him and making way'; 995: *Nes.* offers down his glove (in challenge); 1037 *sd*: 'Go out all. *Vi.* enters with a staff and a bottle or dish and wallet'; 1058 *sd*: '(*Vi.*) Put off the beggar's coat and all thy things'; 1131 *sd*: 'Let *Du.* and *Tru.* take the crown in their right hands'; 1145 *sd*: 'Let *Tru.* and *Du.* crown *Hor.*'; 1163 *sd*.: 'Go out all and let *Tru.* and *Du.* speak'; **Simple entry**: *Rus.*, *Hod.* 21; (*Hor.*) 170; (*Id.*, *Cou.*) 449; (*Mess.*) 607; *Hor.*, *Herm.*, *Nob.*, *Com.*, *Tru.*, *Du.* 1121; **Simple exit**: (*Rus.*, *Hod.*) 170; (*Hor.*) 290; (*Vi.*) 291; (*Nat.*) 448; (*Hor.*) 449; (*Mess.*) 615; *Hera.* 707; (*Cly.*), *Sol.* 739; (*Vi.*) 916; (*Fa.*) 925; (*Vi.*) 1121

Songs and music (w.s. to all songs) 1. *Haltersick* 'Fare well, adieu, that courtly life' (to the tune of 'Have over the water to Floride' or 'Sellenger's Round') 306–29; 2. *Egistus, Clytemnestra* 'And was it not a worthy sight?' (to the tune of 'King Solomon', w. ref.) 538–601; 3. *Vice* 'Stand back, ye sleeping jacks at home' (to the tune of 'The Painter') 648–79; 4. *Vice* 'A new master, a new' 849–60. **Instrumental** a drum 399 *sd*, 451 *sd*, 453 *sd*, 754 *sd*, 768 *sd*; a trumpet 604 *sd* (off stage, to signal an entry), 693 *sd*

Staging and set the title page has a doubling scheme 'for six to play': 1. *Vice, Nature, Duty*; 2. *Rusticus, Idumeus, Soldier, Menelaus, Nobles*; 3. *Hodge, Counsel, Messenger, Nestor, Commons*; 4. *Horestes, a Woman, Prologue*; 5. *Haltersick, Soldier, Egistus, Herald, Fame, Truth, Idumeus*; 6. *Hempstring, Clytemnestra, Provision,*

Hermione. the direction for *Horestes* and his men to go 'about the stage' may either suggest that they march across the acting area, or walk around the perimeter of a raised stage (679 *sd*); a siege and battle on stage and reference in a stage direction to the 'city' (693 *sd*), represented by a 'wall' (695 *sd*); *Horestes* makes a triumphal entry apparently through the city gates (698 ff.); there is a hanging on stage, with a ladder and scaffold (790 *sd*); a coronation is staged towards the end of the play (1145 *sd*); otherwise the action is either unlocalized or locations are identified by the presence and dialogue of characters; *Provision* clears a space for *Nestor, Horestes* and *Menelaus* to enter through the audience (926)

Stage properties a blade 60; staffs 154 *sd*; the soldier's weapons 643 *sd*; a scaffold ('ladder') 790 *sd*; *Provision*'s cap 947 *sd*; *Nestor*'s glove 995; a staff, bottle or dish and wallet 1037 *sd*; a crown 1131 *sd*

PLACENAMES

Athens 909, 911, 1101; the Canaries 882; Crete 25, 844, 946; Cythera 567; Greece 298, 540, 544, 908, 971; Mycene 612, 969, 994; Portugal 882; Spain 881; Troy 300, 541, 544; Venice 882

ALLUSIONS

Achilles 299; Charon and the Styx 236; Cupid 560, 570; Juvenal 808; Livy 486; Mars 209, 602; Nero 804, 899; Oedipus 804; Ovid 894; Ovid *Tristia V.12.37* 861–2, *V.1.75* 863–4; Paris and Helen 538–601; Plato 484, 518; Pluto and Hades 237; Priam 539, 578; Protegeus 522; Pythagoras 432; Socrates 485, 806, 1092; Socrates and Xantippe 1101–7; Publius Syrus 914, 917–21; Hermes Trismegistus 984; Venus 539, 547, 602

REPORT ON MODERN PRODUCTION

University of Dundee 15 February 1977, dir. K. Nelson [*RORD* 37 (1998) pp. 125–7]

BIBLIOGRAPHY

Brie, F. '*Horestes* von John Pickeryng', *EngS* 46 (1912) pp. 66–72
Broude, 1973, pp. 489–502
Burns, 1990, pp. 58–64
Glickfield, L. '*Horestes*: A Bridge to Shakespearian Comic Forms', *Komos* 3:1–4 (1973) pp. 1–9
Hallett and Hallett, 1980, pp. 246–54
Happé, 1965, pp. 207–27
Kipka, 1907, pp. 9–15
Knapp, R. '*Horestes*: The Uses of Revenge', *ELH* 40:2 (1973) pp. 205–20
Merritt, K. 'The Sources of John Pikeryng's *Horestes*', *RES* n.s. 23:91 (1972) pp. 255–66
Phillips, J. E. 'A Re-evaluation of *Horestes*', *HLQ* 18:3 (1955) pp. 227–44
Phillips, 1964, pp. 46–9, 126–7

Robertson, K. 'The Natural Body of a Queen: Mary, James, *Horestes*', *R&R* 14 (1990) pp. 25–36
Ruys, C. 'John Pickering – Merchant Adventurer and Playwright', *Costerus* 9 (1973) pp. 145–58
Shapiro, M. 'John Pickering's *Horestes*, Auspices and Theatricality' in Elton and Long, 1989, pp. 211–26
Southern, 1973, pp. 494–506
Woolf, 1973, pp. 99–103

40   Impatient Poverty

DATE, AUTHORSHIP AND AUSPICES

1547–58 (*SR* 10 June 1560); anonymous; offered for acting; Greg 30

TEXT AND EDITIONS

Extant originals

1560 printing by John King: BL; *STC* 14112.5
1561 (?) printing by William Copland: Huntington (imp.); *STC* 14113

Editions

1994	CHD (CD-Rom and online transcription of King printing, l.l., OS)*
1984	Tennenhouse (NS)*
1911	McKerrow (King printing, OS)
1909	Farmer (n.l., OS)
1907	Farmer (9) (n.l., NS)
1907	'Lost' Tudor Plays, TFT (privately printed facsimile, n.l.)

SOURCES

No sources have been identified.

CHARACTERS

Peace	Impatient Poverty (Prosperity)	Conscience	Colhazard
Envy	Abundance	Misrule	Summoner

PLOT SUMMARY

Peace delivers a sermon against envy and malice, which is interrupted by *Envy* who engages in a debate with him, arguing that peace is ruinous to many such as soldiers or surgeons. *Peace* eventually becomes angry and threatens to call a constable, at which *Envy* retreats, and *Impatient Poverty* enters. He is an aggressive young man who, however, learns patience from *Peace*'s teaching and is then renamed *Prosperity*. They both go out and are replaced on stage by *Abundance* and *Conscience*, who also debate, this time about *Abundance*'s crooked commercial dealings through which he has amassed wealth. *Conscience* brings him initially to some sort of repentance, but *Abundance* refuses to make restitution, and he departs unconverted. *Envy* then comes to *Conscience* and introduces himself as *Charity*. When he learns who *Conscience* is he tells him that he (*Conscience*) has been replaced in many areas of the realm, including the administration of justice, by *Covetise*. When *Conscience* departs sorrowfully, *Envy* pretends to weep in sympathy, but as soon as *Conscience* is out of sight this turns to gleeful laughter as he reflects on all the discord he has sown. *Prosperity*, whom *Envy* knows by his previous name, now comes in and *Envy* (introducing himself as *Charity*) claims kinship with him. *Prosperity* is at first disdainful, until *Envy* claims to have three hundred pounds, which he would like *Prosperity* to look after for him. On *Prosperity*'s departure, *Envy* conspires with another companion, *Misrule*, to bring him to grief. *Prosperity* then re-enters, upon which *Misrule* introduces himself as *Mirth* and invites him to revelry. *Peace* comes in and tries to intervene, but *Prosperity* now refuses to listen to him and they drive him off before going to gamble and dine. *Peace* returns to the stage briefly to lament what has happened, after which *Envy* and *Misrule* enter with *Colhazard*, a gambler who has just won two thousand pounds from *Prosperity*. *Misrule* and *Colhazard* end up fighting, and all three go off. *Prosperity*, now *Poverty* again, comes in poorly dressed and he is followed by his erstwhile companions, *Misrule* and *Envy*, who at this point scorn him. They leave him to lament his folly when he is called by a *Summoner* to appear in court and they go off. There is then a brief episode in which *Abundance* is able to escape a summons with a bribe, after which the *Summoner* leads *Poverty* in and clears a space for him to do public penance. *Peace* arrives to enquire whether due process of law has been followed, but the *Summoner* reveals that the only principle that operates is bribery and corruption. *Peace* then rescues *Poverty*, giving him fresh clothes, pointing out to the audience the perils of corruption and offering a prayer for the queen and the kingdom.

PLAY LENGTH

1,083 lines

COMMENTARY

This interlude specifically targets the potential for corruption afforded by wealth. The fall and redemption of the central figure, and indeed his changes of name, all relate predominantly to the dangers posed to material rather than spiritual well-being. There is more interest, anyway, in the airing of complaints about judicial corruption than in the moral progress of the humanity figure. The play is episodic, poorly organized and lacking in consistent focus.

Other social ills plays: **2, 15, 24, 38, 52, 53, 71, 72** (frag.), **76, 94, 96, 98, 100**.

SIGNIFICANT TOPICS AND NARRATIVE ELEMENTS

the failings of youth; wealth and its pitfalls; peace and war; dishonest trading; extortion and usury; bribery and corruption in the judiciary; bad companions; gambling

DRAMATURGICAL AND RHETORICAL FEATURES

Verbal and general the renaming of *Impatient Poverty–Prosperity–Foolish Poverty* 218, 816; Vices' aliases: *Envy–Charity* 557, *Misrule–Mirth* 633; *Misrule*'s French greeting on first entry 607–9; the *Summoner* and *Poverty* probably enter through the audience 978; stage directions mainly in English, with some brief ones in Latin

Costume and dress *Envy* removes *Prosperity*'s outer garment 681; *Poverty* is poorly clad 723; the reclothing of *Poverty* 217; *Poverty* enters again in poor dress 873

Actions and stage directions 409 *sd*: 'Here comes *En.* running in laughing, and says to *Con.*'; 504 *sd*: 'And he (*En.*) weeps' (L); 603 *sd*: 'Here *Mis.* sings without, coming in'; 690–3: *Mis., En.* and *Pro.* dance; 742 *sd*: 'And here they (*En., Mis., Pro.*) face *Pe.* out of the place'; 855 *sd* 'Here they (*Mis., Col.*) fight and run all out of the place, and then enters *Pro.* poorly and says'; 977 *sd*: 'Here enters the *Sum.* again, and *Pov.* follows him with a candle in his hand doing penance about the place. And then says the *Sum.*'; **Simple entry:** *I. Pov.* 100; *Pe.* 693; *Sum.* 927; *Ab.* 936; **Simple exit:** 'Both' (*Pe., Pro.*) 239; (*Ab.*) 402; *Mis.* 777; 'Both' (*En., Pro.*) 787; (*Pe.*) 807; (*Mis.*) 903; (*En.*) 905; 'Both' (*Ab., Sum.*) 977; *Sum.* 1038

Songs and music (w.n.s. to either song) 1. *Misrule* 603 *sd*; 2. *Misrule, Envy, Prosperity* 676/690 (with dance); **Instrumental:** music for the dance at 690–3? (a French round)

Staging and set the title page states that 'four men may well and easily play this Interlude' and a doubling scheme given as follows: 1. *Peace, Colhazard, Conscience*; 2. *Abundance, Misrule*; 3. *Impatient Poverty, Prosperity, Poverty*; 4. *Envy, the Summoner*. the action is unlocalized and there are no indications as to set; references to the 'place' may indicate the hall; the *Summoner* asks the audience to make room for *Poverty*'s entry (978–9)

Stage properties a sword 716; a dagger 742; a bag of gold 830; a penance candle 977 *sd*

PLACENAMES

Fleur de Lys (tavern) 754; Jerusalem 568; Marshalsea (prison) 869; Newgate (prison) 83, 712; Tyburn 497; Woolpit (Suffolk) 80

ALLUSIONS

Ahab and Naboth 373–84; St Augustine, *Epistle* 153 350–1; King David 1049; Elijah 381; *Ephesians 4:26* 77; *Luke 3:34* 193; *Matthew 5:3* 195, *25:34* 197; *Psalm 17:26* (V)/*18:26* (AV) 1049

BIBLIOGRAPHY

Bevington, 1962, pp. 141–4
Mackenzie, 1914, pp. 105–10
Takemoto, 1989, pp. 1–18

41   Jack Juggler

DATE, AUTHORSHIP AND AUSPICES

1553–8 (*SR* 1562/3 *c*. Nov.); anonymous; offered for acting, and performed by boys ('an interlude for children to play') possibly at court and probably at Christmas; Greg 35

TEXT AND EDITIONS

Extant originals

1562 printing by William Copland: Rosenbach; *STC* 14837
1565 printing by William Copland: Huntington; *STC* 14837a
1570 printing by John Allde: Folger; Huntington (frag.); *STC* 14837a.5

Editions

1994	CHD (CD-Rom and online transcription of fragmentary Allde printing, l.l., OS)
1984	Tydeman (OS)*
1982	Axton (OS)*
1937	Evans and Greg (1937a) (OS)
1933	Smart and Greg (OS)
1914	Williams (OS)*
1913	Farmer (facsimile, n.l.)
1912	TFT (facsimile, n.l.)
1906	Farmer (5) (n.l., NS)
1876 (?)	Ashbee (1876a) (facsimile, n.l.)
1874–6	Dodsley, vol. II (n.l., NS)
1870–2	Grosart, vol. IV (n.l., OS)
1848	Child (n.l., OS)
1820	Haslewood (n.l., OS)

SOURCES

The narrative is drawn from the first part of Plautus's *Amphitruo*.

CHARACTERS

Prologue   Jenkin Careaway, a lackey   Alice Trip and Go, a maid
Jack Juggler, the Vice   Dame Coy, a gentlewoman   Master Boungrace, a gallant

PLOT SUMMARY

The *Prologue* talks of the restorative value of recreation and says that this play, based on Plautus's first play, is designed to provide no serious matter but simply honest mirth. *Jack Juggler*, the Vice, opens the action with a long speech in which he announces his intention to play a trick on *Jenkin Careaway*, the reprobate servant of *Master Boungrace*. This will be to confuse *Jenkin* about his own identity by persuading him that he is someone else. *Jenkin* enters complaining of his shrewish mistress, *Dame Coy*, and his stern master, *Boungrace*. *Jenkin* has squandered time idly while supposedly on errands and seeks to cover this up by resolving to tell *Dame Coy* that he has been occupied spying on *Boungrace* flirting with women, and that a man *Dame Coy* had entertained the previous week has sent her some apples (which *Jenkin* has, in fact, stolen). As he is congratulating himself on his ingenuity, *Jack Juggler* accosts him and pretends that he himself is *Jenkin*. He accuses *Jenkin* of being an impostor and strikes him several times. *Jack* is able to recite all of *Jenkin*'s movements, and he is dressed exactly like him. When *Jack* finally leaves, *Jenkin* is left in confusion about his own identity and goes off to look for *Dame Coy*. *Coy* herself enters next, with *Alice Trip and Go*, who tells her mistress about *Jenkin*'s pranks. On *Jenkin*'s entry she is unsympathetic about the problem he has over his identity and angrily sends him off to attend on *Boungrace*. *Jack* comes in briefly to inform the audience of his resumption of his own identity and he is followed by *Boungrace* and *Jenkin*, the master refusing to believe the events that *Jenkin* relates and reprimanding him for his mischief. *Jenkin* lets slip the story of how he has stolen the apples, at which *Boungrace* beats him, encouraged by his wife who has just entered. They go off to dine, leaving *Jenkin* both to muse on the events which have befallen him and to wonder about his *doppelgänger*. The *Epilogue* then concludes the play with a discussion about truth and deception, with negative implications for the doctrine of transubstantiation.

PLAY LENGTH

1,062 lines

COMMENTARY

This is a school play and despite the claim in the prologue that it contains no serious matter, the epilogue (which may be a later addition) does reflect seriously on issues of truth and deception. The play does not have the five-act structure of classical comedy, and the classical element is principally evident in the farce involving the antics of servants, though *Jack Juggler* as a Vice not endowed with psychological motivation is a native element.

Other plays based on classical or Italian models: **5, 7, 32, 37, 43, 88, 91, 92.**
Other secular comedies: **5, 30, 46, 47, 75, 88, 91, 92, 95.**

SIGNIFICANT TOPICS AND NARRATIVE ELEMENTS

recreation and relaxation; shrewish wives; a coquettish maid; truth and deception; transubstantiation; deceitful servants

DRAMATURGICAL AND RHETORICAL FEATURES

Verbal and general *Jenkin* makes a remark about the strong smell of the audience 866; a servant is the focus of the action; costume is used in the deception of *Jenkin*; only two stage directions, both in Latin
Costume and dress *Jenkin* wears a 'short coat' 138; *Jack* wears identical clothes to *Jenkin*'s 'garments, cape and other gear' 174–6, 574–5
Actions and stage directions 249 *sd*: 'Here let him (*Jen.*) sit as though musing'; 329 *sd*: 'Here let him (*Jen.*) strike the door'; 347: *Ja.* pulls up his *sleeves; 384: Ja.* waves his hands; 442, 456, 460, 464: *Ja.* strikes *Jen.*; 694: *D. Co.* strikes *Jen.*; 907: *Bou.* beats *Jen.*
Staging and set the action takes place in a street in London, but there is little indication as to set apart from the door to *Boungrace*'s house, upon which *Jenkin* knocks (329 *sd*)
Stage properties a stick 910; possibly apples (in *Jenkin*'s sleeve) 902

PLACENAMES

Bedlam 975; Calicut 974; England 288, 361, 570, 711; Jerusalem 976; London 117, 225

ALLUSIONS

Cato 9, 40; Cicero *Cato Major* (*De Senectute*) 1–2; Cicero *De Officiis* I.*xxix.104* 42–67; Ovid *Heroides IV.89* 27–8; Plato 41; Plautus 56, 64; Plutarch 41; Socrates 41

BIBLIOGRAPHY

Cope, 1973, pp. 107–11
Dudok, 1916, pp. 50–62
Kuya, T. 1985, pp. 75–114
Marienstras, R. 'Jacke Jugeler: Aspects de la conscience individuelle dans une farce du 16e siècle', EA 16:4 (1963) pp. 321–3
Petersen, D. L. 'The Origins of Tudor Comedy: Plautus, Jack Jugeler and the Folk Play as Mediating Form' in Allen and White, 1991, pp. 105–15
Voisine, J. and R. Marienstras, 'A propos de Jack Juggler', EA 18:2 (1965) pp. 166–8
White, 1992, pp. 124–9
Williams, W. H. 'The Date and Authorship of Jacke Jugeler', MLR 7:3 (1912), pp. 289–95

42   Jacob and Esau

DATE, AUTHORSHIP AND AUSPICES

1550–7 (SR 1557/1558 c. Oct./Nov.); anonymous; auspices unknown, but probably performed by boys at court; Greg 51

TEXT AND EDITIONS

Extant originals

1557/8 printing by Henry Sutton (?): BL (frag.); STC 14326.5
1568 printing by Henry Binneman: BL; Bodleian; Huntington; Folger; Pforzheimer; Eliz. Club; Newberry; STC 14327

Editions

1994	CHD (CD-Rom and online transcription of Binneman printing, l.l., s.l., OS)
1992	White (OS)*
1956	Crow and Wilson (facsimile, OS)
1913	Farmer (facsimile, n.l.)
1908	TFT (facsimile, n.l.)
1906	Farmer (4) (n.l., NS)
1874–6	Dodsley, vol. II (n.l., NS)

SOURCES

The principal source is *Genesis* 25:27, but Calvin's *Institutes* may also be a source; see White, 1993, pp. 186–8.

CHARACTERS

Prologue (Poet)	Esau	Zethar	Jacob	Mido	Deborra
Ragau	Hanan	Rebecca	Isaac	Abra	

PLOT SUMMARY

The *Prologue* announces the *Genesis* story of Jacob and Esau as the subject of the action. *Esau*'s servant *Ragau* opens the play complaining of his master's excessive devotion to hunting, and *Esau* then enters to chase him up to get ready for the hunt. When *Ragau* suggests they call *Jacob* too, *Esau* is scornful of what he sees as his milksop brother, though when *Ragau* echoes this scorn, he is beaten for it. When they set off, the neighbours, *Hanan* and *Zethar*, complain of the noise *Esau* makes going off in the mornings and compare *Jacob* favourably with him. They leave and the boys' mother *Rebecca* enters with *Jacob*, talking of *Esau*'s coarse ways. She expresses the wish that *Jacob* had been the elder and had the right of ascendancy. Though he is reluctant, she urges him to try to acquire *Esau*'s birthright. He departs and she meets *Isaac*, her blind husband, being led by his boy servant *Mido*. When *Isaac* remarks that blindness is an affliction of old age, *Mido* imagines himself (and imitates) being old and blind, but is reprimanded by *Rebecca*, who thinks he is mocking his master. She then talks to *Isaac* about *Esau*'s reckless passion for hunting, and pleads for *Jacob* to be given the rights of an elder son, but to no avail. She afterwards leads *Isaac* off and *Ragau* enters complaining of hunger, followed by an equally ravenous *Esau*. They cannot find food but *Ragau* comes to *Jacob*, who offers his brother pottage in exchange for his birthright, to which *Esau* readily agrees. When they go into *Jacob*'s tent, *Mido* enters to give *Ragau* a comic account of *Esau*'s greedy eating and the story of the birthright. On *Esau*'s appearance, *Ragau* confronts him about the issue, but he laughs it off, saying that *Isaac* would never agree to it. The scene then changes to *Jacob*, who informs his mother of what he has done. She devises a plan to get *Jacob* *Isaac*'s blessing by subterfuge, and swears the servants to secrecy. She later overhears *Isaac* asking *Esau* to prepare some venison for him, after which he will give him the blessing. *Rebecca* then hastens to prepare a dish for *Isaac*, *Abra* the maid going to collect herbs. When all is prepared with the help of the servants, *Rebecca* puts sleeves of kid's fleece on *Jacob*'s arms to simulate the hairiness of *Esau*, he dresses in fine clothing, and he goes to his father thus disguised. *Isaac* eats, then kisses and blesses his son whom he takes to be *Esau*, *Rebecca* offering thanks to God. The scene now switches to *Ragau*, who carries venison killed by *Esau*, but all is then revealed to both *Esau* and *Isaac*. *Esau* wants the blessing reversed, but *Isaac* says he cannot undo it. *Esau* rages and chastises the servants for their part in the subterfuge, while *Rebecca* sends *Jacob* away to avoid his brother's wrath. At length she persuades *Esau* to forgive both herself and *Jacob* and all then sing a final song. The *Poet* speaks an epilogue, and the actors playing *Jacob* and *Rebecca* offer a prayer for the queen, government and realm.

PLAY LENGTH

1,780 lines, including a prologue of 21 lines

COMMENTARY

Though this is a biblical morality, the issue at the heart of the play is a source of contemporary social concern: reprobate heirs. *Esau* is identifiably a riotous son of a noble household who fails to take his responsibilities seriously. Ideas of predestination also underlie the play. The role of the servants is extensive and dramatic interest in them extends beyond the strict demands of the narrative. The part of *Mido* may have been written with a particular actor possessed of a talent for comic mimicry in mind. The playwright has attempted to create a representation of the biblical world of his characters and the play has one of the earliest indications in English drama of period costume (Hebrew dress).

Other biblical plays: **10, 11, 16, 34, 44, 48, 63, 77, 90, 93.**

SIGNIFICANT TOPICS AND NARRATIVE ELEMENTS

hunger and gluttony; masters and servants; neighbour comments; primogeniture and sibling relations; education and predestination; the afflictions of age; irresponsible youth; cooking with herbs

DRAMATURGICAL AND RHETORICAL FEATURES

Verbal and general passages of stichomythia: 398–423 (*Rebecca* and *Isaac*), 655–69 (*Ragau* and *Mido*), 1471–8 (*Isaac* and *Esau*); *Ragau*'s rhetorical list of adjectives describing *Esau* 562–9; *Abra*'s list of herbs 1156–9; four instances of mimicry: *Ragau* 25 *sd*, and *Mido* 333–7, 649, 857; five acts with scene divisions (this being one of the earliest interludes to be thus divided); stage directions in English
Costume and dress the title page states that the characters 'are to be considered to be Hebrews, and so should be apparelled with attire'; *Jacob* dresses as *Esau* (donning fine clothing) and puts on false body hair 1242–5, 1248 *sd*, 1253
Actions and stage directions 21 *sd*: '*Ra.* enters with his horn at his back, and his hunting staff in his hand, and leads 3 greyhounds or one as may be gotten'; 25 *sd*: 'Here he (*Ra.*) counterfeits how his master calls him up in the mornings, and of his answers'; 71 *sd*: 'Here *Es.* appears in sight, and blows his horn ere he enters'; 91 *sd*: 'Here *Es.* blows his horn again'; 94 *sd*: 'Here he (*Es.*) speaks to his dogs'; 131–2: *Es.* beats *Ra.*; 137: *Es.* beats *Ra.*; 292–5: *Reb.* prays with her hands in the air; 333–7: *Mi.* mimics *Isa.*'s movements as a blind man; 495 *sd*: '[*Es.*] Comes in so faint that he can scarce go'; 510: *Es.* lies down; 628 *sd*: '*Es.* entering into *Ja.*'s tent, shakes *Ra.* off'; 640 *sd*: '*Mi.* comes in clapping his hands, and laughing'; 649: *Mi.* mimics Esau's greedy eating; 743 *sd*: 'He (*Es.*) comes forth wiping his mouth'; 857: *Mi.* mimics

Es.; 871 *sd*: 'Here they (*Reb.*, *Ja.*, *Ab.*, *Mi.*) kneel down to sing all four, saving that *Ab.* is slackest, and *Mi.* is quickest'; 917: *Mi.* leads *Isa.*; 975 *sd*: 'She (*Reb.*) kneels down and prays'; 982 *sd*: 'Here he (*Ra.*) comes forth with a hunting staff and others and a bag of victuals'; 1102 *sd*: 'Then let her (*Ab.*) sweep with a broom, and while she does it, sing this song, and when she has sung, let her say thus'; 1128: *Ab.* gives *Deb.* her broom; 1172: a kid bleats (off stage); 1248 *sd*: 'Here she (*Reb.*) does the sleeves on *Ja.*'s arms'; 1260 *sd*: '*Ja.* stands and looks on himself'; 1332 *sd*: '*Ja.* kisses *Isa.* and then kneels down to have his blessing'; 1372 *sd*: 'Then she (*Reb.*) speaks kneeling, and holding up her hands'; 1382 *sd*: '*Ra.* brings in venison at his back'; 1580 *sd*: 'This he (*Es.*) speaks to *Deb.*'; 1642: *Ja.* kisses *Isa.*; 1643: *Ja.* kisses *Reb.*; 1646: *Ja.* shakes hands with *Mi.*; 1723 *sd*: '*Ra.* calls all to sing. This song must be sung after the prayer'; 1739 *sd*: 'Then enters the *Poet*, and the rest stand still, until he have done. The *Poet* enters'; 1767 *sd*: 'All the rest of the actors answer "Amen". Then follows the prayer'; **Simple exit**: 'Both' (*Es.*, *Ra.*) 142; *Ja.* 274; (*Mi.*) 686; 'All' (*Reb.*, *Ja.*, *Mi.*, *Ab.*) 912; 'Both' (*Es.*, *Ra.*) 1003; *Ja.* 1362

Songs and music (w.s. to all songs) 1. *Rebecca, Jacob, Mido, Abra* 'Blessed be thou O the God of Abraham' (w. ref.) 872–88; 2. *Abra* 'It hath been a proverb before I was born' (w. ref.) 1103–121; 3. Whole cast (?) 'O Lord the God of our father Abraham' 1724–39

Staging and set several of the characters have tents that function as entrances and exits, at least one of which is represented on stage (628 *sd*)

Stage properties *Ragau*'s horn, hunting staff and three greyhounds ('or one, as may be gotten') 21 *sd*; *Esau*'s horn 71 *sd*; a bench 919; a bag of victuals 982 *sd*; *Jacob*'s shepherd's crook 1045; *Abra*'s broom 1102 *sd*; a kid 1182; Jacob's kidskin sleeves 1242–5, 1248 *sd*; venison 1382 *sd*

PLACENAMES

Canaan 1637; Haran 1651; Mesopotamia 1638, 1651

ALLUSIONS

Cain 1684; Cain and Abel 1504; St Paul 1758

RECORDED PRODUCTION

LP Record: BBC, *The First Stage*, dir. J. Barton (1970)

BIBLIOGRAPHY

Aoki, N. 'Construction of a Biblical Comedy: Characteristics of *Jacob and Esau*', *MFLAE* 29 (1978) pp. 17–24
Blackburn, 1971, pp. 148–51

Ephraim, M. K. 'Jewish Matriarchs and the Staging of Elizabeth I in *The History of Jacob and Esau*', *SEL* 43:2 (2003) pp. 301–21

Greene, 1974, pp. 357–65

Pasachoff, 1975, pp. 16–56

Scheurweghs, G. 'The Date of *The History of Jacob and Esau*', *ES* 15:4 (1933) pp. 218–19

Southern, 1973, pp. 361–74

Stopes, C. C. 'The Interlude, or, Comedie of Jacob and Esau', *Athenaeum*, 28 April 1900, pp. 538–40

Thomas, H. 'Jacob and Esau – rigidly Calvinistic?', *SEL* 9:2 (1969), pp. 199–213

White, P. W. 'Predestination Theology in the Mid-Tudor Play *Jacob and Esau*', *R&R* 24 (1988) pp. 291–302

43   Jocasta

DATE, AUTHORSHIP AND AUSPICES

1566; George Gascoigne and Francis Kinwelmershe; presented at Gray's Inn; Greg 61

TEXT AND EDITIONS

Extant originals

Manuscript: British Library Add. MS 34063

1572 printing by Henry Binneman (and Henry Middleton?): BL; Bodleian; Cambridge (imp.); Emmanuel; Eton; Folger; Harvard (imp.); Huntington; Illinois (imp.); Pforzheimer; further copies extant; *STC* 11635

1575 printing by Henry Binneman for Richard Smith: Bodleian; Folger (two copies); Huntington; Pforzheimer; PML; private collector; *STC* 11636

1575 printing for Richard Smith: BL (imp.); Bodleian (imp.); Cambridge (imp.); Harvard; Huntington; Illinois; Newberry; Lichfield; Rylands; Yale; *STC* 11637

1587 printing by Abel Jeffes: BL; Chapin; Dyce; Eton (imp.); Folger; Huntington; Newberry; Trinity; Worcester; Yale; (further copies extant); *STC* 11638

1587 printing by Abel Jeffes (variant): Bodleian (imp.); Dartmouth; Folger (imp.); NLS; Peterborough (deposited at Cambridge; imp.); Pforzheimer; Rylands; *STC* 11639

Editions

1994   CHD (CD-Rom and online transcription of Smith printing, l.l., s.l., OS)

1912   Cunliffe (s.l., OS)*

1907   Cunliffe, vol. 1 (n.l., OS)

1906   Cunliffe (with Italian originals, s.l., OS)

1869   Hazlitt, vol. 1 (n.l., OS)

1848   Child (n.l., OS)

SOURCES

The play is based on Lodovico Dolce's *Giocasta*; see the introduction to Cunliffe's 1912 edition, pp. lxxxiii–lxxxvi.

CHARACTERS

Jocasta, the Queen
Servus, a noble man of the Queen's train
Bailo, governor to the Queen's sons
Antigone, daughter to the Queen
Polynices, son to Oedipus and the Queen
Eteocles, son to Oedipus and the Queen
Creon, the Queen's brother
Menetius, son to Creon
Tiresias, the divine priest
Manto, the daughter of Tiresias
Sacerdos, the sacrificing priest
Nuntii, three messengers from the camp
Oedipus, the old king, son and husband to Jocasta
Epilogue
Chorus, four Theban dames
Mute: sixteen Bacchanales attending on Sacerdos; several figures in the dumbshows: kings, mourners, attendants, gentlemen, slaves

PLOT SUMMARY

Jocasta tells a servant the story of the consigning to death by exposure by her husband Laius of their son shortly after his birth, as the result of a prophecy that the boy would kill his father. She describes how the boy was found by a shepherd and taken to the court of King Polibus of Corinth, who raised him as his own son, named *Oedipus*. *Jocasta* goes on to relate how *Oedipus* unwittingly slew his real father in battle and, coming to Thebes, unknowingly married Laius's widow and his own mother. She bore him two sons and two daughters, but when he discovered the truth, he tore out his own eyes. His sons then cast their father into a dungeon, and afterwards fell into strife. They initially agreed to rule alternately as kings but *Eteocles*, having tasted power, refused to give up the crown after his year and this led to a civil war with his brother, *Polynices*. *Jocasta* then asks her servant to go to *Eteocles*, to urge him to keep his promises. The scene now switches to *Antigone*, the sister of the warring brothers, who anxiously enquires about *Polynices* of their erstwhile governor *Bailo*, and is told that he has brought a powerful force to besiege Thebes. In the second act *Jocasta* is told by *Polynices* that he has won in marriage the daughter of King Adrastus of Greece, who is supporting him in his fight to claim the Theban throne. *Eteocles* then arrives and proudly reaffirms his refusal to give up power. *Jocasta* chastises both her sons, who, to her distress, fall into debate between themselves until all finally depart. *Eteocles* then discusses strategies with his uncle, *Creon*, and the prospective marriage of *Creon*'s son, *Hæmone*, to *Antigone*. In the third act the blind prophet *Tiresias* performs a divination ceremony and predicts victory for the Thebans, but that *Creon* will slay his own son as a sacrifice for his country and will end up as king of Thebes. *Creon*'s son *Menetius* declares himself prepared to die, but his father sends him away to the land of Thesbeoita. In the fourth act a messenger gives *Jocasta* a description of the battle and reports that the Greeks have failed to take the city. He relates further that her sons have agreed to engage in a single combat fight to the death, but *Jocasta* afterwards tells *Antigone* that she intends to plead with her sons to forsake this pact. The act ends with a messenger bringing *Creon* the news that his son has killed himself for the sake of his country. In the final act *Creon* is brought a report that *Jocasta*'s sons have killed each other, and that she in grief has cut her own throat. *Antigone* enters uttering a lamentation and she then relays news of the events to her father. *Creon*, to whom the throne has now passed, banishes *Oedipus* his realm for the reason that *Tiresias* had predicted that sorrow would remain in the city as long as *Oedipus* did. He now gives orders for the funerals of *Jocasta* and *Eteocles*, and tells *Antigone* to prepare for her marriage to *Hæmone*. However, he orders that *Polynices* is to remain unburied, despite the protests of *Antigone*, who then refuses to marry *Hæmone* and chooses instead to accompany her father into exile. The play ends with their preparing for a life of poverty and hardship, and the epilogue discusses the dangers posed by aspiring minds.

PLAY LENGTH

2,895 lines, including choruses and epilogue but excluding descriptions of dumb-shows

COMMENTARY

This is a formal, neoclassical tragedy with Senecan elements very much along the lines of Norton and Sackville's *Gorboduc*, another Inns of Court play, with which it shares several characteristics. These include reported, off-stage action, allegorical dumbshows preceding each act, a narrative that involves fraternal conflict leading to civil war, and a chorus concluding each act. Acts 1 and 4 are by Kinwelmershe, the rest by Gascoigne, with an epilogue by Francis Yelverton, a fellow Innsman.

Other secular tragedies: **7, 32, 37.**

Other plays featuring prominent women characters: **3, 6, 30, 32, 46, 51, 63, 70, 75, 87, 95, 97.**

Other plays based on classical or Italian models: **5, 7, 32, 37, 41, 88, 91, 92.**

Other plays with classical settings: **19, 29, 39, 57** (frag.), **91, 92.**

SIGNIFICANT TOPICS AND NARRATIVE ELEMENTS

the Oedipus story; civil war; fraternal conflict; patriotic self-sacrifice; the vicissitudes of fortune; the uncertainty of royal power; political ambition and its dangers

DRAMATURGICAL AND RHETORICAL FEATURES

Verbal and general a formal reflection on pomp and fortune by a servant 1.1.221–60; *Tiresias*, aided by *Sacerdos*, performs a divination ceremony on stage 3.1.70–228; several passages of stichomythia, principally 2.1.550–69, 581–9, 2.2.46–85, 3.1.182–99, 208–19, 3.2.70–87, 100–10, 5.5.87–136; each act is closed by the Chorus, who also takes a significant role in the final act; five acts with scene divisions

Costume and dress (dumbshows listed first) d.s. 1: *Sesostres* enters 'an imperial crown on his head, very richly apparelled' 4–5, and four kings with crowns and in doublets and hose with crowns on their head 7–8; d.s. 2: the attendants are in 'mourning weed' 4, *Polynices*'s six attendants wear gorgets 17; d.s. 3: the gentlemen are in doublets and hose 4; d.s. 5: *Fortune* is clothed in white, with white lawn about her eyes, and her legs naked 2–6, the kings despoiled of their rich robes which are given to the slaves, and the 'vile clothes' of the slaves given to the kings 11–14; *Main text*: *Jocasta* and her train are in 'clothes of grisly black' 2.1.19–20; *Eteocles* and his twenty attendants are in armour 2.1.240 sd; Tiresias wears a crown 3.1.36; *Oedipus* is clad in 'ragged ruthful weeds' 5.5.243

Actions and stage directions (the very extensive directions for the action of the dumbshows are not included, except those directions attached to the dumbshows pertaining to actions of characters in the main narrative); d.s 1. 18–27: '*Joc.* the queen issues out of her palace before her twelve gentlemen, following after her eight gentlewomen, whereof four be the Chor. that remain on the stage after her departure. At her entrance the trumpets sounded, and after she had gone once about the stage, she turns to one of her most trusty and esteemed servants, and unto him she discloses her grief, as follows'; 1.220 sd: '*Joc.* goes off the stage into her palace, her four handmaidens follow her, the four Chor. also follow her to the gates of her palace, after[wards] coming on the stage, take their place, where they continue to the end of the tragedy'; 1.1.262 sd: '*Serv.* goes off the stage by the gates called Electræ. *Ant.* attended with iii gentlewomen and her governor comes out of the qu. her mother's palace'; 1.2.192 sd: '*Ant.* with her maids returns into her mother's palace, her governor goes out by the gates Homoloydes'; d.s. 2.15–20: 'Immediately by the gates Homoloydes entered *Pol.* accompanied with vi gentlemen and a page that carries his helmet and target: he and his men unarmed saving their gorgets . . . and *Pol.*, after good regard taken about him, speaks as follows'; 2.1.240 sd: '*Ete.* comes in here by the gates Electræ, himself armed, and before him xx gentlemen in armour, his two pages, whereof one bears his target, the other his helmet'; 2.1.602 sd: '*Ete.* here goes out by the gates Electræ'; 2.1.615 sd:

'*Pol.* here goes out by the gates Homoloydes'; 2.1.626 *sd:* '*Joc.* goes into her palace'; 2.1.635 *sd:* 'While the Chor. is thus praying to Bacchus, *Ete.* returns by the gates called Electræ'; 2.2.8 *sd:* 'Here *Cre.* attended by four gentlemen, comes in by the gates Homoloydes'; 2.2.135 *sd:* '*Cre.* attends *Ete.* to the gates Electræ. He returns and goes out by the gates called Homoloydes'; 3 d.s. 18–20: 'This done, blind *Tir.* conducted by *Men.* the son of *Cre.*, enters by the gates Electræ, and says as follows'; 3.1.13 *sd:* '*Cre.* returns by the gates Homoloydes'; 3.1.69 *sd:* '*Sac.* accompanied by xvi Bacchanales and all his rites and ceremonies, enters by the gates Homoloydes'; 3.1.130 *sd:* '*Sac.* returns with the Bacchanales, by the gates Homoloydes'; 3.1.228 *sd:* '*Tir.* with *Man.* his daughter, returns by the gates called Electræ'; 3.2.116 *sd:* '*Cre.* goes out by the gates Homoloydes'; 3.2.125 *sd:* '*Men.* departs by the gates Electræ'; 4 s.d. 26–8: 'Also came in a mess. armed from the camp, seeking the qu. and to her spoke as follows'; 4.1.0p. *sd:* '*Nun.* comes in by the gates Homoloydes'; 4.1.6 *sd:* 'The queen with her train comes out of her palace'; 4.1.178 *sd:* '*Nun.* returns to the camp by the gates Homoloydes'; 4.1.185 *sd:* '*Ant.* comes out of her mother's palace'; 4.1.233 *sd:* '*Joc.* with *Ant.*, and all her train (except the Chor.) go towards the camp by the gates Homoloydes'; 4.1.chor.26 *sd:* '*Cre.* comes in by the gates Homoloydes'; 4.2.14 *sd:* '*Nun.* comes in by the gates Electræ'; 4.2.52 *sd:* '*Nun.* returns by the gates Electræ'; 4.2.78 *sd:* '*Cre.* goes out by the gates Homoloydes'; 5 d.s. 20–22: 'After her departure came in Duke *Cre.* with four gentlemen waiting upon him and lamented the death of *Men.* his son in this manner'; 5.2.200 *sd:* '*Cre.* exit'; 5.3.58 *sd:* '*Oed.* enters'; 5.5.134 *sd:* 'Pointing to *Oed.*'; 5.5.139 *sd:* '*Cre.* exit'; 5.5.191 *sd:* 'She (*Ant.*) gives him (*Oed.*) a staff and stays him herself also'

Songs and music (no songs, music only occurs in dumbshows) d.s. 1: 'a doleful and strange music of viols, cythers, bandurion and such like' 2–3, and trumpets at the queen's entry 21–2; d.s. 2: 'a very doleful noise of flutes' 1–2; d.s. 3: 'a very doleful noise of cornets' 2; d.s. 4: 'the trumpets, drums and fifes sounded' 1–2; d.s. 5: 'from the stillpipes sounded a very mournful melody' 1

Staging and set almost all entrances and exits are signalled through the gates 'Electræ' or 'Homoloydes' (two of the four gates of Thebes), or *Jocasta*'s palace, all of which may have been indicated by stage structures; except for the ceremonial movement of characters, and *Tiresias*'s divination ceremony (3.1.70–228), the actions occur off stage and the principal visual elements are contained in the allegorical dumbshows, which precede each act as follows: 1. *Sesostres* in his chariot as *Ambition*; 2. two coffins buried in one tomb and consumed by flames to signify fraternal discord; 3. a gulf which only closes when a knight jumps in, signifying love of country; 4. a battle betokening conflict between brothers; 5. a figure of *Fortune* who clothes slaves in the apparel of kings and vice versa

Stage properties (dumbshows listed first) d.s. 1: a sceptre, orb and chariot 5–6; d.s. 2: two coffins covered with haircloths, a grave and flames 3–7, *Polynices*'s target and helmet 16; d.s. 3: baskets of earth 5, chains and jewels 7–8, the knight's sword 9; d.s. 4: firing ordnance 2–3, the knights' swords 10; d.s. 5: *Fortune*'s double-faced pillar, jewels, ball and chariot 3–6; **Main text:** *Polynices*'s sword 2.1.10; *Eteocles*'s target and helmet 2.1.240 *sd*; *Tiresias*'s crown 3.1.30; a sacrificial kid and entrails, salt, a knife 3.1.76–84; *Oedipus*'s staff 5.5.191 *sd*

PLACENAMES

Argos 4.1.149; Athens 3.1.33, 5.5.179; Corinth 1.1.73; Greece 1.2.141 *passim*; Phocis 1.1.89, 100; Thebes 1.1.35 *passim*; Thesbeoita 3.2.103

ALLUSIONS

Apollo 3.1.226, 5.5.178; Bacchus 1.2.chor.57 ('son of Semele'), 2.1.13, 2.1.629, 2.2.chor.7, 3.1.78, 3.1.95; Bellona 3.1.99; Charon 5.2.181; Dodona 3.2.104; Horatii and Curiatii d.s. 4.22–3; Jove 1.1.237 *passim*; Juno 5.2.46; Mars 1.2.chor.55, 2.2.chor.1, 3.1.99, 3.1.138; Medusa 2.1.275; Phoebe 1.2.chor.33; Phoebus 2.1.427; Semele 1.2.chor.57; Sphinx 1.1.116; Stygian lake 1.1.158, 4.1.136, 5.2.164; Titan 4.2.chor.20; Venus 2.2.chor.12; Ver 4.2.chor.22; Vestal Virgins 4.2.40

BIBLIOGRAPHY

Corti, C. 'A proposito di *Jocasta*: Indagine su une rielabroazione elisabettiana'. *RLMC* 30 (1977) pp. 85–104
Förster, M. T. 'Gascoigne's *Jocasta* a Translation from the Italian'. *MP* 2:1 (1904) pp. 147–50
Johnson, 1972, pp. 142–7
Mehl, 1965, pp. 41–9
Schelling, 1892, pp. 259–66

44   John Baptist's Preaching

DATE, AUTHORSHIP AND AUSPICES

1538; John Bale; St Stephen's, Canterbury and Kilkenny (see **35**)

TEXT AND EDITIONS

Extant originals

Earliest printing, *c.* 1547 by Dirik van der Straten, not extant; earliest edition: BL, *The Harleian Miscellany* vol. I (1744) pp. 97–110; STC 1279

Editions

2000	Walker (OS)*
1994	CHD (CD-Rom and online copy of Happé, 1985/6, l.l. OS)
1985/6	Happé, vol. II (OS)*
1907	Farmer (8) (n.l., NS)

SOURCES

The principal scriptural sources are *Luke 3:1–22, John 1:15–42* and *Matthew 3.*

CHARACTERS

Bale as Prolocutor	The Publican	The Sadducee
John the Baptist	The Soldier	Jesus Christ
The Common People	The Pharisee	The Heavenly Father

PLOT SUMMARY

The prologue spoken by *Bale* summarizes the action of the play and urges submission to the teachings of the Gospel. *John the Baptist* begins the play with a sermon to the audience, received with joy by three on-stage characters, the *Common People*, the *Publican* (also called the *Tax Gatherer*) and the *Soldier*. Each of these characters gives an account of himself, acknowledges his sin, and is given baptism by *John*. *John* then preaches a sermon to the audience on baptism, while a *Pharisee* and a *Sadducee* enter. *John* rounds on these, calling them hypocrites, and falls into dispute with them. The *Pharisee* and *Sadducee* claim the authority of (Mosaic) Law and their descent from Abraham, but *John* stresses instead the importance of true faith. The *Pharisee* and *Sadducee* see *John* as a heretic who is likely to foment insurrection, and they go off to ponder action against him. *Jesus Christ* now enters declaring his divine nature and his role of redemption, and is immediately recognized and accepted by *John* as the Messiah. *Christ* requests baptism from *John*, who, however, is reluctant to administer it as he considers himself unworthy, but *Christ* persists, saying that he wishes to submit himself to the laws of his father and to become one of the common people. *John* baptizes *Christ*, who kneels in a prayer of thanks to *God*. The Holy Spirit then descends upon him and *God* speaks from heaven declaring that *Christ's* new order will replace the old traditions of men and the Mosaic law. *John* rejoices and ends the play with a song, after which *Bale* delivers an epilogue urging adherence to the teachings, not of the Fathers of the Church, but of *John* and *Christ*.

PLAY LENGTH

492 lines, including prologue and epilogue but excluding 'Praefacio' of 35 lines

COMMENTARY

John the Baptist is presented here as a Protestant campaigner striking against the old order of the Pharisees and Sadducees. Though the analogy is not made fully explicit, the reference to Christ's Gospel replacing the old traditions, the claim to ancient authority by the Pharisee and Sadducee, and the reference by the Sadducee to the 'new learning', are all significant. The point is driven home even further in the epilogue. Almost all the actions in the play are ritual ones. *God* may be present for much of the play on an elevated scaffold.

Other biblical plays: **10, 11, 16, 34, 42, 48, 63, 77, 90, 93.**
Other Protestant and anti-Catholic plays: **14, 24, 45, 49, 50, 53, 58, 66, 85, 86** (frag.), **90, 93.**

SIGNIFICANT TOPICS AND NARRATIVE ELEMENTS

Protestant 'new learning' and Christian versus Mosaic doctrine; John the Baptist as prophet of Christ; baptism; the baptism of Christ

DRAMATURGICAL AND RHETORICAL FEATURES

Verbal and general the play is described as 'a brief comedy or interlude'; stage directions and names of characters in Latin
Actions and stage directions 113 *sd*: 'The *Co. P.* is turned to *God* and confesses his sins thus'; 120 *sd*: 'He (*Co. P.*) then kneels, and *Jo.* baptizes him'; 138 *sd*: 'When he (*Co. P.*) has gone out, the *Pu.* acknowledges his sins in *God*'s presence'; 145 *sd*: 'Then he (*Pu.*) kneels and *Jo.* baptizes him'; 163 *sd*: 'He (*Pu.*) leaves and the *Sol.* confesses his sins'; 170 *sd*: 'He (*Sol.*) falls to his knees and *Jo.* baptizes him'; 188 *sd*: 'As he (*Sol.*) leaves the place, the *Pha.* and the *Sad.* enter. Meanwhile *Jo.* addresses the people'; 206 *sd*: 'They (*Pha., Sad.*) speak together privately'; 212 *sd*: 'And turning towards *Jo.*, he (*Pha.*) speaks to him craftily'; 382 *sd*: 'Here with hands extended, *Jo.* withholds baptism from him (*Je.*)'; 421 *sd*: 'Here *Je.* raises *Jo.* and submits to him in baptism'; 424 *sd*: 'Falling to his knees, *Je.* then speaks his thanks to *God*'; 431 *sd*: 'Then the Holy Spirit descends upon *Chr.* in the form of a dove and from heaven the voice of the *Father* is heard in this way'; 445 *sd*: 'Then, looking towards heaven, *Jo.* kneels down'; 453 *sd*: 'And, stretching his hands to heaven, *Jo.* sings'
Songs and music John 'Glory be to the Trinity' (w.s.) 454–7
Staging and set there is likely to be a scaffold with an elevated platform for *God*; the Holy Spirit descends in the form of a dove, requiring appropriate technology; the action is unlocalized and there are no further indications as to set; the River Jordan needs to be represented at *Christ*'s baptism, but there is no indication as to how this is done
Stage properties water for the baptisms 138 *sd*, 163 *sd*, 170 sd. 421 *sd*; a dove as the Holy Spirit 431 *sd*

PLACENAMES

Galilee 378; Nazareth 378

ALLUSIONS

Abraham 279, 283–92; St Albert 489; 'Robin Bell' (proverbial?) 297; St Benedict 488; St Bruno 488; King David 43; St Dominic 489; St Francis 488; Isaiah 61; *Isaiah 40:3* 203; Ismael 285; Jacob 45; *Luke 3:2–3* (preceding preface); Moses 23, 229, 234, 442; the Pentateuch 234

BIBLIOGRAPHY

Blackburn, 1971, pp. 58–63
Blatt, 1968, pp. 95–7
Happé, 1995/6, pp. 108–24
Harris, 1940, pp. 81–4
McCusker, 1942, pp. 73–85
Sperk, 1973, pp. 53–72
White, 1993, pp. 158–60

45   John the Evangelist

DATE, AUTHORSHIP AND AUSPICES

1520–57; anonymous; auspices unknown; Greg 26

TEXT AND EDITIONS

Extant originals

c. 1550 printing by William Copland for John Waley: BL (two copies); *STC* 14643

Editions

1994   CHD (CD-Rom and online transcription of Copland printing, l.l., OS)
1907   Farmer (9) (n.l., NS)
1907   Greg and Esdaile (OS)*
1907   TFT (facsimile, n.l.)
1907   *'Lost' Tudor Plays*, TFT (privately printed facsimile, n.l.)

SOURCES

John's account in his sermon of the Pharisee and the Publican is from *Luke 18*, but see also Carpenter's essay below.

CHARACTERS

St John the Evangelist   Eugenio   Irisdision   Actio   Evil Counsel   Idleness

PLOT SUMMARY

St John opens the play with a sermon advocating holy meditation. Two characters listening to it then fall into discussion with one another, *Eugenio* a gallant and *Irisdision*, who elaborates an allegorical account of the paths to heaven and hell. *Eugenio* is sceptical about *Irisdision*'s teaching and prefers mirth and revelry to the stricter paths of the elect. *Irisdision* loses patience with him and leaves, followed soon after by *Eugenio*, while *St John* enters again to preach once more, this time about redemption. He goes out and a roisterer, *Actio*, enters, soon joined by *Eugenio*. They quickly find common ground in worldly interests. Despite this disposition, however, they go off in search of *St John*, and seek to avoid *Evil Counsel* (a Vice figure), who enters after their departure. He boastfully describes to the audience how he encourages mischief throughout England, and he is shortly joined by a companion, *Idleness*. He tells *Idleness* that he is seeking a position as a serving man, and goes on to talk of the seduction of other men's wives and also of other bawdy matters. They fall to quarrelling, but in the end go off to enjoy themselves at the house of an acquaintance, *Unthrift*, while *Eugenio* and *Actio* return. They are followed by *St John*, who begins to preach, taking as his text the story of the Pharisee and the Publican. *Eugenio* and *Actio* are then both converted from their idle ways and the play ends.

PLAY LENGTH

653 lines

COMMENTARY

This short Calvinist play contains three sermons preached directly to the audience by *St John*, and a further passage of religious instruction delivered by *Irisdision*, which is full of Bunyanesque allegory. There is little plot development in the play. There may be missing sections.

Other Protestant and anti-Catholic plays: **14, 24, 44, 49, 50, 53, 58, 66, 85, 86** (frag.), **90, 93.**

SIGNIFICANT TOPICS AND NARRATIVE ELEMENTS

cuckoldry and sexual dalliance; the biblical story of the Pharisee and the Publican; bad servingmen; good and bad companionship

DRAMATURGICAL AND RHETORICAL FEATURES

NOTE: line numbering includes character names
Verbal and general *St John* preaches directly to the audience 1–25, 576–629; *Irisdision*'s allegorical narrative 82–183; no stage directions
Costume and dress *Eugenio* clearly has his name written on his person, which *Irisdision* reads 72–9
Staging and set no clear indications as to set, but the amount of preaching in the play suggests the need for a pulpit on stage for *St John*

PLACENAMES

Babylon 148; Calais 299; Cornwall 394; Coventry 373; England 222, 384, 415; Jerusalem 82; St Katherine's (hospital in London) 395; Kent 394; London 378; Paul's Cross 33; Rochester 371; Salisbury Plain 457; Trentham 228; Westminster 395; Zion 83

ALLUSIONS

Cain 610; Cato (q.n.t.) 41–2; King David 106; *Jeremiah 4:6* (q.a.) 153; Longinus 246; Mary Magdalene 15; Martha 15; *Psalm 37:10* (V)/*38:9* (AV) (q.a.) 2–3, *83:5* (V)/*84:4* (AV) 25; Venus 390

BIBLIOGRAPHY

Bradley, H. 'Textual Notes on *The Enterlude of Johan the Evangelist*', *MLR* 2:4 (1907) pp. 350–2
Carpenter, S. 'Source of *John the Evangelist*', *N&Q* 223 (1978) pp. 501–3
Dahlström, C. E. 'The Name Irisdision in the *Interlude of John the Evangelist*', *MLN* 58:1 (1943) pp. 44–6
Holthausen, F. 'Zum älteren englischen Drama: *Johan the Evangelyst*', *Beiblatt zur Anglia* 29 (1918) pp. 372–5
Williams, W. H. '"Irisdision" in the Interlude of *Johan the Evangelyst*', *MLR* 3:4 (1908) pp. 369–71

46   John John the Husband

DATE, AUTHORSHIP AND AUSPICES

1520–33; John Heywood; auspices unknown; Greg 13

TEXT AND EDITIONS

Extant originals

1533 printing by William Rastell: Bodleian; Pepys; STC 13298

Editions

1994   CHD (CD-Rom and online transcription of Rastell printing, l.l., OS)
1991   Axton and Happé (OS)*
1975   Bevington (OS)*
1972   Denny (n.l., NS)
1967   Proudfoot (OS)
1966   Creeth (OS)*
1962   Hopper and Lahey (n.l., NS)
1937   De la Bère (n.l., OS)
1935   Parks and Beatty (NS)
1924   Adams (OS)*
1909   TFT (facsimile, Pepys Library copy, n.l.)
1908   Farmer (11) (n.l., NS)
1905   Farmer (1) (n.l., NS)
1903   A. W. Pollard in Gayley, vol. 1 (OS)*
1898   Brandl (OS)

SOURCES

The main source is the fifteenth-century French *Farce nouvelle du Pasté* of *c.* 1500; see Craik's essay below. See also Maxwell, 1946, listed below.

CHARACTERS

John John, the Husband   Tyb, the Wife   Sir John, the Priest

PLOT SUMMARY

John the husband opens the play with a long speech declaring his intention to give his wife a good beating because of her gadding about, and he voices his suspicions about the nature of her friendship with *Sir John* the priest. When she appears, however, he becomes submissive. She tells him she has been making a pie with her friends *Margaret* and *Sir John* and, guessing her husband's suspicion of her, protests *Sir John*'s holiness and innocence. They put the pie on the hearth to warm and she announces that she has invited *Sir John* to dine with them. In asides to the audience *John* expresses his suspicions and she her awareness of these. He takes off his gown and they make preparations, *John* all the while continuing to mutter his doubts and annoyance. She sends him to fetch the priest, which he does. *Sir John* claims that *Tyb* dislikes him for the penances he imposes on her, and relates that tests he has made of her virtue have proven her blameless. This temporarily pacifies *John* and he repents of his doubts. *Sir John* goes on to relate how they had planned the meal together, and they return to *John*'s house, where the greeting between the priest and *Tyb* rekindles the husband's concerns. *Tyb* sends *John* to fetch water and while he is gone *Sir John* tells her how he has mollified her husband. *John* enters with an empty pail that is found to have a leak, and *Tyb* gives him some wax candles with which to repair it. *John* continues to express his suspicions in asides while he heats the wax by the fire. *Sir John* tells three tales of 'miraculous' births of children, all recognized by the grumbling *John* to be the result of sexual impropriety. *John* then finds that *Tyb* and the priest have eaten the whole pie while he has been mending the pail and, when he complains, his wife feigns incomprehension. *John* then throws back the pail and, when she attacks him for breaking it, he loses his temper and begins to fight with her and the priest. They retreat and, left alone, he prepares to go in pursuit of them to check that they are not cuckolding him.

PLAY LENGTH

678 lines

COMMENTARY

This is a secular farce, and is one of a small number of plays to deal with marriage and its problems. The comedy is based principally on the henpecked figure of *John* the husband, whose opening bravado is largely belied by his actions. *John's* weakness in the face of his wife's aggressiveness is something that Heywood emphasizes, by comparison with the source. The play is firmly rooted in an English, rural, middle-class world, incorporating many details of domestic life, including the preparations for a meal and the mending of a pail. There is more stage action than is generally found in Heywood's plays, which tend to be dialogue-based.

Other secular comedies: **5**, **30**, **41**, **47**, **75**, **88**, **91**, **92**, **95**.
Other marital strife plays: **73**, **84**, **95**.
Other plays featuring prominent women characters: **3**, **6**, **30**, **32**, **43**, **51**, **63**, **70**, **75**, **87**, **95**, **97**.

SIGNIFICANT TOPICS AND NARRATIVE ELEMENTS

marital infidelity; marital strife; a corrupt priest; domestic chores and activities

DRAMATURGICAL AND RHETORICAL FEATURES

Verbal and general *John* opens the play with an address to the audience 1–110; *Sir John* relates three tales or 'miracles' 537–82; though there are only two stage directions (both in English) there is a great deal of action implied or described in the verbal exchanges
Costume and dress *John* takes off his gown and leaves it in the keeping of an audience member (asking him/her to scrape off the dirt) 250–7

Actions and stage directions 442 *sd*: 'Then he (*Jo.*) brings the pail empty'; 262–3: *Jo.* sets the table; 467, 491, 507, 523: *Jo.* chafes the wax; 664 *sd*: 'Here they (*Jo., Tyb*) fight by the ears a while, and then the priest and the wife go out of the place'

Staging and set this is a hall play; the action is set in a two locations, briefly Sir *John*'s house (probably just a door), but mainly *John*'s house, which is set up as a proper domestic interior; the fireplace needs to be placed at some distance from the table

Stage properties a table and dining accoutrements 262; candlesticks 264; a stool 273; a pie 278; two cups 279; a pot for ale 287; candles 291; trestles 292; bread 297; a pail 420; a fire 458; a distaff and shears 649; a shovel full of coal 654

PLACENAMES

Coventry 164; Crome 10; London 563; St Paul's Church 153; Thames Street 114

ALLUSIONS

St Anthony the swineherd 6; St Modwin 561

REPORTS ON MODERN PRODUCTIONS

1. New York (Seventh Heaven Players), dir. J. Elliott, spring/summer 1977 [*RORD* 20 (1977) pp. 103–4]
2. York Minster (Lords of Misrule, University of York), 6–30 June 1980 [*RORD* 23 (1980) pp. 89–90]
3. Toronto (PLS), dir. L. Phillips, August 1996 [*RORD* 36 (1997) pp. 184–5]
4. Towson University, Maryland, March 1998, University of Toronto, 20 June 1998 (Towson University Theatre Department), dir. S. Tairstein [*RORD* 38 (1999) pp. 133–4]

RECORDED PRODUCTION

LP Record: BBC, *The First Stage*, dir. J. Barton (1970)

BIBLIOGRAPHY

Ash, M. 'John John' in Brydges and Haslewood, 1814, pp. 118–22
Bolwell, 1921, pp. 112–15
Craik, T. W. 'The True Source of John Heywood's *Johan Johan*'. *MLR* 45:3 (1950) pp. 289–95
De la Bère, 1937, pp. 83–7
Elton, W. 'Reply to "*Johan Johan* and Its Debt to French Farce"'. *JEGP* 53:2 (1954) pp. 271–2 (response to Sultan's essay below)
Johnson, R. C. 'A Textual Problem in *Johan Johan*'. *N&Q* 215 (1970) pp. 210–11

Johnson, 1970, pp. 102–7

Maxwell, 1946, pp. 56–69

Mori, H. 'On *Johan Johan*', *Sagami Journal* 1 (1981) pp. 3–22 (in Japanese)

Norland, H. B. 'Formalizing English Farce: *Johan Johan* and its French Connection', *CD* 17:2 (1983) pp. 141–52, and in Davidson and Stroupe, 1991, pp. 356–67

Norland, 1995, pp. 255–66

Southern, 1973, pp. 244–50

Sultan, S. 'The Audience Participation Episode in *Johan Johan*', *JEGP* 52:4 (1953) pp. 491–7

Sultan, S. '*Johan Johan* and its Debt to French Farce', *JEGP* 53:1 (1954) pp. 23–37

Young, 1904, pp. 98–124

47   July and Julian

DATE, AUTHORSHIP AND AUSPICES

1547–53, anonymous; auspices unknown, but manifestly a play for boys

TEXT AND EDITIONS

Extant originals

Manuscript: Folger MS 448.16

Editions

1955   Dawson and Brown (OS)*

SOURCES

No sources have been identified.

CHARACTERS

Prologue	Wilkin, a servant
Fenell	Chremes, an old man
Maud, wife of Chremes	Julian
Pierpinte, her brother	Misis
Dick, younger son of Chremes	Messenger
Grammar school master	Bamford
Song school master	Undersheriff
Nan, daughter of Chremes	Bettrice
July, elder son of Chremes	

Mute: scholars

Menedemus (father of Misis) is mentioned but does not appear

PLOT SUMMARY

The *Prologue* tells the story of the play, and the action is opened by *Fenell*, a servant complaining about his lot as a slave and resolving to try to obtain his liberty. He comes upon his mistress, *Maud*, with her brother and younger son, *Dick*, who complains to *Fenell* about the hardships of his life at school. In the next scene *Maud* is seen chastening her daughter, *Nan*, who also afterwards complains to *Fenell* about her treatment. The scene then switches to the elder son, *July*, who is bewailing to another servant, *Wilkin*, the fact that he will have to give up his lover. *Wilkin* reveals in the scene following that this lover is a slave girl, *Julian*, whom *July* would like to marry. When *Dick* comes to complain again about his sorrows, *Wilkin* advises him to co-operate with his brother so that they can help each other. On *Dick*'s departure, *July* reappears disclosing that he has been overheard by his mother talking to *Julian*, and he decides to appeal to his mother to accept the situation. *Wilkin*, however, suggests that instead he get *Julian* to go and tell the mother that *July* has bid her to a tryst, in order to endear her to the mother and gain her confidence. *Wilkin* asserts that the mother might then disguise herself to take *Julian*'s place, and on her arrival *July* can then berate the supposed *Julian*, saying he was only testing her loyalty to his parents, thus himself regaining his mother's trust. However, in the following scene *Maud* tells *Chremes* about overhearing her son and the maid and what she suspects their intentions are. They resolve to spy on the next meeting of the pair. *Maud* then summons *Julian* and pretends to ask her advice over a match supposedly proposed by a gentleman between his daughter and *July*. *Julian* confesses that *July* has paid court to her, advising that he be chastised for this and that the marriage should go ahead. *Maud* applauds her loyalty and pledges to trust her forever more. They send for *Fenell* to get him to fetch *Misis*, a neighbour's daughter, to meet *July* in *Julian*'s place, as she is very like her. *Fenell* goes off to speak to *Misis* but he meets *Wilkin* outside her door and enlists his aid to further his plans for *July*'s marriage, by which means both slaves hope to achieve their freedom. In the next scene *Wilkin* reveals *Chremes*'s plan to *July*, who is in the process of retrieving his brother from school so that the boy can have a day off. He tells *July* that *Chremes* is going to substitute another for *Wilkin* when he attends on *Julian* at the meeting, and advises him to take a cudgel to drive off the fellow. At the tryst *July* accuses the substitute *Julian* of being untrue to his parents, and having sent her off counterfeits repentance before his parent that he undertook this 'test' without their knowledge, the ruse finally convincing them of his probity. At this point a letter arrives from a merchant with an offer to buy *Julian* and the servants now have to develop a further scheme to frustrate this sale. They resolve to substitute *Fenell*'s niece, *Bettrice*, for *Julian*, and then win her back by law. The substitution made, *Bettrice*'s father, *Bamford*, comes and claims his daughter from the messenger of the merchant, who has been detailed to make the purchase. The next stage of the play involves *Bamford*'s making *Chremes* drunk to facilitate the final execution of the plot. As *Chremes* drinks, *Bamford* tells him that he has staying with him a gentlewoman whose father has lands adjoining those of *Chremes*, and that she must marry within a twelvemonth in order to qualify for a grant of these lands. *Chremes* orders *July* to marry her, to which he acquiesces. In the following scene he brings his bride and asks his father in return to pardon both him and *Julian* for all they ever did, to release *Fenell* and *Wilkin* from bondage, and thirdly to forgive him, *Bamford* and the two slaves for all they did that might be amiss. *Chremes* agrees and the bride is then revealed to be *Julian*. The play ends with *Chremes* accepting the situation, and an epilogue is spoken by *Wilkin*.

PLAY LENGTH

1,340 lines, including epilogue

COMMENTARY

This is a crudely constructed play, imitative of Roman comedy, with a somewhat haphazard servant-intrigue plot. The scene involving the schoolmasters, and more generally the role of the younger brother, are gratuitous elements which may have been included because of the play's clear school auspices. Curiously, despite the obvious involvement of boys and the presence of a song schoolmaster as a character, the play contains no clearly defined songs, though lines 133–6 may have been sung, as the first two lines are the opening lines of a Redford song (see Halliwell's edition of *Wit and Science*, 1848b, p. 62). The prologue states that the play is for boys to 'show wit'.

Other marriage quest plays: **29, 57** (frag.), **61, 62, 101**.
Other secular comedies: **5, 30, 41, 46, 75, 88, 91, 92, 95**.
Other plays with foreign (non-biblical, non-classical) settings: **5, 6, 7, 12, 13, 32, 33, 70, 74, 83, 88**.

SIGNIFICANT TOPICS AND NARRATIVE ELEMENTS

slavery and the rigours of servitude; a love intrigue; the cruelty of schoolmasters; servant intriguers; marriage and parental coercion; drinking and drunkenness

DRAMATURGICAL AND RHETORICAL FEATURES

Verbal and general a play clearly conceived of in five acts, but after 4.6 (line 793) the numbering of the acts and scenes is discontinued; no stage directions
Costume and dress *Pierpinte* complains that as a poor countryman he cannot be as 'gay' (well-dressed) as city people 105; *Maud* admits that her she and her family 'go gay' 106; *Julian* changes her dress 942; *Julian* is dressed in 'fine apparel' 1045

Actions 202–3: *Maud* beats *Nan*; 526: *Misis* knocks *Fenell*'s shins with the door
Staging and set locations are indicated by the dialogue and presence of characters, but there may have been some attempt to demarcate the identified locations: *Chremes*'s house (103), a schoolroom (180–91, 592–621), *Menedemus*'s
house, with an opening door (520), and possibly *Bamford*'s house (referred to in
1153)
Stage properties *July*'s 'wand' or cane 620; money 917; a pot of wine 1087

PLACENAMES

Brabant 671, 736, 913; Bristol 964; Kent 895

BIBLIOGRAPHY

Grantley, D. '"Promisse me my liberty": Conventions of Roman Comedy and the Representation of
    Oppression and Resistance in the Tudor Interlude *July and Julian*', *EnterText* 3:1 (2003, Renaissance
    Issue) pp. 13–30

48   The Killing of the Children (Candlemas Day)

DATE, AUTHORSHIP AND AUSPICES

1480–90, though the date 1512 appears on the manuscript; anonymous (the John
Parfre named on the manuscript is likely to have been the scribe); an East Anglian
play to celebrate the feast day of St Anne

TEXT AND EDITIONS

Extant originals

Manuscript: Bodleian MS Digby 133, fos. 146r–157v

Editions

1994   CHD (CD-Rom and online copy of Baker, Murphy and Hall, 1982, l.l., OS)
1993   Coldewey (OS)*
1982   Baker, Murphy and Hall (OS)*
1976   Baker, Murphy and Hall (facsimile, n.l.)
1896   Furnivall (OS)*
1867   Hawkins (n.l., OS)
1838   Marriott (n.l., OS)
1835   Sharp (OS)

SOURCES

The scriptural sources are the accounts of the slaughter of the innocents in *Matthew* 2 and the bringing of the infant Christ to Simeon in *Luke 2:27–39*.

CHARACTERS

Poet	4th Knight	3rd Woman
Herod	Angel	4th Woman
Watkyn, the messenger	Joseph	Simeon
1st Knight	Mary	Anna the Prophetess
2nd Knight	1st Woman	A Virgin
3rd Knight	2nd Woman	

Mute: a number of virgins 'as many as a man will'

PLOT SUMMARY

The *Poet* delivers the prologue, announcing the play to be for the feast of St Anne, mother of the Virgin Mary and descended from the house of David and Solomon. He mentions a play of the shepherds and three kings performed the previous year, and announces the two current plays as being the Purification of the Virgin and a Herod play (the reverse of their order in the manuscript), before calling for minstrel music and a dance by 'virgins'. *Herod* commences the action with a 'boast' about his power and worldly prosperity, then summons his messenger *Watkyn*, ordering him (in a passage cancelled in the manuscript) to look throughout the realm for any rebels, and relating how the three kings had deceived him. He summons his knights and commands them to kill the children throughout the land. They go off and *Watkyn* now asks to be made a knight, which *Herod*, doubtful of his courage, promises to do only if he acquits himself well in the field. *Watkyn* makes his way to the knights and, while they walk about the place, an angel tells *Joseph* and *Mary* to flee into Egypt, at which they depart. The knights then launch an attack on mothers, killing their children. In the affray, the women turn on *Watkyn* and beat him with their distaffs, until he has to be rescued by the knights. When the returning knights tell *Herod* that the women have cursed him, he expresses some remorse at the slaughter and doubt that it has achieved its purpose. As a result of all this he falls into a state of distress, runs mad and soon after dies. *Simeon* opens the next sequence with a prophecy of the coming of Christ, after which *Mary* and *Joseph* appear bringing the infant *Jesus* and two doves to *Simeon*. *Simeon* pronounces the 'nunc dimittis' and prophesies Christ's redemption of mankind. *Anna the Prophetess* then enters to summon virgins for a procession in honour of Christ. Led by *Simeon*, they process about the temple with tapers, singing the 'nunc dimittis', and *Simeon* preaches a short sermon before handing the child back to *Mary*. *Mary* and *Joseph* depart and *Simeon* then prophesies the Crucifixion before dismissing *Anna* and the virgins. The *Poet* concludes the play, begging the audience's patience for the players' lack of eloquence, promising a play of the disputation of the doctors for the following year, and calling on the minstrels for music and a dance.

PLAY LENGTH

566 lines

COMMENTARY

These two dramatic episodes are possibly part of a cycle or an occasional sequence celebrating a saint's day. The Simeon episode is purely ritual, with little narrative content. In 1911 the play was translated into German by a Dr Fricke as *Lichtmess oder der Bethlehemitische Kindermord: Heiligenspiel von John Parfre*.

Other biblical plays: **10, 11, 16, 34, 42, 44, 63, 77, 90, 93.**
Other plays with probable place and scaffold staging: **9, 23, 63, 72** (frag.), **83, 85.**

SIGNIFICANT TOPICS AND NARRATIVE ELEMENTS

Herod as an irascible tyrant; the toppling of pagan idols; knighthood and cowardice; women and physical conflict; women cursing; Herod's madness and death; the story of Simeon in the temple

DRAMATURGICAL AND RHETORICAL FEATURES

Verbal and general *Herod* enters with a vaunting, alliterative 'boast' 57–80; *Herod*'s rage and death throes are graphically played out 365–88; at the foot of the final page is the inscription 'John Parfre did write this book'; shorter stage directions in Latin and longer ones in English
Costume and dress the knights arm themselves in 'steel shining bright' 106, 306; *Herod* tears his clothes 383
Actions and stage directions 56 *sd*: 'And they (*An.*, virgins) busy themselves (dance)' (L); 133 *sd*: 'Here the knights shall depart from *He.* to Israel, and *Wa.* shall abide, saying to *He.*' (E); 216 *sd*: 'And he (*He.*) must go out' (L); 232 *sd*: 'Here the knights and *Wa.* walk about the place till *Ma.* and *Jos.* be conveyed into Egypt. The *Ang.* says' (E/L); 276 *sd*: 'And they (*Ma.*, *Jo.*) must go out' (L); 280 *sd*: 'Here *Ma.* and *Jos.* shall go out of the place, and the gods shall fall, and then shall come in the women of Israel, with young children in their arms, and then the knights shall go to them, saying as follows' (E); 314 *sd*: 'Here they (knights) kill the children' (L); 349 *sd*: 'Here they (women) shall beat *Wa.*, and the knights shall come to rescue him, and then they go to *He.*, saying' (E); 388 *sd*: 'Here dies *He.*, and *Sim.* says as follows' (E); 412 *sd*: 'Here shall *Our Lady* come forth, holding *Jes.* in her arms, and say this language following to *Jos.*' (E); 428 *sd*: 'Here *Ma.* and *Jos.* go toward the

temple with *Jes.* and two doves, and *Our Lady* says unto *Sim.*' (E); 436 *sd*: 'Here shall *Sim.* receive of *Ma. Jes.* and two doves, and hold *Jes.* in his arms, expounding "Nunc dimittis" et cetera, saying thus' (E); 444 *sd*: 'Here (*Sim.*) declare "Nunc dimittis"' (E); 460 *sd*: 'Here shall *An.* say thus to the virgins' (E); 464 *sd*: 'Here virgins, as many as a man will, shall hold tapers in their hands, and the first says' (E); 484 *sd*: 'Here shall *Sim.* bear *Jes.* in his arms, going in a procession round about the temple, and all this while the virgins sing "Nunc dimittis" and when that is done, *Sim.* says' (E); 516 *sd*: 'Here she (*Ma.*) receives her son, thus saying' (E); 524 *sd*: 'Here *Ma.* and *Jos.* going from the temple, saying' (E); 550 *sd*: '*An.* and [the virgins] busy themselves (dance)' (L)

Songs and music the virgins sing the 'nunc dimittis' (w.n.s.) 484 *sd*; **Instrumental**: the minstrel music and dance of the virgins 53–4; concluding music and dance from the minstrels 565–6

Staging and set this appears to be a simple place and scaffold play; it is in two relatively separate dramatic sequences, the second of which (beginning 389) has the direction 'vacat ab hinc' ('omitted from here') written at the outset, suggesting that at times it may have been omitted; the action is localized, principally in *Herod*'s palace and the temple, which are likely to have had scaffolds or wagons; the former includes a pagan temple with gods that fall (280 *sd*)

Stage properties *Joseph*'s bag of tools 273; an ass 280; gods (pagan idols) 280 *sd*; the knights' swords 292; dolls (as the children) 314 *sd*; distaffs 330, 347; a doll (as Christ) 412 *sd*; two doves 428 *sd*; the virgins' tapers 464 *sd*

PLACENAMES

Bethlehem 95, 237, 285, 357, 370, cancelled pass.18; Mt Calvary 536; Egypt 48, 232 *sd*, 234, 256; Israel 41, 123, 133 *sd*, 170, 280 *sd*, 353, cancelled pass. 23; Jericho 13; Jerusalem 82, 118, 351; Judea 351

ALLUSIONS

St Anne 2, 9, 18, 51, 550, 558; King David 4; Phoebus 492; Solomon 4

REPORTS ON MODERN PRODUCTIONS

1. Winchester Cathedral (King Alfred's College Drama Department), dir. J. Marshall, 26–9 May 1983 [*METh* 5:1 (1983) pp. 51–2; *RORD* 26 (1983) pp. 119–20]
2. Columbia University (Medieval Guild), dir. J. Crosby and N. Magarill, 14 October 1995 [*RORD* 35 (1996) pp. 140–1]

CONCORDANCE

Preston, 1977

BIBLIOGRAPHY

Baker and Murphy, 1967, pp. 153–66
Coletti, T. '"Ther be but women": Gender Conflict and Gender Identity in the Middle English Innocents
   Play', *Mediaevalia* 18 (1995 for 1992) pp. 245–61
Coletti, T. 'Genealogy, Sexuality and Sacred Power: The Saint Anne Dedication of the Digby *Candlemas
   Day and the Killing of the Children of Israel*', *JMEMS* 29:1 (1999) pp. 25–59
Harrington, G. 'The Dialogism of the Digby Mystery Play', *Mediaevalia* 18 (1995 for 1992) pp. 67–80
Marshall, 1994, pp. 111–48
Patch, H. R. 'The *Ludus Coventriae* and the Digby *Massacre*', *PMLA* 35:3 (1920) pp. 324–43
Scherb, 2001, pp. 84–94

49 King Darius

DATE, AUTHORSHIP AND AUSPICES

published 1565 (*SR* 1565/6 *c.* Oct.); anonymous; offered for acting; Greg 40

TEXT AND EDITIONS

Extant originals

1565 printing by Thomas Colwell: BL (three copies), Huntington; Newberry; Pepys;
   Pforzheimer; Rosenbach; *STC* 6277
1577 printing by Hugh Jackson: BL; *STC* 6278

Editions

1994 CHD (CD-Rom and online transcription of Colwell printing, l.l., OS)*
1909 TFT (facsimile of 1577 Jackson printing, n.l.)
1907 TFT (facsimile of 1565 Colwell printing, n.l.)
1906 Farmer (5) (n.l., NS)
1898 Brandl (OS)*
1860 Halliwell (n.l., OS)

SOURCES

The play is based on the third and fourth chapters of the first *Book of Esdras* (V).

CHARACTERS

Prolocutor	King Darius	Preparatus	Persia	Optimates	Zorobabell
Iniquity	Partiality	Perplexity	Juda	Anagnostes	
Charity	Equity	Curiosity	Media	Stipator Primus	
Importunity	Agreeable	Ethiopia	Constancy	Stipator Secundus	

PLOT SUMMARY

The *Prolocutor* relates those parts of the play's narrative that involve the king: a banquet and a wit contest. He then gives way to the Vice, *Iniquity*, soon joined by *Charity*, who attempts to convert him from his errant ways, but fails and leaves. *Iniquity* is later approached by new companions, *Importunity* and *Partiality*, and the three plot against *Charity*. *Equity* then enters to continue the attempt at reformation, but with no success, and after his departure the three reprobates sing a song. The scene now changes to *Darius*'s court, where the king gives a banquet at which his guests, *Ethiopia*, *Persia*, *Juda* and *Media* consume rapidly and then depart, thanking him for his generosity. Another scene switch has *Iniquity* entering singing, joined by his erstwhile companions, and they fall first to debating and then to quarrelling about which has the most elevated birth. Once again they are accosted by *Equity*, who is soon joined by *Constancy* and *Charity*, and together they attempt to convert *Iniquity*, but, having failed, they drive him off and sing a song. The scene then changes back to *Darius*'s court, where the king announces that he has overheard some of his attendants debating, and he has them summoned to a formal wit contest that will involve their attempting to identify the strongest thing in the world. There are three contestants. *Stipator Primus* argues for the potency of wine, *Stipator Secundus* for the might of the king, and *Zorobabell* for the power of women and men's love for them, but he goes on to say that wine, the king and women are unrighteous and that the real power is that of God and truth. *Zorobabell* wins and as a reward the king accedes to his request to be allowed to rebuild Jerusalem. The play ends with a prayer for the queen and a final song.

PLAY LENGTH

1,605 lines, including final song

COMMENTARY

This is a Protestant morality with a strong range of social referents. The play has two strands of plot that minimally connect and there is little relationship either between the two sequences in which the king is involved. The *Iniquity* sequences contain the religious debate, the Vices embodying Catholicism. The argument of the successful candidate in the wit contest, about the power of women, may be an oblique compliment to Queen Elizabeth. There are no female characters in the play.

Other Protestant and anti-Catholic plays: **14, 24, 44, 45, 50, 53, 58, 66, 85, 86** (frag.), **90, 93**.

SIGNIFICANT TOPICS AND NARRATIVE ELEMENTS

rank and social competition; the oppression of the poor; the role and identity of women; alcohol and drinking; kingship; court life; religious conflict

DRAMATURGICAL AND RHETORICAL FEATURES

Verbal and general a wit contest or debate 1302–493; a form of epilogue ('sublocutio') is delivered by *Constancy* within the play 1548–71; few stage directions, all in English

Actions and stage directions 486 *sd*: 'Here he (*Equ.*) kneels down and prays'; 689 *sd*: 'They (*Eth., Per., Ju., Me.*) sit down all'; 707 *sd*: 'They (*Eth., Per., Ju., Me.*) rise from meat'; 738 *sd*: 'They (*Cur., Per.*) go out, and *In.* comes in singing'; 922 *sd*: 'He (*In.*) casts (a piece of brass pan) at *Con.*'; 928 *sd*: (*In.* casts a fig) 'At *Cha.*'; 934 *sd*: (*In.* casts a taper and beads) 'At *Equ.*'; 1226 *sd*: 'They (*Con., Cha.*) go out and the ki. enters and says'; 1155 *sd*: 'Here somebody must cast fire to *In.*'; 1547 *sd*: 'Here they (*Ana., Opt., Zor.*) go out, and then enters *Con.* saying as it were a Sublocutio';

Simple entry: *In.* 34; *Cha.* 46; *Imp., Par.* 178; *Equ.* 285; ki.'s two servants 610; ki., council 628; *Eth., Per., Ju., Me.* 675; *Imp., Par.* 746; *Equ.* 806; *Con., Cha.* 873; *Pre., Agr.* 1228; *Ana., Opt.* 1238; *Sti. P., Sti. S., Zor.* 1288; *Equ., Cha.* 1571; **Simple exit:** *Prol.* 34; *Cha.* 169; *Equ.* 523; *Imp., Par.* 590; *In.* 610; *Pre., Agr.* 664; *Eth., Per., Ju., Me.* 780; (*Imp., Par.*) 845; (*In.*) 1159; (*Pre., Agr.*) 1238; *Sti. P., Sti. S., Zor.* 1538

Songs and music (w.s. to all): 1. *Partiality, Iniquity, Importunity*, 'Let the knaves take heed' 568–86; 2. *Iniquity* (scales only) 'La, so, so, fa, mi, re, re' 739; 3. *Equity, Constancy, Charity* 'Sing we together' 1202–19; 4. *Equity, Charity* (?) 'Let the truth, let the truth' 1582–1605

Staging and set the title page states that 'six may easily play it' but no doubling scheme is offered; a (very short) feast, with trappings, is held on stage (689 *sd*–707 *sd*); there are pyrotechnics in the form of the 'fire' thrown at *Iniquity* (1155 *sd*); apart from *Darius*'s court, for which there are no indications as to set, the action is unlocalized

Stage properties *Importunity*'s bread 195; *Iniquity*'s dagger 359; a table with a banquet 689; a 'piece of a brass pan' 924; a fig 930; a taper 936; beads 937; pyrotechnic material 1155 *sd*; *King Darius*'s 'writings' 1255

PLACENAMES

Babylon 1525; Buckingham 67; Gomorrah 1005; Jerusalem 1516, 1528; Newgate (prison) 851; Peterborough 232; Rome 770; Sodom 1005; Southampton 777

ALLUSIONS

Antichrist 858; 'King Bartacus' (?) 1445; Cyrus the Great 1524; *Ecclesiasticus* (V) (q.n.t.) 384, 817; *Genesis* 2:7(?) 391–2, 827–9; *James* 4:4 148–9; *Jeremiah* 23:5(?)

325–6; *Luke 1:51* 819–20; St Matthew 1054; *Matthew 23:16–22* 1055–6; Midas 1168; St Paul *Romans* (q.n.t) 134–6, 150, 319; *I Peter 5:5* 823–4; *Proverbs 31:30* 395–6; Zachariah 1045; *Zechariah 5:2–3* 1046–53

BIBLIOGRAPHY

Bevington, 1962, pp. 175–8
Blackburn, 1971, pp. 125–8

50   King John

DATE, AUTHORSHIP AND AUSPICES

1538, revised later by the author in 1558–62; John Bale; performed at St Stephen's, Canterbury, Cranmer's House, also in Canterbury, and offered for acting

TEXT AND EDITIONS

Extant original

Manuscript: Huntington Library MS HM3

Editions

1994	CHD (CD-Rom and online copy of Happé, 1985/6, l.l., OS)
1985/6	Happé, vol. 1 (OS)*
1979	Happé (OS)*
1969	Adams (OS)*
1966	Creeth (a.l., OS)
1965	Armstrong (n.l., NS)
1931	Pafford and Greg (OS)
1909	Bang (facsimile, n.l.)
1907	Farmer (8) (n.l., NS)
1897	Manly, vol. 1 (OS)
1838	Collier (n.l., OS)

SOURCES

Likely sources include Robert Barnes's *A Supplicacion unto the Most Gracyous Prynce H. the VIII* (1534), Simon Fish's *A Supplicacyon of the Beggers* (1524) and William Tyndale's *The Obedience of Christen Man* (1528); see the introduction to Happé's 1985/6 edition, pp. 14–16.

CHARACTERS

King John

Widow England

Sedition (also Steven Langton/ Monk)

Nobility

Clergy

Civil Order

Dissimulation (also Raymundus/ Simon of Swinsett)

Usurped Power, also the Pope

Private Wealth (also Pandulphus)

The Interpreter

Treason

Commonality

Veritas

Imperial Majesty

PLOT SUMMARY

The *Widow England* complains to *King John* that she is suffering abuse at the hands of the corrupt clergy, encouraged by the *Pope. Sedition*, a cleric, tries to intervene, but she complains of him too. *John* resolves to call his nobles, clerics and judges to a parliament to discuss the matter and, when *Sedition* proceeds to reveal his corrupt nature, *John* decides to suppress the monasteries. On *Sedition's* departure, *Nobility, Clergy* and *Civil Order* come in and *John* lays *Widow England's* charges before them, affirming strongly that he will defend her cause. *Clergy* ostensibly submits to *John's* rule, though in a slip of the tongue he reveals his continued allegiance to the *Pope*, while *Nobility* and *Civil Order* pledge their loyalty to the king. When *John* leaves, *Clergy* and *Nobility* engage in a discussion, but *Nobility* admits he is unlearned and decides to leave matters of religious politics to the clergy. On their exit, *Sedition* reappears and is soon joined by *Dissimulation*, who comes in singing the litany. They revel in their clerical corruption and plot to defend their position against *John*, fetching their friends *Usurped Power* (the *Pope*) and *Private Wealth* to help them. *Sedition* is borne aloft by the other three to signify his leadership. *Dissimulation* brings letters to *Usurped Power* from the bishops, telling of *King John's* assumption of control over the Church. *Usurped Power* appoints *Sedition* Archbishop of Canterbury under the name *Steven Langton, Dissimulation* reasserts the power of the *Pope* over the Church, and the *Pope* excommunicates *John*. After *Dissimulation* and *Private Wealth* are given the names *Raymundus* and *Cardinal Pandulphus* respectively, they are despatched to encourage foreign kings to attack *John* and to offer absolution to anyone who kills him. The *Interpreter* then enters to summarize *John's* quarrel with the Church and to introduce the action of the second act. This act opens with *Sedition* offering *Nobility* remission of penance in exchange for taking the Church's part in the dispute with *John*, and he also hears *Nobility's* confession, absolving him from duty to the king. *Sedition* next encounters *Clergy* and *Civil Order*, to whom he also gives absolution, and they promise to stir up insurrection in the realm against the king. When they hear *John* coming they run off to hide and he appears, recalling his father's killing of Thomas Becket. *Private Wealth* enters as a cardinal, demanding the king's restitution of Church property and acceptance of *Steven Langton* as Archbishop of Canterbury. The king agrees to readmit the exiled monks on the condition of their reformation, but refuses to accept *Langton*, at which *Private Wealth* curses him and absolves his subjects from loyalty to him. *Sedition* makes a noise off stage which *Private Wealth* explains as the sound of enemies preparing to invade *John's* realm, but the king remains scornful and defiant and chases him off. *Civil Order* and *Clergy* then enter to confront *John*, followed by *Nobility*, all declaring the king to be accursed. *John* takes issue with them but *Clergy* and *Civil Order* soon depart, leaving *Nobility* to pursue the argument. *John* cites the Scriptures to prove that the Church ought to be subject to royal authority, but *Nobility* remains unconvinced and he too goes off. *Widow England* next appears, accompanied by *Commonality*, who has been made poor and both physically and spiritually blind through lack of teaching. *England* encourages *John* in his campaign against the Church, but when the papal legate *Pandulphus* arrives to castigate *Commonality* for coming to the king, he quickly obeys the cleric and leaves. *Pandulphus* tells *England* that foreign forces are mustering against *John*, and *Sedition* comes in to restate the remission of penance granted to those engaging in insurrection against the king. *Pandulphus* and *Sedition* insist that *John* give up the crown, which, to *England's* sorrow, he consents to do in order to prevent civil disorder, and he also agrees to pay heavy taxes to the *Pope*. *Langton* comes to absolve *John* of his sins and the king accepts him as primate. *Treason* now enters, as a priest under charge of treason, defiantly giving an account of Catholic perversion of religion, promotion of superstition, and undermining of the realm. When *John* sentences him to death, he claims benefit of clergy and the king's refusal of this brings him once again into conflict with *Sedition* and *Pandulphus*, until the priest is finally released. *Pandulphus* and *Sedition* then demand that *John* give up a third of his realm to be ruled by his sister-in-law Juliana, something which is only avoided by *England's* pointing out that the woman is dead. They then make him promise no longer to defy the Church, and the king departs with *England*. When *Dissimulation* reappears, *Sedition* plots with him *John's* death by poison and gives him absolution to commit the deed. They go off and *John* re-enters with *England*, depressed at the insurrection against him, though *England* consoles him with the news that the *Pope* no longer supports his enemies. *Dissimulation*, as *Simon of Swinsett*, administers a drink to the king, who soon afterwards falls ill and dies. *Verity* comes in to deliver a paean to the historical figure of *King John*, convincing *Nobility* and *Civil Order* of his worth. *Imperial Majesty* then arrives to confirm the rejection of Catholicism from the realm for ever. When *Sedition* reappears, he is apprehended and taken off to be hanged. To end the play, *Clergy*, *Civil Order* and *Nobility* join *Imperial Majesty* in a tirade against not only Catholicism but also the Anabaptists.

PLAY LENGTH

2,691 lines

COMMENTARY

Though not strictly speaking a history play, this Protestant morality is one of the earliest plays to take as its subject matter a topic from English history. Bale is careful to weave into his play aspects of Catholic religious practice, such as absolution, remission of penance and excommunication, which are all used as devices in a process of corrupt political manoeuvring. The doubling in the play goes beyond simply being a matter of economy of resources, as it dovetails with the conventional practice of Vices taking on aliases and certain of the doubled characters (such as *Dissimulation* and *Simon of Swinsett*) carry over characteristics one to the other. The convention of Vices taking on other names is also used by Bale to introduce figures from the historical narrative into the play.

Other Protestant and anti-Catholic plays: **14, 24, 44, 45, 49, 53, 58, 66, 85, 86** (frag.), **90, 93**.

SIGNIFICANT TOPICS AND NARRATIVE ELEMENTS

the suppression of the monasteries; Catholic ecclesiastical corruption; the conflict between King John and Pope Innocent III; Protestantism and Reformation; relics; excommunication; the murder of Thomas Becket; benefit of clergy; treason and punishment; Anabaptists

DRAMATURGICAL AND RHETORICAL FEATURES

Verbal and general aliases: 1. *Sedition–Steven Langton–Good Perfection* 983 *sd*, 1057, 1136; 2. *Usurped Power–the Pope* 983 *sd*; 3. *Dissimulation–Raymundus* 1057; 4. *Private Wealth–Cardinal Pandulphus* 983 *sd* 1056. *Sedition*'s Skeltonic list of his guises repeating 'sometime' 194–210; *Sedition*'s list of places he has visited as the *Pope*'s ambassador 214–17; *Clergy*'s list of monastic orders and clerical ranks 442–60; *Sedition* addresses *Dissimulation* in French 668; *Dissimulation*'s list of corrupt Catholic practices 699–719; *Dissimulation*'s list of monastic orders 726–30; *Usurped Power* shrives *Dissimulation* 847 *sd*–864; a bell, book and candle ceremony to excommunicate *John* 1034–52; the *Interpreter*'s speech is interpolated into the text in Bale's own hand 1086–120; *Sedition* hears *Nobility*'s confession and absolves him 1148 *sd*–1189; a satirical list of mock relics 1215–30 (containing allusions to several saints); *Sedition* makes a noise off stage 1378–9; *Sedition*'s violent laughter 1700–1; *Langton*'s Latin absolution of the king 1789–800; two acts, with no scene division, and the ending talks of the 'two plays of King John'; stage directions in English, except for a few short ones in Latin
Costume and dress a description 'vidua' *on England*'s entry suggests that she should be dressed like a widow 21 *sd*; *Sedition* changes his apparel for that of a bishop 296–7; *Usurped Power*'s apparel is 'light' 864; *Sedition* puts on a 'stole' to hear *Nobility*'s confession 1148; *Private Wealth* comes in 'like a cardinal' 1303 *sd*;

Dissimulation is dressed as a 'religious man' (monk) 2093; the doubling instructions require actors to 'dress for' the next roles they are taking

Actions and stage directions 154 *sd*: 'Go out *Eng.* and dress for *Cle.*'; 312 *sd*: 'Here go out *Sed.* and dress for *Civ. O.*'; 506 *sd*: '(*Cle.*) kneel'; 556 *sd*: 'Here *K. Jo.* and *Civ. O.* go out, and *Civ. O.* dress him for *Sed.*'; 636 *sd*: '(*Dis.*) Sing the litany' (off stage); 638 *sd*: 'Here come *Dis.* singing of the litany. *Dis.* sing'; 639 *sd*: '*Sed.* sing'; 640 *sd*: '*Dis.* sing'; 649 *sd*: '(*Dis.*) Here sing this'; 763 *sd*: 'Here come in *Us. P.* and *Pri. W.*, singing one after another. *Us. P.* sing this'; 764 *sd*: '*Pri. W.* sing this'; 768 *sd*: 'Here (*Dis.*) go and bring them (*Us. P.*, *Pri. W.*)'; 802 *sd*: 'Here they (*Us. P.*, *Pri. W.*, *Dis.*) shall bear him (*Sed.*) in, and *Sed.* says'; 828 *sd*: 'Here (*Us. P.*, *Pri. W.*, *Sed.*) sing'; 847 *sd*: '(*Dis.*) kneel'; 890 *sd*: 'Here *Dis.* shall deliver writings to *Us. P.*'; 983 *sd*: 'Here go out *Us. P.* and *Pri. W.* and *Sed.*, *Us. P.* shall dress for the *Po.*, *Pri. W.* for a cardinal, and *Sed.* for a monk. The *Car.* shall bring in the cross, and *Ste. La.* the bell, book and candle'; 1027 *sd*: '(*Dis.*) Kneel and knock on thy breast'; 1051 *sd*: 'Say this all three (*Po.*, *Dis.*, *Sed.*)'; 1055 *sd*: 'Here they (*Po.*, *Dis.*, *Sed.*) shall sing'; 1061 *sd*: 'Here (*Pri. W.*) go out and dress for *Nob.*'; 1120 *sd*: '[*Sed.*] and *Nob.* come in and say'; 1148 *sd*: 'Here (*Sed.*) sit down and *Nob.* shall say Benedicite'; 1190 *sd*: 'Here enter *Cle.* and *Civ. O.* together. *Sed.* shall go up and down a pretty while'; 1192 *sd*: '(*Cle.*, *Civ. O.*) Kneel and say both'; 1303 *sd*: '[*Pri. W.*] come in like a cardinal'; 1377 *sd*: (*Sed.* calls) 'Out of the place' (off stage) (L); 1397 *sd*: '(*Pri. W.*) Go out and dress for *Nob.*'; 1490 *sd*: 'Here go out *Cle.* and dress for *Eng.*, and *Civ. O.* for *Com.*'; 1533 *sd*: 'Here *Nob.* go out and dress for the *Car.* Here enter *Eng.* and *Com.*'; 1597 *sd*: 'Here enter *Pan.* the cardinal and says'; 1728 *sd*: 'Here the *Ki.* deliver the crown to the *Car.*'; 1778 *sd*: 'Here *K. Jo.* shall deliver the obligation'; 1956 *sd*: 'Falling to his knees he (*Jo.*) praises the Lord, saying' (L); 2061 *sd*. 'He (*K. Jo.*) bends his knees' (L); 2645 *sd*: 'Here the *Ki.* kisses them all' (L); **Simple entry**: *Eng.* 21; *Sed.* 626; *Jo.* 1275; *Ste. L.* 1782; *Sed.* 2456; **Simple exit**: *Nob.*, *Cle.* 626; *Po.* 1085; *Nob.* 1189; 'All' (*Sed.*, *Civ. O.*, *Cle.*) 1275; *Com.* 1609; (*Sed.*, *Dis.*) 2137; (*Jo.*, *Eng.*) 2192

Songs and music 1. *Dissimulation*, *Sedition* the litany (incipit supplied) 636 *sd*, 639–41, 650; 2. *Usurped Power*, *Private Wealth* 'Super flumina Babilonis' (parody of the Vespers for the dead, two lines supplied, each singing one) 764–5; 3. *Dissimulation*, *Usurped Power*, *Private Wealth*, *Sedition* a 'merry song' (w.n.s.) 828 *sd*; 4. *Pope*, *Sedition*, *Dissimulation*, *Private Wealth* sing 'merrily' (w.n.s.) 1055 *sd*; 5. *King John*, *Steven Langton* (chanting) 'Confiteor Domine Pape et omnibus cardinalibus' 1789–800; 6. *Dissimulation* 'Wassail, wassail, wassail, out of the milk pail' (off-stage, w.s.) 2086–91, 7. *Sedition* 'Pepe I se ye, I am glad I have spied ye' (incipit and a bar of music supplied) 2457

Staging and set doubling is indicated in the text as follows: 1. *England–Clergy* (154 *sd*); 2. *Sedition–Civil Order–Commonality–Steven Langton* (312 *sd*, 983 *sd*); 3. *Private Wealth–Nobility–Cardinal* (983 *sd*, 1061 *sd*, 1533 *sd*); 4. *Usurped Power–Pope* (983 *sd*), but considerably more doubling is likely. the action is localized by the presence of characters and also through props, there being no particular indications as to set; off-stage speech or singing is indicated in 1377 *sd* and 2086–92

Stage properties 'writings' delivered to *Usurped Power* 890 *sd*; a cross, bell, book and candle 983 *sd*; John's crown 1728 *sd*; money as John's obligation 1778 *sd*; the captive priest's chains 1917; poison for *John* 2020

PLACENAMES

Anjou 16, 579; Aragon[1] 216; Babylon 369, 2414; Bohemia?[1] 215; Bury St Edmunds 2212; Canterbury 937,[2] 948, 1123, 1191,[2] 1312,[2] 1741,[2] 2132; Denmark[1] 215; Dover 312; Dunwich 2212; Ely[2] 932; England 9 *passim* (also a character name); France 13, 182, 216,[1] 569, 577, 595, 1606; Germany[1] 216; Hertford[2] 933; Ipswich 2212; Ireland 16, 571, 574, 1367, 1730, 1734; Italy[1] 214; Jerusalem 1297, 2264; Lewes 2070; Llandaff 1366;[2] Lombardy[1] 215; London 932,[2] 2071, 2214, 2528; London Bridge 2584; Marshalsea (prison) 2535; Munster 2629; Naples[1] 214; Newgate (prison) 2535; Normandy 16, 596; Norwich 943,[2] 1362;[2] Orleans 596; Persia 2263; Poland[1] 215; Portugal 2114; Prague 1903; Prussia (? 'Spruse')[1] 215; Reading 2071; Rochester 1364,[2] 2070; Rome 71 *passim*; Salisbury 1364;[2] Scotland 217,[1] 571, 1365; Sicily[1] 214; Sodom 370; Spain 182, 216,[1] 2114; Swinsett Abbey 2043, 2102; Tower of London 1635; Tyburn 2579; Venice[1] 214; Wales 16, 571, 574, 1367; Winchester 933,[2] 1362,[2] 2071; Windsor 2071

1 Part of a list of places *Sedition* claims to have visited as the Pope's ambassador.
2 As part of episcopal or archiepiscopal titles.

ALLUSIONS

Abraham 2613; Absolom 2606; Achilles 234; Adam 2611; St Ambrose 807; Annas 1855; St Anthony the Swineherd 1976; Argus 244; Aristotle *Historia animalium* 605.b.11 2252; St Asaph 1366; St Augustine 729,[1] 807; Balaam 1436; Thomas Becket 2590, 2597; Bel (idol) 1354; St Benedict[1] 726; St Bernard[1] 726; Hector Boethius 2203; Marcus Junius Brutus 2605; Caesar 609, 1411; Caiaphas 1855; Caius Cassius 2606; Sergius Catiline 2606; St John Chrysostom 2273; Daniel 2400, 2678; Dathan and Abiram 1528; King David 433, 436, 462–3, 1114, 1510, 1652, 1957, 2261, 2292, 2367–8, 2614; St David 1366; Diomedes 233; St Dominic[1] 728; *Ecclesiastes 10:20* 1404–7, 2227–30; Ehud and Eglon 2262; Elena of Tadcaster 729; Elijah 2129, 2689; Enoch 2129; Ezra 2263; St Francis[1] 728; St Gilbert[1] 727; Giraldus Cambrensis 2202; St Gregory 807; Hector 233; Hezekiah 1513; Homer 2616; *Isaiah 1:17* 130–2; Ish-bosheth 2372; Jehosophat 1512; St Jerome 807, 2231; St Joanna of Toulouse[1] 727; St John 1416, 2675; *John 1:1* 117–18; John the Baptist 1415; Judas 1852, 2144; John Leland 2198; St Leodegerius 1975; Lot's Wife 522; St Louis 1975; *Luke 20:46–7* 64–5; *1 Maccabees 4: 41–51*(V) 1515–8; Johan Major 2203; Baptista Mantuanus *Bucolica* 2268; *Mark 12:38* 65; St Matthew 2249; *Matthew 6:19* 97, *15:14* 34, *16:17* 2417; Maurice Morganensis 1899–905; Moses 1107, 1827, 2410, 2614; John Nauclerus 2201; Nestor 2686; Noah 2613; Matthew Paris 2202; St Patrick[1]

729; St Paul 4, 53, 1408, 1416, 1498, 1502, 2124, 2400; St Paul *Colossians 4:6* 54; St Paul *Romans 13:1–2* 2349–57, *13:2* 1409, *13:4* 1503–4; St Peter 4, 1412, 1416, 1849, 2417; Paulus Phrigio 2203; Plato 2259; Peter Pomfrete 1883; *Proverbs 16: 9–10* 1343–4, 2237–8, *22:11* 2243; *Psalm 2:10*(V and AV) 1467, *44:10*(V)/*45:9*(AV) 434–5, *79:14*(V)/*80:13*(AV) 86, *136:1–4*(V)/*137:1–5*(AV) 764–5; Quirinius 1410; *Revelation 7:2–4* 2675; 2 *Samuel* ('*Kings*') *7:25–9* 1957–8, *1:2–16* 2291–4, *4:5–12* 2364–72; Saul 2291–3, 2367; Anneus Seneca 2279; Sigbert of Gemblours 2201; Solomon 1343, 1510, 2238, 2243; Solon 1698; Susanna 1460; Polydore Vergil 2195, 2204; Vincent of Beauvais 2201

1 Part of a list of saints reeled off by *Dissimulation*.

RECORDED PRODUCTION

LP Record: BBC, *The First Stage*, dir. J. Barton (1970)

BIBLIOGRAPHY

Adams, B. B. 'Doubling in Bale's *King Johan*', *SP* 62:2 (1965) pp. 111–20
Barke, 1937
Bevington, 1968, pp. 97–105
Blatt, 1968, pp. 99–129
Bryant, 1984, pp. 45–81
Burns, 1990, pp. 54–60
Carpenter, S. 'John Bale's *Kynge Johan*: The Dramatisation of Allegorical and Non-Allegorical Figures' in Muller, 1981, pp. 263–9
Cason, C. 'Additional Lines for Bale's *King Johan*', *JEGP* 27:1 (1928) pp. 42–50
Cavanagh, D. 'The Paradox of Sedition in Bale's *King Johan*', *ELR* 31:2 (2001) pp. 171–91
Dillon, 1998, pp. 95–105
Duncan, R. 'The Play as Tudor Propaganda: Bale's *King John* and the Authority of Kings', *UDR* 16:3 (1983/4) pp. 67–74
Ebihara, H. 'The English Political Morality from *Magnyfycence* to *Wealth and Health*, with Special Attention to Bale's Treatment in *King Johan* of the Doctrine of Absolutism', *SELL* English Number 47:2 (1971) pp. 141–64
Ebihara, H. 'Theme and Structure in John Bale's *King Johan*', *SELL* 19 (1969) pp. 1–13 (in Japanese with English abstract)
Elson, J. 'Studies in the King John Plays' in McManaway, 1948, pp. 191–7
Forest-Hill, 2000, pp. 165–96
Griffin, 2001, pp. 37–45
Grosse, 1935, pp. 32–9
Happé, P. 'Sedition in *King Johan*: Bale's Development of a "Vice"', *METh* 3:1 (1981) pp. 3–6
Happé, 1996, pp. 89–107
Happé, 1999, pp. 246–51
Harris, 1940, pp. 91–9
Johnson, 1959, pp. 157–71
Kamps, 1996, pp. 51–66
Kastan, D. S. '"Holy Wurdes" and "Slypper Wit": John Bale's *King Johan* and the Poetics of Propaganda' in Herman, 1994, pp. 267–82
Levin, C. 'A Good Prince: King John and Early Tudor Propaganda', *SCJ* 11:4 (1980) pp. 23–32

McCusker, 1942, pp. 73–85

Mackenzie, 1914, pp. 217–26

Mattsson, 1977, pp. 21–7, 60–71, 95–9, 122–30

Miller, E. 'The Roman Rite in Bale's *King John*', *PMLA* 64:4 (1949) pp. 802–22

Morey, J. H. 'The Death of King John in Shakespeare and Bale', *SQ* 45:3 (1994) pp. 327–31

Norland, 1995, pp. 188–98

Pafford, J. H. 'Bale's *King John*', *JEGP* 30:2 (1931) pp. 176–8

Pineas, R. 'William Tyndale's Influence on John Bale's Polemical use of History', *Archiv für Reformationsgeschichte* 53:1–2 (1962) pp. 79–96

Potter, 1975, pp. 94–104

Ribner, I. 'Morality Roots of the English History Play', *Tulane Studies in English* 4 (1954) pp. 21–43

Sperk, 1973, pp. 105–38

Uéno, Y. 'An Essay on the King John Plays: From History to Romance', *ShS(J)* 12 (1973–4) pp. 1–30

Walker, 1991, pp. 169–221

Whall, 1988, pp. 60–96

51   The Life and Repentance of Mary Magdalene

DATE, AUTHORSHIP AND AUSPICES

1550–66 (*SR* 1566/7 *c.* Dec./Jan.); Lewis Wager; offered for acting (for touring players); Greg 47

TEXT AND EDITIONS

Extant originals

1566 printing by John Charlewood: Huntington; *STC* 24932
1567 printing by John Charlewood: BL (two copies, one imp.); *STC* 24932a

Editions

1994   CHD (CD-Rom and online transcription of 1566 Charlewood printing, l.l., OS)

1992   White (OS)*

1914   Farmer (1914a) (facsimile, n.l.)

1908   TFT (facsimile, n.l.)

1902   Carpenter (OS)

SOURCES

The scriptural source is *Luke 7–8*. Calvin's *Institutes of the Christian Religion* may also have been drawn upon; see the introduction to White's edition, pp. xxxii–iv.

CHARACTERS

Prologue	Cupidity	The Law	Repentance
Infidelity	Carnal Concupiscence	Knowledge of Sin	Justification
Mary Magdalene	Simon the Pharisee	Jesus Christ	Love
Pride of Life	Malicious Judgement	Faith	

PLOT SUMMARY

Citing both classical authorities and Scripture, the *Prologue* advocates the learned pursuit of virtue and announces the topic of the play. The action commences with the entry of *Infidelity*, the Vice, singing. He introduces himself in terms of his attachment to Mosaic law and to the seven deadly sins. *Mary* then comes in complaining about her tailor, and *Infidelity* begins ingratiating himself with her by talking about the tricks of tailors and by praising her beauty. He claims to have known her family and says that her noble status demands that she be materially well provided for. She talks about her upbringing by virtuous but indulgent parents and he urges her to use her wealth for worldly pleasure, promising also to introduce her to good companions. When she goes off he reveals his intention to corrupt her, and welcomes his old friends, the Vices *Pride*, *Cupidity* and *Carnal Concupiscence*. He tells them about *Mary* and they each give a description of themselves, detailing the evil they bring about. They are then given new names to disguise their true identities. When *Mary* reappears, *Infidelity* introduces his friends to her under their new names and she kisses them all. They encourage her to be arrogant and to think of herself as a goddess, to be vain and wear make-up, to dress extravagantly, to be boastful about her family connections, and to give herself to sexual pleasure and idle pursuits. She agrees to all this and sings a song with them, before *Infidelity* takes her off to a banquet. *Simon the Pharisee* then enters looking for *Christ*, whom his companion *Malicious Judgement* describes as a blasphemer and friend of sinners. *Simon* sends him to spy on *Christ* and when he meets *Infidelity*, *Malicious Judgement* tells him that *Simon* is intending to invite *Christ* to dinner under pretence of friendship. In turn, *Infidelity* tells him about *Mary* and *Malicious Judgement* invites him to come to the dinner. *Infidelity* now returns to *Mary*, who complains to him that she has found a young man in her bed. They are then confronted by the *Law of God*, who preaches a sermon that pricks *Mary*'s conscience. *Infidelity* attempts to shrug off the preaching by suggesting that women have no souls, but the *Law of God* insists that the doctrine applies to everyone. *Knowledge of Sin* joins him and his exhortations make *Mary* even more aware of her sin. Finally *Christ* himself enters and completes *Mary*'s conversion, driving seven devils from her, and *Infidelity* runs away. *Faith* and *Repentance* enter and together deliver a sermon on their respective qualities, until *Christ* thanks God for the salvation of *Mary*. *Simon* now arrives with *Malicious Judgement* to invite *Christ* to dinner, which he accepts. *Malicious Judgement* vows to prepare the gallows for *Christ*, while *Infidelity* complains bitterly to him about the conversion of *Mary*. *Infidelity* puts on Pharisee's clothing to attend the feast and helps *Malicious Judgement* in its preparation. When *Christ* arrives they question him about his teachings and, as they are about to eat, *Mary* appears with a long lament for her sins. She brings ointment and anoints the feet of *Christ*, at which *Infidelity* and *Malicious Judgement* express outrage to each other that he should allow himself to be touched by a sinner. When he perceives similar doubts in the mind of *Simon*, *Christ* relates the biblical parable of the two debtors. He also points out that *Simon*'s banquet was for motives of self-display, whereas *Mary* has shown true humility. He dismisses *Mary* with an absolution, and when she leaves *Christ* is rounded on by *Malicious Judgement* and *Infidelity* as a blasphemer and consorter with sinners. *Christ* counsels *Simon* to expel both of them from his presence, but when he leaves, *Simon* asks them to follow *Christ* and report on any heretical teaching he might deliver. In a final scene *Mary* re-enters talking to *Justification* and *Love*, who emphasize the value of penitence, faith and the love of God.

PLAY LENGTH

2,138 lines, including a prologue of 86 lines

COMMENTARY

The final scene involving *Justification* and *Love* underlines the play's Protestant orientation. The piece comes close to being a Protestant saint play, though what is emphasized is not the element of miracle, which is a prominent feature of hagiographical drama, but rather redemption through repentance. The casting out of the seven demons is not staged (unlike in the Digby *Mary Magdalen*). Another difference with the Digby play is that no use is made here of the legendary life of Mary Magdalene either. The very Protestant preoccupation with the proper and disciplined upbringing of youth is a significant motif. Other elements of interest include the representation of Simon the Leper as an enemy of Christ, and reference to the idea that women have no souls.

Other conversion plays: **16, 63, 66, 83.**

Other plays featuring prominent women characters: **3, 6, 30, 32, 43, 46, 63, 70, 75, 87, 95, 97.**

SIGNIFICANT TOPICS AND NARRATIVE ELEMENTS

the seven deadly sins; tailors and women's apparel; education and the upbringing of youth; cosmetics and personal ornamentation; extravagance of dress; social ascendancy; sexual dalliance; economic oppression; Mosaic law versus Christian doctrine; the nature of women; Mary in the house of Simon; the parable of the two debtors; the ministry of Christ

DRAMATURGICAL AND RHETORICAL FEATURES

Verbal and general the players solicit money from the audience 43; *Infidelity* gives his name among the Jews as *Mosaical Justice* 107, Vices' aliases: *Pride–Nobility and Honour* 453–4, *Cupidity–Utility* 460, *Carnal Concupiscence–Pleasure* 465, *Infidelity–Legal Justice* 473 (also *Counsel* and *Prudence* 480); the Vices coach *Mary* in coquettish behaviour, dress and appearance 612–830; stage directions in English

Costume and dress *Mary* plays with her garments on entry 142 *sd*; *Mary* wishes to change into other attire 'that according to my birth I may appear' 299–300; *Infidelity* has a garment 'correspondent to my name' (*Legal Justice*) 477, 485; *Infidelity* puts on a gown and cap 490 *sd*; *Mary* 'trims' her clothing 507; *Infidelity* wears garments appropriate to his company 1025–6; *Knowledge of Sin* frightens *Mary* with his horrible appearance 1197–212; *Infidelity* dons a Pharisee's gown (bordered with the Commandments) and cap 1625–30; *Mary* appears 'sadly (soberly) apparelled' 1764 *sd*

Actions and stage directions 142 *sd*: 'Here enters *Ma. M.*, trifling with her garments'; 311–14: *Ma.* kisses *Inf.*; 490 *sd*: '(*Inf.*) Put on a gown and cap'; 526–7: *Ma.* kisses *Inf.*; 530: *Ma.* kisses *Pri., Cu.* and *C. Con.*; 564: *Ma.* kisses *Inf.*; 574: *Inf.* prevents *Pri.* embracing *Ma.*; 577–8: *Ma.* embraces *Inf.*; 618: *Ma.* adopts a pose; 656: *Ma.* blushes; 734: *Infidelity* whispers in *Mary*'s ear; 829: *Mary* embraces the Vices; 898–900: *Ma.* kisses the Vices; 1089: *Inf.* whispers in *Ma.*'s ear; 1289–90: *Inf.* takes *Ma.*'s pulse; 1372 *sd*: '*J. Chr.* speaks to *Ma.*'; 1388 *sd*: '*Inf.* runs away. *Ma.* falls flat down. Cry all thus without the door, and roar terribly'; 1393–7: *Ma.* rises; 1564 *sd*: 'Here enters *Si. the Ph.*, and *Mal. Ju., Si.* bids *Chr.* to dinner'; 1764 *sd*: '*Ma. M.* (enters) sadly apparelled'; 1828 *sd*: 'Let *Ma.* creep under the table, abiding there a certain space behind, and do as it is specified in the Gospel. Then *Mal. Ju.* speaks these words to *Inf.*'; **Simple entry**: *Inf.* 86; *Pri., Cu., C. Con.* 332; *Si., Mal. Ju.* 928; *Kno.* 1188; *Chr.* 1316; *Fa., Rep.* 1414; *Ma., Just.* 2048; *Lo.* 2092; **Simple exit**: (*Ma.*) 312; (*Pri., Cu., C. Con.*) 898; (*Ma., Inf.*) 928; (*Mal. Ju.*) 1074; (*Law*) 1288; (*Ma., Fa., Rep.*) 1540; (*J. Chr.*) 2020; (*Si., Inf., Mal. Ju.*) 2048

Songs and music (w.s. to both songs) 1. *Infidelity* 'With a heigh down down' (scraps) 87–90; 2. *Mary, Infidelity, Pride, Cupidity, Carnal Concupiscence* 'Hey dery dery, with a lusty dery' 869–88 (*Infidelity*–treble, *Cupidity*–bass, *Pride*–mean 861–4)

Staging and set on the title page is stated 'Four may easily play this interlude', but no doubling scheme is offered; the action is mostly localized by the speech and presence of the characters, except for the house of *Simon*, where a banquet is staged (1661–2012), with a table under which *Mary* hides herself (1828 *sd*)

Stage properties *The Law of God*'s tablets 1110; trenchers, spoons, salt and bread 1649; water for *Christ* 1665; a cushion and stool 1669; a table 1670; *Mary*'s ointment 1809

PLACENAMES

Calvary 100; Egypt 1120; Jerusalem 103, 195, 275, 913, 1638; Nain 931, 936

ALLUSIONS

Abraham 1118, 1383; Adam 1188; Cicero, *De Finibus I.xvi* 728–9; King David 1167, 1433; Helen of Troy 874; Horace *Epistles I.xviii.39* 16; Juvenal *Satires V.66* 517, *VI.269* (q.a.) 740–1; Lais 871; St Luke 69; *Luke 7* 60; St Mark 69; Moses 1214, 1341; Ovid, *Amores II.xvi.45* 207; Ovid, *De Arte Amandi II.113* 793–6; Ovid, *Metamorphoses IV.64* 546; Solomon 1165; Thais 873; Valerius Maximus, *Factorum ac dictorum memorabilium IV.vii* 1–2, 9

BIBLIOGRAPHY

Badir, P. '"To allure vnto their loue": Iconoclasm and Striptease in Lewis Wager's *The Life and Repentance of Marie Magdalene*', *TJ* 51:1 (1999) pp. 1–20
Bevington, 1962, pp. 171–5
Blackburn, 1971, pp. 131–6
Happé, P. 'The Protestant Adaptation of the Saint Play' in Davidson, 1986, pp. 205–40
White, P. W. 'Lewis Wager's *Life and Repentaunce of Mary Magdalene* and John Calvin', *N&Q* 28 (1981) pp. 508–12
White, 1993, pp. 80–8

52   Like Will to Like

DATE, AUTHORSHIP AND AUSPICES

1562–8 (*SR* 1568/9 c. Sept.); Ulpian Fulwell; offered for acting, and it seems probable that this is a travelling play; Greg 50

TEXT AND EDITIONS

Extant originals

1568 printing by John Allde: Bodleian; *STC* 11473
post-1568 (?) printing by John Allde: Folger; *STC* 11473.5
1587 printing by Edward Allde: BL; Eliz. Club; Huntington; *STC* 11474

Editions

1994	CHD (CD-Rom and online transcription of 1587 Allde printing, l.l., OS)
1991	Happé, Woudhuysen and Pitcher (facsimile)
1974	Somerset (NS)

1972   Happé (OS)*
1909   TFT (facsimile, n.l.)
1906   Farmer (7) (n.l., NS)
1874–6 Dodsley, vol. III (n.l., NS)

SOURCES

No sources have been identified but the play is part of a tradition of Protestant interludes.

CHARACTERS

Nicol Newfangle (Vice)	Haunce	Good Fame
Devil/Lucifer	Philip Fleming	God's Promises
Tom Collier	Cuthbert Cutpurse	Honour
Tom Tosspot	Pierce Pickpurse	Severity
Rafe Roister	Virtuous Living	Hankin Hangman

PLOT SUMMARY

After the opening 'boast' of the vice, *Newfangle*, *Lucifer* charges him to infect men with a desire for worldliness and to ensure that men stick with people of their own kind. The first companion *Newfangle* finds is for *Lucifer* himself, a dishonest coalman, *Tom Collier*. After their departure *Newfangle* encounters *Tom Tosspot* and *Rafe Roister*, whom he designates as fit companions for each other. He attempts to judge which of the two is the greater knave, but ends up declaring them equal and promising both the 'lands' of St Thomas-a-Watering or Tyburn Hill (both places of execution). The next pair to be teamed up are the drunkards *Haunce*, who dances around drunkenly before falling asleep, and *Peter Fleming*. When they go on their way a pair of thieves enters, *Cuthbert Cutpurse* and *Pierce Pickpurse*, recounting their criminal exploits. *Newfangle* also promises them a piece of land 'of the two legged mare' (unbeknownst to them, implying the gallows). They are briefly joined by *Virtuous Living* who, however, quickly deserts them for his true companions, *Good Fame*, *God's Promises* and *Honour*, and *Honour* crowns *Virtuous Living* before they exit. *Tosspot* and *Roister* then re-enter in a state of destitution brought about by their roistering. *Newfangle* packs them off to a life of begging, in response to which they beat him up and leave him groaning on the ground. He is helped up by a judge, *Severity*, and he in turn assists the judge to capture and tie up *Cutpurse* and *Pickpurse*, who are duly led off to execution by *Hankin Hangman*. Of the remaining pair, *Haunce* and *Fleming*, *Newfangle* relates that they are in a paupers' hospital ill with gout. The *Devil* enters again to carry *Newfangle* off on his back to Spain, while *Virtuous Life*, *Good Fame* and *Honour* enter to conclude the play and offer a prayer for the queen and her government.

PLAY LENGTH

1,243 lines and a song of 36 lines

COMMENTARY

This is one of several proverb plays and proverbial statements are found not only in the title but scattered through the play. There is no single, central humanity figure and the play's action is dominated and orchestrated by the Vice. It is noteworthy that one of the drunkards is identified as a Fleming and the other has a Dutch- or Flemish-sounding name too, as excessive drinking was a vice commonly imputed to people from the Low Countries. The play is one of a number presenting a negative image of immigrants from the Continent.

Other proverb plays: **24, 53, 94.**
Other social ills plays: **15, 24, 38, 40, 53, 71, 72** (frag.), **76, 94, 96, 98, 100.**

SIGNIFICANT TOPICS AND NARRATIVE ELEMENTS

appropriate companionship; education and the upbringing of youth; roistering and financial decline; drinking and drunkenness; criminality and judicial punishment; apparel and fashion; foreigners, especially Flemings; hangman's booty; gambling

DRAMATURGICAL AND RHETORICAL FEATURES

Verbal and general rustic speech: *Tom Collier* 144 ff.; *Newfangle*'s 'catechism' 206–15; drunken behaviour and speech is represented in *Haunce* 449 *sd* ff.; *Virtuous Living*'s coronation by *Honour* 847 *sd*–854; there is final song instead of an epilogue, reflecting on the theme of the play; stage directions in English
Costume and dress the *Devil* has his name (Lucifer) written on his back and breast 76 *sd*; *Tom Tosspot* has a feather in his hat 227 *sd*; *Newfangle*'s dress is 'gay and brave' (well appointed) 333; *Rafe Roister* and *Tom Tosspot* enter in doublet and hose and a night cap 924 *sd*; *Newfangle* and *Hankin* take *Pickpurse*'s and *Cutpurse*'s coats 1158 *sd*
Actions and stage directions 36 *sd*: 'Here enters N. New. the Vice, laughing, and has a knave of clubs in his hand which, as soon as he speaks, he offers unto one of the men or boys standing by'; 70 *sd*: 'Here the *Dev.* enters but speaks not yet'; 76 *sd*: 'This name "Lucifer" must be written on his (*Dev.*'s) back and on his breast'; 78 *sd*: '(*New.*) Pointing to one standing by'; 168 *sd*: 'He (*Luc.*) takes him (*Toss.*) by the hand'; 176 *sd*: 'N. New. must have a gittern or some other instrument, if he may, but if they have none they must dance about the place all three, and sing this song that follows, which must be done [as] though they have an instrument'; 204 *sd*: 'He (*New.*) kneels down'; 227 *sd*: 'T. Toss. comes in with a feather in his hat';

335 sd: 'He (New.) fights'; 340 sd, 345 sd: 'He (New.) fights again'; 449 sd: 'Here enters Hau. with a pot, and sings as follows. He sings the first two lines, and speaks the rest as stammering as may be'; 456 sd: 'He (Hau.) seats him[self] in the chair'; 461 sd: 'He (Hau.) drinks'; 496 sd: 'He (Hau.) dances as evil favoured as may be devised, and in the dancing he falls down, and when he rises he must groan'; 501 sd: 'He (Hau.) rises'; 513 sd: 'Hau. sits in the chair and snorts as though he were fast asleep'; 521 sd: 'P. Fle. enters with a pot in his hand'; 523 sd: 'P. Fle. sings these few lines following'; 566 sd: 'They three (Ha., Fle., Toss.) are gone together, and N. New. remains behind, but he must not speak till they be within'; 599 sd: 'Here enters C. Cut. and P. Pic., C. Cut. must have in his hand a purse of money or counters in it, and a knife in one hand and a whetstone in the other, and Pierce must have money or counters in his hand and jingle it as he comes in'; 743 sd: 'Exeunt they three (New., Pic., Cut.). They sing this song as they go out from the place'; 757 sd: 'When this is spoken he (V. Liv.) must pause and say as follows'; 847 sd: 'V. Liv. sits down in the chair; 850: Hon. crowns V. Liv.; 877 sd: 'They (V. Liv., G. Pro., Hon.) sing this song following. This must be sung after every verse'; 894 sd: 'Go out all (V. Liv., G. Pro., Hon.). Here enters N. New. and brings in with him a bag, a staff, a bottle and two halters, going about the place showing it to the audience, and singing this'; 895 sd: 'He (New.) may sing this as oft as he thinks good'; 924 sd: 'Here enters R. Roi. and T. Toss. in their doublet and hose, and no cap nor hat on their head, saving a night cap because the strings of the beards may not be seen, and R. Roi. must curse and swear ('ban') as he comes in'; 963 sd: 'He (New.) gives the bag to R. Roi., and the bottle to T. Toss.'; 1030 sd: 'R. Roi. beats him (New.) with the staff, and T. Toss. with the bottle'; 1037 sd: 'They (Roi., Toss.) have him (New.) down and beat him. He cries for help'; 1041 sd: 'R. Roi.and T. Toss. go out, and Sev. the Judge enters. N. New. lies on the ground groaning'; 1075 sd: 'He (New.) rises'; 1111 sd: 'He (New.) puts about each of their (Cut., Pic.) necks a halter'; 1120 sd: 'He (New.) helps to tie them (Cut., Pic.)'; 1158 sd: 'They (Cut., Pic.) take off their coats and divide them'; 1166 sd: 'Hank. goes out and leads the one in his right hand, and the other in his left (Cut., Pic.) having halters about their necks'; 1212 sd: 'He (New.) rides away on the Dev.'s back. Here enter V. Liv. and Hon.'; **Simple entry**: Col. 136; Roi. 273; V. Liv. 665; G. Fa. 795; G. Pro., Hon. 832; Cut., Pic. 1085; Hank. 1154; Dev. 1202; G. Fa. 1228; **Simple exit**: Col. 193; Luc. 219; Roi. 469; G. Fa. 864; 'All' (G. Fa., G. Pro., Hon.) 894; (Sev.) 1121

Songs and music (w.s. to all): 1. Newfangle, Collier, Lucifer 'Tom Collier of Croydon hath sold his coals' 177–88; 2. Haunce 'Quas in hart and quas again, and quas about the house' 450–55; 3. Phillip Fleming 'Troll the bole and drink to me, and troll the bole again-a' 524–7; 4. Newfangle, Cutpurse, Pickpurse 'Good hostess, lay a crab in the fire, and broil a mess of sous-a' 744–9; 5. God's Promises, Honour, Virtuous Living 'Life is but short, hope not therein' (with a refrain to be sung after every verse) 878–94; 6. Newfangle 'Trim merchandise, trim trim' (a jingle only, see 895 sd) 895; 7. Final song (whole cast?) 'Where like to like is matched so' 1243–79; **Instrumental**: first song (and others?) accompanied by a gittern or other instrument 176 sd

Staging and set the action is unlocalized and there are no indications as to set
Stage properties *Newfangle*'s playing card 36 *sd*; *Haunce*'s and *Fleming*'s pots 449
sd, 521 *sd*; a chair 456 *sd*; *Cuthbert*'s purse, knife and whetstone, and *Pierce*'s money
or counters 599 *sd*; *Honour*'s sword and crown 848–9; *Newfangle*'s bag, staff, bottle
and two halters 894 *sd*; *Newfangle*'s rope ('string') 917; *Roister*'s bag and *Tosspot*'s
bottle 963 *sd*; *Roister*'s staff 1030 *sd*

PLACENAMES

Calais 211; Croydon 175, 177; England 143, 254, 257, 545, 648; Flanders 557; France
491, 557; London 1079; Salisbury Plain 428; Spain 1212; St Thomas-a-Watering
383, 391; Tyburn Hill 383, 391; Walsingham (shrine) 97

ALLUSIONS

St Augustine *De Civitatis Dei* 758; Balaam 1181; Cicero ('Tully') 679, 1052;
Cicero ('Tully') *De Amicitia* 1; Haman and Mordecai 359–65; Isidore of Seville 1048;
Matthew 11:38 820; Phalaris 351–5

BIBLIOGRAPHY

Adams, 1943, pp. 63–6
Bevington, 1962, pp. 155–8
Brown, 1999, pp. 56–68
Jones, R. C. 'Jonson's *Staple of News* Gossips and Fulwell's *Like Will to Like*: "The Old Way" in a "New"
    Morality Play', *YES* 3 (1973) pp. 74–7
Mackenzie, 1914, pp. 180–7
Neuss, 1984, pp. 1–18
Sabol, A. J. 'A Three-Man Song in Fulwell's *Like Will to Like* at the Folger', *Renaissance News* 10 (1957)
    pp. 139–42

53   The Longer Thou Livest the More Fool Thou Art

DATE, AUTHORSHIP AND AUSPICES

1559–68 (*SR* 1568/9 *c.* Apr.); William Wager; offered for acting; Greg 53

TEXT AND EDITIONS

Extant originals

1569 printing by William How for Richard Jones: BL; *STC* 24935

Editions

SOURCES

No sources have been identified, but this is a play about errant youth in the 'Christian Terence' tradition; see Spengler, 1888, for an account of this tradition.

CHARACTERS

Prologue	Exercitation	Fortune	People
Moros	Idleness	Ignorance	God's Judgement
Discipline	Incontinence	Impiety	Confusion
Piety	Wrath	Cruelty	

PLOT SUMMARY

The *Prologue* stresses the value of a good education, especially for the children of the ruling class, and cites the subject of the play, *Moros*, as a negative example. When *Moros* then enters singing idle songs taught to him by a servant, *Discipline* upbraids him, but his teachings and those of the other Virtues, *Piety* and *Exercitation*, have no effect on the reprobate young man, despite a beating. They give up and he is soon joined by the Vices *Idleness*, *Incontinence* and *Wrath*, whose companionship proves much more congenial to him. *Moros* swaggeringly prepares to take on *Discipline*. However, when he does arrive *Moros* runs and hides on recognizing his erstwhile instructor, and *Discipline* delivers a sermon on the laxity of parents. He goes off and is succeeded on stage by *Fortune* who talks of her power over the fates of men. She encounters *Incontinence* who tells her about *Moros*, whom she perversely resolves to endow with material wealth despite his folly. They leave and *Piety* enters to bemoan *Moros*'s dissolute ways, but *Wrath* comes along to taunt him about *Moros*'s enrichment by *Fortune*. When *Piety* leaves, *Ignorance* comes in looking for *Moros* and *Wrath* goes off to fetch him. Soon, however, *Moros* enters dressed colourfully and accompanied by *Cruelty* and *Impiety*. *Ignorance* and the other Vices warn him against the influence of *Discipline* and the other Virtues, at which he readily embraces their suggestions for a life of revelry and depravity. *Discipline* at length returns to confront *Moros* and exhort him to virtue, but he proves recalcitrant, especially as he now claims responsibility for himself as an adult, and he goes off with *Ignorance*. *Discipline* complains that folly in the ruling class has detrimental consequences in the realm, and when he leaves *People* enters to cite instances of the sort of abuses in society of which *Discipline* has been talking.

On his departure *Moros* comes in as an old man with an aggressive manner, but he is confronted with his evil deeds by *God's Judgement*, who strikes him down. *Confusion* then comes in foully dressed and, on the order of *God's Judgement*, despoils *Moros* of his good clothing, puts a fool's coat on him, and eventually carries him off to the Devil. *God's Judgement*, followed by *Exercitation*, *Piety* and *Discipline*, draw moral conclusions from *Moros*'s life and fate until they conclude the play by offering prayers for the queen and council.

PLAY LENGTH

1,988 lines

COMMENTARY

This is an 'upbringing of youth' play clearly aimed at the elite, as the title page advertises that it is especially pertinent 'for such as are like to come to dignity and promotion' and the prologue stresses the value of education particularly for those who 'are like to have gubernation'. The central figure ages in the course of the play, and his life ends without redemption. He is orientated towards vice from the start, being constructed around Protestant notions of predestination, and there is no real sense of his being corrupted by the Vices. These thus tend to fulfil the role of vicious companions.

Other Protestant and anti-Catholic plays: **14, 24, 44, 45, 49, 50, 58, 66, 85, 86** (frag.), **90, 93**.

Other youth and education plays: **21, 33, 56, 58, 61, 62, 64, 67, 68, 73** (frag.), **101, 103, 104**.

Other social ills plays: **2, 15, 24, 38, 40, 52, 71, 72** (frag.), **76, 94, 96, 98, 100**.

Other proverb plays: **24, 52, 94**.

SIGNIFICANT TOPICS AND NARRATIVE ELEMENTS

education and the upbringing of youth; a well-born fool; bad companions; slang terms; the vicissitudes of fortune; braggadocio and cowardice; a satire of Catholicism and scholasticism; the ages of man; wealth and responsibility; corruption in the social and economic life of the realm

DRAMATURGICAL AND RHETORICAL FEATURES

Verbal and general *Discipline*'s teaching passage with Latin sayings and English translations 126–41; *Moros* mindlessly repeats the words of *Discipline* and *Exercitation* 340–75; *Moros* mangles the names of *Discipline* and *Piety* (and later *Exercitation*) 497–507; Vices' aliases: *Idleness–Pastime* 683, *Incontinence–Pleasure*

686, *Wrath–Manhood* 688, *Impiety–Philosophy* 1262–3, *Cruelty–Prudence* 1264, *Ignorance–Antiquity* 1264; *Moros* mangles the Vices' names 755–6, 806, 1310–25; *Moros* tests for pitch before the song 888–93; *Moros* mangles the Vices' teaching 978–85; *Fortune*'s speech describing herself 1038–69; *People*'s alphabetical and alliterative list of corrupt social types 1715–34; stage directions in English

Costume and dress *Moros* is 'gaily disguised with a foolish beard' 1292 *sd*; *Moros* gets a feather for his cap 1541–3; *Moros* wears his clothes in an 'unseemly' fashion, hanging all to one side 1564–5; *Moros*'s grey beard 1742 *sd*; *God's Judgement* has 'a terrible visure' 1758 *sd*; *Confusion* has 'an ill-favoured visure and all things beside ill favoured' 1806 *sd*; *Confusion* takes away *Moros*'s good clothing and gives him a fool's coat 1819–21

Actions and stage directions 70 *sd*: 'Here enters *Mo.*, counterfeiting a vain gesture and a foolish countenance [and] singing the foot of many songs as fools were wont'; 339 *sd*: '(*Mo.*) Say after him (*Di.*)'; 375 *sd*: '(*Di.*, *Pi.*, *Ex.*) Hold and him (*Mo.*) and beat him'; 388 *sd*: '(*Di.*) Repeat them (lessons) again'; 432 *sd*: 'Here let *Mo.* between every sentence say, "Gay gear", "good stuff", "very well", "fin-ado", with such mockish terms'; 515 *sd*: 'Go before him and yet say' (unclear *sd* because of two missing lines); 535 *sd*: 'Between whiles let *Mo.* put in his head'; 593 *sd*: '(*Mo.*) Cry without the door, making the noise of beating'; 694 *sd*: 'Here enters *Mo.* looking upon a book and oftentimes look behind him'; 702 *sd*: '(*Mo.*) Read as fondly as you can devise. Laugh all three (*Wra.*, *Inc.*, *Id.*) at his reading'; 750 *sd*: '*Mo.* take them (*Wra.*, *Inc.*, *Id.*) by the hand'; 769 *sd*: '(*Id.* Have a pair of cards ready'; 782 *sd*: '(*Mo.*) Make a curtsey backward'; 835 *sd*: '(*Mo.*) Flourish with your sword'; 948 *sd*: 'Let *Mo.* let fall his sword and hide him'; 1085 *sd*: '(*Inc.*) Semble a going out'; 1292 *sd*: '*Mo.* enter gaily disguised and with a foolish beard'; 1512 *sd*: '(*Mo.*, *Ign.*, *Cru.*, *Imp.*) Sing some merry song'; 1551 *sd*: '(*Mo.*) Look upward to see the feather. Stumble and fall'; 1742 *sd*: '(*Mo.*) Enter furiously with a grey beard'; 1752 *sd*: '(*Mo.*) Fight alone'; 1758 *sd*: '(*Go. Ju.*) Enter with a terrible visure'; 1791 *sd*: '(*Go. Ju.*) Strike *Mo.* and let him fall down'; 1806 *sd*: 'Enter *Con.* with an ill-favoured visure and all things besides ill-favoured'; **Simple entry:** *Ex.*202; *Id.* 581; *Inc.* 605; *Wra.* 635; *Di.* 945; *Di.* 1576; *Pe.* 1684; 'All three' (*Di.*, *Pi.*, *Ex.*) 1890; **Simple exit:** *Pi.*, *Mo.* 521; 'Both' (*Ex.*, *Di.*) 581; *Inc.* 911; 'All three' (*Mo.*, *Wra.*, *Id.*) 1005; (*Di.*) 1037; 'Both' (*Fo.*, *Inc.*) 1164; *Wra.* 1272; 'Both' (*Cru.*, *Imp.*) 1524; 'Both' (*Mo.*, *Ign.*) 1664; (*Di.*) 1684; *Pe.* 1742; (*Go. Ju.*) 1890

Songs and music 1. *Moros* 'Broom, broom on a hill' (w.s., 'the foot of many songs') 71–101; 2. *Moros*, *Idleness*, *Incontinence*, *Wrath* 'I have a pretty titmouse' (w.s.) 898–913; 3. *Moros*, *Ignorance*, *Cruelty*, *Impiety* ('some merry song', w.n.s.) 1512 *sd*

Staging and set the action is unlocalized and, aside from a reference to a door (593 *sd*) there are no indications as to set

Stage properties *Moros*'s book 694 *sd*; *Idleness*'s cards 769 *sd*; *Idleness*'s dice 788; a sword 830; a dagger 831; a feather 1541–3; *Moros*'s chain and staff 1821

PLACENAMES

Eastcheap 252; England 1027; St Katherine's (hospital in London) 252; Kent 78, 80, 82; London 1032; St Nicholas parish 251

ALLUSIONS

Aristophanes 1; Aristotle 1915; Arius 297; St Augustine, *City of God* 1919; Cicero ('Tully') 1915; *Ezekiel 16:18* 1901; Hercules 1896; Robin Hood 954, 966, 1474; Isaiah 1010; King Midas 1827; St Paul 1404; Pericles 2; Plato 1915; *Psalm 13:1* (V)/*14:1*(AV) 1610–11; Solomon 1816, 1941; Theophylactus, Archbishop of Achrida 1899; Valerius Maximus 1915; Valerius Maximus, *De factorum dictorum quoque memorabilium exemplis* 1–14

BIBLIOGRAPHY

Bevington, 1962, pp. 91–9, 163–5
Dillon, 1998, pp. 132–40
Eccles, 1981, pp. 258–62
Farnham, 1936, pp. 234–9
Mackenzie, 1914, pp. 131–7
Southern, 1973, pp. 474–81

54   (The Play of) Love

DATE, AUTHORSHIP AND AUSPICES

1520s or early 1530s; John Heywood; possibly for performance at Inns of Court revels; Greg 16

TEXT AND EDITIONS

Extant originals

1534 printing by William Rastell: Pepys; BL (frag.); *STC* 13303
c. 1550 printing by William Copland for John Waley: Bodleian (no t.p.); *STC* 13304

Editions

1994   CHD (CD-Rom and online transcription of Rastell printing, l.l., OS)
1991   Axton and Happé (OS)*
1979   LaRosa (OS)
1977   Somerset, Mares and Proudfoot (facsimile)
1974   Somerset (NS)

1944   Cameron (OS)
1937   De la Bère (n.l., OS)
1909   TFT (facsimile, n.l.)
1905   Farmer (1) (n.l., NS)
1898   Brandl (OS)

SOURCES

The play may owe something to the French love debate tradition, though no specific source has been identified; see the introduction to the edition by Axton and Happé, pp. 45–7. See also the introduction to LaRosa's edition, pp. xviii–cxxxi, for a discussion of the humanist and dramatic traditions that inform the play, and Maxwell, 1946, for a suggestion that it may bear some relationship to the fifteenth-century collection, *Le Jardin de plaisance*.

CHARACTERS

A Man a Lover not Beloved (Lover-not-loved)
A Man a Lover and Beloved (Lover-loved)
A Woman Beloved not Loving (Loved-not-loving)
The Vice Neither Lover nor Beloved (No-lover-nor-loved)

PLOT SUMMARY

Lover-not-loved complains of his great grief in not having his love for a woman of great beauty requited, whereas *Loved-not-loving* argues that her pain in being loved by someone whose feelings she cannot return is equal. They are unable to resolve the debate about who suffers most, and go out to find someone who is able to judge impartially the measure of their pain. *Lover-loved* then enters with a song and declares that lovers are to be commended for the fact that they are unable to conceal their feelings and thus dissemble. He is joined by the jaunty Vice, *No-lover-nor-loved*, and they commence a debate about which enjoys the more pleasant situation, each claiming it for themselves. They, too, fail to resolve their disagreement and also decide that they need an independent judge. Then *Lover-loved* leaves and *No-lover-nor-loved* delivers a long speech in which he tells of having once feigned to woo a woman. When he was convinced she was in love with him, he discovered that she was being unfaithful to him, and concluded that it was futile to try to be more wily than a woman. He decides to play a trick on the *Lover-loved* to remedy his besottedness. The *Lover-loved* then re-enters, followed shortly by *Lover-not-loved* and *Loved-not-loving* who explain their need for a judge. *Lover-loved* suggests that each pair should judge the other's case. They each then present their cases but, before judgement can be given, *No-lover-nor-loved* suddenly departs and comes running in again with squibs shouting that a fire has destroyed the house of *Lover-loved*'s mistress. *Lover-loved* runs out, only to return when he realizes it is a trick. *No-lover-nor-loved* claims victory saying his lie would have been ineffective had *Lover-loved* not been in the grip of love, but *Lover-loved* replies that without pain there can be no pleasure. The two pairs then adjudge the other to be equal in pleasure or pain, resolving that each should be contented with his lot and should seek to love God.

PLAY LENGTH

1,577 lines

COMMENTARY

This is a complicated disputation or debate play involving two pairs of opposing positions. It is not, as many such debates are, structured so that the invalidity of one position provides a foil for the veracity of the other. Rather, there is recognition of the complexities present in human amorous relations. The 'Vice' is one of the debaters and his position of Vice is largely determined by his role in attempting deception through a trick and involvement with pyrotechnics, though he is also the most cynical of the four. The play's incorporation of several legal terms has a satirical thrust.

Other debate plays: **28, 29, 31, 69, 99, 102.**

SIGNIFICANT TOPICS AND NARRATIVE ELEMENTS

the nature of women; fidelity; the administration of justice; the complexities of love

DRAMATURGICAL AND RHETORICAL FEATURES

Verbal and general *No-lover-nor-loved*'s alliterative list of types of women 351–62; *No-lover-nor-loved*'s descriptive love lyric 427–70; considerable use of legal terminology and the play has a debate structure; few stage directions, all in English
Costume and dress the Vice's 'coppintank' hat 1297 *sd*
Actions and stage directions 245 *sd*: 'Here they (*Bel.-n.-l., L.-n.- loved*) go both out and the *L.-beloved* enters with a song'; 1297 *sd*: 'Here the Vi. comes in running suddenly about the place among the audience with a high coppintank on his head full of squibs crying "Water, water, fire, fire, fire, water, water, fire" till the fire in the squibs be spent'; **Simple entry:** *Bel.-n.-l.* 63; *N.-l.-nor.l.* 301; *L-loved* 690; *L.-n.-loved, Bel.-n.-l.* 697; **Simple exit:** *L-loved* 398; *L-loved* 1335
Songs and music *Lover-loved* 245 *sd* (w.n.s.)
Staging and set this is a debate play with little action and no indications as to set
Stage properties squibs 1297 *sd*

PLACENAMES

St Saviour's (church) 425; Westminster Hall 1424

ALLUSIONS

St Catherine of Alexandria 467

BIBLIOGRAPHY

Bolwell, 1921, pp. 85–90

Greg, W. W. 'An Unknown Edition of Heywood's *Play of Love*', *Archiv* 106 (1901) pp. 141–3

Johnson, 1970, pp. 69–71, 75–81

Maxwell, 1946, pp. 102–3

Mullini, R. 'Il dibattito sull'amore in *A Play of Love* di John Heywood', in Papetti and Visconti, 1997, pp. 67–83.

Schoeck, R. J. 'Satire of Wolsey in Heywood's *Play of Love*', *N&Q* 196 (1951) pp. 112–14

Schoeck, R. J. 'A Common Tudor Expletive and Legal Parody in Heywood's *Play of Love*', *N&Q* 201 (1956) pp. 375–6

Schoeck, R. J. 'Heywood's Case of Love: A Legal Reading of John Heywood's *Play of Love*', *SN* 39:2 (1967) pp. 284–301

Southern, 1973, pp. 231–5

Walker, 1998, pp. 85–9

55   Love Feigned and Unfeigned (fragment)

DATE, AUTHORSHIP AND AUSPICES

1540–60; anonymous; auspices unknown

TEXT AND EDITIONS

Extant originals

Manuscript: British Library MS I.B.2172

Editions

1994   CHD (CD-Rom and online copy of Esdaile and Greg, 1907, l.l., OS)

1907   Esdaile and Greg (OS)*

SOURCES

No sources have been identified.

CHARACTERS

Familiarity   Love Unfeigned   Falsehood   Love Feigned   Fellowship

PLOT SUMMARY

Love Unfeigned is introduced to *Fellowship* by *Familiarity*, and he expresses satisfaction at having two such companions to help him withstand vice. He represents virtuous love without cruelty and he cites various biblical authorities on the value of pure love. When the trio departs, *Falsehood* enters boasting of his power to deceive and he is shortly joined by *Love Feigned*. They resolve to corrupt *Fellowship*, who thereupon makes his appearance. They feign sorrow that he has been mixing with what they deem to be unprofitable companions and they start instructing him in the ways of deceit and hypocrisy. They suggest that *Love Unfeigned* and *Familiarity* are only interested in using their friendship with him to acquire his lands by trickery. *Fellowship* is won over by these arguments and he joins them in a song, after which they go off to a banquet, intending to spare no expense. Here the fragment ends.

PLAY LENGTH

243 lines extant

COMMENTARY

This fragment of an interlude about the dangers of evil friendship refers to scriptural writing in ways that suggest it is Protestant in orientation. Though it takes a moral approach, there is also present an economic dimension in the concern about the dangers to heirs from unscrupulous companions. The choice between the paths of virtue and vice is not as clear-cut in this play as it is in many other moral interludes.

SIGNIFICANT TOPICS AND NARRATIVE ELEMENTS

biblical writings on love; good and bad friendship; the gulling of heirs

DRAMATURGICAL AND RHETORICAL FEATURES

Verbal and general extant stage directions in English except 228 (*sd*)
Actions and stage directions 228 (*sd*): 'They (*Fel., Fal. L. Fei.*) sing' (L); **Simple entry**: *L. Unf.* 5; *Fal.* 73; *L. Fei.* 105; *Fel.* 120; **Simple exit**: (*L. Unf., Fel., Fam.*) 73; (*Fel., Fal.*) 243
Songs and music *Fellowship, Falsehood, Love Feigned* 'Sing we sing we, with joyful heart' (w.s.) 229–36

PLACENAMES

Corinth 42; 'St Quintin's Hall' (?) 171

ALLUSIONS

Ecclesiasticus (V) *13:19* 52; Jacob and Esau 211–12; St John, *3rd Epistle* 49; St Paul 41; St Peter 50; Rebecca 211; Solomon 51, 79, 175; Solomon, *Proverbs 1:7* 79; Solomon, *Sapientia* (V) 80

BIBLIOGRAPHY

Daw, B. '*Love Feyned and Unfeyned* and the English Anabaptists', *PMLA* 32:2 (1917) pp. 267–91
Scragg, L. L. '*Love Feigned and Unfeigned*: A Note on the use of Allegory on the Tudor Stage', *ELN* 3:4 (1966) pp. 248–52

56   Lucidus and Dubius (fragment)

DATE, AUTHORSHIP AND AUSPICES

mid-fifteenth-century dialogue, anonymous; possibly for school performance

TEXT AND EDITIONS

Extant originals

Manuscript: Winchester College MS 33, fos.54v–64v

EDITIONS

1979   Davis (facsimile and transcription)*

SOURCES

The writer appears to draw on the *Elucidarium* of Honorius of Autun, and other texts based on it; see Lee's essay noted below.

CHARACTERS

Lucidus   Dubius

PLOT SUMMARY

Lucidus, a doctor of law and divinity, opens the dialogue with an address to the audience, before he is approached by *Dubius* who asks him a series of questions about the creation of man and about the fall of man and Lucifer. *Dubius* informs him that he had been *Lucidus*'s pupil as a boy and expresses resentment about the fact that the master had beaten him. *Lucidus* replies that the punishment was given because *Dubius* did not take his studies seriously enough. *Dubius*, however, wishes to get revenge by posing a question which *Lucidus* will not be able to answer, and asks how Judas could be deemed culpable in betraying Christ if this helped to bring about the Crucifixion, thus fulfilling God's purpose. *Lucidus* responds that Judas's covetousness in accepting the silver made him guilty. *Dubius* asks further questions about the Crucifixion, Christ's sacrifice and other doctrinal matters in the hope of tripping *Lucidus* up, but this simply affords *Lucidus* the opportunity for doctrinal teaching and exposition. The fragment ends with his explanation that absolution is not affected by the moral state of the administering priest, since it comes from Christ and not the cleric.

PLAY LENGTH

612 lines extant, excluding Latin quotations of around 13 lines

COMMENTARY

The nature of this dialogue suggests that it was written for educational contexts. Its interest in the topic of education is something that occurs repeatedly in later interludes. It is really an opportunity for doctrinal exposition rather than a true debate. There is nothing dramatic in it, but the idea of an errant pupil trying to trick his master enlivens the didactic project of the dialogue. It may be a companion piece to the dialogue that follows it in the Winchester manuscript, *Occupation and Idleness* (**68**).

   Other youth and education plays: **21, 33, 53, 58, 61, 62, 64, 67, 68, 73** (frag.), **101, 103, 104**.

SIGNIFICANT TOPICS AND NARRATIVE ELEMENTS

the creation of man; the fall of man; the doctrine of the fortunate fall; the nature of paradise; the envy of Satan; punishment and the upbringing of youth; the Crucifixion; original sin; the inviolability of the sacraments; sinful priests

DRAMATURGICAL AND RHETORICAL FEATURES

Verbal and general this is a dialogue with no action and no stage directions
Costume and dress *Lucidus* wears a 'great hood' 332
Staging and set the action is unlocalized and there are no indications as to set

PLACENAMES

Bath (?) 325 ('a child of Bathe' – proverbial?)

ALLUSIONS

NOTE: Quotations are not included in line numbering, and are marked +
Acts 5:29 593+; Adam 97 *passim*; Eve 113, 177, 185, 429, 443; Judas 353, 356, 358, 361, 365, 367+; *Matthew 23:2–3* 593+; Moses 593+; *Romans 8:32* (q.a.) 350+

BIBLIOGRAPHY

Davis, 1969, pp. 461–72
Lee, B. S. '*Lucidus and Dubius*: A Fifteenth-Century Theological Debate and its Sources', *MÆ* 45:1 (1976) pp. 79–96

57   (The Play of) Lucrece (fragment)

DATE, AUTHORSHIP AND AUSPICES

early sixteenth century, anonymous, auspices unknown; Greg 1

TEXT AND EDITIONS

Extant originals

c. 1530 printing possibly by John Rastell: BL (frag.: two leaves); *STC* 17778

Editions

1994   CHD (CD-Rom and online copy of Greg, 1908, l.l., OS)*
1908   Greg (OS)*
1905   Bang and McKerrow (facsimile)*

SOURCES

Buonaccorso da Montemagno's *De vera nobilitate* (*c.* 1428), translated by John Tiptoft and printed by Caxton in 1481, is a possible source, but the play also probably bears some relationship to Medwall's version, *Fulgens and Lucres*, as it has besides Cornelius and Lucrece the servant B, who appears to occupy a similarly dominant role to the servants in Medwall's play.

CHARACTERS

B   Publius Cornelius   Lucrece

PLOT SUMMARY

The fragment opens with B talking to *Cornelius*, whom he advises that it is beneath his dignity to wait for the people they are expecting but rather that he should withdraw and reappear after their arrival. *Cornelius* tells B to commend him to *Lucrece* when she arrives and B asks for a 'token' so that *Lucrece* can be assured that the messenger does come from *Cornelius*. By way of providing the token, *Cornelius* relates an anecdote of *Lucrece* and himself walking in her garden, when she asked him to see if he could scare away a bird. As he had no stone to throw she gave him her must ball which he threw into the hole of a hollow tree. The story over, he departs and B goes off to *Lucrece*, declaring *Cornelius*'s love for her and saying that his master had related to him several anecdotes as tokens. The fragment breaks off with *Lucrece* enquiring as to what they are.

PLAY LENGTH

132 lines extant

COMMENTARY

This is a version of the Fulgens and Lucrece story and the fragment centres on the use of anecdotes (possibly emphasizing intimacy) as love tokens. The servant figure apparently plays a major part in the proceedings and here he gives his master a lesson in social strategy and etiquette before going off to become his go-between.
   Other marriage quest plays: **29, 47, 61, 62, 101.**
   Other wooing plays: **6, 75, 84, 87.**
   Other plays with classical settings: **19, 29, 39, 43, 91, 92.**

SIGNIFICANT TOPICS AND NARRATIVE ELEMENTS

wooing and courtship; social precedence and manners; love-tokens; go-betweens

DRAMATURGICAL AND RHETORICAL FEATURES

Verbal and general the servant as romantic go-between; the anecdote as an identifying token 50–76; stage directions in Latin
Actions and stage directions 88 *sd*: 'And *Cor.* shall go out'; 102 *sd*: '*Lu.* enters'
Staging and set the action is unlocalized and there are no indications as to set

BIBLIOGRAPHY

Creizenach, W. 'Die Quelle des *Play of Lucrece*', *JDSG* 47 (1911) pp. 200–1

58   Lusty Juventus

DATE, AUTHORSHIP AND AUSPICES

1547–53 (*SR* 14 Aug. 1560); Richard Wever; offered for acting; Greg 41

TEXT AND EDITIONS

Extant originals

c. 1550 (?) printing by John Wyer for Abraham Vele: Bodleian; *STC* 25148
c. 1565 printing by John Awdley: BL; Huntington (imp.); *STC* 25149
c. 1565 (?) printing by William Copland (in Lothbury): BL; Huntington; Pforzheimer; *STC* 25149.5

Editions

1994	CHD (CD-Rom and online transcription of Copland printing, l.l., OS)
1982	Thomas (OS)
1974	Somerset (NS)*
1971	Nosworthy (OS)
1914	Farmer (1914a) (facsimile, n.l.)
1907	TFT (facsimile, n.l.)
1905	Farmer (2) (n.l., NS)
1874–6	Dodsley, vol. ii (n.l., NS)

SOURCES

No sources have been identified, but the play is part of a range of Protestant interludes on youth which owe something to the continental Christian Terence tradition; see Spengler, 1888, for an account of this tradition.

CHARACTERS

Messenger (Prologue)	Knowledge	Fellowship
Lusty Juventus (Youth)	The Devil	Abominable Living
Good Counsel	Hypocrisy	God's Merciful Promises

PLOT SUMMARY

The *Messenger* delivers the prologue, partly a sermon on the frailty of youth and partly an account of the play's narrative. *Lusty Juventus* then enters singing about the pleasures of youth and seeking merry company. He meets *Good Counsel*, who converts him to piety, after which they are joined by *Knowledge*, who coaches *Juventus* further in religion with a distinctly Protestant slant. They then all quit the stage and the *Devil* enters complaining of his loss of power because the young are following Scripture rather than the old (Catholic) tradition. He enlists the help of his 'son' *Hypocrisy* in the project of perverting *Juventus*. Calling himself *Friendship*, *Hypocrisy* accosts *Juventus* who is on his way to hear a sermon. Despite initial resistance, *Juventus* is at last won over by *Hypocrisy*'s Catholic and fleshly blandishments, at which point they are joined by *Fellowship*, whom *Hypocrisy* introduces as a fit companion. They immediately start talking about a whore who soon joins them. Although addressed by *Hypocrisy* as *Unknown Honesty*, she is in fact *Abominable Living*. She flirts with *Juventus*, who kisses her twice, and the companions all sing a song together before going off. *Good Counsel* reappears and laments the fall of *Juventus*, who re-enters shortly after. *Good Counsel* reproves him at length, which makes *Juventus* fall into despair. However, *God's Merciful Promises* enters to promise him forgiveness and grace, and *Juventus* recovers to deliver a sermon on the snares of the flesh and the *Devil*. He concludes the play by praying for the nobility of the realm.

PLAY LENGTH

1,168 lines

COMMENTARY

This is probably the first fully extant native play on the theme of youthful prodigality. No parental figures are present, however, and the youth character enters with an existing predilection for fleshly pleasure. There is a strong anti-Catholic bias in the interlude, and at one point Catholic practices are listed in a way that stresses their superstitious nature. The play has a simple narrative scheme of a single fall and redemption. Lines from the interlude in adapted form occur in the play of *Sir Thomas More* (c. 1594).

Other youth and education plays: **21, 33, 53, 56, 61, 62, 64, 67, 68, 73** (frag.), **101, 103, 104.**

Other Protestant and anti-Catholic plays: **14, 24, 44, 45, 49, 50, 53, 66, 85, 86** (frag.), **90, 93.**

SIGNIFICANT TOPICS AND NARRATIVE ELEMENTS

education and the rearing of youth; the Devil's trickery; Protestant versus Catholic doctrine; bad companionship; Catholic superstition; relics; whores and sexual dalliance

DRAMATURGICAL AND RHETORICAL FEATURES

Verbal and general *Hypocrisy*'s Skeltonic list of Catholic superstitions, repeating 'holy' 408–43; the Vices' aliases: *Hypocrisy–Friendship* 484, *Abominable Living–Unknown Honesty* 518; stage directions in English
Actions and stage directions 36 *sd*: 'Here enters L. *Juv.*, or *Yo.*, singing as follows'; 69 *sd*: 'Here enters G. *Cou.* to whom *Yo.* yet speaks'; 155 *sd*: 'He (*Juv.*) kneels'; 162 *sd*: 'He (*Juv.*) rises'; 276: G. *Cou.* gives *Juv.* a copy of the New Testament; 530 *sd*: 'Here enters *Yo.* to whom *Hyp.* yet speaks'; 817 *sd*: 'He (*Juv.*) kisses (*Ab. Li.*)'; 844 *sd*: 'He (*Juv.*) kisses (*Ab. Li.*)'; 883 *sd*: 'They (*Juv.*, *Hyp.*, *Ab. Li.*, *Fell.*) sing as follows'; 1011 *sd*: 'He (*Juv.*) lies down'; 1067 *sd*: 'He (*Juv.*) rises'; **Simple entry:** *Kno.* 166; *Dev.* 323; *Hyp.* 358; *Fell.* 716; G. *Cou.* 901; *Juv.* 936; G. *M. Pr.* 1045; **Simple exit:** (G. *Cou.*) 319; (*Kno.*) 321; (*Juv.*) 323; (*Dev.*) 488; (*Hyp.*, *Ab. Li.*, *Juv.*) 901; **Simple speech:** *Juv.* 48
Songs and music (w.s. to both songs) 1. *Lusty Juventus* 'In a herber green asleep where as I lay' 37–48; 2. *Juventus, Hypocrisy, Abominable Living, Fellowship* 'Why should not youth fulfil his own mind?' 884–901 (w. ref.)
Staging and set the title page gives a direction on doubling: 'four may play it easily, taking such parts as they think best; so that any one take of those parts that be not in place at once'; the action is unlocalized and there are no indications as to set
Stage properties a book for the New Testament 276

PLACENAMES

Flanders 388

ALLUSIONS

King David 194; *Deuteronomy 29:10–11* 104; *Ecclesiasticus 30:1–15* (V) 5; *Ezekiel 18:32* 1050, *33:9* 1046–7; *Genesis 8:21* 1–2; *Hosea 4:1–2* 959; *Luke 15:11–32* 1075; *Matthew 7:12* 272–3; Moses 103; St Paul 96, 205, 211, 213, 987, 1002; St Paul, *Ephesians 5:15–16* 96; St Paul, *Galatians 5:16–17* 990, *5:22–3* 205; St Paul, *Hebrews 10:26–7* 1003, *11:6* 211–14; St Paul *Romans 4:5* 228, *14:23* 213; St Peter 236; *1 Peter 1:18* 236–7; *Psalm 1:1–2* (V and AV) 196–7, *93:12* (V)/*94:12* (AV) 198–200, *110:10* (V)/*111:10* (AV) 263; Solomon 263

BIBLIOGRAPHY

Bevington, 1962, pp. 143–6
King, 1993, pp. 87–102
Mackenzie, 1914, pp. 95–9
Takemoto, 1989, pp. 1–18
Young, 1979, pp. 87–92

59   **Magnificence**

DATE, AUTHORSHIP AND AUSPICES

1520–2; John Skelton; auspices unknown, but written for indoor performance in London; Greg 11

TEXT AND EDITIONS

Extant originals

1530 (?) printing by P. Treveris for John Rastell: BL (no t.p.), Bodleian (frag.); Cambridge; *STC* 22607

Editions

2000	Walker (OS)
1994	CHD (CD-Rom and online copy of Dyce, 1856, l.l., OS)
1980	Neuss (NS)*
1979	Happé (OS)
1948	Henderson (n.l., NS)
1910	Farmer (n.l., OS)
1910	Farmer TFT (facsimile, n.l.)
1908	Ramsay (OS)
1843	Dyce, vol. III (OS)
1821	Littledale (facsimile, n.l.)

SOURCES

Skelton is likely to have drawn on Lydgate's poems 'A Song of Just Mesure' and 'Mesure is Tresour'. The idea of the play may also have been based on the lost *Speculum Principis* and other 'advice to princes' literature; see the introduction to Neuss's edition, pp. 19–22, and to Ramsay's edition, pp. lxxi–lxxxix.

CHARACTERS

Felicity	Fancy	Courtly Abusion	Despair	Circumspection
Liberty	Counterfeit Countenance	Folly	Mischief	Perseverance
Measure	Crafty Conveyance	Adversity	Good Hope	
Magnificence	Cloaked Collusion	Poverty	Redress	

PLOT SUMMARY

In the debate that opens the play, *Felicity* argues that wealth can only bring happiness if used with prudence, while *Liberty* contends that it is best used with total freedom. *Measure* arrives and arbitrates, until they all finally agree that moderation is necessary. The prince, *Magnificence*, appears and they enter his service, before *Measure* and *Liberty* go off. *Fancy* then comes in, calling himself *Largesse*, and bringing *Magnificence* a letter (purportedly from *Sad Circumspection* but actually forged by *Counterfeit Countenance*). *Fancy* urges *Magnificence* to be more free with his spending and while they go off to talk further *Counterfeit Countenance*, who has been skulking to one side, now comes forward to tell the audience that *Magnificence* has been caught by *Fancy*, and he rejoices in his own promotion of deceitfulness throughout the realm. He is then joined by *Fancy* and *Crafty Conveyance*, and as they begin to plot to bring about the removal of *Measure* from *Magnificence*'s service, *Cloaked Collusion* also arrives. After brief comments on *Collusion*'s clothing, they all continue their plotting, *Countenance* and *Collusion* taking on the names *Good Demeanance* and *Sober Sadness* respectively. Three of the Vices depart, leaving *Collusion* to boast about his role in sowing double-dealing and dissension in England. *Courtly Abusion* next makes his appearance 'huffing' and singing, and proceeds to reveal his aspirations for courtly promotion, requesting *Collusion*'s help. *Conveyance* now returns and the three engage in mock-aggressive banter before two go off to leave *Abusion* strutting about the stage drawing attention to his own dress and talking about fashions imported from France. He is interrupted by *Fancy* who returns carrying a hawk (which is likely, in fact, to be an owl). They are old friends and *Fancy* tells *Abusion* what has been going on in *Magnificence*'s court. Finally, *Abusion* departs leaving *Fancy* to parade about the stage showing off his 'hawk' until he is joined by *Folly* and his dog. They eventually agree to swap both their pets and their purses, an exchange from which *Folly* comes off the better, despite his apparent foolishness. When they are joined by *Conveyance* there is more verbal horseplay, in the course of which *Folly* delivers several satirical observations on abuses and follies in society. He and *Fancy* then go off to try and dislodge *Measure* from *Magnificence*'s household, while *Conveyance* is left to comment to the audience about his companions' and his own mischief in the realm. *Magnificence* now enters with *Liberty* and *Felicity*, having dismissed *Measure* and fallen fully under the influence of the Vices. He despatches *Conveyance* to fetch *Fancy* or '*Largesse*', to whose care he commits his wealth despite *Felicity*'s objections. *Magnificence* is left alone to deliver a boasting speech claiming sovereignty over all the earth, until *Abusion* re-enters to flatter him and encourage him to sexual indulgence. *Collusion* then brings *Measure* in and pretends to press *Magnificence* to grant him an audience. However, *Measure* is speedily dismissed and forcibly removed by *Abusion*, while *Collusion* continues to flatter *Magnificence* and give him bad advice. When *Collusion* leaves he is replaced on stage by *Folly*, who entertains *Magnificence* with a narrative of comic incongruities. *Fancy* then arrives to deliver the sorrowful news to *Magnificence* that he has been reduced to poverty by his vicious companions, and he is swiftly followed by *Adversity*, who knocks *Magnificence* down, takes his goods and clothing from him, and addresses to the audience a moral account of his vengeance on folly and excess. He is succeeded by *Poverty*, who lifts *Magnificence* on to a bed where he bewails his lot, accompanied by *Poverty*'s chastisement. After a long solo complaint by *Magnificence*, *Liberty* enters with a jolly song until he is interrupted by *Magnificence* who reminds him he was once his master. *Liberty* then comments to the audience using *Magnificence*'s downfall as an example, while *Conveyance* and *Collusion* enter to gloat. They finally fall to fighting until *Countenance* comes in to stop and upbraid them. When *Magnificence* curses them from his bed, they show him scant respect and leave him to sorrow until *Despair* enters. He is followed by *Mischief* with a halter and knife for *Magnificence* to kill himself. As he is about to do this, *Good Hope* comes in to point out to him that this would be a mortal sin and to remind him of God's grace. *Magnificence* finally rises and is brought a new garment by *Redress*, after which *Sad Circumspection* and *Perseverance* enter successively to strengthen and confirm him in his conversion, both uttering rhetorically highly formal speeches. *Magnificence* echoes their language in his own final speech which has acquired the authority of a sermon.

PLAY LENGTH

2,568 lines

COMMENTARY

This is a moral play with a classic *psychomachia* scheme and a single fall and redemption, but with the specific theme of the use of moderation in the handling of wealth. It uses a *speculum principis* or 'advice to princes' model but, though there are reflections on abuses in the state, the fall of *Magnificence* himself is presented as an individual crisis. The play may have been a satire on Wolsey. Notable is the succession of 'boasting' speeches in which each of the Vices, and *Magnificence* himself, get the opportunity to parade their particular forms of corruption in solo performance on stage.

Other political comment and state of the realm plays: 1 (frag.), 14, 37, 38, 71, 76.

SIGNIFICANT TOPICS AND NARRATIVE ELEMENTS

wealth and its management; excess and moderation – the 'golden mean'; good and bad servants; rulers and flatterers; the nature of nobility; corruption and deception in the state; apparel and (foreign) fashion; folly in high places; lust and sexual dalliance; poverty; the wheel of fortune; adversity as a scourge of God; despair and suicide

DRAMATURGICAL AND RHETORICAL FEATURES

Verbal and general *Conveyance*'s (corrupt) French expression as an example of 'counterfeit language' 441; the Vices (and *Magnificence*) have a series of solo 'boasting' speeches on their entries 401–93, 688–744, 828–916, 1458–515; *Courtly*

Abusion enters as a 'huffing' gallant 744 *sd*; *Collusion* addresses *Abusion* in French 748–50; *Collusion* asks the audience to make room for *Abusion* 753; aliases of the Vices: *Fancy–Largesse* 270, *Crafty Conveyance–Sure Surveyance* 525, *Counterfeit Countenance–Good Demeanance* 674, *Cloaked Collusion–Sober Sadness* 681, *Courtly Abusion–Lusty Pleasure* 963; *Folly*'s series of comic incongruities 1807–41; *Adversity*'s Skeltonic speech detailing the afflictions he visits on mankind, repeating 'and some' 1902–18; *Magnificence*'s 'ubi sunt' speech 2049–62; *Redress*'s, *Circumspection*'s and *Perseverance*'s Skeltonic speeches on life's uncertainty, repeating 'now', 'suddenly' and 'today' 2513–17, 2522–33, 2537–47; some stage directions in Latin and some in English

Costume and dress *Collusion*'s cape, possibly an ecclesiastical garment 601; *Abusion*'s boots and his fashionable French attire, which he describes to the audience 833–82; *Fancy*'s fool's outfit 1045; *Conveyance* puts off his gown 1204 *sd*; *Magnificence*'s new garment 2407 *sd*

Actions and stage directions   28: *Fel.* and *Lib.* shake hands; 239 *sd*: 'So let *Me.* leave the place with *Lib.*, and *Mag.* remain with *Fel.*' (L); 324 *sd*: 'Here let him (*Mag.*) make as if he were reading the letter silently. Meanwhile let *C. Cou.* come on singing, who on seeing *Mag.* should softly retreat on tiptoe. At the right moment, after a while, let *C. Cou.* approach again looking out and calling from a distance, and *Fa.* motions silence with his hand' (L); 493 *sd*: 'Here let *Fa.* come in hurriedly with *Cr. Con.*, gabbling many things together; finally on seeing *C. Coun.* let *Cr. Con.* say' (L); 572 *sd*: 'Here let *C. Coll.* come in with a haughty expression, strolling up and down' (L); 688 *sd*: 'Here he (*Coll.*) walks about' (L); 744 *sd*: 'Here let *Co. Ab.* come in singing' (L); 748 *sd*: 'And here let him (*Coll.*) doff his cap ironically' (L); 778 *sd*: 'Here comes in *Cr. Con.* pointing with his finger, and says: "Hem *Collusion*"' (E); 827 *sd*: '*Co. Ab.* alone in the place' (E); 910 *sd*: 'Here comes in *Fa.* crying "Stow, Stow"' (E); 1041 *sd*: 'Here let *Fol.* enter, shaking a bauble and making a commotion, beating on tables and suchlike' (L); 1199 *sd*: 'Here *Fol.* makes semblant to take a louse from *Cr. Con.* shoulder' (E); 1204 *sd*: 'Here *Cr. Con.* puts off his gown' (E); 1208 *sd*: 'Here *Fol.* makes semblant to take money of *Cr. Con.*, saying to him' (E); 1327 *sd*: '*Cr. Con.* alone in the place' (E); 1457 *sd*: '*Mag.* alone in the place' (E); 1515 *sd*: 'Here comes in *Co. Ab.* doing reverence and courtesy' (E); 1631: *Coll.* kneels; 1693 *sd*: 'Here let *Coll.* bring *Me.* forward, *Mag.* looking on with a very haughty expression' (L); 1709: *Coll.* kneels; 1797 *sd*: 'Here goes *C. Coll* away and leaves *Mag.* alone in the place' (E); 1876 *sd*: 'Here *Mag.* is beaten down and spoiled from all his goods and raiment' (E); 1967 *sd*: 'Here let him (*Pov.*) set about lifting *Mag.* and he will place him on a bed' (L); 2038 *sd*: 'Despairingly let him (*Mag.*) say these words' (L); 2048 *sd*: 'Here *Mag.* dolorously makes his moan' (E); 2151 *sd*: 'Here someone blows a horn from the back behind the audience' (L); 2160 *sd*: 'Here come in *Cr. Con.* [and] *C. Coll.* with a lusty laughter' (E); 2179: *Coll.* throws down his glove; 2189: *Con.* pulls out a dagger; 2190: *Coll.* threatens *Con.* with a sword; 2200: *Coll.* and *Con.* hand over their weapons to *Coun.*; 2277 *sd*: 'And let them (*Con.*, *Coun.*, *Coll.*) leave the place hurriedly' (L); 2323 *sd*: 'Here *Mag.* would slay himself with a

knife' (E); 2325 *sd*: 'Here enters *G. Ho.* while *Des.* and *Mis.* are running away. Let *G. Ho.* suddenly snatch the sword from him (*Mag.*) and say' (L); 2407 *sd*: Let *Mag.* receive the garment' (L); 2419 *sd*: 'Here comes in *Cir.* saying' (E); **Simple entry:** *Me.* 80; *Mag.* 162; *Fa.* 250; *Coun.* 395; *Con.* 1159; *Mag., Lib., Fel.* 1375; *Fa.* 1409; *Coll., Me.* 1629; *Fol.* 1803; *Fa.* 1843; *Adv.* 1873; *Pov.* 1955; *Des.* 2284; *Mis.* 2309; *Red.* 2385; *Per.* 2457; **Simple exit:** *Mag., Fa.* 395; (*Coll., Con.*) 823; *Con.* 1401; *Fel., Lib., Fa.* 1457; *Me.* 1725; *Fol.* 1851; (*G. Ho.*) 2402
Songs and music 1. *Conveyance* (w.n.s.) 324 *sd*; 2. *Abusion* 'Taunderum taunderum tayne' (possibly a corruption of a Flemish song, w.s.) 745–51; 3. *Liberty* 'With yea marry sirs, thus should it be' (passage likely to have been sung, w.s.) 2064–78; **Instrumental:** a horn 2151 *sd*
Staging and set this is a hall play, the action is only vaguely localized in *Magnificence*'s palace, and there are no indications as to set apart from a bed for *Magnificence* (1967 *sd*)
Stage properties *Fancy*'s letter 312; *Fancy*'s 'hawk' (an owl) 921; *Folly*'s bauble 1041 *sd*; 'tables' (possibly a board or instrument) 1041 *sd*; *Folly*'s dog 1053; *Folly*'s and *Fancy*'s purses 1103–4; the shoe buckle in *Folly*'s purse 1107; *Magnificence*'s bowl 1729; *Magnificence*'s bed or 'place to stretch out' ('locus stratum') 1967 *sd*; *Collusion*'s glove 2179; *Conveyance*'s sword (dagger) 2189; *Collusion*'s broad sword ('falchion') 2190; *Mischief*'s halter and knife 2318

PLACENAMES

Alnwick 1121; Anjou or Angers ('Angey') 1121; Babylon 1474; Britain ('Albion') 1503; Calais 675; Carthage 1513; Cockermouth 1061–2; Doncaster 293; England 715, 882, 1099; France 280, 877, 1502; the Half Street (in Bankside) 2264; Kent 981; Macedon 1467; Persia 1489; Pontoise 343; Rennes 2017; Rome 1512; Stroud 981; Taylor's Hall (in Threadneedle St) 1405; Tower Hill 2141; Trent 980; Troy 1577; Turkey 1481; Tyburn 423, 909; Tyne 980; Woodstock 1211

ALLUSIONS

Alaric the Goth 1505; Alexander the Great 1467; King Arthur 1503; Julius Caesar 1483; Caracalla 1504; Cato 1488; Cerberus 1496; Charlemagne 1502; Cyrus the Great 1474; Darius I of Persia 1489; Servius Sulpicius Galba 1509; Hannibal 1512; Hercules 1495; Horace *Odes II,x* 114; King Louis (XII ?) of France 280; Nero 1510; Pluto 1497; Lars Porsenna 1481; Scipio Africanus Major 1513; Theseus 1497; Friar Tuck 357; Vespasian 1511

REPORT ON MODERN PRODUCTION

Edinburgh (Salford University Theatre Co), 13–23 August 1984 [*METh* 6:2 (1984) pp. 162–3]

RECORDED PRODUCTION

LP Record: BBC, *The First Stage*, dir. J. Barton (1970)

BIBLIOGRAPHY

Anderson, J. 'John Skelton's *Magnificence*', *METh* 6:2 (1984) pp. 162–3
Bevington, 1968, pp. 54–63
Carpenter, N. C. 'Skelton and Music: Roty Bully Boys', *RES* n.s. 6:23 (1955) pp. 279–84
Carpenter, 1967, pp. 75–82
Edwards, 1949, pp. 169–78
Forest-Hill, 2000, pp. 108–35
Gordon, 1943, pp. 135–46
Haller, 1916, pp. 122–8
Happé, P. 'Fansy and Foly: The Drama of Fools in *Magnyfycence*' *CD* 27:4 (1993–4) pp. 426–52
Happé, 1998, pp. 27–44
Harris, W. O. 'The Thematic Importance of Skelton's Allusion to Horace in *Magnyfycence*', *SEL* 3:1 (1963) pp. 99–125
Harris, W. O. 'Wolsey and Skelton's *Magnyfycence*: a Revaluation' *SP* 57:2 (1960) pp. 99–122
Harris, 1965
Heiserman, 1961, pp. 66–125
Hogrefe, 1959, pp. 309–13
Kinsman, R. S. 'Skelton's *Magnyfycence*: The Strategy of the "Olde Sayde Sawe"', *SP* 63:2 (1966) pp. 99–125
Levitsky, R. '*Timon*: Shakespeare's *Magnyfycence* and an Embryonic *Lear*', *ShS* 11 (1978) pp. 107–21
Lloyd, 1938, pp. 76–98
Lombardo, 1954, pp. 9–39
Neuss, P. 'Proverbial Skelton', *SN* 54 (1982) pp. 237–46
Norland, 1995, pp. 175–87
Pollet, 1971, pp. 83–103
Potter, 1975, pp. 67–77
Scattergood, J. 'Skelton's *Magnyfycence* and the Tudor Royal Household', *METh* 15 (1993) pp. 21–48
Southern, R. 'The Technique of Play Presentation' in *Revels II*, pp. 80–9
Southern, 1973, pp. 180–201
Spinrad, P. S. '"Too Much Liberty": *Measure for Measure* and Skelton's *Magnificence*', *MLQ* 60:4 (1999) pp. 431–49
Walker, 1991, pp. 60–101
Winser, L. 'Skelton's *Magnyfycence*', *RenQ* 23:1 (1970) pp. 14–25
Winser, L. '*Magnyfycence* and the Characters of *Sottie*', *SCJ* 12:3 (1981) pp. 85–94

60   Mankind

DATE, AUTHORSHIP AND AUSPICES

between 1465 and 1470; anonymous; an East Anglian play likely to have been for a touring company

TEXT AND EDITIONS

Extant originals

Manuscript: Folger Shakespeare Library MS V.a.354, fos.1–13

Editions

2000	Walker (OS)
1997	Meredith (NS)
1995	Knittel and Fattic (OS)
1994	CHD (CD-Rom and online copy of Eccles, 1969, l.l., s.l., OS)
1993	Coldewey (OS)
1985	Gray (OS)*
1981	Lester (NS)
1976	Wickham (NS)
1975	Bevington (OS)*
1972	Bevington (facsimile with transcription)*
1974	Somerset (NS)
1969	Eccles (OS)*
1924	Adams (OS, bowdlerized)
1914	Markoe (n.l., OS)
1914	Farmer (1914a) (facsimile, n.l.)
1907	Farmer (9) (n.l., NS)
1907	TFT (facsimile, n.l.)
1907	'Lost' Tudor Plays, TFT (facsimile, n.l.)
1904	Furnivall and Pollard (repr. 1924, OS)
1898	Brandl (OS)
1897	Manly, vol. 1 (OS, bowdlerized)

SOURCES

There are some folk play elements, but no single or major source has been identified.

CHARACTERS

Mercy   Mischief   Nought   New Guise   Nowadays   Mankind   Titivillus

PLOT SUMMARY

A standard sermon by *Mercy* opening the play about the 'corn' that is saved and the 'chaff' that is lost, is interrupted by *Mischief* who mocks his aureate language. He is soon joined by his fellow Vices, *New Guise*, *Nought* and *Nowadays*, accompanied by minstrels, and they all dance. When *Mercy* tries to intervene he is again mocked in obscene language. The Vices depart singing and *Mercy* is joined by *Mankind*, who talks of the dichotomy of his body and soul and his fear of falling into sin. *Mercy* counsels him to avoid sin and embrace 'measure'. The Vices return and *Mercy* warns *Mankind* against them before leaving, at which *Mankind* hangs a moral slogan around his neck. He then apparently goes to one side while the Vices lead the yeomen in the audience in what proves to be an obscene song. When they turn their attention back to *Mankind* and try to distract him from his work in the fields he chases them off with his spade, after which he prays and reaffirms to the audience his determination to resist vice. The Vices bewail their beating and decide to bring in *Titivillus*, who duly enters after the audience has been induced to pay for his appearance, though the Vices do not hand over the money to him. He sends the Vices out to do mischief in the local population, some of whom are specifically named by them. *Titivillus* himself sets about harassing *Mankind* by putting a board under the ground to make it hard to dig, by hiding his spade, by making him interrupt his prayers for a call of nature, and by stealing his rosary. When *Mankind* returns he falls asleep and *Titivillus* makes him dream that *Mercy* has been hanged for horse theft. *New Guise* enters with a halter and marks on his neck, himself having narrowly escaped hanging. The other Vices reappear too, *Mischief* with fetters, newly escaped from prison. *Mankind* then comes in to beg the Vices' forgiveness for his earlier violence to them, and telling them of his dream, which they gleefully recognize as the work of *Titivillus*. They set up a mock court in which legal language is parodied, and *Mankind* is divested of his coat, that is then twice cut down before being returned to him. They also lead him through a catechism embracing vice and sin, and when *Mercy* returns *Mankind* rejects him before going off to a tavern with the Vices. *Mercy* delivers a sorrowful soliloquy, for which he is mocked by the returning Vices. *Mankind* then enters in despair, wishing to commit suicide, for which purpose the Vices bring him a gibbet shaped tree. *Mercy* intervenes however, chasing the Vices off with a whip before finally being reconciled with *Mankind*. He delivers another sermon, and finally the epilogue.

PLAY LENGTH

914 lines

COMMENTARY

This is an early play in which the Vices have a vigorous theatrical presence, also taking on social characteristics beyond their strictly allegorical role. *Mankind* also has some social identity as a peasant farmer, though this is largely symbolic. The main target of the play is idle language, and it contains considerable obscenity. *Mankind*'s change of linguistic register when he is under the influence of either

Mercy or the Vices signals his moral state. The device of theatrically attractive Vices who engage and trick the audience as part of the moral message is well developed here, especially in having the audience pay to see *Titivillus*. A leaf is missing from the manuscript after line 70.

SIGNIFICANT TOPICS AND NARRATIVE ELEMENTS

language and piety; the body and soul debate; good and bad companionship; money; crime; punishment and hanging; taverns and drinking; despair and suicide; the infernal trinity: World, Flesh and Devil

DRAMATURGICAL AND RHETORICAL FEATURES

Verbal and general the Vices' mock-Latin 57–63, 398–9, 680–1; *Titivillus* enters through the audience 474; several named local figures are referred to by the Vices 503–15; *Titivillus* demonstrates a trick to the audience 569–71; the mock court of the Vices 664–725; *Nowadays*'s proclamation 667–9; *Mankind*'s 'oath' or catechism with the Vices 702–18; *Mankind*'s language varies under influence of *Mercy* (aureate speech) and the Vices (coarse language); stage directions (mostly Latin) are minimal, most of the indications for action being present in the dialogue

Costume and dress *Titivillus* probably wears a mask 465; *Mankind* wears a long 'side gown' 671; *Mankind*'s jacket is cut down 674–6, 718–19

Actions and stage directions 74–81: *Nou.* enters whipped into a dance by *Now.*; 81 *sd*: 'Here they (*Now.*, *Nou.*) dance. *Me.* says' (E); 113: *Nou.* trips *Me.*; 161 *sd*: 'They (Vices) exit together. They sing' (L); 213–18: *Man.* prays and rises; 315–18: *Man.* writes; 342 *sd*: '(Vices) All sing' (L); 380: *Man.* drives the Vices off with his spade; 392: *Man.* kneels to pray; 424 *sd*: 'They (Vices) cry' (L); 457–74: the Vices collect money for *Tit.*'s appearance; 477 *sd*: '*Tit.* says to *N. Gui.*' (L); 522: *Tit.* blesses the Vices with his left hand; 530: *Tit.* hangs his net before *Man.*'s eyes; 533 *Tit.* places a board in the earth; 537: *Tit.* adulterates *Man.*'s seed; 549 *sd*: 'Here *Tit.* goes out with the spade' (E); 553: *Man.* kneels down to pray; 557: *Tit.* whispers in *Mankind*'s ear; 588: *Man.* lies down to sleep; 593: *Tit.* whispers in *Man.*'s ear; 658–61: *Man.* kneels before the Vices; 672 *sd*: '*Nou.* writes' (L); 730: *Mis.* trips and falls; 783–4: *Nou.* urinates on his foot; 807: *Me.* threatens the Vices with a whip; **Simple exit:** (Vices) 400; (*Man.*) 564; *Mis.* 798; (*Now.*, *N. Gui.*) 810; *Man.* 902; **Simple speech:** 'All' (Vices, *Man.*) 725

Songs and music 1. *Nowadays*, *New Guise*, *Nought*, (w.n.s.) 161 *sd*; 2. *Nowadays*, *New Guise*, *Nought*, audience 'It is written with a coal' (an obscene 'round', w.s.) 335–43; **Instrumental:** minstrel music for the *Nowadays*'s dance, and the Vices' dance 72; 81 *sd*; *Nought* plays a flute (a 'Walsingham whistle') to bring in *Titivillus* 452–3

Staging and set open air production may possibly be suggested by the fact that a collection is taken from the audience (457–74), which is clearly socially mixed

(29); the action is unlocalized except for *Mankind*'s agricultural work (348–549) and to an extent the makeshift court scene (664–725); there are no indications as to set, but several portable stage properties

Stage properties *Nowadays*'s whip 73; a paper hung around *Mankind*'s neck 315, 322; *Mankind*'s spade 377; the Vices' purses 479, 488; *Titivillus*'s net 530; *Titivillus*'s board 533; *Mankind*'s bag of seed 537; *Mankind*'s rosary 564; *Newguise*'s halter 617; *Nowadays*'s stolen church plate; 633–4; *Mischief*'s fetters 641; *Mischief*'s dish and platter 647; *Nowadays*'s proclamation 665; *Mischief*'s court book and pen 672 *sd*; a rope and gibbet tree 801–2; *Mercy*'s whip 807

PLACENAMES

Bottisham 514; Bury 274; Canaan 848; France 597; Fulbourn 511; Gayton 510; Hauxton 506; Massingham 513; St Patrick's Purgatory (in Donegal) 614; Sawston 505; Swaffham 515; Trumpington 507; Walsingham 452; Walton 509

ALLUSIONS

St Audrey 628; Cicero ('Tully') 692; King David 397; Job 286; *Job 1:21* 292–3, *7:1* 228, *34:15* (q.a.) 321; *John 8:11* 850, 852; St Paul, *2 Corinthians 6:2* 866; *Proverbs 12:7* (q.a.) 826b; *Psalm 17:26* (V)/*18:26* (AV) (q.a.) 324, *76:11* (V)/*77:10* (AV) 826a; *120:7* (V)/*121:7* (AV) 901–2, *131:1* (V)/*133:1* (AV) 325–6; *1 Samuel 17:47* 397

REPORTS ON MODERN PRODUCTIONS

1. Trinity Hall, Cambridge (Trinity Hall Preston Society), dir. C. Heap, 19–25 July 1976 [*RORD* 19 (1976) p. 83]
2. Syracuse, New York (Seventh Heaven Players), dir. J. Elliott, 5 December 1976 [*RORD* 20 (1977) pp. 102–3]
3. University College, Dublin (PLS), dir. D. Parry, 10 July 1980 [*RORD* 23 (1980) pp. 85–6]
4. Mt Allison University, New Brunswick, dir. R. Knowles, 19–21 February 1981 [*RORD* 24 (1981) pp. 193–4]
5. York (PLS), 4 May 1981 [*METh* 3:1 (1981) pp. 58–60]
6. Australia (Tour, Medieval Players), spring 1985 [*METh* 7:1 (1985) pp. 57–61]
7. University of Toronto (PLS), dir. L. Phillips, October 1995 [*RORD* 35 (1997) pp. 183–4]
8. University College, Cork, dir. A. Ryan, 3 January 1996 [*RORD* 36 (1997) pp. 181–2]
9. University of Camerino (Leeds University Drama Department), dir. P. Meredith, 28–30 June 1996 [*see* Batty, Boon, Price and Meredith below]
10. University of Leeds, dir. P. Meredith, 7 July 1996 [*RORD* 36 (1997) pp. 182–3]

11. Atlanta, Georgia (Duquesne University Medieval and Renaissance Players), dir. M. Butler, 16, 22–24, 29–31 October 1998 [*RORD* 38 (1999) pp. 145–8]
12. University of Illinois, 4–5 December 1998, dir. K. Moranski and C. Risdon [*RORD* 39 (2000) pp. 253–5]
13. Pittsburgh (Duquesne University Medieval and Renaissance Players), dir. M. Butler, 10, 12, 17, 19 July, 1999 [*RORD* 39 (2000) pp. 247–8] (Revival of 11 above)
14. University of California, Santa Barbara, dir. M. Shaw 2–4, 6 June 2000 [*RORD* 40 (2001) pp. 203–5]

CONCORDANCE

Preston, 1975

BIBLIOGRAPHY

Ashley, K. M. 'Titivillus and the Battle of Words in *Mankind*', *AM* 16 (1975) pp. 128–50
Baker, D. C. 'The Date of *Mankind*', *PQ* 42:1 (1963) pp. 90–1
Batty, M. 'Playing Mischief: Clown, Rogue or Dramatic Necessity', *STP* 15 (1977) pp. 73–8
Beadle, R. 'Monk Thomas Hyngham's Hand in the Macro Manuscript' in Beadle and Piper, 1995, pp. 315–37
Beene, L. D. 'Language Patterns in *Mankind*', *USFLQ* 21:3/4 (1983) pp. 25–9
Billington, S. '"Suffer fools gladly": The Fool in Medieval England and the Play *Mankind*' in Williams, 1979, pp. 36–54, 125–33
Boon, R. 'Begging for Mercy', *STP* 15 (1977) pp. 62–72
Bowers, J. M. '*Mankind* and the Political Interests of Bury St Edmunds', *Æstel* 2 (1994) pp. 77–103
Brooke, 1996, pp. 99–107
Chaplan, R. E. 'Farewell, Jentyll Jaffrey: Speech-Act Theory and *Mankind*', *METh* 11 (1989) pp. 140–9
Castle, 1990
Clopper, L. M. '*Mankind* and its Audience', *CD* 8:4 (1974–5) pp. 347–55, and also in Davidson and Stroupe, 1991, pp. 240–8
Coogan, 1947
Davenport, 1982, pp. 36–78
Davenport, W. 'Peter Idley and the Devil in *Mankind*', *ES* 64:2 (1983) pp. 106–12
Davidson, 1989, pp. 15–45
Denny, N. 'Aspects of the Staging of *Mankind*', *MÆ* 43:3 (1974) pp. 252–63
Dillon, J. '*Mankind* and the Politics of "Englysch Laten"', *M&H* 20 (1994) pp. 41–64
Dillon, 1998, pp. 54–69
Fifield, 1967, pp. 27–35
Fifield, 1974, pp. 12–34
Forest-Hill, L. '*Mankind* and the Fifteenth-Century Preaching Controversy', *MRDE* 15 (2003) pp. 17–42
Forstater, A and J. Baird, '"Walking and Wending": Mankind's Opening Speech', *TN* 26:2 (1971–2), pp. 60–64
Garner, 1987, pp. 272–85
Garner, 1989, pp. 71–9

Gash, A. 'Carnival against Lent: Ambivalence of Medieval Drama' in Aers, 1986, pp. 74–98

Haller, 1916, pp. 99–101

Heap, C. 'On Performing *Mankind*', *METh* 4:2 (1982) pp. 93–103

Jack, 1989 pp. 165–73

Jambeck, T. J. and R. L. Lee, '"Pope Pokett" and the Date of *Mankind*', *MS* 39 (1977) pp. 511–13

Jones, R. C. 'Dangerous Sport: The Audience's Engagement with the Vice in the Moral Interludes', *RenD* n.s. 6 (1973) pp. 45–64

Keiller, M. M. 'The Influence of *Piers Plowman* on the Macro Play of *Mankind*', *PMLA* 26:2 (1911) pp. 339–55

Kelley, 1979, pp. 64–93

Keppel, 2000, pp. 76–7, 103–10

Lombardo, 1954, pp. 9–39

MacKenzie, R. W. 'A New Source for *Mankind*', *PMLA* 27:1 (1912) pp. 98–105

Marshall, J. '"O ȝe souerens þat sytt and ȝe brothern þat stond right wppe": Addressing the Audience of *Mankind*' in Higgins, 1997, pp. 189–202

Meredith, P. 'Playing the Very Devil and other Matters', *STP* 16 (1997) pp. 84–92

Miyajima, 1977, pp. 73–83

Neuss, P. 'Active and Idle Language: Dramatic Images in *Mankind*' in Denny, 1973, pp. 41–68

Pettit, T. '*Mankind*: an English Fastnachtspiel?', in Twycross, 1996, pp. 190–202

Price, A. 'Dramatising the Word', *STP* 16 (1997) pp. 77–83 and *LSE* 29 (1998) pp. 293–303

Raftery, M. 'Cosmic Signs: the Representation of Go(o)d and (the) (D)evil in the Medieval Morality Play *Mankind*', *SAJMRS* 10 (2000) pp. 13–33

Rendall, 1981, pp. 255–69

Richardson and Johnston, 1991, pp. 128–38

Scherb, 2001, pp. 108–30

Sikorska, L. '*Mankind* and the Question of Power Dynamics: Some Remarks on the Validity of Sociolinguistic Reading', *NM* 97:2 (1996) pp. 201–16

Smart, W. K. 'Some Notes on *Mankind*', *MP* 14:1 (1916) pp. 45–58, 14:4, pp. 293–313

Smart, W. K. '*Mankind* and the Mumming Plays', *MLN* 32:1 (1917) pp. 21–5

Southern, 1973, pp. 21–44

Sponsler, 1997, pp. 84–9

Stock, L. K. 'The Thematic and Structural Unity of *Mankind*', *SP* 72:4 (1975) pp. 386–407

Taylor, A. '"To pley a pagyn of þe devyl": *Turpiloquium* and the *Scurrae* in Early Drama', *METh* 11 (1989) pp. 162–74

Tydeman, 1986, pp. 31–52

Wenzel, 1967, pp. 47–66

61   The Marriage of Wit and Science

DATE, AUTHORSHIP AND AUSPICES

c. 1569 (*SR* 1569 *c.* Aug.); anonymous; performed by boys at court; Greg 55

TEXT AND EDITIONS

Extant originals

1570 printing by Thomas Marshe: Bodleian; *STC* 17466

Editions

1994   CHD (CD-Rom and online transcription of Marshe printing, l.l., s.l., OS)
1975   Lennam (OS)*
1961   Brown, Crow and Wilson (facsimile)
1914   Farmer (1914a) (facsimile, n.l.)
1909   TFT (facsimile, n.l.)
1908   Farmer (10) (n.l., NS)
1874–6   Dodsley, vol. II (n.l., NS)

SOURCES

The play is based on John Redford's play, the *Play of Wit and Science* (see 101).

CHARACTERS

Nature	Reason	Diligence	Ignorance
Wit	Experience	Tediousness	Shame
Will	Instruction	Recreation	
Science	Study	Idleness	

'With three other women singers'

PLOT SUMMARY

Wit announces to his mother, *Nature*, his desire to win the hand of *Science*, the daughter of *Reason* and *Experience*, and she tells him he must embark on a journey of self-improvement through education in order to become worthy. *Wit* gives his servingman, *Will*, a picture of himself to take to *Lady Science*, though *Will* declares himself doubtful about the pleasures of marriage. *Science* in the next scene also expresses to her parents her misgivings about marriage, but they persuade her that she should be open to the idea, and *Will* then enters to present his master's suit. With her parents' approval she agrees to meet him. When *Wit* goes to the House of Science he is told that he must prepare himself further if he is to be an acceptable suitor, and *Experience* assigns him *Instruction, Study* and *Diligence* as retainers and instructors. *Will* continues to express his doubts and he is also hostile to the new retainers. When they tell *Wit* that he has to study for several years he rejects them, with *Will*'s encouragement, and they depart. *Wit* continues to burn with love however, and when he again meets *Science*, she tells him she has a mortal enemy called *Tediousness* who must be killed. Accompanied by *Will* and *Diligence*, *Wit* attacks *Tediousness* but is struck down. He is then revived by *Recreation* and *Will*, who sing a song. Having been revived, *Wit* dances a galliard with *Recreation* and *Will*, but when *Recreation* leaves he falls into the company of *Idleness* and *Ignorance*. *Wit* is lulled to sleep with song in the lap of *Idleness*, who dresses him in *Ignorance*'s clothes, and when he wakes and visits *Science* she does not recognize him. Comparing his present state with the picture he gave her, even *Wit* finds his own face blotted and his clothes changed. He departs and in the next scene is physically chastised by *Shame* and admonished by *Reason*, to whom he expresses his repentance. After coaching by *Instruction*, and with the help of *Will*, *Instruction*, *Study* and *Diligence*, he attacks *Tediousness* again, this time killing him and hoisting his head upon his spear. He is then reconciled with *Science* and the marriage is able to proceed.

PLAY LENGTH

1,563 lines

COMMENTARY

This play is very similar to the Redford interlude on which it is based, though there are some variations in both plot and character. As with that play, the narrative is basically a chivalric love quest. There is less physical action than in the Redford piece, but the psychological allegory is just as carefully worked out. This interlude provides a fuller role for *Experience*, the mother of *Science*, and introduces the figure of *Will*, which does not occur in the earlier play.

Other youth and education plays: **21, 33, 53, 56, 58, 62, 64, 67, 68, 73** (frag.), **101, 103, 104**.

Other marriage quest plays: **29, 47, 57** (frag.), **62, 101**.

SIGNIFICANT TOPICS AND NARRATIVE ELEMENTS

estates; education and social mobility; Parnassus; marriage and social mobility; the difficulties of and challenges to study

DRAMATURGICAL AND RHETORICAL FEATURES

NOTE: character names and stage directions included in line numbering
Verbal and general *Science*'s Skeltonic series of questions on effort and ambition, repeating 'how many' 382–8; *Wit*'s Skeltonic passage repeating 'this same' 1301–5; there is some textual corruption, requiring a transposition of lines 557–728 and 729–925 (in the equivalent lines of the Marshe text) to allow the narrative to proceed logically; a five-act play with scene divisions; stage directions in English
Costume and dress *Wit* is dressed in *Ignorance*'s clothes 1175–7; *Shame* is given *Wit*'s coat as payment for his chastisement of *Wit* 1382
Actions and stage directions 962 (*sd*): '(*Ted.*) Fight, strike at *Will*'; 965: *Wit* strikes at *Ted.*; 967–9: *Ted.* strikes down *Wit*; 983 (*sd*): '(*Will*) Rub him and chafe him (*Wit*)'; 986 (*sd*) 'Sing (*Rec.*, *Will*)'; 999 (*sd*): 'Both (*Will*, *Rec.*) sing "Give a leg" as is before'; 1006 (*sd*): 'Sing both (*Will*, *Rec.*)'; 1013 (*sd*): 'Sing (*Will*, *Rec.*) "Give a

leg" etc'; 1017 (sd): 'Wit lifting himself up, sitting on the ground'; 1093 (sd): 'Let Will call for the dances, one after another'; 1121–2 (sd): 'Let him (Wit practise in dancing all things to make himself breathless'; 1131 (sd): 'Id. sings'; 1147 (sd): '(Wit) Fall down in her (Id.) lap'; 1152 (sd): '(Id.) Lull him (Wit)'; 1180: Id. blackens Wit's face; 1494 (sd): '(Wit, Ted.) Fight'; 1536 (sd): 'Say all (Will, Ins., Stu., Dil.) at once'; **Simple exit:** (Nat.) 211; (Will, Wit) 227; Sci., Rea., Exp. 506
Songs and music (w.s. to both songs) 1. Recreation, Will 'Give a leg, give an arm, arise, arise' (w. ref.) 987–1019; 2. Idleness 'Come, come lie down, and thou shalt see' 1132–46 **Instrumental:** music for the dance (minstrels piping – a galliard) 1090 **Staging and set** the action is either unlocalized or suggested by the presence and dialogue of character; Lady Science's house may have had a door or gate, referred to in 373, though the house is not seen exclusively from the outside as actions take place inside it; Tediousness's cave may have been represented 'in drowsy darkness hid' (948); there is a closet into which Science retires to watch Wit's fight with Tediousness (1428); otherwise there are no indications as to set; a false head is used for decapitation (1524)
Stage properties Wit's picture 481–2; Wit's looking-glass 1283; Tediousness's club 1486; Wit's club 1496; Tediousness's false head and Wit's spear 1524

ALLUSIONS

Robin Hood 571; Parnassus 170

BIBLIOGRAPHY

Habicht, 1965, pp. 73–88
Hauke, 1904, pp. 2–37
Hogrefe, 1959, pp. 324–8
Lennam, 1975
Mackenzie, 1914, pp. 167–73
Race, S. 'The Moral Play of Wit and Science', N&Q 198 (1953) pp. 96–99
Varma, R. S. 'Act and Scene Divisions in The Marriage of Wit and Science', N&Q 10 (1963) pp. 95–6
Varma, R. S. 'Philosophical and Moral Ideas in The Marriage of Wit and Science', PQ 44:1 (1965) pp. 120–2
Withington, R. 'Experience the Mother of Science', PMLA 57:2 (1942) p. 592

62   The Marriage of Wit and Wisdom

DATE, AUTHORSHIP AND AUSPICES

1571–9; Francis Merbury; possibly a university play (Cambridge), but offered for acting

TEXT AND EDITIONS

Extant originals

Manuscript: British Library Add. MS 26782

Editions

1994 CHD (CD-Rom and online copy of Lennam, 1971, l.l., OS)
1976 Wickham (NS)*
1971 Lennam (OS)
1914 Farmer (1914a) (facsimile, n.l.)
1909 TFT (facsimile, n.l.)
1908 Farmer (10) (n.l., NS)
1846 Halliwell (n.l., OS)

SOURCES

The play is based on the anonymous *Marriage of Wit and Science* (see **61**).

CHARACTERS

Prologue	Wantonness	Irksomeness	Lob
Severity	Good Nurture	Wisdom	Mother Bee
Indulgence	Honest Recreation	Search	Inquisition
Wit	Snatch	Fancy	Epilogue
Idleness (Vice)	Catch	Doll	

PLOT SUMMARY

The *Prologue* warns against the snares that lie in the path of the young in the pursuit of *Lady Wisdom*. *Severity* and *Indulgence* then enter and exhort their son, *Wit*, to prepare himself to win *Wisdom* as a wife, avoiding the Vices *Idleness* and *Irksomeness*. When they all go off *Idleness* comes in declaring his intention to lead *Wit* astray, and he is soon joined by *Wantonness*, a loose woman. On *Wit's* re-entry, *Idleness* introduces himself as *Honest Recreation* and *Wantonness* as *Modest Mirth*. She makes overtures to *Wit* and eventually lulls him to sleep in her lap with a song, at which *Idleness* steals his purse, while she paints his face black and puts a dunce's cap on his head. He is found thus and rescued by *Good Nurture*. In the next scene, *Idleness* resolves to take the new name of *Due Disport*. He meets up with *Snatch* and *Catch*, sailors returned from the Netherlands, who steal money from his purse, tie him up with a sheet, and later beat him. *Wit* enters attended by the true *Honest Recreation*, and unties *Idleness*, now introducing himself as *Due Disport*. *Wit* is reconciled with him, dismisses *Honest Recreation*, and accompanies *Idleness* to the den of *Irksomeness*, who beats him and leaves him for dead on stage. *Wit* is helped up by *Lady Wisdom* and after her departure he calls for *Irksomeness*, fights him and decapitates him. In the next scene *Idleness* enters disguised as a rat-catcher, as he is being pursued by the law for the tricking of *Wit*. He meets *Search*, a court messenger who unwittingly coaches *Idleness* in the reading out of the very proclamation that pertains to himself, before going on to trick him out of sixpence and running off. *Dame Fancy* then enters pretending to be a messenger from *Lady Wisdom*, finds *Wit* and delivers him a letter purportedly from her arranging an assignation. *Fancy* leads him to a house where he is suddenly held fast, to his alarm. The scene changes to *Idleness* dressed as a beggar, a porridge pot hung about his neck, and when he goes off *Doll* and *Lob* enter to complain about the theft of the pot while they were kissing. *Mother Bee* now arrives and beats them for their negligence until *Inquisition* brings *Idleness* in with the pot, and takes him off to justice. *Good Nurture* then comes in looking for *Wit*, who cries out from his prison, and she proceeds to release him as it is his wedding day. *Idleness* appears as a priest to perform the ceremony, regretting the loss of his control over *Wit* but consoling himself that if he is rejected by men, women will still entertain him. The final scene sees the uniting of *Wit* and *Wisdom*, who sing a song together and this is followed by the *Epilogue* offering formal excuses for the rudeness of the play's style.

PLAY LENGTH

770 lines, including prologue

COMMENTARY

This play engages the issue of the appropriate education of youth for access to a proper social position, which is represented through marriage. It thus articulates concerns that are secular and humanist rather than primarily theological. Implicit attitudes to women are signalled by the name of the mother, *Indulgence* (as opposed to the father, *Severity*), the role of *Wantonness*, the woman who impedes *Wit's* educational progress, and the remark of *Idleness* that he can ultimately be assured of being entertained by women. The comic business of the play is fairly well integrated into the development of the principal narrative, though the episodes involving *Snatch* and *Catch*, *Doll* and *Lob* and *Idleness* and *Search* seem to have been included mainly for additional comic effect. The susceptibility of the Vice to duping, theft and beating by others is notable.

Other youth and education plays: **21, 33, 53, 56, 58, 61, 64, 67, 68, 73** (frag.), **101, 103, 104.**

Other marriage quest plays: **29, 47, 57** (frag.), **61, 101.**

SIGNIFICANT TOPICS AND NARRATIVE ELEMENTS

learning and the upbringing of youth; marriage and social position; sexual temptation; good and bad companionship; the nature of women

DRAMATURGICAL AND RHETORICAL FEATURES

Verbal and general *Idleness* engages with several individual members of the audience on his entry 87–117; aliases of the Vices: *Idleness–Honest Recreation* 113, later *Due Disport* 256, *Wantonness–Modest Mirth* 166; *Idleness* pretends to be foreign 258–65; (pretended) rustic speech: *Snatch* and *Catch* 345 ff.; *Search* teaches *Idleness* to read out a proclamation 494–531; the Vice in this play made a victim, being beaten and robbed by *Catch* and *Snatch*, and duped by *Search* 266–356, 535–535 sd; the play is in ten scenes, though the printer has added the words 'the second act' after scene 3; extensive stage directions, all in English

Costume and dress *Wantonness* blackens *Wit*'s face and puts a fool's cap on his head 201 *sd*; *Idleness* is 'arrayed like a physician' 253; *Irksomeness* enters 'like a monster' (i.e. with a mask) 414 *sd*; *Idleness* adopts beggar's 'gear' 592; *Idleness* is dressed 'like a priest' 680 *sd*

Actions and stage directions 18 *sd*: 'Enter *Sev.* and his wife *Ind.*, and their son *Wit*'; 117 *sd*: '*Wa.* enters and says'; 181: *Wit* kisses *Wa.*; 201 *sd*: 'Here shall *Wa.* sing this song to the tune of "Attend thee, go play thee"; and having sung him (*Wit*) asleep in her (*Wa.'s*) lap, let him snort; then let her set a fool's bauble on his head, and blacking ('colling') his face; and *Id.* shall steal away his purse from him and go his ways'; 223 *sd*: 'Enter *G. Nur.* speaking this'; 229 *sd*: 'Here he (*G. Nu.*) stays, stumbling at *Wit* as he lies asleep'; 231 *sd*: 'Here he (*G. Nu.*) awakes him (*Wit*)'; 233 *sd*: 'Here he (*Wit*) rises, rubbing his eyes, and saying'; 235 *sd*: 'Here he (*Wit*) washes his face and takes off the bauble'; 237 *sd*: 'He (*G. Nu.*) delivers him (*Wit*) *H. Rec.*'; 267 *sd*: '(*Id.*) Lay down the purse in a corner'; 267 *sd* (2): 'The song that *Sna.* and *Ca.* sing together'; 297 *sd*: 'Here they (*Ca., Sna.*) espy him (*Id.*)'; 321 *sd*: 'Now he (*Ca.*) shall find the purse. Here after they have sc[r]ambled for the money, they shall spit in the purse and give it him (*Id.*) again'; 338 *sd*: 'Here they (*Ca., Sna.*) turn him (*Id.*) about, and bind his hands behind him, and tie the sheet about his face'; 342 *sd*: 'Here they (*Ca., Sna.*) run to one corner of the stage, and the other to the other, and speak like countrymen to beguile him (*Id.*)'; 352 *sd*: 'Here they (*Ca., Sna.*) beat him (*Id.*)'; 366 *sd*: 'Enter *Wit*, and *H. Rec.* waiting on him'; 374 *sd*: 'Here he (*Wit*) steps back, having espied *Id.*'; 393 *sd*: 'Here shall *Wit* pull off the sheet saying'; 414 *sd*: 'Here *Id.*, having brought him (*Wit*) to the den of *Irk.*, shall leap away, and *Irk.* shall enter like a monster, and shall beat down *Wit* with his club, saying'; 415 *sd*: 'Here they (*Wit, Irk.*) fight. *Wit* falls down'; 419 *sd*: 'Exit (*Irk*). *Irk.* leaves him (*Wit*) dead on the stage. Enter *Wis.* and says'; 423 *sd*: 'Here she (*Wis.*) helps him (*Wit*) up'; 449 *sd*: 'Exit *Wis. Wit* calls forth *Irk.*'; 451 sd: 'Enter *Irk.* saying'; 455 *sd*: 'Here they fight awhile, and *Irk.* must run in a-doors, and *Wit* shall follow, taking his (*Irk.'s*) visor off his head, and shall bring it in upon his sword, saying'; 459 *sd*: 'Enter *Id.*, halting with a stilt, and shall carry a cloth upon a staff, like a rat-catcher, and say'; 469 *sd*: 'Here he (*Id.*) espies *Se.* coming in, and goes up and down, saying "Have you any rats or mice?" as in the first five lines'; 491 *sd*: 'Here shall *Se.* take out a piece of paper and look on it'; 493 *sd*: 'Here shall *Se.* reach a chair, and *Id.* shall go up

and make the proclamation'; 497 *sd*: 'He (*Id*.) cries too often'; 501 *sd*: '(*Id*. to cry) Very often'; 505 *sd*: 'Here he (*Id*.) shall cry well'; 531 *sd*: '(*Se*.) Pull him (*Id*.) down'; 535 *sd*: 'Now shall *Se*. run away with his (*Id*.'s) money, and he shall cast away his stilt, and run after him'; 562 *sd*: 'Here he (*Wit*) receives the letter, and reads it to himself'; 566 *sd*: 'Here, *Wit* going in, one shall pull him by the arm, whereupon he shall cry on this manner'; 587 *sd*: 'He (*Id*.) goes in, and brings out the porridge pot about his neck'; 607 *sd*: 'Here enters *M. Bee* with a stick in her hand'; 617 *sd*: 'Here she (*M. Bee*) beats them (*Doll, Lob*) up and down the stage'; 627 *sd*: 'Enter *Inqu*., bringing in *Id*., with the pottage-pot about his neck'; 651 *sd*: 'Here *Wit* cries out in prison, and says this'; 664 *sd*: 'He (*G. Nur*.) comes near the prison'; 673 *sd*: 'Here enters and releases him (*Wit*) *G. Nur*.; 680 *sd*: 'Enter *Id*. like a priest'; 713 *sd*: 'Enter *G. Nur*.and *Wis*., and *Wis*. and *Wit* singing this song'; 745 *sd*: 'Here ends the song';
Simple entry: *Id*. 86; *Wit* 130; *Id*. 244; *Sna*., *Ca*. 265; *Fa*. 535; *Wit* 546; *Id*. 572; *Doll, Lob* 597; *G. Nur*. 641; *Sev. Wit* 705; *Epil*. 758; **Simple exit**: (*Prol*.) 18; *Sev*., *Ind*. 84; (*Wit*) 86; (*Id*.) 130; (*Wa*.) 223; (*G. Nur*.) 241; 'Both' (*H. Rec*., *Wit*) 244; *Sna*., *Ca*. 356; *H. Rec*. 411; (*Wit*) 459; (*Fa*., *Wit*) 572; *M. Bee* 635; 'All' (*Doll, Lob, Id*., *Inqu*.) 641; (*G. Nur*., *Wit*) 680; (*Id*.) 705; 'All' (*Sev*., *Wit*, *Wis*., *G. Nur*.) 758
Songs and music (w.s. to all songs) 1. *Wantonness* 'Lie still and here nest thee' (to the tune of 'Attend thee, go play thee'; w. ref.) 203–23; 2. *Snatch*, *Catch* 'It hath been told, been told, in proverbs old' 268–80; 3. *Wisdom*, *Wit* 'My joy hath overgrown my grief' 714–45
Staging and set the title page has a doubling scheme for six actors: 1. the *Prologue*, *Idleness*, *Epilogue*; 2. *Severity*, *Irksomeness*, *Snatch*, *Honest Recreation*; 3. *Indulgence*, *Wisdom*, *Mother Bee*; 4. *Wantonness*, *Fancy*, *Doll*; 5. *Wit*, *Search*, *Inquisition*, 6: *Good Nurture*, *Catch*, *Lob*. The action is partly unlocalized (sc. 1, 4, 9, 10) while it is possible to double the scenic structures needed for other scenes: *Wantonness*'s house (sc. 2)–*Mother Bee*'s house (sc. 6); *Irksomeness*'s den (sc. 3)–*Wit*'s prison (sc. 5, 8). *Wit*'s 'decapitation' of *Irksomeness* is effected with a mask and false head (455 *sd*); the 'corner' of the stage is mentioned in 267 *sd* and 342 *sd*
Stage properties *Wit*'s purse and dunce's cap, blacking for *Wit*'s face 201 *sd*; *Idleness*'s purse 267 *sd*; a rope and sheet to bind *Idleness* 338 *sd*; *Irksomeness*'s club 414 *sd*; *Wit*'s sword ('Perseverance') 443; *Irksomeness*'s visor 455 *sd*; *Idleness*'s crutch ('stilt') and cloth upon a staff 459 *sd*; *Search*'s proclamation 491 *sd*; a chair 493 *sd*; *Wisdom*'s letter 562 *sd*; *Idleness*'s porridge pot 587 *sd*; *Mother Bee*'s stick 607 *sd*

PLACENAMES

'Dawe's Cross' 324; Flushing 283; 'Harlowe-bery' 102; Kent 99; Musselburgh 487; St Paul's 255; 'St Quintin's' 486

ALLUSIONS

King Amasis of Egypt 698; Jove 660; Mount Parnassus 6

REPORT ON MODERN PRODUCTION

University of Jerusalem 15–17 June 1987 [*METh* 9:1 (1987) pp. 64–9]

BIBLIOGRAPHY

Greg. W. W. 'The Date of *Wit and Wisdom*', *PQ* 11:4 (1932) p. 410
Habicht, 1965, pp. 73–88
Haller, 1916, pp. 133–7
Hogrefe, 1959, pp. 328–31
Mackenzie, 1914, pp. 173–9
Race, S. '*The Marriage of Wit and Wisdom*', *N&Q* 198 (1953) pp. 18–20
Scolnicov, H. 'To Understand a Parable: The Mimetic Mode of *The Marriage of Wit and Wisdom*', *CE* 29 (1986) pp. 1–11
Tannenbaum, S. A. 'Comments on *The Marriage of Wit and Wisdom*', *PQ* 9 (1930) pp. 321–40
Tannenbaum, S. A. 'Dr Tannenbaum Replies', *PQ* 12:1 (1933) pp. 88–9
Tilley, M. P. 'Notes on *The Marriage of Wit and Wisdom*', *Shakespeare Association Bulletin* 10 (1935) pp. 45–57, 89–94

63   Mary Magdalen (Digby)

DATE, AUTHORSHIP AND AUSPICES

late fifteenth or early sixteenth century, anonymous; likely monastic or civic auspices, possibly to celebrate a saint's day

TEXT AND EDITIONS

Extant originals

Manuscript: Bodleian MS Digby 133, fos. 93–143

Editions

1994   CHD (CD-Rom and online copy of Baker, Murphy and Hall, 1982, l.l., OS)*
1993   Coldewey (OS)*
1982   Baker, Murphy and Hall (OS)*
1976   Baker, Murphy and Hall (facsimile, n.l.)
1975   Bevington (OS)
1929   *Sancta Maria Magdalena. Reproduced from MS Digby 133, fols 95–145 (recto)*, in the Bodleian Library, Oxford, New York, MLA Photographic Facsimiles no. 116 (facsimile, n.l.)
1896   Furnivall (reprinted from 1882 edition, OS)
1835   Sharp (OS)

SOURCES

The play draws on scriptural references to Mary Magdalene from *Luke 7* and also from the legendary accounts of the life of Mary Magdalene in Jacobus de Voragine's *Golden Legend* or in the *South English Legendary*; see the introduction to the edition by Baker, Murphy and Hall, pp. xl–xliii, and the essays by Davidson (1972) and Grantley below.

CHARACTERS

Emperor Tiberius
Scribe
Provost
Cyrus (Syrus)
Lazarus
Mary Magdalen
Martha
The Messenger (Nuncius)
Herod
First Philosopher
Second Philosopher
First Soldier (Primus Miles)
Second Soldier (Secundus Miles)
Pilate
First Sergeant-at-law
Second Sergeant-at-law
King of the World (Mundus)
Pride
Covetise
King of the Flesh
Lechery (Luxuria)
Sloth (mute)
Satan
Wrath
Envy
Sensuality (World's Messenger)
Bad Angel (Spiritus Malignus)
Taverner

Curiosity, a gallant
Simon Leprous
Jesus
Belfagor (Secundus Diabolus)
Good Angel (Bonus Angelus)
Belzabub (Tertius Diabolus)
Disciple of Jesus
Jew
King of Marcyll
Queen of Marcyll
A Devil
Mary Jacobe
Mary Salome
First Angel (at the tomb)
Second Angel (at the tomb)
St Peter
St John
Morell (pagan priest)
Hawkyn (Morell's acolyte)
Pilate's Messenger
Mary's Disciple
Raphael
Shipman
Grobbe (shipman's boy)
Soldier (of Marcyll)
Prince of Marcyll (mute)
Priest (Christian)

In addition there are several groups of attendants, the 'people', Jews, disciples and mourners. The seven devils cast out of Mary are the Seven Deadly Sins.

PLOT SUMMARY

The *Emperor Tiberius Caesar* opens the play with a 'boast' about his temporal power, and this is followed by another from *Cyrus*, father of *Mary Magdalen*, stressing his worldly well-being. The *Emperor* then resumes the action, sending a messenger from his scaffold to that of *Herod* to ensure that his laws are being kept. *Herod* is being told by his philosophers about the coming of *Christ*; he reacts irascibly to the news and, when the messenger arrives, *Herod* affirms his intention to rule ruthlessly. He sends the messenger on to *Pilate*, who makes similar undertakings when he receives the *Emperor*'s letters. On his scaffold, *Cyrus* suddenly falls ill and dies, to the sorrow of his children. Successively on their respective stages the *World*, *Flesh* and *Devil* then introduce themselves with appropriate 'boasts', after which the *Devil* goes to the *World* and they summon the *Flesh* to a council to plot an assault on the virtue of *Mary Magdalen*. *Lady Lechery* is detailed to do this and, after the Seven Deadly Sins besiege the castle of Magdalen, she befriends *Mary*, who is still grieving over her father's death. *Lechery* takes her off to a tavern in Jerusalem where *Mary* meets a gallant, *Curiosity*, who woos her and gives her drink. The *Devil* rejoices in his new victim, but when *Mary* falls asleep in an arbour, the *Good Angel* prompts her to virtue and when she wakes she resolves to follow *Christ*. She encounters him at the house of *Simon Leprous* and when *Christ* blesses her, seven devils exit from her body and make their way to Hell, where they are beaten for dereliction of duty. They afterwards set *Simon*'s house on fire. *Mary* returns to the castle of Magdalen where her brother *Lazarus* falls ill and dies. *Christ* is summoned and he raises *Lazarus* from the dead, while giving notice of his own impending death by crucifixion. They all then go off and (possibly after an interval) the *King of Marcyll* (Marseilles) introduces himself on his scaffold with a 'boast' about his own power and the beauty of his wife, after which a devil enters lamenting and telling of *Christ*'s harrowing of hell. The three Marys approach *Christ*'s sepulchre to ask for his body, to be told by the angels guarding it that he has risen. They fetch *Peter* and *John*, who fear that his body has been stolen. *Mary* goes to one side and is addressed by a man she thinks is the gardener, but he reveals himself as *Christ*. He sends her to fetch the other Marys and tells them to break the news to the disciples. He then departs, as do the Marys, and the *King of Marcyll* reappears to do a sacrifice to his pagan god. Back on his stage *Pilate*, who has been having some doubts about the justice of *Christ*'s death, nevertheless sends a message to *Herod* and the *Emperor* to report that he has done his duty. *Christ* then appears in heaven and sends the angel *Raphael* down to instruct *Mary* to convert the kingdom of Marcyll. She travels by ship and preaches to the *King*, who, however, proves resistant to her message. When he seeks to worship his idol *Mary* offers up a prayer, as a result of which a cloud comes down from heaven and sets the temple on fire. The *Pagan Priest* and his *Boy* sink and the disgruntled *King* retires to bed, while *Mary* seeks shelter in an old lodge. She prays further to *Christ*, who sends an angel to help her. She is able to appear to the *King* in a dream, prompting a change of heart which causes him to send for her and to request conversion. When he is converted, the *Queen* suddenly and miraculously falls pregnant, to their joy. *Mary* despatches them off to *St Peter* in the Holy Land to be baptized and they travel by boat. On the journey the *Queen* dies in childbirth and her body is placed on a rock with her child beside her.

The *King* then continues and receives baptism from *Peter*. On the return journey the *King* visits the rock where his wife has been laid, finding her resurrected and the child alive. On their arrival in Marcyll, the family is welcomed home by *Mary*, who has been regent in their absence. She then departs to live as a hermit in the desert where she is nourished by angels and visited by a priest who administers communion to her. Finally her soul is received into heaven accompanied by the singing of angels.

PLAY LENGTH

2,139 lines, with a further 4-line address by the scribe to readers of the play

COMMENTARY

This play is of interest as one of the few extant English saint plays, and also for the technical and scenic complexity of its staging. It is a place and scaffold play with a large number of stages as well as other minor though iconic locations. It is likely that several of these were doubled, such as Lazarus's tomb and Christ's tomb. The plot is a hybrid blend of allegorical sequences, elements of scriptural narrative and the life of Mary Magdalene drawn from legendary sources. It is notable among early plays in having a strong female central figure whose prominence resides in action and authority rather than in obedient passivity. The staging requires a considerable number of technical devices, including pyrotechnics.

Other biblical plays: **10, 11, 16, 34, 42, 44, 48, 77, 90, 93.**
Other conversion plays: **16, 51, 66, 83.**
Other female virtue plays: **3, 6, 34, 70, 87, 97.**
Other plays featuring prominent women characters: **3, 6, 30, 32, 43, 46, 51, 70, 75, 87, 95, 97.**
Other plays with probable place and scaffold staging: **9, 23, 48, 72** (frag.), **83, 85.**

SIGNIFICANT TOPICS AND NARRATIVE ELEMENTS

Old Testament, Mosaic law versus Christian teaching; the infernal trinity; the seven deadly sins; bad companionship; taverns, drinking and dancing; sexual dalliance; the raising of Lazarus; the crucifixion and resurrection; a *Quem Quaeritis* sequence; a *Hortulanus* sequence; miracles; paganism and conversion; the scriptural narrative of Mary Magdalene; the apocryphal life of Mary Magdalene; Mary as a female disciple; an assumption into heaven

DRAMATURGICAL AND RHETORICAL FEATURES

Verbal and general formal 'boasts' introduce several characters: *Emperor* 1–18, *Cyrus* 49–84, *Herod* 140–66, *Pilate* 229–43, *World* 305–25, *Flesh* 334–51,

Devil 358–76, *King of Marcyll* 925–62; *Herod*'s geographical list of places over which he claims sovereignty 157–9; the *World*'s list of metals and planets 313–22; the *Flesh*'s list of herbs and spices 339–43; the *Taverner*'s list of wines 476–9; a 'huffing' gallant 491 ff.; two dream appearances 588–601, 1610–17; a formal *planctus* by the three Marys 993–1004; comic folk play sequences involving mischievous servants: the priest's boy 1143–248; the shipman's boy 1395–422; the pagan priest's boy's passage of mock-Latin 1186–97; the heathen priest's relics 1232–41; there are several instances of the use of aureate speech; extensive and detailed stage directions, mostly in English with some in Latin (clustering mostly in the latter part of the play)

Costume and dress *Cyrus* is 'glistering in gold' 53; *Herod* has magnificent attire with pearl and rubies 153–4; *Pilate* has 'robes of richesse' 229; *Flesh* is 'flourished in my flowers' 334; *Curiosity* has elegant dress, including a shirt of Rennes linen with wide pendant sleeves, a doublet and hose 496, 501–5; the mourners are 'arrayed in black' 841 *sd*; *Lazarus* enters 'trussed with towels, in a sheet' (from the tomb) 910 *sd*; a devil enters 'in horrible array' 962 *sd*; the three Marys are 'arrayed as chaste women with signs of the Passion printed on their breasts 992 *sd*; two angels in white appear at *Christ*'s grave 1022 *sd*; the heathen priest dons his vestments 1183; *Mary* visits the king clad in white 1607; *Mary* and the *Angel* change their clothing 1617 *sd*

Actions and stage directions 44 *sd*: 'Here answer the people at once: "3a, my lord," 3a'; 48 *sd*: 'Here enter *Sy.*, the father of *M. M.*'; 113 *sd*: 'Here shall they (*Cy.*, *M. M.*, *Mar. Laz.*) be served with wine and spices'; 139 *sd*: 'Here goes the *Mess.* toward *Her.*'; 208 *sd*: 'Here comes the *Emp.*'s [*Mess.*], thus saying to *Her.*'; 216 *sd*: 'Here shall he (*Mess.*) take the letters unto the *Ki.*'; 248 *sd*: 'Here comes the *Emp.*'s *Mess.* to *Pil.*'; 256 *sd*: 'Here *Pil.* takes the letters with great reverence'; 264 *sd*: 'Here avoids (departs) the *Mess.*, and *Cy.* takes his death'; 276 *sd*: 'Here avoids *Sy.* suddenly, and then saying *Laz.*'; 304 *sd*: 'Here shall enter the *K. of the Wo.*, the *Fle.*, and the *Dev.* with the Seven D. Sins, a *B. An.* an[d] a *G. An.*, thus saying the *Wo.*'; 333 *sd*: 'Here shall enter the *K. of Fle.* with *Slo.*, *Glu.*, *Lec.*'; 357 *sd*: 'Here shall enter the prince of devils in a stage, and hell underneath that stage, thus saying the *Dev.*'; 380 *sd*: 'Here shall the *Dev.* go to the *Wo.* with his company'; 397 *sd*: 'Here he (*Mess.*) goes to the *Fle.*, thus saying'; 408 *sd*: 'Here comes the *Ki. of Fle.* to the *Wo.*, thus saying'; 439 *sd*: 'Here shall the Seven D. Sins besiege the castle till [*Mary*] agree to go to Jerusalem. *Lec.* shall enter the castle with the *B. An.*, thus saying *Lec.*'; 469 *sd*: 'Here takes *Mary* her way to Jerusalem with *Lux.*, and they shall resort to a *Tav.*, thus saying the *Tav.*'; 490 *sd*: 'Here shall enter a gallant, thus saying'; 546 *sd*: 'Here shall *Mary* and the gallant avoid, and the *B. An.* goes to the *Wo.*, the *Fle.* and the *Dev.*, thus saying the *B. An.*'; 559 *sd*: 'Here goes the *B. An.* to *Mary* again'; 563 *sd*: 'Here shall *Sat.* go home to his stage, and *Mary* shall enter into the place alone, save the *B. An.*, and all the Seven D. Sins shall be conveyed into the house of *S. Lep.* They shall be arrayed like seven devils, thus kept close; *Mary* shall be in an arbour, thus saying'; 571 *sd*: 'Here shall *Mary* lie down and sleep in the arbour'; 587 *sd*: 'Here enter *Sim.* into the place, the *G. An.* thus saying to *Mary*'; 614 *sd*: 'Here shall enter the Prophet with his disciples, thus saying *S. Lep.*'; 630 *sd*: 'Here shall *Mary* follow along, with this lamentation'; 640 *sd*: 'Here shall *Mary* wash the feet of the Prophet with the tears of her eyes, wiping them with her hair, and then anoint them with a precious ointment. *Jes.* says' (E/L); 691 *sd*: 'With this word seven devils shall devoid (exit) from the woman and the *B. An.* enter into hell with thunder'; 704 *sd*: 'Here devoids *Jes.* with his disciples, the *G. An.* rejoicing of *Magd.*'; 725 *sd*: 'Here appear two devils before the master'; 730: the *B. An.* prostrates himself before the *Dev.*; 735–6: the *B. An.* is beaten; 739 *sd*: 'Here shall they serve all the seven (devils) as they do the first'; 743 *sd*: 'Here shall the other devils set the house on fire, and make a soot, and *Mary* shall go to *Laz.* and to *Mart.*'; 775 *sd*: 'Here shall *Laz.* take his death, thus saying'; 793 *sd*: 'Here go *Mary* and *Mart.*, and meet with *Jes.*, thus saying'; 818 *sd*: 'Here go *Mary* and *Mart.* homeward, and *Jes.* devoids'; 823 *sd*: 'He (*Laz.*) dies' (L); 841 *sd*: 'Here the one kn. make ready the stone, and the other bring in the weepers, arrayed in black'; 845 *sd*: 'Lay him (*Laz.*) in. Here all the people resort to the castle, thus saying *Jesus*'; 868 *sd*: 'Here shall *Jes.* come with his disciples, and one Jew tells *Mart.*'; 872 *sd*: 'Here *Mart.* shall run against *Jes.*, thus saying'; 888 *sd*: 'Here *Mary* shall fall to *Jes.*, thus saying *Mart.*'; 902 *sd*: 'Here shall *Mart.* put off the grave stone'; 910 *sd*: 'Here shall *Laz.* arise, trussed with towels, in a sheet'; 920 *sd*: 'Here all the people and the Jews, *Mary* and *Mart.*, with one voice say these words: We believe in you, Saviour, Jesus, Jesus, Jesus'; 924 *sd*: 'Here devoids *Jes.* with his disciples; *Mary* and *Mart.* and *Laz.* go home to the castle, and here [*Ki. of Mar.*] begins his boast'; 962 *sd*: 'Here shall the knights get spices and wine, and here shall enter a devil in horrible array, thus saying'; 992 *sd*: 'Here shall enter the three Marys arrayed as chaste women, with signs of the passion printed upon their breast[s], thus saying *Magd.*'; 1004 *sd*: 'All the Marys with one voice say this following'; 1022 *sd*: 'Here shall appear two angels in white at the grave'; 1030 *sd*: 'Here shall the Marys meet with *Pe.* and *Jo.*'; 1046 *sd*: 'Here *Pe.* and *Jo.* go to the sepulchre and the three Marys following'; 1060 *sd*: 'Here appears *Jes.*' (L); 1095 *sd*: 'Here avoids *Jes.* suddenly, thus saying *M. Magd.*'; 1124 *sd*: 'Here *Jes.* devoids again'; 1132 *sd*: 'Here devoid all the three Marys and the *K. of Mar.* shall begin a sacrifice'; 1142 *sd*: 'Here shall enter a heathen priest and his boy'; 1177 *sd*: '(*Pri.*) Beat him (*Boy*)'; 1178 *sd*: 'The *Ki.* says' (L); 1210 *sd*: 'The *Ki.* says' (L); 1227 *sd*: 'Sing both (*Pri.*, *Boy*)'; 1280 *sd*: 'Here goes the *Mess.* to *Her.*'; 1292 *sd*: 'Here goes the *Mess.* to the *Emp.*'; 1335 *sd*: 'Here enter *Magd.* with her disciple, thus saying'; 1348 *sd*: 'Here shall heaven open, and *Jes.* shall show'; 1375 *sd*: 'Then the *Ang.* descends' (L); 1394 *sd*: 'Here shall enter a ship with a merry song'; 1418 *sd*: '(*Shi.*) Beat him (*Boy*); 1438 *sd*: 'Now shall the shipmen sing'; 1445 *sd*: 'Here goes the ship out of the place'; 1453: 'Here shall *Mary* enter before the *Ki.*'; 1537 *sd*: 'Here goes the *Ki.* with all his attendant to the temple'; 1153 *sd*: 'Here shall the idol ('mament') tremble and shake'; 1561 *sd*: 'Here shall come a cloud from heaven, and set the temple afire, and the priest and the clerk shall sink, and the *Ki.* goes home, thus saying'; 1577 *sd*: 'Here the *Ki.* goes home to bed in haste, and *Mary* goes into an old lodge without the gate, thus saying'; 1597 *sd*: 'Then the angels descend. The first one says' (L); 1609 *sd*: 'Here goes *Mary*, with the angels before her, to the *Ki.*'s bed, with lights bearing, thus saying *Mary*'; 1617 *sd*: 'Here *Mary* voids (exits), and the angel and *Mary* change their clothes, thus saying the *Ki*'; 1641 *sd*: 'Then the *Kn.* goes to *Mary*' (L); 1645 *sd*: 'Then *Mary* goes to the *Ki.*'; 1715 *sd*: 'And then the ship comes into the place, and the *Shi.* says' (L); 1724 sd: 'And then the *Ki.* goes to the ship, and the *Ki.* says' (L); 1744 *sd*: 'The *Qu.* lamenting' (L); 1780 *sd*: '(Shipmen) Make ready for to cast her (*Qu.*) out'; 1790 *sd*: 'Then they (shipmen) row to the rock, and the *Ki.* says' (L); 1796 *sd*: 'Then they row from the rock, and the *Shi.* says' (L); 1842 *sd*: 'Then (*St Pe.*) sprinkles him (*Ki.*) with water' (L); 1862 *sd*: 'Then the *Ki.* goes to the ship and the *Ki.* says' (L); 1878 *sd*: 'Then the ship comes around the place. The *Ki.* says' (L); 1914 *sd*: 'Then they row from the rock, and the *Shi.* says' (L); 1922 *sd*: 'Here goes the ship out of the place, and *Magd.* says'; 1938 *sd*: 'Here shall the *Ki.* and the *Qu.* kneel down. The *Ki.* says' (E/L); 1971 *sd*: 'Here goes *Mary* into the wilderness, thus saying the *Ki.*'; 1988 *sd*: '*Mary* in the wilderness' (L); 2018 *sd*: 'Here shall two angels descend into wilderness, and another two shall bring an offering, openly appearing aloft in the clouds; the two beneath shall bring *Mary*, and she shall receive the bread and then go again into the wilderness'; 2030 *sd*: 'Here shall she (*Mary*) be saluted ('halsyd') by angels with reverent song. *Mary* is assumed into the clouds. The heavens rejoice, angels praising the son of God, and *Mary* says' (E/L); 2038 *sd*: 'Here shall speak a holy priest in the same wilderness, thus saying the *Pri.*'; 2044 *sd*: 'Here he (*Pri.*) shall go in the wilderness, and spy *Mary* in her devotion, thus saying the *Pri.*'; 2072 *sd*: 'Here shall the *Pri.* go to his cell, thus saying *Jes.*'; 2084 *sd*: 'Here shall two angels go *Mary* and to the *Pri.*, thus saying to the *Pri.*'; 2092 *sd*: '(*Mary*) In the wilderness' (L); 2100 *sd*: 'Here appears the *Angel* and the *Priest* with the Host' (L); 2108 *sd*: 'Here she (*Mary*) receives it (Host)'; 2122 *sd*: 'They rejoice in the heavens' (L)

Songs and music (w.n.s. to any songs) 1. *Priest*, *Boy* (boy singing the treble) 1227 *sd*; 2. *Shipman*, *Boy* 'a merry song' 1394 *sd*; 3. *Shipman*, *Boy* 1438 *sd*; 4. Angels 'reverent song' 2030 *sd*; 5. Angels' 'merry song' 2122 *sd*; 6. whole cast (?) 'Te Deum Laudamus' 2139

Staging and set this is a place and scaffold play for open air production, with very elaborate staging requirements; scaffolds are needed for *Emperor Tiberius*, the Castle of Magdalen, the *World*, the *Flesh*, Hell (the lower part of the *Devil*'s scaffold, 337 *sd*), a tavern, *Pilate*, *Simon*, *Herod*, Heaven (opening, 1348 *sd*), Marcyll and Jerusalem, and there are likely to have been lesser locations, such as *Mary*'s arbour, *Lazarus*'s and *Christ*'s tombs, the pagan temple, *Mary*'s lodge, an island, and *Mary*'s hermitage; several of the locations could have been doubled, however, since the play divides naturally into two halves, allowing this; there is a moving ship which travels around the *platea* (1445 *sd*); several mechanical and pyrotechnic effects are used, such as the trembling and collapse of the pagan gods (1553 *sd*), the firing of both *Simon*'s house (743 *sd*) and the temple (with a cloud which descends from the Heaven stage in 1561 *sd*), and the ascents and descents from the Heaven

stage (*sds* after 1375, 1597, 2018); a trick is used to represent devils emerging from *Mary* (691 *sd*); there is a siege of the castle of Magdalen (439 *sd*); messengers traverse the *platea* to take messages between the scaffolds
Stage properties wine and spices 113 *sd*, 962 *sd*; the *Emperor*'s letters 216 *sd*, 256 *sd*; *Curiosity*'s lace sash for his lover 497; *Simon*'s feast 630; *Mary*'s ointment 640 *sd*; the *Devil*'s whip 735; the *Devil*'s pan of pitch 738; *Lazarus*'s gravestone 841 *sd*; a winding sheet ('sudare cloth') 1049; the heathen priest's relics: a bone and an eyelid 1233, 1237; *Pilate*'s letter 1313; a moving ship 1394 *sd*; a heathen idol 1553 *sd*; lights 1609 *sd*; a bread offering for *Mary* 2018 *sd*; a communion wafer 2100 *sd*

PLACENAMES

Aleppo[1] 158; Antalya ('Satyllye') 1437; Arimathea 1260; Asia[1] 158; Beersheba ('Berȝaby')[1] 159; Bethany 62, 82; Bethlehem[1] 159; Galilee 982, 1122; Hebron ('Abyron')[1] 159; Israel 181; Jerusalem 61 *passim*; Judea 170, 849; Castle of Magdalo ('Maudleyn') 59; Marseilles ('Marcyll') 938 *passim*; Troy 368; Turkey 1435; Tyre[1] 158;

1 Part of *Herod*'s alliterative list of places over which he claims sovereignty.

ALLUSIONS

Dagon 1244; King David 1010; *Genesis 49:10* 184–5; Gideon 1351; Goliath 1243; Isaiah 697; *Isaiah 44:22* 757, *60:3* 175–6; *John 1:1* 1483; Joseph of Arimathea 1260; Judah 184; Jupiter (pl.) 320; *Luke 7:43* 661, *7:50* 691, 924; Mars (pl.) 317; Mercury (pl.) 318; Noah 1351; Phoebus 1353; *Psalm 26:1* (V)/*27:1* (AV) 1552–3, *143:5* (V)/*144:5* (AV) 1011; Saturn (pl.) 321; Solomon 1349; Venus (pl.) 319

REPORTS ON MODERN PRODUCTIONS

1. St Bartholomew the Great Church, Smithfield, London, dir. H. Gates, 26–9 May 1976 [*Daily Telegraph*, 28 May 1976, RORD 19 (1976) pp. 83–4]
2. University of Colorado, Boulder (Whitsun Productions), dir. J. D. Schuchter, 23–5, 31 July, 1 August 1977 [*RORD* 21 (1978) p. 96]
3. University of Durham, dir. J. McKinnell, 27–8 June, 3–4 July 1982 [*METh* 4:1 (1982) pp. 63–70; see also McKinnell's essay listed below]
4. Amherst (University of Massachusetts, English Department), dir. J. Gates and M. Otter, 15, 18 May 1983 [*RORD* 26 (1983) pp. 120–1]

RECORDED PRODUCTION

LP Record: BBC, *The First Stage*, dir. J. Barton (1970)

CONCORDANCE

Preston, 1977

BIBLIOGRAPHY

Baker and Murphy, 1967, pp. 153–66

Bennett, J. 'The *Mary Magdalene* of Bishop's Lynn', *SP* 75:1 (1978) pp. 1–9

Boehnen, S. 'The Aesthetics of "Sprawling Drama": The Digby *Mary Magdalene* as Pilgrim's Play', *JEGP* 98:3 (1999) pp. 325–52

Bowers, R. H. 'The Tavern Scene in the Middle English Digby Play of *Mary Magdalene*' in Bryan, Alton and Murphree, 1965, pp. 15–32

Bush, J. 'The Resources of *Locus* and *Platea* Staging: The Digby *Mary Magdalene*', *SP* 86:2 (1989) pp. 139–65

Coldewey, J. 'The Digby Plays and the Chelmsford Records', *RORD* 18 (1975) pp. 103–21

Coletti, T. 'The Design of the Digby Play of *Mary Magdalene*' *SP* 76:4 (1979) pp. 313–33

Coletti, T. '*Paupertas est donum Dei*: Hagiography, Lay Religion and the Economics of Salvation in the Digby *Mary Magdalene*', *Speculum* 76:2 (2001) pp. 337–78

Craymer, S. L. 'Margery Kempe's Imitation of Mary Magdalene and the Digby Plays', *MQ* 19:4 (1993) pp. 173–81

Davidson, C. 'The Digby *Mary Magdalen* and the Magdalene Cult of the Middle Ages', *AM* 8 (1972) pp. 70–87

Davidson, C. 'The Medieval English Saint Play' in Davidson, 1986, pp. 71–97

Dixon, M. '"Thys Body of Mary": "Femynyte" and "Inward Mythe" in the Digby *Mary Magdalene*', *Mediaevalia* 18 (1995 for 1992) pp. 221–44

Dobson, E. J. 'The Etymology and Meaning of "Boy"', *MÆ* 9 (1940) pp. 139–47

Godfrey, R. 'Survivals of "Place and Scaffold" Staging in the Sixteenth Century' in Lascombes, 1998, pp. 163–84

Godfrey, R. 'The Machinery of Spectacle: The Performance Dynamic of the *Play of Mary Magdalen* and Related Matters' in Higgins, 2000, pp. 145–59

Grantley, D. 'The Source of the Digby *Mary Magdalen*', *N&Q* n.s. 31:4 [229] (1984) pp. 457–9

Jeffrey, 1973, pp. 68–89

Jones, M. K. 'How the Seven Deadly Sins "Dewoyde from the Woman" in the Digby *Mary Magdalen*', *ANQ* 16:8 (1978) pp. 118–19

Jones, M. K. 'Sunlight and Sleight of Hand in Medieval Drama', *TN* 32:3 (1978) pp. 118–26

Maltman, N. 'Light in and on the Digby *Mary Magdalene*' in King and Stevens, 1979, pp. 257–80

McKinnell, J. 'Staging the Digby *Mary Magdalen*', *METh* 6:2 (1984) pp. 126–52

Mead, S. X. 'Four-Fold Allegory in the Digby *Mary Magdalene*', *Renascence* 43:4 (1991) pp. 269–82

Milner, S. 'Flesh and Food: The Function of Female Asceticism in the Digby *Mary Magdalene*', *PQ* 73:4 (1994) pp. 385–401

Ritchie, H. 'A Suggested Location for the Digby "Mary Magdalene"', *TS* 4 (1963) pp. 51–8

Scherb, V. I. 'Worldly and Sacred Messengers in the Digby *Mary Magdalene*', *PQ* 73:4 (1994) pp. 385–401

Scherb, V. I. 'Blasphemy and the Grotesque in the Digby *Mary Magdalene*', *SP* 96:3 (1999) pp. 225–40

Scherb, 2001, pp. 172–90

Schmidt, 1885, pp. 371–93

Velz, J. W. 'Sovereignty in the Digby *Mary Magdalene*', *CD* 2:1 (1968) pp. 32–43

Velz, 1981–2, pp. 311–26

Wickham, 1972, pp. 99–119

Womack, P. 'Shakespeare and the Sea of Stories', *JMEMS* 29:1 (1999) pp. 169–87

64   Misogonus

DATE, AUTHORSHIP AND AUSPICES

1564–77; anonymous, though it is likely it was written by one or a combination of three of the men whose names appear on the manuscript: Anthony Rudd, Laurentius Bariona or Thomas Rychardes; possibly written for university performance at Trinity College, Cambridge

TEXT AND EDITIONS

Extant original

Manuscript: Huntington Library MS 542

Editions

1994   CHD (CD-Rom and online copy of Bond, 1911, l.l., s.l., OS)
1979   Barber (s.l., NS)*
1911   Bond (s.l., OS)
1906   Farmer (4) (n.l., NS)
1898   Brandl (OS)

SOURCES

The idea derives from the biblical parable of the prodigal son, but the narrative also owes something to the continental Christian Terence tradition; see the introduction to Barber's edition, pp. 44–60, and Spengler, 1888, for an account of this tradition. The lost child motif may owe something to the Roman comedy of Terence and Plautus.

CHARACTERS

Prologue
Philogonus, the father
Eupelas, the father's faithful neighbour
Cacurgus, the fool
Misogonus, the son of the household
Orgalus, servant to Misogonus
Oenophilus, servant to Misogonus
Liturgus, servant to Philogonus
Melissa, a courtesan
Sir John, a priest

Jack, a clerk
Custor Codrus, a rustic
Alison, wife to Codrus
Isbell Busby, witness, old woman
Madge Caro, witness, old woman
Eugonus, absent son
Crito, a foreigner
Epilogue

PLOT SUMMARY

After a prologue which calls on the Muses and introduces the narrative, the play opens with *Philogonus*'s complaint about his son's prodigality to his friend *Eupelas*, who offers to exhort the young man to virtue. *Philogonus* is called to supper by a servant, *Cacurgus*, who affects verbal incompetence and the manner of a professional fool. When *Philogonus* goes off, *Cacurgus* expresses a Vice-like glee in the corruption of the son, *Misogonus*, and goes off to inform him of *Eupelas*'s impending attempt to convert him. *Misogonus*'s corruption is demonstrated in scenes of his carousing and brawling with his servingmen, *Oenophilus* and *Orgalus*. On two missing pages of the manuscript, *Eupelas* duly makes his attempt to reform *Misogonus* but is beaten for his pains. When *Misogonus* goes off to fetch his servingmen, *Eupelas* hastily retreats, while the young man goes on to engage in more scenes of revelry and gambling with the servingmen, a whore *Melissa*, and a corrupt priest *Sir John*. In a scene that is interspersed with these, *Philogonus* hears more about his son from *Cacurgus* and discusses his sorrows with another servant, *Liturgus*, who tells him what has happened to *Eupelas*. When *Philogonus* and his friends arrive to confront *Misogonus*, he is defiant even when his father threatens to disinherit him, knowing that he is the only heir. On the departure of all the other characters, *Philogonus* sings a song of sorrow, signalling the lowest point in his fortunes. Soon afterwards, an old rustic and tenant of *Philogonus*, *Codrus*, comes to pay his rent and, when he hears his landlord's complaints about his son, reveals to him that he has another son sent away at birth by *Philogonus*'s now deceased wife. This is confirmed by *Codrus*'s wife, who relates that *Philogonus*'s wife bore him twins, but on the advice of a wise man sent one away to her brother to be reared. *Liturgus* is sent to fetch the boy but *Cacurgus*, urged by *Misogonus* to whom he has communicated the news, works out a plan to foil *Philogonus*. He pretends to be a doctor and tries to bribe some rustic women to deny the truth of *Codrus*'s account, though they prove too foolish and disorganized to do this. The lost son, *Eugonus*, is brought in and his identity confirmed by the fact that he has six toes on one foot. After *Alison* and *Codrus* reiterate the circumstances of *Eugonus*'s birth, he and his father are reunited. *Misogonus* attacks his brother as a land-grabber, but he refuses to express sorrow for his past deeds in exchange for the reconciliation which *Philogonus* offers him. Instead he turns on his servingmen for allegedly leading him astray. After a passage in which *Cacurgus* delivers a long lament about his situation, *Misogonus* re-enters, accompanied by *Liturgus*, who persuades him to repent. He does this and is reconciled to his father, but the manuscript ends prematurely at this point.

PLAY LENGTH

1,950 lines extant

COMMENTARY

This is one of the most important and substantial 'profligate youth' interludes of the sixteenth century. As in the case of most of these plays, there is only one parent. The figure of *Cacurgus* is of interest as a combination of a Vice figure, a scheming servant of classical comedy, and a quick-witted professional Fool. *Cacurgus* affects rustic speech when he considers it politic to do so, and rusticity is also exploited for comic potential elsewhere in the piece. The use of songs to denote either moral states or states of mind is noteworthy. The play uses the classic romance device of a distinguishing physical mark to identify the lost son.

Other youth and education plays: **21, 33, 53, 56, 58, 61, 62, 67, 68, 73** (frag.), **101, 103, 104.**

SIGNIFICANT TOPICS AND NARRATIVE ELEMENTS

friendship; the education of and upbringing of youth; inheritance and profligate heirs; a prodigal son narrative; bad companions; drink and drunkenness; whores and sexual dalliance; corrupt clergy; gambling; Will Summer; Catholicism and popular religious practice; herbs and popular medicine; comic rusticity; a lost child motif

NOTE: line numbering is by scene; references are therefore to act/scene/line

DRAMATURGICAL AND RHETORICAL FEATURES

Verbal and general rustic speech: *Cacurgus* (pretended) 1.1.193–217, *Codrus* 3.1.1 ff., *Alison* 3.1.130 ff., *Isbell* 3.2.73 ff., *Madge* 3.2.77 ff.; *Orgalus* appears to enter through the audience 1.1.393; *Cacurgus* interacts with the audience, giving his laces to them 1.1.274–7; a gambling scene 2.2.135–208; a bell sounds off stage 2.2.209; *Madge Mumblecrust* speaks with a stutter (because of toothache) 3.2.77 ff.; *Cacurgus*'s list of ailments (as a pretended doctor) 3.2.121–4; *Cacurgus*'s list of his skills as a professional Fool 4.2.21–69; four acts with scene divisions, which are scribal or done by a later Corrector, and it is likely this was originally conceived as a standard five-act play on the classical model; a leaf is missing from the manuscript between folios 6 and 7, and at least one at the end; several lines elsewhere are wholly or partly missing; Greek names for the principal characters and English ones for the rustics; a comic subplot element; lower-class figures have a central role in resolving the plot; the play is set in Italy; stage directions in Latin

Costume and dress *Cacurgus* wears long ears 1.1.282; *Cacurgus* wears jester's dress, 'foolish weed' 1.1.321; *Cacurgus* pulls off the priest's gown 2.2.143–4; *Codrus* complains that his wife looks as though she has been lying in ash 3.1.129; *Cacurgus*'s garment is 'pied' (multicoloured) 3.2.100

Actions and stage directions 1.1.208: 'Someone (speaking) within' 2081.1.274–7: *Cac.* throws his laces to the audience; 2.1.op. *sd*: 'The servants shout within'; 2.1.67–70: *Mis.* beats *Oen.*; 2.1.74: *Mis.* beats *Cac.*; 2.1.283–5: *Phil.* gives *Cac.* 'ding dongs' or embellishments from his own hose; 2.2.209: A bell rings off stage; 2.2.263–99: *Mel., Org., Oen.* and *S. Jo.* dance (a cinquepace); 3.1.9: A hen cackles off stage; 4.1.45–62: *Phil.* and *Eup.* eavesdrop on *Isb.* and *Mad.* talking to *Cod.*; 4.1.125–6; *Ali.* cuts *Eug.*'s hose; 4.1.195: *Mis., Org.* and *Oen.* threaten *Eug.* and bar him from entering *Phil.*'s house; 4.1.220–22: *Mis.*, threatens to beat *Org.*and *Oen.*; 4.2.1 *sd*: *Cac.* calls 'in a high voice' and 'in a low voice' (repeated exclamations); 4.2.4 *sd*: 'Like a castrator of pigs he (*Cac.*) blows his nose and calls out in sobs for a time'; **Simple entry:** *Mis.* 1.1.285; *Cac.* 2.1.70; *Phil., Lit.* 2.1.183; *Cac.* 2.2.72; *Oen.* 2.2.92; *Phil., Eup., Lit.* 2.2.299 (2); *Phil.* 3.1.49; *Isb. Bus., Mad.* 3.2.72; *Lit., Eug.* 4.1.62; *Cri.* 4.1.82; *Mis., Org., Oen.* 4.1.193; *Cac.* 4.2.op. *sd*; *Lit., Mis.* 4.3.op. *sd*; *Phil., Lit.* 4.3.40; **Simple exit:** (*Prol.*) pr. 44; *Phil., Eup.* 1.1.217; *Cac.* 1.1.388; (*Org.*) 1.1.437; (*Lit.*) 2.1.261; 'All' (*Phil., Lit., Cac.*) 2.1.304; *Cac.* 2.2.299; *Phil.* 2.2.476; (*Phil.*) 3.1.281; *Phil., Eup., Eug., Lit., Cri., Cod., Ali.* 4.1.219; *Org., Oen.* 4.1.237; *Mis.*4.1.249; (*Cac.*) 4.2.89

Songs and music (w.s. to both songs) 1. *Cacurgus, Oenophilus, Orgalus, Misogonus*: 'Sing care away with sport and play' (to the tune of 'Hearts Ease') 2.1.140–79 (*Cacurgus* first gives out the parts according to voices 2.1.126–38); 2. *Philogonus*: 'O mighty Jove, some pity take' (to the tune of 'Labondoso Hoto') 2.2.417–77; **Instrumental:** possibly music for the dance at 2.2.263–99

Staging and set a doubling scheme is given beside the character list as follows: 1. *Philogonus*, 2. *Eupelas*, 3. *Misogonus*, 4. *Cacurgus, Prologus, Eugonus*, 5. *Codrus, Sir John, Epilogus*, 6. *Orgalus, Isbell*, 7. *Oenophilus, Madge*, 8. *Melissa, Crito*; where the action is localized, it is done through the presence and dialogue of the characters and there are no particular indications as to set, apart from the fact that *Misogonus* bars *Eugonus* from entering *Philogonus*'s house

Stage properties *Cacurgus*'s laces ('points') 1.1.274; coins 2.2.27; cards 2.2.139; dice 2.2.133; *Codrus*'s baskets of capons 3.1.26; *Codrus*'s penknife 4.1.125; weapons for *Misogonus* and his companions 4.1.195

PLACENAMES

Apollonia (fict.) 3.1.170 *passim*; 'Baul's bush' (?) 4.1.133; Cambridge 3.2.145; India 3.2.106, 120; Italy pr. 22, 1.1.26; Laurentum pr. 21, 1,1.56, 4.1.63; London 3.1.37; St Paul's 3.2.3; 'Piper's Hill' (?) 4.1.136; Troy 2.2.442; Walsingham (shrine) 3.1.150

ALLUSIONS

Aeolus 4.1.184; Aganippe fountain pr. 3; Apollo pr. 15; Balaam 1.1.283; St Clement 4.1.146; King David 4.1.175; Fates 1.1.58; Hercules 4.1.242; Homer pr. 19; Robin Hood 1.1.291; Icarus and Daedalus 2.2.439–40; Jove 2.2.417; Mercury 2.2.167;

King Midas 1.1.285; Muses pr. 3–5; Neptune 4.1.184; Nestor 4.1.175; St Nicholas 4.1.147; Parnassus pr. 1; St Paul 4.3.12; Phaeton and Phoebus 2.2.437–8; Phoebus pr. 12; Pilate 4.1.230; Priam 2.2.441; Solomon 2.1.252; St Stephen 4.1.148; Venus 3.2.207; Nine Worthies 2.1.81

BIBLIOGRAPHY

Barber, L. E. 'Anthony Rudd and the Authorship of *Misogonus*', *ELN* 12:4 (1975) pp. 255–60
Bevington, D. '*Misogonus* and Laurentius Bariωna' *ELN* 2:1 (1964) pp. 9–10
Bond, 1911, pp. xiii–cxviii
Kittredge, G. L. 'The *Misogonus* and Laurence Johnson' *JEGP* 3:3 (1901) pp. 335–41
Manly, J. M. untitled (corrections and additions to the notes in Brandl's edition), *JEGP* 2:3 (1899) pp. 395–410
Miller, E. S. 'Magnificat nunc dimittis in *Misogonus*', *MLN* 60:1 (1945) pp. 45–7
Tannenbaum, S. A. 'A Note on *Misogonus*' *MLN* 45:4 (1930) pp. 308–10
Tannenbaum, S. A. 'The Author of *Misogonus*' in Tannenbaum, 1933, pp. 129–41
Young, 1979, pp. 117–27

65   Nature

DATE, AUTHORSHIP AND AUSPICES

c. 1496; Henry Medwall; probably for production in the Great Hall at Lambeth Palace (under the patronage of John Morton); Greg 17, 18

TEXT AND EDITIONS

Extant originals

1530–4 printing by William Rastell: BL (one copy and one frag.) Bodleian (frag.); Cambridge; Huntington (frag.); State Library of Victoria, Melbourne (frag.); *STC* 17779

Editions

1994   CHD (CD-Rom and online copy of Nelson, 1980, l.l., OS)
1981   Moeslein (OS)
1980   Nelson (OS)*
1914   Farmer (1914a) (facsimile, n.l.)
1908   TFT (facsimile, n.l.)
1908   '*Lost*' *Tudor Plays*, TFT (facsimile, n.l.)
1907   Farmer (9) (n.l., NS)
1905   Bang and McKerrow (fragment, facsimile)
1898   Brandl (OS)

SOURCES

No specific sources have been firmly identified, but Alan Nelson considers the play to be reminiscent of the mid-fifteenth-century *Liber Apologeticus* of Thomas Chaundler; see the introduction to his edition, p. 23. See also Mackenzie's and Macauley's essays below.

CHARACTERS

Nature	World (Mundus)	Bodily Lust	Meekness	Abstinence
Man	Worldly Affection	Sloth	Charity	Chastity
Sensuality	Pride	Gluttony	Patience	
Reason	Boy	Wrath	Good Occupation	
Innocency	Shamefastness	Envy	Liberality	

PLOT SUMMARY

Nature opens the play with a sermon which exhorts *Man* to follow *Reason*, though he recognizes that *Sensuality* is natural to him. *Sensuality* steps in to take issue with *Nature*, claiming the right to dominance over *Man*, and then going on to debate with *Reason*, *Innocency* also participating. *Reason* hands *Man* over to the *World*, requesting that he be looked after as *Nature* commands. The *World* clothes him and invests him with authority and power. He also seeks to provide *Man* with servants; he designates *Worldly Affection* and *Sensuality* as worthy attendants and advises him to dismiss *Innocency*, which *Man* duly does. *Sensuality* undertakes to find another servingman for *Man* and he advises him to observe *Pride*, who enters richly apparelled. *Pride* asks *Sensuality* to engage him in *Man's* service, which he agrees to do in exchange for a bribe. On becoming *Man's* servingman, *Pride* (now calling himself *Worship*) proceeds to counsel him against *Reason*, exhorting him also to change his fashion of dress. While *Sensuality* leads *Man* off to a tavern, *Pride* resolves to find his new master fine clothes. *Sensuality* then reappears to tell of *Man's* encounter with whores and to say that he has summoned as company for his master the other deadly sins, who are *Pride's* kinsmen, each changing their names to disguise their natures. *Man*, in youth, embraces all readily except *Covetise* (who does not actually appear) (a vice of old age). When *Sensuality* goes out, *Reason* comes in bemoaning *Man's* abandonment of him. *Man* appears with *Worldly Affection*, but is visited by *Shamefastness* and this provokes in him a desire for *Reason*, with whom he is then reconciled. This ends the first part of the play. In Part II, *Man* enters in the company of *Reason*, who exhorts him to hold out against the Vices, like a castle against a siege. However, *Man* is sorrowfully reminded of his old companionship by *Sensuality*, especially the whores, and he soon falls into the company of *Bodily Lust*. He goes off with *Worldly Affection* to find whores and when he returns *Pride* is there to tell him his new garments are ready. *Sloth* is also in his company, and they are soon joined successively by *Gluttony*, *Bodily Lust*, *Envy* and

Wrath. *Pride* is later shocked to be informed by a gleeful *Envy* that his expenditure on clothing has ruined him, and he departs. *Sensuality* tells *Envy* that *Man* has become old and has been abandoned by *Gluttony* and *Bodily Lust*, while *Covetise* has joined his company. They leave and *Man* then enters with *Reason*, who lectures him about his fall into sin and advises him to repent, which he does, thereafter to be visited successively by *Meekness*, *Charity*, *Patience*, *Good Occupation*, *Liberality*, *Chastity* and *Abstinence* before *Reason* comes to reclaim him. The play ends with a song.

PLAY LENGTH

2,850 lines (Part I, 1438; Part II, 1412)

COMMENTARY

This is a two-part play that involves a double fall and redemption scheme. *Nature's* opening sermon is strongly humanistic in tone and subject matter. The role of the seven deadly sins is well integrated and the independent interaction of the Vices in *Envy's* telling *Pride* about his ruin is noteworthy. The visitation of the Virtues at the end of the play, in which each counsels *Man* on how to counteract an opposing vice, is a well-developed example of the 'remedia' trope. It is also an 'ages of man' play (see also **103**), and while *Man* embraces pride and lust in youth, he is later prey to covetousness, typically a sin of old age.

SIGNIFICANT TOPICS AND NARRATIVE ELEMENTS

the processes of nature; Aristotle's teaching; free will; a debate between body and soul (*Reason* and *Sensuality*); apparel, sartorial fashion and identity; youth and age; servingmen and companions; gallants; bribery; taverns; the stews and sexual dalliance; the seven deadly sins; the infernal trinity: World, Flesh and Devil; 'remedia'

DRAMATURGICAL AND RHETORICAL FEATURES

Verbal and general *Nature's* sermon on the processes of Nature I.1–105; *Garcius* greets *Pride* with a French expression I.826; *Sensuality* mistranslates 'radix viciorum' as 'root of virtue' I.840; Vice's alias: *Pride–Worship* I.937; *Sensuality* gives an account of the aliases taken by the seven deadly sins I.1208–27; *Reason* delivers a sermon against the World, Flesh and Devil II.1–56; *Reason's* verbal image of the assault of sin as the siege of a castle II.2–7; *Sensuality* refers to a popular song, 'Come kiss me John' II.150; *Man* and *Bodily Lust* have an exchange in French II.257; *Pride* asks the audience for directions II.401–7; *Reason* sets out 'remedia' against the Vices II.1066–75 (subsequently enacted in the successive appearances of the Virtues); the play is in two parts, with no further act or scene division; the language of the Vices is peppered with slang terms; there is considerable conflict among the Vices; stage directions in English, except for one in Latin (for speech: 511 *sd*)

Costume and dress *Man* wears a 'garment of innocency' I.438; the *World* gives *Man* a garment, cap and girdle I.463–5; *Pride* is 'well apparelled at each point of his array' I.722; *Pride* points out and describes his fine clothing in detail: a red bonnet, an unlaced doublet, a satin stomacher, a short gown with wide sleeves I.739–70; *Pride* complains of *Man*'s 'array' which is 'not the fashion that goes nowadays' I.1023–4; *Man* comes in with new, fashionable clothing II.574 (described by *Pride* in I.1058–75); *Wrath* is 'defensibly arrayed' (in armour) II.642

Actions and stage directions op. *sd*: 'First comes in *Mundus* and sits down and says nothing, and with him *W. Aff.* bearing a gown and cap and a girdle for *Man.* Then comes in *Na., Man, Rea.,* [*Sen.*], and *Inn.,* and *Na.* sits down and says'; I.471: *Man* sits on the *Wo.*'s throne; I.511 *sd*: '(*Wo.*) speaks to *Man*' (L); I.706: *W. Aff.* apparently makes to depart; I.834 *sd*: 'Then *Pri.* speaks to *Sen.* in his ear that all may hear'; II.80 *sd*: 'Then he (*Sen.*) weeps; II.757 *sd*: 'Then comes in *Glu.* with a cheese and a bottle'; II.1412 *sd*: 'Then they (*Rea., Man*) sing some goodly ballad'; **Simple entry**: *Pri.* I.722; *W. Aff., Sen.* I.1034; *Rea.* I.1291; *Man* I.1319; *Rea., Man* II.op. *sd*; *Sen.* II.63; *B. Lu., W. Aff.* II.164; *Pri.* II.302; *Man, W. Aff.* II.408; *Rea., Man* II.1002; *Mee.* II.1096; *Abs., Chas.,* II.1320; *Rea.* II.1370; **Simple exit**: *Na.* I.238; *Inn.* I.654; (*Sen.*) I.921; *Man., Sen.* I.1050; *W. Aff.* I.1291; *Sha.* I.1389; *Rea.* II.63; *B. Lu.* II.219; 'They three' (*Man, B. Lu., W. Aff.*) II.302; *Sen.* II.364; *Slo.* II.503; *Man, Pri.* II.511; *W. Aff.* II.541; *Man* II.627; *Bo. Lu.* II.686; *Man, Glu., Wra.* II.813; 'They' (*Sen., En.*) II.1002; *Rea.* II.1096; *Mee.* II.1152; *Char.* II.1201; *G. Occ.* II.1255; *Lib.* II.1320; 'They' (*Lib., Abs., Chas.*) II.1370

Songs and music *Man* and *Reason* (end of play, 'some goodly ballad', w.n.s.)

Staging and set there are several verbal images, but the action is unlocalized and there are no indications as to set, beyond the seats indicated at the start; *Worldly Affection*, when left alone, talks of 'this good fire', likely to refer to the hall fire (II.513), and he calls for a stool or chair, probably from the audience (II.516–17)

Stage properties thrones for the *World* and *Nature* op. *sd*; *Pride*'s dagger I.773; a stool or chair for *Worldly Affection* II.516–17; *Gluttony*'s cheese and bottle II.757 *sd*

PLACENAMES

Cheapside II.279; the Cotswolds II.649; Court of Common Pleas (in Westminster) I.877; Paris I.738; St Paul's II.278; Westminster Hall II.744

ALLUSIONS

Adam II.1104; Aristotle I.59; Diana I.15; Ovid, *Metamorphoses* I.78; St Paul II.1161

REPORT ON MODERN PRODUCTION

(Part II) University of Salford, 3 February 1984 [*METh* 6:1 (1984) pp. 40–42]

RECORDED PRODUCTION

Videotape: Durham Medieval Theatre Company, dir. J. McKinnell, University of Durham (2001)

BIBLIOGRAPHY

Alford, J. A. "'My Name is Worship'": Masquerading Vice in Medwall's *Nature*' in Alford, 1995, pp. 151–77
Bevington, 1968, pp. 51–3
Crupi, C. W. 'Christian Doctrine in Henry Medwall's *Nature*', *Renascence* 34:2 (1982) pp. 100–12
Debax, 1994, pp. 15–36
Fifield, M. 'Medwell's [*sic*] Play and Non-Play', *SMC* 6 (1974) pp. 532–6
Haller, 1916, pp. 105–12
Hogrefe, 1959, pp. 257–62
Macauley, E. R. 'Notes on the Sources for Medwall's *Nature*', *MLN* 32:3 (1917) pp. 184–5
McCutchan, J. W. 'Similarities between Falstaff and Gluttony in Medwall's *Nature*', *Shakespeare Association Bulletin* 24 (1949) pp. 214–19
Mackenzie, W. R. 'A Source for Medwall's *Nature*', *PMLA* 29:2 (1914) pp. 189–99
Ozawa, 1984, pp. 1–23
Potter, 1975, pp. 58–67
Southern, 1972, pp. 55–94

66   New Custom

DATE, AUTHORSHIP AND AUSPICES

1550–73; anonymous; offered for acting; Greg 59

TEXT AND EDITIONS

Extant originals

1573 printing by William How for Abraham Vele: BL; Bodleian; Folger; Huntington; Newberry; NYPL; Worcester; Yale; (further copies extant); *STC* 6150

Editions

1994   CHD (CD-Rom and online transcription of How printing, l.l., s.l., OS)
1914   Farmer (1914a) (facsimile, n.l.)
1908   TFT (facsimile, n.l.)
1906   Farmer (5) (n.l., NS)*
1874–6   Dodsley, vol. III (n.l., NS)

SOURCES

No sources have been identified.

CHARACTERS

Prologue

Perverse Doctrine, an old Popish priest

Ignorance, another but elder

New Custom, a minister

Light of the Gospel, a minister

Hypocrisy, an old woman

Cruelty, a ruffler

Avarice, a ruffler

Edification, a sage

Assurance, a virtue

God's Felicity, a sage

PLOT SUMMARY

The *Prologue* announces that the play will demonstrate that things are not always as they appear, and that the (Protestant) religious doctrine deemed new is actually based on original principles, while that which claims authority through antiquity is actually a perversion. In the first scene the aged priests *Ignorance* and *Perverse Doctrine* bemoan what they see as the illegitimate meddling in divinity by upstarts, and the fact that many young people regard the practices of the old religion as superstitious. They are especially concerned about *New Custom*, a young minister who encourages Bible reading and services in English. They resolve to fight against him and as part of their strategy they change their names to 'Simplicity' and 'Sound Doctrine' respectively. In the next scene, they hear a sermon by *New Custom* and then debate with him. He affirms that Catholicism is actually a perversion of God's word, and declares himself to be 'Primitive Constitution', a promoter of the original truth. Later *New Custom* is joined by *Light of the Gospel* while *Hypocrisy* joins *Perverse Doctrine* and *Ignorance* in scenes in which their doctrinal positions are restated. *Perverse Doctrine* and *Ignorance* are worried by the appearance of the 'Genevan doctor' *Light of the Gospel* in England, and resolve to seek the help of their friends *Cruelty* and *Avarice*. They first eavesdrop to hear these two 'rufflers' (bullying vagabonds) talking with pleasure about physical persecution of followers of the new religion, and they then proceed to enlist their support. For the purpose, *Cruelty* will become 'Justice with Severity' and *Avarice* 'Frugality'. The four then seal the pact by singing a song. In the next scene *Perverse Doctrine* engages in a debate with *New Custom* and *Light of the Gospel* and is converted by them, thereafter becoming *Sincere Doctrine*, and changing his garments in token of this. He is then joined by *Edification*, *Assurance* and *God's Felicity* and the play ends with a prayer for Queen Elizabeth and a final song.

PLAY LENGTH

1,076 lines

COMMENTARY

This is a strongly Protestant play that seeks to expose Catholicism as reposing on perversion of the Gospel and on superstition. It advocates, however, an attack on Catholicism through conversion rather than persecution, and features the rare conversion of a Vice figure at a climactic point. There is clear interest in the scholarly dimensions of the conflict. It is sophisticated in its approach to doctrinal issues (particularly in relation to religious practice) and is also a good example of drama as an effective medium of propaganda. However the play consists mainly of debate and discussion, with little action and few stage directions.

Other Protestant and anti-Catholic plays: **14, 24, 44, 45, 49, 50, 53, 58, 85, 86** (frag.), **90, 93.**

Other conversion plays: **16, 51, 63, 83.**

SIGNIFICANT TOPICS AND NARRATIVE ELEMENTS

youth and age; religious conflict and Catholic practice; superstition; religious persecution in the state; clerical dress; learning and religious authority; Genevan Protestant scholars; judicial punishment; the doctrine of election; the conversion of a Catholic

NOTE: no hard-copy lineated editions and references are thus to page numbers

DRAMATURGICAL AND RHETORICAL FEATURES

Verbal and general aliases of the Vices: *Ignorance–Simplicity, Perverse Doctrine–Sound Doctrine* 165, *Cruelty–Justice with Severity, Avarice–Frugality* 190; *New Custom* takes the name *Primitive Constitution* 174; *Hypocrisy* is a woman 181; a three-act play with scene divisions; minimal stage directions, in English

Costume and dress *New Custom* has 'a gathered frock, a polled head and a broad hat' (as a Protestant) 163; *Perverse Doctrine* is dressed like a Catholic priest, with gown, cap and surplice 180, 198

Actions and stage directions 185 *sd*: '*Cru.* and *Av.* enter. *P. Do.* and *Ig.* tarry'; *Simple entry*: *P. Do., Ig.* 161; *N. Cu.* 166; *L. Gos., N. Cu.* 176; *Hyp., P. Do., Ig.* 178; *L. Go., N. Cu., P. Do.* 192; *Edi.* 199; *Ass.* 200; *G. Fe.* 201; *Simple exit*: (*N. Cu.*) 175; (*P. Do., Ig.*) 176; (*N. Cu.*) 199; (*L. Go.*) 200

Songs and music (w.n.s. to either song) 1. *Cruelty, Avarice, Ignorance, Perverse Doctrine* 'the first song' 191; 2. Final song 'the second song' (whole cast?) 202

Staging and set a doubling scheme on the title page states that 'four may play this interlude': 1. *Perverse Doctrine, 2. Ignorance, Hypocrisy, Edification, 3. New Custom, Avarice, Assurance, 4. Light of the Gospel, Cruelty, God's Felicity*, the *Prologue*; the action is unlocalized and there are no indications as to set

Stage properties rosary ('beads') 175; a breviary ('portas') 175; a 'testament book' 200

PLACENAMES

England 184, 185, 186, 202; London 161; Rome 173

ALLUSIONS

Antichrist 194; Duns Scotus 171, 172; *John 14:13* 177; Judas 187; Queen Mary 186; · St Paul 172, 197; St Paul *2 Corinthians* (but q.n.t.) 167; St Paul *Hebrews 11:1* 197; St Peter 173

BIBLIOGRAPHY

Bevington, 1962, pp. 146–9
Oliver, L. M. 'John Foxe and the Drama *New Custom*', *HLQ* 10:4 (1947) pp. 407–10
Mackenzie, 1914, pp. 46–50
White, 1993, pp. 89–92

67   Nice Wanton

DATE, AUTHORSHIP AND AUSPICES

1547–53 (*SR* 10 June 1560); the play is likely to have been written in Edward VI's reign though the extant form is a revision for performance by boys before Queen Elizabeth; anonymous; probably a school play performed by boys at court; Greg 31

TEXT AND EDITIONS

Extant originals

1560 printing by John King: BL; *STC* 25016
1565 (?) printing by John Allde: BL; Huntington; *STC* 25017

Editions

1994	CHD (CD-Rom and online transcription of King printing, l.l., OS)
1984	Tennenhouse (NS)
1978	Parry and Pearl (NS)
1977	Kruse (NS)
1976	Wickham (NS)*
1914	Farmer (1914a) (facsimile of 1560 King printing, n.l.)
1909	TFT (facsimile of 1560 King printing, n.l.)
1908	TFT (facsimile of 1565 Allde printing, n.l.)
1905	Farmer (2) (n.l., NS)
1897	Manly, vol. I (OS)
1874–6	Dodsley, vol. II (n.l., NS)

SOURCES

The central idea is based on Proverbs 13:24 but no narrative sources have been identified, though it has sometimes, erroneously, been thought to be drawn from the Latin play *Rebelles* by the Dutch schoolmaster and writer, Georgius Macropedius.

CHARACTERS

Messenger	Ismael	Daniel (judge)
Barnabas	Eulalia	Quest (Jury)
Dalilah	Iniquity (later disguised	Worldly Shame
Xantippe	as Baily Errand)	

PLOT SUMMARY

The prologue, spoken by the *Messenger*, cites Solomon's apophthegm about sparing the rod and spoiling the child, and recounts the narrative of the play. The 'good' child, *Barnabas*, commences the action, complaining of the laxity of his mother towards his siblings, *Ismael* and *Dalilah*. They then enter singing, quarrel with him, complain about the rigours of school and cast away their schoolbooks. After they exit, again singing, their mother, *Xantippe*, is accosted by her neighbour, *Eulalia*, who attempts to warn her about her children's behaviour. When *Xantippe*, however, responds by becoming defensive and aggressive, they quarrel and both go their separate ways. *Dalilah* and *Ismael* return, accompanied by the Vice *Iniquity*, all singing. They engage in gambling and sexually charged banter, but all end up quarrelling over alleged cheating before leaving the stage for an interval in the play. In the second half, *Dalilah* enters visibly afflicted with venereal disease, and is exhorted to repentance by her brother, *Barnabas*, who initially fails to recognize her. They exit and the scene changes to a court in which *Ismael* is being indicted for theft. He is sentenced to death, upon which he also implicates *Iniquity*, who had come in dressed as the court official *Baily Errand*. *Ismael* is led out, as is the now exposed *Iniquity* in a halter, fighting, concluding the matter of the court. *Worldly Shame* then enters to remind *Xantippe* that her son has been executed and her daughter has died of the pox, both as a consequence of her failings as a parent. She falls into despair and almost stabs herself with a knife left for the purpose by *Worldly Shame*, but is saved by *Barnabas*, who urges her to repentance. The epilogue exhorts parents in the audience to strictness in disciplining their children, and a prayer is offered for the queen. There is a final song to end the play.

PLAY LENGTH

552 lines, excluding final song of 20 lines

COMMENTARY

This is an 'upbringing of youth' play with, characteristically, only one parent present, in this case the mother. The importance of learning is particularly stressed.

The play is unusual in having two errant children and the sins into which they fall are defined by their gender, the daughter's sin being sexual transgression. It is a secular interlude and has a partly tragic conclusion; though the repentance of the two miscreant children is reported, it is not dramatized and no emphasis is given to it. The actors include a jury of twelve in the court scene, only one of whom speaks; these are possibly choristers. The play has two parts, with an interval signalling the passage of time.

Other youth and education plays: **21, 33, 53, 56, 58, 61, 62, 64, 68, 73** (frag.), **101, 103, 104.**

SIGNIFICANT TOPICS AND NARRATIVE ELEMENTS

education and the rearing of youth; neighbourly advice; sexual dalliance; gambling; venereal disease; crime and punishment; judicial bribery; bad companionship, despair and suicide

DRAMATURGICAL AND RHETORICAL FEATURES

Verbal and general a gambling scene 170–244; a court scene with a judge, clerk and jury 343–431; the play is divided into two parts of equal length; stage directions in English

Costume and dress *Ismael* and *Dalilah* initially 'go handsomely' (are well dressed) 125; *Dalilah* comes in 'ragged' 260 *sd* (2); *Iniquity* is dressed as *Baily Errand*, the court messenger 346 *sd*

Actions and stage directions 38 *sd*: 'Is. and Da. come in singing'; 78 *sd*: 'They (Is. and Da.) cast away their books'; 140 *sd*: 'Ini., Is. and Da. come in together singing'; 145 *sd*: '(Ini., Is., Da. singing) All together'; 161–2: Is. strikes Da.; 172 *sd*: 'He (In.) casts dice on the board'; 189 *sd*: 'He (Ini.) kisses her (Da.)'; 191 *sd*: 'Ini. and Da. sing'; 209 *sd*: 'They (Da. and Is.) set him (Ini.)'; 212 *sd*: '(Is.) Casts dice'; 215 *sd*: 'She (Da.) casts and they set'; 218 *sd*: 'He (Is.) loses'; 237 *sd*: 'They (Da., Ini.) tell it (the winnings)'; 244 *sd*: He (Ini.) gives her (Da.) a box (blow)'; 260 *sd*: 'Da. comes in ragged, her face hid or disfigured, halting on a staff'; 346 *sd*: 'Ini. [dressed as] the B. Err. comes in; the Ju. sits down'; 353 *sd*: 'He (Ba.) tells him (Ju.) in his ear that all may hear'; 360 *sd*: 'Ini. goes out; the Ju. speaks still'; 364 *sd*: 'They bring Is. in, bound like a prisoner'; 371 *sd*: 'One of them speaks for the Quest (jury)'; 379 *sd*: 'One (jury member) [speaks] for the rest'; 409 *sd*: 'He (Ini.) would go'; 412 *sd*: 'They (officers) take him (Ini.) in a halter: he fights with them'; 429 *sd*: 'They (officers) lead them (Is., Ini.) out'; 471 *sd*: 'She (Xa.) would swoon'; 488 *sd*: 'She (Xa.) would stick herself with a knife'; 545 *sd*: 'He (Epi.) kneels down'; 552 *sd*: 'He (Epi.) makes curtsey and goes out'; **Simple entry:** Bar. 24; Ju. 342; Xa. 456; **Simple exit:** Bar. 55; (Eul.) 134; Is. 231; Da. 253; Ini. 260; 'They' (Bar., Da.) 342; Ju. 431; Xa. 522; **Simple speech:** Ini. 146

Songs and music (mostly brief snippets, w.s. to all) 1. *Ismael, Dalilah* 'Here we comen, and here we loven' 39–40; 2. *Ismael, Dalilah* 'Farewell our school' 77–81;

3. *Iniquity, Ismael, Dalilah* 'Lo, lo, here I bring her' 141–5; 4. *Iniquity, Dalilah* 'Gold locks' 192–203; 5. final song (after epilogue) 'It is good to be merry' (20 lines), no singer(s) specified, but with the following marginal instruction (clear in Allde printing, partly cut off in King): 'Three sing one answering another, but alway ye fourth line they sing together'

Staging and set the gambling scene early in the play (170–244), and the court-room scene later on (343–431) are dramatized with the help of stage properties; otherwise the action is unlocalized or the localities signalled by the presence or dialogue of characters, and there are no indications as to set

Stage properties schoolbooks 78 *sd*; dice and a gaming board 172 *sd*; *Dalilah*'s staff 260 *sd* (2); the judge's seat 346 *sd*; a halter for *Iniquity* 412 *sd*; a knife 488 *sd*

PLACENAMES

England 205

ALLUSIONS

Ecclesiastes (not *Ecclesiasticus*) 11:10 (but cf. *Genesis 8:21*) 26–7; Job 236; St Paul 53; *Proverbs 13:24* 2; Solomon 1, 120, 362

REPORTS ON MODERN PRODUCTIONS

1. Windsor, Ontario (St Caecilia Society, dir. C. Atkinson and E. Kovarik) 26–27 November 1982 [*RORD* 26 (1983) pp. 74–5]
2. University College, Cork, dir. A. Corbett 15–16 January 1999 [*RORD* 39 (2000) pp. 249–50]

RECORDED PRODUCTION

LP Record: BBC, *The First Stage*, dir. J. Barton (1970)

BIBLIOGRAPHY

Adams, 1943, pp. 59–63
Dean, W. 'Some Aspects of the Law of Criminal Procedure in the Trial of Ismael in *Nice Wanton*', *METh* 13:1/2 (1991) pp. 27–38
Dean, W. '*Nice Wanton* (*c.* 1550): A Witness to Virulent Syphilis in the Tudor Age', *NQ* 39:3 (1992) pp. 285–9
Hogrefe, 1959, pp. 321–4
King, 1993, pp. 87–102
Southern, 1973, pp. 354–8
Young, 1979, pp. 92–102

68   Occupation and Idleness

DATE, AUTHORSHIP AND AUSPICES

mid-fifteenth century; anonymous; possibly for university or school performance

TEXT AND EDITIONS

Extant originals

Manuscript: Winchester College MS 33, fos. 65r–73v

Editions

2001   Beadle (OS)*
1979   Davis (facsimile and transcription)*

CHARACTERS

Occupation   Idleness (later Cleanness)   Doctrine

PLOT SUMMARY

The piece begins with a prayer by *Occupation* for relief from the sorrows of the world and this soon turns into a speech of self-introduction. *Occupation*'s devotion to work contrasts with the attitude of *Idleness*, who enters and declares his aversion to labour. When *Occupation* asks who he is, *Idleness* becomes fearful of 'blame' and thus claims to be called *Busyness*. *Occupation* engages him in his service and gives him a purse containing £10, warning him to keep it well, before making his exit. *Idleness*, however (probably addressing a member of the audience), declares his intention to waste the money in taverns. He goes off and *Occupation* reappears asking (probably the audience again) who has seen his man *Busyness*. *Idleness* now returns, reveals to the audience that he has spent the money on food and drink, and confesses to *Occupation* that the money is gone. *Occupation* castigates him, saying that he will only gain honour if he pays attention to *Occupation*'s words and follows the teachings of *Doctrine*, a master of divinity at the university. *Doctrine* duly appears and is welcomed by *Occupation*. He declares himself ready to undertake the instruction of the young man, who, however, would rather flee. *Doctrine* preaches that children should be set to school and *Idleness* is put to learning but finds it difficult. *Occupation* then poses a series of questions to *Doctrine*, which gives him the opportunity for teaching and doctrinal explanation, but *Idleness* remains disengaged and yearns for a drink of ale. He spills water on his book and starts to threaten *Occupation* and *Doctrine*, but is finally brought to heel by *Doctrine*.

He ultimately accepts *Doctrine*'s teaching and *Occupation* remarks that it is easiest to teach people while they are young. On *Idleness*'s request, *Doctrine* delivers a sermon on the Virgin Mary and he is thanked by both *Occupation* and *Idleness* in his new identity of *Cleanness*. *Doctrine* ends the piece with a blessing on the audience.

PLAY LENGTH

877 lines

COMMENTARY

Though this is not a fully-fledged play, there is a clear sense of an audience and some limited dramatic action. It is obvious that *Idleness* is a young man and this is something of a debate between youth and age. The interest in education and the idea of questions allowing an opportunity for doctrinal teaching are topics that link it to the fragment which follows in the Winchester manuscript, *Lucidus and Dubius* (see **56**). The introduction of the figure of *Doctrine* permits an element of drama to emerge, especially in the characterization of *Idleness* as a recalcitrant prodigal. Though brief, the text appears to be complete.

Other youth and education plays: **21, 33, 53, 56, 58, 61, 62, 64, 67, 73** (frag.), **101, 103, 104**.

SIGNIFICANT TOPICS AND NARRATIVE ELEMENTS

hindrances to learning; prodigal youth; idle pursuits and taverns; the infernal trinity: the World, the Flesh and the Devil; education; simony; the Virgin Mary

PLACENAMES

Bread Street 175; Gomorrah 387; Lebanon 851; Sodom 387

DRAMATURGICAL AND RHETORICAL FEATURES

Verbal and general alias: *Idleness–Busyness* 109; *Idleness*'s name is later changed to *Cleanness* 813; sole stage direction in Latin
Costume and dress *Idleness* wears 'simple weed' (denoting poverty) 62; *Idleness* dons the 'cloth of cleanness' 812
Actions and stage directions 318 *sd*: 'Then come *Doctrine*'; 719–21: *Idleness* 'washes' his book; 750: *Idleness* threatens *Occupation* and *Doctrine*
Staging and set unlocalized action, though the latter part appears to be in a schoolroom; there is one stage direction (for *Doctrine*'s entry) after 318
Stage properties *Occupation*'s purse 145, 152; *Idleness*'s schoolbook 468; water 719–21; *Idleness*'s dagger 751

ALLUSIONS

Adam 383, 647; Eve 383; John the Baptist 576; *Matthew 5:14* 596, *25:13* (q.a.)
779–80; *Song of Songs 4:8* (q.a.) 850–1

BIBLIOGRAPHY

Beadle, R. '*Occupation and Idleness*', LSE n.s. 32 (2001) pp. 7–11
Davis, 1969, pp. 461–72

69   The Pardoner and the Friar

DATE, AUTHORSHIP AND AUSPICES

1513–21; John Heywood; auspices unknown; Greg 14

TEXT AND EDITIONS

Extant originals

1533 printing by William Rastell: Huntington; Pepys; STC 13299

Editions

1994	CHD (CD-Rom and online transcription of Rastell printing, l.l., OS)
1991	Axton and Happé (OS)*
1984	Proudfoot (facsimile)
1937	De la Bère (n.l., OS)
1914	Farmer (1914a) (facsimile, n.l.)
1909	TFT (facsimile, n.l.)
1906	Farmer (1906b) (n.l., NS)
1905	Farmer (1) (n.l., NS)
1874–6	Dodsley, vol. 1 (n.l., NS)
1848	Child (n.l., OS)

SOURCES

The principal known sources are Chaucer's *Pardoner's Prologue* and a French farce, *La Farce d'un pardonneur, d'un triacleur, et d'une tavernière*; see the introduction to the edition by Axton and Happé, pp. 38–9, and Maxwell, 1946.

CHARACTERS

A Friar   A Pardoner   The Curate (Parson)   Neighbour Pratt

PLOT SUMMARY

The *Friar* opens the play with a lengthy defence of friars and their work, and a plea for their acceptance, before finally kneeling down to say his prayers while a *Pardoner* enters. The *Pardoner* displays his relics, for which he claims a variety of spiritual, magical and healing properties, and invites his audience to make offerings to them. He shows a papal bull on which he bases the authority to pursue his activities. The *Friar* then commences a sermon and at the same time, alternating with him line by line, the *Pardoner* delivers a speech promoting his pardons. Each begins to be irritated by the other's presence and they eventually confront one another. They then compete for the audience's attention, in both cases their addresses leading to a solicitation for alms, and each delivers an extended advertisement of the benefits of their respective services. They begin to threaten each other, ending up engaging in physical combat until the *Curate* enters and intervenes. The *Curate* summons his neighbour, *Pratt*, to help apprehend the two for making an affray in his church. When, however, the *Pardoner* and the *Friar* resist vigorously, *Pratt* refuses further help and the *Curate* is forced to let them depart, which they do cursing.

PLAY LENGTH

641 lines

COMMENTARY

The main thrust of the play is a competitive dialogue between the *Pardoner* and the *Friar*, in which both are satirically treated. The audience of the play is used as the congregation addressed by the two.
  Other debate plays: **28, 29, 31, 54, 99, 102.**

SIGNIFICANT TOPICS AND NARRATIVE ELEMENTS

the ministry of friars; pardons and pardoners; relics and relic worship; a papal bull; corrupt practices in the Church

DRAMATURGICAL AND RHETORICAL FEATURES

Verbal and general the *Friar*'s rhetorical passage of Skeltonic repetition 6–14; concurrent addresses of the *Pardoner* and the *Friar* 189–255, 316–407; a verbal duel between the *Pardoner* and the *Friar* (mostly in stichomythia) 407–538; stage directions in English

Actions and stage directions 78 *sd*: 'And then kneels down the *Fr.* saying his prayer, and in the meanwhile enters the *Pard.* with all his relics, to declare what each of them be, and the whole power and virtue thereof'; 188 *sd*: 'Now shall the *Fr.* begin his sermon, and even at the same time the *Pard.* begins also to show and speak of his bulls and authorities come from Rome'; 538 *sd*: 'Then they (*Pard., Fr.*) fight; 544 *sd*: 'The *Cu.* [enters]'; 627 *sd*: '*Pra.* [fights] with the *Pard.* and the *Pars.* with the *Fr.*

Staging and set the single setting for the action is a church, though there are no indications as to set

Stage properties the *Pardoner*'s bulls 98; the *Pardoner*'s relics: a bone 106, a mitten 128, an arm 134; a toe 140, a veil ('bongrace') 146; a jawbone 154, a skull ('brayn pan') 162; the *Pardoner*'s stool 512

PLACENAMES

Rome 97, 188 *sd*

ALLUSIONS

Pope Boniface IX 223; Dives and Lazarus 228–34; St Dominic ('Sondaye')[1] 134; Pope Julius (?) 225; Pope Leo X 193; St Leonard 79, 207; *Luke 6:38* 189; St Michael[1] 162

1 Part of the *Pardoner*'s list of relics.

REPORTS ON MODERN PRODUCTIONS

1. King's College, London 23 June 1977 [*RORD* 20 (1977) p. 64]
2. Winchester Great Hall (Medieval Players, dir. C. Heap) 11 June 1982 [*RORD* 25 (1982) pp. 147–8]

BIBLIOGRAPHY

Blocker, D. 'Heywood's Indulgent Pardoner', *ELN* 29:2 (1991) pp. 21–30
Bolwell, 1921, pp. 105–12
Bryant, J. G. '*The Pardoner and the Friar* as Reformation Polemic', *RenP 1971* (1972) pp. 17–24
De la Bère, 1937, pp. 69–73
Furnivall, F. J. 'John Heywood and Geoffrey Chaucer', *N&Q* 45 (1872) pp. 177–8
Johnson, 1970, pp. 96–102
Kittredge, G. L. 'John Heywood and Chaucer', *AJP* 9:4 (1888) pp. 473–4
Lines, 2000, pp. 406–13
Long, R. A. 'John Heywood, Chaucer, and Lydgate', *MLN* 64:1 (1949) pp. 55–6
Maxwell, 1946, pp. 70–86
Ozawa, 1984, pp. 1–23
Walker, 1998, pp. 80–5
Young, 1904, pp. 97–124

70   Patient and Meek Grissell

DATE, AUTHORSHIP AND AUSPICES

1558–61 (*SR* 1565/6 *c.* Apr. and 1568/9 *c.* Feb); John Phillip; offered for acting, and performed by boys at court; Greg 52

TEXT AND EDITIONS

Extant originals

1566 (?) printing by Thomas Colwell: Eliz. Club; *STC* 19865

Editions

1994   CHD (CD-Rom and online copy of McKerrow and Greg, 1909, l.l., OS)
1909   McKerrow and Greg (facsimile)*

SOURCES

This version of the story is drawn from Boccaccio's final novel of the fourth day of *The Decameron*.

CHARACTERS

Politic Persuasion, the Vice	Nurse
Gautier, Marquis of Salutia	Maid to Grissell
Fidence	Countess of Pango
Reason	Maid to Countess
Sobriety	Midwife
Grissell	Rumour
Grissell's Mother	Vulgus, a citizen of Salutia
Janicle, Grissell's Father	Patience
Indigent Poverty	Constancy
2 Lackeys	Daughter to Grissell
2 or 3 Ladies	Son to Grissell
Diligence	Epilogue (and Preface speaker)

There is one named non-speaking part, *Sansper*. This may be an alternative name for another character, as no provision is made for him in the doubling scheme. The 'preface' was clearly intended for delivery in the theatre, as its speaker is provided for in the doubling scheme.

PLOT SUMMARY

The preface explains the genesis of the play and briefly introduces the topic. The play is opened by *Politic Persuasion*, who tells a tall story about his adventures until he encounters *Gautier*, the Marquis of Salutia, out hunting with his courtiers *Reason* and *Sobriety*. *Gautier* invites him to join his household and he readily accepts. *Gautier*'s companions urge their master to choose a wife, which he agrees to do, and they all go on their way. *Grissell* enters with her parents and a neighbour, *Indigent Poverty*. In the next few scenes there is a discussion about women and marriage by *Gautier* and his court, the death of *Grissell*'s mother is reported and lamented, *Grissell* assumes the care of her father, and *Gautier* encounters *Grissell* and seeks her hand in marriage. She is initially reluctant because of her own poverty, but accedes to her father *Janicle*'s granting of her hand to *Gautier* and is taken off to be dressed as a bride. Despite the joy of the courtiers at their new mistress, *Politic Persuasion* argues that *Grissell*'s base blood makes her inappropriate to produce heirs for *Gautier*, and privately resolves to cause problems for her. He persuades *Gautier* to test *Grissell*'s patience by claiming that his courtiers have demanded either the death of their first-born, a daughter, or *Gautier*'s own exile. The apparent killing of the child by *Diligence* is then staged, though in reality she is sent to be kept by *Gautier*'s sister, the *Countess of Pango*. *Grissell* patiently endures her loss and when she goes on to give birth to a son, the 'test' is repeated, also on *Politic Persuasion*'s instigation. This child is also apparently taken from its protesting nurse by *Diligence* and killed, though again it is in reality sent to its aunt. When *Grissell* bears this too with patience, *Politic Persuasion* devises yet another affliction for her, this time that *Gautier* will send her home to her father and take a new wife. She accepts her lot with resignation and concern for her husband's well-being, but the court and people are sorrowful, as is her father. After being comforted by *Patience* and *Constancy*, she is sent for by *Gautier*, purportedly to serve his new wife, but when she arrives at court, the 'wife' turns out to be her daughter, and *Gautier* reveals all to her. To general joy she is reunited with her husband and children, and the court praises her virtue. An actor then speaks an epilogue which requests the audience's kind judgement, and offers a prayer for the queen and council.

PLAY LENGTH

2,120 lines, excluding a preface of 21 lines, but stage directions are included in the lineation

COMMENTARY

This is a standard version of the Patient Griselda story. Though *Politic Persuasion* is called a Vice and has something of the appropriate role of managing the narrative, he is not actually morally subversive and functions more as a malicious counsellor. Songs provide regular punctuation points, particularly serving to underscore heightened emotion. Though secular, the play is strongly Protestant in orientation.

Other female virtue plays: 3, 6, 34, 63, 87, 97.

Other plays featuring prominent women characters: 3, 6, 30, 32, 43, 46, 51, 63, 75, 87, 95, 97.

Other plays with foreign (non-biblical, non-classical) settings: 5, 6, 7, 12, 13, 32, 33, 47, 74, 83, 88.

SIGNIFICANT TOPICS AND NARRATIVE ELEMENTS

courtiers and advisers; marriage; the nature of women; idealization of female submissiveness; poverty; the rearing of children; filial obedience; a protective nurse; motherhood; the wheel of fortune

DRAMATURGICAL AND RHETORICAL FEATURES

Verbal and general there is a spoken preface rather than a prologue; *Politic Persuasion* claims his name is *Dunstable* 154; the lackey's formal dialogue 529–50; stage directions in English

Costume and dress *Grissell* has ragged clothes 694; *Grissell* is dressed in 'costly robes' 822; *Grissell* gives up her rich apparel 1533, 1624; *Grissell* is given a 'simple smock' 1649, 1655; *Grissell* is dressed in her old, poor clothing 1750; *Janicle's* ragged clothes are exchanged for silken ones 2070

Actions and stage directions 55–7 (*sd*): 'Here let there be a clamour, with whooping and hallowing, as though ye were hunting, or chasing the game'; 216–18 (*sd*): 'Here enter Gri. singing and spinning with her parents and Ind. P.'; 493–4 (*sd*): 'Here Gri. singing a song to the tune of "Damon and Pithias"'; 564 (*sd*): 'Enter marquis with his lords'; 581 (*sd*): '(Gau.) Turn to the ladies'; 591 (*sd*): 'Let there be 2 or 3 ladies'; 750 (*sd*): '(Gau.) Turn to Jan.'; 838–9 (*sd*): '(Gri., Gau.) Sing and then go out to the tune of "Malkin"'; 968 (*sd*): 'Enter marquis singing to the tune of "The latter Almain"'; 1184 (*sd*): '(Dil.) Make as you would kill it (the child)'; 1370 (*sd*): 'Enter the Nur., bearing the child in her arms'; 1383 (*sd*): 'The Nur. sings'; 1400 (*sd*): 'Enter Dil., his sword drawn'; 1671 (*sd*): 'Enter Rum. blowing and puffing'; 1835–8 (*sd*): 'Go once or twice about the stage (Dil.? Jan.?). Let Gri. sing some song, and sit spinning. A song for Gri., when the Mess. comes to her'; 1956 (*sd*): '(Gri.) Fall down'; **Simple entry**: Pol. 1; Gau., San., Fid., Rea., Sob. 58; 2 lackeys 528; Gau., lords 565; Rea., Sob. 903; Vul. 1688; Pat., Con. 1786; **Simple exit**: (Gau., San., Fid., Rea., Sob.) 213; (Gri., Jan., Mot., Ind. P.) 347; (Gau., San., Fid., Rea., Sob.) 468; (Pol.) 478; (Gri.) 527; (2 lackeys) 550; (Gri., ladies) 777; (Jan.) 888; (Nur., Dil.) 1192; (Gau., Gri.) 1218; (Pol.) 1234; (Dil.) 1280; (Cou., Ma.) 1292; (Pol., Mid.) 1323; (Gau.) 1341; (Dil.) 1349; (Pol.) 1369; (Dil.) 1447; (Nur.) 1471; (Gau., Gri.) 1664; (Pol.) 1670; (Vul.) 1718; (Rea., Sob.) 1743;

(*Pat., Con.*) 1820; (*Gri., Dil.*) 1876; (*Gau., Cou., Gri., Rea., Sob., Son., Dau.*) 1976; (*Gau., Rea., Sob., Jan.*) 2043; (*Gau., Cou., Gri., Son., Dau., Jan.*) 2091
Songs and music (w.s. to all songs) 1. *Grissell* 'God by his providence divine' (w. ref.) 219–66; 2. *Grissell* 'Can my poor breast be still' ('to the tune of "Damon and Pithias"') 495–526; 3. *Grissell, Gautier* 'Sith fate and fortune thus agree' ('to the tune of "Malkin"', w. ref.) 840–75; 4. *Gautier* 'Live in joyful jollity' ('to the tune of "the latter Almain"') 969–78; 5. *Nurse* 'Lulla by baby' (w. ref.) 1384–99; 6. *Grissell* 'How greatly I am bound to praise' 1839–62
Staging and set the title page gives a doubling scheme for eight players as follows: 1. *Politic Persuasion*, the *Epilogue*, 2. *Preface, Marquis* 3. *Fidence, Indigence, Second Lackey, Grissell's Son*, 4. *Reason, Diligence*, the *Countess's Maid, Patience* 5. *Sobriety*, the *Countess of Pango, Vulgus, Constancy* 6. *Rumour, Janicle* 7. *Janicle's Wife, First Lackey, Nurse* 8. *Grissell, Midwife*; the action is localized by the presence and dialogue of the characters, and there are no particular indications as to set, though it is likely that some attempt was made to suggest the contrast between the domestic settings of *Janicle's* and *Gautier's* residences (e.g. certain stage properties are present)
Stage properties *Grissell's* spinning wheel 216–18 (*sd*); a doll or bundle (as both babies) 1184 (*sd*), 1370 (*sd*); *Diligence's* sword 1149; *Grissell's* jewels and ring 1624–6

PLACENAMES

'Bullin Lagras' 1026, 1478, 1822; Charing Cross[1] 50; Cheapside Cross[1] 54; Europe 71; Gomorrah 386; 'Pango' 1027 *passim*; St Paul's[1] 51; 'Salutia' (town) 73 *passim*; Sodom 386; Westminster Hall[1] 49

1 Part of a nonsense speech by *Politic Persuasion*.

ALLUSIONS

Alcestis 865; Apollo pref. 15; Appian 858; Atropos 511; Aurora 61; Bellona 27,[1] 410; Calliope 490; Cassandra 988; Cleopatra 2053; Clio pref. 12, 490; Croesus 870; Cupid 5,[1] 645, 651; Diana 62, 872; Dido 986, 1942; Eccho 59; the Furies 1893; Helen of Troy 203, 362, 702, 1824; Helicon pref. 11; Hymeneus 1892; Iphis and Anaxarete 688–9, 691, 712; Juno[1] 24; Jupiter/ Jove 11,[1] 19,[1] 36,[1] 1895; Kay Citheria (?) pref. 12; Luna 1758; Mars[1] 26; Mercury[1] 16; Midas 870; Muses 410, 489, 1880; Nestor 151, 2107; Orpheus[1] 15; Pallas pref. 1; Pan pref. 14; Parcae – the Fates (? 'Parchas') 497; Paris 1825; Parnassus 489, 1880; St Paul 173; Penelope 860, 986, 1942; St Peter[1] 18; Phoebus 61; Phyllis (Constant Truth) 364; Priam 1826; Pyramus and Thisbe 697, 987; 'Tarquin's knight' (?) 858; Terpsichore 490; 'Teucer's son' (?) 690; Thisbe 364, 848; Venus 3,[1] 652, 660, 873; Vesta 176

1 Part of a nonsense speech by *Politic Persuasion*.

BIBLIOGRAPHY

Bliss, L. 'The Renaissance Griselda: A Woman for All Seasons', *Viator* 23 (1992) pp. 301–5
Comensoli, 1996, pp. 54–6
Greg, W. W. 'John Phillip, Notes for a Bibliography', *Library*, 3rd series 1 (1910) pp. 396–423
Potter, U. 'Tales of Patient Griselda and Henry VIII', *EaT* 5:2 (2002) pp. 11–28
Southern, 1973, pp. 445–62
Swaen, A. E. 'The Songs of John Phillip's *Patient Grissell*', *Archiv* 168 (1935) pp. 77–9
Wright, 1957, pp. 173–84
Wright, L. B. 'A Political Reflection in Phillip's *Patient Grissel*', *RES* 4:16 (1928) pp. 424–8

71   The Pedlar's Prophecy

DATE, AUTHORSHIP AND AUSPICES

1561–3 (SR 1594 *c.* 13 May); anonymous, possibly by Robert Wilson; auspices unknown; Greg 134

TEXT AND EDITIONS

Extant originals

1595 printing by Thomas Creede, to be sold by William Barley: BL; Bodleian (no t.p.); Dyce (no t.p.); Folger; Harvard; Huntington; Pepys (no t.p); Pforzheimer; private collector; *STC* 25782

Editions

1994   CHD (CD-Rom and online transcription of Creede printing, l.l., OS)
1914   Greg (facsimile)*
1911   TFT (facsimile, n.l.)

SOURCES

No sources have been identified.

CHARACTERS

Prologue	Maid's Father	A Landlord
Pedlar	A Mariner	An Interpreter
A Maid	A Traveller	A Justice
Maid's Mother	An Artificer	A Judge

PLOT SUMMARY

The *Prologue* discusses prophecy and divination, warning against superstition, and introduces the play. The *Pedlar* opens the action with a fanciful account of his travels, and telling of the prophecy stones he has acquired. A *Maid* approaches seeking pins, but the *Pedlar* is more interested in persuading her of his power of prophecy. When he learns from her *Mother* that the *Maid* is a good needlewoman, he advises her to learn some other occupation as an impending eclipse of the sun will shortly put an end to society's current obsession with fashion and her work will dry up. The *Father* then appears and when the *Pedlar* asks him why he refuses to let his daughter marry, he expresses his fear that she may marry a foreigner and help adulterate English blood. The *Pedlar* tells the family the story of a huge devouring beast, and he predicts universal calamity which will occur in the coming July. Against the wishes of the *Maid*, her parents invite him to dine with them, and they all sing a song about a pedlar. The *Mother* and *Maid* then go off to prepare the meal, while the *Pedlar* regales the *Father* with more fantastic observations about the world. They eventually depart and a *Mariner* enters complaining of the scarcity of good sailors. He is joined by a *Traveller* and they talk about trade, travel and bankruptcy. They are approached by an *Artificer* who is seeking the *Pedlar*, whom he accuses of being a sorcerer. The *Pedlar* then reappears and tries to overcome their initial scepticism of him with more display of his supposed learning. He utters more prophecies and stories, and fulminates against the invasion of foreigners in the realm, especially London. He offers to sell his prophecy stones to his companions, and they are won round. Before he departs, they agree to later meetings, and all sing a song together. The *Pedlar*, *Traveller* and *Mariner* having gone their various ways, the *Artificer* is left on stage and he is joined by the *Landlord* coming to claim his rent. The *Pedlar* returns once again and this time tells of various disasters that have befallen the *Landlord*'s household. The *Artificer* warns the *Pedlar* that he should leave quickly as the *Landlord* is inclined to accuse him of necromancy, but the *Pedlar* simply promises to produce wonders. They are joined by the *Interpreter*, who has come to hear the *Pedlar*'s speech, and shortly afterwards by the *Justice*. The *Pedlar*, pretending now to be a priest, gives a third-person account of his own pronouncements, especially against Justices. Soon the *Judge* arrives and questions the 'priest' further. Without revealing his true identity, he reports that the *Pedlar* does not involve himself with religion but rather makes pronouncements on the social ills of the realm, such as the oppression of the poor and judicial corruption. The *Judge* agrees, though refusing to pay attention to the prattling of pedlars, that there are matters that need amendment, and they end the play with a song, after which the *Pedlar* delivers an epilogue.

PLAY LENGTH

1,592 lines

COMMENTARY

This rather rambling play centres on the idea of a plebeian character who lives by his wits and is able to make observations on the state of the realm and its ills. The figure of the pedlar varies between that of a charlatan and one endowed with gifts of real perception. The play is carelessly constructed and it is not always clear which characters have left the stage. There is little action and the situations seem simply to be opportunities to make a range of social comments, which are themselves not always coherent.

Other political comment and state of the realm plays: 1 (frag.), 14, 37, 38, 59, 76.

Other social ills plays: 2, 15, 24, 38, 40, 52, 53, 72 (frag.), 76, 94, 96, 98, 100.

SIGNIFICANT TOPICS AND NARRATIVE ELEMENTS

a plebeian commentator figure; prophecy and divination; astrology; dress and fashion; Englishness and foreigners in the realm; travel; commerce and bankruptcy; rack-renting; false erudition and heresy; judicial corruption; religious conflict

DRAMATURGICAL AND RHETORICAL FEATURES

Verbal and general *Pedlar*'s list of necromantic practices 37–43; most stage directions are in English, including all except one for simple entry

Costume and dress most of the characters are defined by their occupations and would have been attired accordingly

Actions and stage directions 461 (*sd*): 'Here they (*Ped., Ma., Mo., Fa.*) sing' (L); 990 (*sd*): 'Here they (*Mar., Tra., Art., Ped.*) sing' (L); 1301 (*sd*): 'Let the *Ped.* be going out' (when he is stopped by the *Jus.*) (E); 1574–6 (*sd*): 'Here they (*Jus., Int., Ped.*) sing an heavenly song. And after they be out, the *Ped.* speaks as follows' (E); **Simple entry**: *Ma.* 142; *Fa.* 305; *Mar.* 530; *Tra.* 555; *Art.* 603; *Ped.* 643; *Lan.* 1049; *Ped.* 1090; *Int.* 1194; *Jus.* 1211; *Jud.* 1410; **Simple exit**: *Mo., Ma.* 470; (*Fa., Ped.*) 529; (*Mar.*) 1015; (*Ped.*) 1040; (*Ped.*) 1193; (*Ped.*) 1593

Songs and music (w.n.s.) 1. *Pedlar, Maid, Mother, Father* 461 (*sd*); 2. *Pedlar, Mariner, Traveller, Artificer* 990 (*sd*) (voice parts apportioned 987); 3. *Pedlar, Justice, Judge* 'a heavenly song' 1574 (*sd*)

Staging and set the action is unlocalized and there are no indications as to set

Stage properties the *Pedlar*'s pack 79; the *Pedlar*'s ballad books 986

PLACENAMES

Africa 373; Alexandria 473; Antarctic 93; Armenia 764; Asia ('Inde') 682; 'River Awroer' (?) 1096; 'Carowse Ferry' 82; Crete 754; Dover 374; 'Droppe' (?) 378; Dunwich 376; England 204; River Euphrates 1440; 'Fangringosse Wood' 249; France 396; 'Jason's Wood' 92; Little Witham 481; London 882; 887; 889; Ludgate 71; 'Marybosse Ferry' 1101; Naxos 790; Orcades 1180; Portsmouth 376; Spain 90; Thule 1179; Troy ('Ilion') 934, 937, 1457, 1519, 1523; Tyre 785, 831, 837, 930, 1458, 1523; Wade 374

ALLUSIONS

Acheron 772; Actaeon 1147, 1149; Arthur (King ?) 849; Artophilos 847; Atlas 94, 201, 1008; St Augustine *De Civitate Dei* 17; Bacchus 790, 794; Cain 358; St Clement 1195; Dryostarydes (?) 118; Egistheus 355; Eli 1329; Enoch 1329; Euclid 1026; Helios 203; Isaiah 49, 863, 1249; St James 1195; Jeremiah 863, 1439; St Jerome 23; Job 49; John the Baptist 233; Juno 743, 750, 755; Jupiter 124 (pl.), 743, 750, 754; Lactantius 51; Mars 125 (pl.); Mercury 128 (pl.); Micah 23; Midas 772; Moses 49; Nebuchadnezzar 1190; St Paul 1425; Phoebus 425; Pleiades 199; Pluto 771; Rhamnusia 432; Saturn 122 (pl.), 401 (pl.), 755; Socrates 1442; Sol 126; Titan 1158; Venus (pl.) 128; King Vortigern 353; Charles Wane 846; Zephyrus 766

BIBLIOGRAPHY

Kittredge, G. L. 'The Date of *The Pedler's Prophecie*', HSNPL 16 (1934) pp. 97–118
Pineas, R. 'Polemical Technique in *The Pedlers Prophecie*', ELN 6.2 (1968) pp. 90–4

72   The Pride of Life (fragment)

DATE, AUTHORSHIP, AUSPICES

first half of the fifteenth century or as early as the middle of the fourteenth century (see introduction to Davis's edition, pp. xcviii–xcix); anonymous; possibly an Anglo-Irish or a Kentish play, but auspices not known

TEXT AND EDITIONS

Extant originals

The manuscript was destroyed by fire in 1922 and there were no early printed editions. See the introduction to Davis's edition, pp. lxxxv–lxxxvi.

Editions

1994   CHD (CD-Rom and online copy of Davis, 1970, l.l., OS)
1972   Happé (OS)*
1979   Davis (facsimile, n.l.)
1970   Davis (OS)*
1909   Waterhouse (OS)*
1902   Holthausen (OS)*
1898   Brandl (OS)*

SOURCES

No sources have been identified.

CHARACTERS

Prologue	Strength, first soldier	Mirth, messenger
King of Life	Health, second soldier	Bishop
Queen		

PLOT SUMMARY

The *Prologue* tells the whole story of the play, so it is possible to fill in the narrative of the missing sections. The play opens with a conventional 'boast' of the *King of Life* claiming great earthly ascendancy. He is supported in this by his knights, *Strength* and *Health*, but the *Queen* warns him of the inevitability of death and the need to take care of his soul. He dismisses her words as woman's speech and his knights pledge to defend him against *Death*. His messenger, *Mirth*, announces that he has travelled the length of the realm, and there is no one as powerful as the *King*, at which he is granted lands in reward. A *Bishop*, who is sent for by the *Queen* using the messenger, takes up her argument but the *King* rejects his advice too. The *King* sends his messenger to track down *Death* so that he can send his armies against him, and with the vaunting speech of *Mirth* moving round the *platea* the fragment ends. The *Prologue* account tells of the conquest of the *King* by *Death*, and of his subsequent salvation through the intercession of the Virgin Mary.

PLAY LENGTH

502 lines extant, including prologue of 112 lines

COMMENTARY

This is a 'coming of death' play, like *Everyman*, and it also has elements of the 'debate of the body and soul' motif found mostly in religious lyrics. The 'boasting' speeches of the *King* about earthly well-being predate similar speeches by Herod in various plays and Cyrus or the King of Marcyll in the Digby *Mary Magdalen*. The presence of a woman in a morally authoritative role is noteworthy, even if her gender is cited as a factor in the *King*'s rejection of her argument. The *Prologue* suggests that the play may be addressed to a specifically elite audience.

Other social ills plays: **2, 15, 24, 38, 40, 52, 53, 71, 76, 94, 96, 98, 100.**
Other plays with probable place and scaffold staging: **9, 23, 48, 63, 83, 85.**

SIGNIFICANT TOPICS AND NARRATIVE ELEMENTS

'dance of death' motif; death as a leveller; the ruthlessness of rich men; the 'twelve abuses of the age'

DRAMATURGICAL AND RHETORICAL FEATURES

Verbal and general an opening 'boast' by the *King* claiming universal sovereignty 113–26; *Bishop*'s sermon at first apparently directly to audience, preceding his address to the *King* 327–90; the messenger makes a proclamation 471–502; the play has a debate structure; stage directions in Latin

Costume and dress the *King*'s knights wear bright helmets 140; the *King* wears a gold crown 155, 176, 446; the *Bishop* wears a mitre 324

Actions and stage directions 112 *sd*: 'The *K. of Li.* begins, thus saying'; 306 *sd*: 'And then, with the booth closed, the *Qu.* shall secretly say to the mess.'; 322 *sd*: 'And he (*Mi.*) sings'; 390 *sd*: 'Then he (*Bish.*) says to the *Ki.*'; 450 *sd*: 'Here he (*Ki.*) shall add'; 470 *sd*: 'And he (*Mi.*) shall go about the place ('*platea*')'

Songs and music *Mirth* (w.n.s.) 322 *sd*

Staging and set this appears to be for open air 'place and scaffold' production; extensive use is made of the messenger who walks around the *platea* to indicate travel; there is a closed booth in which the *Queen* is seated (306 *sd*)

Stage properties swords for the *King*'s knights 139; the *King*'s sword 277

PLACENAMES

Berwick-on-Tweed 285; 'Gailispire-on-the-Hill' (?) 301; Kent 302

REPORT ON MODERN PRODUCTION

Southwark Cathedral, 12 Dec. 1981 [*METh* 4:1 (1982) pp. 61–2]

RECORDED PRODUCTION

LP Record: BBC, *The First Stage*, dir. J. Barton (1970)

BIBLIOGRAPHY

Axton, 1974, pp. 166–8
Brown, C. 'The *Pride of Life* and the "Twelve Abuses"', *Archiv* 128 (1912) pp. 72–8
Davenport, 1982, pp. 15–20
Fifield, 1967, pp. 19–22
Fifield, 1974, pp. 12–34
Haller, 1916, pp. 102–5
Hengstebeck, I. 'The *Pride of Life*, Vers 444', *NM* 72 (1971) pp. 739–41
Mackenzie, W. R. 'The Debate over the Soul in *The Pride of Life*', *Washington University Studies* 9:2 (1921) pp. 263–74
Miyajima, 1977, pp. 83–7
Spinrad, 1987, pp. 61–4

73   The Prodigal Son (Pater, Filius et Uxor) (fragment)

DATE, AUTHORSHIP AND AUSPICES

early sixteenth century; anonymous; auspices unknown, but possibly a play for boys; Greg 19

TEXT AND EDITIONS

Extant originals

1530 (?) printing by William Rastell: Cambridge (frag., 1 leaf); *STC* 20765.5

Editions

1994   CHD (CD-Rom and online transcription of Rastell printing, l.l., OS)
1907   Greg (1907a) (OS)*

SOURCES

The play is likely to have been a version of Ravisius Textor's *Pater, Filius et Uxor.*

CHARACTERS

. The Wife (Uxor)   The Father (Pater)   The Son (Filius)   The Servant (Servus)

PLOT SUMMARY

The fragment starts with the *Wife* declaring her intention to cuckold her husband with several lovers, and she ends up singing a song on the subject. All the while *Father* (her husband) complains about and curses her, without apparently being in direct communication with her. In the meantime (and presumably on yet another part of the stage) the *Son* is hawking faggots, a trade into which he has been forced by his neglect of learning and his marrying of a shrewish wife. When the *Servant* comes in speaking a strange tongue, the *Son* expresses his bewilderment and ascribes this to the fact that he has not been to university. The servant introduces himself by means of a comic nonsense rhyme and says that his master is Humphrey Heartless, beaten by his wife twice a day. Here the fragment ends.

PLAY LENGTH

84 lines extant

COMMENTARY

This brief fragment manages to incorporate representations of a bad marriage and cuckoldry, as well as a recurrent source of anxiety in several Tudor interludes, the upbringing of children. The situation of the son here bears considerable similarity to that of the son in *The Disobedient Child*. The servant appears to be a type of lively professional fool figure.

Other youth and education plays: **21, 33, 53, 56, 58, 61, 62, 64, 67, 68, 101, 103, 104**.

Other marital strife plays: **46, 84, 95**.

SIGNIFICANT TOPICS AND NARRATIVE ELEMENTS

bad marriage; cuckoldry; education and the upbringing of youth

DRAMATURGICAL AND RHETORICAL FEATURES

Verbal and general the *Son*'s mispronunciation of 'university' as 'insteynste', corrected by the servant 58–9; the *Servant*'s list of rhyming names 70–8; the extant stage directions in English

Actions and stage directions 13–14 (*sd*): 'Here she (*Wife*) must sit down and sew, and let her sing this song following'; 26–7 (*sd*): 'Here the *Son* comes in again lamentably saying as follows'; 52–4 (*sd*): 'Here the *Ser.* comes in speaking some strange language, and the *Son* says to him as follows'

Songs and music *Wife* 'A husband I have' (w.s.) 15–20

Staging and set it is possible that actors are performing at the same time on stage without direct communication with each other; the action is not clearly localized and there are no indications as to set

Stage properties the *Son*'s faggots 5; a needle and thread 7; a napkin 8; the *Servant*'s penny 63

PLACENAMES

Oxford ('Oxynby' – University) 57; Cambridge (University) 58

BIBLIOGRAPHY

Takemoto, 1989, pp. 1–18

74   Promos and Cassandra

DATE, AUTHORSHIP AND AUSPICES

1578 (*SR* 31 July 1578); George Whetstone; auspices unknown, possibly a closet play: Greg 73, 74

TEXT AND EDITIONS

Extant originals

1578 printing by John Charlewood for Richard Jones: BL; Bodleian (imp.); Folger (two copies, one imp.); Huntington; Trinity; *STC* 25347

Editions

1994   CHD (CD-Rom and online transcription of Charlewood printing, l.l., s.l., OS)
1958   Bullough, vol. II (n.l., OS)
1910   TFT (facsimile, n.l.)
1889   Cassel (part 2 only, n.l., OS)
1875   Hazlitt vol. VI (n.l., OS)*

SOURCES

Sources include Giraldo Cinthio, *Ecatommithi* (1565), II, Ded. 8, Nov. 8, and Rouillet, *Philanira* (1556). See Budd's and Prouty's essays below.

PLAY LENGTH

The play is in two parts, the first part having approximately 1,290 lines, and the second approximately 1,490 lines.

COMMENTARY

The necessity for making a two-part play of this story was possibly occasioned by Whetstone's very expansive and minutely episodic narrative style. He uses a very large number of characters, many of whom appear only briefly and several only once. He builds the narrative of a large number of small sequences, most of which involve characters giving accounts of developments in the story, frequently single characters addressing the audience. The subplot involving *Phallax* and *Lamia* is strongly developed, the low life elements allowing Whetstone a more detailed, trenchant and colourful exploration of the relationship between sexual and political corruption than the main plot figuring *Promos*. The subplot also introduces economic dimensions in the oppression of the poor, which picks up social concerns that occur recurrently in sixteenth-century interlude drama. The play is the principal source for Shakespeare's *Measure for Measure*.

Other plays with foreign (non-biblical, non-classical) settings: **5, 6, 7, 12, 13, 32, 33, 47, 70, 83, 88**.

a   The first part of Promos and Cassandra

CHARACTERS

Promos	2. Second Hackster
Phallax, Promos's man	3. A Woman
Mayor	4. A Scoffing Catchpole
Sheriff	5. One Like a Giptian
A Sword Bearer	6. A Poor Rogue
A Key Carrier	A Preacher
Lamia, a Courtesan	A Churlish Officer
Rosko, Lamia's man	Ganio, Andrugio's boy
Lamia's maid	A Beadle
Cassandra, a Maiden	A Bill Carrier
Andrugio, Cassandra's brother	A Gaoler
Gripax, a Promoter	Grimbal
Rapax, a Promoter	Polina, Andrugio's lover
A Hangman	Rowke
Six Prisoners:	Boy
1. First Hackster	

Mute: Officers

PLOT SUMMARY

Promos is appointed judge by royal proclamation and he receives the sword and key of office. The scene then switches to a courtesan, *Lamia*, who rejoices in her wantonness until she hears that, as a result of the new, strict regime, one *Andrugio* has been sentenced to death for making his lover pregnant. She sends her man, *Rosko*, to seek protection from *Phallax*, the servant of *Promos* who has imposed the new regime. In the following scenes the condemned man *Andrugio* asks his sister *Cassandra* to intercede with *Promos* on his behalf, which she proceeds to do. *Promos* grants a temporary reprieve but finds himself smitten with desire for *Cassandra*. After *Phallax* is shown revealing his own corrupt nature by sending promoters to incite wrongdoing so that he can fleece the malefactors when they are caught, *Promos* confides to him his intention to exploit for his own sexual motives *Cassandra*'s desire to save her brother. A brief episode follows in which a group of prisoners passes over the stage pointing to themselves as examples of the sorrowful outcome of crime, and then *Promos* is again seen expressing his lustful intentions. When *Cassandra* comes to plead once more he offers her a pardon for her brother in exchange for her sexual favours, but she resists. He, however, gives her time to think about his proposal, saying that she should return to his court in two days' time disguised as a page if she changes her mind. *Cassandra* tells her brother that she cannot accede to *Promos*'s wishes, but he at length persuades her to comply with them. The scene now switches back to *Phallax*, before whom *Lamia* and *Rosko* are brought accused of lewdness. He initially makes sexual overtures to her but she says she needs his advice in a law case, and she finally goes off assured of his protection. *Cassandra* appears briefly, dressed as a page on her way to *Promos*'s court, and then *Promos* is seen alone, having satisfied his lust with her but deciding to renege on his side of the bargain. He resolves to have *Andrugio* beheaded and to have the head sent to *Cassandra*. The gaoler presents a head to her, announcing that this is the way *Promos* has decided to release her brother from prison, at which she falls into lamentation and decides to kill herself. However, unbeknown to her the gaoler in fact releases *Andrugio*, revealing that he had substituted the head of a man executed earlier. After a brief exchange involving *Dalia* and *Grimbal*, *Phallax* muses on his master's tortured conscience since the supposed execution of *Andrugio*, but his reflections are interrupted by an invitation to supper with *Lamia* and he goes off. *Andrugio*'s lover, *Polina*, now comes in grieving over his supposed death and resolving to remain in mourning until the end of her own life. After an episode in which *Lamia*'s servants dupe and rob *Grimball*, *Cassandra* is seen in mourning black with a knife in her hand, intending to do away with herself. She ends with a song by which she means her 'knell to ring'.

SIGNIFICANT TOPICS AND NARRATIVE ELEMENTS

prostitution; sexual transgression; judicial corruption; *agents provocateurs*; tyrannical rule; crime and punishment; a corpse substitution

NOTE: As lines are not numbered, references are to act/scene/page number

DRAMATURGICAL AND RHETORICAL FEATURES

Verbal and general rustic speech: *Grimball* 4.7.248 ff.; a five-act play with scene divisions; a fully developed subplot in the story of *Lamia*; servant episodes separate strands of the main narrative or signify the passage of time; stage directions in English

Costume and dress *Lamia* wears 'brave weeds' 2.1.211; *Cassandra* initially wears 'virgin's weeds' 3.4.235; *Lamia* wears 'costly' clothes 3.6.236; *Cassandra* enters 'apparelled like a page' 3.7.241 *sd*; *Polina* appears in a blue gown (a mark of shame) 5.3.252 *sd*; *Cassandra* enters dressed in mourning black 5.6.258 *sd*

Actions and stage directions 1.1.209 *sd*: '*Pha*. reads the King's Letters Patents, which must be fair written in parchment, with some great counterfeit seal'; 1.2.211 *sd*: '*La*. a courtisan, enters singing'; 1.2.211 *sd*: 'She (*La*.) speaks'; 2.3.219 *sd*: '*Cas*. (speaking) to herself'; 2.3.219 *sd*: 'She (*Cas*.) kneeling speaks to *Pro*.'; 2.4.222 *sd*: '*Pha*. (speaks) alone'; 2.6.225 *sd*: '(Enter) The *Han*. with a great many ropes about his neck'; 2.7.226 *sd*: '(Enter) Six prisoners bound with cords. Two Hacksters, one Woman, one like a Giptian, the rest poor rogues, a *Pre*. and other Officers'; 2.7.226 *sd*: 'They (prisoners) sing'; 2.7.228 *sd*: 'They (prisoners) leisurably depart singing, the *Pre*. whispering some one or other of the prisoners still in the ear'; 2.7.228 *sd*: 'They (prisoners) sing'; 3.2.229 *sd*: '*Cas*. speaks to herself'; 3.2.229 *sd*: 'She (*Cas*.) kneeling speaks to *Pro*.'; 3.2.231 *sd*: '*Cas*. (speaking) to her self'; 3.2.232

sd: '(*Pro.* speaking) To himself'; 3.2.233 *sd*: 'At these words *Ga.* must be ready to speak'; 3.4.233 *sd*: 'And. out of prison. *Cas.* on the stage'; 3.6.236 *sd*: '*Pha.*, *Grip.*, *Rap.*, a *Bea.*, and one with a brown bill, bring in *La.*, and *Ro.* her man'; 3.7.241 *sd*: '*Cas.*, apparelled like a page'; 4.1.241 *sd*: '*Da.*, *La.*'s maid, going to the market'; 4.4.243 *sd*: '[Enter] *Gao.* with a dead man's head on a charger'; 4.6.247 *sd*: '*Da.* from market'; 4.6.248 *sd*: 'She (*Da.*) feigns to go out'; 4.7.248 *sd*: '*Grim.*, *Da.*, either of them (with) a basket'; 4.7.248 *sd*: 'She (*Da.*) feigns to look in his (*Grim.*'s) basket'; 4.7.248 *sd*: 'She (*Da.*) takes out a white pudding'; 5.3.252 *sd*: '*Pol.* (the maid that *And.* loved) in a blue gown'; 5.5.256: the *Boy* brings water; 5.5.256 *sd*: '*Ro.* cuts *Grim.*'s purse'; 5.5.257 *sd*: '*Boy* (calls) within'; 5.6.258 *sd*: '*Cas.* in black'; **Simple exit**: (*Pro.*, *May.*, *She.*, *Pha.*, attendants) 1.1.210; (maid) 1.4.216; (*La.*) 1.4.216; (*Cas.*) 2.3.221; (*Pro.*, *She.*, officers) 2.3.221; (*Pro.*, *Gri.*, *Rap.* officers, promoters) 2.4.222; (*Pha.*, *Pro.*) 2.5.225; (*Han.*) 2.6.226; (*Cas.*, *Ga.*) 3.3.233; (*Cas.*) 3.4.235; (*Gri.*, attendants) 3.6.238; (*Pha.*) 3.6.239; (*La.*, *Ro.*) 3.6.240; (*Cas.*) 3.7.241; (*Da.*) 4.1.241; (*Cas.*) 4.4.246; (*And.*) 4.5.247; (*Gao.*) 4.5.247; (*Da.*) 4.7.250; (*Ro. Pha.*) 5.2.252; (*Pol.*) 5.3.254; (*Boy*) 5.5.256; (*Ro.*) 5.5.256; (*Boy*) 5.5.257; (*Grim.*) 5.5.258; (*Ro.*) 5.5.258; (*Cas.*) 5.6.259

Songs and music (w.s. to all songs) 1. *Lamia* 'All aflaunt now vaunt it, brave wench cast away care' (13 lines, w. ref.) 1.2.211; 2. Prisoners 'With heart and voice to thee O Lord' (8 lines, w. ref.) 2.7.226; 3. Prisoners 'Our secret thoughts, thou Christ dost know' (7 lines, w. ref. – a continuation of the previous song) 2.7.228; 4. *Lamia* 'Adieu, poor care, adieu' (16 lines) 3.6.240; 5. *Grimball, Dalia* 'Come smack me, come smack me, I long for a smooch' (a duet, 14 lines) 4.7.250; 6. *Cassandra* 'Sith fortune thwart, doth cross my days with care' (12 lines, w. ref.) 5.6.259

Staging and set the action is only vaguely localized (apart from being set in the city of Julio), and this through the presence and dialogue of characters, sometimes with the help of stage properties; there are no indications as to set

Stage properties a sword (heading to 1.1); a bunch of keys 1.1.209 *sd*; a parchment letter 'with some great counterfeit seal' 1.1.209 *sd*; the *Hangman*'s ropes 2.6.225 *sd*; cords binding the prisoners 2.7.226 *sd*; a 'brown bill' 3.6.236 *sd*; a false head on a charger 4.4.243 *sd*; baskets for *Grimball* and *Dalia* 4.7.248 *sd*; a white pudding 4.7.248 *sd*; a bowl of water 5.5.256; *Grimball*'s purse 5.5.256 *sd*; a toothpick 5.5.256; a porringer 5.5.257; comfits 5.5.257; *Cassandra*'s knife 5.6.259

PLACENAMES

Hungary 1.1.209; 'Julio' (city) 1.1.209, 4.1.241

ALLUSIONS

Chaucer 1.3.215; Cupid 3.2.230; Diana 4.4.245; Pope Joan 4.6.248; Ovid *Metamorphoses* 3.3.12, 2.5.224; Samson 2.5.224; Solomon 2.5.224; Venus 2.1.217, 3.2.233

b   The second part of *Promos and Cassandra*

CHARACTERS

Polina	A Sergeant
King's Messenger	An Officer
Rosko	A Crier
Phallax	Sir Ulrico
Dowson, a carpenter	First Poor Citizen
Beadle of the Tailors	Second Poor Citizen
Two men as 'green men'	Pimos
Corvinus, King of Hungary and Bohemia	Gripax, a promoter
Cassandra	Rapax, a promoter
Two Counsellors	John Adroynes, a clown
Udislao, a young nobleman	Gonsago
Promos	A Poor Man
Mayor	Gresco, a good substantial officer
Three Aldermen	First Beadle
The King's gentleman usher	Second Beadle
Lamia	Andrugio
Apio, a gentleman stranger	Three Men with bills
Bruno, a gentleman stranger	Cassandra's Maid
Lamia's four women	Ganio
Five singers	

Mute: A Swordbearer, Two Attendants, Marshal, Three or Four with halberds

PLOT SUMMARY

Polina opens the second part of the play mourning on *Andrugio*'s supposed tomb. A messenger appears briefly declaring that he has come from the *King* to summon *Promos*, before the scene switches to *Rosko*, who reveals that *Lamia* has become enamoured of *Phallax*. *Phallax* is then seen giving instructions to a carpenter for the construction of a stage, and the *Beadle of the Tailors* (Company) comes to give him an account of the pageant to be staged. *Phallax* gives further instructions for the entertainment of the *King*, who duly arrives with his train, including *Cassandra*, to whom he promises punishment for *Promos*. The *King* is then formally received into the city by the *Mayor* and *Promos*, after which the scene switches to *Lamia* rejoicing in the licence she enjoys to practise her trade because of her liaison with *Phallax*, and her women are seen singing a song. The *King*'s officer now issues a proclamation offering royal redress for anyone unjustly treated by the judiciary, something about which *Rosko* privately expresses misgivings. The *King*'s officer receives complaints about *Phallax* from wronged citizens, before the scene switches to *Phallax* himself expressing his sense of guilt but then proceeding to help the promoters *Gripax* and *Rapax* fleece a poor man, *John Adroynes*. The *King* enters and despatches an attendant to seek out instances of injustice, after which

Phallax is accused, confesses and is stripped of his office. Because he expresses his contrition, however, he is not given further punishment than this. *Cassandra* now arrives and accuses *Promos*, who promptly confesses his wrongdoing. He is sentenced to marry *Cassandra* in order to recover her honour, and then be executed the following day. The *King* then goes off, taking a petition from a poor man as he departs. A search is mounted for *Lamia*, while *Andrugio* now appears disguised as a woodsman, still fearful of punishment. He learns from *John Adroynes* what has happened to *Promos* and, though rejoicing, resolves to continue his disguise for the moment. *Lamia* is at length apprehended and taken off for judgement. *Cassandra* now reappears bewailing the dilemma in which she finds herself of both desiring redress for her brother's death, but at the same time wishing to save her new husband's life. *Phallax* arrives and gives a description of the disgracing of *Lamia* and the purging of courtesans from the city, regretfully bidding farewell to the benefits he derived from them. After *Andrugio* reappears briefly, still disguised, the order is given for *Promos*'s execution and *Cassandra* asks an officer to lead her to the *King* so that she can request mercy for him. *Andrugio* is aware of her dilemma and decides to risk revealing to the *King* that he still lives. *Promos* is led out for execution and *Cassandra* bids him a sorrowful farewell, accompanied by *Polina* who has also forgiven him. They all go off and *Ganio* comes in to reveal to *Cassandra* that her brother is still alive, and her husband reprieved. The *King* re-enters with them both, and there is a joyous reunion. *Andrugio* is reunited with *Polina* and reconciled to *Promos*, who is reinvested with his legal authority but warned to use it justly.

Other plays with foreign (non-biblical, non-classical) settings: **5, 6, 7, 12, 13, 32, 33, 47, 70, 83, 88.**

SIGNIFICANT TOPICS AND NARRATIVE ELEMENTS

a royal entry and civic entertainments; royal redress of injustice; the oppression of the poor; disguised identity; forgiveness and reconciliation; an idealized dutiful wife

NOTE: As lines are not numbered, references are to act/scene/page number

DRAMATURGICAL AND RHETORICAL FEATURES

Verbal and general *Promos* makes an oration 1.9.268–9; the *Officer* delivers a proclamation (aided by a *Crier*) 2.2.272–3; several passages of stichomythia, most notably 3.2.277; rustic speech: *John Adroynes* (*Clown*) 3.2.276 ff.; *Promos* makes a scaffold speech 5.4.298–9; a five-act play with scene divisions; stage directions in English

Costume and dress *Polina* enters 'with a blue gown, shadowed with a black sarsenet' 1.1.261 *sd*; two men are 'apparelled like green men' 1.6.265 *sd*; the three aldermen are in red gowns 1.9.268 *sd*; *Lamia*'s women are 'bravely apparelled' 2.2.271 *sd*; *Cassandra* has a blue gown, lined with black 3.2.283 *sd*; two

Beadles come in 'in blue coats' 4.1.287 *sd*; *Andrugio* enters 'as out of the woods' (dressed as a woodsman) 4.2.288 *sd*; *Andrugio* is 'disguised in some long black cloak' 5.1.296 *sd*

Actions and stage directions 1.1.261 *sd*: '*Pol.* in a blue gown, shadowed with a black sarsenet, going to the Temple to pray, upon *And.*'s tomb'; 1.2.263 *sd*: 'Enter a *Mess.* From the *Ki.*'; 1.6.265 *sd*: 'Two men, apparelled like green men at the *May.*'s feast, with clubs of fireworks'; 1.9.268 *sd*: '*Pro.*, *May.*, three Aldermen in red gowns, with a *Swo.*, awaits the *Ki.*'s coming'; 1.9.269 *sd*: 'The *Ki.* delivers the sword to one of his Counsel'; 1.9.269 *sd*: 'The *May.* presents the *Ki.* with a fair purse'; 1.9.269 *sd*: 'Five or six, the one half men, the other women, near unto the Music, singing on some stage erected from the ground. During the first part of the song, the *Ki.* feigns to talk sadly with some of his Counsel'; 1.9.270 *sd*: 'They (*Ki.*, train) go out leisurably while the rest of the song is made at an end'; 2.2.271 *sd*: 'Four women bravely apparelled, sitting singing in *La.*'s window, with smocks and cauls in their hands, as if they were working'; 2.2.272 *sd*: 'Enter a *Serg.*, bearing a mace, another *Off.* with a paper, like a proclamation, and with them the *Cri.*'; 2.2.272 *sd*: '(*Cri.* cries) And so thrice'; 2.2.272 *sd*: 'The *Off.* reads the Proclamation'; 2.4.274 *sd*: '*Sir Ul.* with diverse papers in his hand, two poor citizens, soliciting complaints'; 2.4.275 *sd*: 'As he (*Ul.*) is going out, *Pi.*, a young gentleman, speaks to him'; 3.2.277 *sd*: 'They (*Jo. Ad.* and the Promoters) fall a-fighting'; 3.2.280 *sd*: '*Gon.* does reverence and departs'; 3.2.281 *sd*: '*Ul.* delivers the *Ki.* a writing with names on it'; 3.2.283 *sd*: '*Cas.* in a blue gown, shadowed with black'; 3.2.286 *sd*: 'As the *Ki.* is going out, a poor man shall kneel in his way'; 4.1.287 *sd*: '(Enter) *Gre.*, a good substantial officer, two Beadles in Blue Coats, with Tipstaffs'; 4.2.288 *sd*: '(Enter) *And.*, as out of the woods, with bow and arrows, and a cony at his girdle'; 4.2.290 *sd*: 'He (*Jo. Ad.*) whistling looks up and down the stage'; 4.2.293 *sd*: '(Enter) *Gre.*, with three other, with bills, bringing in *La.* prisoner'; 5.1.296 *sd*: '*And.*, disguised in some long black cloak'; 5.4.298 *sd*: '(Enter) The *Mar.*, three or four with halberds, leading *Pro.* to execution'; **Simple entry:** Ki., Pro., Ul., May., Gon., Pha., two attendants 3.2.280; Jo. Ad., Clo. And. 4.2.289; Ul., Mar. 5.2.296; And. 5.3.297; Cas., Pol., one maid 5.4.299; Ga. 5.4.301; Ki., And., Pro., Ul., Mar. 5.4.302; **Simple exit:** Pol. 1.1.263; (Dow.) 1.4.264; (Bea.) 2.5.265; (men) 1.6.266; (Pha.) 1.7.266; (Ro.) 1.7.266; (Cas.) 1.8.267; (La.) 2.1.270; (Ro.) 2.2.271; (Ro., Ap., Bru., officers) 2.2.273; (Ro.) 2.3.274; (citizens) 2.4.275; (Ul., Pi.) 2.5.276; (Rap., Grip.) 3.2.279; (Pha.) 3.2.279; (Jo. Ad.) 3.2.280; (Ki, Pro., Ul., May., Gon., Pha., Cas., two attendants) 3.2.286; (Clo.) 3.2.287; (beadles) 4.1.288; (Gre.) 4.1.288; (Jo. Ad.) 4.2.292; (And.) 4.2.293; (La., bills) 4.2.294; (Cas.) 4.2.295; (Mar.) 5.2.296; (Cas., Ul.) 5.3.297; (And.) 5.3.298; (Mar., Pro., attendants) 5.4.300

Songs and music 1. *Polina* 'Amid my bale, the lightning joy that pining care doth bring' (w.s. 8 lines) 1.1.262–3; 2. 'The choir of 'five or six singers, one half men and one half women' (w.n.s.) 1.9.269 *sd*; 3. *Lamia*'s women 'If pleasure be treasure' (a part-song w. ref., w.s. 17 lines) 2.2.271–2; 4. *Clown* 'You barons bold, and lusty lads' (w.s. 14 lines, w. ref.) 3.2.287; 5. *Andrugio* 'To thee O Lord, with heart and voice

I sing' (w.s. 12 lines) 4.2.292–3; 6. *Cassandra* 'Dear dames divorce your minds from joy, help to bewail my woe' (w.s. 12 lines) 5.4.301; **Instrumental:** there appears to be a group of instrumentalists, the 'Music' 1.9.269 *sd*

Staging and set the singers perform 'on some stage, erected from the ground' (1.9.269 *sd*); there may be a tomb for *Andrugio* at the outset, and a scaffold for *Promos* at the end, but no further indications as to set, the action being localized by the presence and dialogue of characters; the play, like Part I, is set in the 'city of Julio'; there is considerable ceremony, especially in the reception of the *King*

Stage properties 'clubs of fireworks' for the green men 1.6.265 *sd*; a sword 1.9.269 *sd*; a purse 1.9.269 *sd*; 'smocks and cauls' for *Lamia*'s women 2.2.271 *sd*; the *Sergeant*'s mace 2.2.272 *sd*; the *Officer*'s proclamation 2.2.272 *sd*; *Sir Ulrico*'s papers 2.4.274 *sd*; *John Adroynes*'s money 3.2.279; *Ulrico*'s list for the *King* 3.2.281 *sd*; tipstaffs for the beadles 4.1.287 *sd*; *Andrugio*'s bow and arrow and cony on his girdle 4.2.288 *sd*; bills for *Gresco*'s attendants 4.2.293 *sd*; halberds for the *King*'s officers 5.4.298 *sd*

PLACENAMES

Bohemia 2.2.272; 'Cock Lane' 4.1.287; 'Duck Alley' 1.5.265, 4.1.287; Hungary 2.2.272; 'Julio' (city) 2.2.272, 2.2.273, 4.2.290, 4.2.291, 4.2.292, 4.2.296; 'Scold's Corner' 4.1.287

ALLUSIONS

Apollo 3.2.279; Hercules 1.5.265; Pan 3.2.279; Phalaris and Perillus 2.4.275

BIBLIOGRAPHY

Budd, F. E. 'Materials for a Study of the Sources of *Measure for Measure*', RLC 11 (1931) pp. 711–36

Budd, F. E. 'Rouillet's *Philanira* and Whetstone's *Promos and Cassandra*', RES 6:21 (1930) pp. 31–48

Eccles, M. 'Emendations on Whetstone's *Promos and Cassandra*', N&Q 216 (1971) pp. 12–13

Eccles, M. 'George Whetstone in Star Chamber', RES n.s. 33:132 (1982) pp. 385–95

Foth, K. 'Shakespeare's *Masz für Masz* und die Geschichte von Promos und Cassandra', JDSG 13 (1878) pp. 163–85

Hunter, 1965, pp. 52–64

Izard, 1942, pp. 52–79

Kott, J. 'Head for Maidenhead, Maidenhead for Head: The Structure of Exchange in *Measure for Measure*' in Conejero, 1980, pp. 93–113

Prouty, C. T. 'George Whetstone and the Sources of *Measure for Measure*', SQ 15:2 (1964) pp. 131–45

Sandmann, P. 'Shakespeare's *Measure for Measure* und Whetstone's *Historie of Promos and Cassandra*', Archiv 68 (1882) pp. 263–94

Stroup, T. B. '*Promos and Cassandra* and *The Law against Lovers*', RES 8:31 (1932) pp. 309–10

Wilson, R. H. 'The Mariana Plot of *Measure for Measure*', PQ 9:4 (1930) pp. 341–50

75   Ralph Roister Doister

DATE, AUTHORSHIP AND AUSPICES

1552–4 (*SR* 1566/7 *c.* Oct.); Nicholas Udall; auspices unknown, but probably for performance by boys at Windsor; Greg 46

TEXT AND EDITIONS

Extant originals

1566–7 printing by Henry Denham for Thomas Hackett: Eton (no t.p.); *STC* 24508

Editions

1994	CHD (CD-Rom and online transcription of Denham printing, l.l., s.l., OS)
1984	Tydeman (OS)*
1984	Whitworth (s.l., NS)
1966	Creeth (s.l., OS)
1963	Gassner (s.l., NS)
1958	Thorndike, vol. II (a.l., NS)
1939	Scheurweghs (OS)
1935	Parks and Beatty (NS)
1935	Greg (facsimile)
1934	Baskervill, Heltzel and Nethercot (s.l., NS)
1934	Boas (s.l., NS)
1928	Schweikert (NS)
1924	Adams (s.l., OS)
1912	Child (s.l., NS)
1907	Farmer (n.l., NS)
1903	E. Flügel in Gayley, vol. I (s.l., OS)
1901	Williams and Robins (s.l., NS)
1897	Manly, vol. II (s.l., OS)
1874–6	Dodsley, vol. III (n.l., NS)
1869	Arber (n.l., OS)
1847	Cooper (n.l., OS)

SOURCES

These include Plautus's *Miles Gloriosus* and possibly the Thraso plot of Terence's *Eunuchus*; see Hinton's, Chislett's and Williams's essays listed below, and also the introduction to Child's edition, pp. 43–52.

CHARACTERS

Prologue
Matthew Merrygreek, a parasite
Ralph Roister Doister, a braggart
Madge Mumblecrust, Custance's former nurse
Tibet Talkapace, Custance's maid
Annot Alyface, Custance's maid
Dobinet Doughtie, Ralph's servant

Harpax, Ralph's servant
Christian Custance, a widow
Tom Truepenny, Custance's servant
Parish Clerk
Scrivener
Sim Suresby, Gawyn's servant
Gawyn Goodluck
Tristram Trusty, Gawyn's friend

PLOT SUMMARY

The prologue is in praise of mirth, of which interludes are reckoned a source. *Matthew Merrygreek* then enters telling of his own idle ways and of his wealthy friend *Ralph Roister*. He is joined by *Ralph* who announces his desperate love for *Christian Custance*, a widow betrothed to *Gawyn Goodluck*. *Ralph* is a braggart with a very positive view of his own attractive qualities and he is bolstered in this by *Merrygreek*'s flattery (rewarded with gold). *Merrygreek* proposes that *Ralph* pursue his wooing with the help of minstrels. In the next scene *Ralph* comes upon a group of *Custance*'s servant women spinning, and flirts with them while enquiring about their mistress. Her former nurse, *Madge Mumblecrust*, suggests that *Custance* will be favourably disposed to his suit and he whispers to her what to say to her mistress. When *Merrygreek* enters he takes *Mumblecrust* for the object of *Ralph*'s affections, and there is more comic play. *Madge* delivers a letter from *Ralph* to *Custance* but *Custance* demands she bring no more and when *Ralph*'s servant *Dobinet Doughtie* enters with a further token, a ring, *Madge* turns him away. He then turns to *Custance*'s maids, who agree to take the package in the expectation of a rich husband for their mistress. *Custance* is furious and warns her maids not to accept any more tokens for her. Finally *Merrygreek* approaches *Custance* on *Ralph*'s behalf, but she remains adamant. *Ralph* is in despair when he hears of her response and says he will die. *Merrygreek* arranges a mock funeral mass for him, but encourages him to revive and continue his wooing. They then go and sing before *Custance*'s house. She comes out and when asked why she is so scornful of his suit, she shows them the letter from him which, when *Merrygreek* proceeds to read it aloud, proves to be highly insulting. *Ralph* is appalled and together with *Merrygreek* they go and demand an explanation from the scrivener, who takes out his copy and reads it out to them with very different punctuation so that the meaning is entirely altered. *Ralph* is angry that *Merrygreek* read it in the way he did and strikes him, at which he promises to rectify the situation. At this point *Gawyn Goodluck*'s servant, *Sim Suresby*, arrives to tell *Custance* that his master, her betrothed, is on his way home. They are interrupted by *Matthew* and *Ralph*, who try to explain about the letter, but she continues to reject *Ralph*. However, *Sim* is left with some doubt as to her fidelity and he departs to report back to his master. When *Merrygreek*, and *Ralph* depart,

Custance warns her servant to chase off any further advances from them and asks *Tristram Trusty*, a friend of *Gawyn*, to go and correct any false impression which *Sim* might have gained. *Merrygreek* returns to say that *Ralph* is on his way to compel her to yield by force and, confessing his earlier mischief with the letter, conspires to help her surreptitiously in the coming conflict. *Ralph* arrives and battle eventually commences, *Custance*'s servants being armed with household implements. *Ralph* is driven off with the help of *Merrygreek*, who continually strikes him while pretending to aid him. *Gawyn* then arrives with *Sim*, and after initially expressing his doubts he is reassured by *Tristram*, and the lovers embrace. They are then also reconciled with *Merrygreek* and *Ralph*, and all sing a song before a prayer is offered for the queen and her government.

PLAY LENGTH

2,014 lines

COMMENTARY

This is loosely based on Roman comedy, with adaptations of the braggart and the parasite, but *Merrygreek* also has all the manipulative skill of the native Vice, though substantially without the moral dimension. Minor figures are also strong and the servants not only play a major role in the action but also have defined personalities. The action has a three-part Terentian structure across five acts. The reference to St Paul's steeple (786) suggests that the action is set in London.

Other secular comedies: **5, 30, 41, 46, 47, 88, 91, 92, 95.**

Other wooing plays: **6, 57** (frag.), **84, 87.**

Other plays featuring prominent women characters: **3, 6, 30, 32, 43, 46, 51, 63, 70, 87, 95, 97.**

SIGNIFICANT TOPICS AND NARRATIVE ELEMENTS

reflections on drama as entertainment; wooing and go-betweens; love tokens; unrequited love; wealthy fools and parasites; women's work, banter and song; a mock funeral; a comic battle; servants

DRAMATURGICAL AND RHETORICAL FEATURES

Verbal and general *Merrygreek*'s two Skeltonic passages repeating 'Sometime' 44–53 and 'I can' 85–90; rustic speech: *Mumblecrust* 281 ff.; *Merrygreek*'s mock funeral mass for *Ralph* 964–1004; *Merrygreek* coaches *Ralph* in deportment 1029–54; *Merrygreek* mischievously misplaces the punctuation in reading *Ralph*'s letter, changing the meaning 1126–60 (later read correctly 1289–323); *Ralph*'s Skeltonic passage repeating 'a thousand' 1223–30; a five-act play with scene divisions; a few stage directions in Latin, otherwise in English

Actions and stage directions 28 sd: 'He (*Mer.*) enters singing'; 280 sd: 'M. *Mum.* spinning on the distaffs, T. *Tal.* sewing, A. *Aly.* knitting', R. *Roi.*; 296 sd: '(*Tib.*) Sings' (L); 330 sd: '*Tib., An.* and *Ma.* do sing here'; 337 sd: 'Then they (as above) sing again'; 344 sd: 'They (as above) sing a third time'; 351 sd: 'They (as above) sing a fourth time'; 356 sd: 'Let her (*Tib.*) cast down her work'; 377: *Ma.* wipes her mouth; 378–9: *Ra.* kisses *Ma.*; 417 sd: 'Here let him (*Ra.*) tell her (*Ma.*) a great long tale in her ear'; 513–14, 517–18, 519–20: *Mer.* strikes *Ra.*; 530 sd: 'They (*Ra., Mer.,* servants) sing' (L); 558 sd: 'Here they (*Ra., Mer.*) sing, and go out singing'; 673: *Tru.* and *Do.* shake hands; 704 sd: 'Here they (*An., Tru., Do., Tib.*) sing'; 993 sd: 'The peal of bells rung by the parish clerk, and R. *Doi.*'s four men'; 1007–8: *Mer.* slaps *Ra.*; 1064 sd: 'They (*Ra., Mer.,* servants) sing' (L); 1177: *Ra.* weeps; 1266: *Ra.* threatens to hit the *Scri.*; 1268–9: the *Scri.* threatens *Ra.*; 1331–2: *Mer.* strikes *Ra.*; 1565–6: *Cu.* weeps; 1669–70: *Mer.* and *Ra.* fight; 1760–61: *Ra.* fires his gun; 1780–93: general fighting; 1790, 1793, 1812: *Mer.* strikes *Ra.*; 1817 sd: 'All (speaking) together (*Tib., Ma., An.*)'; 1989–90: *Ra.* shakes hands with *G. Go.*; 2000 sd: 'Here they (whole cast?) sing'; **Simple exit**: (*Mer.*) 276; (*An.*) 360; 'Both' (*Tib., An.*) 402; (*Ma.*) 641; (*Tib.*) 742; 'All' (*Al., Tru.*) 744; (*Do.*) 746; (*Tru.*) 762; (*Cu.*) 790; (*Tib.*) 833; (*Cu.*) 902; (*Mer.*) 1056; (*Cu.*) 1175; (*Mer.*) 1240; 'Both' (*Mer., Ra.*) 1351; (*Sim*) 1440; (*Tru.*) 1504; *Ra., Mer.* 1516; (*An., Tib., Ma.*) 1540; (*Tru.*) 1558; (*Mer.*) 1640; 'All' (*Ra., Mer.* servants) 1814; (*Tri.*) 1823; (*Cu.*) 1824; (*Ga., Sim*) 1882; (*Sim*) 1926; (*Mer.*) 1951

Songs and music 1. *Merrygreek* (w.n.s.) 28 sd; 2. *Tibet* 'Old brown bread crusts' (a snippet, w.s.) 297–8; 3. *Tibet, Annot, Madge* 'Pipe merry Annot' (a work song w. ref., w.s.) 331–56; 4. *Dobinet, Harpax, Madge, Ralph, Merrygreek* (?) 'Whoso to marry a minion wife' (w.s.) 531–42; 5. *Dobinet, Harpax, Madge, Ralph, Merrygreek* (w.n.s. . possibly a reprise of 4) 558 sd; 6. *Tibet, Annot, Truepenny, Dobinet* 'A thing very fit' (w.s., w. ref.) 705–36; 7. *Merrygreek* 'Placebo dilexi' (mock funeral rites, chanted, w.s.) 955–99; 8. *Ralph's* four men (chanting) 'When died he, when died he?' (w.s.) 995–8; 9. *Ralph, Merrygreek, Dobinet, Harpax* 'I mun be married a Sunday' (w.s., w. ref.) 1065–88; 10. Whole cast (?) 'The Lord preserve our most noble Queen of renown' (w.s.?: possibly 2001–14 are words sung); full texts of 4, 7 and 9 printed after main body of play, with some variation from version within the play; **Instrumental**: *Dobinet* and *Harpax* play instruments to accompany some (or all of) the songs 529; the Parish Clerk rings a peal of bells 993 sd (peal of bells noted after main body of play, connected to lines of text); drums Act 4, sc. 7 and sc. 8 headings

Staging and set the action is localized either by stage properties, as in the distaffs used by the women, or the presence and dialogue of the characters, though *Custance*'s house is likely to have been represented on stage, with an opening door (1091); the whole cast wages a comic battle on stage (1767–1815); the peal of bells rung by the Parish Clerk (993 sd) may require an appropriate structure

Stage properties distaffs, sewing and knitting implements 280 sd; a letter for Custance 543; a package for Custance (ring and token) 623; a cross 1009; kitchen implements for the battle: a distaff 1533, a broom 1534, a club 1535; a skimmer 1536, a firefork 1537, a spit 1538; two ensigns for the drummers Act 4, sc. 7 heading; a pail for Ralph 1706; Ralph's 'potgun' (possibly a popgun) 1708

PLACENAMES

'Alie' land (Holy Land ?) 218; Calais 1162, 1695; Cotswolds 1638; (Court of) Exchequer 1975; Greece 1706; Naples 499; St Paul's (steeple) 786; Rome 499, 644; Tower of London 141; Troy 215; Warwick 213

ALLUSIONS

Alexander the Great 219; Brute 218; Cato 223; Charlemagne 219; Colbrand (giant) 217; Esther 1895; St George 1407, 1720; Goliath 217; Guy of Warwick 213; Hector 215; Hercules 148, 214; Juno 908; Sir Lancelot du Lake 212; Lazarus 999; Marsyas 610; Neptune 1356; Nine Worthies 222; Plautus 19; Samson 217; Susanna 1893; Terence 19

RECORDED PRODUCTION

LP Record: BBC, *The First Stage*, dir. J. Barton (1970)

BIBLIOGRAPHY

Aoki, N. 'Roister Doister: The Comic Principle and the Play', *MFLAE* 28 (1977) pp. 10–19 (in Japanese)

Baldwin, T. W. and M. C. Linthicum, 'The Date of *Ralph Roister Doister*', *PQ* 6:4 (1927) pp. 379–95

Chislett, W. 'The Sources of *Ralph Roister Doister*', *MLN* 29:3 (1914) pp. 166–7

Dudok, 1916, pp. 50–62

Edgerton, W. L. 'The Date of *Roister Doister*', *PQ* 44:4 (1965) pp. 555–60

Edgerton, 1965, pp. 89–107

Faust, R. 'Das erste englische Lustspiel in seiner Abhängigkeit vom "Moral-Play" und von der römischen Komödie' in *Jahresbericht des Neustädter Realgymnasium zu Dresden* (Dresden, C. Heinrich, 1889) pp. 1–22

Habersang, O. '*Ralph Royster Doyster* von Nicholas Udall, die erste englische Comödie' in *Programm des Gymnasiums zu Bückeburg, Ostern 1875* (Bückeburg, Grimmeschen, 1875) pp. 1–24

Hales, J. W. 'The Date of "The First English Comedy"', *EngS* 18 (1893) pp. 408–21

Hinton, J. 'The Source of *Ralph Roister Doister*', *MP* 11:2 (1913) pp. 273–8

Maulsby, D. L. 'The Relation between Udall's *Roister Doister* and the Comedies of Plautus and Terence', *EngS* 38 (1907) pp. 251–77

Miller, E. S. 'Roister Doister's "Funeralls"', *SP* 43:1 (1946) pp. 42–58

Möller, F. 'Remarks on the First Regular Comedy of English Literature and its Author' in *Jahresbericht des Königlichen Christianeums zu Altona über das Schuljahr 1889/90* (Altona, Peter Mener, 1890) pp. i–xxi

Norland, 1995, pp. 267–79

Peery, W. 'The Prayer for the Queen in *Roister Doister*', *UTSE* 27 (1948) pp. 222–3

Pittenger, E. '"To Serve the Queere": Nicholas Udall, Master of the Revels' in Goldberg, 1994, pp. 162–89

Plumstead, A. W. 'Satirical Parody in *Roister Doister*: A Reinterpretation', *SP* 60:2 (1963) pp. 141–54

Reed, A. W. 'Nicholas Udall and Thomas Wilson', *RES* I:3 (1925) pp. 275–83

Scheurweghs, 1964, pp. 84–9

Towne, 1950, pp. 175–80

Udal, J. S. '*Ralph Roister Doister*: Nicholas Udall', *N&Q* 140 (1921) pp. 281–4

Walter, M. 'Beiträge zu *Ralph Royster Doyster*', *EngS* 5 (1882) pp. 67–74

Webster, H. T. '*Ralph Roister Doister* and the Little Eyases', *N&Q* 196 (1951) pp. 135–6

Wheat, C. H. '*A Pore Helpe, Ralph Roister Doister*, and *Three Laws*', *PQ* 28:2 (1949) pp. 312–19

Williams, W. H. '*Ralph Roister Doister*', *EngS* 36 (1906) pp. 179–86

Williams, W. H. '*Ralph Roister Doister* and *The Wasps*', *MLR* 7:2 (1912) p. 235

Willson, 1975, pp. 12–26

76   Respublica

DATE, AUTHORSHIP AND AUSPICES

1553; anonymous, possibly by Udall; a Christmas play for boys, perhaps performed at court

TEXT AND EDITIONS

Extant originals

Manuscript: Pforzheimer Library MS 40 A

Editions

1994 CHD (CD-Rom and online copy of Greg, 1952, l.l., s.l., OS)
1969 Schell and Schuchter (NS)
1952 Greg (OS)*
1914 Farmer (1914a) (facsimile, n.l.)
1908 TFT (facsimile, n.l.)
1907 Farmer (9) (n.l., NS)
1907 '*Lost*' *Tudor Plays*, TFT (facsimile, n.l.)
1905 Magnus (OS)
1898 Brandl (s.l., OS)
1866 Collier, vol. 1 (n.l., OS)

SOURCES

No sources have been identified.

CHARACTERS

Prologue, a Poet	Oppression	Veritas
Avarice, the Vice	Respublica	Peace
Adulationn	People	Justice
Insolence	Misericordia	Nemesis

PLOT SUMMARY

The *Prologue* celebrates the accession of Mary to the throne to address the abuses the realm has suffered in the years prior to her reign. The action of the play is then opened by the Vice, *Avarice*, who declares his intention to fleece *Lady Respublica* (representing the realm of England) taking the name *Policy* to conceal his true nature. In the next scene a group of gallants, *Insolence, Oppression* and *Adulation* dream of power and they resolve to seek out *Avarice* for counsel and leadership. He is at first suspicious of them, but at length agrees that they should all insinuate themselves into *Respublica*'s service for their own gain. They all change their names for the purpose, and have to be rehearsed in their new identities, partly through the use of song. They also decide to acquire new clothes to complete the disguise. *Avarice* approaches *Respublica*, who is lamenting the sorrowful state into which she has fallen, and she readily agrees to put the management of her estate into his hands. He quickly introduces his fellow Vices and she charges them to vanquish the foes who have brought her into the current crisis. These are, unbeknown to her, the very people to whom she is talking, in their concealed identities. They exit singing and *Respublica* expresses the hope of recovery. Very soon *People* arrives, representing the 'poor Commons', to complain to a sympathetic *Respublica* of the poverty and oppression he is suffering. *People* inveighs against the Vices who control the realm, citing their original names. He also starts to expose her current advisers for what they are, but she defends them as trying to repair the harm already done the realm. *People* remains sceptical and *Avarice*, who joins them, vows worse oppression for him. The Vices convene to compare notes on their villainous activities and ill-gotten gains, and *Avarice* lists the corrupt practices in which he has been able to engage in the name of church reform. They decide that they need to speed up their activities as Time is hastening upon them and has a daughter, *Veritas*, who is likely to expose them. They need to get hold of the goddess Occasion who only has one tuft of hair which can be grasped as she passes by. They all depart and *Respublica* comes in complaining that she is unable to relieve *People*'s woes. She is joined by *People*, followed soon after by *Avarice* and the other Vices, and the acrimonious debate between *People* and the Vices continues. *Respublica* tries to mediate, though she is really in sympathy with *People*, pointing out that the realm had been in better shape some years previously when the Church was prosperous. They all leave and *Misericordia* enters talking of God's mercy and announcing that she has come to relieve the plight of *Respublica*. *Misericordia* comforts *Respublica* and goes off to fetch *Veritas*, who proceeds to reveal the true identities of the Vices. *Justicia* and *Pax* are then summoned, and they pledge their support in *Respublica*'s recovery. The Vices are alarmed at the turn events have taken and *Avarice* comes to justify himself to *Respublica* who, however, rejects him and his companions. *People* is summoned to be told of the justice about to be done and, after *Veritas* forces the Vices to expose their true natures, they are given into the custody of *People* while *Nemesis* is fetched. *Veritas, Pax, Justicia* and *Misericordia* advise her on the judgement to be imposed and *Nemesis* then proceeds to deliver it. *Adulation* repents and is pardoned, and while the other three are given over to officers for justice to be administered, *Nemesis* promises *People* protection from oppression and *Pax* ends the play with a prayer for Queen Mary and her ministers.

PLAY LENGTH

1,937 lines, including a prologue of 58 lines

COMMENTARY

This is a mildly anti-Reformation play which, however, deals principally with social and economic rather than doctrinal matters. The focus is more on corruption in the state than on moral or theological issues, and the central character *Respublica* is not a humanity figure as such but represents the state. Though shown to be in error, she never herself falls into corruption. This is one of the earliest extant interludes to deal with historical matter.

Other political comment and state of the realm plays: **1** (frag.), **14, 37, 38, 59, 71**.

Other social ills plays: **2, 15, 24, 38, 40, 52, 53, 71, 72** (frag.), **94, 96, 98, 100**.

SIGNIFICANT TOPICS AND NARRATIVE ELEMENTS

Edwardian ecclesiastical reform; (Protestant) corruption in the state; the appropriation of land; the plundering of the Church; inflation; poverty; flatterers and bad advisers; the Four Daughters of God; Queen Mary as Nemesis, redressing corruption resulting from the reform; a 'wise' plebeian (*People*)

DRAMATURGICAL AND RHETORICAL FEATURES

Verbal and general aliases of the Vices: *Avarice–Policy* 80–4, *Insolence–Authority* 378, *Oppression–Reformation* 380, *Adulation–Honesty* 389; *Avarice*'s rhetorical list of trash in the realm 93–105; several passages of stichomythia especially 173–231; the Vices rapid-fire exchange of brief exclamations 245–50; *Adulation* has the alternative name of Flattery 345–6; *Respublica*'s 'ubi sunt' passage 439–56; rustic dialect: *People* 636 ff.; *Misericordia*'s sermon 1169–208; *Veritas*'s list of corrupt practices with endings playing on 'rye' 1740–3; the Vices as gallants; dialogue is frequently in part lines; a five-act play with scene divisions; stage directions in either Latin or English

Costume and dress the Vices' change of dress (as disguise) 417; the reapparelling of *Respublica* (her clothing having earlier fallen into disrepair) 1500, and she is 'gorgeously decked' 1502; *People* is able to buy a new coat 1599; the Vices are forced to remove their outer garments to expose their true identities 1752

Actions and stage directions 122 sd: '(*Ad., Ins., Op.*) Enter singing' (L); 337 sd: '(Vices) Go forward, one after other' (E); 338 sd: 'He (*Av.*) whistles'; 460 sd: '*Av.* enters musing and playing' (L); 531 sd: 'Enter *Av.* leading *Ins., Op.* and *Ad.*' (L); 597 sd: 'They (Vices) sing "Bring ye to me and I to ye" and thus go out' (L/E); 898 sd: 'They (Vices) sing "Hey nony nony, houghe for money" and so on' (L/E); 949 sd: '(*Op., Ad., Ins.*) Let them depart running' (L); 1430 sd: 'They (*Mis., Ver., Jus., Pax*) sing "The mercy of God" etc. and let them depart' (L/E); 1938 sd: 'They (*Pe., Nem., Pax, Ver., Jus., Res.*) sing and let them depart' (L); **Simple entry**: *Av.* 154; *Pe.* 983; *Mis., Ver.* 1337; *Res.* 1482; *Pe.* 1574; *Av.* 1631; **Simple exit**: (*Av.*) 122; (*Ins., Op., Ad.*) 434; *Av.* 438; (*Av.*) 524; *Res.* 588; (*Res., Pe.*) 739; (*Av.*) 968; *Res.* 1141; (*Pe.*) 1166; (*Ins.*) 1167; (*Op.*) 1167; (*Av.*) 1168; *Mis.* 1260; *Ad.* 1324; (*Ad.*) 1481; (*Av.*) 1572; (*Pe.*) 1610

Songs and music (w.n.s. to any songs except 6) 1. *Adulation, Insolence, Oppression* no title 122 sd; 2. *Avarice* teaches *Adulation* a 'sol fe' on 'Reformation' 410–13; 3. *Adulation, Insolence, Oppression* 'Bring ye to me and I to ye' 597 sd; 4. *Oppression, Adulation, Insolence, Avarice* 'Hey, nony, nony, houghe for mony' 898 sd; 5. *Pax, Misericordia, Justitia, Veritas* 'The Mercy of God' 1430 sd; 6. *Avarice* 'Haye, haie, haie, haie' (a catch, two lines) 1661–2; 7. Whole cast? final song (no title) 1938 sd

Staging and set the action is unlocalized and there are no indications as to set

Stage properties *Avarice*'s 'gaping purses' 421; the Vices' bags 829; *Avarice*'s hidden bag 1725; purses 1758

PLACENAMES

Athens 449; Babylon 449; Barwick 1550; Calais 782; Corinth 449; Cumberland 1548; England 45; Jerusalem 42; Kent 1547; Newgate (prison) 1634; Northumberland 1547; St Paul's steeple 635; 'Prickingham' (Priory?) 884; Somerset 1548; Troy 446; Warwickshire 1549; Westminster Hall 1695

ALLUSIONS

Amos 5:7 1532; *Job* 1527; *Matthew 21:16* 41; *Psalm 8:3* (V)/*8:2* (AV) 41; *84:11* (V)/*85:10* (AV) 1284; *84:12* (V)/*85:11* (AV) 1706, *144:9* (V)/*145:9* (AV) (q.a.) 1182–4; *Sapientia 1:15* (V) 1530

BIBLIOGRAPHY

Bevington, D. M. 'Drama and Polemics under Queen Mary'. *RenD* 9 [1966] (1967) pp. 105–24
Bevington, 1968, pp. 115–20

Broude, 1973, pp. 489–502

Debax, J.-P. 'Respublica: Pièce Catholique?', Caliban 24 (1987) pp. 27–47

Haller, 1916, pp. 138–43

Kuya, T. 1985, pp. 75–114

Mackenzie, 1914, pp. 226–34

Mullini, 1984

Norland, 1995, pp. 199–209

Potter, 1975, pp. 89–94

Rutledge, D. F. 'Respublica: Rituals of Status Elevation and the Political Mythology of Mary Tudor', MRDE 5 (1991) pp. 55–68

Scheurweghs, 1964, pp. 84–9

Southern, 1973, pp. 375–94

Starr, G. A. 'Notes on Respublica', N&Q n.s. 8 (1961) pp. 290–2

Traver, 1907, pp. 141–4

Walker, 1998, pp. 163–95

77   The Resurrection of Our Lord (fragments)

DATE, AUTHORSHIP AND AUSPICES

1530–60; anonymous; auspices unknown

TEXT AND EDITIONS

Extant originals

Manuscript: Folger Shakespeare Library MS V.b.192

Editions

1994   CHD (CD-Rom and online copy of Dover Wilson, Dobell and Greg, 1913, l.l., OS)

1913   Dover Wilson, Dobell and Greg (OS)*

SOURCES

The play is based on the relevant Resurrection sequences in the Gospels, principally Matthew 27–28, Mark 16, Luke 24 and John 19–21.

CHARACTERS

Pilate	Mary Salome	Luke
Centurion	Mary Jacobe	Andrew
Caiphas	Mary Jose	James
Annas	Peter	Thomas
1st Soldier	John	James the Less

2nd Soldier	1st Angel	Philip
3rd Soldier	2nd Angel	Bartholemew
4th Soldier	Jesus Christ	Matthew
Appendix (Expositor)	Senior	Simeon
Mary Magdalene	Cleophas	Jude

PLOT SUMMARY

The first fragment starts with *Pilate* discussing with a centurion the circumstances of *Christ's* death and burial. *Pilate* is concerned to verify that *Christ* was indeed dead when he was taken down for burial. When they are joined by *Caiphas* and *Annas*, these mention their fear that *Christ's* body will be stolen by the disciples in order to claim a resurrection, and they assert the importance of maintaining Mosaic law. They appoint four soldiers to watch the tomb who, however, are struck down with terror by thunder as *Christ* rises. They then fear being accused of dereliction of duty and go off to discuss their strategy of defence. The *Appendix* (or expositor) enters to comment on events, using the idea of resurrection as a metaphor for personal spiritual renewal, and introduces the next sequence. The four Marys appear, seeking *Christ's* body in order to anoint it, but to their sorrow they find the tomb empty, and they are joined by *Peter* and *John* who are equally dismayed. When *Peter* and *John* leave, the Marys encounter two angels whom they ask about *Christ* and are told about the Resurrection, though *Mary Magdalene* remains doubtful. She is then addressed by *Christ* himself, who she takes to be the gardener and the fragment ends here, four leaves being missing. The next sequence has *Caiphas* paying a bribe to the soldiers to spread the tale that the disciples have stolen *Christ's* body. The *Appendix* again begins a comment on the narrative, but two more leaves are missing from the manuscript at this point. The following sequence has *Christ* reprimanding *Peter* for not believing *Mary Magdalene*'s news of the Resurrection, but then appointing him chief of the disciples. When *Christ* leaves, *Peter* experiences remorse for his lack of faith. The *Appendix* next comments on the play's extrapolation of this narrative from brief references in Scripture, requesting indulgence for the use of imagination, and goes on to introduce the next sequence. This is the journey to Emmaus. The travellers *Luke* and *Cleophas* voice their doubts about the Resurrection for which Christ, appearing as a stranger in their midst, castigates them. He draws comparisons between Moses's deliverance of his people and *Christ's* saving of mankind, citing Old Testament prophecies of the coming of the Messiah. They welcome the stranger's teaching and he breaks bread, distributing it to them. When he then suddenly disappears, they realize to whom they have been speaking and resolve to go and inform the disciples. The *Appendix* preaches on how *Christ* reveals himself to individuals, and makes way for the following sequence, which involves *Cleophas* and *Luke* informing the disciples of their experience. Two leaves are missing here, and the next section starts with the *Appendix* arguing against delusion, before bringing in the final sequence, which is the story of *Thomas*'s doubt. The section ends with the appearance of *Christ* to *Thomas*.

PLAY LENGTH

1,321 lines extant

COMMENTARY

This is a Resurrection play divided into several sequences to be played over two days. A total of eight leaves of text are missing, from three points in the play. The comments and expositions on the action by the *Appendix* have a strongly Protestant slant.

Other biblical plays: **10, 11, 16, 34, 42, 44, 48, 63, 90, 93**.

SIGNIFICANT TOPICS AND NARRATIVE ELEMENTS

the dream of Pilate's wife; Pilate's doubts about execution of Christ; Mosaic law versus Christian doctrine; a 'Quem Quaeritis' sequence; a 'Hortulanus' sequence; the journey to Emmaus; Doubting Thomas

DRAMATURGICAL AND RHETORICAL FEATURES

Verbal and general the *Appendix* comments on the play's expansion of scriptural narrative 292–321, 511–20, 590–617, 1062–99; the apostles speak in a numbered sequence 1208–43; there are four Marys instead of three visiting the tomb
Costume and dress *Christ* is apparelled 'like a gardener' 443 *sd*
Actions and stage directions 148 *sd*: 'Here let the *Cen.* and his soldiers make sign of valour'; 242 *sd*: 'Here they (soldiers) fall down as dead on hearing the guns shot off and thunder. *Je.* rises throwing off death and the *Ang.*'; 243 (*sd*): 'The *1st Soldier* [says] after his astonishment'; 370 *sd*: 'Here (*Ma. M.*) look towards Jerusalem'; 383 *sd*: 'Let *Ma.* here lament'; 406 *sd*: 'Here do the women go to the sepulchre'; 417 *sd*: '*Ma. M.* laments'; 418 (*sd*): 'Both angels speak'; 443 *sd*: '*Chr.* (dressed) like a gardener'; 997–8 (*sd*): 'Here *Chr.* takes the bread, breaks it and gives it unto them (*Lu., Cle.*), and so suddenly departs'; 999–1000 (*sd*): 'Here they (*Lu., Cle.*) make gestures of wonder a while'; 1099 *sd*: 'Here they (*Lu., Cle.*) walk aside and *Pe.* with the Apostles comes in'; **Simple entry:** *Pe., Jo.* 345; *Tho.* 1189; **Simple exit:** (?) 8; (*Pil.*) 163; *Cai., An.* 205; (*1st Sol.*) 221; (soldiers) 291; *Pe., Jo.* 363; (*Cai., An.,* soldiers) 510; (*Je.*) 568; (*Lu., Cle.*) 1061; (*Ap.*) 1100; (*Lu., Cle.*) 1111
Staging and set the action is localized by the presence of the characters rather than by any direction for setting or set, but *Christ*'s tomb is clearly a structure which is present on stage; there is a gunshot or device for making a noise of thunder (242 *sd*)

Stage properties *Mary Magdalene*'s box of ointment 345; money paid by *Annas* and *Caiphas* as a bribe 488; bread broken by *Christ* 997–8 *sd*

PLACENAMES

Arabia 852; Bethlehem 840; Emmaus 609, 621, 662, 1141, 1150, 1158; Galilee 414, 428, 536, 599, 1182; Jerusalem 370 *sd*, 667, 775, 1053, 1060, 1102; Judea 840; Nazareth 410, 674; Saba 852; Mount Sion 771, 800

ALLUSIONS[1]

King David 778, 779, 784, 808, 840, 842, 851, 880, 886, 902, 929; Elijah 815; *Exodus 37* 893m; *Genesis 22:6* 919m; Isaac 919; Isaiah 760, 902, 907, 913, 942; *Isaiah 7:14* 843m, *60* 851m, *61* 858m; Jeremiah 853; *Jeremiah 31:15* 853m; John the Baptist 863, 865–6; Jonah 935–40; Joseph 846–7; Judas 879; St Luke 593, 610; *Matthew 11* 863m, *27:19* 27m; Melchidesek 811; *Micah 5:2* 840m; Moses 132 *passim*; Nathan 777, 779; *Numbers 21:8* 921m; St Paul 593; *Psalm 15:10* (V)/*16:10* (AV) 930m, *71:10* (V)/*72:10* (AV) 851m; Rachel 854; Solomon 769, 777, 781, 784, 785, 791, 799, 805; Zachariah 883; *Zachariah 9:9* 870m

1 Some allusions occur in the margins and are marked m.

BIBLIOGRAPHY

Revels II, pp. 184–5

78   The Reynes Extracts (fragments)

DATE, AUTHORSHIP AND AUSPICES

latter half of the fifteenth century; anonymous; auspices unknown

TEXT AND EDITIONS

Extant originals

Manuscript: Bodleian Library MS Tanner 407 fos. 43v–44v

Editions

1994   CHD (CD-Rom and online copy of Davis, 1970, l.l., OS)*
1993   Coldewey (OS)*
1979   Davis (facsimile, n.l.)
1970   Davis (OS)*
1916   Calderhead (OS)*

CHARACTERS

Delight   Epilogue speaker

PLOT SUMMARY

The extracts consist of a speech by a character, *Delight*, rejoicing in various worldly pleasures. The next speech is the epilogue thanking the audience for its attentiveness and good behaviour, and offering a conventional apology for any faults. It ends by announcing an ale for the benefit of the Church.

PLAY LENGTH

Two speeches extant: *Delight* (60 lines), *Epilogue* (30 lines)

COMMENTARY

The speech of *Delight* is clearly uttered by a youthful figure, very probably early in the play. A point of interest in the epilogue is the connection of the performance with a church ale.

SIGNIFICANT TOPICS AND NARRATIVE ELEMENTS

nature; country sports; great houses; fine apparel; female beauty; audience behaviour; a church ale

BIBLIOGRAPHY

1949: R. H. Robbins, 'A Sixteenth-Century English Mystery Fragment', *ES* 30:3, pp. 134–6

79   The Rickinghall (Bury St Edmunds) Fragment

DATE, AUTHORSHIP AND AUSPICES

early fourteenth century; anonymous; auspices unknown

TEXT AND EDITIONS

Extant originals

Manuscript: (British Library) British Museum Add. Roll 63481 B

Editions

1994   CHD (CD-Rom and online copy of Davis, 1970, l.l., OS)*
1979   Davis (facsimile, n.l.)
1970   Davis (OS)*
1923   Brandl (n.l., OS)
1921   Gilson (n.l., OS)

CHARACTERS

A King   A Messenger

PLOT SUMMARY

A *King* (possibly Herod) asserts his authority over his court, which includes counts, barons and knights, and he summons his *Messenger*.

PLAY LENGTH

15 lines in Anglo-Norman, and a partial translation in English of 10 lines extant

COMMENTARY

This is part of a conventional 'boasting' speech by a tyrant figure. There is one direction for speech by a messenger, but what follows appears to be a continuation of the *King*'s speech. See also the commentary on the *Cambridge Prologue* above.

SIGNIFICANT TOPICS AND NARRATIVE ELEMENTS

a 'boasting' speech; a list of ranks

BIBLIOGRAPHY

Greg, W. W. 'A Fourteenth-Century Fragment', *TLS*, 2 June 1921, p. 356
Sisam, 1921, p. xxvi
Studer, P. 'A Fourteenth-Century Fragment', *TLS*, 9 June 1921, p. 373

80   Robin Hood and the Friar

DATE, AUTHORSHIP AND AUSPICES

1560 (probable *SR* entry 30 Nov. 1560, erroneously dated 30 Oct.); anonymous; folk play for May games, offered for acting; Greg 32

TEXT AND EDITIONS

Extant originals

c. 1560 (?) printing by William Copland (in *A Mery Geste of Robyn Hoode and of hys lyfe*, H2v–H4v): BL; *STC* 13691

c. 1565 (?) printing by William Copland: All Souls College (frag., 1 leaf): *STC* 13691.3

1590 printing for Edward White (appended to *A Merry Jest of Robin Hood*): Bodleian; Chapin; *STC* 13692

Editions

1994   CHD (CD-Rom and online copy of Greg, 1908, n.l., OS)
1981   Wiles (n.l., OS)
1981   Blackstone (NS)*
1978   Parfitt (n.l., NS)
1977   Knight and Ohlgren (OS) pp. 281–95 (continuous with *Robin Hood and the Potter*)
1924   Adams (OS, bowdlerized lines 118–20)*
1914   TFT (facsimile, n.l.)
1908   Greg (n.l., OS, printed as one play with *Robin Hood and the Potter*)
1897   Manly, vol. 1 (OS, bowdlerized lines 118–20)*

SOURCES

The play is probably based on a version of the ballad, *Robin Hood and the Curtal Friar* (Child, 1888, no. 123).

CHARACTERS

Robin Hood   Little John   Friar Tuck
Mute: Robin Hood's men, Friar Tuck's men, a maid

PLOT SUMMARY

Robin Hood opens the play complaining that he has been robbed of his purse by a friar, and asking who among his men will avenge him. *Little John* volunteers and they all go off. When *Friar Tuck* appears, *Robin* returns and sets upon him, but is thrown off. He attacks again and *Tuck* this time carries him on his back and throws him into water. They fight until *Robin* blows his horn and his men appear. At this, *Tuck* whistles and his men appear. They all fight until *Robin* proposes that *Tuck* join his band, offering him a lady to whom he can become chaplain. *Tuck* responds with lustful glee and the play concludes with a dance.

PLAY LENGTH

122 lines

COMMENTARY

This exemplifies one strand of the folk play tradition, another being that of St George. The ritualized game element is very evident and the dialogue is simple, serving merely to introduce the combative action that constitutes the substance of the play.

SIGNIFICANT TOPICS AND NARRATIVE ELEMENTS

the Robin Hood legend; Tuck as a lustful friar; May combat games

DRAMATURGICAL AND RHETORICAL FEATURES

Verbal and general at the start is the comment: 'Here begins the play of Robin Hood, very proper to be played in May games'
Costume and dress *Tuck* wears a 'long coat' 46; *Robin* and his men are 'clothed in Kendal green' 98
Actions (no stage directions) 47–8: *Robin* seizes *Tuck* by the throat; 76–9: *Robin* gets on *Tuck*'s back; 80: *Tuck* throws *Robin* into the water; 85–7: *Robin* and *Tuck* fight; 95–6: *Robin* blows his horn; 103–4: *Tuck* whistles; 105–7: all the men fight (?)
Songs and music music is likely for the dance
Staging and set this is for open air performance; little indication as to set, except that a body of water is used in the performance (72)
Stage properties *Tuck*'s quarter staff 28; *Tuck*'s three dogs 45; *Robin*'s horn 93; 'clubs and staves' for the combat 106

PLACENAMES

Barnsdale 39; Kendal 98

REPORTS ON MODERN PRODUCTIONS

1. Bloomington, Indiana (PLS), 18 October 1979 and tour [*RORD* 22 (1979) pp. 141]
2. Leeds (PLS) 3 May 1981 [*METh* 3:1 (1981) pp. 60–1]

RECORDED PRODUCTIONS

Videotape: PLS, Scotiabank Information Commons (1983)
Videotape: Insight Media, produced by M. Edmunds (1990)

BIBLIOGRAPHY

Knight, 1994, pp. 98–115
Simeone, 1951, pp. 265–74
Wiles, 1981, pp. 1–63
Wiles, 1999, pp. 77–98

81   Robin Hood and the Potter (fragment)

DATE, AUTHORSHIP AND AUSPICES

1560 (probable *SR* entry 30 Nov. 1560, erroneously dated 30 Oct.); anonymous; folk play for May games, offered for acting; Greg 32

TEXT AND EDITIONS

Extant originals

c. 1560 (?) printing by William Copland (in *A Mery Geste of Robyn Hoode and of hys lyfe*, H2v–H4v): BL; *STC* 13691
1590 printing for Edward White (appended to *A Merry Jest of Robin Hood*): Bodleian; Chapin; *STC* 13692

Editions

1994   CHD (CD-Rom and online copy of Greg, 1908, n.l., OS)
1981   Wiles (n.l., OS)
1978   Parfitt (n.l., NS)
1977   Knight and Ohlgren pp. 281–95 (OS, continuous with *Robin Hood and the Friar*)
1926   Tickner (n.l., NS)
1914   TFT (facsimile, n.l.)
1908   Greg (OS, continuous with *Robin Hood and the Friar*)
1897   Manly, vol. 1 (OS)*

SOURCES

The play is based on the ballad of *Robin Hood and the Potter*, *c.* 1500 (Child, 1888, no. 121)

CHARACTERS

Robin Hood   Little John   Jack, the Potter's boy   The Potter

PLOT SUMMARY

Robin Hood tells of a *Potter* who has consistently avoided his tolls and asks who of his men would be bold enough to extract payment from him. *Little John*, despite initial reluctance, agrees to do so for a reward of £20. He then goes off and the *Potter*'s boy, *Jack*, enters with some pots on his way to market. *Robin* apprehends him and, to the boy's consternation, smashes the pots. When the *Potter* himself arrives to reprimand *Jack* for not being at the market, the boy reports what has happened to the pots and also that *Robin* has called his master a cuckold. *Robin* reappears and demands a toll from the *Potter*, which he robustly refuses. The *Potter* challenges him to sword combat, and *Robin* summons *Little John*. The fragment ends with *Little John*'s preparing for the fight.

PLAY LENGTH

202 lines extant

COMMENTARY

Copland prints this with *Robin Hood and the Friar* as one play. This play has a strong similarity in its formula to that one, though there is a discernible narrative element in the episode with the boy.

SIGNIFICANT TOPICS AND NARRATIVE ELEMENTS

the Robin Hood legend; a cuckoldry accusation; May game combats

DRAMATURGICAL AND RHETORICAL FEATURES

Costume and dress the *Potter* is referred to as wearing a 'rose garland' 126
Actions (no stage directions) 156–9: *Robin* smashes the pots
Songs and music music is likely for the morris dances that, while not specified here, traditionally accompany these plays
Staging and set the only indication as to set is *Robin*'s reference to 'the green wood tree' (187)
Stage properties pots 154; *Robin*'s bow 190; swords and bucklers 191

PLACENAMES

Nottingham 151

BIBLIOGRAPHY

Knight, 1994, pp. 98–115
Simeone, 1951, pp. 265–74
Wiles, 1981, pp. 1–63
Wiles, 1999, pp. 77–98

82   Robin Hood and the Sheriff or Robin Hood and the Knight (fragment)

DATE, AUTHORSHIP AND AUSPICES

c. 1475; anonymous; folk play for May games

TEXT AND EDITIONS

Extant originals

Manuscript: Cambridge, Trinity College MS R.2.64

Editions

1994   CHD (CD-Rom and online copy of Greg, 1908, n.l., OS)
1981   Wiles (n.l., OS)
1979   Davis (facsimile, n.l.)
1978   Parfitt (n.l., NS)
1977   Knight and Ohlgren (OS) pp. 275–85*
1924   Adams (OS)*
1908   Greg (n.l., OS)
1897   Manly, vol. 1 (OS)

SOURCES

The ballad of *Robin Hood and Guy of Gisborne* is the likely source (Child, 1888, no. 118).

CHARACTERS

A Knight   Sheriff   Robin Hood   One of Robin's Men   Friar Tuck
           Mute: Robin's men; Sheriff's men

PLOT SUMMARY

A *Knight* undertakes to challenge *Robin Hood* on behalf of the *Sheriff*. He and *Robin* first have a shooting contest, then a stone-throwing competition, and finally a wrestling match, all of which *Robin* wins. *Robin* kills the *Knight* and dons his clothes as a disguise. A man comes to report that the *Sheriff* has attacked *Robin*'s men and they come upon the scene to see the men, including *Friar Tuck*, being led to prison. The fragment ends here.

PLAY LENGTH

42 lines extant

COMMENTARY

As in the other Robin Hood plays, the tournament element is suggested by the volunteering of a 'champion' to undertake the contest. Here there is a varied contest of three activities and Robin's assumption of the knight's clothes may also be a ritual feature.

SIGNIFICANT TOPICS AND NARRATIVE ELEMENTS

the Robin Hood legend; May game combats

DRAMATURGICAL AND RHETORICAL FEATURES

Costume and dress *Robin* dons the *Knight*'s clothes and hood 23–4
Actions (no stage directions) 9–10: *Robin* and the *Knight* shoot arrows; 11–12: *Robin* and the *Knight* cast stones; 13: *Robin* and the *Knight* cast the axle tree; 14–15: *Robin* and the *Knight* wrestle; 22: *Robin* severs the *Knight*'s neck; 35: Robin's men are bound; 40: Robin's men are led to prison
Songs and music music is likely for the morris dances that, while not specified here, traditionally accompany these plays
Staging and set the only indications of set are the references to the linden tree (13) and the prison gates that are apparently openable (41)
Stage properties bows and arrows and a target 9–10; stones 11; a caber or axle ('axletree') 13; the *Knight*'s horn 17; ropes to bind the men 35

BIBLIOGRAPHY

Knight, 1994, pp. 98–115
Simeone, 1951, pp. 265–74
Wiles, 1981, pp. 1–63
Wiles, 1999, pp. 77–98

83   (The Play of the) Sacrament (Croxton)

DATE, AUTHORSHIP AND AUSPICES

second half of the fifteenth century; anonymous; offered for acting, probably for a touring company

TEXT AND EDITIONS

Extant originals

Manuscript: Trinity College, Dublin MS F.4.20, Catalogue no. 652, fos. 338r–356r

Editions

2000	Walker (OS)
1994	CHD (CD-Rom and online copy of Davis, 1970, l.l. OS)*
1993	Coldewey (OS)*
1970	Davis (OS)*
1979	Davis (facsimile, n.l.)
1975	Bevington (OS)*
1924	Adams (OS)
1909	Waterhouse (OS)*
1860–1	Stokes (OS)
1897	Manly, vol. 1 (OS)

SOURCES

No direct sources have been identified, but the story appears in Italy in Villani's *Cronaca Figurata* dating from before 1348. There are records of several similar continental plays including a Dutch play performed in Breda in around 1500, and sixteenth-century Italian and French versions.

CHARACTERS

Primus Vexillator (1st Standard-bearer)
Secundus Vexillator (2nd Standard-bearer)
Aristorius, a Christian Merchant
The Priest, Sir Isoder
The Clerk, Peter
Jonathas, 1st Jew
Jason, 2nd Jew

Jasdon, 3rd Jew
Masphat, 4th Jew
Malchus, 5th Jew
Colle, the Doctor's Boy
Master Brundyche, the Doctor
Jesus
Bishop

PLOT SUMMARY

The banns are spoken by the first and second standard-bearers, giving the story of the play, relating that it dramatizes events which took place in the forest of Aragon in the year 1461, as well as announcing that it will be performed 'on Monday' at Croxton. *Aristorius* the merchant, attended by a flattering *Priest* and *Clerk*, opens the action with a 'boast' about the extensiveness of his trading activities. They then exit and are followed by *Jonathas*, a Jewish merchant, who exultantly describes his merchandise, which includes precious stones and spices. He plots with a group of fellow Jews to get hold of the Eucharist or Host, the 'cake' worshipped by Christians. *Jonathas* next approaches the Christian merchant proposing a transaction, and requests that he procures the Host for him. *Aristorius* at first refuses but is induced by the offer of £100 to steal it. He approaches the *Priest* and *Clerk* and drinks with them. With the connivance of the *Clerk* but without the knowledge of the *Priest* he enters the church, steals the Host, and takes it to the Jews. They lay it on the table and, after some discussion about the beliefs of the Christians, stab it with their daggers and when it bleeds they begin to panic. *Jonathas* tries to throw it into a cauldron of oil, but it sticks to his hand. The other Jews nail the Host to a post and attempt to pull *Jonathas's* arm apart from it, but the hand comes off. He retires with them to his chamber to recover and *Colle*, a doctor's assistant, enters advertising his master's skills and then issuing an insulting proclamation about him. The physician, a quack called *Master Brundyche*, now enters and the boy quickly assures him that he has been promoting him to the audience. He then issues a proper proclamation detailing the ailments his master can cure, and brings him to *Jonathas* to offer his services. The Jews drive them away, however, and instead throw the hand with the Host into the cauldron, which immediately bubbles up with blood. They then decide to cast the Host into an oven, and they kindle the fire. With pincers they take the Host and push it into the oven, at which the oven splits open, bleeding at the crevices, and the image of *Christ* appears asking why they are tormenting him. They immediately fall to their knees, expressing their contrition, and *Jesus* exhorts them to cleanse their hearts. He tells *Jonathas* to retrieve his hand from the cauldron, at which it becomes whole again. *Jonathas* praises *Christ* and goes to fetch the *Bishop*, to whom he confesses his deeds and requests absolution. The image of *Christ* changes back into the Host and the *Bishop* takes it to the church in procession with the Jews, all singing. When the *Priest* sees this he asks *Aristorius* what is going on and the merchant confesses his part in the affair, for which the *Priest* promises to work to procure him absolution. The *Bishop* preaches a sermon against the devil and gives penance to *Aristorius* and a warning to the *Priest* for his negligence. The Jews once more confess their deeds and are christened by the *Bishop*. *Aristorius* goes off to perform his penance and the play ends with a blessing from the *Bishop* and the singing of the *Te Deum*.

PLAY LENGTH

1,007 lines

COMMENTARY

The play deals with the idea of the cruelty of the Jews towards Christ, a motif which is found recurrently in the plaints of the Marys at the Cross in the liturgical plays. The comic episode of the quack doctor and his boy is a folk play element that does not exist in continental versions of the story, and may have been interpolated as it has very little connection with the main narrative. The play shares with the small range of hagiographical drama in English an interest in dramatizing miracle, which is the principal focus of the stage action. As such, one major feature is the use of complex stage devices, including the Jew's detachable hand to which the Host adheres, the cauldron that boils over with blood, the oven that rives asunder bleeding at the crevices, and the (speaking) image of Christ that turns back into the Host.

Other conversion plays: **16, 51, 63, 66.**

Other plays with foreign (non-biblical, non-classical) settings: **5, 6, 7, 12, 13, 32, 33, 47, 70, 74, 88.**

Other plays with probable place and scaffold staging: **9, 23, 48, 63, 72** (frag.), **85.**

SIGNIFICANT TOPICS AND NARRATIVE ELEMENTS

the selling of Christ; merchants and trade; bribery; ecclesiastical corruption; the Jews' tormenting of Christ; the Eucharist and miracle; a folk play quack doctor; medicine; religious conversion

DRAMATURGICAL AND RHETORICAL FEATURES

Verbal and general *Aristorius* has an opening 'boast' including an alliterative list of geographical places where he trades 81–124; *Jonathas*'s alliterative lists of precious stones and spices 158–88; *Jonathas* calls 'out harrow' (traditionally a devil's exclamation) 481; the physician's boy issues two proclamations 565–72, 608–21; one stage direction in Latin (607 *sd*), the rest in English

Costume and dress the doctor wears a threadbare gown and torn hose 570

Actions and stage directions 148 *sd*: 'Now shall the merchant's man withdraw him and the Jew *Jon*. shall make his boast'; 228 *sd*: 'Here shall *Sir Is*. the priest speak unto *Sir Ar*. saying in this wise to him; and *Jon*. go down off his stage'; 236 *sd*: 'Here shall the merchant men meet with the Jews'; 248 *sd*: 'Here shall the *Cle*. go to *Sir Ar*., saluting him thus'; 265 *sd*: 'Here shall the Jew merchant and his men come to the Christian merchant'; 335 *sd*: 'Here go the Jews away and the *Pri.* comes home'; 355 *sd*: 'Here shall *Ar.* call his clerk to his presence'; 367 *sd*: 'Here shall he (*Ar.*) enter the church and take the Host'; 384 *sd*: 'Here shall *Ar.* go his way and *Jon.* and his servants shall go to the table, thus saying'; 392 *sd*: 'Now the Jews go and lay the Host on the table, saying'; 468 *sd*: 'Here shall the 4 Jews prick their daggers in 4 quarters, thus saying'; 480 *sd*: 'Here the Host must bleed'; 503 *sd*: 'Here he (*Jon.*) runs mad with the Host in his hand'; 515 *sd*: 'Here shall they pluck the arm, and the hand shall hang still with the Sacrament'; 524 *sd*: 'Here shall the leech's man come into the place, saying'; 564 *sd*: 'Here shall he (*Co.*) stand up and make proclamation, saying this'; 607 *sd*: 'Here he (*Co.*) should make a proclamation in the meanwhile' (L); 652 *sd*: 'Here shall the 4 Jews beat away the leech and his man'; 660 *sd*: 'Here shall *Jas.* pluck out the nails and shake the hand into the cauldron'; 670–1: the Jews kindle the fire; 672 *sd*: 'Here shall the cauldron boil, appearing to be as blood'; 676 *sd*: 'Here shall *Jas.* and his company go to *Sir Jon.*, saying'; 695 *sd*: 'Here they (Jews) kindle the fire'; 700 *sd*: 'Here shall *Jas.* go to the cauldron and take out the Host with his pincers and cast it into the oven'; 712 *sd*: 'Here the oven must rive asunder and bleed out at the crannies, and an image appear out with wounds bleeding'; 716 *sd*: 'Here shall the image speak to the Jews, saying thus'; 745 *sd*: 'Here shall they (Jews) kneel down on their knees, saying'; 777 *sd*: 'Here shall *Sir Jon.* put his hand into the cauldron, and it shall be whole again, and then say as follows'; 797 *sd*: 'Here shall the master Jew go to the *Bis.* and his men kneel still'; 813 *sd*: 'Here shall the *Bis.* enter into the Jew's house and say'; 825 *sd*: 'Here shall the image change again into bread'; 841 *sd*: 'Here shall the priest, *Sir Is.*, ask his master what this means'; 865 *sd*: 'Here shall the merchant and his priest go to the church and the *Bis.* shall enter the church and lay the Host on the altar, saying thus'; 900: *Ar.* kneels before the *Bishop*; 930 *sd*: 'Here the [Jews] must kneel all down'; 951 *sd*: 'Here shall the *Bis.* christen the Jews with great solemnity'

Songs and music (w.n.s. to either song) 1. *Bishop*, Jews 'O Sacrum Convivum' 840, 2. Cast (and audience ?) 'Te Deum Laudamus' 1007

Staging and set this appears to be a play conceived for place and scaffold production as 228 *sd* mentions *Sir Jonathas*'s 'stage'; though the action is only vaguely localized (apart from the church), the set includes a table and an altar (384 *sd*, 865 *sd*); there is a range of potentially complicated and sophisticated mechanical stage devices: the Host bleeds (481 *sd*), *Jonathas*'s hand becomes detached (515 *sd*), the cauldron boils over, apparently with blood (672 *sd*), the oven breaks open, bleeding at the crevices, revealing an image with wounds bleeding (712 *sd*), and the image changes again back into bread (825 *sd*); with the list of players at the end is the statement: '9 may play it at ease' but no doubling scheme is supplied

Stage properties *Jonathas*'s £100 315; the priests' wine and bread 340–2; a Host wafer 367 *sd*; cloth to wrap the Host 383; a table 384 *sd*; the Jews' daggers 462; a post 507; a hammer and nails 508; a false hand 515 *sd*; pincers 657; a cauldron 660; an oven 692; straw and thorns 693; an image of Christ 712 *sd*; an altar 865 *sd*

PLACENAMES

Alexandria[1] 101; Antioch[1] 97; Aragon 11, 60, 87, 130, 267, 341; 'Babwell Mill' 621; Bethlehem 781; Bozrah 443; Brabant 98[1], 533, 566; Britain[1] 98; Calabria[1] 99; Calais 590; Calvary 214, 449; Chelidonia (? 'Shelysdown') 140,[1] 148; Cologne[1] 99; Croxton 74; Denmark[1] 100; Dordrecht[1] 100; Dover 590; Eraclea 12, 86, 138, 194; Faroe (? 'Farre')[1] 102; France[1] 102; Galicia[1] 103; Gelderland[1] 103; Geneva[1] 95; Genoa[1] 95; Germany ('Almayn')[1] 97; Hamburg[1] 104; Holland[1] 104; 'Jenyse' (?)[1] 95; Jericho[1] 105; Jerusalem 105,[1] 779; Judah 780; Lombardy[1] 113; Luxembourg[1] ('Lachborn') 113; Maine[1] 109; Milan[1] 109; Naples[1] 110; Navarre[1] 110; Orleans (? 'Oryon')[1] 115; St Peter's (in Rome)[1] 107; 'Pondere' (?)[1] 111; Portugal[1] 111; Prussia ('Spruce')[1] 112; Rheims[1] 107; Rome 56, 57, 107;[1] Romney 340; Saba[1] 96, 140,[1] 148; Salerno[1] 96; Spain[1] 112; Syria 19, 96,[1] 140;[1] Tharsia[1] 114; Turkey[1] 114

1 Part of *Aristorius*'s alliterative list of places in which he trades.

ALLUSIONS

Alexander the Great 432; Gabriel (angel) 412; *Isaiah 63:1* 448; Joachim 411; *Lamentations 1:2* (q.a.) 717–18; *Luke 17:14* (q.a.) 765; Mary Magdalene 422; *Matthew 26:26* 404; St Peter 107, 405; *1 Peter 4:5* or *2 Timothy 4:1* 440; Philip (apostle) 438; *Psalm 26:1* (V)/*27:1* (AV) 741, *50:9* (V)/*51:7* (AV) 761; *Revelation (Apocalypsis) 20:2* (q.a.) 866–7; the Sibyl 431; Doubting Thomas 422

REPORT ON MODERN PRODUCTION

Alençon (Cambridge Medieval Players), dir. C. Heap, 13 July 1977 [*RORD* 20 (1977) p. 101]

RECORDED PRODUCTION

LP Record: BBC, *The First Stage*, dir. J. Barton (1970)

BIBLIOGRAPHY

Axton, 1974, pp. 195–9

Beckwith, S. 'Ritual, Church and Theatre: Medieval Dramas of the Sacramental Body' in Aers, 1992, pp. 65–89

Clark, R. L. and C. Sponsler, 'Othered Bodies: Racial Cross-Dressing in the *Mistère de la Sainte Hostie* and the Croxton *Play of the Sacrament*', *JMEMS* 29:1 (1999) pp. 61–87

Cutts, C. 'The Croxton Play: An Anti-Lollard Piece', *MLQ* 5:1 (1944) pp. 45–60

Dillon, J. 'What Sacrament?' in Higgins and Paino, 2000, pp. 187–200

Dox, D. 'Medieval Drama as Documentation: "Real Presence" in the Croxton *Conversion of Ser Jonathas the Jewe by the Myracle of the Blissed Sacrament*', *TS* 38:1 (1997) pp. 97–115

Erler, M. C. 'Spectacle and Sacrament: A London Parish Play in the 1530s', *MP* 91:4 (1994) pp. 449–54

Gibson, 1989, pp. 32–40

Groeneveld, L 'Christ as Image in the Croxton *Play of the Sacrament*', *RORD* 40 (2001) pp. 177–95

Hill-Vasquez, H. '"The precious body of Christ that they tretyn in their hondis": "Miraclis Pleyinge" and the *Croxton Play of the Sacrament*', *EaT* 4 (2001) pp. 53–72

Homan, R. L. 'Devotional Themes in the Violence and Humor of the *Play of the Sacrament*', *CD* 20:4 (1986) pp. 327–40

Homan, 1991, pp. 199–209

Jones, M. 'Theatrical History in the Croxton *Play of the Sacrament*', *ELH* 66:2 (1999) pp. 223–60

Kruger, S. 'The Bodies of Jews in the Late Middle Ages' in *The Idea of Medieval Literature: New Essays on Chaucer and Medieval Culture in Honor of Donald R. Howard*, ed. J. Dean and C. Zacher (Newark, Delaware University Press, 1992) pp. 301–23

Lascombes, A. 'Revisiting *The Croxton Play of the Sacrament*: Spectacle and the Other's Voice' in Higgins, 1998, pp. 261–75

Maltman, Sister N. 'Meaning and Art in the Croxton *Play of the Sacrament*', *ELH* 41:2 (1988) pp. 149–64

Muir, L. 'Further Thoughts on the Tale of the Profaned Host', *EDAM Newsletter* 21 (1999) pp. 88–97

Nichols, A. E. 'The Croxton *Play of the Sacrament*: A Re-Reading', *CD* 22:2 (1988) pp. 117–37

Nichols, A. E. 'Lollard Language in the Croxton *Play of the Sacrament*', *N&Q* 36 (1989) pp. 23–5

Reid-Schwartz, A. 'Economics of Salvation: Commerce and the Eucharist in *The Profanation of the Host* and the Croxton *Play of the Sacrament*', *Comitatus* 25 (1994) pp. 1–20

Scherb, V. I. 'The Earthly and Divine Physicians: Christus Medicus in the Croxton *Play of the Sacrament*' in Clarke and Aycock, 1990, pp. 161–71

Scherb, V. I. 'Violence and the Social Body in the Croxton *Play of the Sacrament*' in Redmond, 1991, pp. 69–78

Scherb, 2001, pp. 68–84

Spector, S. 'Time, Space and Identity in *The Play of the Sacrament*' in Knight, 1997, pp. 189–200

Tydeman, 1986, pp. 53–77

84   A Satire of the Three Estates (Cupar banns)

Date, authorship and auspices
1552; Sir David Lindsay; public performance of banns in Cupar, Fife

TEXT AND EDITIONS

Extant originals

Manuscript: National Library of Scotland (Advocates Library) Bannatyne MS

Editions

2000	Walker (OS)*
1998	Mace (NS)
1989	Lyall (OS)*
1979	Happé (OS)*
1931–6	Hamer, vol. II (1554 version, OS)
1928	Ritchie, vol. III (OS)*

CHARACTERS

Nuntius (Messenger)	Fool	Merchant
Cotter	Old Man	Clerk
Cotter's Wife	Bessy	
Findlaw of the Foot Band	Courtier	

PLOT SUMMARY

The banns involve not just the announcement of the main play, in a proclamation made by the *Messenger*, but a series of comic scenes. The first is one of domestic conflict between the *Cotter* and his shrewish wife, which ends in her beating him. This is followed by the appearance of *Findlaw*, a braggart who boasts of his prowess in battle but whose cowardice is exposed by the *Fool*. The *Old Man* then brings in *Bessy*, his young wife, leading her in a dance, and he locks up her chastity belt before going to sleep, after which she is courted by a *Courtier*, a *Merchant*, a *Clerk* and the *Fool*. She goes off with the last of these when he is able to steal the key from under her husband's head. *Findlaw* then reappears recruiting for war in France and he falls into dispute with the *Clerk*, who advocates peace. They are followed by the *Old Man* looking for his wife, whom he accuses of infidelity. She, however, claims that she has been spending her time sewing him a shirt, which she puts over his head while the *Fool* slips the key back. *Findlaw* now makes yet another swaggering appearance until he is frightened by the *Fool* carrying a sheep's head on a stick, and he runs away, after which the *Messenger* takes up again the announcement of the play to be performed on Whitsun Tuesday, the 7th of June.

LENGTH OF BANNS

277 lines, including the proclamation of 24 lines

COMMENTARY

The banns merit an entry separately from the main play because of their substantial dramatic content and the fact that none of the characters in them reappears in the play proper. The banns are of considerable interest in being replete with a number of folk play motifs whose inclusion in this bit of theatrical advertising implies recognition of their popular appeal. The interest in estates manifests itself here in the wooing of *Bessy* by the *Courtier*, *Merchant* and *Clerk*, with some implicit satire present in the fact that it is the *Fool* who succeeds in winning her.

Other marital strife plays: **46**, **73** (frag.), **95**.
Other wooing plays: **6**, **57** (frag.), **75**, **87**.

SIGNIFICANT TOPICS AND NARRATIVE ELEMENTS

domestic strife and husband beating; a cowardly braggart soldier – 'miles gloriosus'; a 'January and May' marriage; cuckoldry; peace and war; social estates; a wily fool

DRAMATURGICAL AND RHETORICAL FEATURES

Verbal and general the *Messenger* makes a proclamation announcing the main play 1–24; stage directions in English

Costume and dress the *Fool* probably has a large codpiece 161; *Bessy* puts a sark on her husband 225 *sd*

Actions and stage directions 94 *sd*: 'Here shall the *Wi.* ding the Carl (*Cot.*) and he shall cry God's mercy'; 133 *sd*: 'Here he (*Fin.*) shall lie down'; 141 *sd*: 'Here shall the *O. Man* come in leading his wife in a dance'; 147 *sd*: 'Here shall he (*O. Man*) lock her (*Be.*'s) cunt and lay the key under his head: he shall sleep and she sit beside him'; 175 *sd*: 'Here shall they (*Be., Fo.*) go to some quiet place'; 207 *sd*: 'Here shall the *Goodman* (*O. Man*) waken and cry for *Be.*'; 225 *sd*: 'Here shall she (*Be.*) put the sark over his (*O. Man*'s) head and the *Fo.* shall steal in the key again'; 247 *sd*: 'Here shall the *Fo.* come in with a sheep's head on a staff and *Fin.* shall be frightened'; 269: *Fin.* runs away (through the audience?)

Songs and music music for the dance of the *Old Man* and *Wife?* (not specified) 141 *sd*

Staging and set this is a dramatic sequence rather than a full play; the action is unlocalized and there are no indications as to set

Stage properties *Bessy*'s chastity belt and the *Old Man*'s key 147 *sd*; a shirt or 'sark' 225 *sd*; a sheep's head on a stick 247 *sd*; *Findlaw*'s sword 260; *Findlaw*'s armoured gloves and headpiece 262; *Findlaw*'s purse, belt and knife 264

PLACENAMES

Castle Hill (in Cupar) 17; Cupar 6, 28, 67, 98, 203; France 176, 196; Fyfe 234; Holland 224; Kinneil 243; Pinkie Crags/Cleuch 125, 139, 182; Scotland 185; Southampton 245; Troy 246

ALLUSIONS

Sir Bevis of Hampton 245; Gyr Carling 253; Sir Gawain 246; Goliath 240, 246; Sir Greysteel 242; Guy of Alet 251; Hector 246; Gow MacMorne 257; Merlin 252

BIBLIOGRAPHY

See **85**.

85   A Satire of the Three Estates

DATE, AUTHORSHIP AND AUSPICES

Version 1: 1540 (lost), version 2: 1552, version 3: 1554; Sir David Lindsay; performed before the court (and elswhere); the text of the 1540 production is not extant; Greg 193, 194

TEXT AND EDITIONS

Extant originals

Manuscript: Scottish National Library (Advocates Library) Bannatyne MS fos. 164a–210a (version of 1552–4, MS *c.* 1568)

1602 printing by Robert Charteris, Edinburgh: Bodleian; Huntington; *STC* 15681

1602 printing by Robert Charteris, Edinburgh (a variant): Bodleian; Folger; Lincoln Cathedral; NLS; *STC* 15681.5

1604 printing by Robert Charteris for sale in London 'The Works': BL; *STC* 15682

A contemporary account (by Sir William Eure) of a performance of the 1540 version exists in British Library MS Reg. 7. C. xvi, fos. 137r–138r

Editions

2000 Walker (OS)*
1998 Mace (NS)
1994 CHD (CD-Rom and online transcription of Charteris 1602 printing, l.l., OS)
1989 Lyall (OS)*
1979 Happé (OS)
1969 'The English Experience' no. 137 (facsimile of Charteris 1602 printing, n.l.)
1954 Kinsley (n.l., OS)
1951 Kemp (NS)
1931 Hamer, vol. II (both extant versions of the play in parallel texts, OS)
1928 Ritchie, vol. III (OS)
1879 Laing, vol. II (OS)
1869 Hall, vol. IV (Charteris 1602 printing, OS)
1806 Chalmers, vol. I (Part I), vol. II (Part II) (n.l., OS)

SOURCES

The play may have been influenced by French dramatic traditions and has analogues in early English Protestant drama; see the introduction to Lyall's edition, pp. xxii–xxvi.

CHARACTERS

Diligence, the Messenger	Abbot	John the Common Weal
Rex Humanitas	Parson	1st Sergeant
Wantonness	Chastity	2nd Sergeant
Placebo	Prioress	Covetise
Solace	Temporality	Abbess
Sensuality	Soutar ('a Carl')	Scribe
Homeliness	Tailor	(Common) Theft
Danger	Jennie	(Public) Oppression

Fund-Jonet	Tailor's Wife	Doctor
Good Counsel	Soutar's Wife	1st Licenciate
Flattery	Correction's Varlet	2nd Licenciate/ Bachelor
Falset	Divine Correction	Folly
Deceit	Pauper/Poor Man	Glaiks (Folly's daughter)
Verity	Pardoner	Stult (Folly's son)
Spirituality/Prelate	Merchant	

Mute: Sapience, Devotion, Dempster, further members of the spiritual and temporal estates, Minstrels, Trumpet(er)

PLOT SUMMARY

The Messenger, *Diligence*, summarizes the narrative of the play, the corruption and ultimate reformation of the *King of Humanity*. The *King* then commences the action with a 'boast' and he is quickly joined by *Wantonness*, *Placebo* and a little later *Solace*, who offer him worldly comfort and companionship. The *King* is at first resistant to their efforts to lead him into sin, but they assure him the Catholic Church condones lechery, and *Lady Sensuality* soon enters with her retinue. The *King* sends *Wantonness* to find out about her, and when he receives a report about her beauty he is filled with desire and despatches *Solace* and *Wantonness* to procure her. *Sensuality* is at length brought to the *King*, whom she addresses graciously, and she is taken to his chamber. *Good Counsel* now appears and expresses his sorrow at the *King*'s fall. When he retires, *Flattery* comes in newly arrived from France, soon to be joined by his companions *Falset* and *Deceit*, all seeking the *King of Humanity*. They decide to change their clothes and identities, *Flattery* becoming a friar, and they take on new names. They introduce themselves in these guises to the *King* when he emerges from his chamber, and he engages them in his service. When *Good Counsel* reappears trying to gain access to the *King*, and perceiving the true identity of the Vices, they drive him off. They now plot to help each other to maintain their influence over the *King*, and return to his presence. The *King* is being entertained by *Sensuality* and her ladies, who sing a song. *Verity* now arrives, preaches a sermon, and seeks the *King* to try to convert him to rectitude, but the Vices enlist the help of the Catholic clergy to help prevent her access to him. The *Parson* threatens her with burning if she does not recant her position, but she remains defiant and the Vices take her into captivity. They put her in the stocks, for which they are rewarded by the clergy. *Chastity* next appears, complaining that she has been abandoned by the lords temporal and spiritual, and also by princes. She seeks refuge successively with nuns, the clergy and the lords temporal, but is rejected by all. Finally she is taken in by a tailor and a shoemaker, until chased away by their shrewish wives who then set about beating their husbands. *Chastity* meets *Diligence* who tries to take her to the *King*, but *Sensuality* intervenes and has the Vices put her in the stocks alongside *Verity*. *Correction's Varlet* now enters to issue a proclamation that his master intends to reform the realm, including the three estates, something which strikes fear into the hearts of the Vices. They decide to make off, stealing the *King*'s box as they go. They then fall into dispute about the box, fight, and *Deceit* runs off with it. *Correction* himself finally enters preaching a long sermon, and he is welcomed by *Good Counsel* who reports to him what has gone on. They release *Verity* and *Chastity* and all make their way to the *King*, to whom *Correction* delivers a vigorous admonition. *Sensuality* takes refuge with the clergy, and the *King* receives instead *Good Counsel*, *Verity* and *Chastity*. He humbly embraces *Correction*, following which *Wantonness*, *Placebo* and *Solace* also confess their faults. The *King* is informed of the deceit practised on him by the Vices and *Good Counsel* addresses a speech of advice to him while *Diligence* delivers a proclamation summoning all the members of Parliament to the court. He ends the first part of the play exhorting the audience to go and take refreshment and relieve themselves. In the interlude between Parts I and II, a *Pauper* comes in and sits in the *King*'s chair. *Diligence*, who is outraged by this, pulls away the ladder and commands the man to jump down, which he does. He explains that his livestock have been taken by his landlord and the vicar, which has reduced him to penury, and he is seeking justice for which he will pay with his remaining groat. He lies down to rest and a *Pardoner* enters, displaying his pardons and relics for sale. The shoemaker or *Soutar* and his wife arrive and express their discontent with one another, she because of his impotence. For the payment of a couple of shirts, the *Pardoner* gives them dispensation to part, after each has kissed the other's arse. The *Pardoner's Boy* briefly arrives to bring him a horse bone to use as a relic and to warn him that the only welcome he can expect in the town will be from a whore. When he departs, the *Pauper* rises and the *Pardoner* inveigles him to part with his groat. When the *Pauper* learns that all he will receive in return is a pardon, he becomes angry, fights with the *Pardoner*, and ends the interlude by throwing all the relics into the water. Part II is opened by *Diligence* with a call to attention and the three Estates are led in backwards by the Vices, suggesting their persistently errant ways. They are brought before the *King*, who declares his intention to reform them. *Diligence* calls for all who are oppressed to come forward and testify, and the first to arrive is *John the Common Weal*. As a result of his testimony, the Vices are led to the stocks and *John* continues his complaint at length, particularly aimed at the Catholic Church. The temporal estates express their contrition and are forgiven, but the clergy remain intransigent, despite the voices of the *Pauper*, *Verity* and *Chastity* being added to *John*'s complaints. The clergy claim exemption through authority of the Pope, but when the financial abuses of the Church are detailed, *Good Counsel* reminds them that the duty of the clergy is to preach. *John* is now joined by the temporal estates in opposition to the Catholic clergy. There is a brief episode in which *Oppression*, having been put in the stocks, tricks his friend *Common Theft* into taking his place and makes off. *Diligence* then brings in three scholars to pursue the argument against the spiritual estate, and more corruption comes to light, particularly of a sexual nature. The *Doctor* delivers a long speech or sermon with a strongly Protestant slant which gives rise to further debate with the clergy, until finally judgement is given that the miscreants should be punished. *Flattery* escapes hanging by volunteering to help hang his fellow Vices, and the prelates are stripped of their habits and sent off, while *John the Common Weal* is gorgeously arrayed and set in Parliament. *Diligence* proclaims fifteen acts of ecclesiastical reform, and the prisoners are led off to be hanged. *Theft* and *Deceit* are hanged and, after a long satirical diatribe against craftsmen, *Falset* too. A comic episode then ensues involving *Folly*, who, after some foolish banter, delivers a mock sermon. *Diligence* finally closes the play with a blessing on the audience and calling for music.

PLAY LENGTH

4,671 lines, including an interlude of 366 lines and *Diligence's* prologues to Parts I and II, 77 and 22 lines respectively

COMMENTARY

Despite the elaborateness of this large place and scaffold play, there are known to have been three productions in the lifetime of its author: Linlithgow (1540), Cupar (1553) and Edinburgh (1554), the first and last before the king and court. The structure is rambling and episodic, with a generous use of characters. Though the play is strongly anti-Catholic and delivers serious doctrinal points, the tone is leavened by comic episodes, including folk play elements. It is notable for a large number of stage directions, some quite complex. Several actions are designated 'with silence', presumably indicating dumbshow.

Other Protestant and anti-Catholic plays: **14, 24, 44, 45, 49, 50, 53, 58, 66, 86** (frag.), **90, 93.**

Other 'estates' plays: **29, 31, 94, 98.**

Other plays with probable place and scaffold staging: **9, 23** (frag.), **48, 63, 72** (frag.), **83.**

SIGNIFICANT TOPICS AND NARRATIVE ELEMENTS

bad companions; lechery; Catholic corruption; Friars; the New Testament in English; shrews and domestic violence – husband beating; celibate clergy; the oppression of the poor; the sale of pardons; relics; impotence; marital separation; royal versus papal authority; judicial inefficiency and corruption; religious reform; dishonest craftsmen

DRAMATURGICAL AND RHETORICAL FEATURES

Verbal and general several pauses are indicated in the action, with the direction 'pausa' after 13, 2335, 2497, 2539, 3006, 3464, 3816, 4015; the Vices' mock-christening 778–99; *Flattery* enters through the audience 602; the Vices' aliases: *Deceit–Discretion* 785, *Falset–Sapience* 793, *Flattery–Devotion* 797; *Deceit's* alliterative list of place names 906–11; the council of the Vices 991 *sd*–1017; *Correction's Varlet's* proclamation 1482–515; the Vices fight among themselves 1571 *sd*; *Diligence's* proclamations 1910–33, 2301–22, 3823–981 (the fifteen Acts of Reform); there is a direction for the people (audience) to 'make collation' during the interval before the Interlude 1933 *sd*, and a reference to people's need to relieve themselves 1926–30; the *Pardoner's* list of relics 2087–128; the *Pauper's* list of legal processes 3076–91; the *King* holds a court of enquiry into abuses 2398–477; *Common Theft* enters through the audience 3214–15; *Common Theft's* and *Deceit's* lists of Borders families 4030–8, 4094–8; *Folly* refers to a member of the audience 4440; *Folly's* mock sermon 4502–48; *Folly's* nonsense Latin jingle 4631–4; the play is divided into two parts, with an interlude; several local people are named in the Cupar performance of the play; stage directions are in English

Costume and dress *Lady Sensuality* has 'gay attire' 279; *Flattery* is 'begirt with sundry hues' 604; *Deceit* wears noble garb 675–6; the Vices change into clerical clothing 721; *Falset* dons a hood 727, and has a 'gay garment' 734; *Flattery* puts on a 'cowl of Tullilum' (Carmelite monastery) 767; the Vices discard their 'counterfeit clothes' 1559 *sd*; *Flattery* has a 'hood and heavy gown' 3655; *Flattery's* friar's garment is removed 3672 *sd*; the *Prioress* has a silk gown under her habit 3682 *sd*; the scholars are clothed in the habits taken from the prelates 3752 *sd*; the prelates have fool's garb under their habits 3765; *John the Common Weal* is clothed 'gorgeously' with a 'gay garment' of satin, damask or fine velvet 3800–1 *sd*; *Divine Correction* wears wings 4359–61

Actions and stage directions Directions marked [1] occur only in the 1552 version (Bannatyne MS), while those marked [2] only in the 1554 version (Charteris printing). Unmarked directions occur in both, albeit frequently in variant forms. The directions below follow Walker's edition (Lyall's varying slightly.) 101 *sd*:[1] 'Here the *Ki.* shall pass to royal seat and sit with a grave countenance until *Wan.* come'; 189 *sd*:[1] 'Here shall *Pla.* give *Sol.* a drink'; 270 *sd*:[1] 'Here shall enter *Dame Sen.* with her maidens *Ho.* And *Da.*'; 334 *sd*:[1] 'Here shall *Wan.* go spy them (*Sen.*, and ret.) and come again to the *Ki.*'; 416 *sd*:[1] 'Here shall they (*Wan.*, *Sol.*) depart singing merrily'; 451: *Wan.* dances; 498 *sd*:[1] 'Here shall *Sen.* come to the *Ki.* and say'; 525 *sd*:[1] 'Here shall she (*Sen.*) make reverence and say'; 533 *sd*:[1] 'Here shall she (*Sen.*) pass to the chamber and say'; 553 *sd*:[1] 'Here shall they all (*Ki.*, *Wan.*, *Ho.*) pass to the chamber and *G. Co.* shall say'; 601 *sd*:[1] 'Here enters *Fla.* newly landed out of France and storm-bound at the May (on the Isle of May)'; 657 *sd*:[1] 'Here shall *Dec.* enter'; 727 *sd*:[1] 'Here shall *Fla.* help his two companions'; 807 *sd*: 'Now shall the *Ki.* come from his chamber'; 847 *sd*: 'Now the Vices come and make salutation, saying'; 937 *sd*: 'Here shall *G. Co.* show himself in the field'; 985 *sd*: 'Here shall they (*Fla.*, *Dec.*, *Fal.*) hurl away *G. Co.*'; 991 *sd*: 'Now the Vices go to a council'; 1017 *sd*:[2] 'Now they (*Fla.*, *Dec.*, *Fal.*) return to the *Ki.*'; 1033 *sd*:[2] 'Here shall the ladies sing a song, the *Ki.* shall lie down among the ladies, and then *Ver.* shall enter'; 1076 *sd*: 'Here shall *Fla.* spy *Ver.* with a dumb countenance'; 1084 *sd*:[2] 'Here shall *Ver.* pass to her seat'; 1096 *sd*:[2] 'Here they (Vices) come to the *Spi.*'; 1135 *sd*:[2] 'Here shall they (Vices) pass to *Ver.*'; 1151 *sd*:¹ 'Here the Vices go to the spiritual estate and lie upon *Ver.* desiring her to be put in captivity which is done with diligence'; 1167 *sd*: '*Ver.* sits down on her knees and says'; 1179 *sd*:² 'They put *Ver.* in the stocks and return to *Spi.*'; 1199 *sd*:¹ 'Here shall enter *Cha.* and say'; 1225 *sd*:² '*Cha.* passes to the *L. Prio.* and says'; 1245 *sd*:² '*Cha.* passes to the lords of spirituality'; 1307 *sd*:¹ 'Here shall they (*Tai.*, *Sou.*) make *Cha.* sit down and drink'; 1341 *sd*:² 'Here the wives shall chase away *Cha.*'; 1355 *sd*:² 'Here shall they (wives) speak with their goodmen and ding them'; 1365 *sd*: 'Here shall they (wives) ding their goodmen with silence'; 1375 *sd*: 'Here the wives stand by the water side and say'; 1391 *sd*:² 'She (*Sou.'s Wi.*) lifts up her clothes above her waist and enters in the water'; 1395 *sd*: 'Here shall they (wives) depart and pass to the Pavilion'; 1411 *sd*:² 'Here shall they (*Dil.*, *Cha.*) pass to the *Ki.*'; 1451 *sd*: 'Here shall they (*Sol.*, *Dec.*) drag *Cha.* to the stocks and she shall say'; 1473 *sd*: 'Here they (*Sol.*, *Dec.*) put her (*Cha.*) in the stocks'; 1481 *sd*: 'Here shall enter *Co.'s V.*'; 1551 *sd*: 'Here shall *Fal.* steal the *Ki.*'s box with silence'; 1559 *sd*:¹ 'Here shall they (*Fla.*, *Fal.*, *Dec.*) cast away their counterfeit clothes'; 1571 *sd*: 'Here shall they (*Fla.*, *Dec.*, *Fal.*) fight with silence'; 1579 *sd*:² 'Here shall *Dec.* run away with the box through the water'; 1668 *sd*: 'They (*Cor.*'s attendants?) take the ladies forth of the stocks, and *Ver.* shall say'; 1676 *sd*: '*Cor.* passes towards the *Ki.*, with *Ver.*, *Cha.* and *G. Co.*'; 1740 *sd*:² 'Here shall she (*Sen.*) pass to *Spi.*'; 1752 *sd*:² 'Here shall the bishops, abbots and parsons kiss the ladies'; 1760 *sd*: 'Here shall the *Ki.* receive *G. Co.*, *Ver.* and *Cha.*'; 1784 *sd*:² 'The *Ki.* embraces *Cor.* with a humble countenance'; 1909 *sd*: 'Here shall the mess. *Dil.* return and cry "a Hoyzes, a Hoyzes, a Hoyzes" and say'; 1933 *sd*:² 'Now shall the people (audience) make collation, then begins the Interlude, the kings, bishops, and principal players being out of their seats'; (**Interlude**) 1949 *sd*: 'Here shall the *Carl* climb up and sit in the *Ki.*'s chair'; 1957 *sd*: 'Here *Dil.* casts away the ladder'; 1961 *sd*: 'Here shall the *Carl* leap off the scaffold'; 2043 *sd*: '*Pau.* lies down in the field. *Par.* enters'; 2086 *sd*: 'Here he (*Par.*) shall lay down his gear upon a board and say'; 2180 *sd*: 'Here shall she (*Sou.'s Wi.*) kiss his (*Sou.*'s) arse with silence'; 2182 *sd*: 'Here shall the *Carl* kiss her (wife's) arse with silence'; 2186 *sd*: 'Here shall the *Boy* cry off the hill'; 2226 *sd*: 'Here shall the *Pau.* rise and rax (stretch?) him[self]'; 2238 *sd*: 'Here he (*Par.*) shall bless him (*Pau.*) with his relics'; 2296 *sd*: 'Here shall they (*Pau.*, *Par.*) fight together with silence, and *Pau.* shall cast down the board, and cast the relics into the water'; (**Part II**) 2300 *sd*:² 'Here shall *Dil.* make his proclamation'; 2322 *sd*:² 'Here shall the 3 estates come from the Pavilion, going backward led by their Vices'; 2358 *sd*:² 'Here shall the three estates come and turn their faces to the *Ki.*'; 2397 *sd*:² 'They (3 Est.) are set down and *G. Co.* shall pass to his seat'; 2437 *sd*: 'Here shall *Jo.* leap the ditch or else fall into it'; 2493 *sd*: 'Here shall the Vices be led to the stocks'; 2519 *sd*:² 'Here shall the sergeants chase them (*Spi.*, *Sen.*) away and they shall go to the seat of *Sen.*'; 2703 *sd*:² 'Here shall the bishops come with the *Fri.*'; 2711 *sd*: 'Here shall the temporal estate sit down on their knees and say'; 2721 *sd*: 'Here shall the temporal estates, to wit the lords and merchants embrace *Jo. the C. W.*'; 2787 *sd*:² 'Here *Spi.* foams and rages'; 2915 *sd*:² '*G. Co.* shall read their words in a book'; 3115 sd:² 'Here shall *Ver.* and *Cha.* make their plaint at the bar'; 3193 sd:² 'Here shall *Dil.* pass to the Pavilion'; 3213 sd: 'Here shall enter *C. The.*'; 3293 sd: 'Here shall *C. The.* put his feet in the stocks and *Op.* shall steal away and betra[y] him'; 3333 sd:² 'Here shall *Dil.* convey the three clerks'; 3472 sd:² 'Here shall the *Doc.* pass to the pulpit and say'; 3586 sd:² 'Here *Dil.* spies the *Fri.* rounding (whispering) to the *Prel.*'; 3672 sd: 'Here shall they (sergeants) spoil (strip) *Fla.* of the friar's habit'; 3682 sd:² 'Here shall they (sergeants) spoil (strip) the *Prio.* and she shall have a gown of silk under her habit'; 3716 sd: 'Here shall *Fla.* sit beside his companions'; 3734 sd:² 'Here shall the *Ki.* and Temporal Estate round (whisper) together'; 3744 sd:² 'The *Ki.*'s servants lay hands on the three prelates and says'; 3752 sd:² 'Here shall they (*Ki.*'s servants) spoil (strip) them (prelates) in silence and put their habit on the three clerks'; 3762 sd:² 'Here shall they (prelates) pass to *Sen.*'; 3792 sd:² 'The *Bis.*, *Ab.*, *Par.* and *Prio.* depart all together'; 3802 sd:² 'Here shall they (sergeants) clothe *Jo. the C. W.* gorgeously and set him down among them in the Parliament'; 3822 sd:² 'Here shall *Dil.* with the *Scri.* and the *Tru.* pass to the pulpit and proclaim the Acts'; 3981 sd:² 'Here shall *Pau.* come before the *Ki.* and say'; 3999 sd: 'Here shall the sergeants loose the prisoners out of the stocks and lead them to the gallows'; 4045 sd: 'Here shall *The.* be drawn up or his figure'; 4117 sd: 'Here shall *Dec.* be drawn up or his figure'; 4219 sd: 'Here shall he (*Fal.*) look up to his fellows hanging'; 4231 sd: 'Here shall they (sergeants) fasten the cord to his (*Fal.*'s) neck with a dumb countenance. Thereafter he shall say'; 4271 sd: 'Here shal he (*Fal.*) be hoisted up, and not his figure, and a crow or jackdaw shall be cast up, as it were his soul'; 4301 sd: 'Here shall enter *Fo.*'; 4425 sd:² 'Here shall the bairns cry keck like a jackdaw, and he (*Fo.*) shall put meat in their mouths'; 4489 sd: 'Here shall *Fo.* hang his hats on the pulpit and say'; 4501 sd: 'Here shall *Fo.* begin his sermon, as follows';

Additional directions (omitted from editions selected) 815 sd:¹ 'Here the *Ki.* has been with his concubine and thereafter returns to his young company'; 1215 sd:¹ 'Here shall she (*Cha.*) pass to the whole spiritual estate and she shall not be received but put away'; 1288 sd:¹ 'Here shall *D. Cha.* pass and seek lodging athort all the spiritual estate and temporal estate while she come to the *Sou.* and *Tai.* and say'; 1732 sd:¹ 'Here shall *Sen.* depart from the *Ki.*'; 1933 sd:¹ 'Here shall enter the *Po. M.*'

Songs and music (w.n.s. to any song) 1. *Sensuality* and her ladies 326; 2. *Wantonness*, *Solace* 416 sd; 3. *Sensuality* and her ladies 1033 sd; **Instrumental:** a trumpet (probably) sounds for *Diligence*'s proclamation 3822 sd; minstrel music and 'a brawl of France' at the end of the play 4666

Staging and set the 1540 Linlithgow performance was likely to have been an indoor one, while the 1552 and 1554 Cupar and Edinburgh performances were outdoor productions; the play is fairly clearly for 'place and scaffold' production; where the action is localized it is effected largely through the presence of characters and the dialogue, but there are several furnishings (see stage properties) and more substantial structures including a throne for the *King* with a ladder to it (1949 sd, 1957 sd), a pulpit (3472 sd), and a gallows (3999 sd); there is also a body of water (1375 *sd*, the Lady burn possibly being used in the Cupar production); three hangings are performed on stage, using either the actors or 'figures' (4045 *sd*, 4117 *sd*) and in the third definitely an actor (4271 *sd*); various characters pass to a 'pavilion' or tent (1395 *sd*, 2322 *sd*, 3193 *sd*), presumably a form of tiring house **Stage properties** the *King*'s crown, sword and sceptre 22; a drink for *Solace* 189 *sd*; stocks 1179 *sd*; ten crowns for the Vices 1183; a drink for *Chastity* 1307 *sd*; the *King*'s box 1551 *sd*; the *Pardoner*'s pardons sealed with oyster shells 2087–9 and relics: a jaw bone 2094–5, cow horn 2096, cord 2099, cow's arse 2105, pig's snout 2106, and bell 2107–8; a horse bone 2190; the *Pauper*'s groat bound in a rag 2246; ropes to bind the Vices 2491; *Counsel*'s book (Bible) 2915 *sd*; dummies to hang as the Vices 4045 *sd*, 4117 *sd*; a live crow or jackdaw as *Falset*'s soul 4271 *sd*; food for *Folly*'s children 4425 *sd*; *Folly*'s fools' hats 4489 *sd*

PLACENAMES

St Andrews 1937, 1971, 2266; Angus 4150; River Annet 3268; Ayr 1987, 3434; Balmerino Abbey (in Fife, 'Bamirrinoch') 261; Balquidder 2098, 3307; Calvary 3506; Carrick 3425; Corstorphine (in Edinburgh)[1] 911; Crail 3425; Cupar 4095, 4166; Danzig[1] 906; Denmark[1] 906; Dumbarton 2198, 3147; Dysart Moor 3261; Edinburgh 1972, 3881, 4104; Elgin 3857; England 576, 1154, 2588, 4600; Ewesdale 3226, 4038; Ewes-durris 3256; Ferny Mire (near Cupar) 1813; Fife 3153, 3324, 4150, 4473; Flanders 4610; France 452, 576, 601 *sd*, 723, 909,[1] 3097, 3594, 3682, 3790, 3841, 4078, 4601, 4606, 4666; Germany ('Almane')[1] 906, 4609; Inverness 3857, 4369; Israel 3600, 4261; Italy 576, 914, 4610; St John's Town 761; Kinnoul 761; Liddisdale 3293, 3319, 4223; Loch Leven 4646; Loretto (chapel near Musselburgh) 4300; Lothian 1969; Isle of May 611; the Merse (in Berwickshire) 3320; Paris 3435; Peebles 156; Renfrew[1] 909; Rome 241, 286, 910,[1] 1462, 1730, 2848, 2853, 2865, 2867, 2869, 2884, 3945; Rothes 3250; Rutherglen[1] 910; Scotland 578, 2443, 2977, 3752, 3865, 3989, 4599; 'Shoegate' 4315; Spain 907,[1] 4610; Spittalfields (in Perthshire)[1] 907; Struthers 3263; Tranent 1817, 1969; Tullilum (monastery) 767, 4420

1 Part of *Deceit*'s alliterative list of place names.

ALLUSIONS

St Andrew 4615; Annas and Caiphas 3972–3; St Anthony[1] 2106; St Bridget 2105,[1] 2194, 2230; Heinrich Bullinger 2079; Claudian *Panegrycus de Quarto Consolatii Honorii Augusti I.302* 1059; Emperor Constantine 1458; Cupid 373, 527, 3953; David I of Scotland 2965; Diogenes 2633; Isaiah 1184, 3917; *Isaiah 56:10* 3918, *59:14* (not 55) 1186–7; James I of Scotland 2989; Jezebel 4261; St John 1196; St John *Revelation 22:18* 1197; *John 3:16* 3482; Judas 32, 1344; the Tartar Khan (?)[1] 2088; *Luke 9:58* 3605–8; Martin Luther 2078; Finn MacCoul[1] 2094; Mary Magdalene 2644; Mary of Egypt 2645; *Matthew 5:6* 1580, *5:16* 1068, *7:20* (q.a.) 4578, *19:17* 3473, 3535, 22:39–40 3524–5; Melancthon 2079; Merlin 4626, 4628; Noah 1709; St Paul 1190, 2082, 2317, 2602, 2849, 2913, 2928, 2930, 2931, 3474, 3950, 4615; St Paul *1 Corinthians 3:19* 4528; St Paul *1 Thessalonians 5:21* 269, *2 Thessalonians 3:10* 2605; St Paul *1 Timothy 3:1–3* 2916–24, *2 Timothy 4:4* 1191; Paul the Hermit 2646; St Peter 2317, 2849, 3950, 4615; Pontius Pilate 3026, 4247; Pluto 3069, 3981; *Psalm 110:10* (V)/*111:10* (AV) 1883, *129:7* (V)/*130:7* (AV) 3507; *Sapientia 1:1* (V) 1034; King Sardanapalus (of Assyria) 1705; Sodom and Gomorrah 1712; Tarquin and Lucretia 1769–74; Venus 272 *passim*

1 Mentioned in the *Pardoner's* list of relics.

REPORTS ON MODERN PRODUCTION

Edinburgh, August 1984, dir. T. Fleming [*METh* 6:2 (1984) pp. 163–8; *Times*, 14 August 1984, p. 8; *Sunday Times*, 19 August 1984, p. 37; *TLS*, 24 August 1984, p. 945]

BIBLIOGRAPHY

Aoki, N. 'Structural Unity of the Quarto Version of Sir David Lindsay's *Satire of the Three Estates*', *MFLAE* 27 (1976) pp. 11–20 (in Japanese)

Carpenter, S. 'Drama and Politics: Scotland in the 1530s', *METh* 10:2 (1988) pp. 81–90

Dessen, A. C. 'The Estates Morality Play', *SP* 62:2 (1965) pp. 121–36

Edington, 1994, pp. 128–41

Eva, R. '*Ane Pleasant Satyre of the Thrie Estaitis in Commendation of Vertew and Vituperation of Vyce*' 1540–1554', *Filológiai közlöny* 4 (1957) pp. 359–72 (in Hungarian)

Graf, C. 'Sottise et folie dans la *Satire des trois états*', *RAA* 3 (1970) pp. 5–27

Graf, C. 'Theatre and Politics: Lindsay's *Satire of the Thrie Estaitis*' in Aitken, McDairmid and Thomson, 1977, pp. 143–55

Graf, C. 'Audience Involvement in Lindsay's *Satyre of the Thrie Estaitis*' in Strauss and Drescher, 1986, pp. 423–35

Harward, V. '*Ane Satyre of the Thrie Estaitis* Again', *SSL* 7:3 (1970) pp. 139–46

Henderson, 1910, pp. 216–30

Houk, R. 'Versions of Lindsay's *Satire of the Three Estates*', *PMLA* 55:2 (1940) pp. 396–405

Kantrowitz, J. S. 'Encore: Lindsay's *Thrie Estaitis*, Date and New Evidence', *SSL* 10:1 (1972) pp. 18–32

Kantrowitz, 1975

Lester, J. H. 'Some Franco-Scottish Influences on Early English Drama' in *Haverford Essays: Studies in Modern Literature Prepared by Some Former Pupils of Professor Francis Gummere* (Haverford, PA, privately printed, 1900) pp. 129–52

McClure, J. D. 'A Comparison of the Bannatyne MS and the Quarto Texts of Lindsay's *Ane Satyre of the Thrie Estaitis*' Estaitis' in Strauss and Drescher, 1986, pp. 409–22

Maclaine, A. H. '*Christis Kirk on the Grene* and David Lindsay's *Satyre of the Thrie Estaitis*', *JEGP* 56:4 (1957) pp. 596–601

McGavin, J. 'The Dramatic Prosody of Sir David Lindsay' in Jack and McGinley, 1993, pp. 39–66

MacQueen, J. '*Ane Satyre of the Thrie Estaitis*', *SSL* 3:3 (1966) pp. 129–43

Mill, A. J. 'The Influence of the Continental Drama on Lyndsay's *Satyre of the Thrie Estaitis*', *MLR* 25:4 (1930) pp. 425–42

Mill, A. J. 'The Original Version of Lyndsay's *Ane Satyre of the Thrie Estaitis*', *SSL* 6:1 (1969) pp. 67–75
Mill, A. J. 'The Records of Scots Medieval Plays: Interpretations and Misinterpretations', in Aitken, McDairmid and Thomson, 1977, pp. 136–42
Mill, A. J. 'Representations of Lyndsay's *Satyre of the Thrie Estaitis*', *PMLA* 47:2 (1932) pp. 636–51
Mill, A. J. 'Representations of Lyndsay's *Satyre of the Thrie Estaitis*: Corrigenda to *PMLA* 1932, 636–51', *PMLA* 48:1 (1933) pp. 315–16
Millar, 1903, pp. 97–110
Miller, E. S. 'The Christening in the *Thrie Estaitis*', *MLN* 60:1 (1945) pp. 42–4
Murison, 1938, pp. 38–74
Norland, 1995, pp. 210–29
Potter, 1975, pp. 81–9
Reid, D. 'Rule and Misrule in Lindsay's *Thrie Estaitis* and Pitcairne's *Assembly*', *SLJ* 11 (1984) pp. 5–24
Schwend, J. 'Demokratie und Rationalismus in David Lyndsays *Ane Pleasant Satyre of the Thrie Estaitis*' in Schwend, Hagemann and Völkel, 1992, pp. 3–17
Smith, 1934, pp. 124–30
Van Heijnsbergen, 1996
Walker, G. 'Sir David Lindsay's *Ane Satire of the Thrie Estaitis* and the Politics of Reformation', *SLJ* 16:2 (1989) pp. 5–17
Walker, 1998, pp. 117–62

86 Somebody and Others, or The Spoiling of Lady Verity (otherwise Somebody, Avarice and Minister) (fragment)

DATE, AUTHORSHIP AND AUSPICES

1547–50; anonymous; auspices unknown; Greg 25

TEXT AND EDITIONS

Extant originals

c. 1550 printing by William Copland (?): Lambeth (frag.); *STC* 14109.3

Editions

1977   Houle (alongside *La Vérité cachée*, OS)*
1931   Greg (OS, with photographic facsimile)*
1843   Maitland (n.l., OS)

SOURCES

This is an adaptation of a French morality, *La Vérité cachée*; see Houle's essay below.

CHARACTERS

Somebody   Avarice   Minister   Verity

PLOT SUMMARY

The fragment opens with a speaker (probably *Minister*) promising a curse on *Somebody*, who shrugs it off saying that learning is needed for proper ministry. *Somebody* then goes off and *Avarice* approaches *Minister* to ask what the argument was about. *Minister* replies that he has always pursued his ministry in the interests of self-enrichment, but complains that he has now been opposed in this by *Verity*. He asks *Avarice* to provide him with another patron, which *Avarice* agrees to do. He proposes *Lady Simony*, who says that *Minister* will not lack goods if he enters her service. *Simony* needs to be disguised as *Verity* to retain the support of the people, so *Minister* and *Avarice* proceed to despoil *Verity* of her clothes, proposing then to throw her into a pit. *Verity* says that she prophesied that this would happen and that for many years lies and false doctrine would reign. The fragment breaks off here.

PLAY LENGTH

140 lines extant (2 leaves only)

COMMENTARY

The prophecy of *Verity* suggests a period of perceived religious corruption, and W. W. Greg conjectured that the play was written at a time of increased enforcement of Protestantism or its reinstatement following a period of Catholic rule, either under Edward VI in 1547–50, or Elizabeth in 1558–60.

   Other Protestant and anti-Catholic plays: **14, 24, 44, 45, 49, 50, 53, 58, 66, 85, 90, 93**.

SIGNIFICANT TOPICS AND NARRATIVE ELEMENTS

ecclesiastical ignorance; simony; religious conflict

DRAMATURGICAL AND RHETORICAL FEATURES

Costume and dress *Verity* has her clothes removed 98 (*sd*) to disguise *Simony* 81–2
Actions and stage directions 98 (*sd*): 'Here they (*Min., Av.*) [de]spoil *Ver.*'
Staging and set the action is unlocalized and there no indications as to set apart, possibly, from the pit in which the *Verity* may be cast (117)

ALLUSIONS

Antichrist 92; St Lawrence 89

BIBLIOGRAPHY

Houle, P. J. 'A Reconstruction of the English Morality Fragment *Somebody and Others*', *PBSA* 71:3 (1977) pp. 259–69 (introductory essay)

87   The Student and the Girl (Interludium de Clerico et Puella) (fragment)

DATE, AUTHORSHIP AND AUSPICES

1290–1335; anonymous; auspices unknown

TEXT AND EDITIONS

Extant originals

Manuscript: British Library Add. MS 23986

Editions

1994   CHD (CD-Rom and online transcription of Wright and Halliwell, 1843, l.l., OS)*
1979   Davis (n.l., facsimile)
1976   Wickham (OS with parallel text in modern English)*
1968   Bennett and Smithers (OS)*
1958   Kaiser (OS)*
1931   Dickins and Wilson (OS)*
1915   Cook (OS)
1907   Heuser (OS)*
1903   Chambers, vol. II (n.l., OS)
1843   Wright and Halliwell, vol. I, London (n.l., OS)

SOURCES

The interlude is possibly based on the thirteenth-century fabliau, *Dame Sirith*, or shares a common source with it.

CHARACTERS

A Student (Clerico)   A Girl (Malkyn)   Mother Heloise (Helwis)

PLOT SUMMARY

The extract begins with an exchange between the student and the girl in which he attempts to woo her, but she rejects him. He then attempts to enlist the help of an old woman in pursuing his suit and offers her a reward if she will help him. She, however, affirms herself to be a poor, God-fearing woman and the fragment ends with her declaration of her piety.

PLAY LENGTH

84 lines extant

COMMENTARY

The most significant feature of this extract is that it is a secular piece of a very early date.

Other female virtue plays: **3, 6, 34, 63, 70, 97.**
Other wooing plays: **6, 57** (frag.), **75, 84.**
Other plays featuring prominent women characters: **3, 6, 30, 32, 43, 46, 51, 63, 70, 75, 95, 97.**

SIGNIFICANT TOPICS AND NARRATIVE ELEMENTS

a university student; wooing and rejection; female chastity; an attempted bribe; a go-between

DRAMATURGICAL AND RHETORICAL FEATURES

Staging and set no indications as to set, but there may be houses for *Malkyn* and *Mother Heloise*; the girl mentions that there is no one 'here at home' (4)

BIBLIOGRAPHY

Lancashire, I. '"Ioly Walte and Malkyng": A Grimsby Puppet Play in 1431', *REEDN* 4:2 (1979) pp. 6–8
Miller, B. D. 'Further Notes on *Interludium de Clerico et Puella*', *N&Q* 208 (1963) pp. 248–9
Moore, B. 'The Narrator within the Performance: Problems with Two Medieval "Plays"', *CD* 22:1 (1988) pp. 21–36
Nicoll, 1931, pp. 171–5
Richardson, F. E. 'Notes on the Text and Language of the *Interludium de Clerico et Puella*', *N&Q* 207 (1962) pp. 133–4

88   Supposes

DATE, AUTHORSHIP AND AUSPICES

1566; George Gascoigne; presented at Gray's Inn; Greg 60

TEXT AND EDITIONS

Extant originals

1572 printing by Henry Binneman (and Henry Middleton?): BL; Bodleian; Cambridge (imp.); Emmanuel; Folger; Harvard (imp.); Huntington; Illinois (imp.); Pforzheimer; (further copies extant); *STC* 11635

1575 printing by Henry Binneman for Richard Smith: Bodleian; Folger (two copies); Huntington; Pforzheimer; PML; private collector; *STC* 11636

1575 printing for Richard Smith: BL (imp.); Bodleian (imp.); Cambridge (imp.); Lichfield; Rylands; Huntington; Harvard; Illinois; Newberry; Yale; *STC* 11637

1587 printing by Abel Jeffes: BL; Dyce; Worcester; Trinity; Eton (imp.); Folger; Huntington; Chapin; Newberry; Yale; (further copies extant); *STC* 11638

1587 printing by Abel Jeffes (variant): Bodleian (imp.); NLS; Rylands; Peterborough (imp.); Folger (imp.); Dartmouth; Pforzheimer; *STC* 11639

Editions

1976   Fraser and Rabkin, vol. I (s.l., NS)*
1957   Bullough, vol. I (n.l., OS)*
1934   Baskervill, Heltzel and Nethercot (s.l., NS) *
1934   Boas (s.l., NS) *
1924   Adams (s.l.; OS) *
1911   Bond (s.l., OS)*
1907   Cunliffe vol. II (OS)*
1906   Cunliffe (with Italian originals, s.l., OS)*
1869   Hazlitt, vol. I (n.l., OS)*

SOURCES

The play is a translation of Ariosto's *Gli Suppositi*; see the introduction to Cunliffe's 1906 edition.

CHARACTERS

Balia, the nurse
Polinesta, the young woman
Cleander, the doctor
Pasiphilo, the parasite
Carion, the doctor's man
Dulipo, feigned servant
Erostrato, feigned master
Dalio, servant to feigned Erostrato
Crapino, servant to feigned Erostrato
The Sienese, a gentleman stranger

Paquetto, the Sienese's servant
Petrucio, the Sienese's servant
Damon, father to Polinesta
Nevola, his servant
Two other servants to Damon
Psiteria, an old hag in his house
Philogano, father to Erostrato
Litio, his servant
Ferrarese, an innkeeper

PLOT SUMMARY

The prologue explains that the term 'supposes' relates to mistaken or supposed identities. The play opens with *Polinesta* being castigated by her nurse, *Balia*, for sleeping with one of her father's servants, *Dulipo*, instead of making a more socially advantageous match. *Polinesta* reveals, however, that her lover is in fact a noble Sicilian who has come to Ferrara to study, but through love of her has swapped identities with his servant and has entered the service of *Polinesta*'s father in order to gain access to her. In the next scene a middle-aged doctor, *Cleander*, who is a suitor to *Polinesta*, expresses to a parasite *Pasiphilo* his desire to win her and his concern that she might prefer his rival suitor, called *Erostrato*. He sends *Pasiphilo* to tell *Polinesta*'s father that he does not require a dowry. However, *Pasiphilo* is as willing to promote *Erostrato*'s cause as he is *Cleander*'s. *Dulipo* (the real *Erostrato*) reveals that he has put his servant, the ostensible *Erostrato*, up to stand as a rival to *Cleander* in order to stall the doctor's suit. The servant reveals that he has enlisted *Pasiphilo* to spy, and that he has asked him to request *Damon*, *Polinesta*'s father, to delay his consent to *Cleander* for two weeks until his 'father' *Philogano* can visit Ferrara. The servant goes on to disclose that, in order to produce the father, he has played a trick on a Sienese he had encountered about to arrive in Ferrara. He has told the Sienese that a diplomatic incident between Ferrara and Siena has made Sienese citizens unwelcome in the city, but he has offered him safe lodging on condition that he would pretend to be *Philogano*. The pretended *Dulipo* then encounters *Cleander* and proceeds to allege that *Pasiphilo* has betrayed him and denigrated him to *Damon*. *Damon* has, in the meantime, been told by a malicious old woman of the pretended *Dulipo*'s relations with his daughter, discovers them in bed, and has him bound and cast into a dungeon. Now the feigned *Erostrato* is placed in a dilemma about whether to reveal the whole deception, since he has also seen the real *Philogano* arrive in the city. *Philogano* remarks to the keeper of the inn where he is staying that he has come to fetch his son home, as he has missed him too much. When he goes to *Erostrato*'s house, however, he is met by the *Sienese*, who claims to be him, and a quarrel ensues until the *Sienese* retires. *Philogano* then encounters the feigned *Erostrato*, whom he recognizes as his son's servant. The servant persists in maintaining his pretence and retreats indoors, leaving *Philogano* to wonder what has happened to his son. He decides to take his case to the authorities, while the feigned *Erostrato*'s problems are increased when *Pasiphilo* informs him of the real *Erostrato*'s discovery and confinement in the dungeon. *Cleander* meets *Philogano*, but is sceptical of his claims as to his own and the false *Erostrato*'s identities. In discussion, however, it turns out that the real *Dulipo* is the long-lost son of *Cleander*, separated from him when they fled the Turkish seizure of Otranto. *Damon* is seen sorrowing over the turn of events, and despairing of being able to marry off his daughter, but *Pasiphilo* then reveals the supposed *Dulipo*'s real identity as *Erostrato*, and the supposed *Erostrato* as the son of *Cleander*. All is resolved with a marriage agreed between the real *Erostrato* and *Polinesta*, and having found a son and heir, *Cleander* is happy to renounce his pursuit of a wife.

PLAY LENGTH

thirty-one scenes in five acts; the play is in prose and lineation differs widely in the various editions

COMMENTARY

This translation of Ariosto's modernization of the Roman comedy is a good example of the reformulation of classical (Plautine) comedy, first by Ariosto and further by Gascoigne, who anglicizes the comic tone. In the 1575 printing, Gascoigne muses on the possible confusion which the title of his play might cause and explains a 'suppose' as 'nothing else but a mistaking or imagination of one thing for another'. The characters are very much stock figures, but with refined and witty dialogue, and the dramatic interest otherwise lies in the complications of the plot. The play is a likely source for Shakespeare's *The Taming of a Shrew*.

Other plays based on classical or Italian models: **5, 7, 32, 37, 41, 43, 91, 92.**

Other secular comedies: **5, 30, 41, 46, 47, 75, 91, 92, 95.**

Other plays with foreign (non-biblical, non-classical) settings: **5, 6, 7, 12, 13, 32, 33, 47, 70, 74, 83.**

SIGNIFICANT TOPICS AND NARRATIVE ELEMENTS

clandestine love; a superannuated lover; disguise and presumed identity; masters and servants; servant intrigue; a lost child motif

NOTE: as the play is in prose, line references are inappropriate and reference to the play is by act and scene only

DRAMATURGICAL AND RHETORICAL FEATURES

Verbal and general the play is set in Ferrara; a five-act play with scene divisions; most stage directions in English, with a few in Latin

Costume and dress *Pasiphilo* has three laces to his hose, with a codpiece point 1.3; *Cleander* wears a side bonnet 2.3

Actions and stage directions 1.1 *sd*: '*Pol.* goes in and *Ba.* stays a little while after, speaking a word or two with the *Doc.*, and then departs'; 1.2: *Pas.* reads *Cle.*'s palm; 1.2 *sd*: '*Cle.* goes out, *Pas.* remains' (L); 1.3. *sd*: '*Pas.* enters, *Dul.* remains' (L); 1.3. *sd*: 'Here must *Cra.* be coming in with a basket and stick in his hand'; 1.4. *sd*: '*Cra.* departs, and *Dul.* also; after[wards] *Dul.* comes in again seeking *Ero.*'; 2.1 *sd*: '*Ero.* espies the *Sie.* and goes towards him. *Dul.* stands aside'; 2.2 *sd*: 'They (*Sie., Paq., Pet.*) go in. *Dul.* tarries and espies the Doc. coming in with his man'; 2.3 *sd*: '*Dul.* espies the *Doc.* and his man coming'; 3.1: *Dal.* strikes *Cra.*; 3.1 *sd*: '*Ero.* and *Dul.* [enter] unexpectedly' (L); 3.1 *sd*: '*Dul.* is espied by *Ero.*'; 3.1 *sd*: '*Dul.* tarries. *Ero.* goes out'; 3.2 *sd*: '*Dam.* coming in, espies *Dul.* and calls him'; 3.3. *sd*: 'The servants come in'; 3.3. *sd*: '*Dam.*'s servants come to him again'; 3.4. *sd*: '*Dam.* goes out'; 3.4 *sd*: '*Pas.* enters suddenly and unexpectedly' (L); 3.4 *sd*: '*Pas.* espies *Psi.* coming'; 4.1 *sd*: '*Ero.* espies *Psi.* coming and sends his lackey to her'; 4.2 *sd*: '*Ero.* espies *Phil.* coming, and runs about to hide him[self]'; 4.3: *Ferr.* knocks on *Ero.*'s door; 4.3 *sd*: '*Dal.* comes to the window, and there makes them (*Phil.*, *Ferr.*, *Lit.*) [an] answer'; 4.4. *sd*: '*Dal.* draws his head in at the window'; 4.4. *sd*: 'The *Sie.* comes out'; 4.5: *Dal.* threatens *Phil.* with his sword; 4.5 *sd*: '*Dal.* pulls the *Sie.* in at the doors'; 4.6 *sd*: '*Ero.* is espied upon the stage running about'; 4.7 *sd*: '*Ero.* takes all his servants in at the doors'; 5.1 *sd*: '*Ero.* espies *Pas.* running towards him'; 5.2 *sd*: '*Pas.* goes in, *Ero.* tarries'; 5.3 *sd*: '*Pas.* returns to *Ero.*'; 5.4 *sd*: '*Ero.* exit'; 5.4 *sd*: '*Cle.* and *Phil.* come in, talking of the matter in controversy'; 5.5 *sd*: '(*Cle.*, *Phil.*, *Lit.*) Exeunt. *Dam.* and *Psi.* come in'; 5.6 *sd*: '*Pas.* comes out of the house laughing'; 5.7 *sd*: '*Dam.* goes in. *Sie.*, *Cle.* and *Phil.* come upon the stage'; 5.8 *sd*: '*Pas.* stays their (*Phil.*'s, *Sie.*'s, *Cle.*'s) going in'; 5.9 *sd*: 'Here they (*Cle. Phil.*, *Dam.*, *Ero.*, *Pas.*, *Pol.*) come all together'; 5.10 *sd*: 'And they (audience) will applaud' (L)

Staging and set the action occurs in one location, the street between the houses of *Damon* on one side, and the feigned *Erostrato* on the other, from and into which characters enter and exit; *Erostrato*'s house has an openable window through which a character speaks (4.3); little action takes place on stage; the direction for *Erostrato* to be running about 'on the stage' (4.6 *sd*) may suggest a raised platform

Stage properties *Crapino*'s basket and stick 1.3 *sd*; a key to the dungeon 3.4; *Dalio*'s sword 4.5; *Nevola*'s fetters and bolts 5.10

PLACENAMES

Ancona 4.3; 'St Anthony's gate' 2.1, 3.4; Cathanea 2.1, 2.2, 4.4, 4.5, 5.5, 5.7, 5.10; Ferrara 2.1, 4.6, 5.5; Naples 2.1; Otranto 1.2, 5.5, 5.7, 5.10; Padua 1.2, 2.1, 2.2; Palermo 5.5; Ravenna 4.3; Sicily 1.1, 2.2, 2.4, 4.3, 4.4, 4.5, 4.7, 4.8, 5.3, 5.7; Siena 2.1; Turkey 5.5; Venice 2.1

ALLUSIONS

Argus 2.1; Cupid 1.3; Melchisedech 1.2; Methuselah 1.2; St Nicholas 1.3; Venus 1.2; Virgil 1.2

BIBLIOGRAPHY

Bevington, D. 'Cultural Exchange: Gascoigne and Ariosto at Gray's Inn in 1566' in Marrapodi and Hoenslaars, 1998, pp. 24–40

Bond, 1911, pp. xiii–cxviii

Hosley, R. 'The Formal Influence of Plautus and Terence' in Russell Brown and Harris, 1966, pp. 130–45
Johnson, 1972, pp. 138–42
Jordan, S. M. 'The Captivi and Gascoigne's Supposes', Classical Bulletin 45 (1969) pp. 37–41, 47
Sammut, 1971, pp. 85–90
Schelling, 1892, pp. 259–66
Schücking, 1901, pp. 19–35
Seronsy, C. C. 'Supposes as the Unifying Theme in The Taming of the Shrew', SQ 14:1 (1963) pp. 15–30

89   Temperance and Humility or Disobedience, Temperance and Humility (fragment)

DATE, AUTHORSHIP AND AUSPICES

1521–35; anonymous; auspices unknown; Greg 7

TEXT AND EDITIONS

Extant originals

c. 1528 printing by Wynkyn de Worde: Huntington (frag.: single leaf); STC 14109.5

Editions

1994   CHD (CD-Rom and online transcription of de Worde printing, l.l., OS)*
1909   Greg (1909b) (OS)*

SOURCES

No sources have been identified.

CHARACTERS

Temperance   Disobedience   Humility

PLOT SUMMARY

Disobedience exults in his economic might and his power in the realm, something deplored by *Temperance* and *Humility*. He boasts that they will never prevail against him, helped as he is by his companions *Audacity* and *Adversity*. When *Temperance* and *Humility* charge him with fomenting mischief and wilfulness in the realm, he declares his intention to induce these in more people with the help of his brother *Adversity*, who goes under the counterfeit names of *Prosperity* and *Audacity*. The fragment ends here.

PLAY LENGTH

62 lines extant

COMMENTARY

This appears to be a fragment of a Catholic play, repining against the redistribution of Church lands in the line 'royally provided of land and fee' (4). There seems, however, to be an admonition against monastic corruption of the type which provided the pretext for the suppression of religious houses by Henry VIII's administration, warning that they will 'stand in dread' if they vary from obedience.

SIGNIFICANT TOPICS AND NARRATIVE ELEMENTS

illegitimate wealth; power and corruption; order and obedience

DRAMATURGICAL AND RHETORICAL FEATURES

Verbal and general *Disobedience* takes the alias *Prosperity* 5–6

BIBLIOGRAPHY

Craik, 1953, pp. 98–108

90   The Temptation of Our Lord

DATE, AUTHORSHIP AND AUSPICES

1538; John Bale; St Stephen's, Canterbury and Kilkenny (see entry for *God's Promises*); Greg 23

TEXT AND EDITIONS

Extant originals

c. 1547 (?) printing by Dirik van der Straten, Wesel: Bodleian; *STC* 1279

Editions

1994	CHD (CD-Rom and online copy of Happé, 1986, l.l., OS)
1985/6	Happé, vol. II (OS)*
1976	Wickham (NS)
1919	Schwemmer (OS)

1914   Farmer (1914a) (facsimile, n.l.)
1909   TFT (facsimile, n.l.)
1907   Farmer (8) (n.l., NS)
1870–2 Grosart, vol. i, London (n.l., OS)

SOURCES

The title page identifies *Matthew 4* as the source of the narrative. The Corpus Christi cycles may also have been drawn upon; see Happé's edition, vol. i, p. 13.

CHARACTERS

Prologue (Bale)   Jesus Christ   Satan   First Angel   Second Angel

PLOT SUMMARY

The prologue spoken by *Bale* stresses the importance of the Holy Ghost as man's guide and introduces the story of Christ's temptation by Satan. *Christ* opens the action of the play telling of his forty-day fast, and he is followed by a self-revelatory speech by *Satan*, who declares his intention to tempt *Christ*. *Satan* then proceeds with the temptation, challenging *Christ* first to turn stones into food to break his fast, then to avoid official persecution by denying his divine parentage, and finally to cast himself off a mountain top. When none of these temptations succeeds, *Satan* offers *Christ* secular power over the kingdoms of the world in exchange for abandoning the belief that he is the son of God, but again he is rejected. He finally resolves to conspire in *Christ*'s downfall with the Pharisees, scribes, false clerics and (in a deliberate anachronism) the Pope. *Christ* is comforted by two angels and finally takes food, after which the angels conclude the play's narrative with a song. *Bale* speaks the epilogue, illustrating the value of the Scriptures in resisting the snares of the Devil.

PLAY LENGTH

433 lines, including prologue of 35 lines

COMMENTARY

This is part of a sequence of four Protestant plays by Bale which place an emphasis on Scripture as the route to redemption. It is essentially a debate play, the angels coming in at the end to provide a ceremonial and homiletic conclusion. Its anti-Catholicism can be seen most clearly in the anachronistic inclusion of the Pope in the list of *Satan*'s allies.

Other biblical plays: **10, 11, 16, 34, 42, 44, 48, 63, 77, 93.**
Other Protestant and anti-Catholic plays: **14, 24, 44, 45, 49, 50, 53, 58, 66, 85, 86** (frag.), **93.**

SIGNIFICANT TOPICS AND NARRATIVE ELEMENTS

the scriptural story of the temptation of Christ in the desert; Protestantism and Scripture; the Pope as Antichrist; fasting; religious persecution

DRAMATURGICAL AND RHETORICAL FEATURES

Verbal and general stage directions in Latin
Costume and dress *Satan* is dressed as a monk or hermit: 'devout and sad in my gear' 75, 'under appearance of religion' 77 *sd*, and a 'brother' 83
Actions and stage directions 77 *sd*: 'Here, under appearance of religion, he (*Sa.*) approaches *Chr.*'; 350 *sd*: 'Here the angels approach to administer comfort'; 364 *sd*: 'Here in the presence of the angels standing near him he (*Chr.*) eats'; 380 *sd*: 'He (*F. Ang.*) speaks to the people (audience)'; 398 *sd*: 'Here they (angels) perform a sweet song in the presence of *Chr.*'
Songs and music the angels' song at the end (w.n.s.) 398 *sd*
Staging and set the locations (desert, temple, mountain) are all signalled in the dialogue (36, 184, 268); there are no indications as to set
Stage properties food for *Christ* 362

PLACENAMES

Africa 274; Arabia 273; Asia 274; Europe 274; Jerusalem 167, 374; Jordan 64; Rome 337

ALLUSIONS

Aaron 315; Adam 133, 314; Daniel 139; *Deuteronomy 6:16* 249–50, *8:3* 128–30, *10:12–14* 318–22; Elijah 139; Eve 314; Job 407; *Matthew 4:6* 209–11; Moses 51, 137, 315; St Paul 407; *1 Peter 5:8* 413; the Pope 337; *Psalm 90:11–12* (V)/*91:11–12* (AV) 223–8, *90:13* (V)/*91:13* (AV) 243–4

BIBLIOGRAPHY

Blatt, 1968, pp. 97–9
Greg, W. 'Bale's Plays on the Baptism and Temptation' ('Notes on Some Early Plays'), *Library*, 4th series 11 (1930) pp. 53–6
Happé, P. 'The *Temptation of Our Lord*: Bale's Adaptation of the Structural Narrative' in Lascombes, 1995b, pp. 57–78
Happé, 1996, pp. 108–24

Sperk, 1973, pp. 53–72
Strietman, E. 'Representations of *The Temptation of Christ* in Medieval Dutch and English Drama' in
    Bitot, Mullini and Happé, 1996, pp. 148–75

91   Terence in English (Andria)

DATE, AUTHORSHIP AND AUSPICES

1516–33; translation anonymous; possibly a closet play or for school production;
Greg 12

TEXT AND EDITIONS

Extant originals

c. 1520 (?) printing by Phillipe LeNoir, Paris: BL; *STC* 23894

Editions

1994   CHD (CD-Rom and online transcription of LeNoir printing, l.l., s.l., OS)
1987   Twycross (s.l., NS)*

SOURCES

The play is a translation of Terence's *Andria*, which is itself based on two Menander
comedies, *The Girl from Andros* and *The Girl from Perinthos*.

CHARACTERS

Poet (Prologue and Epilogue)	Mysis, maid to Glycery
Simo, a merchant of Athens	Charinus, friend to Pamphilus
Chremes, another merchant	Byrria, slave to Charinus
Sosia, Simo's male cook	Lesbia, a midwife
Pamphilus, Simo's son	Crito
Davus, slave to Pamphilus	Dromo, Simo's slave-driver

Several characters are mentioned but never appear, including Glycery and Pam-
phila, with whom Pamphilus and Charinus are in love respectively.

PLOT SUMMARY

The *Poet* in the prologue discusses the issue of literary translation before going on
to a summary of the play's narrative. *Simo* opens the action expressing to *Sosia*
his disquiet about his son, *Pamphilus*, whom he suspects of attraction to a loose

woman neighbour from Andros, despite having been betrothed by his father to the daughter of *Chremes*. He relates that the woman in question has died, but that he noted *Pamphilus*'s extreme grief at the funeral and that the boy seemed to pay great attention to her sister *Glycery*, intervening to stop her throwing herself on the pyre. *Chremes* had also noticed this and expressed his concern. *Simo* details *Sosia* to keep an eye on *Pamphilus*. In the next scene *Simo* warns the slave *Davus* not to help prevent his son's marriage, and when he leaves *Davus* reveals to the audience the fact that *Glycery* is pregnant by *Pamphilus*. The scene now changes to *Pamphilus* himself, who expresses his fears about being made to marry, and he talks to *Glycery*'s maid, who informs him that she is on her way to fetch the midwife. Act 2 begins with *Charinus* describing to his slave his love for *Philumena*, *Chremes*'s daughter, to whom *Philumenus* is betrothed. He is joined by *Philumenus* who, after they have discussed the problem of their thwarted desires, promises *Charinus* he will find a way to prevent the marriage. *Davus* arrives to report his discovery that *Chremes*, having learned of *Glycery*'s pregnancy, no longer wishes to marry his daughter to *Pamphilus*. *Davus* urges *Pamphilus* therefore to appear to accede to his father's wishes about the marriage, secure in the knowledge that it will now not go ahead anyway. He now goes to *Simo* and tells him his son has agreed to the marriage. *Simo* has, however, himself got somewhat abreast of events and he remains suspicious, thinking that *Glycery*'s pregnancy is feigned and a ruse. Despite the midwife's activity in *Glycery*'s house, and *Davus*'s assurances, he remains unconvinced. *Simo* next meets *Chremes* and manages to persuade him that there is no longer anything between his son and *Glycery*, securing his agreement to the marriage again and thus foiling *Davus*'s plot. *Pamphilus* is wretched when he hears the news, and *Charinus* is equally distraught, accusing *Pamphilus* of breaking his promise. *Davus* begs *Pamphilus*'s forgiveness for botching the plan, and he vows to use his wits to find a remedy. He now goes to *Glycery*'s maid and tells her to lay the newly born baby before *Simo*'s gates, in which act she is discovered by *Chremes*. Despite *Simo*'s subsequent attempts to argue that it is simply a ploy to prevent the marriage, and that it is not *Pamphilus*'s child at all, *Chremes* remains unconvinced. The final scene of the fourth act sees the arrival of *Crito*, the cousin of *Chrysis*. The last act begins with a quarrel between *Simo* and *Chremes* over the aborted marriage, and in the next scene *Crito* reveals that *Glycery* is not an Andrian, but an Athenian citizen after all, which legally obliges *Pamphilus* to marry her, having made her pregnant. Despite his anger, *Simo* finally agrees to this marriage. *Crito* then goes on to reveal in the final scene that *Glycery*, having been left behind in Athens when her father fled from the city during time of war, had subsequently been taken by her uncle in search of him, but that they had been shipwrecked in Andros, where she had been left in the care of *Chrysis*. *Chrysis* afterwards moved to Athens, taking her protegée with her. This story enables *Chremes* to recognize *Glycery* as none other than his long-lost daughter, Pasibula. All now happily resolved, *Davus*, having been released on *Pamphilus*'s request from the prison to which he has been confined for his activities, ends the play with the confirmation that both *Pamphilus* and *Charinus* will after all have the brides they want, and the *Poet* apologizes for any deficiencies in the translation.

PLAY LENGTH

1,593 lines, including prologue of 105 lines and epilogue of 28 lines

COMMENTARY

This is a theatrically sophisticated Roman comedy of bluff and counter-bluff, in which the central problem is nonetheless resolved by the device of a *deus ex machina* character. As in other Roman comedy, the action is largely off stage, and some characters important in the narrative do not appear at all. There is considerable self-consciousness and reflexivity with respect to conventions of both character construction and the use of the stage. This, along with the reflections on translation found in the prologue and epilogue, is derived from the original text.

Other plays based on classical or Italian models: **5, 7, 32, 37, 41, 43, 88, 92**.
Other secular comedies: **5, 30, 41, 46, 47, 75, 88, 92, 95**.
Other plays with classical settings: **19, 29, 39, 43, 57** (frag.), **92**.

SIGNIFICANT TOPICS AND NARRATIVE ELEMENTS

literary translation; youth and education; a formal parent–child conflict intrigue; forced marriage; a servant intrigue; a lost child narrative

DRAMATURGICAL AND RHETORICAL FEATURES

Verbal and general a five-act play with scene divisions; characters frequently speak to themselves, even with other characters present on stage; no directions for music or songs, and no indications of dress; stage directions all in English, but these may simply be indications to the reader if this is a closet play
Actions and stage directions (occur only at the start of scenes) 1.2 *sd*: 'Here *Si.* and *Da.* speak each of them to himself a while'; 1.3 *sd*: 'Here *Da.* speaks all to himself'; 1.4 *sd*: 'Here *My.* speaks to *Arc.*, being within the house'; 1.5 *sd*: 'Here *Pam.* and *My.* speak each of them to themselves a while'; 2.2 *sd*: 'Here *Da.* speaks to himself a while'; 2.4: 'Here *Si.* speaks to himself'; 2.5 *sd*: 'Here *By.* stands in a corner and speaks to himself'; 3.1 *sd*: 'Here *Si.* stands in a corner and speaks to himself'; 3.2 *sd*: 'Here *Les.* speaks to *Arc.*, being within the house'; 3.5 *sd*: 'Here *Da.* stands in a corner being afeared'; 4.1 *sd*: 'Here *Pam.* and *Da.* stand in a corner a while'; 4.2 *sd*: 'Here *My.* speaks to *Gly.*, being within the house'; 4.3 *sd*: 'Here *My.* speaks to herself a while'; 4.4 *sd*: 'Here *Chr.* stands still and hears *My.* and *Da.* talk together'; 5.2 *sd*: 'Here *Da.* speaks a while to himself'; 5.4 *sd*: 'Here *Cri.* speaks to *Pam.* a while'; 5.5 *sd*: 'Here speaks *Cha.* and *Pam.* each to himself a while'

Staging and set the action takes place off stage; apart from the fact that the play is set in Athens the dialogue on stage is largely unlocalized, though some of it takes place outside *Glycery*'s house, which may have been represented; several characters stand 'in a corner' (2.5, 3.1, 3.5)
Stage properties a doll as *Glycery*'s child 4.3.9

PLACENAMES

Andros pr. 48 *passim*; Asia 5.4.54; Athens pr. 36 *passim*

ALLUSIONS

Apollo 4.2.26; Chaucer pr. 10; Gower pr. 8; Lydgate pr. 13; Oedipus 1.2.37

RECORDED PRODUCTION

Videotape: JL, dir. M. Twycross (Lancaster University Television, 1988)

BIBLIOGRAPHY

Brodie, A. H. '*Terens in Englysh*: Towards the Solution of a Literary Puzzle', *C&M* 27 (1966) pp. 397–416

92   Thersites

DATE, AUTHORSHIP AND AUSPICES

1537; author unknown, possibly Nicholas Udall; auspices unknown: it is likely to have been an Oxford play but it was possibly performed by Eton boys at court in October 1537; Greg 37

TEXT AND EDITIONS

Extant originals

c. 1562 printing by John Tysdale: Huntington; Johns Hopkins University Library, Pforzheimer; *STC* 23949

Editions

1994   CHD (CD-Rom and online copy of Axton, 1982, l.l., OS)
1982   Axton (OS)*
1913   Farmer (facsimile, n.l.)

1912   TFT (facsimile, n.l.)
1906   Farmer (3) (n.l., NS)
1876 (?) Ashbee (1876b) (facsimile, n.l.)
1874–6   Dodsley, vol. 1 (n.l., NS)
1848   Child (n.l., OS)
1847   Cooper (n.l., OS)

SOURCES

The narrative is drawn from Ravisius Textor's *Dialogi Aliquot Festuissimi* (printed in an appendix to Axton's edition with parallel text in English).

CHARACTERS

Thersites, a boaster   Mulciber, a smith   Mater   Miles, a knight   Telemachus, a child

PLOT SUMMARY

Thersites brags of his brave deeds and reports that he has lost all his equipment except his club in the Trojan War. He approaches the blacksmith *Mulciber* to ask him to make him a 'sallet', by which he means military headgear, though the smith comically misunderstands this as 'salad'. At length *Thersites* gets his helmet and continues his boasting, comparing himself favourably to King Arthur's knights. He gets *Mulciber* to make him more armour, and also procures a sword from him. *Mulciber* returns to his shop and *Thersites* then meets his mother, who responds to his vaunting speeches with alarm, begging him not go into battle. When she goes off, he encounters a snail, which terrifies him until he recognizes what it is. He calls for his servants to help him fight it. They do not appear, but *Thersites* is scornfully watched by *Miles*, a genuine soldier. *Thersites* takes on the snail by himself, first with his club and then his sword, finally giving up when she draws her horns in. *Miles* now emerges and challenges him, at which *Thersites* runs and hides behind his mother's back, claiming that a thousand horsemen have set upon him. When *Miles* departs, *Thersites* resumes his bragging until *Telemachus*, the young son of Ulysses, comes in with a letter from his father. In it Ulysses apologizes for his former contempt for *Thersites* and asks him to request his mother to cure his son of worms. The mother, mindful of Ulysses's past attitude, is unwilling to do so until *Thersites* coerces her with threats. She recites a charm over the child, who then thanks her and goes back with a message for his father that *Thersites* will visit him. When the mother also leaves, *Thersites* delivers a long speech expressing his contempt for her, before continuing his vaunting claims that he will vanquish *Miles*. *Miles* now reappears and strikes at *Thersites*, causing him to run off leaving his club and sword behind. *Miles* concludes the play with an epilogue decrying boasting and the sin of pride. He exhorts the audience to obedience to parental and state authority, and offers a prayer for the king, queen and prince.

PLAY LENGTH

915 lines

COMMENTARY

The plot is relatively shapeless, the narrative principally determined by the antics of the bragging coward, *Thersites*. This is a classical comedy without a Vice. There are no songs.

Other plays based on classical or Italian models: **5, 7, 32, 37, 41, 43, 88, 91.**
Other secular comedies: **5, 30, 41, 46, 47, 75, 88, 91, 95.**
Other plays with classical settings: **19, 29, 39, 43, 57** (frag.), **91.**

SIGNIFICANT TOPICS AND NARRATIVE ELEMENTS

a 'miles gloriosus', braggadoccio and cowardice; heroes from classical, Arthurian and Robin Hood legend; the snail combat; magical folk healing; relics; a mother–son relationship

DRAMATURGICAL AND RHETORICAL FEATURES

Verbal and general *Thersites* enters through the audience 3–4; *Mater*'s internally rhyming series of exclamations 622–7; *Thersites*'s list of alliterative and tongue-twisting popular names 659–82; *Mater*'s charm to cure *Telemachus*, including a mostly alliterative list of ridiculous religious relics 697–754; stage directions in English

Costume and dress *Thersites*'s headdress and armour 103–11, with a 'red thong' 56

Actions and stage directions op. sd: '*The.* comes in first having a club upon his neck'; 21 *sd*: '*Mu.* must have a shop made in the place and *The.* comes before it saying aloud'; 34 *sd*: 'And then he (*Mu.*) must do as he would go away'; 80 *sd*: 'And then he (*Mu.*) goes in to his shop and makes a sallet (helmet) for him (*The.*); at the last he says'; 83 *sd*: 'Then *Mu.* goes into his shop until he is called again'; 119 *sd*: 'Then he (*Mu.*) goes in to his shop again'; 233 *sd*: '*Mu.* goes into his shop again and *The.* says forth'; 265 *sd*: '*Ma.* comes in'; 304: *Ma.* begs *The.* on her knees; 381 *sd*: 'Then the mother goes in the place which is prepared for her'; 387 *sd*: 'Here a snail must appear unto him (*The.*) and he must look fearfully upon the snail, saying'; 406 *sd*: 'Here *Mi.* comes in'; 444 *sd*: 'Then he (*The.*) must fight against the snail with his club'; 448 *sd*: 'And he (*The.*) must cast his club away'; 455 *sd*: 'Here he (*The.*) must fight then with his sword against the snail and the snail draws her horns in'; 478 sd: 'And he (Mi.) begins to fight with him but The. must run away and hide him behind his mother back, saying'; 507 sd: 'Then he (The.) goes out and the mother says'; 509 sd: 'Then he (The.) looks about if he (Mi.) be gone or not at the last he says'; 523 sd: 'Then comes in Tel. bringing a letter from his father Ulysses, and The. says'; 531 sd: 'Here he (Tel.) must deliver him (The.) the letter'; 533 sd: 'Here he (The.) must read the letter'; 594 sd: 'Then The. goes to his mother, saying'; 611: The. threatens his mother with a club; 621 sd: 'Then he (The.) must take her (Ma.) by the arms, and she cries out as follows'; 696 sd: 'Then he (Tel.) must lay him down with his belly upward and she (Ma.) must bless him from above to beneath, saying a[s] follows'; 764 sd: 'Tel. goes out and the mother says'; 781 sd: 'The mother goes out and The. says forth'; 831: The. holds up ten fingers; 875 sd: 'Then Mi. comes in saying'; 885 sd: 'Then he (Mi.) must strike at him, and The. must run away, and leave his club and sword behind'

Staging and set Mulciber has a shop 'in the place' into which he withdraws (21 sd); the action is otherwise unlocalized and there are no further indications as to set; the mother retires to a place 'which is prepared for her' (381 sd, possibly off stage)

Stage properties Thersites's club, opening sd; Thersites's helmet ('sallet') 80 sd; Thersites's arm armour ('briggen irons') 188; a snail (with retracting horns) 387 sd, 455 sd; Thersites's sword 455 sd; Telemachus's letter 531 sd

PLACENAMES

Antwerp[1] 681; Birmingham[2] 721; Broken Heys (in Oxford) 155; Buckingham[2] 723; Calais 411; Mount Calvary[1] 712; Chertsey[2] 746; Comberton[2] 697; Cotswolds 124; Cumnor[1] 660; Demon's Dale (? in Derbyshire, 'Dymmings dale')[2] 747; Elba ('Ilva') 30; Hampton 116; Hinksey[2] 745; Jordan[2] 751; Kent 314; Lemnos 30; London 160, 742;[2] Malvern Hills 114; St Michael's Mount[2] 735; Moreton[2] 740; Newmarket Heath 794; Oxford[2] 745; Rome 430; Sudeley[1] 669; Tavistock[2] 727; Tewkesbury[2] 667; Thruxton (? 'Thrutton')[2] 746; Troy 8, 716;[2] Wales 314

1 Part of Thersites's alliterative list of names.
2 Part of Mater's alliterative recited charm.

ALLUSIONS

Abraham[1] 701; Adam[1] 710; Aeolus[1] 722; Ahasuerus[1] 737; Aman 638; Amazons 192; King Arthur 126; Balaam[1] 717; Beelzebub 517; Bevis of Hampton 116, 724;[1] Busyris 324; Cacus 239–42; Cerberus 89; Dares and Entellus 421–2; King David 828; David and Goliath 94–6, 734;[1] Li Biaus Desconneus 132; Enceladus 201; Eve[1] 701; Sir Gawain 130; Guy of Warwick and Colebrand 116; Hercules 88, 190, 241, 323, 513; Robin Hood and Little John 318; the Hydra 90; Isaac[1] 709; Isumbras 316; Juno 310; Jupiter 23 passim; Sir Kay 130; Sir Lancelot de Lake 136; Mary Magdalene

639; Mars 202; St Michael[1] 735; Minerva 311; Moses[1] 711; Noah 99, 715;[1] St Peter 185; Phaeton 209; Samson 92, 190, 472; Samuel 743; Tantalus[1] 730; Tobias (Book of Tobit, V)[1] 720; Friar Tuck 450; Typhoeus 200; Venus 40; Virgil 421; Xerxes 192

1   Part of *Mater's* alliterative recited charm.

BIBLIOGRAPHY

Holthausen, F. 'Studien zum älteren englischen Drama: I *Thersites*', *EngS* 31 (1902) pp. 77–90
Moon, A. R. 'Was Nicholas Udall the Author of *Thersites?*', *Library* 4th series 7 (1926) pp. 184–93
Southern, 1973, pp. 290–304
Swaen, A. E. 'Thersytes', *Neophilologus* 5:2 (1920) pp. 160–2 (in Dutch)
Willson, 1975, pp. 4–8
Yamakawa, T. 'The Comical Elements in *Thersytes*', *ELR (Kyoto)* 15 (1971) pp. 23–40 (in Japanese)

93   Three Laws

DATE, AUTHORSHIP AND AUSPICES

1538, and revised by the author in *c.* 1547 and 1562; John Bale; St Stephen's, Canterbury and offered for acting; Greg 24

TEXT AND EDITIONS

Extant originals

1548 (?) printing by Dirik Van der Straten, Wesel: BL (no t.p.), Bodleian (two copies, one imp.); Marsh Library, Dublin; *STC* 1287
1562 printing by Thomas Colwell: BL; Huntington (imp.); Illinois; *STC* 1288

Editions

2000	Walker (OS)
1994	CHD (CD-Rom and online copy of Happé, 1985/6, a.l., OS)
1985/6	Happé, vol. II (OS)*
1914	Farmer (1914a) (facsimile, n.l.)
1908	TFT (facsimile, n.l.)
1907	Farmer (8) (n.l., NS)
1882	Schroeer (OS)

SOURCES

The play is broadly based on Old and New Testament history; for a discussion of other possible sources see the introduction to Happé's edition, vol. I, pp. 13–14.

CHARACTERS

Bale, the Prolocutor	Infidelity	Christ's Gospel
God the Father	Sodomy	Hypocrisy
The Law of Nature	Idolatry	False Doctrine
Mosaic Law	Avarice	Vengeance of God
The Law of Christ	Ambition	Christian Faith

PLOT SUMMARY

Bale speaking the prologue stresses the importance of law in the commonwealth and then introduces the topic of the play. *God* opens the action summoning the laws of *Nature, Moses* and *Christ* to guide mankind. The *Law of Nature* is to instruct man in the time of his exile from Paradise, *Mosaic Law* from Moses to the exile of the Jews and the coming of Christ, and *Christ's Law* from then on perpetually. *God* gives them a heart, stone tablets and a copy of the New Testament respectively as their signs. In the second act the *Law of Nature* is approached by *Infidelity*, who enters as a pedlar selling brooms, and who treats him with mocking contempt. When the *Law of Nature* claims that it is only man who deviates from obedience to him, *Infidelity* cites natural disasters, but the *Law of Nature* replies that these are for the punishment of errant humanity. *Infidelity* announces that he will summon his henchmen *Idolatry* and *Sodomy* to keep the *Law of Nature* from mankind; when the *Law of Nature* leaves these two duly enter, *Sodomy* as a monk and *Idolatry* as a necromancer. *Idolatry* tells how he inducts women into magical practice and he gives a lengthy description of the Catholic superstition surrounding relics. *Sodomy* then recounts a history of biblical and ecclesiastical sexual deviation, for which he claims responsibility, and connects it with the corruption of *God*'s image by Catholic religious practice. *Infidelity* equips them with the appropriate religious artefacts and sends them to corrupt men with Catholic ritual. He then details their work with satisfaction before himself departing. The *Law of Nature* next re-enters in a leprous state, having been abused by both *Idolatry* and *Sodomy*, and warns against the Pope. In the third act the *Law of Nature*, having been corrupted, is replaced by *Mosaic Law*. Again *Infidelity* makes an appearance, this time talking with enjoyment of the 'stories' told in church instead of the preaching of the Gospel. On being questioned, *Mosaic Law* tells *Infidelity* that he is concerned to ensure obedience to the Ten Commandments, which he lists. When *Infidelity* reveals his identity he is dismissed by *Mosaic Law* and immediately goes off to recruit the Vices *Avarice* and *Ambition* to his cause. They are initially arrogant in their attitude, but come to order when *Infidelity* beats them, and they agree to go about corrupting the leaders and people of the world so that they will come to deviate from the laws of Moses. They reveal that their methods are the religious practices of the Catholic Church, and finally exit singing while *Infidelity* rejoices in their work. When he too goes off, *Mosaic Law* re-enters blind and lame, having been attacked by *Ambition* and *Avarice*. *Christ's Gospel* opens the fourth act by announcing *God's* mercy to all believers. Once again, *Infidelity* comes along to mount an attack, and they dispute the merits of married as opposed to a celibate priesthood. *Christ's Gospel* accuses the Catholic priesthood of sexual impropriety and issues a warning against following the ways of *Infidelity*. After he goes off, *Infidelity* summons his companions *False Doctrine* and *Hypocrisy*, Catholic clergy who take great delight in their own and others' sexual incontinence. They declare that they will pursue their subversive ends through scholasticism and Catholic clerical powers. *Christ's Gospel* now reappears, at which *Infidelity* slips quietly away. When he desires to preach, *False Doctrine* and *Hypocrisy* try to prevent him by demanding he follow the Catholic ritual patterns of worship, but he dismisses these as having no scriptural authority. They are rejoined by *Infidelity*, who comes in trying to sell pardons. *Christ's Gospel* then launches a vigorous verbal attack on them all, and reveals himself as the Holy Ghost. At this, *False Doctrine* and *Hypocrisy* lay hands on him, despoil him of his clothes, deck him in shabby garments, and take him off intending to burn him. *Infidelity* exults in his defeat of *God's* laws, before himself departing to visit a tavern. The final act has the *Vengeance of God* (formerly *God the Father*) threatening *Infidelity*, who vainly seeks to ward him off with conjuration. He throws water on *Infidelity* in token of the Flood, and chases him off with fire to signify the consuming of the world in flame in the final days. As *God the Father* he then preaches a sermon and restores the three Laws to their former vigour. They sing a song glorifying him, after which they are joined by *Christian Faith*. The Laws each restate their functions and the play is ended by *Christian Faith* with a prayer for Queen Katherine (Parr) and the Lord Protector. There is a final song 'upon Benedictus'.

PLAY LENGTH

2,041 lines, exclusive of the final song

COMMENTARY

This play bears some relationship to another of Bale's plays, *God's Promises*, in respect of its structure and material. In both plays the narrative development is clearly structured according to the doctrinal ideas being explored. The notion of the three laws of God, the central idea of this play, is also strongly present in the other one. This play contains the earliest extant dramatic treatment of homosexuality, which is represented not only as a practice among Catholic clergy and monastic orders, but also as a subversion of the natural order. The use of a pyrotechnic device to drive out *Infidelity* is a notable feature.

Other biblical plays: **10, 11, 16, 34, 42, 44, 48, 63, 77, 90**.

Other Protestant and anti-Catholic plays: **14, 24, 44, 45, 49, 50, 53, 58, 66, 85, 86** (frag.), **90**.

SIGNIFICANT TOPICS AND NARRATIVE ELEMENTS

providence; Old and New Testament doctrine; necromancy; transvestism; sexual deviation; relics; Catholic liturgy and religious practice; leprosy as a metaphor for corruption; blindness and lameness as metaphors for corruption; the Ten Commandments; married versus celibate clergy; scholasticism; the sale of pardons

DRAMATURGICAL AND RHETORICAL FEATURES

Verbal and general *Infidelity* 'conjures' *Sodomy* and *Idolatry* by tetragrammaton 392–4; *Infidelity*'s list of men who donned women's clothing 432–5; *Idolatry*'s list of charms and relics 507–45; *Sodomy*'s list of sexual transgressors 611–18; *Infidelity* delivers a mock Latin prayer 699–703; *Ambition*'s list of tyrants 1038–46; *Avarice*'s list of covetous sinners 1072–8; *Hypocrisy*'s list of pagans and proponents of Catholic corruption 1578–84; a five-act play with no further scene division; if Bale is identified as Prolocutor, the doubling scheme for the first production suggests he took a fuller part in the play as well; names of characters and stage directions in Latin

Costume and dress *Sodomy* is described as 'knavebald and pie-pecked' (tonsured with a multicoloured habit) 625; the Vices exchange *Christ's Gospel*'s garments for more shabby ones 1726 *sd*; there is an instruction at the end of the play for 'the apparelling of the six Vices, or fruits of *Infidelity*': 'Let *Idolatry* be decked like an old witch (see also 399 *sd*), *Sodomy* like a monk of all sects (see also 389 *sd*), *Ambition* like a bishop, *Covetousness* (*Avarice*) like a Pharisee or spiritual lawyer (see also 967 *sd*), *False Doctrine* like a popish doctor, and *Hypocrisy* like a grey friar. The rest of the parts are easy enough to conjecture'

Actions and stage directions 112 *sd*: 'Here he (*God*) shows him (*L. of Na.*) a heart for his sign'; 122 *sd*: 'Here he (*God*) gives him (*Mos. L.*) stone tables for a sign'; 134 *sd*: 'Here he (*God*) gives him (*Chr. L.*) the New Testament for a sign'; 389 *sd*: '(*Sod.* dressed as) A Monk'; 394 *sd*: 'They (*Sod., Ido.*) enter together'; 399 *sd*: '(*Ido.* dressed as) A Necromantic'; (*Inf.* instructing and handing out relics and other items): 656 *sd*: 'To *Sod.*', 657 *sd*: 'To *Ido.*', 663 *sd*: 'To *Ido.*', 671 *sd*: 'To *Sod.*', 679 *sd*: 'To *Ido.*'; 698 *sd*: 'After the song, *Inf.* says in a high voice'; 801: *Inf.* enters laughing; 967 *sd*: '(*Av.* dressed as) Jurisconsultus'; 981–2: *Inf.* beats *Amb.* and *Av.*; 1219 *sd*: 'The little song being finished, they (*Amb., Av.*) both leave'; 1608 *sd*: '(*Inf.*) Exit secretly'; 1726 *sd*: 'Here having removed his (*Chr. Go.*'s) garment, they put more shabby ones on him'; 1744 *sd*: 'They (*F. Doc., Hyp.*) go out with him (*Chr. Go.*)' 1818 *sd*: 'Here he (*V. of God*) throws water on *Inf.*'; 1829 *sd*: 'He (*V. of God*) strikes *Inf.* with a sword a second time'; 1851 *sd*: 'The flame of the fire forces *Inf.* to leave the place'; 1913 *sd*: 'Here they (*L. of Nat., Mos. L., Chr. L.*) will sing to the glory of God, "In exitu Israel de Aegypto", or something similar'; **Simple entry:** (*F. Doc., Hyp.*) 1431; (*Inf.*) 1664; **Simple exit:** (*God, Mos. L., Chr. L.*) 161; (*L. of Nat.*) 372; (*Inf.*) 751; (*Inf.*) 1251; (*Chr. Go.*) 1419; (*Inf.*) 1853

Songs and music 1. *Infidelity* 'Brom, brom, brom' (w.s.) 176–80; 2. *Infidelity, Idolatry, Sodomy* 'some merry song' (w.n.s.) 696; 3. *Infidelity* 'Lapides preciosi' (two words only) 814, and 'Saepe expugnaverunt me a iuventute mea' (one line only) 819; 4. *Infidelity, Avarice, Ambition* ('a little song', w.n.s.) 1219; 5. *Law of Nature, Mosaic Law, Christ's Law* 'In exitu Israel de Aegypto' ('or some similar song', w.n.s.) 1913 *sd*; 7. Whole cast (?) final song (possibly sung after the play) 'Benedictus Dominus' (attached to play, w.s., 60 lines); music for a version of the first song is extant

Staging and set at the end of the play a doubling scheme divides the roles as follows: 1. The *Prolocutor, Christian Faith, Infidelity*; 2. *Law of Nature, Covetousness* (*Avarice*), *False Doctrine*; 3. *Law of Moses, Idolatry, Hypocrisy*; 4. *Law of Christ, Ambition, Sodomy*; 5. *God the Father, Vengeance of God. Sodomy* speaks off stage before entering (389–91); the action is unlocalized and though there are several stage properties there are no indications as to set

Stage properties a heart 112 *sd*; stone tablets 122 *sd*; a book as the New Testament 134 *sd*; broaches, beads, pins and rings 660; a staff and bag 667; a stool 675; a box of creams and oil 678; a purse of relics 679; water 1818 *sd*, a sword 1829 *sd*; pyrotechnic material 1851 *sd*

PLACENAMES

Babylon 602, 1914; Boston 1667; Bungay 1576; Bury St Edmunds 831; Crete 1027; Egypt 602, 1791, 1793, 1913 *sd*; England 1212, 1483, 2029; Gomorrah 562, 779, 1408, 1788; Hailes Abbey 833; Ingham 957, 1667; Jerusalem 745, 1868; Kent 494; Leipzig 1486; Lyons 1451, 1461; the Minories 807–8; Nantes 650; Norwich 1575; Paris 1451, 1453; Queenhithe 538, 1305; Rome 576, 643, 738, 1208, 1210; Sodom 562, 779, 1408, 1788; Southampton 809; Spain 1476; R. Tiber 1599; Viterbo 1210; Wrest (Bedfordshire) 1624

ALLUSIONS

Abraham 107, 1096, 1364; Absolom[4] 1042; Achitophel[4] 1042; Adam 107, 1034, 1288, 1363; Adonisedech[4] 1043; Agathocles[3] 612; Ahab[5] 1072; Alanus de Insulis *Doctrinale Minus*[6] 1584; St Albertus Magnus, *De secretis mulierum*[6] 1582; Alchimus[4] 1046; Alexander the Coppersmith 1834; Amram 108; Andronicus[5] 1078; St Anthony 1668, 1679; St Thomas Aquinas 521 (?),[2] 569, 1579;[6] Aristo[3] 615; Aristotle 613,[3] 1582;[6] Averroes[6] 1583; Avicenna[6] 1583; Babel 1037; Roger Bacon[6] 1580; Priests of Bel[5] 1073; St Blaise[2] 534; St Blythe[2] 534; Caiaphas 1564; Chrysippus 8; Cicero *De Legibus III .2.3* 3–7; Pope Clement VII 1204; Clisthenes[1] 433; Clodius[1] 434; Crathes[3] 617; Johannes Cremona 1481; St Cyriacus of Jerusalem[2] 536; Dagon 1703; Daniel 596; King David 117, 591, 1844; Demetrius 1834; Diotrephes[5] 1076; Duns Scotus 1579; Durandus of St Pourcain[6] 1579; Eckius 1485; 'Sons of Eli'[5] 1074; Elimas 1834; Euclides[1] 434; Eve 1034; Ezechiel 595; King Ferdinand of Spain 1476;

Formosus 1597; St Francis of Assisi 540,[2] 1168, 1495, 1497, 1501, 1503; Franciscus de Paola 1200; Fulvius[3] 615; Gehazi[5] 1074; *Genesis 26:14–18* 1096, *37:2* 589–90; St Germain of Auxerre[2] 507; St Guthlac of Crowland[2] 535; Ham 583, 1820; Henry of Ghent 1581; Henry VIII 2022; Hercules[1] 435; St Herman 1593; Hieoroboam[4] 1045; Hortensius[3] 616; Hyliscus[3] 617; Isaiah 595, 1344, 1637; *Isaiah 1:4* 1637–8, *1:12* (q.a.) 1640; *1:13–15* 1643–6, *29:13* 1344–5; Jambres[5] 1076; Jannes[5] 1076; Jeremiah 596, 1697; Jezebel[4] 1042; Job 1070; St John 1861, 1868, 1901; St John *Revelation 14:9–11* 609–10, *21:1* 1861–2, *21:2* 1868–9; Joseph (son of Jacob) 589; Judah 1223; Judas 523,[2] 1074;[5] Pope Julius II[3] 647; St Leger[2] 511; St Leonard of Limoges[2] 512; St Louis 1453; Martin Luther 1486; Mantuan 1050; Mantuan *De Suorum Temporum Calamitatibus* (*Opera III. f.154*) 1848–52; Petrus Mendoza 1477; Menelaus[5] 1078; King Minos 1027; Moses (aside from *Law of Moses*) 108, 117, 513,[2] 1104, 1244; Nabal[5] 1072; Nadab[5]1072; Nebuchadnezzar[4] 1045; Nero[3] 612; Nicholas de Orbelis[6] 1579; Nimrod[4] 1038; Noah 107, 583; Onan 587; St Paul 603, 853, 942, 1156, 1371, 1377, 1379, 1392, 1649, 1653, 1657; St Paul *I Corinthians 1:17* 1655–8, *4:15* 1369–72; St Paul *Hebrews 8:8–10* 942–3, *13:9* 1653; St Paul *Romans 1:22–7* 603–6; Bartolomeo Platina 1600; Reginald Pole 2005; Pontius[3] 617; *Psalm 31:9* (V)/*32:9* (AV) 592–4, *51:3* (V)/*52:2* (AV) 1769, *96:3* (V)/*97:3* (AV) 1844–5; Roboam[4] 1044; 'Sons of Samuel'[5] 1075; Sardinapalus[1] 435; Saul[4] 1042; Semiramus[3] 616; Simon Magus 1046,[4] 1833; Solomon 2001; Sophocles[3] 611; Pope Sylvester II 1603; Thalon[3] 611; Thamiras[3] 612; Johan Thessecclius (?) 1459; Tiberius[3] 613; Triphon[4] 1046; St Uncumber[2] 532; Venus 439; St Wilfrid of York[2] 520

1　Part of *Infidelity*'s list of men who donned women's clothing.
2　Part of *Idolatry*'s list of charms and relics associated (mostly) with saints.
3　Part of *Sodomy*'s list of lechers and sexual deviants.
4　Part of *Ambition*'s list of tyrants.
5　Part of *Avarice*'s list of covetous sinners.
6　Part of *Hypocrisy*'s list pagans and of proponents of Catholic corruption.

BIBLIOGRAPHY

Bevington, 1962, pp. 128–32
Blackburn, 1971, pp. 41–7
Blatt, 1968, pp. 65–86, 133–48
Broude, 1973, pp. 489–502
Epp, G. P. '"Into a Wommanys Lyckenes": Bale's Personification of Idolatry – A Response to Alan Stewart', *METh* 18 (1996) pp. 63–73
Happé, 1996, pp. 71–88
Harris, 1940, pp. 85–90
McCusker, 1942, pp. 73–85
Mackenzie, 1914, pp. 43–6
Mager, D. A. 'John Bale and Early Tudor Sodomy Discourse' in Goldberg, 1994, pp. 141–61
Schroeer, A. '*A Comedy Concernynge Thre Lawes* von Johan Bale', *Anglia* 5 (1882) pp. 232–64 (essay)
Sperk, 1973, pp. 73–104
Stewart, A. '"Ydolatricall Sodometrye": John Bale's Allegory', *METh* 15 (1993) pp. 3–20

94   The Tide Tarrieth No Man

DATE, AUTHORSHIP AND AUSPICES

printed 1576 (*SR* 22 Oct. 1576); George Wapull; offered for acting; Greg 70

TEXT AND EDITIONS

Extant originals

1576 printing by Hugh Jackson: BL; Cambridge (frag.); Eliz. Club; Folger; Huntington; Pforzheimer; *STC* 25018

Editions

1994   CHD (CD-Rom and online transcription of Jackson printing, l.l., OS)
1969   Schell and Schuchter (NS)
1913   Farmer (facsimile, n.l.)
1910   TFT (facsimile, n.l.)
1907   Rühl (OS)*
1863   Collier, vol. II (n.l., OS)

SOURCES

No sources have been identified.

CHARACTERS

Prologue	No Good Neighbourhood	Debtor
Courage, the Vice	Willing to Win Worship	Christianity
Hurtful Help	Tenant	Faithful Few
Painted Profit	Wilful Wanton	Despair
Feigned Furtherance	Wastefulness	Authority
Greediness, the Merchant	Sergeant	Correction

PLOT SUMMARY

The *Prologue* talks about the corrupt people in the commonwealth who spoil the whole, and more specifically about the greedy who oppress the poor. *Courage*, the Vice opens the play with a long speech listing dishonest types and declaring his intention to corrupt as many people as possible in the short time he has available. His friends, *Hurtful Help*, *Painted Profit* and *Feigned Furtherance* arrive and greet him. They fall to discussing and then quarrelling about who should be leader of their band until, by threatening them with violence, *Courage* assumes leadership. They also drop the negative aspects of their names, becoming *Help*, *Profit* and *Furtherance* respectively. After a song, the others go off, leaving *Courage* to give a nonsensical account of their doings. He is then joined by *Greediness*, a rich landlord who complains about a priest who has pricked his conscience about greed. *Courage* dismisses this, saying that life is too short to dispense with material comfort, an argument which *Greediness* accepts readily. He departs and *Help* now re-enters with *No Good Neighbourhood*, who has come to seek *Courage*'s advice since he covets a piece of land belonging to his neighbour, *Greediness*, but tenanted. *Courage* introduces him to *Furtherance* who reappears and who promises help. When *Neighbourhood* leaves with *Help*, *Furtherance* resolves to take bribes from both *Neighbourhood* and *Greediness*'s tenant, whom he is trying to displace. *Courage* is next approached by a courtier, *Willing to Win Worship*, who seeks honour and preferment. *Courage* encourages him to borrow money with which to effect his advancement and when *Help* and *Furtherance* return, he explains the predicament to them. *Help* points the courtier to *Furtherance*, as one who can help him, since he is a friend of a merchant who can lend money. *Willing to Win Worship* departs with *Help* and *Furtherance*, while *Courage* reflects on the way he promotes both aspirations in men and discord in marriage. *Courage* encounters *Greediness* again and enquires about a loan on behalf of the *Courtier*, to which he readily agrees. Asked about the matter of *No Good Neighbourhood* and the tenant, *Greediness* asserts he will have nothing to do with that, but discloses that he has been paid a substantial sum by *No Good Neighbourhood*. *Profit* comes in seeking *Wealthiness* (as whom *Courage* identifies *Greediness*) and says his master requests a visit from him. *Greediness* agrees and they go off. *Tenant* then reappears complaining that he has been thrust off his land by *Greediness*, and *Courage* rejoices at the evil brought about by his followers. A young woman, *Wantonness*, next enters expressing her frustration that her mother will not let her marry, and *Courage* agrees to help her. *Help* comes in to report that the *Courtier* is now hopelessly ensnared in debt, and soon afterwards *Profit* and *Furtherance* arrive revealing that they have received bribes from *Greediness*. When *Courage* then encourages them to theft, they all go off and the *Courtier* enters bewailing his ruin through debt. *Courage* returns and starts to beat him, afterwards claiming it is by mistake, and the courtier exits. *Greediness* now comes in briefly with *Help*, rejoicing in his gains through extortion and preying on his debtors. When he leaves, *Courage* demands his part of *Help*'s bribes and, on being refused, starts fighting with him. *Wastefulness*, the new husband of *Wantonness*, makes an appearance expressing pleasure in marriage, but this is cut short when his wife enters to complain of his spendthrift ways. They quarrel and she weeps, but they end up singing a song before departing revelling in their current youthful life. A *Sergeant* passes across the stage escorting to court a *Debtor* who has fallen victim to *Greediness* and, when they go off, *Christianity* appears preaching against the deceptiveness of wealth, but carrying a deformed sword and shield. He is approached by *Faithful Few*, who promises to arm him properly for his task. *Greediness* reappears, accompanied by *Courage* but not seeing *Christianity*, and he is rounded on by *Faithful Few* with *Christianity* joining in, until *Courage* leads him away. *Wastefulness* comes back, this time sorrowing and poorly dressed, followed by *Despair*, who encourages him to kill himself. However, *Faithful Few* rescues him and they pray together, whereupon *Despair* flees. When *Wastefulness*, having repented, goes off with *Faithful Few*, *Courage* comes in weeping and reporting that *Greediness*, prompted by *Despair*, has taken his own life and gone straight to hell. *Faithful Few* returns, accompanied by *Authority* and they accuse *Courage* of provocation to vice. When *Correction* appears he apprehends *Courage* who, despite resistance and a fight, is taken off. On *Christianity*'s return, his estate is reformed by turning around his title and his shield to reveal theological slogans.

PLAY LENGTH

1,879 lines, including a prologue of 56 lines

COMMENTARY

There is very much an economic and social orientation to this play though the issues are dressed up in moral terms, and it deals principally with social competition and the ambition that proceeds from it, a phenomenon commonly perceived as problematic in the period. While the 'reformation' of Christianity at the end of the play clearly makes reference to religious change, what is really involved is the assertion of Christian principles over economic corruption. The consequences of the Vices' actions are represented in essentially material terms. The discursive nature of the piece is underlined by a large number of soliloquies.

Other 'estates' plays: **29, 31, 85, 98**.
Other social ills plays: **2, 15, 24, 38, 40, 52, 53, 71, 72** (frag.), **76, 96, 98, 100**.
Other proverb plays: **24, 52, 53**.

SIGNIFICANT TOPICS AND NARRATIVE ELEMENTS

conflict between Vices; land envy; foreigners in the realm; economic and social aspiration; courtiers and court life; usury and debt (a merchant usurer); bad marriage; bribery; despair and suicide; crime and punishment

DRAMATURGICAL AND RHETORICAL FEATURES

Verbal and general *Courage* has a long self-introductory opening speech of short lines 1–158; aliases of the Vices: *Hurtful Help–Help* 179, *Painted Profit–Profit* 189, *Feigned Furtherance–Furtherance* 224, *No Good Neighbourhood–Neighbourhood* 446–7; *Greediness* has the alternative name *Wealthiness* 765; *Wastefulness* repeats *Faithful Few*'s prayer line by line 1702–9; stage directions in English; 'exiunt' is routinely used even for single departures

Costume and dress *Willing to Win Worship* enters (dressed) 'courtier like' 587 *sd*, and has attire that is 'costly and gay' 633; *Wastefulness* enters 'poorly (dressed)' 1660 *sd*; *Despair* enters 'in some ugly shape' 1681

Actions and stage directions 161 *sd*: '(*He.*) Salute *Cou.*'; 192 *sd*: '(*F. Fur.*) Feign a going out'; 200 *sd*: '(*Cou.*) Out quickly with his dagger'; 215 *sd*: 'And (*Cou., Fur.*) shake hands'; 587 *sd*: 'W. to W. Wor. enter courtier like'; 678 *sd*: '(*He.* speaks) Pointing to *Fur.*'; 697 *sd*: '(*Court.*) Speaking to *Cou.* and goes out with *Fur.* and *He.*'; 750 *sd*: '(*Gre.*) feign a going out'; 766 *sd*: '(*Cou.*) Speaking to *Gre.*'; 768 *sd*: '(*Cou.*) Turning to *Pro.*'; 793 *sd*: 'The *Ten.* tormented enters'; 993 *sd*: '*Pro.* and *Fur.* enter together'; 1069: *Cou.* pats *Pro.* on the back; 1120 *sd*: 'And (*Cou.*) smites the gentleman (*W. to W. Wor.*)'; 1138 *sd*: 'He. and Gre. enter together'; 1172 *sd*: '(*Gre.*) Feign a going out'; 1214 *sd*: 'And (*Cou., He.*) fight to prolong the time, while *Wan.* makes her[self] ready'; 1220 *sd*: 'Enter *Was.* the husband of *Wan.*'; 1305 *sd*: 'She (*Wan.*) weeps'; 1364 *sd*: '(*Was.*) Pause (in speech)'; 1392 *sd*: 'The *Serg.* and the *Deb.* [ar]rested enter'; 1439 *sd*: '*Chr.* must enter with a sword, with a title of policy, but on the other side of the title, must be written "God's Word", also a shield, whereon must be written "Riches", but on the other side of the shield must be "Faith"'; 1487 *sd*: 'He (*F. Few*) goes towards him (*Chr.*)'; 1501 *sd*: 'He (*F. Few*) turns the titles'; 1520 *sd*: '*Cou.* and *Gre.* enter as though they saw not *Chr.*'; 1660 *sd*: 'Enter *Was.* poorly [dressed]'; 1681 *sd*: '*Des.* enters in some ugly shape, and stands behind him (*Was.*)'; 1693 *sd*: '(*Was.*) Feign a going out. *F. Few* plucks him again'; 1700 *sd*: 'They both kneel, and *Was.* says after *Fai.*'; 1709 *sd*: '*Des.* flies, and they (*F. Few, Was.*) arise'; 1751 *sd*: 'Enter *Cou.* weeping'; 1760 *sd*: '(*Cou.*) reasoning with himself'; 1795 *sd*: '(*Cou.*) Feign to go out'; 1799 *sd*: '(*Cou.*) Still feign to go out'; 1820 *sd*: 'And (*Cor.*) begins to lay hands on him (*Cou.*)'; 1821 *sd*: 'They (*Cou., Cor.*) strive, he draws his dagger and fights'; 1822 *sd*: 'And (*Cor.*) catches him (*Cou.*)'; 1857 *sd*: '*Chr.* enter in as at the first'; 1871 *sd*: 'He (*F. Few*) turns the titles'; **Simple entry:** *Cou.* 56; *He. Pro. Fur.* 158; *Gre.* 340; *He., Nei.* 427; *Fur.* 519; *He., Fur.* 663; *Gre.* 725; *Pro.* 763; *Cou.* 835; *Wan.* 855; *He.* 967; *Court.* 1081; *Cou.* 1116; *Wan.* 1246; *F. Few* 1467; *Auth., F. Few* 1775; *Cor.* 1812; **Simple exit:** 'They three' (*He. Pro. Fur.*) 316; (*Gre.*) 421; (*He., Nei.*) 551; (*Gre., Pro.*) 789; (*Cou.*) 793; (*Wan.*) 951; (*He. Pro. Cou.*) 1081; (*Court.*) 1134; (*Gre.*) 1198; (*Cou., Wan.*) 1362; (*Was.*) 1392; 'They two' (*Deb., Serg.*) 1439; 'They two' (*Cou., Gre.*) 1620; (*Chr.*) 1636; (*Was.*) 1737; (*F. Few*) 1751; (*Cou.*) 1827

Songs and music (w.s. to all songs) 1. *Courage, Feigned Furtherance, Painted Profit, Hurtful Help* 'First Courage causes minds of men' (w. ref.) 291–311; 2. *Courage, Feigned Furtherance, Painted Profit, Hurtful Help* 'We have great gain, with little pain' (w. ref.) 1028–52; 3. *Wastefulness, Wantonness* 'Though Wastefulness and Wantonness some men have us two named' (w. ref.) 1337–58

Staging and set on the title page is a doubling scheme with the remark that 'Four persons may easily play it'– 1. the *Prologue, Hurtful Help*, the *Tenant, Faithful Few*; 2. *Painted Profit, No Good Neighbourhood*, the *Courtier* (*Willing to Win Worship*), *Wastefulness, Christianity, Correction*; 3. *Courage* the Vice, *Debtor*; 4. *Feigned Furtherance, Greediness* the Merchant, *Wantonness* the Woman, the *Sergeant, Authority, Despair*.

Courage and *Help* use stage business to give another character time to prepare (1214 *sd*); the action is unlocalized and there are no indications as to set

Stage properties *Courage*'s dagger 200 *sd*; *Christianity*'s sword, title of policy and shield 1439 *sd*

PLACENAMES

Paul's Cross 1175, 1177, 1400; Tyburn 1071, 1073

ALLUSIONS

St Ambrose 26; Antisthenes (q.n.t.) 1573–4; Aristotle 1591; St Augustine 23; 'Hyemes' (?) 415; Juvenal 1107, 1801; St Paul 1453, 1504; Paul *Romans 8:31* 1509; Periander 624, (q.n.t.) 626; Plato 1652; Plautus 616; Plautus, *Aulularia, 380–1* 618–19; Pythagoras 1584; St Sallust 394; Seneca 1654; Socrates 614, 1840

BIBLIOGRAPHY

Beckerman, B. 'Playing the Crowd: Structure and Soliloquy in *Tide Tarrieth No Man*' in Gray, 1984, pp. 128–37

Bevington, 1962, pp. 149–51

Mackenzie, 1914, pp. 187–95

Mann, 1991 pp. 23–5

Weimann, R. '"Moralize Two Meanings in One Play": Divided Authority on the Morality Stage', *Mediaevalia* 18 (1995 for 1992) pp. 426–50

95   Tom Tiler and his Wife

DATE, AUTHORSHIP AND AUSPICES

c. 1561; anonymous; performed by boys at court (Chapel?, Pauls?)

TEXT AND EDITIONS

Extant originals

1661 printing by Francis Kirkman, 'the second impression': BL; Bodleian; Eton; Folger; Glasgow; Harvard; Huntington; Illinois; Worcester; Yale (further copies extant); *STC* 13354

Editions

1994   CHD (CD-Rom and online transcription of Kirkman printing, n.l., OS)
1912   Farmer (n.l., OS)

1912   Farmer TFT (facsimile, l.l.)
1910   Moore Smith and Greg (facsimile)
1908   Farmer (11) (n.l., NS)
1906   Farmer (4) (n.l., NS)
1900   Schelling (OS)*

SOURCES

No sources have been identified.

CHARACTERS

Prologue	Tom Tiler, a labouring man	Tipple, an ale-wife
Desire, the Vice	Strife, Tom Tiler's wife	Tom Tayler, an artificer
Destiny, a sage parson	Sturdy, a gossip	Patience, a sage parson

PLOT SUMMARY

The *Prologue* tells of the play's being 'set out by pretty boys' and prays silence, after which *Destiny* and *Desire* start the action by discussing the bad marriage of *Tom Tiler*, whom they had helped to find a wife. When they leave, *Tiler* himself comes in singing a song about his marital woes and proceeds to describe his shrewish wife, *Strife*, who herself enters when he departs the stage. She affirms her dominance over him and is then joined by a gossip *Sturdy* and an ale-wife *Tipple*, who support her in her tyranny. On *Tiler's* return his wife beats him until he is forced to retire, and the women sing two songs while joking about *Tiler*. When they at length go off, *Tiler* returns to complain about the abuse he suffers, and is shortly joined by *Tom Tayler*, a friend who offers to impersonate *Tiler* and deal with his wife. They exchange clothing, *Tiler* withdraws and when *Strife* reappears *Tayler* gives her a sound beating until she finally has to take to her bed. *Tayler* subsequently reports the event to *Tiler* and they sing a song before exiting. *Sturdy* and *Tipple* then enter to comment on the turn of events and they are joined by a sorrowful *Strife* nursing her injuries. When the friends leave, *Tiler* approaches his now submissive wife and chastises her for her past behaviour, but foolishly confesses the trick of *Tayler's* impersonation to her. At this she revives and becomes so aggressive to *Tiler* that he retreats, and she is again joined by her friends who take up their earlier robust attitude, ending up with the women singing another song together about *Tiler*. On their departure, *Tiler* enters with *Tayler* and *Destiny*. *Tayler* says *Tiler* was destined to be beaten and strikes him a blow on the cheek, while *Destiny* says he should accept his lot and make the best of it. *Strife* enters to berate *Tiler* again, until *Patience* arrives to urge the couple to a more harmonious marriage. To end the play, *Patience* leads the others in a dance and they sing two final songs together.

PLAY LENGTH

875 lines, including final songs

COMMENTARY

This is one of the few plays in the interlude tradition to deal with the subject of marriage, and it is one of a number to portray a wife who is shrewish or has the upper hand in the marriage. The protagonists are clearly placed as members of the artisan class, and much of the action borders on farce. The Vice *Desire*'s role is not at all the classic one, and there seems little to distinguish him from *Destiny*, 'a sage parson' with whom he makes an entrance. He certainly has no direct interaction with any historical figure in the play. The piece is remarkable for the large number of songs that occur in it.

Other secular comedies: **5, 30, 41, 46, 47, 75, 88, 91, 92.**

Other plays featuring prominent women characters: **3, 6, 30, 32, 43, 46, 51, 63, 70, 75, 87, 97.**

Other marital strife plays: **46, 73** (frag.), **84.**

SIGNIFICANT TOPICS AND NARRATIVE ELEMENTS

female shrewishness; bad marriage and domestic violence; female friendship; male friendship; an ale-wife

DRAMATURGICAL AND RHETORICAL FEATURES

Verbal and general a popular song, 'John come kiss me' is possibly being referred to (but not sung) in 159; the large number of extensive songs suggest that the play was designed for choristers; stage directions in English, some printed in the margin
Costume and dress *Tom Tiler* has 'simple array' 63; *Tiler* and *Tayler* exchange garments (for disguise) 347–9
Actions and stage directions 62 *sd*: 'T. Ti. comes in singing'; 87 *sd*: 'The song ended, T. Ti. speaks'; 140 *sd*: 'Here enters Tip. with a pot in her hand, and a piece of bacon'; 186 *sd*: 'She (Str.) beats him (T. Ti.)'; 208 *sd*: 'Here they (Str., Tip., Stu.) sing'; 211 *sd*: 'Str. sing this staff'; 216 *sd*: 'Tip. sing this staff'; 222 *sd*: 'Stu. sing this staff'; 228 *sd*: 'Here they end singing, and Tip. speaks'; 244 *sd*: 'Here they (Str., Tip., Stu.) sing again'; 266 *sd*: 'Here they end singing, and Tip. speaks first'; 364 *sd*: 'Here T. Ti. goes in a while'; 379–90: T. Ta. beats Str.; 384–8: Str. kneels to ask forgiveness; 402 *sd*: 'He (T. Ta.) fires in'; 440 *sd*: 'Here they (T. Ti., T. Ta.) sing'; 443 *sd*: 'T. Ti. sings'; 447 *sd*: 'T. Ta. sings'; 451 *sd*: 'T. Ti. sings'; 455 *sd*: 'T. Ta. sings'; 459 *sd*: 'Here they (T. Ta., T. Ti.) end singing, and T. Ta. first speaks'; 493 *sd*: 'Enter Str. fair and softly, wailing and weeping'; 505: Str. lies down; 597–9: Str. strikes T. Ti.; 647 *sd*: 'Here they (Str., Tip., Stu.) sing'; 674 *sd*: 'Here they (Str., Tip., Stu.) end

singing'; 727 *sd*: 'He (*T. Ta.*) strikes him (*T. Ti.*) on the cheek'; 823–5: *Str.* kisses *T. Ti.*; 837 *sd*: 'Now all (*Des.*, *Str.*, *T. Ti.*, *T. Ta.*) speak together, except *Pat.*'; 840: a final dance led by *Patience*; 841 *sd*: 'Here they (*Pat.*, *Des.*, *Str.*, *T. Ti.*, *T. Ta.*) sing this song'; 857 *sd*: 'Here they all go in, and one comes out, and sings this song following all alone with instruments, and all the rest within sing every staff the first two lines'; **Simple entry**: *Dest.*, *Des.* 18; *Str.* 103; *Stu.* 123; *T. Ti.* 176; *T. Ti.* 272; *T. Ta.* 294; *Str.* 366; *Stu.*, *Tip.* 477; *T. Ti.* 516; *Stu.*, *Tip.* 614; *T. Ti.*, *T. Ta.*, *Des.* 697; *Str.* 765; *Pat.* 779; *Des.* 835; **Simple exit**: 'They both' (*Dest.*, *Des.*) 62; *T. Ti.* 103; *T. Ti.* 197; 'They all' (*Str.*, *Tip.*, *Stu.*) 272; *T. Ta.* 469; *T. Ti.* 477; *Stu.*, *Tip.* 516; *T. Ti.* 623; (*Str.*, *Tip.*, *Stu.*) *T. Ta.*, *T. Ti.* 697; *Des.* 769

Songs and music (w.s. to all songs) 1. *Tiler* 'I am poor Tiler in simple array' (w. ref.) 63–87; 2. *Strife*, *Sturdy*, *Tipple* 'As many as match themselves with shrews' (w. ref., parts apportioned among the women) 209–28; 3. *Strife*, *Sturdy*, *Tipple* 'Let us sip and let it slip' (w. ref.) 245–66; 4. *Tiler*, *Tayler* 'Tom might be merry, and well might fare' (2 part, w. ref., see stage directions) 441–59; 5. *Strife*, *Sturdy*, *Tipple* 'Tom Tiler was a trifler' (w. ref.) 648–74; 6. *Patience*, *Destiny*, *Tiler*, *Strife*, *Tayler* 'Patience entreateth good fellows all' 842–57; 7. One (unspecified) member of cast on stage, and rest off stage singing ref. 'Though pinching be a privy pain' (concluding song, w. ref.) 858–75 **Instrumental**: music for songs and dance with 'instruments' 857 *sd*
Staging and set the action is set in the single location of *Tom Tiler*'s house, which is likely to have been set up as a domestic interior, with a bed for *Strife* (505); several of the exit directions call for characters to 'go in'
Stage properties *Tipple*'s pewter pot and bacon 140 *sd*; a cudgel 354–5; a bandage for *Strife* 506

PLACENAMES

Dunmow 115, 717

ALLUSIONS

St John 421

REPORTS ON MODERN PRODUCTIONS

1. Magdalen College, Cambridge (PLS), dir. D. Parry, 23 April 1981 [*RORD* 24 (1981) pp. 194–5]
2. Bedford College London (PLS), dir. D. Parry, 7 May 1981 [*METh* 3:1 (1981) pp. 61–3]

BIBLIOGRAPHY

Greene, 1974, pp. 357–65

96   The Trial of Treasure

DATE, AUTHORSHIP AND AUSPICES

published 1567; anonymous, possibly by William Wager; offered for acting;
Greg 49

TEXT AND EDITIONS

Extant originals

1567 printing by Thomas Purfoote: BL (imp.); Bodleian (imp.); Huntington (imp.)
Pforzheimer; Rosenbach; *STC* 24271

Editions

1994	CHD (CD-Rom and online transcription of Purfoote printing, l.l., OS)
1914	Farmer (1914a) (facsimile, n.l.)
1908	TFT (facsimile, n.l.)
1906	Farmer (5) (n.l., NS)*
1874–6	Dodsley, vol. III (n.l., NS)
1850	Halliwell (n.l., OS)

SOURCES

No sources have been identified.

CHARACTERS

Preface	Sturdiness	Trust, a Woman	God's Visitation
Lust	Elation	Contentation	Time
Just	Greedy-gut	Treasure, a Woman	
Inclination, the Vice	Sapience	Pleasure	

PLOT SUMMARY

The *Preface* cites the story of Diogenes and Alexander to illustrate the vanity of
material pleasure, the subject of the play. *Lust* then opens the action singing and
embracing the pleasures of youth, but he is opposed by *Just*. They debate and
quarrel, *Lust* drawing his sword at first, but they end up wrestling and *Just* drives
him out before himself making an exit. *Inclination* enters with a self-declaratory
speech and he is followed by *Lust* and *Sturdiness*, singing. They attack *Inclination*
with a sword, but quickly come to an accord with him and *Lust* puts himself under
the guidance of *Inclination*, who counsels him to follow Epicurus. He promises
him companions, *Elation* and *Greedy-gut*, who duly come in singing. *Lust* develops

cramp suddenly, which *Inclination* explains as inspired by subjection to himself (i.e. forcing *Lust* to bow). *Lust* is inspired to greed and the Vices sing as they all depart. *Just* and *Sapience* then appear talking of their abjuration of material wealth, when they encounter *Inclination*. He attacks them, but they overcome him and tie him up. He is subsequently found by *Greedy-gut* and released by *Lust*, who tells him that he desires a lady called *Treasure*, and they go off to seek her in the house of Carnal Cogitation. *Just* enters with *Trust*, a soberly dressed woman, and *Contentation*, these latter two proceeding to sing a song. The three discuss the dangers of the snares of the world, citing historical precedent and eventually exit singing, apparently a hymn. *Inclination* reappears followed shortly after by *Lust* with *Lady Treasure*, richly apparelled, and they call for a drink. *Treasure*'s brother, *Pleasure*, arrives singing and promises them enjoyment, at which they all sing another song. *God's Visitation* suddenly comes in to ordain that *Pleasure* cannot remain with the ungodly, and leads him away. *Time* then enters to turn *Treasure* to rust, *Inclination* exits, and he is later brought in in shackles by *Just*. *Trust* and *Contentation* arrive to celebrate the victory of *Just* and when *Inclination* is led out grumbling, *Time* reappears with dust and rust to show what *Lust* and *Treasure* have turned into. The play ends with a moral exhortation addressed to all estates.

PLAY LENGTH

1,148 lines

COMMENTARY

The play has no one central mankind figure, but is constructed around the dichotomy of *Lust* and *Just*. This dominates the piece, which is made up more of demonstrative scenes than of any strong narrative development. There is a strong visual dimension, including physical conflicts and contrasts of dress, and the play also has abundant singing.

Other social ills plays: **2, 15, 24, 38, 40, 52, 53, 71, 72** (frag.), **76, 94, 98, 100**.

SIGNIFICANT TOPICS AND NARRATIVE ELEMENTS

philosophy and material life; bad companions; errant youth; age and decay; women and the power of sexual attraction; obligations of nobility and power; apparel and moral states; alcohol and drinking; wealth; the doctrine of election; Time as an emblematic figure

NOTE: no hard-copy line-numbered edition; all location references are page rather than line numbers

DRAMATURGICAL AND RHETORICAL FEATURES

Verbal and general there is a 'Preface' instead of a prologue; rustic speech: *Greedy-gut* 216 ff.; *Sapience*'s Skeltonic passage repeating 'sometime' 221; *Inclination*

speaks French and Dutch to try to trick his adversaries 221; *God's Visitation's* Skeltonic passage repeating 'sometime' 238; a final exhortation 'for all estates' 246; stage directions in English

Costume and dress *Lust* is dressed 'like a gallant' 207 *sd*; *Just* describes *Lust*'s dress as 'disguised and jagged, of sundry fashion' 208; *Trust* is 'plainly' dressed, but with a crown 227 *sd*; *Treasure* is 'finely apparelled 233 *sd*; *Lust* receives a 'gay' crown 243–4

Actions and stage directions 207 *sd*: 'Enter *Lu.*, like a gallant, singing this song'; 209 *sd*: '(*Lu.*) Draw out his sword'; 209 *sd*: '(*Lu.*) Put it (sword) up'; 210 *sd*: '(*Lu.*, *Ju.*) Wrestle and let *Lu.* seem to have the better at the first'; 210 *sd*: '(*Lu.*) Stay, and then speak'; 210 *sd*: '(*Ju.*) Cast him (*Lu.*) and let him rise again'; 210 *sd*: '(*Lu.*) Go out. He (*Ju.*) must drive him out'; 210 *sd*: '(*Ju.*) Pause (in speech)'; 212 *sd*: 'Enter *Lu.* and *Stu.*, singing this song'; 213 *sd*: '(*Stu.* speaks) Braggingly'; 213 *sd*: '(*Stu.*) Draw out the sword; make him put it up; and then strike him (*Inc.*). (*Inc.*) Look in your spectacles'; 215 *sd*: 'Enter *El.* and *Gr.-g.* They sing'; 217 *sd*: '(*Lu.*) Bow to the ground'; 217 *sd*: '(*Gr.-g.*) Gape, and the Vice (*Inc.*) gape'; 218 *sd*: 'They (*Lu.*, *Inc.*, *Gr.-g.*, *Stu.*) sing'; 221 *sd*: '(*Inc.*) Make as going back'; 222: *Inc.* threatens *Ju.* with his dagger; 222 *sd*: '(*Ju.*, *Sap.*, *Inc.*) Struggle two or three times'; 223 *sd*: '(*Ju.*, *Sap.*) Bridle him (*Inc.*)'; 223 *sd*: '(*Ju.*, *Sap.*) Bridle him (*Inc.*) shorter'; 224 *sd*: 'Enter *Gr.-g.* running, and catch a fall'; 226 *sd*: '(*Lu.*) Unbridle him (*Inc.*)'; 226 *sd*: '(*Inc.*) Whisper (in *Lu.*'s ear)'; 227 *sd*: 'Enter *Ju.*, *Tru.* and *Cont. Tru.*, a woman plainly [apparelled] and *Cont.* kneel down and sing, she have a crown'; 232 *sd*: 'Here if you will (*Tru.*, *Ju.*, *Cont.*) sing "The man is blest that feareth God" etc. Go out. Enter *Inc.* laughing'; 233 *sd*: 'Enter *Lu.* and *Tre.*, a woman finely apparelled'; 234 *sd*: 'Enter *Ple.*, singing this song'; 237 *sd*: '(*Lu.*, *Ple. Tre.*) Sing this song'; 239 *sd*: '(*Tre.* speaks) To *Vis.*'; 242 *sd*: 'Enter *Ju.*, leading *Inc.* in his bridle, shackled'; 243: *Inc.* struggles and *Ju.* tightens his rein; 243: *Ju.* receives a 'crown of felicity'; 244 *sd*: '(*Ju.*) Lead him (*Inc.*) out. Enter *Ti.*, with a similitude of dust and rust'; **Simple entry:** *Ju.* 208; *Inc.* 211; *Ju.*, *Sap.* 220; *Inc.* 221; *Lu.* 225; *G. Vis.* 238; *Ti.* 241; *Tru.*, *Cons.* 243; *Ju.* 244; **Simple exit:** (*Ju.*) 211; (*Lu.*, *Inc.*, *Gr.-g.*, *Stu.*) 220; 'Both' (*Ju.*, *Sap.*) 224; (*Lu.*, *Inc.*) 227; *G. Vis.*, *Ple.* 240; (*Inc.*) 241; (*Ti.*, *Tre.*, *Lu.*) 242

Songs and music (w.s. to all but one song): 1. *Lust* 'Heigho, care away, let the world pass' (4 lines inc. ref.) 207; 2. *Lust*, *Sturdiness* 'Where is the knave that did so rave' (8 lines, *Lust* sings last four lines alone) 212; 3. *Elation*, *Greedy-gut* 'With Lust to live is our delight' (4 lines) 215, 4. *Lust*, *Sturdiness*, *Greedy-gut*, *Inclination* (singing treble) 'Lust shall be led by Inclination' (14 lines, some lines sung alone by individual singers) 218–19; 5. *Trust*, *Contentation* 'So happy is the state of those' (12 lines) 227, 6. *Just*, *Trust*, *Contentation* 'The man is blest that feareth God' (w.n.s.) 232; 7. *Pleasure* 'O happy days and pleasant plays' (4 lines) 234, 8. *Lust*, *Pleasure*, *Treasure*, (poss. *Inclination*) 'Am I not in blessed case?' (24 lines including refrain) 237–8

Staging and set the characters on the title page are listed in a doubling scheme: 1. *Sturdiness*, *Contentation*, *Visitation*, *Time*; 2. *Lust*, *Sapience*, *Consolation*; 3. *the Preface*, *Just*, *Pleasure*, *Greedy-gut*; 4. *Elation*, *Trust*, *Treasure*; 5. *Inclination*. the action is unlocalized and there are no indications as to set, though significant use is made of stage properties.

Stage properties Lust's sword 209 *sd*; *Sturdiness*'s sword and *Inclination*'s spectacles 213 *sd*; *Inclination*'s dagger 222; a bridle for *Inclination* 223 *sd*; shackles for *Inclination* 242 *sd*; *Just*'s 'crown of felicity' 243; 'a similitude of dust and rust' (a model?) 244 *sd*

PLACENAMES

Athens 205; St Mary-le-Bow ('Bow-bell') 211; St Paul's 211; Salisbury Plain 211; Smithfield 210; Troy 221

ALLUSIONS

Adam 212; Adrastia 229; Aesop 216; Alexander the Great 205, 213, 230; Amphion 207; Antisthenes 205; Aristippus 220; Balaam 224; Caesar 230; Cain 212; Ceres 234; Cicero 209, 215 ('Tully'); Chronos 241; Circe 229; 'Cock Lorel's Barge' (poem) 207; Cressida 237; Croesus 216, 221, 228; Diana 234; Diogenes 205, 206; Dionysius 230; Epicurus 215; Eve 212; Felix 215; Galen 240; Goliath 213, 240; Haman 209; Hector 213; Helen of Troy 221, 234; Heliogabalus 230; Hercules 212; Hydra 211; St James 206; Juno 226, 234; Mars 226; Minerva 237; Morpheus 208; Musonus 220; Noah 211; Orpheus 207, 234; Pallas 226, 234; Paris 226; St Paul 215, 229; Pegasus 207; Prometheus 226; Pythagoras 206; 'Samies' (?) 216; Samson 210; Samson and Dalilah 212; Solomon 230; Solon 228; Tarquinius Superbus 230; Thales 235, 238; Venus 226, 234, 238; Vulcan 211, 242

BIBLIOGRAPHY

Bevington, 1962, pp. 153–5
Brown, 1999, pp. 127–34
Daw, E. B. 'Two Notes on *The Trial of Treasure*', *MP* 15:1 (1917) pp. 53–5
Greg, W. W. '*The Trial of Treasure*, 1567: A Study in Ghosts', *Library* 3rd series 1 (1910) pp. 28–35
Haller, 1916, pp. 129–33
Mackenzie, 1914, pp. 121–31
Oliver, L. 'William Wager and *The Trial of Treasure*', *HLQ* 9:4 (1946) pp. 419–29
Spinrad, 1987, pp. 93–8

97   Virtuous and Godly Susanna

DATE, AUTHORSHIP AND AUSPICES

1563–9 (*SR* 1568/9 *c*. Apr./May); Thomas Garter; offered for acting; Greg 76.5

TEXT AND EDITIONS

Extant originals

1578 printing by Hugh Jackson: Folger; *STC* 11632.5

Editions

1994   CHD (CD-Rom and online transcription of Jackson printing, l.l., OS)
1937   Evans and Greg (1937b) (facsimile)*
(forthcoming) M. Twycross, *Medieval English Theatre*, Modern Spelling Texts no. 5

SOURCES

The narrative is drawn from the scriptural account of Susanna and the elders in the *Book of Daniel 13* (V).

CHARACTERS

Prologue	Sensualitas	Ancilla	Helchia's Wife
Satan/Devil	Joachim	Servus	Gaoler/Bayly
Ill Report	Susanna	True Report	Iudex/Judge
Voluptas	Serva	Helchia	Daniel

PLOT SUMMARY

The *Prologue* summarizes the biblical story of Susanna and points out its exemplary nature. *Satan* commences the action by expressing frustration about a virtuous Babylonian woman he has been unable to corrupt, and he summons his son, the Vice *Ill Report*, instructing him to find a way to bring her down. *Ill Report* encounters two elders (also called judges) *Voluptas* and *Sensualitas* and, posing as a doctor, he undertakes to relieve their indisposition by procuring for them the sexual favours of *Susanna* in return for the sum of £5 each. He goes on his way and *Joachim*, *Susanna*'s pious husband, enters to meet the elders on judicial business. When *Susanna* later comes to call her husband for dinner, the elders are inflamed with lust at the sight of her. On *Ill Report*'s next appearance, they apprehend him to remind him of his undertaking and he assures them that he will fulfil his promises. After a brief further entry by *Joachim*, *Susanna* and two maids pass across the stage, one maid talking of what she has heard about life at court. *Sensualitas* and *Voluptas* come in and hide in an orchard, into which *Susanna* and her maids soon after come walking. The maids leave and the elders emerge to accost *Susanna*, but she rejects their advances. When servants arrive and break open the orchard door, the elders accuse *Susanna* of being a whore. They all go off leaving a servant distressed at his mistress's plight, but *True Report* appears and assures the servant that *Susanna* will be delivered from the unjust accusation, and the elders punished. *Joachim* and *Susanna*'s parents make successive appearances to decry the wickedness of the elders who have wrongfully accused her, after which *Ill Report* and the *Gaoler* come in followed by the judge, *Iudex*, the elders and *Susanna*. *Susanna* is tried, on the false allegation of the elders that she consorted with a young man, and found guilty. She is led off to execution but the spirit of *Daniel* then arises to condemn the injustice and the court is reconvened. *Susanna* is exonerated and the two elders condemned and led off to execution by stoning. After they are dead, *Ill Report* is also apprehended on *True Report*'s accusation and hanged. The *Devil* takes *Ill Report* to punishment in hell, while *Susanna* appears with her husband and parents to give thanks to God. The *Prologue* then closes the play by entreating the indulgence of the audience.

PLAY LENGTH

1,453 lines, including a prologue of 25 lines and epilogue of 10 lines

COMMENTARY

Described in its title as a 'comedy', this is one of a number of plays on virtuous women and it draws on a scriptural narrative. *Ill Report* exhibits the versatility often shown by the interlude Vice, in that he not only adopts the role of crier for the trial of *Susanna*, and takes part in the execution of the elders, but also intersperses the play with vigorous verses serving a variety of purposes. *Susanna*'s servants have a fairly prominent role at certain points, exceeding narrative necessity. The play is rather unusual in having no prescription for music or songs.

Other female virtue plays: **3, 6, 34, 63, 70, 87.**

Other plays featuring prominent women characters: **3, 6, 30, 32, 43, 46, 51, 63, 70, 75, 87, 95.**

SIGNIFICANT TOPICS AND NARRATIVE ELEMENTS

female chastity; slander and reputation; corrupt rulers/judges; lust; servant life; court life; a trial; punishment and execution

DRAMATURGICAL AND RHETORICAL FEATURES

Verbal and general *Voluptas*'s formal paean on *Susanna*'s beauty 409–20; the Vice enters to deliver a nonsense address to the audience without reference to the other characters on stage 461 (*sd*)–485; *Ill Report* gives a clue to his name with reference to three English towns 518; *Ill Report* and the *Bayly* simultaneously make their cries 958–76; a courtroom scene 941–1060, 1093–217; *Daniel* appears as a *deus ex machina* 1061–2 (*sd*)–1205; *Daniel* preaches to the audience 1118–33; *Ill Report* plays rhetorically on his name, including reference to figures of rhetoric

1308–47; *Ill Report* intersperses the action with verses, partly narrative, partly commentatory and partly comically nonsensical; stage directions in English
Costume and dress the elders wear 'garments sad and grave' 445; *Ill Report* refers to *Sensualitas*'s 'bloody' (scarlet) gown 529; the Vice dons one of the scarlet gowns of the executed elders 1253–4 (*sd*)
Actions and stage directions 51–2 (*sd*): 'Here the *Dev.* sits down in a chair and calls for *Ill R.*, who enters in'; 137–8 (*sd*): 'Here the *Dev.* goes out and *Evil R.* tarries still'; 186–7 (*sd*): 'Herewith comes in *Vol.*, and calls *Sen.* in this sort'; 236 (*sd*): 'Here he (*Ill R.*) offers to run out'; 247 (*sd*): 'Here he (*Vol.*) lets his purse fall'; 266 (*sd*): 'Here they (elders) go out and *Ill R.* speaks still'; 330–2 (*sd*): 'With that *Sen.* and *Vol.* sit down at a table turning of books, while *Joa.* kneeling on his knees says'; 352 (*sd*): 'With that she (maid) goes to him (*Joa.*) and makes curtsey'; 359–61 (*sd*): 'Note that from the entrance of *Sus.*, the Judges eyes shall never be off her, till her departure, whispering between themselves, as though they talked of her'; 364–5 (*sd*): 'With this *Joa.*, *Sus.* and her two maids go to the table to the elders'; 384–5 (*sd*): 'Here *Joachim*, *Sus.*, and her two maids depart, and the Judges make up their books and rise, and *Vol.* speaks'; 388 (*sd*): 'And so (elders) shut their books'; 461 (*sd*): 'The Vice enters and looks not at them (elders)'; 486 (*sd*): 'The Vice running out, is stayed by *Sen.*, who says'; 534: *Ill R.* shakes hands with the elders; 581 (*sd*): 'Here go out the Judges, and the Vice tarries still'; 594 (*sd*): '*Joa.* enters, and the Vice runs out'; 672–3 (*sd*): 'Here they (elders) go afore into the orchard, and *Sus.* and her two maids come upon the stage'; 692 (*sd*): 'Here they (*Sus.*, maids) go into the orchard'; 701 (*sd*): 'Here they (servants) go out and shut the orchard door'; 726–7 (*sd*): 'Here they (servants) go out and the two Judges that lie hidden talk in this wise'; 774–5 (*sd*): 'Here the two servants of the house run out, and break open the orchard door, and ask what is the matter, and then *Vol.* speaks'; 797 (*sd*): 'Here go out the two judges and *Sus.*, and says as she goes'; 802 (*sd*): 'They (*Sus.*, judges) be gone'; 814 *sd*: '*Ser.* kneel down'; 835 (*sd*): '*Joa.* enters looking about him'; 904–5 (*sd*): 'Here they (*Hel.*, *Wife*) go out and the Vice enters and says "in my best petticoat" etc. with a bell in his hand'; 910 *sd*: '(*Ill R.*) 'Ring bell'; 941–2 (*sd*): 'Here enter *Iud.*, *Sen.*, *Vol.* and *Sus.* and *Iud.* speaks'; 951 (*sd*): 'Here the *Ju.* sits down'; 956 (*sd*): 'Then *Ill R.* goes up (on stage)'; 977–8 (*sd*): 'Here shall the *Cri.*, the *Ba.*, and the rest go stand before the *Ju.* and tell him the cry is made'; 991 (*sd*): '*Vol.* shall seem to whisper in the other's ear'; 1013 *sd*: 'They (elders) kiss the book'; 1061–2 (*sd*): 'Here the *Ju.* rises, and *Sus.* is led to execution, and God raises the spirit of *Dan.*'; 1079–80 (*sd*): '*Sus.* for joy shall seem to sound (swoon), and the Vice shall call for vinegar and mustard to fetch her again, the *Ba.* shall say'; 1093 (*sd*): 'Here they return all back to judgement'; 1099–100 (*sd*): 'Here the *Cri.* goes up again, and makes an oyez, *Iud.* speaks'; 1117 (*sd*): '*Dan.* [speaks] to the people'; 1139 (*sd*): 'Here he (*Iud.*) takes aside *Vol.* and says'; 1216–17 (*sd*): 'Here goes out *Iud.* and *Dan.*, and *Ill R.* and the *Ba.* lead the two judges to execution'; 1223 (*sd*): 'Then he (*Ill R.*) brings them (elders) to the stake'; 1251–4 (*sd*): 'Here they stone them, and the Vice lets a stone fall on the *Ba.*'s foot, and fall together by the ears, and when the judges are dead, the Vice puts on

one of their gowns'; 1367–8 (*sd*): 'Here they struggle together, the *Gao.* casts the rope about *Ill R.*'s neck'; 1382–3 (*sd*): 'Here they have him (*Ill. R.*) to hanging, the *Dev.* enters saying "oh, oh, oh"'; **Simple entry**: *Sat.* 26; *Joa.* 285–6; *Judges* 295; *Sus.*, two maids 343; *Sus.*, two maids 611; *Sen.*, *Vol.* 646; *Hel.*, *Wife* 852–3; *Gao.* 927; *Ser. Tr. R.* 1265; *Joa.*, *Sus.*, *Hel.*, *Wife* 1404; *Prol.* 1443; **Simple exit**: *Prol.* 26; *Ill R.* 285; *Joa.* 611; (*Sus.*, two maids) 646; *Joa.* 852; *Dev.* 1404; *Joa.*, *Sus.*, *Hel.*, *Wife* 1443
Staging and set a doubling scheme on the title page arranges the characters for eight players: 1. the *Prologue* and *Gaoler*, 2. *Joachim* and *Iudex*, 3. *Satan* and *Voluptas*, 4. *Sensualitas* 5. *Susanna*, 6. *Helchia*, *True Report*, *Ancilla* 7. *Ill Report*, 8. *Helchia's Wife*, *Daniel*, *Servus*, *Serva*; a section of the stage is demarcated as the orchard, with an opening door (672–701), and the playing area may have been divided in two by a partition; the Vice goes up on to a raised stage at one point (956–7); there is a court scene which is fully staged (941–1060, 1093–217), and two scenes of execution with a stake (1251–4) and gallows (1366–7, 1382–3)
Stage properties a chair for the *Devil* 51 (*sd*); *Voluptas's* purse 247 (*sd*); a table, chairs and books for the elders 330–2 (*sd*); *Ill Report's* bell 905 (*sd*); a stake 1223 (*sd*); the stones for the elders' execution 1251 (*sd*); the rope for *Ill Report's* execution 1367 (*sd*)

PLACENAMES

Babylon 36, 78, 151; Baddingham Quay[1] 471; Canaan 1179; Daubeny[1] 462; Dover[1] 462; Dunington[1] 462; Faversham[1] 468; Framlington[1] 465; Freshingfield[1] 468; Ilford[2] 518; Kent[1] 462; London[1] 465; Ludham[1] 469; Nineveh 125; Norwich[1] 469; Oxford (university) 1351; St Paul's[1] 465; Portsmouth[2] 518; Reading[2] 518; Rome[1] 485; Romney[1] 485; Shooter's Hill[1] 477

1 Part of *Ill Report's* nonsense verse.
2 Part of *Ill Report's* riddling identification of his name.

ALLUSIONS

Bacchus 549; Cain and Abel 123; Ceres 549; Cicero ('Tully') 3; Cupid 391, 730; Eve 121; Jonah 125; Pluto 1129; Tobias 890–3; Venus 389, 549

REPORTS ON MODERN PRODUCTION

University of Lancaster 29 April–1 May, Rufford Old Hall, Burscough, 10 May, Perpignan 10 July 1986 (JL), dir. M. Twycross [*METh* 8:1 (1986) pp. 67–71; *RORD* 29 (1986–7) pp. 110–11; *CE* 30 (1986) pp. 101–3]

BIBLIOGRAPHY

Blackburn, 1971, pp. 136–42
Happé, P. 'Aspects of Dramatic Technique in Thomas Garter's "Susanna"', *METh* 8.1 (1986) pp. 61–3

Herrick, M. T. 'Susanna and the elders in Sixteenth Century Drama' in Allen, 1958, pp. 125–35

Horner, O. 'Susanna's Double Life', *METh* 8:2 (1986) pp. 76–102

Hunter, 1965, pp. 49–52

Kerr, H. 'Thomas Garter's *Susanna*: "Policie" and "True Report"', *AULLA* 72 (1989) pp. 183–202

Pasachoff, 1975, pp. 142–53

Pilger, R. 'Die Dramatisierung der Susanna im 16 Jahrhundert', *ZDP* 11 (1889) pp. 129–217

Roston, 1968, pp. 87–100

Sexton, J. H. 'The Theme of Slander in *Much Ado about Nothing* and Garter's *Susanna*', *PQ* 54:2 (1975) pp. 419–33

98   Wealth and Health

DATE, AUTHORSHIP AND AUSPICES

1553–5 (*SR* 1557 *c*. Aug. Sep.); anonymous; offered for acting and possibly performed at court; Greg 27

TEXT AND EDITIONS

Extant originals

1565 (?) printing by William Copland for John Waley: BL (two copies); *STC* 14110

Editions

1994   CHD (CD-Rom and online transcription of Copland printing, l.l., OS)
1914   Farmer (1914a) (facsimile, n.l.)
1908   Holthausen (l.l., OS)*
1907   Farmer (9) (n.l., NS)
1907   Greg and Simpson (facsimile)*
1907   TFT (facsimile, n.l.)
1907   *'Lost' Tudor Plays* (facsimile, n.l.)

SOURCES

No sources have been identified.

CHARACTERS

Wealth   Health   Liberty   Ill Will   Shrewd Wit   Hance   Remedy

PLOT SUMMARY

Wealth and *Health* debate vigorously about which of the two is more important, though the thrust of the discussion is really about the advantages and problems associated with wealth. *Liberty* enters and insists on his own importance over both of them, and they at this stage not only incline to be reconciled to each other, but recognize his value as well. *Ill Will*, the Vice, now makes his appearance, calling himself *Will* and claiming kinship with *Liberty*. *Liberty* and the others welcome him before departing, at which point he reveals (to the audience) his intention to deceive them. He is joined by his friend *Shrewd Wit*, a pickpocket, and they spy a drunken Fleming, *Hance*, with whom they engage in a scarcely comprehensible exchange of words before he goes on his way. On the reappearance of *Health* and *Wealth* the Vices now enter their service, and are entrusted with the care of their household. When *Ill Will* and *Shrewd Wit* (now calling himself *Wit*) depart, *Good Remedy* comes in and warns *Wealth* and *Health* about their new stewards, saying that they are harmful to the realm. He agrees to help them and talks of the well-being of the commonwealth. They leave and the Vices return to be confronted by *Good Remedy* declaring that he intends to deal with them. On his departure, *Wealth* and *Health* arrive and ask their stewards how their household is doing, only to be told that revelry and mayhem rule. They react angrily at first, especially since they remember the admonition of *Good Remedy*, but are soon pacified by the Vices and reconciled to them. They all go out and *Good Remedy* appears again in search of *Wealth*, *Health* and *Liberty*. He comes upon *Hance*, whom he reproves as a foreigner for dissipating England's wealth. *Hance* goes on his way and *Health* enters with a kerchief on his head. He is unwell and reports that *Wealth* is in decay and *Liberty* in captivity, all the consequence of their bad servingmen's actions. *Health* and *Good Remedy* then confront *Ill Will* and *Shrewd Wit* and send them to prison, after which *Good Remedy* restores their masters to health, wealth and liberty respectively. He finally closes the play with a prayer for Queen Elizabeth and her government.

PLAY LENGTH

964 lines

COMMENTARY

This play articulates concerns both about the management of wealth and about foreign workers in the realm. Xenophobia is suggested not only by the portrayal of the drunken Fleming *Hance* (whose appearance is entirely incidental to the narrative) but also possibly by *Shrewd Wit*'s French greeting on his first entry, and *Ill Will*'s adoption of a form of mangled Spanish when confronted by *Good Remedy* and *Health*. Concern about the dangers of bad servingmen was a recurrent theme in the period, and the good-natured naïveté of the virtuous figures contrasts with the cunning malevolence of the servingmen.

Other 'estates' plays: **29, 31, 85, 94.**

Other social ills plays: **2, 15, 24, 38, 40, 52, 53, 71, 72** (frag.), **76, 94, 96, 100.**

SIGNIFICANT TOPICS AND NARRATIVE ELEMENTS

wealth, its value and pitfalls; drunken Flemings; foreigners in the realm; wealth and estates of the realm; bad servingmen; crime; the management of wealth and property

DRAMATURGICAL AND RHETORICAL FEATURES

Verbal and general Shrewd Wit's first entry is with a French greeting 350; the Vices' aliases: Ill Will–Will 284, 657, Shrewd Wit–Wit 481, 657; Hance's partly Flemish speech 390 ff.; Ill Will's mangled Spanish 845–52; stage directions in English
Costume and dress Health's kerchief on his head to signify ill health 781 (sd); Remedy apparently wears a rich gown 625–7; Remedy evidently wears a red cap 834
Actions and stage directions op. sd: 'Here enter We. and He., singing together a ballad of two parts, and after speaks We.'; 196 (sd); 'Here enters Li. with a song, and afterwards speaks'; 281 (sd): 'Here enters with some jest Ill W.'; 349 (sd): 'Enters Shr. W. with a song'; 389 (sd): 'Enters Han. with a Dutch song'; 466 (sd): 'Li. and He. return back with We.'; 519 (sd): 'They (Ill W., Shr. W.) sing'; 528 (sd): 'Here comes Rem. in and to him says (We.)'; 613 (sd): 'Will returns'; 681 (sd): 'He. turns him[self]'; 690 (sd): 'Li. turns him[self]'; 781 (sd): 'He. comes in with a kercher on his head'; 821 sd: 'Will turns'; **Simple exit:** (Li.) 326; We., He. 330; (Han.) 429; (Ill W., Shr. W.) 520; (He.) 610; (Rem.) 663; (He.) 737; (Han.) 778; (Shr. W.) 891; (Ill. W.) 894
Songs and music (w.n.s. to any songs) 1. Wealth, Health 'a ballad of two parts' op. sd, 2. Liberty 196 (sd), 3. Shrewd Wit 349 (sd), 4. Hance 389 (sd), 5. Ill Will, Shrewd Wit 519 (sd)
Staging and set the title page contains the direction: 'Four may easily play this play', though no doubling scheme is offered, and at least five are actually needed; the action is unlocalized and there are no indications as to set
Stage properties Shrewd Wit's groats 354

PLACENAMES

England 395 ('Angliter'), 545, 549, 773; Flanders 424, 426; St Katherine's (hospital in London) 428, 753, 775

BIBLIOGRAPHY

Craik, 1953, pp. 98–108
Greg, W. W., W. Bang and L. Brandon, 'Notes on the Society's Publications', MSC 1:1 (1907) pp. 3–15
Holthausen, F. 'Zum älteren englischen Drama: Wealth and Health', Beiblatt zur Anglia 29 (1918) pp. 369–72
Hunter, M. 'Notes on the Interlude of Wealth and Health', MLR 3:4 (1907) pp. 366–9
Pineas, R. 'The Revision of Wealth and Health', PQ 44:4 (1965) pp. 560–2
Swaen, A. E. 'Wealth and Health', EngS 41 (1910) p. 456

99   (Play of the) Weather

DATE, AUTHORSHIP AND AUSPICES

1527–33; John Heywood; performed by boys at court; Greg 15

TEXT AND EDITIONS

Extant originals

1533 printing by William Rastell: Pepys; St John's, Oxford (imp.); *STC* 13305
1544 (?) printing by William Middleton: Cambridge (imp.); *STC* 13305.5
c. 1560 (?) printing by John Tisdale for Anthony Kitson: Bodleian; *STC* 13306
c. 1573 printing by John Awdley: BL; *STC* 13307

Editions

2000 Walker (OS)*
1994 CHD (CD-Rom and online transcription of Rastell printing, l.l., OS)
1991 Axton and Happé (OS)*
1987 Robinson (OS)*
1977 Lennam (facsimile of Rastell printing)
1975 Bevington (OS)*
1972 Happé (OS)
1924 Adams (OS)*
1914 Farmer (1914a) (two: facsimiles of Rastell and Awdeley printings, n.l.)
1909 TFT (facsimile of Rastell printing, n.l.)
1908 TFT (facsimile of Awdeley printing, n.l.)
1905 Farmer (1) (n.l., NS)
1903 A. W. Pollard in Gayley, vol. 1 (OS)
1898 Brandl (OS)

SOURCES

No single source has been clearly identified, but see the introduction to the edition by Axton and Happé, pp. 47–50; see also Cameron, 1941, pp. 9–27 and Holthausen's essay (both listed below).

CHARACTERS

Jupiter	Merchant	Wind Miller	Boy
Merry Report (the Vice)	Ranger	Gentlewoman	
Gentleman	Water Miller	Launder	

PLOT SUMMARY

Jupiter declares that there is discord among those of his gods and goddesses responsible for the weather: Saturn (cold and frost), Phebus (sun), Eolus (wind) and Phebe (rain). To resolve this they have asked *Jupiter* to ordain what weather is acceptable, and he in turn expresses the wish to assemble a range of people to help him decide on this. He calls for a messenger and *Merry Report* appears, claiming to be a gentleman, though he looks like a jester. Despite the doubts about his appearance, he persuades *Jupiter* of his suitability for the task because of his indifference to the weather. *Merry Report* first summons a *Gentleman* (entering blowing a horn) who pleads for dry, calm weather for hunting, which is necessary for the health and preservation of the 'heads of the commonwealth'. A *Merchant* is next admitted who asks for moderate winds suitable for travel and the pursuit of trade, through which the wealth of the nation will be enhanced. A *Ranger* (estate keeper) then requests to speak to *Jupiter*, but *Merry Report* says he will carry the message. The *Ranger* asks for wild, windy and thundery weather to stir up game. A *Water Miller* appears now to ask for rain to fill the rivers, but no wind. *Merry Report* takes issue with him for his familiarity of tone, at which he apologizes, explaining that he took the messenger for a person of his own rank. They are joined by a *Wind Miller* who requests wind but no rain. The two millers debate their positions vigorously before *Merry Report* intervenes, revealing that his wife owns a mill of each sort, before dismissing them. A *Gentlewoman* now enters but *Merry Report* says that *Jupiter* is busy making a new moon, and he receives her suit himself, which is for close, temperate weather that will not spoil her complexion. She describes her idle life, full of dancing and singing, and she and *Merry Report* end up singing a song together. She is followed by a *Launder* (laundry woman) who contrasts her more arduous life with that of the *Gentlewoman*, asking for sunshine to dry her clothes. She and *Merry Report* engage in banter, which includes passages of proverbial word play, before she departs. The final suit is from a *Boy* who requests snow to make snowballs. *Merry Report* then sums up the petitions and *Jupiter* sends him to summon all the suitors to appear. He announces that to be fair to everyone there will be all kinds of weather, a decision applauded by all.

PLAY LENGTH

1,254 lines

COMMENTARY

Though not fully an 'estates' play, this introduces a range of social types, including a child. There are two women, one working and neither defined in sexual terms, though there is considerable sexual innuendo and the *Gentlewoman* is the object of *Merry Report*'s libidinous attentions. It is notable that only the

two most socially elevated males actually gain access to *Jupiter* to present their suit.
Other debate plays: **28, 29, 31, 54, 69, 102**.

SIGNIFICANT TOPICS AND NARRATIVE ELEMENTS

apparel, hunting, trades, the benefits and disbenefits of various types of weather; sexual dalliance, cuckoldry; rank and courtesy

DRAMATURGICAL AND RHETORICAL FEATURES

Verbal and general *Jupiter* appears to wish to recruit a messenger from the audience 94–7; *Merry Report* exits through the audience 176–8; *Merry Report's* alliterative list of place names 198–211; *Merry Report* and the *Launder* engage in an alliterative verbal contest 960–9; *Merry Report* makes a proclamation 1057–64; the messenger figure controls the action; stage directions in English
Costume and dress *Merry Report* wears 'light' (frivolous) array 110, possibly of 'frise' (coarse woollen cloth) and feathers 134
Actions and stage directions 178 *sd*: 'M. Rep. goes out. At the end of this staff the god has a song played in his throne before *M. Rep.* comes in'; 215 *sd*: 'Here the *G/man.* before he comes in he blows his horn'; 249 *sd*: 'Here he (*M. Rep.*) points to the women'; 321: the *G/man.* shakes *M. Rep.*'s hand; 853 *sd*: 'Here they (*M. Rep., G/wom.*) sing'; 1001 *sd*: 'The *Boy* comes in, the least (smallest) that can play'; 1252–4: a song is sung as *Jup.* ascends his throne at the end; **Simple entry:** *M. Rep.* 97; *M. Rep.* 185; *Merc.* 328; *Ran.* 399; *Wat.* M. 441; *Win.* M. 505; *M. Rep.* 709; *G/wom.* 765; *Lau.* 867; *M. Rep.*, all suitors 1138; **Simple exit:** *Merc.* 395; *Ran.* 441; *M. Rep.* 551; 'Both millers' 761; *G/wom.* 954; *Boy* 1049; *M. Rep.* 1131
Songs and music (w.n.s. to any song) 1. singers unnamed (poss. instrumental only) 178 *sd*, 2. *Merry Report, Gentlewoman* 853 *sd*, 3. Final song (whole cast?) 1252
Staging and set there is a throne for *Jupiter*, possibly a mobile one (178 *sd*) but no other indications as to set; either most of the dialogue takes place at a remove from *Jupiter's* throne, or he may be present on stage only in the scenes that involve him; the list of characters stipulates the smallest actor who can play (for the *Boy*)
Stage properties an attendant's torch 98; the *Gentleman's* horn 215 *sd*

PLACENAMES

Baldock 199; Barfold 199; Berwick 209; Boston 209; Bristol 209; Butsbury 211; Canterbury 200; Chios ('Syo')[1] 385–6, 389; Colchester 200; Coventry 200; Faleborne 202; Fenlow 202; Fulham 202; Glastonbury 210; Gloucester 205; Gotham 205; Gravelines 210; Gravesend 210; Guildford 205; Harrow-on-the-Hill 206; Harwich

206; Hertford (or Hartford End) 206; Lombardy 198; London 198; Louvain 198; North Africa ('Barbary') 199; Shooters Hill 207; Southampton 207; Sudbury 207; Taunton 204; Tiptree 204; Tottenham 204; Wakefield 203; Wallingford 203; Walsingham 208; Walthamstow 203; Wandsworth 201; Warwick 208; Welbeck 201; Westchester 201; Witham 208

1 All form part of *Merry Report*'s alliterative list of place names, except.

ALLUSIONS

Noah 805

REPORT ON MODERN PRODUCTION

University of Missouri, dir. P. Williams, 30 April and 3 May 1980 [*RORD* 23 (1980) pp. 87–8]

RECORDED PRODUCTION

LP Record: BBC, *The First Stage*, dir. J. Barton (1970)

BIBLIOGRAPHY

Adams, J. Q. 'Heywood's *Play of the Weather*', *MLN* 22:8 (1907) p. 262
Axton, R. 'Royal Throne, Royal Bed: John Heywood and Spectacle', *METh* 16 (1994) pp. 66–76
Bevington, D. M. 'Is John Heywood's *Play of the Weather* Really About the Weather?', *RenD* 7 (1964) pp. 11–19
Bevington, 1968, pp. 64–70
Bolwell, 1921, pp. 95–101
Cameron, 1941c
Canzler, D. G. 'Quarto Editions of *Play of the Wether*', *PBSA* 62:3 (1968) pp. 313–19
De la Bère, 1937, pp. 61–8
Forest-Hill, L. 'Lucian's Satire of Philosophers in Heywood's *Play of the Wether*', *METh* 18 (1996) pp. 142–60
Forest-Hill, 2000, pp. 136–64
Greg, W. W. 'The *Play of the Weather*: An Alleged Edition by Robert Wyer' ('Notes on Some Early Plays'), *Library* 4th series 11 (1930) pp. 50–3
Happé, 1999, pp. 239–46
Hogrefe, 1959, pp. 305–9
Holthausen, F. 'Zu John Heywood's *Wetterspiel*', *Archiv* 116 (1906) pp. 103–4
Johnson, 1970, pp. 81–7
Lanahan, W. F. 'John Heywood's *The Play of the Wether*: Creative Innovation in the Tudor Interlude', *Nassau Review* 3:1 (1975) pp. 72–9
Lancashire, I. 'Robert Wyer's alleged Edition of Heywood's *Play of the Weather*: The Source of the Error', *Library* 5th series 29:4 (1974) pp. 441–6
Lines, 2000, pp. 421–30
Walker, 1991, pp. 133–68

Whall, 1988, pp. 34–59
Yamakawa, T. 'The Boy Dick and *The Play of the Wether*', *ELR (Kyoto)* 18 (1974) pp. 55–63 (in Japanese)
Yamakawa, T. 'The Elements of Water and Wind in *The Play of the Wether*', *Letters and Essays* (Kyoto) 16 (1973) pp. 32–8 (in Japanese)
Yamakawa, T. '*The Play of the Wether* as a Comedy', *ELR (Kyoto)* 16 (1972) pp. 33–53 (in Japanese)

100   Wisdom, Who is Christ (Mind, Will and Understanding)

DATE, AUTHORSHIP AND AUSPICES

1460–70; anonymous; an East Anglian play, but auspices unknown

TEXT AND EDITIONS

Extant originals

Manuscripts: Folger Shakespeare Library MS Macro V.a.354, fos. 14–37; Bodleian Library MS Digby 133, fos. 158–69 (frag.)

Editions

2000   Walker (OS)
1998   Riggio (OS/NS – parallel texts)
1994   CHD (CD-Rom and online copy of Eccles, 1969, l.l., s.l., OS)
1993   Coldewey (OS)*
1982   Baker, Murphy and Hall (Digby fragment, OS)
1976   Baker, Murphy and Hall (Digby fragment, facsimile, n.l.)
1972   Bevington (facsimile with transcription)*
1969   Eccles (OS)*
1926   Tickner (Digby fragment) (n.l., NS)
1907   TFT (facsimile, n.l.)
1904   Furnivall and Pollard (OS)
1896   Furnivall, reissued 1967 (Digby fragment, OS)
1837   Collier and Turnbull (a printing of the section of the Macro version com-
          plementing Digby fragment, line 753 onwards, OS)
1835   Sharp (Digby fragment, OS)

SOURCES

The play draws on various devotional texts; see Smart's essay below.

CHARACTERS

Wisdom   Anima (the Soul)   Mind   Will   Understanding   Lucifer
Mute: Five Wits; A Shrewd Boy; Six Dancers with Mind (seven named) – Indignation,
Sturdiness (Stubborness), Malice, Hastiness, Wreche (Vengeance), Discord,
Maintenance (Unjust Support in Law); Six Dancers with Understanding – Wrong,
Sleight (Trickery), Doubleness, Falseness, Ravine (Robbery), Deceit; Six Dancers
with Will (seven named) – Recklessness, Idleness, Surfeit, Greediness,
Spousebreach (Adultery), Mistress, Fornication; seven small boys as devils

PLOT SUMMARY

Wisdom and the *Soul* enter with speeches of self-identification after which *Wisdom*
introduces the *Soul* to the Five Wits, who appear as virgins, and he brings in *Mind*,
Will and *Understanding*, whom he invites to give an account of themselves. They
each describe themselves as parts of the *Soul* instrumental in the understanding and
love of God. *Wisdom* exhorts the *Soul* to keep these three uncorrupted, and warns
against the threats posed by the World, the Flesh and the Devil. They all then exit
processionally, the Five Wits singing. *Lucifer* now enters expressing his discontent at
being cast down from heaven, and he plots the downfall of the *Soul*. He then goes out
and comes in again dressed as a gallant, and approaches *Mind*, *Understanding* and
Will, who are engaged in religious contemplation. *Lucifer* decries the contemplative
life on the grounds of its rigour, and argues instead for material enrichment. They
quickly succumb to his persuasion and decide to embrace worldly ways, at which
he sends them off to change their dress. After expressing his satisfaction, *Lucifer*
exits carrying off a naughty *Boy*. The components of the *Soul* soon re-enter with
new apparel and describe their new life of pride, covetousness, lechery, material
self-advancement and judicial and financial corruption. Each then introduces a
troupe of six dancers, composed of named Vices, *Mind's* with crests, *Understanding's*
as jurors and *Will's* as gallants and matrons. (Here the Digby fragment ends.) After
the dances, they fall to quarrelling and fighting, but then come to agreement
again to plan their future. *Understanding* announces that he will pursue his career
at Westminster, *Mind* that he will practise in St Paul's, and *Will* that he will resort
to the stews. They vow to spend their lives in ease and self-indulgence, and at
length all go off together to drink. *Wisdom* then enters and confronts them, also
bringing in the *Soul*, who is now in a disfigured state, with devils running in and
out from under her cloak. This, *Wisdom* points out, is the result of their fall into
sin. *Mind*, *Understanding* and *Will* are horrified by this and immediately resolve
to convert and forsake their reprobate ways. The *Soul* bewails her state and calls
for mercy, at which point the devils retreat. The *Soul* expresses her contrition in
song as she goes off, and *Wisdom* preaches a sermon on nine points essential to
a Christian life. The *Soul* then re-enters processionally with *Mind*, *Understanding*,
Will and the Five Wits, with further expressions of repentance, while *Wisdom's*
account of his sufferings reveal him to be Christ. *Mind*, *Understanding* and *Will*

respectively announce the *Soul's* renunciation of worldly pomp, reformation of reason and acquisition of charity and the *Soul* ends the play by joyfully embracing *Wisdom* as Christ.

PLAY LENGTH

1,163 lines (Digby fragment 752 lines extant)

COMMENTARY

Though this is not a particularly dramatic play, it is a very visual one, with processions, dancing and spectacular dress. Changes in moral states are signalled visually, and the appearance of the visibly degraded *Soul* as beset by devils is a striking image of chaos and decay. This play is possibly the most important example of the atomization of the human moral psyche, which is a tendency found especially in the early interludes. In fact the *Soul* is a nominal figure who takes little part in the action. Rather than being Vices, *Mind, Will* and *Understanding* are legitimate aspects of the psyche which become corrupted, the Vices being confined to the troupes of dancers and having no significant part in the action. Social referents are realized, not through the progress of a humanity figure as such, but by the tendency of the different aspects of the moral mind to embrace different varieties of sin.

Other social ills plays: **2, 15, 24, 38, 40, 52, 53, 71, 72** (frag.), **76, 94, 96, 98**.

SIGNIFICANT TOPICS AND NARRATIVE ELEMENTS

the infernal trinity: World, Flesh and Devil; the Devil's grudge; monastic life; France and lechery; sexual dalliance; social climbing; judicial corruption; demonic possession, Christian life

DRAMATURGICAL AND RHETORICAL FEATURES

Verbal and general *Understanding* uses a French expression 511; each of *Mind's* dancers answers for his name in the dance 692 *sd*; a named dance: 'Madam Regent' is performed 707; *Wisdom's* sermon 997–1064; substantial stage directions in English and some briefer ones in Latin

Costume and dress *Wisdom* wears purple and gold cloth, furred mantle, wig and crown, op. *sd*; *Anima* has a white cloth bordered with fur, a black mantle and a rich headdress with gold tassels 16 *sd*; the five virgins have white kirtles and mantles, wigs and headdresses, *Mind, Will* and *Understanding* are dressed identically in white and gold 324 *sd*; *Lucifer* has devil's dress over gallant's clothing 324 *sd* (2); *Lucifer* is disguised as a gallant 380 *sd*; *Mind, Will* and *Understanding* enter in 'new array' after their fall 551, 558, 566; *Mind* is devoted to 'curious' (elaborate) dress 609; *Mind's* dancers are dressed in his livery, with red lions rampant 692 *sd*; *Understanding*'s dancers are dressed as jurors in livery, gowned, with hoods, retainers' hats, and visors 724 *sd*; three of *Will*'s dancers are disguised as gallants and three as matrons with appropriate visors 752 *sd*; *Anima* appears in foul dress 902 *sd*; the *Soul*, Five Wits, *Mind, Understanding, Will* enter in their original dress, headdresses and crests, and with crowns 1064 *sd*

Actions and stage directions op. *sd*: 'First entered *Wis.* in a rich purple cloth of gold with a mantle of the same ermined within, having about his neck a splendid hood furred with ermine, upon his head a chevelure (wig) with brows, a beard of gold of curled gold cloth, a rich imperial crown thereupon set with precious stones and pearls, in his left hand a ball of gold with a cross thereupon and in his right hand a regal sceptre, thus saying'; 16 *sd*: 'Here enters *An.* as a maid, in white cloth of gold handsomely bordered with miniver, a mantle of black thereupon, a wig like *Wis.*'s, with a rich chapelet (headdress) laced behind hanging down with two knots of gold and side tassels, kneeling down to *Wis.*, thus saying'; 164 *sd*: 'Here entered five virgins in white kirtles and mantles, with chevelures and chapelets and sing "Nigra sum sed formosa, filia Jerusalem, sicut tabernacula cedar et sicut pelles Salamonis"'; 324 *sd*: 'Here in the going out the Five Wits sing "Tota pulcra es" et cetera, they going before, *An.* next, and her following *Wis.*, and after him *Mi., Wi.* and *Und.*, all three in a white cloth of gold, chevelured and crested, in suit (identical dress)'; 324 *sd* (2): 'And after the song enters *Luc.* in a devil's array without and within as a proud gallant, saying thus in this wise'; 380 *sd*: 'Here *Luc.* devoids (exits) and comes in again as a goodly gallant'; 518 *sd*: 'They (*Mi., Wi., Und.*) go out' (L); 550 *sd*: 'Here he (*Luc.*) takes a shrewd boy with him and goes his way crying'; 620 sd: 'And they (*Mi., Wi., Und.*) sing' (L); 692 *sd*: 'Here enter six disguised in the suit (livery) of *Mi.* with red beards, and lions rampant on their crests, and each a warder (staff) in his hand, here minstrels, trumpets. Each answer for his name'; 724 *sd*: 'Here enter six jurors in a suit (identical dress), gowned, with hoods about their necks, hats for retainers thereupon, visored diversely; here minstrel, a bagpipe'; 752 *sd*: 'Here enter six women in suit (identical dress), three disguised as gallants and three as matrons, with wonderful visors congruent; here minstrel[s], a hornpipe'; 776 *sd*: 'They (dancers) go out' (L); 902 *sd*: 'Here *An.* appears in the most horrible wise, fouler than a fiend'; 912 *sd*: 'Here run out from under the horrible mantle of the *Soul* seven small boys in the likeness of devils and so return again'; 978 *sd*: 'Here the devils retreat' (L); 996 *sd*: 'Here they go out, and in the going the *Soul* sings in the most lamentable wise, with drawn out ("drawte") notes as it is sung in the Passion week'; 1064 *sd*: 'Here enters *An.*, with the Five Wits going before, *Mi.* on the one side and *Und.* on the other side and *Wi.* following, all in their first clothing (previous costume), their chapelets and crests, and all having on crowns, singing in their coming in, "Quid retribuam Domino pro omnibus que retribuit mihi? Calicem salutaris accipiam et nomen Domini invocabo"'

Songs and music 1. Five Wits 'Nigra sum sed formosa' (w.s., bib. text) 164 *sd*; 2. Five Wits 'Tota pulchra es' (w.n.s.) 324 *sd*; 3. *Mind, Will, Understanding* (w.n.s.)

620 sd (parts apportioned: Mind–tenor, Understanding–mean, Will–treble); 4. The Soul 'Magna velud mare contricio' (w.s. two lines, 'in most lamentable wise, with drawn out notes as it is sung in Passion Week') 996 sd; 5. the Soul, the Five Wits, Mind, Understanding, Will 'Quid retribuam Domino pro omnibus' (w.s. bib. text, 'on their coming in') 1064 sd; **Instrumental**: minstrel music and trumpets for Mind's dancers 692 sd; minstrels and a bagpipe for Understanding's dancers 724 sd; minstrels and a hornpipe for Will's dancers 752 sd

Staging and set no indications as to set; the considerable ceremonial action and dancing suggest hall or institutional production

Stage properties Wisdom's orb and sceptre op. sd; staffs ('warders') for Mind's dancers 692 sd

CONCORDANCES

Preston, 1975
Preston, 1977 (Digby fragment)

PLACENAMES

the Admiralty (court) 854; Ely 832; France 516, 767; Holborn 721, 731; Jerusalem 164, 164 sd, 165; Marshalsea (court) 853; St Paul's 794; Westminster 789

ALLUSIONS

Adam 106, 110; Ecclesiasticus (V) 24:12 276; Jove 170; Mary Magdalene 414; Malachi 4:2 (q.a.) 1154–5; Martha 413; Matthew 25:2 173, 20:6 394; St Paul 1148; St Paul Colossians 3:9 (q.a.) 1135; St Paul Ephesians 4:23, 24 1127–8; St Paul Romans 5:1 (q.a.) 1151, 12:2 (q.a.) 1119–20; Proverbs 1:7 1153; Psalm 85:13 (V)/86:13 (AV) (q.a.) 1081, 115:12–13 (V)/116:12–13 (AV) 1064 sd, 144:9 (V)/145:9 (AV) 1142–3; Liber Sapientiae (V) 8:2 17–20, 7:29 27–9, 7:26 30–2; Solomon 168, 1152; Song of Songs 1:4 (q.a.) 164, 164 sd, 1:5 (q.a.) 169–70, 4:9 (q.a.) 1083–4

REPORTS ON MODERN PRODUCTIONS

1. Winchester College (King Alfred's College Drama Dept) dir. J. Marshall, 21–23 May 1981 [METh 3:1 (1981) pp. 53–5; RORD 24 (1981) pp. 196–7]
2. Hartford, CT (Trinity College), dir. R. Shoemaker, 12–14 April 1984 [see Coletti and Sheingorn essay below]

RECORDED PRODUCTION

LP Record: BBC, The First Stage, dir. J. Barton (1970)

BIBLIOGRAPHY

Baker, D. C. 'Is *Wisdom* a "Professional" Play?' in Riggio, 1986, pp. 67–86

Baker, Murphy and Hall, 1967, pp. 153–66

Beadle, R. 'Monk Thomas Hyngham's Hand in the Macro Manuscript' in Beadle and Piper, 1995, pp. 315–37

Beadle, R. 'The Scribal Problem in the Macro Manuscript', *ELN* 21:4 (1984) pp. 1–13

Bevington, D. '"Blake and wyght, fowll and fayer": Stage Picture in *Wisdom, Who is Christ*', *CD* 19:2 (1982) pp. 136–50, and Riggio, 1986, pp. 18–38

Bevington, 1968, pp. 28–34

Bevington, D. 'Political Satire in the Morality *Wisdom Who is Christ*', *RenP* [1963] (1964) pp. 41–51

Clark, M., S. Kraus and P. Sheingorn, '"Se in What Stat Thou Dost Indwell": The Shifting Construction of Gender in *Wisdom*' in Paxson, Clopper and Tolmasch, 1998, pp. 43–57

Coletti, T. and P. Sheingorn, 'Playing *Wisdom* at Trinity College', *RORD* 27 (1984) pp. 179–84

Davenport, 1982, pp. 79–105

Davidson, 1989, pp. 83–111

Fifield, M. 'The use of Doubling and "Extras" in *Wisdom, Who is Christ*', *BSUF* 6 (1965) pp. 65–8

Fifield, 1967, pp. 23–6

Fifield, 1974, pp. 12–34

Gatch, M. McC. 'Mysticism and Satire in the Morality of *Wisdom*', *PQ* 53:3 (1974) pp. 342–62

Gibson, G. M. 'The Play of *Wisdom* and the Abbey of St Edmund', *CD* 19:2 (1985) pp. 117–35 and in Riggio, 1986, pp. 39–66

Gibson, 1989, pp. 108–13

Green, 1938

Haller, 1916, pp. 96–9

Happé, P. 'The Devil in the Morality Plays: The Case of *Wisdom*' in Bitot, Mullini and Happé, 1996, pp. 115–24

Hill, E. D. 'The Trinitarian Allegory of the Moral Play of *Wisdom*', *MP* 73:2 (1975–6) pp. 121–35

Jack, 1989, pp. 159–64

Johnston, A. F. '*Wisdom* and the Records: Is there a Moral?' in Riggio, 1986, pp. 87–102

Jones, M. ('Souls in Jeopardy') *Revels I*, pp. 251–8

Kelley, 1979, pp. 94–118

Koontz, C. 'The Duality of Styles in the Morality Play *Wisdom Who is Christ*: A Classical-Rhetorical Analysis', *Style* 7:3 (1973) pp. 251–70

Marshall, J. 'Marginal Staging Marks in the Macro Manuscript of *Wisdom*', *METh* 7:2 (1985) pp. 77–82

Marshall, J. '"Fortune in Worldys Worschyppe": The Satirising of the Suffolks in *Wisdom*', *METh* 14 (1992) pp. 37–66

Marshall, 1994, pp. 111–48

Miyajima, 1977, pp. 68–73

Molloy, 1952

Riehle, W. 'English Mysticism and the Morality Play *Wisdom Who is Christ*' in Glasscoe, 1986, pp. 202–15

Riggio, 1986

Riggio, 1998

Riggio, M. C. 'The Staging of *Wisdom*', *RORD* 27 (1984) pp. 167–78, and in Riggio, 1986, pp. 1–17

Riggio, M. C. '*Wisdom* Enthroned: Iconic Stage Portraits', *CD* 23:3 (1989) pp. 228–54, and in Davidson and Stroupe, 1991, pp. 249–79

Scherb, 2001, pp. 130–45

Schmidt, 1885, pp. 390–93

Smart, 1912

Smith, 1935, pp. 151–7

101   (The Play of) Wit and Science

DATE, AUTHORSHIP AND AUSPICES

1539, John Redford, performed by boys, probably at court

TEXT AND EDITIONS

Extant originals

Manuscript: British Library Add. MS 15233

Editions

1994   CHD (CD-Rom and online copy of Brown, Wilson, Greg and Sisson, 1951, l.l., OS)
1975   Bevington (OS)*
1972   Happé (OS)
1969   Schell and Schuchter (NS)
1951   Brown, Wilson, Greg and Sisson (OS)
1924   Adams (OS)*
1908   TFT (facsimile, n.l.)
1907   Farmer (9) (n.l., NS)
1897   Manly, vol. I (OS)
1853   Dodsley (Supplement, vol. II, n.l., NS)
1848   Halliwell (1848b) (n.l., OS)

SOURCES

No sources have been identified.

CHARACTERS

Reason	Diligence	Idleness	Worship
Instruction	Tediousness	Ignorance	Experience
Confidence	Honest Recreation	Fame	Lady Science
Wit	Quickness	Favour	
Study	Strength	Riches	

PLOT SUMMARY

It is evident that, in the missing leaves of the manuscript, *Wit* has requested the hand of *Lady Science* and *Reason*, her father, has agreed on condition that he journeys to Mount Parnassus and defeats the giant *Tediousness*. *Reason* gives *Instruction* a glass in which the worth or otherwise of *Wit* will be reflected, and sends him off. Though a man of substance, he declares his intention to wed his daughter to the base-born but worthy *Wit*. When he departs, *Confidence* passes across the stage with a picture of *Wit* for *Lady Science*, assured that it will please her. The scene changes to *Wit* in the company of *Study*, and he is also soon joined by *Instruction*, who warns him against the enemy, *Tediousness*. However, *Wit* chooses to go on his way without *Instruction*, is soon assailed by *Tediousness* and is slain. He is found and revived by *Honest Recreation*, *Comfort*, *Quickness* and *Strength*, and later reprimanded by *Reason* for not following *Instruction*. However, he strays again, this time falling into the company of *Idleness*, a woman who lulls him to sleep, paints his face and summons *Ignorance*, whose coat she puts on *Wit*. When she leaves him, *Confidence* passes across the stage in search of *Wit* and sorrowfully goes on his way. The scene switches to an attempt by *Fame*, *Favour*, *Riches* and *Worship* to entertain *Lady Science* with music, but she takes no pleasure in them. When *Wit* appears before her, she does not recognize him from his picture, takes him for *Ignorance*, rejects him and departs. *Wit* is then joined by *Shame*, to whose physical chastisement he submits himself, and *Reason* to whom he repents his straying and folly. When *Instruction*, *Study* and *Diligence* make their appearance, *Reason* orders them to dress *Wit* in new apparel, and *Confidence* then comes in to present him with a token from *Science*, a heart of gold. *Instruction* tells him that he has to climb Mount Parnassus, but he is assailed again by *Tediousness*. Helped this time by his friends, *Wit* defeats him however, and subsequently brings in the giant's head on his sword. *Wit* is then dressed in the gown of knowledge and reconciled with *Lady Science* in song. They prepare for marriage, *Reason* offers a prayer for the king, queen and parliament, and there is a final song.

PLAY LENGTH

1,101 lines

COMMENTARY

This is an early education play that advocates not only the intrinsic importance of learning, but its value for social advancement as well. The double fall and redemption scheme is presented in entirely secular terms and the play addresses particular problems: the difficulties of study and the lure of idle recreations. The narrative is structured as a chivalric love quest. There is no Vice as such, though *Idleness* has something of the Vice's enticing qualities, while *Tediousness* is a straightforward foe. The slaying of the giant is reminiscent of folk play combats.

Other youth and education plays: **21, 33, 53, 56, 58, 61, 62, 64, 67, 68, 73** (frag.), **103, 104.**

Other marriage quest plays: **29, 47, 57** (frag.), **61, 62.**

SIGNIFICANT TOPICS AND NARRATIVE ELEMENTS

education and social advancement; marriage and wealth; the rigours of study; good and bad companionship; the weakness of youth

DRAMATURGICAL AND RHETORICAL FEATURES

Verbal and general rustic speech: *Ignorance* 441 ff.; *Ignorance*'s 'spelling' lesson from *Idleness* 450–545; stage directions in English

Costume and dress *Wit* wears 'garments of science' 89; *Tediousness* wears a visor 140 *sd*; *Wit*'s garment is heavy 321–4; *Wit* discards his gown 329; *Ignorance*'s and *Wit*'s coats are exchanged, *Wit* acquiring a fool's coat 560–70, 579; *Ignorance*'s and *Wit*'s caps are exchanged 583 (*Wit* getting a coxcomb) 813–14; *Wit* changes dress on repentance 876; *Wit* receives the 'gown of knowledge' 971–3

Actions and stage directions 10 *sd*: 'Here all go out save *Rea.*'; 40 *sd*: '*Con.* comes in with a picture of *Wit*'; 49: *Con.* shows the picture to the audience; 62 *sd*: '*Wit* comes in without *Ins.*, with *Stu.* etc.'; 140 *sd*: '*Ted.* comes in with a vizor over his head'; 170–5: *Ted.* apparently makes a foray into the audience; 192 *sd*: '*Wit* speaks at the door'; 208 *sd*: '*Ted.* rises up'; 208–10: *Ted.* fights with *Wit*; 210 *sd*: 'Here *Wit* falls down and dies'; 222: *Ted.* strikes *Wit* again; 224 *sd*: 'Here come in *H. Rec.*, *Com.*, *Qui.* and *Str.*, and go and kneel about *Wit*'; 260 *sd*: 'And at the last verse (*Wit*) raises him[self] up upon his feet, and so make an end (to the song). And then *H. Rec.* says as follows'; 264 *sd*: '*Rea.* comes in and says as follows'; 330 *sd*: 'Here they (*Wit, H. Rec.*) dance, and in the meanwhile *Id.* comes in and sits down, and when the galliard is done, *Wit* says as follows, and so falls down in *Id.*'s lap'; 435–8 (and see 815–16): *Idleness* blackens *Wit*'s face; 440 *sd*: 'Here she (*Id.*) whistles, and *Ign.* comes in'; 591 *sd*: '*Con.* comes in with a sword by his side, and says as follows'; 617 *sd*: 'Here they (*Fame, Fav., Ric., Wor.*) come in with viols'; 625 *sd*: 'Here they (*Fame, Fav., Ric., Wor.*) sing "Exceeding Measure"'; 707 *sd*: '*Wit* comes before'; 839 *sd*: '*Sha.* comes in with a whip'; 857 *sd*: '*Wit* kneels down'; 842, 859: *Sha.* whips *Wit*; 954–60: *Ted.* and *Wit* fight; 960 *sd*: '(*Ted.*) Dies'; 961 *sd*: 'Here *Wit* comes in and brings in the head upon his sword, and says as follows'; 965 *sd*: '*Con.* comes running in'; 981 *sd*: '*Con.* comes running in'; 985 *sd*: 'Here *Wit, Ins., Stu.* and *Dil.* sing "Welcome mine own" and *Sci., Exp., Rea.* and *Con.* come in at l[eft] and answer every second verse'; 1017 *sd*: 'And when the song is done, *Rea.*, sending *Ins., Stu.* and *Dil.* and *Con.* out, and then standing in the middle of the place, *Wit* says as follows'; 1100 *sd*: 'All say'; 1100 *sd* (2): Here come in four with viols and sing "Remember me" and at the last choir (chorus) all make cur[t]sey, and so go forth singing'; **Simple entry:** *Ins.* 69; *Ins., Stu., Dil.* 872; *Con.* 913; *Ins., Wit., Stu., Dil.* 923; **Simple exit:** *Wit, Stu., Dil.* 128; *Ins.* 140; *Ted.* 224; *Com., Qui., Str.* 280; (*Rea.*) 286; (*H. Rec.*) 422; (*Con.*) 617; *Ins., Stu., Wit, Dil.* 879; *Rea.* 913; *Con.* 923

Songs and music (the words of the first three songs are appended after the play in the manuscript) 1. *Honest Recreation, Confidence, Quickness, Strength* 'When travails great in matters thick' (w.s., w. ref., some individual part singing) 225–60; 2. *Fame, Favour, Riches, Worship* 'Exceeding measure and with pains continual' (with viols, w.s.) 626–39; 3. *Wit, Instruction, Study, Diligence, Science, Experience, Reason, Confidence* 'O lady dear' or 'Welcome, my own' (w.s., w. ref., singers in two groups, parts apportioned to each – *Wit's* 'company' and *Science's* 'company') 986–1017; 4. Whole cast (?) Final song with viols 'Remember me' (w.n.s.) **Instrumental:** music for the dance, a galliard 330 *sd* (see 330); viols 617 *sd*, 1100 *sd*

Staging and set the action is localized by the presence and dialogue of characters, and there are no indications as to set, except for the door at which *Wit* speaks (192 *sd*), but there is a reference to a mountain (968) which may have involved a structure; the play requires a minimum of eleven actors, even with doubling

Stage properties *Reason's* glass (mirror) 7; *Wit's* picture 40 *sd*; *Tediousness's* vizor 140 *sd*; *Tediousness's* club 161; *Idleness's* whistle 440; *Confidence's* sword 591 *sd*; *Wit's* sword 790; *Shame's* whip 839 *sd*; *Reason's* written document 843; *Science's* gold heart 919; *Wit's* new sword 932; *Tediousness's* false head on a sword 961 *sd*

PLACENAMES

England 454, 455, 457

ALLUSIONS

Mount Parnassus 946

REPORT ON MODERN PRODUCTION

Kalamazoo (Chicago Medieval Players), 12 May 1990 [*METh* 12:1 (1990) pp. 80–1]

RECORDED PRODUCTIONS

Videotape: JL, dir. M. Twycross (Lancaster University Television, 1993)
Audiotape: University of Chicago, dir. J. W. Velz

BIBLIOGRAPHY

Brown, A. 'The Play of *Wit and Science* by John Redford', *PQ* 28:4 (1949) pp. 429–42
Cartwright, 1999, pp. 49–74
Duffy, R. A. '*Wit and Science* and Early Tudor Pageantry: A Note on Influence', *MP* 76:2 (1978) pp. 184–9
Haller, 1916, pp. 119–22
Hauke, 1904, pp. 2–37
Hogrefe, 1959, pp. 314–20
Lombardo, 1954, pp. 9–39
Norland, 1993, pp. 80–9
Norland, 1995, pp. 161–74

Nunn, H. '"It tak'th but life": Redford's *Wit and Science*, Anne of Cleves, and the Politics of Interpretation', *CD* 33:2 (1999) pp. 270–91

Schell, E. T. '*Scio Ergo Sum*: The Structure of *Wit and Science*', *SEL* 16:2 (1976) pp. 179–99

Schell, 1983, pp. 52–76

Southern, 1973, pp. 312–28

Tannenbaum, S. 'Editorial Notes on *Wit and Science*', *PQ* 14:4 (1935) pp. 307–26

Velz, J. W. and C. P. Dow 'Tradition and Originality in *Wyt and Science*', *SP* 65:4 (1968) pp. 631–46

Watson, T. R. 'Redford's *Wyt and Science*', *Explicator* 39:4 (1981) pp. 3–5

102   Witty and Witless

DATE, AUTHORSHIP AND AUSPICES

1520–33; John Heywood; probably for court production, or possibly closet

TEXT AND EDITIONS

Extant originals

Manuscript: British Library MS Harleian 367

Editions

1994   CHD (CD-Rom and online copy of De la Bère, 1937, l.l., OS)
1991   Axton and Happé (OS)*
1991   Happé, Woudhuysen and Pitcher (OS)
1937   De la Bère (n.l., OS)
1914   Farmer (1914a) (facsimile, n.l.)
1914   Farmer (1914b) (facsimile, n.l.)
1909   TFT (facsimile, n.l.)
1905   Farmer (1) (n.l., NS)
1846   Fairholt (n.l., OS)

SOURCES

No sources have been positively identified, but see Cameron's essay below for an account of analogues. See also Maxwell, 1946, and Young's essay, both listed below, for a discussion of possible links with the French *Dialogue du fou et du sage* and Erasmus's *Encomium moriae* respectively.

CHARACTERS

John   James   Jerome

PLOT SUMMARY

Two 'interlocutors' *John* and *James* are engaged in a discussion, the beginning of which is missing, about whether it is better to be witless or intelligent. *James* argues that the foolish are excused from difficult work, while *John* maintains that they are treated badly and fall prey to flattery and vain pursuits. *James* contends that while physical labour may be taxing it has its rewards, and that mental work is more painful. When *John* replies that the clever can more easily discern opportunities to benefit themselves, *James* says that they will also experience sorrow more intensely and that the foolish are pleased with less. He comes to the view that the variety of dispositions is such that it is as good to be witless as witty, which *John* applauds as a move from his original position that it was better to be witless. However, *James* continues to challenge *John*'s argument, insisting that mental pain is worse than physical. Each maintains that a mixture of pleasure and pain is present in the work of scholars and physical labourers, but *James* points out that physical exertion is healthier and that there is more peril in mental labour, while *John* concedes that mental activity is more difficult. *James* then adds that the intelligent, by virtue of greater imagination, have a greater capacity for pain. When *John* accepts this *James* uses his concession to claim victory, but *John* replies that the intelligent also have more pleasure. *James*, however, points out that the eternal pleasure of salvation outweighs all others and that this, through baptism, remains available to those who through mental incapacity do not come to moral discernment. When *John* argues that this is available to the intelligent too, if they do well, *James* retorts that this proviso does not apply to the foolish, giving them the advantage. At this point *John* concedes the argument but they are then joined by a third man, *Jerome*, who takes up and supports *John*'s original position. He argues that the witless are like unimaginative beasts and points out that there are degrees of honour in heaven, the highest being reserved for those who use God's gifts best, which are the intelligent. He emphasizes God's mercy and the availability of grace, and ends the play with prayers for the king and his government.

PLAY LENGTH

703 lines

COMMENTARY

In common with most of Heywood's work, this is a dialogue rather than properly a play, and its full title advertises it as such. The first few lines of the manuscript are missing, but the dialogue has no prologue and the discussion is joined *in medias*

res. There is no action and even though there are three speakers in all it remains a two-man dialogue throughout, *Jerome* replacing *James*.
Other debate plays: **28, 29, 31, 54, 69, 99.**

SIGNIFICANT TOPICS AND NARRATIVE ELEMENTS

the treatment of fools; the royal jester Will Summer; the strains and pleasures of physical versus intellectual work; the benefits of physical and mental exercise; salvation

DRAMATURGICAL AND RHETORICAL FEATURES

Verbal and general John's Skeltonic passage repeating 'some' 31–42
Staging and set this is a dialogue in an unlocalized space, and there are neither directions for action nor indications as to set; the sole direction (after 675) indicates a slight alteration to the text when the king is not present at the performance: 'These three stave[s] next following (in praise of the king, 676–703) in the King's absence are void'

PLACENAMES

Walsingham 53, 152, 166

ALLUSIONS

St Augustine 562; St John 559; *John 14:2* 560–1; St Paul 570; St Paul *1 Corinthians 14:41–2* 571–2; Solomon 440, 658, 660; Will Summer 43, 440, 522–34, 658, 660

BIBLIOGRAPHY

Bolwell, 1921, pp. 82–5
Cameron, 1941b
De la Bère, 1937, pp. 49–60
Johnson, 1970, pp. 71–5
Maxwell, 1946, pp. 56–69
Young, 1904, pp. 98–124

103   The World and the Child (Mundus et Infans)

DATE, AUTHORSHIP AND AUSPICES

1500–22; anonymous; auspices unknown; Greg 5

TEXT AND EDITIONS

Extant originals

1522 printing by Wynkyn de Worde: Trinity (Dublin); *STC* 25982

Editions

1999	Davidson and Happé (OS)
1994	CHD (CD-Rom and online transcription of De Worde printing, l.l., OS)
1981	Lester (NS)*
1969	Schell and Schuchter (NS)*
1931	Hampden (n.l., NS)
1914	Farmer (1914a) (facsimile, n.l.)
1909	TFT (facsimile, n.l.)
1906	Farmer (3) (n.l., NS)
1897	Manly, vol. 1 (OS)
1874–6	Dodsley, vol. 1 (n.l., NS)
1817	London, Roxburghe Club (n.l., facsimile)

SOURCES

The narrative appears to be based on a fifteenth-century poem, *The Mirror of the Periods of Man's Life*; see Lancashire's and MacCracken's essays below and the introduction to the edition by Davidson and Happé.

CHARACTERS

Mundus (the World)	Conscience
Infans (the Child)/	Folly
Wanton/ Lust and Liking/	Perseverance
Manhood/ Age	

PLAY LENGTH

974 lines

PLOT SUMMARY

The *World* opens the play with a 'boast' about his power, and the *Child* then enters, poor and weak and seeking comfort. He quickly becomes a servant of the *World*, who renames him *Wanton*, clothes him and sends him out to enjoy himself until the age of 14. *Wanton* describes his mischievous ways and disregard of education, finally returning to the *World*, who now renames him *Lust and Liking*. As such he describes his revelry and amorous pursuits before returning to the *World* at the age of 21. He is given the name *Manhood* and urged to follow the *World*'s seven subordinate kings, in fact the seven deadly sins. He is royally dressed and luxuriates in his worldly power and the support he receives from the seven kings. *Manhood* takes a seat triumphantly but is then approached by *Conscience*, who attempts to turn him away from his worldly ways. *Manhood* aggressively resists his teachings but *Conscience* persists, counselling him against each of the sins in turn. He does, however, allow him to maintain allegiance to covetousness, provided that it is covetousness for doing good. He warns him to keep the Ten Commandments, to attend church, be moderate in mirth and to avoid sin and folly. *Manhood* finally recognizes the value of the teaching and *Conscience* takes his leave. *Manhood* is now left wishing to adhere to the teachings of *Conscience* but at the same time unwilling to abandon the *World*. He is approached by *Folly* who declares himself to be a frequenter of the court and who proudly lays claim to a range of corrupt practices. *Manhood*, mindful of *Conscience*'s teaching, at first rejects *Folly* but at length admits him to his service. They decide to visit the taverns of Eastcheap and when *Manhood* expresses fear of being recognized there by *Conscience*, *Folly* gives him the alias of *Shame*. *Folly* then goes off to prepare for the revelry while *Manhood*, left on his own, reaffirms to himself his changed loyalties. When *Conscience* enters again *Manhood* rejects him, refusing to answer to his name and finally going off. *Conscience* reflects on the frailty of humanity before himself making an exit. *Perseverance* now comes in, declaring that he has been summoned by his brother *Conscience* to convert *Manhood*. When he goes off the central figure, now renamed *Age*, comes in bewailing the dissolute life into which *Folly* has led him and decides in his despair to kill himself. However, he meets *Perseverance* and recounts to him the progress of his life. *Perseverance* renames him *Repentance* and exhorts him to contrition, citing scriptural examples of God's forbearance and mercy. He teaches him about the five spiritual wits necessary for salvation and the twelve articles of faith. *Age* thanks *Perseverance* and resolves to find true spiritual knowledge. *Perseverance* concludes the play with a blessing.

COMMENTARY

This is the best example of an 'ages of man' play among the English interludes. The central figure changes identity several times to signal the stages of his progress through life, in addition to being given two further aliases by other characters. There is a stress throughout on the humanity figure's malleability and vulnerability. Though the seven deadly sins are mentioned, *Folly* is the one generic Vice (used for some social satire), and the main target of the play is less the immersion in sin than dependance on the comforts of the world.

Other youth and education plays: **21, 33, 53, 56, 58, 61, 62, 64, 67, 68, 73** (frag.), **101, 104.**

SIGNIFICANT TOPICS AND NARRATIVE ELEMENTS

the ages of man; the seven deadly sins; the court and courtiers; judicial corruption; drinking and taverns; the stews; the five 'spiritual wits'; the twelve articles of faith

DRAMATURGICAL AND RHETORICAL FEATURES

Verbal and general humanity figure's name changes (he takes on names which either reflect his stage of life or his moral state): *Child–Dalliance* 55, *Child–Wanton* 69, *Wanton–Lust and Liking* 125, *Manhood–Shame* 682, *Age (Manhood)–Repentance* 891; *Folly* has the alternative name of *Shame* 640; *Manhood's* list of alliterative geographical place names over which he claims dominance 245–8; *Perseverance* recites the Creed 905–52

Costume and dress the *Child* enters 'naked / not worthily wrapped or went' 45–6; the *World* wears a crown 50; the *World* gives the *Child* 'garments gay' 67; *Lust and Liking* is apparelled in 'garments gay' 134; *Manhood* is dressed in 'robes royal of right good hue' 197, in which he glistens 'like gold' 270; *Folly* removes his cloak (to change identity) 641–2

Actions (no stage directions) 92–3: *Wan.* spins his top; 199: the *Wo.* dubs *Man.* a knight; 285: *Man.* sits; 320–1: *Man.* catches hold of *Con.*; 549–63: *Fo.* and *Man.* fence; 652: *Fo.* gives *Man.* a drink

Staging and set there is little indication as to set and the action is unlocalized; the *World's* throne is likely to double for *Manhood's* seat later in the play (22 and 285)

Stage properties *Wanton's* top and scourge stick 79–80; *Folly's* and *Manhood's* swords 548–63; a drink for *Manhood* 652

PLACENAMES

Artois[1] 247; Asia Minor[1] ('India the Less') 245; Calais[1] 246; Cornwall[1] 246; Eastcheap 671; England 567, 603; Flanders[1] 248; Florence[1] 248; France[1] 248; Gascony[1] 248; Holborn 571; Kent 193, 246[1]; Lombard Street 672; London 569, 570, 583, 702, 708, 787; London Bridge 591; Newgate (prison) 791; Picardy[1] 247; Pontoise[1] 247; the Pope's Head (tavern) 673; Salerno[1] 245; Samer[1] 245; Sicily 350; Westminster 573, 574

1 Part of *Manhood's* alliterative list of places he claims to have conquered.

ALLUSIONS

St James 867; St John 867; Mary Magdalene 868, 871; St Paul 866, 869; St Peter 866, 870; King Robert of Sicily 350; St Stephen 260; St Thomas 867, 872

REPORT ON MODERN PRODUCTION

Bloomington, Indiana (PLS), 18 October 1979 and tour [*RORD* 22 (1979) pp. 141–2]

RECORDED PRODUCTIONS

Audiotape: University of Chicago, dir. A. Fern and A. H Nelson (1967)
LP Record: BBC, *The First Stage*, dir. J. Barton (1970)

BIBLIOGRAPHY

Bevington, 1962, pp. 116–24
Britton, G. C. 'Language and Character in some Late Medieval Plays', *E&S* n.s. 33 (1980) pp. 1–15
Lancashire, I. 'The Auspices of *The World and the Child*', *R&R* 12 (1976) pp. 95–105
Lancashire, I. 'The Provenance of *The Worlde and the Chylde*', *PBSA* 67:4 (1973) pp. 377–88
MacCracken, H. N. 'A Source of *Mundus et Infans*', *PMLA* 23:3 (1908) pp. 486–96
Peterson, J. E. 'The Paradox of Disintegrating Form in *Mundus et Infans*', *ELR* 7:1 (1977) pp. 3–16
Schmitt, N. C. 'The Idea of a Person in Medieval Morality Plays' in Davidson, Gianakaris and Stroupe,
      1982, pp. 304–15
Southern, 1973, pp. 126–42

104   Youth

DATE, AUTHORSHIP AND AUSPICES

1513–14 (SR 1557–8); anonymous; auspices unknown but probably a play of northern provenance evidently written for private household performance, possibly for a festival; Greg 20

TEXT AND EDITIONS

Extant originals

c. 1530 printing by Wynkyn de Worde: Lambeth (frag.: four leaves); *STC* 14111
1557 printing by (John King for?) John Waley: BL; Bodleian (two copies); Eliz. Club;
      Huntington; Pforzheimer; *STC* 14111a
1565 (?) printing by William Copland: BL; Huntington; *STC* 14112

Editions

1994   CHD (CD-Rom and online transcription of Copland printing, l.l., OS)
1980   Lancashire (NS) *
1972   Happé (OS)
1969   Schell and Schuchter (NS)

1931	Hampden (n.l., NS)
1922	Gowans (n.l., NS)
1914	Farmer (1914a) (facsimile, n.l.)
1909	TFT (facsimiles of Waley printing and Lambeth fragment, n.l.)
1908	TFT (facsimile of Copland printing, n.l.)
1906	Farmer (4) (n.l., NS)
1905	Bang and McKerrow (OS, with facsimile of Lambeth fragment)
1874–6	Dodsley, vol. II (n.l., NS)
1849	Halliwell (n.l., OS)
1843	Maitland (Lambeth fragment) pp. 309–16 (n.l., OS)

SOURCES

Ian Lancashire (introduction to his edition, pp. 36–41) suggests that the material drawn upon includes *Everyman*, Medwall's *Nature* and Stephen Hawes's *Example of Vertu* as well as biblical quotations, and that the play contains many allusions to contemporary Tudor politics.

CHARACTERS

Charity   Youth   Riot   Pride   Lechery   Humility

PLOT SUMMARY

Charity preaches a sermon on the virtue his character represents, after which *Youth* enters arrogantly parading his youthful strength and beauty and engages in a defiant dialogue with him. When *Youth* finally threatens him with a dagger *Charity* exits to join *Humility*, while *Youth* then expresses a desire to see his 'brother' *Riot*. *Riot* thereupon enters, saying that he has freshly come from Newgate, and proceeds to give an account of a robbery that he has committed. *Youth* boasts of his birth and his inheritance prospects, saying that he requires a servingman, at which *Riot* engages for him the services of *Pride*. On his entry, *Pride* exhorts *Youth* to scorn the poor, keep company only with gentry, maintain an arrogant bearing and wear extravagant clothes. He then procures his sister *Lechery* as a mistress for *Youth*, and they all set off for a tavern. They are met and confronted by *Charity*, but *Riot* fetches fetters with which he binds him, and the revellers proceed on their way. *Charity* is later released by *Humility*, and they resolve to convert *Youth*. While *Pride* promises *Youth* high social rank, *Humility* exhorts him to virtue. *Youth* resists the conversion, preferring the company of *Riot*, who offers him dicing, drinking and other sports. *Charity* then makes another attempt at converting *Youth* and, helped by *Humility*, finally succeeds. *Pride* and *Riot* are sent on their way while *Charity* and *Humility* take charge of *Youth*, promising him eternal bliss. *Humility* ends the play with a blessing on the audience

PLAY LENGTH

795 lines

COMMENTARY

This is a 'reprobate youth' play in which the central figure is already disposed towards vice at the outset. He is not set upon in innocence by the Vices, but effectively summons them. The social placing of the figure of *Youth* addresses particularly issues of elite interest and concern. The sole clearly female figure is *Lechery*, introduced entirely in the context of sexual transgression.

Other youth and education plays: **21, 33, 53, 56, 58, 61, 62, 64, 67, 68, 73** (frag.), **101, 103**.

SIGNIFICANT TOPICS AND NARRATIVE ELEMENTS

youth, age and mutability; reckless heirs and inheritance; robbery; prisons and execution; upbringing of youth; servants/servingmen; taverns and drinking; apparel; social rank and aspiration; sexuality and transgression; gambling and games; Tudor politics (in allusions)

DRAMATURGICAL AND RHETORICAL FEATURES

Verbal and general *Youth* enters through the audience 40; *Youth*'s description of his youthful body 46–54; *Youth* 'tests' the learning of *Charity* through spurious questioning 115–22; *Riot* enters as a huffing gallant 210; *Riot*'s list of dice and card games 679–89; *Youth* undergoes a sudden conversion at the end, unmotivated by experience, but persuaded by *Charity* 694–754; the sole stage direction is in Latin
Costume and dress *Youth*'s clothing is 'thin' 486; *Youth* receives 'new array' 767
Actions and stage direction 84–5: *Yo.* threatens *Cha.* with a dagger; 389 *sd*: 'Enter *Pri.* with *Lec.*, and let *Pri.* say'; 532–41: *Pri.* and *Ri.* bind *Cha.* with fetters; 576–7: *Hum.* unfetters *Cha.*; 733: *Yo.* kneels before *Cha.*
Songs and music (w.n.s. to either song) 1. *Youth, Pride, Riot* 'a lusty song' 472; 2. *Youth, Pride, Riot* 'a merry song' 543
Staging and set the play is clearly for hall production; the action is not specifically localized though set broadly in London, and *Youth* and his companions go to a tavern off stage; there are no directions as to set
Stage properties a dagger 84; coins 441–2; fetters 525; a rosary 770

PLACENAMES

England 715; Hog's Norton (Oxfordshire) 604; London 253; Newgate (prison) 234, 254, 481; Trumpington (Cambridgeshire) 603; Tyburn 255

ALLUSIONS

Adam 717; *1 John 4:16* 15, *4:18* 26; *Matthew 5:10* 529; *Psalm 144:9* (V)/*145:9* (AV) (q.a.) 110

REPORTS ON MODERN PRODUCTIONS

1. Bloomsbury Hall, London (English Drama Society) 12–14 December 1906 [*Theatre* 6 (1906) p. 50]
2. Lyon (Théatre Lumière, dir. F. Guinle) 9 November 1990 [*CE* 39 (1991) p. 94]
3. University of Toronto PLS Festival (University of Alberta), dir. G. Epp 23–4 May 1992 [*RORD* 32 (1993) pp.165–6]

BIBLIOGRAPHY

De Vocht, H. 'Enterlude of Youth', *Materialien* 25 (1958) pp. 41–6
Guinle, F. '*Youth*: les limites de la parodie et de la satire' in Bitot, Mullini and Happé, 1996, pp. 125–35
Haller, 1916, pp. 116–19
Schell, 1966, pp. 468–74
Sponsler, 1997, pp. 89–95

Index of characters

Numbers after names indicate the entries for the plays in which the characters occur. All names are given in English, but where they occur in Latin, these are entered and cross-referenced with English ones; the Latin are also noted in brackets against each entry in which they occur. Mute characters are indicated by (m). The names of characters are as they appear in the character lists, including changes of names, but other aliases are not recorded here, though they are in the entries. Where characters have surnames, the alphabetical listing uses these, though names of abstract figures are listed according to the first word of the name. If characters are identified solely by association with a place, without any other name (e.g. Queen of Denmark) the place name is used. Occurrences of groups of characters of a type are separately listed below the main list. In the case of *Wisdom, Who is Christ*, the dancers in groups have individual names but are not listed, separately, as they do not operate as distinct characters.

Character groups

(groups of two or more characters of a type)

Index of songs

Songs are listed alphabetically by title/first line (disregarding articles), with the number of the entry in which they occur given after. Only songs with words supplied are listed; for instances of other songs where words are not provided, the entries should be checked.

'Adieu, poor care, adieu' 74a
'Alas, what hap hast thou, poor Pithias, now to die' 19
'All aflaunt now vaunt it, brave wench cast away care' 74a
'Amid my bale, the lightning joy that pining care doth bring' 74b
'Am I not in blessed case?' 96
'And was it not a worthy sight?' 39
'As light as a fly' 15
'As many as match themselves with shrews' 95
'A-spriting, a-spriting, a-spriting go we' 5
'Awake ye woeful wights' 19

'Back and side go bare' 30
'Benedictus Dominus' 93
'Blessed be thou O the God of Abraham' 42
'Brom, brom, brom' 93
'Broom, broom on a hill' 53

'Can my poor breast be still?' 70
'Come, come lie down, and thou shalt see' 61
'Come merrily forth' 13
'Come smack me, come smack me, I long for a smooch' 74a
'Confiteor Domine Pape et omnibus cardinalibus' (chanting) 50

'Dance we, dance we' 27
'Dear dames divorce your minds from joy, help to bewail my woe' 74b
'Down, down, down, down' (a burden, one line) 27

'Exceeding measure and with pains continual' 101

'Fare well, adieu, that courtly life' 39
'Farewell our school' 67
'First Courage causes minds of men' 94

'Give a leg, give an arm, arise, arise' 61
'Glory be to the Trinity' 44
'God by his providence divine' 70
'Gold locks' 67
'Good hostess, lay a crab in the fire, and broil a mess of sous-a' 52

'Have in the ruske' (probably a song) 1
'Haye, haie, haie, haie' (a catch) 76
'Heigho, care away, let the world pass' 96
'Here we comen, and here we loven' 67
'Hey delading, delading' (a catch) 13
'Hey, derry, derry' (a catch) 14
'Hey dery dery, with a lusty dery' 51
'Hope so and hap so, in hazard of threatening' 3
'How can that tree but withered be' (probably a song) 12
'How greatly I am bound to praise' 70
'A husband I have' 73

'I am poor Tiler in simple array' 95
'I fear mine old master shall sing this new note' 5
'If pleasure be the only thing' 15
'If pleasure be treasure' 74b
'I have a pretty titmouse' 53
'I mun be married a Sunday' 75
'In a herber green asleep where as I lay' 58
'It hath been a proverb before I was born' 42
'It hath been told, been told, in proverbs old' 62
'It is good to be merry' 67
'It is written with a coal' 60

'Lapides preciosi' (one line only) 93
'La, so, so, fa, mi, re, re' (scales only) 49
'Lend me you lovers all your pleasant lovely lays' 5
'Let the knaves take heed' 49
'Let the truth, let the truth' 49
'Let us sip and let it slip' 95
'Lie still and here nest thee' 62
'Life is but short, hope not therein' 52
'Live in joyful jollity' 70
'Lo, lo, here I bring her' 67
'The Lord preserve our most noble Queen of renown' 75
'Lulla by baby' 70
'Lustily, lustily let us sail forth' 13
'Lust shall be led by Inclination' 96

'Magna velud mare contricio' 100
'My joy hath overgrown my grief' 62

'A new master, a new' 39
'Nigra sum sed formosa' 100
'Now we will here begin to sing' 27

'O eternal sapience' 35
'O fruitful root of Jesse' 35
'O happy days and pleasant plays' 96
'O high king Emmanuel' 35
'O lady dear' or 'Welcome, my own' 101
'Old brown bread crusts' 75
'O lord God Adonai' 35

'O Lord the God of our father Abraham' 42
'O love I die' 5
'O mighty Jove, some pity take' 64
'O most mighty governor' 35
'O most orient clearness' 35
'O perfect key of David' 35
'Our secret thoughts, thou Christ dost know' 74a

'Patience entreateth good fellows all' 95
'Pepe I se ye, I am glad I have spied ye' (incipit only) 50
'Pipe merry Annot' 75
'Placebo dilexi' (chanted) 75
'The princely heart, that freely spends' 15

'Quas in hart and quas again, and quas about the house' 52
'Quid retribuam Domino pro omnibus' 100

'Reverence, due reverence' 15
'Robin Hood in Barnsdale stood' 27

'Saepe expugnaverunt me a iuventute mea' (one line only) 93
'Sing care away with sport and play' 64
'Sing we sing we, with joyful heart' 55
'Sing we together' 49
'Sith all our grief is turned to bliss' 5
'Sith fate and fortune thus agree' 70
'Sith fortune thwart, doth cross my days with care' 74a
'So happy is the state of those' 96
'Spite of his spite, which that in vain' 21
'Stand back, ye sleeping jacks at home' 39
'The strongest guard that king can have' 19
'Such barbers God send you at all times of need' 19
'Super flumina Babilonis' (two lines only) 50
'Sweet money the minion' 15

'Taunderum taunderum tayne' 59
'A thing very fit' 75
'Though pinching be a privy pain' 95
'Though Wastefulness and Wantonness some men have us two named' 94
'Thou that dost guide the world' 15
'Time to pass with goodly sport' 27
'To men that be heavy and would fain be merry' 34
'Tom Collier of Croydon hath sold his coals' 52
'Tom might be merry, and well might fare' 95
'Tom Tiler was a trifler' 95
'Too nidden' 19
'Tota pulchra es' 100
'To thee O Lord, with heart and voice I sing' 74b
'Trim merchandise, trim trim' (jingle) 52
'Troll the bole and drink to me, and troll the bole again-a' 52
'The trustiest treasure in earth we see' 3

'Victime Paschali' (words partially supplied) 11

'Wassail, wassail, wassail, out of the milk pail' 50
'We have great gain, with little pain' 94
'When Covetous is busy' 24
'When died he, when died he?' 75
'When men will seem misdoubtfully' 3
'When travails great in matters thick' 101
'Where is the knave that did so rave' 96
'Where like to like is matched so' 52
'Whoso to marry a minion wife' 75
'Why doth the world study vain glory to attain?' 21
'Why should not youth fulfil his own mind?' 58
'With a heigh down down' (scraps) 51
'With heart and voice to thee O Lord' 74a
'With huffa, gallant, sing tirl on the berry' (probably sung) 27
'With Lust to live is our delight' 96
'With yea marry sirs, thus should it be' (probably a song) 59

'You barons bold, and lusty lads' 74b

Biographical notes on authors

These brief biographical sketches place emphasis on the education and profession of writers, their literary output aside from the drama, and their engagement in political or religious polemic (where known). Writers to whom plays are uncertainly attributed are excluded. Books and articles on playwrights are listed here only if they have a biographical content.

John Bale (1495–1563) was born in Suffolk and educated in a Carmelite convent at Norwich, subsequently attending Jesus College, Oxford. He converted to Protestantism and was a vicar at Thornden in Suffolk, the county of his birth. Though encountering opposition, he enjoyed the protection of Thomas Cromwell, who had been impressed by his anti-Catholic plays. On Cromwell's fall, Bale took refuge in Germany from 1540–7, where he wrote virulent tracts of religious polemic, earning himself the description 'bilious Bale'. He later returned and, after spells as a vicar in Hampshire and Norfolk, was made Bishop of Ossory in Ireland in 1553. He attempted to flee on the accession of Mary, but his boat was driven on to the coast of Cornwall, he was imprisoned for treason, and only released upon payment of a fine, after which he proceeded to the Netherlands and Switzerland. He returned in Elizabeth's reign and ended his life in Canterbury as a prebendary.

Fairfield, 1976; Happé, 1996; McCusker, 1942

Richard Edwards (1524–66) came from Somerset, was educated at Corpus Christi College and Christ Church College, Oxford, and later entered Lincoln's Inn. He became Master of the Children of the Chapel Royal in 1561. Edwards composed *Palamon and Arcite* for Queen Elizabeth's visit to Oxford in 1566 and wrote several other plays, but *Damon and Pithias* is his only play to survive.

Bradner, 1927

Ulpian Fulwell (fl. 1586) was born in Somerset, educated at St Mary Hall, Oxford, and became rector of Naunton, Gloucestershire, in 1570. *Like Will to Like* is his only known play but he also wrote a chronicle of Henry VIII, *The Flower of Fame* (1575), and a set of comic dialogues, *Ars Adulandi* (1576).

Thomas Garter is known only as the author of *Virtuous and Godly Susanna*.

George Gascoigne (1542–77) grew up in Westmoreland, was probably educated at Trinity College, Cambridge, and later entered the Middle Temple and Gray's Inn. He was MP for Bedford in 1557–9 and Midhurst in 1572. He fled to the Netherlands to avoid creditors in 1572 and there entered the military service of William of Orange (1572–5), during which time he was captured and held prisoner of war by the Spaniards. Gascoigne wrote widely apart from his plays, including a collection of mostly poetical works entitled *The Posies of G. Gascoigne* (1575), which included *Jocasta* and a critical essay. He contributed to *The Princelye Pleasures at Kenilworth* (1576). His other works include *The Steele Glas, The Droomme of Doomesday, A Delicate Diet for Daintie-mouthde Droonkardes* (all 1576) and the *Tale of Hemetes the Heremyte* (published posthumously).

Prouty, 1942; Schelling, 1897

Christopher Hatton (1540–91) was born in Northamptonshire, educated at St Mary Hall, Oxford, and the Inner Temple. He was MP for Northamptonshire and later Lord Chancellor, also becoming a close friend of the queen. *Gismond of Salerne* is the only play in which he had a hand.

John Heywood (1497?–1580?) was London born and bred and became a court entertainer, epigrammatist and ballad writer under Henry VIII. Heywood remained a Catholic but recanted his denial of the royal supremacy in 1544. He enjoyed the favour of Queen Mary but when Elizabeth succeeded to the throne in 1558 he retired to Malines, and it is likely that he died there. Aside from his several comic plays, mostly of a secular nature, he wrote dialogues including one of proverbs and epigrams in 1562 and *The Spider and the Fly* in 1556.

Bolwell, 1921; De la Bère, 1937; Reed, 1969, pp. 29–71

Thomas Ingelend (fl. 1560) is known only for writing *The Disobedient Child* and there is no other biographical information.

John Jefferes (fl. 1560s?) is known only as the probable author of *The Bugbears*.

Francis Kinwelmersh (d. 1580?) was born in Essex and later entered Gray's Inn, where he collaborated with George Gascoigne to write *Jocasta* in 1566. Kinwelmersh also contributed to a collection entitled *The Paradyse of Daynty Devises* in 1576. He may have been MP for Bossiney, Cornwall, in 1572.

Sir David Lindsay (1490–1555) came from Fife and was educated at St Andrews University. He was in royal service as an equerry and later became Lyon king-of-arms in 1529. As a writer he was principally a poet, writing *The Dreme* (1528), *The Complaynt to the King* (1529), *The Testament and Complaynt of our Soverane Lordis Papyngo* (1530), *Ane Dialog betuix Experience and ane Courteour* (1552) and *The Monarchy* (1554). His *Register of Arms of the Scottish Nobility and Gentry*, completed in 1542 but only published in 1821, remains the most significant documentation of early Scottish heraldry. He was an accomplished satirist of courtly abuses. *Ane Satyre of the Three Estaits* is his only dramatic work.

Edington, 1994

Thomas Lupton (fl. 1583) was a miscellaneous writer whose best-known work, *A Thousand Notable Things of Sundry Sortes*, is a collection of enigmatic and grotesque recipes and nostrums, published in 1579. *All for Money* is his only known dramatic work.

Henry Medwall (fl. 1486) was educated at King's College, Cambridge, where he graduated in civil law in 1492. He then became chaplain to John Morton, archbishop of Canterbury, in whose household his plays were performed.

Maclean and Nelson, 1997

Francis Merbury (1555–1611) was born in London and probably educated at Christ's College, Cambridge. He was a preacher and master of the grammar school in Alford, Northamptonshire, and later moved to London when he was granted the living of St Martin's in the Vintry. He was offered, but declined, the post of royal chaplain. *The Marriage of Wit and Wisdom* is his only known play.

Lennam, 1968

Sir Henry Noel (d. 1597) was educated at Oxford, becoming an MA in 1592. Noel became a gentleman-pensioner of the queen and a courtier and was knighted in 1587. *Gismond of Salerne* is the only play in which he had a hand.

Thomas Norton (1532–84) entered the Inner Temple in 1555. He was MP for Galton in 1558, Berwick in 1562, and London in 1571, 1572, and 1580. He was awarded an MA by Cambridge in 1570 and became

Remembrancer of the City of London in 1571. As strongly Protestant, he supported measures against Catholics and in 1579 went to Rome to gather information against them, keeping a diary of his journey which is still extant. In 1581 Norton was appointed an official censor of the queen's Catholic subjects, examining many under torture. However, he himself was briefly imprisoned on an accusation of treason in 1584, having clashed with the Protestant episcopacy. He had strong literary interests, wrote verse in early life and made translations of Calvin's *Institutions of the Christian Religion* in 1559 and Nowell's *Middle Catechism* in 1570. *Gorboduc* is his only known work for the stage.

Graves, 1994

John Phillip (fl. 1550s–60s) is known only for writing *Patient and Meek Grissell*. He was, however, possibly an organist at St Paul's.

Greg, 1910

John Pickering (fl. 1560s) is only known as the author of *Horestes*, though he may have been the individual of the same name who was Speaker of the House of Commons and later Lord Keeper.

Thomas Preston (1537–98) was educated at Eton, where he acted in Latin drama. He went on to Cambridge, where he became a fellow of King's College in 1556, an MA in 1561 and LLD in 1576. While at Cambridge, he acted in a Latin tragedy. Preston became Master of Trinity Hall, Cambridge, in 1584–98 and was vice-chancellor of the university in 1589–90. *Cambises* is his only play.

John Rastell (d. 1536) was born in London and probably educated at Oxford, subsequently entering Lincoln's Inn and practising in law. He was MP for Dunheved, Cornwall 1529–36. Rastell became a printer, mostly of law books but also of plays. He was imprisoned for religious and political dissidence and probably died in prison. He wrote *The Pastyme of the People*, a chronicle, and *A New Book of Purgatory* defending Catholic doctrine. *The Nature of the Four Elements* is his only play.

Baskerville, 1917; Reed, 1900, pp. 1–28, Reed, 1917–19

John Redford (fl. 1535) was a musician and probably organist and almoner at St Paul's. He wrote mostly music and *Wit and Science* is his only play.

Thomas Sackville (1536–1608) son of Sir Richard Sackville, was possibly educated at Hart Hall, Oxford, but became a Cambridge MA in 1571. He was grandmaster of the Order of Freemasons in 1561–7 and was MP for Westmoreland in 1558, East Grinstead in 1559, and Aylesbury in 1563. He was knighted in 1567 and given a peerage, becoming Baron Buckhurst and the first earl of Dorset in 1604. He occupied a number of political and administrative posts, including becoming a commissioner at state trials and communicating to Mary Queen of Scots her sentence of death in 1586, being sent in 1587 to survey affairs in the Netherlands in 1586, being appointed commissioner for ecclesiastical causes, 1588, made ambassador to the Netherlands in 1589, working on the treaty with France of 1591, renewing the treaty with United Provinces in 1598, being appointed Lord Treasurer in 1599, presiding as Lord High Steward, at Essex's trial in 1601, and being appointed a commissioner for peace with Spain in 1604. He was also chancellor of Oxford in 1591. He wrote poetry and contributed the 'Induction' to the *Mirror for Magistrates* compiled by William Baldwin and George Ferrers (1559–63). *Gorboduc* was the only dramatic work in which he had a hand.

Bacquet, 1965; Berlin, 1974; Swart, 1949

John Skelton (1460?–1529) was born in Norfolk, educated at both Oxford and Cambridge and was awarded the degree of 'poet-laureate' by both universities, in 1488 and 1493 respectively, and by the university of Louvain in 1492. He became tutor to Prince Henry (later Henry VIII), and was a favourite at court. He also took holy orders in 1498 and was rector of Diss in Norfolk in 1507 until his death. Skelton had a satirical turn of mind and much of his poetry reflects this. Though Wolsey became his patron. Skelton satirized him in *Colyn Cloute* (1522), *Speake Parrot* (c. 1521) and elsewhere, and may have been imprisoned by him. He died in sanctuary at Westminster. His principal works include *The Bowge of Court* (1499), *Phylyp Sparowe* (earlier than 1508), *The Tunnyng of Elynor Rummynge* (1516) and *The Garlande of Laurell* (c. 1520). Various collections of his works appeared in the sixteenth century, the first complete one in 1568. *Magnificence* is the only dramatic work to his name.

Carpenter, 1967; Edwards, 1949; Gordon, 1943; Walker, 1988

Nicholas Udall (1505–56) was born in Southampton and educated at Winchester College, going on to Corpus Christi College, Oxford, where he gained a degree in 1524 but was only admitted to the MA in 1534 because of his adherence to Protestantism. He became headmaster of Eton in 1534, but was dismissed 1541 for theft of college plate; he also admitted to a sexual relationship with one of the boys. He was vicar of Braintree (1537–44), was later appointed headmaster of Westminster School (1554–6), and became prebendary of Windsor in 1551 and rector of Calborne, Isle of Wight, in 1553. Though he had fallen under suspicion of Lutheranism in 1526 and had been employed by Edward VI to respond in print to the Devonshire Catholic rebels in 1549, he gained the favour of Queen Mary, for whom he wrote plays. He had an interest in promoting drama as a pedagogical tool and in 1533 published selections from Terence with English translations, *Floures for Latine Speakynge*. In 1542 Udall produced an English version of part of Erasmus's *Apophthegms* and also contributed to an English translation of Erasmus's *Paraphrase of the New Testament*, printed in 1548. Further translations were Peter Martyr's *Discourse on the Lord's Supper* in 1550 and Thomas Gemini's *Anatomia* in 1552. *Thersites* and *Respublica* have been claimed as Udall's, but *Ralph Roister Doister* is the only extant play that can be securely attributed to him.

Edgerton, 1965

Lewis Wager (d. 1562) was rector of St James's, Garlickhithe, 1560. Otherwise he is only known as author of *The Life and Repentance of Mary Magdalene*.

William Wager (fl. 1566) is known only as the author of *The Longer Thou Livest, the More Fool Thou Art* and probably *The Cruel Debtor*, though other works have been attributed to him.

George Wapull (fl. 1570s) is only known for his authorship of *The Tide Tarrieth No Man*.

Richard Wever (fl. 1540s–50s?) is only known as the writer of *Lusty Juventus*.

George Whetstone (1544–87) was probably born in London, and was a writer of miscellaneous verse and prose. He fought in the Netherlands against Spain, and was a friend of George Gascoigne. In 1576 he published *Rock of Regard*, a collection of his works to date. This was followed by *Touchstone of the Time* (1584), the *Heptameron of Ciuill Discourses* (1582), *The English Myrror*, a political treatise (1586), and *Censure of a Loyal Subject* (1587) an account of the Babington plot. *Promos and Cassandra* is his only dramatic work.

Izard, 1942

Robert Wilmot (fl. 1568–1608) became vicar of Horndon-on-the-Hill, near Ockenden, Essex. *Gismond of Salerne* (later revised as *Tancred and Gismunda*, written c. 1568 and published 1591) was the only play in which he had a hand. Another work, *Syrophenisia or the Canaanitish Woman*, is not extant.

Nathaniel Woodes (fl. 1570s–80s) is known only as the writer of *The Conflict of Conscience*.

Wine, 1939

Closet plays in English and non-cycle drama not in English

CLOSET PLAYS IN ENGLISH

Abraham's Sacrifice, Arthur Golding	1575
Acolastus, John Palsgrave	1540
Agamemnon, John Studley	1566
Hercules Furens, Jasper Heywood	1561
Hercules Otaeus, Elizabeth I	1561–70
Hercules Oetaeus, John Studley	1566 (SR)
Hippolytus, John Studley	1567 (SR)
Interlude of Minds, anon.	c. 1574
Iphigenia in Aulis, Jane Lumley	1549–77
Medea, John Studley	1566 (SR)
Octavia, Thomas Nuce	1566 (SR)
Oedipus, Alexander Neville	1563
Thyestes, Jasper Heywood	1560
Troas, Jasper Heywood	1559

LATIN PLAYS

Absalom, Thomas Watson (?)	1535–44
Alcestis, George Buchanan	1539–42
Archipropheta, Nicholas Grimald	1546–7
Christus Redivivus, Nicholas Grimald	1540–1
Christus Triumphans, John Foxe	1556
Herodes, William Goldingham	1570–5
Hymenaeus, anon.	1578–80
Jephthah, John Christopherson	1539–44
Jephthes sive Votum, George Buchanan	1539–45
Medea, George Buchanan	1539–44
Palamedes, Renaclus Arduenna	1513
Richardus Tertius, Thomas Legge	1580
Sapientia Solomonis, anon.	1566
Titus et Gisippus, John Foxe	1544–5

CORNISH SAINT PLAY

Life of St Meriasek, anon.	1504

Bibliography

This bibliography is divided into two main sections. The first section contains all the facsimiles, collections and editions of plays referred to in brief in the main text of the individual play entries, the second all the secondary critical material referred to in the bibliographies of the individual play entries.

FACSIMILES, COLLECTIONS AND INDIVIDUAL EDITIONS OF PLAYS

For ease of reference, the twelve anthologies of early plays edited by Farmer are given numbers, as several are published in the same years. His editions of several plays in private printings for subscribers in 1913 and 1914 are grouped together under those years.

Adams, B. B. (1969) *John Bale's King Johan*, San Marino, Huntington Library Publications
Adams, J. Q. (1924) *Chief Pre-Shakespearean Dramas*, London, Harrap
Allen, J. (1953) *Three Medieval Plays*, London, Heinemann
Arber, E. (1869) *Ralph Roister Doister*, Birmingham, English Reprints
Armstrong, W. A. (1965) *Elizabethan History Plays*, Oxford, Oxford University Press
Ashbee, E. W. (1876?a) *The Interlude of 'Jacke Jugeler'*, London, privately printed
Ashbee, E. W. (1876?b) *Thersites*, London, privately printed
Astington, J. (1980) *Everyman*, Toronto, PLS Performance Text no. 2
Axton, M. (1982) *Three Tudor Classical Interludes*, Cambridge, D. S. Brewer
Axton, R. (1979) *Three Rastell Plays*, Cambridge, D. S. Brewer
Axton, R. and P. Happé (1991) *The Plays of John Heywood*, Cambridge, D. S. Brewer
Ayliff, H. K. (1933) *The Malvern Festival Plays*, London, Heath Cranton
Baker, D., J. Murphy and L. Hall (1976) (introd.) *Facsimiles of the Plays in Bodley MSS Digby 133 and E Museo 160*, Leeds, Leeds Texts and Monographs, Medieval Drama Facsimiles 3
Baker, D., J. Murphy and L. Hall (1982) *The Late Medieval Religious Plays of Bodleian MSS Digby 133 and E Museo 160*, EETS 283, Oxford University Press
Bang, W. (1909) *Bale's 'Kinge Johan', nach der Handschrift in der Chatsworth Collection in Faksimile herausgegeben*, Louvain, *Materialien* 25
Bang, W. and R. B. McKerrow (1905) *The Enterlude of Youth*, Louvain, *Materialien* 12
Barber, L. E. (1979) *Misogonus*, New York, Garland
Baskervill, C. R., V. B. Heltzel and A. H. Nethercot (1934) *Elizabethan and Stuart Plays*, New York, Holt, Rinehart & Winston
Beadle, R. (2001) '*Occupation and Idleness*', LSE n.s. 32, pp. 15–47
Benbow, R. M. (1967) *William Wager: The Longer Thou Livest and Enough is as Good as a Feast*, London, Edward Arnold
Bennett, J. A. and G. V. Smithers (1968) *Early Middle English Verse and Prose*, Oxford, Clarendon Press
Bevington D. M. (1972) *The Macro Plays: A Facsimile Edition with Facing Transcriptions*, New York, Johnson Reprint Company
Bevington, D. M. (1975) *Medieval Drama*, Boston, Houghton Mifflin
Blackstone, M. A. (1981) *Robin Hood and the Friar*, Toronto, PLS Performance Text no. 3

Boas, F. S. (1934) *Five Pre-Shakespearean Comedies*, Oxford, World's Classics
Boas, F. S. and A. W. Reed (1926) *'Fulgens and Lucres': A Fifteenth-Century Secular Play*, Oxford, Clarendon Press, Tudor and Stuart Library
Bond, R. W. (1911) *Early Plays from the Italian: Edited, with Essay, Introductions and Notes*, Oxford, Clarendon Press
Brandl, A. (1898) *Quellen des weltlichen Dramas in England vor Shakespeare* (vol. LXXX of *Quellen und Forschungen zur Sprach- und Culturgeschichte der germanischen Völker*, ed. A. Brandl, E. Martin and E. Schmidt, Strasburg, K. J. Trübner
Brandl, A. (1900) *'The Longer Thou Livest the More Fool Thou Art*: Ein Drama aus der ersten Regierungsjahren der Königin Elisabeth', *JDSG* 36, pp. 14–64
Brandl, A. (1923) 'Das Bibelstück-Fragment von Rickinghall Manor', *Archiv* 144, pp. 255–6
Brett-Smith, H. F. (1920) *Gammer Gurtons Nedle*, Oxford, Oxford, Basil Blackwell
Brown, A., F. P. Wilson, W. W. Greg and C. Sisson (1951) *Wit and Science*, Oxford, MSR
Brown, A. and F. P. Wilson (1957) *Damon and Pithias*, Oxford, MSR
Brown, A., J. Crow and F. P. Wilson (1961) *The Marriage of Wit and Science*, Oxford, MSR
Brown, A., W. W. Greg and F. P. Wilson (1951) *Wit and Science*, Oxford, MSR
Bullen, A.H. (1888) *Works of George Peele*, London, John Nimmo, 2 vols.
Bullough, G. (1957–75) *Narrative and Dramatic Sources of Shakespeare*, London, Routledge and Kegan Paul, 8 vols
Calderhead, I. (1916) 'Morality Fragments from Norfolk', *MP* 14, pp. 1–9
Cameron, K. W. (1941a) *Authorship and Sources of 'Gentleness and Nobility'*, Raleigh, NC, Thistle
Cameron, K. W. (1944) *The Play of Love*, Raleigh, NC, Thistle
Carpenter, F. C. (1902) *The Life and Repentaunce of Marie Magdalene*, Chicago, University of Chicago Press
Cassel, J. (1889) *Cassell's National Library*, vol. CCV, 1886
Cauthen, I. B. (1970) *Gorboduc or Ferrex and Porrex*, London, Edward Arnold
Cawley, A. C. (1956) *Everyman and Medieval Miracle Plays*, London, J. M. Dent (Everyman's Library)
Cawley, A. C. (1961) *Everyman*, Manchester, Manchester University Press (rev. 1977)
Chalmers, G. (1806) *Poetical Works of Sir David Lindsay*, London, Longman, Hurst, Rees & Orme
Child, C. G. (1912) *Ralph Roister Doister*, Boston, Riverside Press
Child, F. J. (1848) *Four Old Plays*, Cambridge, G. Nichols
Child, F. J. (1888) *The English and Scottish Popular Ballads*, London, Henry Stevens, Son & Stiles, vol. III
Clark, J. D. (1979) *The Bugbears*, New York, Garland
Clopper, L. M. (1984) *The Four PP*, Oxford, MSR
Coldewey, J. C. (1993) *Early English Drama: An Anthology*, New York, Garland
Coleman, R. (1971) *'The Nature of the Four Elements' as performed at the University Printing House, Cambridge*, privately printed
Collier, J. P. (1838) *Kynge Johan, a play in two parts*, Camden Society o.s. 2, London, John Bowyer Nichols & Sons
Collier, J. P. (1844) *'Albion Knight*: A Moral Play', London, Shakespeare Society's Papers 1, pp. 53–68
Collier, J. P. (1851) *Five Old Plays*, London, Roxburghe Club
Collier, J. P. (1863) *Illustrations of Early English Popular Literature*, London, privately printed
Collier, J. P. (1866) *Illustrations of Old English Literature*, London, privately printed
Collier, J. P. and W. B. D. Turnbull, (1837) *Mind, Will and Understanding: A Morality*, Edinburgh, Abbotsford Club
Concolato, M. G. (1985) *All for Money*, Naples, Liguori
Cook, A. S. (1915) *A Literary Middle English Reader*, Boston, Ginn & Co.
Cooling, J. (1959) 'An Unpublished Middle English Prologue', *RES* n.s. 10, pp. 172–3
Cooper, G. and C. Wortham, (1980) *The Summoning of Everyman*, Nedlands, University of Western Australia Press
Cooper, W. D. (1847) *'Ralph Roister Doister', A Comedy by Nicholas Udall, and 'The Tragedie of Gorboduc' by Thomas Norton and Thomas Sackville*, London, Shakespeare Society
Craik, T. W. (1974) *Minor Elizabethan Tragedies*, London, Dent
Creeth, E. (1966) *Tudor Plays: An Anthology of Early English Drama*, Garden City, NY, Doubleday

Crow, J. and F. P. Wilson (1956) *Jacob and Esau*, Oxford, MSR

Cunliffe, J. W. (1906) *Supposes and Jocasta, two plays translated from the Italian*, Boston, D. C. Heath

Cunliffe, J. W. (1907) *The Complete Works of George Gascoigne*, Cambridge, Cambridge University Press, 2 vols. (vol. II published 1910)

Cunliffe, J. W. (1912) *Early English Classical Tragedies*, Oxford, Clarendon Press

Davidson, C. and P. Happé (1999) *The Worlde and the Chylde*, Kalamazoo, MI, Medieval Institute Publications

Davis, H. and F. P. Wilson (1952) *The Conflict of Conscience*, Oxford, Oxford University Press, MSR

Davis, N. (1970) *Non-Cycle Plays and Fragments*, Oxford, Oxford University Press, EETS, Supplementary Text I

Davis, N. (1979) *Non-Cycle Plays and the Winchester Dialogues*, Leeds, University of Leeds Texts and Monographs, Medieval Drama Facsimiles 5

Dawson, G. and A. Brown (1955) *July and Julian*, Oxford, MSR

De la Bère, R. (1937) *John Heywood, Entertainer*, London, George Allen & Unwin

Denny, N. (1972) *Medieval Interludes*, London, Ginn & Co.

De Ricci, S. (1920a) *Enough is as Good as a Feast*, New York, HFR

De Ricci, S. (1920b) *Fulgens and Lucres*, New York, HFR

Dickins, B. and R. M. Wilson (1931) *Early Middle English Texts*, London, Bowes & Bowes

Dobson, R. B. and J. Taylor (1976) *Rymes of Robin Hood: An Introduction to the English Outlaw*, London, Heinemann

Dodsley, R. (1874–6) *A Select Collection of Old Plays*, London, 1744, 4th edn. by W. C. Hazlitt, London, Reeves & Turner, 15 vols.

Dover Wilson, J., B. Dobell and W. W. Greg (1913) *The Resurrection of Our Lord*, Oxford, MSR

Dyce, A. (1829–39) *Works of George Peele*, London, W. Pickering, 3 vols.

Dyce, A. (1843) *The Poetical Works of John Skelton*, London, Thomas Rodd

Eccles, M. (1969) *The Macro Plays*, Oxford, Oxford University Press, EETS 262

Esdaile, A. and W. W. Greg (1907) *Malone Society Collections* I:1, Oxford, MSR

Evans, B. and W. W. Greg (1937a) *Jack Juggler*, Oxford, MSR

Evans, B. and W. W. Greg (1937b) *Virtuous and Godly Susanna*, Oxford, MSR

Fairholt, F. W. (1846) *A Dialogue on Wit and Folly by John Heywood*, London, Percy Society, vol. XX

Farmer, J. S. (1) (1905) *The Dramatic Writings of John Heywood*, London, EEDS (repr. 1966, Guildford, Charles W. Traylen)

Farmer, J. S. (2) (1905) *The Dramatic Writings of Richard Wever and Thomas Inglelend*, London, EEDS (repr. 1966, Guildford, Charles W. Traylen)

Farmer, J. S. (3) (1906) *Six Anonymous Plays* (1st series) London, EEDS (repr. 1966, Guildford, Charles W. Traylen)

Farmer, J. S. (4) (1906) *Anonymous Plays* (2nd series) London, EEDS (repr. 1966, Guildford, Charles W. Traylen)

Farmer, J. S. (5) (1906) *Anonymous Plays* (3rd series) London, EEDS (repr. 1966, Guildford, Charles W. Traylen)

Farmer, J. S. (6) (1906) *The Dramatic Writings of Richard Edwards, Thomas Norton and Thomas Sackville*, London, EEDS

Farmer, J. S. (7) (1906) *Dramatic Writings of Ulpian Fulwell*, London, EEDS (repr. 1966, Guildford, Charles W. Traylen)

Farmer, J. S. (1906a) *Gammer Gurton's Needle*, London, Museum Dramatists, EEDS

Farmer, J. S. (1906b) *The Pardoner and the Friar/The Four PP*, London, Museum Dramatists, EEDS

Farmer, J. S. (1906c) *The Summoning of Everyman*, London, Museum Dramatists, EEDS

Farmer, J. S. (8) (1907) *The Dramatic Writings of John Bale, Bishop of Ossory*, London, EEDS

Farmer, J. S. (9) (1907) *'Lost' Tudor Plays*, London, EEDS (repr. 1966, Guildford, Charles W. Traylen)

Farmer, J. S. (1907) *Ralph Roister Doister*, London, Museum Dramatists, EEDS

Farmer, J. S. (10) (1908) *Five Anonymous Plays*, London, EEDS, 4th series (repr. 1966, Guildford, Charles W. Traylen)

Farmer, J. S. (11) (1908) *Two Tudor 'Shrew' Plays*, London, Museum Dramatists, EEDS

Farmer, J. S. (12) (1908) *J. Heywood: The Spider and the Fly. Together with an attributed Interlude entitled Gentleness and Nobility*, London, EEDS, privately printed

Farmer, J. S. (1909) *Impatient Poverty*, London, Hazell, Watson & Viney ('The Tudor Reprinted and Parallel Texts', issued privately for subscribers)

Farmer, J. S. (1910) *Magnyfycence: A Goodly Interlude and a Merry*, TFT (and edition the same year for subscribers in a private printing, Amersham)

Farmer, J. S. (1912) *Tom Tyler and his wife, An Excellent Old Play as it was printed and Acted about a hundred years ago*, TFT (and edition the same year for subscribers in a private printing, Amersham)

Farmer, J. S. (1913) Individual facsimile printings of the following (reissues of facsimiles prepared for TFT): *The Contention between Liberality and Prodigality, The Conflict of Conscience, The Longer Thou Livest the More Fool Thou Art, Jack Juggler, Jacob and Esau, Thersites, The Tide Tarrieth No Man,* Amersham, privately printed for subscribers

Farmer, J. S. (1914a) Individual facsimile printings of the following (reissues of facsimiles prepared for TFT): *Calisto and Melebea, Damon and Pithias, Four PP, Gentleness and Nobility, The Life and Repentance of Mary Magdalene, Lusty Juventus, Mankind, Marriage of Wit and Science, Marriage of Wit and Wisdom, Nature, New Custom, Nice Wanton, The Pardoner and the Friar, Respublica, The Temptation of Our Lord, Three Laws, Trial of Treasure, Wealth and Health, Play of the Weather, Witty and Witless, World and the Child, Youth*, Amersham, privately printed for subscribers

Farmer, J. S. (1914b) *Witty and Witless*, London, TFT

Fischer, J. (1903) *Das 'Interlude of the Four Elements'*, Marburg, Universitäts-Buchdrückerei

Fraser, R. A. and N. Rabkin (1976) *The Drama of the English Renaissance*, New York, Macmillan, 2 vols.

Frost, G. L. and R. Nash (1944) 'Good Order or Old Christmas', *SP* 41:4, pp. 483–91

Furnivall, F. J. (1896) *The Digby Plays*, EETS e.s. 70 (reprinted from *The Digby Mysteries*, 1882)

Furnivall F. J. and A. W. Pollard (1904) *The Macro Plays*, EETS e.s. 91 (repr. 1924)

Garbáty, T. (1984) *Medieval English Literature*, Lexington, MA, D. C. Heath

Gassner, J. (1963) *Medieval and Tudor Drama*, New York, Bantam

Gayley, C. M. (1903) *Representative English Comedies*, New York, Norwood Press

Gilson, J. P. (1921) 'A Fourteenth Century Fragment', *TLS*, 26 May, pp. 340–1

Goodman, R. (1961) *Drama on Stage*, New York, Holt, Rinehart & Winston

Gorboduc (1968) Menston, Scolar Press (facsimile)

Gowans, A. L. (1922) *Youth*, London, Gowans & Gray

Grabau, C. (1897) 'The Buggbears', *Archiv* 98: pp. 301–22, 99: pp. 25–58, 311–26

Gray, D. (1985) *The Oxford Book of Late Medieval Verse and Prose*, Oxford, Clarendon Press

Greg, W. W. (1904a) '*Everyman*: Reprinted from the Edition by John Skot Preserved at Britwell Court', Louvain, *Materialien* 4

Greg, W. W. (1904b) *Godly Queen Hester*, Louvain, *Materialien* 5

Greg, W. W. (1907a) *Malone Society Collections* 1:1, Oxford

Greg, W. W. (1907b) *Malone Society Collections* 1:3, Oxford

Greg, W. W. (1908) *Malone Society Collections* 1:2, Oxford

Greg, W. W. (1909a) '*Everyman*: From the Edition by John Skot in the Possession of Mr A. H. Huth', Louvain, *Materialien* 24

Greg, W. W. (1909b) *Malone Society Collections* 1:3, Oxford

Greg, W. W. (1910) '*Everyman*: Reprinted from the Fragments of Two Editions by Pynson Preserved in the Bodleian Library and the British Museum', Louvain, *Materialien* 28

Greg, W. W. (1911) *Malone Society Collections* 1:4 and 1.5, Oxford

Greg, W. W. (1913a) *Clyomon and Clamydes*, Oxford, MSR

Greg, W. W. (1913b) *The Contention between Liberality and Prodigality*, Oxford, MSR

Greg, W. W. (1914) *The Pedlar's Prophecy*, Oxford, MSR

Greg, W. W. (1923) *Malone Society Collections* 2:1, Oxford

Greg, W. W. (1931) *Malone Society Collections* 2.3, Oxford

Greg, W. W. (1935) *Roister Doister*, London, MSR

Greg, W. W. (1952) *Respublica, an Interlude for Christmas 1553*, London, EETS o.s. 226

Greg, W. W. (1956) *Malone Society Collections* 4, Oxford

Greg, W. W. and A. Esdaile (1907) *Johan the Evangelist*, Oxford, MSR
Greg, W. W. and R. B. McKerrow (1911) *Apius and Virginia*, Oxford, MSR
Greg, W. W. and F. Sidgwick (1908) *The Interlude of Calisto and Melebea*, Oxford, MSR
Greg, W. W. and P. Simpson (1907) *Wealth and Health*, Oxford, MSR (corrections and additions to this edition published in *MSC* 1.1, 1908, pp. 3–15)
Grosart, A. (1870–2) *Miscellanies of the Fuller Worthies Library*, London, C. Tiplady, 4 vols.
Hall, F. (1869) *Sir David Lyndesay's Works*, vol. IV, London, EETS o.s. 37, N. Trübner
Halliwell, J. O. (1846) *The Marriage of Wit and Wisdom*, London, Shakespeare Society, F. Shoberl
Halliwell, J. O. (1848a) *Early English Poetry, Ballads and Popular Literature of the Middle Ages*, London, Percy Society
Halliwell, J. O. (1848b) *The Moral Play of Wit and Science*, London, Shakespeare Society, F. Shoberl
Halliwell, J. O. (1849) *Contributions to Early English Literature*, London, privately printed.
Halliwell, J. O. (1850) *The Interlude of The Trial of Treasure*, London, Percy Society
Halliwell, J. O. (1851) *The Literature of the Sixteenth and Seventeenth Centuries*, London, privately printed
Halliwell, J. O. (1860) *A Pretie new Enterlude both pithie & pleasaunt of the Story of Kyng Daryus*, London, Thomas Richards
Hamer, D. (1931–6) *The Works of Sir David Lindsay of the Mount*, Edinburgh, Scottish Text Society, 4 vols.
Hampden, J. (1931) *Everyman, The Interlude of Youth, The World and the Child*, London, Nelson
Happé, P. (1972) *Tudor Interludes*, Harmondsworth, Penguin
Happé, P. (1979) *Four Morality Plays*, Harmondsworth, Penguin
Happé, P. (1985/6) *The Complete Plays of John Bale*, Cambridge, D. S. Brewer, 2 vols.
Happé, P., H. R. Woudhuysen and J. Pitcher (1991) *Two Moral Interludes*, Oxford, MSR
Haslewood, J. (1820) *Two Interludes: 'Jack Jugler' and 'Thersytes'*, London, Roxburghe Club
Hawkins, T. (1867) 'Candlemas Day: A Mystery', *The Journal of Sacred Literature and Biblical Record* n.s. 10, pp. 413–29 (repr. from Hawkins, *The Origins of English Drama*, Oxford, 1773)
Hazlitt, W. C. (1869) *The Complete Poems of George Gascoigne*, London, Roxburghe Club, 2 vols.
Hazlitt, W. C. (ed. J. P. Collier, 1875) *Shakespeare's Library*, London, Reeves & Turner, 6 vols.
Heilman R. B. (1955) *An Anthology of English Drama before Shakespeare*, New York, Rinehart & Co.
Henderson, P. (1948) *The Complete Poems of John Skelton*, London, J. M. Dent
Heuser, W. (1907a) 'Das Interludium de Clerico et Puella und das Fabliau von Dame Siris' *Anglia* 30, pp. 306–19
Heuser, W. (1907b) 'Dux Moraud, Einzelrolle aus einem verlorenen Drama des 14 Jahrhunderts', *Anglia* 30, pp. 180–208
Holthausen, F. (1902) 'The Pride of Life', *Archiv* 108, pp. 32–59
Holthausen, F. (1908) *Enterlude of Welth and Helth. Eine englische Moralität des XVI Jahrhunderts*, Kiel, Festschrift der Universität Kiel (rev. edn 1922), Lipsius & Tischer
Hopper, V. and G. B. Lahey (1962) *Medieval Mystery Plays*, Great Neck, NY, Barron's Educational Series
Houle, P. J. (1977) 'A Reconstruction of the English Morality Fragment *Somebody and Others*', *PBSA* 71:3, pp. 270–75
Johnson, R. C. (1975) *A Critical Edition of Thomas Preston's Cambises*, Institut für Englische Sprache und Literatur, University of Salzburg
Jones, E. E. (1909) *A Tragedye or enterlude manifestyng the chefe promyses of God vnto man*, Erlangen, Junge & Son
Kaiser, R. (1958) *Medieval English: An Old English and Middle English Anthology*, Berlin, privately printed
Kemp, R. (1951) *Ane Satyre of the Thrie Estaites*, London, Heinemann
Kermode, F. and J. Hollander (1973) *The Oxford Anthology of English Literature*, Oxford, Oxford University Press, 2 vols.
Kinsley, J. (1954) *Ane Satyre of the Thrie Estaits*, London, Cassell
Knight, S. and T. Ohlgren (1977) *Robin Hood and Other Outlaw Tales*, Kalamazoo, MI, Medieval Institute Publications
Knittel, F. and G. Fattic, (1995) *A Critical Edition of the Medieval Play Mankind*, Lampeter, Mellen
Kruse, A. (1977) *Nice Wanton*, Sydney, University of Sydney
Laing, D. (1879) *The Poetical Works of Sir David Lyndsay*, Edinburgh, William Patterson, 2 vols.

Lancashire, I. (1980) *Two Tudor Interludes: The Interlude of Youth, Hick Scorner*, Manchester, Manchester University Press

LaRosa, F. E. (1979) *A Critical Edition of John Heywood's Play of Love*, New York, Garland

Lennam, T. N. (1971) *The Marriage of Wit and Wisdom*, Oxford, MSR

Lennam, T. N. (1975) *Sebastian Westcott, the Children of Pauls and the Marriage of Wit and Science*, Toronto, University of Toronto Press

Lennam, T. N. (1977) *The Play of the Weather*, Oxford, MSR

Lester, G. A. (1981) *Three Late Medieval Morality Plays*, London, Benn

Littledale, J. (1821) *Magnificence*, London, Roxburghe Club

Littlejohn, B. J. (1968) *Clyomon and Clamydes: A Critical Edition*, The Hague, Mouton & Co.

Lloyd, L. J. (1938) *John Skelton: A Sketch of his Life and Writings*, Oxford, Basil Blackwell

Loomis, R. S. and H. Willis (1942) *Representative Medieval and Tudor Plays*, New York, Sheed & Ward (repr. 1970)

'Lost' Tudor Plays (1907), London, TFT, privately printed

Lyall, R. (1989) *Ane Satyre of the Thrie Estaitis*, Edinburgh, Canongate

Lyndsay, Sir David (1969) *Ane Satyre of the Thrie Estaitis* (facsimile), 'The English Experience' no. 137, Amsterdam, Orbis Terrarum

Mace, N. (1998) *The Three Estates*, Aldershot, Ashgate, Appendix 1

McIlwraith, A. K. (1938) *Five Elizabethan Tragedies*, Oxford, Oxford University Press

McKerrow, R. B. (1911) *Impacyente Poverte*, Louvain, *Materialien* 33

McKerrow, R. B. and W. W. Greg (1909) *The Play of Patient Grissell*, Oxford, MSR

Maitland, S. R. (1843) *A List of Some of the Early Printed Books in the Archiepiscopal Library at Lambeth* ('Two Curtailed Leaves of a Satirical Interlude', pp. 280–84), London, n.p.

Magnus, L. A. (1905) *Respublica, A Play on the Social Condition of England at the Accession of Queen Mary*, London, EETS e.s. 94

Manly, J. M. (1897) *Specimens of the Pre-Shakespearean Drama*, vol. 1, Boston, Ginn & Co.

Markoe, F. H. (1914?) *Mankynd. A Morality Founded on and in Much Part taken from The Castell of Perseverance, circa 1444 AD*, New York, Premier Press

Marriott, W. (1838) *A Collection of English Miracle Plays*, Basle, Schweighauser

Meredith, P. (1981) *Fulgens and Lucres by Mayster Henry Medwall*, Leeds, University of Leeds School of English

Meredith, P. (1997) *Mankind: An Acting Edition*, Leeds, Alumnus

Moeslein, M. E. (1981) *The Plays of Henry Medwall: A Critical Edition*, New York, Garland

Moore Smith, G. C. and W. W. Greg (1910) *Tom Tiler and his Wife*, Oxford, MSR

Nelson, A. H. (1980) *The Plays of Henry Medwall*, Cambridge, D. S. Brewer

Neuss, P. (1980) *Magnificence*, Manchester, Manchester University Press

Nosworthy, J. M. (1971) *Lusty Juventus*, Oxford, MSR

Pafford, J. H. and W. W. Greg (1931) *King Johan*, Oxford, MSR

Parfitt, G. (1978) 'Early Robin Hood Plays: Two Fragments and a Bibliography', *RMS* 22, pp. 5–12

Parks, E. W. and R. C. Beatty (1935) *The English Drama: An Anthology 900–1642*, New York, Norton

Parry, D. M. and K. Pearl (1978) *Nice Wanton*, Toronto, PLS Performance Text no. 1

Partridge, A. C. and F. P. Wilson (1950) *Gentleness and Nobility*, Oxford, MSR

Pollard, A. W. (1927) *English Mystery Plays, Moralities and Interludes*, Oxford, Clarendon Press, 8th edn

Proudfoot, G. R. (1967) *Johan Johan the Husband*, Oxford, MSR

Proudfoot, G. R. (1984) *The Pardoner and the Friar*, Oxford, MSR

Ramsay, R. (1908) *Magnyfycence, A Moral Play by John Skelton*, EETS e.s. 98, London, Kegan Paul, Trench, Trübner

Rhys, E. (1909) *Everyman and Other Old Religious Plays*, London, J. M. Dent

Riggio, M. C. (1998) *The Play of Wisdom, its Text and Contexts*, New York, AMS Press

Ritchie, W. T. (1928) *The Bannatyne Manuscript Written in Tyme of Pest, 1568*, Edinburgh, Scottish Text Society, 2nd series, vol. 23, William Blackwood

Robbins, R. H. (1950) 'An English Mystery Play Fragment ante 1300', *MLN* 65:1, pp. 31–2

Robbins, R. H. (1954) 'A Dramatic Fragment from a Caesar Augustus Play', *Anglia* 72:1, pp. 31–4

Robertson, D. W. (1970) *The Literature of Medieval England*, New York, McGraw-Hill
Robinson, V. K. (1987) *A Critical Edition of 'The Play of the Wether'*, New York, Garland
Rühl, E. (1907) 'The Tide taryeth no Man: Ein Moralspiel aus Shakespeares Jugendzeit', *JDSG* 43, pp. 13–52
Sackville-West, R. W. (1859) *The Works of Thomas Sackville, Lord Buckhurst*, London, John Russell Smith
Schell E. T. and J. D. Schuchter (1969) *English Morality Plays and Moral Interludes*, New York, Holt, Rinehart & Winston
Schelling, F. E. (1900) 'Tom Tyler and his Wife, an Excellent Old Play as it was *Printed* and *Acted* about a hundred years ago', *PMLA* 15:3, pp. 253–89
Scheurweghs, R. (1939) *Ralph Roister Doister*, Louvain, Materialien n.s. 16
Schroeer, A. (1882) 'A comedy concernynge thre lawes von Johan Bale', *Anglia* 5, pp. 160–225
Schweikert, H. C. (1928) *Early English Plays*, New York, Harcourt, Brace
Schwemmer, P. (1919) *A brefe Comedy or Enterlude concernynge the temptacyon of our lorde and saver Jesus Christ by Sathan in the desart*, Erlangen, University of Nuremberg Press
Seltzer, D., A. Brown and G. E. Bentley (1962) *Horestes*, Oxford, MSR
Sharp, T. (1835) *Ancient Mysteries from the Digby Manuscripts*, Edinburgh, Abbotsford Club
Small, J. (1865, rev. 1883) *Sir David Lyndesay's Works*, London, EETS o.s. 11, N. Trübner (see Hall, 1869, for edition of *Satire of the Three Estates*)
Smart, E. L. and W. W. Greg (1933) *Jack Juggler*, Oxford, MSR
Somerset, J. A. (1974) *Four Tudor Interludes*, London, Athlone Press
Somerset, J. A., F. H. Mares and G. R. Proudfoot (1977) *The Play of Love*, Oxford, MSR
Stokes, W. (1860–1) 'The Play of the Sacrament: A Middle-English Drama', *Transactions of the Philological Society*, Appendix, pp. 101–52
Tennenhouse, L. (1984) *The Tudor Interludes: Nice Wanton and Impatient Poverty*, New York, Garland
Tickner, F. J. (1926) *Earlier English Drama from Robin Hood to Everyman*, London, Thomas Nelson & Sons
Thomas, H. S. (1982) *An Enterlude Called Lusty Iuuentus*, New York, Garland
Thorndike, A. (1958) *Minor Elizabethan Drama*, London, J. M. Dent (Everyman's Library, gen. ed. E. Rhys)
Toulmin Smith, L. (1883) *Englische Sprach- und Literaturdenkmale des 16., 17., und 18. Jahrhunderts* I, Heilbronn, Gebr. Henninger
Trussler, S. (1996) *Everyman*, London, Nick Hern Books
Tucker Brooke, C. F. (1915) *Common Conditions*, Elizabethan Club Reprints, New Haven, Yale University Press
Twycross, M. (1987) *Terence in English, and Early Sixteenth-Century Translation of the Andria*, Lancaster, Medieval English Theatre Modern Spelling Texts no. 6
Tydeman, W. (1984) *Four Tudor Comedies*, Harmondsworth, Penguin
Tydeman, W. (1992) *Two Tudor Tragedies*, Harmondsworth, Penguin
Vogel, E. (1904) 'All for Money, Ein Moralspiel aus der Zeit Shakespeares', *JDSG* 40, pp. 129–86
Walker, G. (2000) *Medieval Drama: An Anthology*, Oxford, Blackwell
Warner Allan, H. (1908) *Celestina, Translated by James Mabbe, 1631, with An Interlude of Calisto and Melebea*, London, Routledge
Waterhouse, O. (1909) *Non-Cycle Mystery Plays, Together with the Croxton Play of the Sacrament and the Pride of Life*, London EETS e.s. 104
White, D. J. (1980) *Richard Edwards's Damon and Pithias: A Critical Old-Spelling Edition*, New York, Garland
White, P. W. (1992) *Reformation Biblical Drama in England: The Life and Repentaunce of Mary Magdalene; The History of Jacob and Esau*, New York, Garland
Whitworth, C. W. (1984) *Three Sixteenth-Century Comedies*, London, New Mermaids
Wickham, G. (1976) *English Moral Interludes*, London, J. M. Dent
Wiles: D. (1981) *The Early Plays of Robin Hood*, Woodbridge, D. S. Brewer
Williams, W. H. (1914) *Jacke Jugeler*, Cambridge, Cambridge University Press
Williams, W. H. and P. A. Robins (1901) *Ralph Roister Doister*, London, J. M. Dent
World and the Child, A Proper New Interlude of the (1917), London, Roxburghe Club
Wright, T. and J. O. Halliwell (1843) *Reliquae Antiquae*, London, William Pickering, 2 vols.

CRITICAL AND BIOGRAPHICAL WORKS

Adams, H. H. (1943) *English Domestic or Homiletic Tragedy 1575–1641*, New York, Columbia University Press

Aers, D. (ed.) (1986) *Medieval Literature Criticism, Ideology and History*, Brighton, Harvester Press

Aers, D. (ed.) (1992) *Culture and History, 1350–1600*, Brighton, Harvester Press

Aitken, A. J., M. P. McDairmid and D. S. Thomson (eds.) (1977) *Bards and Makars: Scottish Language and Literature: Medieval and Renaissance*, Glasgow, University of Glasgow Press

Alblas, J. H. and R. Todd (eds.) (1979) *From Caxton to Becket: Essays Presented to W. H. Toppen on the Occasion of his Seventieth Birthday*, Amsterdam, Rodopi

Alford, J. A. (ed.) (1995) *From Page to Performance: Essays in Early English Drama*, East Lansing, Michigan State University Press

Allen, D. C. (ed.) (1958) *Studies in Honor of T. W. Baldwin*, Urbana, University of Illinois Press

Allen, D. G. and R. A. White (eds.) (1991) *This Work of Dissimilitude*, Newark, University of Delaware Press

Altman, J. (1978) *The Tudor Play of Mind: Rhetorical Enquiry and the Development of Elizabethan Drama*, Berkeley, University of California Press

Anderson, M. D. (1963) *Drama and Imagery in English Medieval Churches*, Cambridge, Cambridge University Press

Ashley, L. R. (1968) *Authorship and Evidence: A Study in Attribution and Renaissance Drama Illustrated by the Case of George Peele (1556–1596)*, Geneva, Librairie Droz

Axton, M. and R. Williams (eds.) (1977) *English Drama: Forms and Development*, Cambridge, Cambridge University Press

Axton, R. (1974) *European Drama of the Early Middle Ages*, London, Hutchinson

Bacquet, P. (1966) *Un Contemporain d'Elisabeth I: Thomas Sackville, l'homme et l'œuvre*, Geneva, Librairie Droz

Baker, D. C. and J. L. Murphy (1967) 'The Late Medieval Plays of MS Digby 133: Scribes, Dates and Early History', *RORD* 10, pp. 153–66

Baker, D. C. and J. L. Murphy (1968) 'The Bodleian MS *e Mus*. 160 *Burial* and *Resurrection* and the Digby Plays', *RES* n.s. 19:75 pp. 290–3

Baker, H. W. (1939) *Induction to Tragedy: A Study in a Development of Form in 'Gorboduc', 'The Spanish Tragedy' and 'Titus Andronicus'*, Baton Rouge, University of Louisiana Press

Barke, H. (1937) *Bales 'Kynge Johan' und sein Verhältnis zur zeitgenössischen Geschichtsschreibung*, Würzburg, Konrad Trilitsch

Beadle, R. and A. J. Piper (eds.) (1995) *New Science out of Old Books: Studies in Manuscripts and Early Printed Books in Honour of A. I. Doyle*, Aldershot, Scolar Press

Bennett, J. W., O. Cargill and V. Hall (eds.) (1959) *Studies in English Renaissance Drama: In Memory of Karl Julius Holzknecht*, New York, New York University Press

Berlin, N. (1974) *Thomas Sackville*, New York, Twayne

Bernard, J. E. (1939) *The Prosody of the Tudor Interlude*, New Haven, Yale University Press

Bevington, D. (1962) *From Mankind to Marlowe: Growth of Structure in the Popular Drama of Tudor England*, Cambridge, MA, Harvard University Press

Bevington, D. (1968) *Tudor Drama and Politics* Cambridge, MA, Harvard University Press

Bevington, D. (1985) *Homo, Memento Finis: The Iconography of Just Judgment in Medieval Art and Drama*, Kalamazoo, Medieval Institute Publications, EDAM Monograph Series 6

Bitot, M., R. Mullini and P. Happé (eds.) (1996) *'Divers Toyes Mengled': Essays on Medieval and Renaissance Culture in Honour of André Lascombes*, Tours, Publication de l'Université François Rabelais

Blackburn, R. H. (1971) *Biblical Drama under the Tudors*, The Hague, Mouton

Blatt, T. (1968) *The Plays of John Bale: A Study of Ideas, Technique and Style*, Copenhagen, C. E. Gad

Bloomfield, M. W. (ed.) (1981) *Allegory, Myth and Symbol*, Cambridge, MA, Harvard University Press

Bolwell, R. W. (1921) *The Life and Works of John Heywood*, New York, Columbia University Press

Bond, R. W. (1911) 'On the Relation of These Plays to Latin and Italian Comedy and the Dutch Education Drama' (introductory essay to *Early Plays from the Italian: Edited, with Essay, Introductions and Notes*, see above, in Editions section), pp. xiii–cxviii

Bradner, L. (1927) *The Life and Poems of Richard Edwards*, New Haven, Yale University Press

Brandl, A. (ed.) (1925) *Anglica: Untersuchungen zur englischen Philologie*, Leipzig, Mayer & Müller

Brooke, N. (1996) 'Emotional Language in *Mankind* and *Cambises*' in *Collection Theta: Essays on Semiotics of Theatre* vol. III, *Emotion in the Theatre*, ed. A. Lascombes, Bern, Peter Lang, pp. 99–107

Brooks, C. and R. Heilman (1961) *Understanding Drama*, New York, Henry Holt

Broude, R. (1973) '*Vindicta Filia Temporis*: Three English Forerunners of the Elizabethan Revenge Play', *JEGP* 72:4, pp. 489–502

Brown, D. H. (1999) *Christian Humanism in the Late English Morality Play*, Gainesville, University of Florida

Bryan, R. A., C. M. Alton and A. A. Murphree (eds.) (1965) *All These to Teach: Essays in Honor of C. A. Robertson*, Gainesville, University of Florida Press

Bryant, D., B. Hewitt, K. Wallace and H. Wichelns (eds.) (1944) *Studies in Speech and Drama in Honor of A. M. Drummond*, Ithaca, NY, Cornell University Press

Bryant, J. C. (1984) *Tudor Drama and Religious Controversy*, Macon, GA, Mercer University Press

Brydges, E. and J. Haslewood (eds.) (1814) *The British Bibliographer*, London, R. Triphook, vol. IV (4 vols.)

Burns, E. (1990) *Character: Acting and Being on the Pre-Modern Stage*, London, Macmillan

Bushnell, R. W. (1990) *Tragedies of Tyrants: Political Thought and Theater in the English Renaissance*, Ithaca, NY, Cornell University Press

Caie, G. D. and H. Norgaard (eds.) (1988) *A Literary Miscellany Presented to Eric Jacobsen*, Copenhagen, University of Copenhagen Press

Cameron, K. W. (1941a) *The Background of John Heywood's 'Witty and Witless'*, Raleigh, NC, Thistle

Cameron, K. W. (1941b) *John Heywood's 'Play of the Wether'*, Raleigh, NC, Thistle

Carpenter, N. (1967) *John Skelton*, New York, Twayne

Carruthers, M. J. and E. D. Kirk (eds.) (1982) *Acts of Interpretation: The Text and Its Contexts 700–1600. Essays in Honor of E. Talbot Donaldson*, Norman, OK, Pilgrim

Cartwright, K. (1999) *Theatre and Humanism: English Drama in the Sixteenth Century*, Cambridge, Cambridge University Press

Castle, D. R. (1990) *The Diabolical Game to Win Man's Soul: A Rhetorical and Structural Approach to Mankind*, Bern, Peter Lang

Chambers, E. K. (1903) *The Mediaeval Stage*, Oxford, Oxford University Press, 2 vols.

Clarke, B. and W. Aycock (eds.) (1990) *The Body and the Text: Comparative Essays in Literature and Medicine*, Lubbock, TX, Technical University Press

Clemen, W. (1961) *English Tragedy before Shakespeare: The Development of Dramatic Speech*, trans. T. S. Dorsch, London, Methuen

Comensoli, V. (1996) *Household Business: Domestic Plays of Early Modern England*, Toronto, University of Toronto Press

Conejero, M. E. (ed.) (1980) *Entorno a Shakespeare: Homenaje a T. J. B. Spenser*, Valencia, University of Valencia, Institución Shakespeare

Coogan, M. P. (1947) *An Interpretation of the Moral Play, 'Mankind'*, Washington, DC, Catholic University of America Press

Cooper, G. and C. Wortham (eds.) (1980) *The Summoning of Everyman*, Nedlands, University of Western Australia Press

Cope, J. I. (1961) '"The Best for Comedy": Richard Edwardes' Canon', *TSLL* 2:4, pp. 501–19

Cope, J. I. (1973) *The Theater and the Dream: From Metaphor to Form in Renaissance Drama*, Baltimore, Johns Hopkins University Press

Cope, J. I. (1984) *Dramaturgy of the Daemonic: Studies in Antigeneric Theatre from Ruzante to Grimaldi*, Baltimore, Johns Hopkins University Press

Cornelius, R. D. (1930) *The Figurative Castle*, Bryn Mawr, Bryn Mawr Press

Craig, H. (1955) *English Religious Drama*, Oxford, Clarendon Press

Craik, T. W. (1953) 'The Political Interpretation of Two Tudor Interludes: *Temperance and Humility* and *Wealth and Health*', *RES* n.s. 4:14, pp. 98–108

Craik, T. W. (1962) *The Tudor Interlude: Stage, Costume, and Acting*, Leicester, Leicester University Press

Davenport, W. A. (1982) *Fifteenth-Century English Drama. The Early Moral Plays and their Literary Relations*, Cambridge, D. S. Brewer, 1982

Davidson, C. (ed.) (1986) *The Saint Play in Medieval Europe*, Kalamazoo, MI, Medieval Institute Publications, EDAM Monograph Series 8

Davidson, C. (1989) *Visualizing the Moral Life: Medieval Iconography and the Macro Moralities*, New York, AMS Press

Davidson, C., C. J. Gianakaris and J. H. Stroupe (eds.) (1982) *Drama in the Middle Ages: Comparative and Critical Essays*, New York, AMS Press

Davidson, C. and J. H. Stroupe (eds.) (1991) *Drama in the Middle Ages: Comparative and Critical Essays (Second Series)*, New York, AMS Press

Davis, N. (1969) 'Two Unprinted Dialogues in Late Middle English and their Language', *RLV* 35:5, pp. 461–72

Davison, P. (1982) *Popular Appeal in the English Drama to 1850*, London, Macmillan

Debax, J.-P. (1994) 'Deux fonctionnements exemplaires du vice: *Nature* et *Fulgens and Lucres* de H. Medwall' in *Tudor Theatre: The Problematics of Text and Character*, Bern, Peter Lang, vol. 1, pp. 15–36

De la Bère, R. (1937) *John Heywood, Entertainer*, London, George Allen & Unwin

Denny, N. (1973) *Medieval Drama*, London, Edward Arnold, Stratford-upon-Avon Studies 16

De Vocht, H. (1947) *Everyman: A Comparative Study of Texts and Sources*, Louvain, Materialien n.s. 20

Dillon, J. (1998) *Language and Stage in Medieval and Renaissance England*, Cambridge, Cambridge University Press

Dudok, G. (1916) 'Has *Jacke Jugeler* been written by the Same Author as *Ralph Roister Doister?*', *Neophilologus* 1:1, pp. 50–62

Eccles, M. (1981) 'William Wager and his Plays', *ELN* 18:4, pp. 258–62

Edgerton, W. L. (1965) *Nicholas Udall*, New York, Twayne

Edington, C. (1994) *Court and Culture in Renaissance Scotland: Sir David Lindsay of the Mount*, Amherst, Massachusetts University Press

Edwards, H. L. R. (1949) *Skelton: The Life and Times of an Early Tudor Poet*, London, Jonathan Cape

Elton, W. R. and W. B. Long (eds.) (1989) *Shakespeare and the Dramatic Tradition: Essays in Honor of S. F. Johnson*, Newark, University of Delaware Press

Fairfield, L. P. (1976) *John Bale: Mythmaker for the English Reformation*, West Lafayette, IN, Purdue University Press

Farnham, W. (1936) *The Medieval Heritage of Elizabethan Tragedy*, Berkeley, University of California Press

Fifield, M. (1967) *The Castle in the Circle*, Muncie, IN, Ball State University, Ball State Monograph 6

Fifield, M. (1974) *The Rhetoric of Free Will*, Leeds, University of Leeds School of English/Scolar Press

Forest-Hill, L. (2000) *Transgressive Language in Medieval English Drama*, Aldershot, Ashgate

Fox, A. (1989) *Politics and Literature in the Reigns of Henry VII and Henry VIII*, Oxford, Blackwell

Garner, S. B. (1987) 'Theatricality in *Mankind* and *Everyman*', *SP* 84:3, pp. 272–85

Garner, S. B. (1989) *The Absent Voice: Narrative Comprehension in the Theatre*, Chicago, University of Chicago Press

Gibson, G. M. (1989) *The Theater of Devotion: East Anglian Drama in the Late Middle Ages*, Chicago, University of Chicago Press

Gilman, D. (ed.) (1989) *Everyman and Company: Essays on the Theme and Structure of the European Moral Play*, New York, AMS Press

Glasscoe, M. (ed.) (1986) *The Medieval Mystical Tradition in England*, Exeter, University of Exeter Press

Goldberg, J. (ed.) (1994) *Queering the Renaissance* Durham, NC, Duke University Press

Goodman, R. (1961) *Drama on Stage*, New York, Holt, Rinehart & Winston

Gordon, I. A. (1943) *John Skelton, Poet Laureate*, Melbourne, University of Melbourne Press

Grantley, D. (2000) *Wit's Pilgrimage: Drama and the Social Impact of Education in Early Modern England*, Aldershot, Ashgate

Graves, M. A. (1994) *Thomas Norton: The Parliament Man*, Oxford, Blackwell

Gray, J. C. (ed.) (1984) *Mirror Up to Shakespeare: Essays in Honour of G. R. Hibbard*, Toronto, University of Toronto Press

Green, J. C. (1938) *The Medieval Morality of Wisdom Who is Christ: A Study in Origins*, Nashville, privately printed by Joint University Libraries

Greenblatt, S. (ed.) (1982) *The Power of Forms in the English Renaissance*, Norman, OK, Pilgrim

Greene, R. L. (1974) 'Carols in Tudor Drama' in *Chaucer and Middle English Studies in Honour of Rossell Hope Robins*, ed. B. Rowland, London, George Allen & Unwin, pp. 357–65

Griffin, B. (2001) *Playing the Past: Approaches to English Historical Drama 1385–1600*, Cambridge, D. S. Brewer

Grosse, F. (1935) *Das englische Renaissancedrama im Spiegel zeitgenössischer Staatstheorien*, Breslau, Priebatsch

Habicht, W. (1965) 'The Wit-Interludes and the Form of Pre-Shakespearean "Romantic Comedy"', *RenD* 8, pp. 73–88

Haller, J. (1916) *Die Technik des Dialogs im mittelalterlichen Drama Englands*, Worms, Wormser Verlags- und Druckereigesellschaft

Hallett, C. A. and E. S. Hallett (1980) *The Revenger's Madness: A Study of Revenge Tragedy Motifs*, Lincoln, University of Nebraska Press

Happé, P. (1965) 'Tragic Themes in Three Tudor Moralities', *SEL* 5:2, pp. 207–27

Happé, P. (1996) *John Bale*, New York, Twayne

Happé, P. (1998) '"Alone in the Place": Soliloquy in *Magnyfycence*, *Apius and Virginia* and *The Spanish Tragedy*' in *Collection Theta: Tudor Theatre 'Let there be covenants': Convention et Théâtre*, ed. A. Lascombes, Bern, Peter Lang, pp. 27–44

Happé, P. (1999) 'Dramatic Images of Kingship in Heywood and Bale', *SEL* 39:2, pp. 239–53

Hardison, O. B. (1989) *Prosody and Purpose in the English Renaissance*, Baltimore, Johns Hopkins University Press

Harris, J. W. (1940) *John Bale: A Study in the Minor Literature of the Reformation*, Illinois Studies in Language and Literature 25, Urbana, University of Illinois Press

Harris, W. O. (1965) *Skelton's 'Magnyfycence' and the Cardinal Virtue Tradition*, Chapel Hill, University of North Carolina Press

Harrison, T. P., A. A. Hill, E. C. Mossner and J. H. Sledd (eds.) (1967) *Studies in Honor of DeWitt T. Starnes*, Austin, University of Texas Press

Hauke, H. (1904) 'John Redfords Moralplay *The Play of Wit and Science* und seine spätere Bearbeitung', *Jahresbericht über die nied.-österreichische Landes-Oberrealschule 41*, pp. 2–37

Heiserman, A. R. (1961) *Skelton and Satire*, Chicago, University of Chicago Press

Helgerson, R. (1976) *The Elizabethan Prodigals*, Berkeley, University of California Press

Henderson, T. F. (1910) *Scottish Vernacular Literature: A Succinct History*, Edinburgh, John Grant

Herman, P. C. (ed.) (1994) *Rethinking the Henrician Era: Essays in Early Tudor Texts and Contexts*, Urbana, University of Illinois Press

Hibbard, G. R. (ed.) (1975) *The Elizabethan Theatre V: Papers Given at the Fifth International Conference on Elizabethan Theatre*, London, Macmillan

Higgins, S. (ed.) (1997) *European Medieval Drama 1997*, vol. 1, Turnhout, Brepols

Higgins, S. (ed.) (2000) *European Medieval Drama 1999*, Camerino, Università degli Studi di Camerino, Centro Linguistico di Ateneo

Higgins, S. and F. Paino (eds.) (1998) *European Medieval Drama 1998*, Turnhout, Brepols

Hogrefe, P. (1959) *The Sir Thomas More Circle: A Program of Ideas and their Impact on Secular Drama*, Urbana, University of Illinois Press

Homan, R. L. (1984) 'Two *Exempla*: Analogues to the Play of the *Sacrament* and *Dux Moraud*', *CD* 18:3, pp. 241–51 and Davidson and Stroupe, 1991, pp. 199–209

Hunter, R. G. (1965) *Shakespeare and the Comedy of Forgiveness*, New York, Columbia University Press

Hunter, R. G. (1976) *Shakespeare and the Mystery of God's Judgments*, Athens, GA, University of Georgia Press

Izard, T. C. (1942) *George Whetstone: Mid-Elizabethan Gentleman of Letters*, New York, Columbia University Press

Jack, R. D. (1989) *Patterns of Divine Comedy: A Study of Mediaeval English Drama*, Cambridge, D. S. Brewer

Jack, R. D. and K. McGinley (eds.) (1993) *Of Lion and of Unicorn*, Edinburgh, Quadriga

Jacquot, J. (ed.) (1964) *Les Tragédies de Sénèque et le theatre de la renaissance*, Paris, Centre National de la Récherche Scientifique

Jeffrey, D. L. (1973) 'English Saints' Plays' in Denny, 1973, pp. 68–89

Johnson, R. C. (1970) *John Heywood*, New York, Twayne

Johnson, R. C. (1972) *George Gascoigne*, New York, Twayne

Johnson, S. F. (1959) 'The Tragic Hero in Early Elizabethan Drama' in Bennett, Cargill and Hall, pp. 157–71

Johnston, A. F. (ed.) (1987) *Editing Early English Drama: Special Problems and New Directions*, New York, AMS Press

Kamps, I. (1996) *Historiography and Ideology in Stuart Drama*, Cambridge, Cambridge University Press

Kantrowitz, J. S. (1975) *Dramatic Allegory: Lindsay's 'Ane Satyre of the Thrie Estaitis'*, Lincoln, University of Nebraska Press

Kelley, M. R. (1979) *Flamboyant Drama: A Study of the Castle of Perseverance, Mankind and Wisdom*, Carbondale, Southern Illinois University Press

Keppel, E. (2000) *Ironie in den mittelenglischen Moralitäten: eine Untersuchung der Dramen The Castle of Perseverance, Mankind und Everyman*, Heildelberg, Universitätsverlag C. Winter

King, M. H. and W. M. Stevens (eds.) (1979) *Saints, Scholars and Heroes: Studies in Medieval Culture in Honor of Charles W. Jones*, Collegeville, MN, Hill Monastic Manuscript Library, vol. I

King, P. (1993) 'Minority Plays: Two Interludes for Edward VI', *METH* 15, pp. 87–102

Kinsman, R. S. (ed.) (1974) *The Darker Vision of the Renaissance: Beyond the Fields of Reason*, Berkeley, University of California Press

Kipka, K. (1907) *Maria Stuart im Drama der Weltliteratur vornehmlich des 17. und 18. Jahrhunderts*, Breslauer Beiträge zur Literaturgeschichte 9, Leipzig, Max Hesse

Knight, A. E. (ed.) (1997) *The Stage as Mirror: Civic Theatre in Late Medieval Europe*, Cambridge, D. S. Brewer

Knight, S. (1994) *Robin Hood: A Complete Study of the English Outlaw*, Oxford, Blackwell

Kuya, T. (1985) 'Determining Authorship based on the Similarities of Rime Words with Special Reference to Dramatic Works often attributed to Nicholas Udall', *SELL* 25, pp. 75–114

Lascombes, A. (1995a) 'Time and Place in Tudor Theater: Two Remarkable Achievements – *Fulgens and Lucres* and *Gorboduc*' in *French Essays in Shakespeare and his Contemporaries*, ed. J.-M. Maguin, and M. Willems, Newark, University of Delaware Press, pp. 66–80.

Lascombes, A. (ed.) (1995b) *Collection Theta: Essays on Semiotics of Theatre*, vol. II, *Narrative and Drama*, Bern, Peter Lang

Lascombes, A. (ed.) (1996a) *Collection Theta: Essays in Semiotics of Theatre*, vol. III, *Emotion in the Theatre*, Bern, Peter Lang

Lascombes, A. (ed.) (1996b) *Tudor Theatre 3*, Bern, Peter Lang

Legge, M. (1963) *Anglo-Norman Literature and its Background*, Oxford, Clarendon Press

Lennam, T. N. (1968) 'Francis Merbury, 1555–1611', *SP* 65:2, pp. 207–22

Lennam, T. N. (1975) *Sebastian Westcott, the Children of Pauls and the Marriage of Wit and Science*, Toronto, University of Toronto Press

Lines, C. (2000) '"To take on them judgemente": Absolutism and Debate in John Heywood's Plays' *SP* 97:4, pp. 401–30

Lloyd, L. J. (1938) *John Skelton*, Oxford, Basil Blackwell

Lombardo, A. (1953) 'Morality Play: *The Castle of Perseverance, Everyman*', *RLMC* 4 pp. 267–83

Lombardo, A. (1954) '"Morality" e "Interlude": *Mankind, Magnificence, Wit and Science*', *English Miscellany* 5, pp. 9–39

McCusker, H. (1942) *John Bale: Dramatist and Antiquary*, Bryn Mawr, privately printed

McDonnell, R. F. (1958) *The Aspiring Mind*, Ann Arbor, University of Michigan Press

Mackenzie, W. Roy (1914) *The English Morality from the Point of View of Allegory*, Boston, Ginn & Co.

Maclean, S.-B. and A. H. Nelson (1997) 'New Light on Henry Medwall', *LSE* 28, pp. 77–98

McManaway, J. G. (ed.) (1948) *Joseph Quincy Adams Memorial Studies*, Washington DC, Folger Shakespeare Library

Mann, D. (1991) *The Elizabethan Player: Contemporary Stage Representation*, London, Routledge

Marrapodi, M. and A. J. Hoenselaars (eds.) (1998) *The Italian World of English Renaissance Drama*, Newark, University of Delaware Press

Marshall, J. (1994) '"Her virgynes, as many as a man wylle": Dance and Provenance in Three Late Medieval Plays, *Wisdom/The Killing of the Children/The Conversion of St Paul'*, LSE 25, pp. 111–48

Matthews, R. and J. Schmole-Rostosky (eds.) (1988) *Papers on Language and Medieval Studies Presented to Alfred Schopf*, Bern, Peter Lang

Mattsson, M. (1977) *Five Plays about King Johan*, Uppsala, Almqvist & Wiksell

Maxwell, I. (1946) *French Farce and John Heywood*, Melbourne, Melbourne University Press

Mehl, D. (1965) *The Elizabethan Dumb Show*, London, Methuen

Millar, J. H. (1903) *A Literary History of Scotland*, London, T. Fisher Unwin

Mills, L. J. (1937) *One Soul in Bodies Twain*, Bloomington, Principia Press

Miyajima, S. (1977) *The Theatre of Man: Dramatic Technique and Stagecraft in the English Medieval Moral Plays*, Clevedon, Clevedon Printing Co.

Molloy, J. (1952) *A Theological Interpretation of the Moral Play, Wisdom, Who is Christ*, Washington DC, Catholic University of America Press

Muller, G. R. (ed.) (1981) *Le Théâtre au moyen age: actes du deuxième colloque de la Société Internationale pour l'Etude du Théâtre Médiéval, Alençon*, Paris, l'Aurore/Univers

Mullini, R. (1984) *'Respublica': testo e intertesto nell'interludio per Mary Tudor*, Bologna, CLUEB

Murison, W. (1938) *Sir David Lyndsay: Poet and Satirist of the Old Church of Scotland*, Cambridge, Cambridge University Press

Neuss, P. V. (ed.) (1983) *Aspects of Early English Drama*, Cambridge, D. S. Brewer

Neuss, P. V. (1984) 'The Sixteenth-Century English "Proverb Play"', *CD* 18:1, pp. 1–18

Nicoll, A. (1931) *Masks, Mimes and Miracles*, London, Harrap

Norland, H. B. (1993) 'The Dramatic Spectacle of Wit's Progress' in *Spectacle and Image in Renaissance Europe*, ed. A. Lascombes, Leiden, E. J. Brill, pp. 80–93

Norland, H. B. (1995) *Drama in Early Tudor Britain 1485–1558*, Lincoln, University of Nebraska Press

Ozawa, H. (1984) 'The Structural Innovations of the More Circle Dramatists', *ShS(J)* 19, pp. 1–24

Papetti, V. and L. Visconti (eds.) (1997) *Le forme del teatro, V. Eros e commedia sulla scena inglese dalle origini al primo Seicento*, Rome, Edizioni di Storia e Letteratura

Pasachoff, N. E. (1975) *Playwrights, Preachers and Politicians: A Study of Four Old Testament Dramas*, Salzburg, Universität Salzburg Institut für Englische Sprache und Literatur

Paster, G. (1993) *The Body Embarrassed: Drama and the Discipline of Shame in Early Modern England*, Ithaca, NY, Cornell University Press

Paxson, J. J., L. M. Clopper and S. Tolmasch (eds.) (1998) *The Performance of Middle English Culture: Essays in Chaucer and the Drama*, Cambridge, D. S. Y. Brewer

Pederson, S. I. (1987) *The Tournament Tradition and the Staging of 'The Castle of Perseverance'*, Ann Arbor, UMI Research Press

Phillips, J. E. (1964) *Images of a Queen: Mary Stuart in Sixteenth-Century Literature*, Berkeley, University of California Press

Pollet, M. (1971) *John Skelton, Poet of Tudor England*, trans. J. Warrington, London, J. M. Dent

Potter, R. (1975) *The English Morality Play: Origins, History and Influence of a Dramatic Tradition*, London, Routledge & Kegan Paul

Preston, M. J. (1975) *A Concordance to Four 'Moral Plays': The Castle of Perseverance, Wisdom, Mankind and Everyman*, Ann Arbor, MI, Xerox University Microfilms

Preston, M. J. (1977) *A Concordance to the Digby Plays and the e Mus. 160 Christ's Burial and Resurrection*, Ann Arbor, MI, Xerox University Microfilms

Prouty, C. T. (1942) *George Gascoigne, Elizabethan Courtier, Soldier and Poet*, New York, Columbia University Press

Redmond, J. (ed.) (1991) *Violence and Drama*, Cambridge, Cambridge University Press

Reed, A. W. (1917–19) 'John Rastell: Printer, Lawyer, Venturer, Dramatist and Controversialist', *Transactions of the Bibliographical Society* 15, pp. 59–82

Reed, A. W. (1919) 'John Rastell's Plays', *Library*, 3rd series 10, pp. 1–17

Reed, A. W. (1969) *Early Tudor Drama: Medwall, the Rastells, Heywood and the More Circle*, New York, Octagon Books

Rendall, T. N. (1981) 'The Times of Mercy and Judgment in *Mankind, Everyman*, and *The Castle of Perseverance'*, *ESC* 7:3, pp. 255–69

Ribner, I. (1965) *The English History Play in the Age of Shakespeare*, London, Methuen (rev. edn)

Richardson, C. and J. Johnston (1991) *Medieval Drama*, London, Macmillan

Richardson, D. A. (ed.) (1976) *Spenser and the Middle Ages*, Cleveland, OH, Cleveland State University

Riggio, M. C. (ed.) (1986) *The Wisdom Symposium: Papers from the Trinity College Medieval Festival*, New York, AMS Press

Riggio, M. C. (1998) *The Play of Wisdom, its Text and Contexts*, New York, AMS Press

Roston, M. (1968) *Biblical Drama in England from the Middle Ages to the Present Day*, London, Faber & Faber

Russell Brown, J. and B. Harris (eds.) (1966) *Elizabethan Theatre*, London, Edward Arnold, Stratford-upon-Avon Studies 9

Sammut, A (1971) *La Fortuna dell'Ariosto nell'Inghilterra Elisabettiana*, Milan, Vita e Pensiero

Schell, E. T. (1966) 'Youth and *Hyckescorner*: Which came first?', *PQ* 45:2, pp. 468–74

Schell, E. T. (1983) *Strangers and Pilgrims: From the Castle of Perseverance to King Lear*, Chicago, University of Chicago Press

Schelling, F. E. (1892) 'Three Unique Elizabethan Dramas', *MLN* 7:5, pp. 259–66

Schelling, F. E. (1897) *The Life and Writings of George Gascoigne*, Philadelphia, University of Pennsylvania Series in Philology, Literature and Archaeology 4:4

Scherb, V. I. (2001) *Staging Faith: East Anglian Drama in the Later Middle Ages*, Madison, WI, Fairleigh Dickinson University Press

Scheurweghs, G. (1964) 'The Relative Pronouns in the XVIth [Century] Plays *Roister Doister* and *Respublica*: A Frequency Study', *ES* 45 supplement, pp. 84–9

Schmidt, K. (1884) *Die Digby Spiele*, Berlin, G. Bernstein

Schmidt, K. (1885) 'Die Digby Spiele', *Anglia* 8, pp. 371–404

Schücking, L. L. (1901) *Studien über die stofflichen Beziehungen der englischen Komödie zur italienischen bis Lilly*, Halle, Max Niemeyer, Studien zur englischen Philologie 9

Schwend, J., S. Hagemann and H. Völkel (eds.) (1992) *Literatur im Kontext/Literature in Context: Festschrift für Horst W. Drescher*, Bern, Peter Lang

Selz, W. A. (ed.) (1969) *Medieval Drama: A Collection of Festival Papers*, Vermillion, University of South Dakota Press

Simeone, W. E. (1951) 'The May Games and the Robin Hood Legend', *Journal of American Folklore* 64, pp. 265–74

Sisam, K. (1921) *Fourteenth Century Verse and Prose*, Oxford, Oxford University Press

Smart, W. K. (1912) *Some English and Latin Sources and Parallels for the Morality of Wisdom*, Kenosha, WI, George Banta Publishing

Smith, J. M. (1934) *The French Background of Middle Scots Literature*, Edinburgh, Oliver & Boyd

Smith, M. F. (1935) *Wisdom and Personification of Wisdom Occurring in Middle English Literature before 1500*, Washington DC, Catholic University of America Press

Southern, R. (1957) *The Medieval Theatre in the Round: A Study of the Staging of the Castle of Perseverance*, London, Faber & Faber

Southern, R. (1973) *The Staging of Plays before Shakespeare*, London, Faber & Faber

Spengler, F. (1888) *Der verlorene Sohn im Drama des XVI Jahrhunderts*, Innsbruck, Verlag der Wagner'schen Universitäts-Buchandlung

Sperk, K. (1973) *Mittelalterliche Tradition und reformatorische Polemik in den Spielen John Bales*, Heidelberg, Carl Winter Universitätsverlag

Spinrad, P. S. (1987) *The Summons of Death on the Medieval and Renaissance English Stage*, Columbus, Ohio State University Press

Spivack, B. (1958) *Shakespeare and the Allegory of Evil*, New York, Columbia University Press

Sponsler, C. (1997) *Drama and Resistance: Bodies, Goods and Theatricality in Late Medieval England*, Minneapolis, University of Minnesota Press, Medieval Cultures 10

Sticca, S. (ed.) (1972) *The Medieval Drama*, New York, State University of New York Press

Stilling, R. J. (1976) *Love and Death in Renaissance Tragedy*, Baton Rouge, Louisiana State University Press

Strauss, D. and H. W. Dreschler (eds.) (1986) *Scottish Language and Literature, Medieval and Renaissance*, Bern, Peter Lang

Swart, J. (1949) *Thomas Sackville*, Groningen, J. B. Wolters' Uitgeversmaatschappij

Symonds, J. (1900) *Shakespere's Predecessors in the English Drama*, London, Smith, Elder & Co.

Takahashi, G. (1953) *A Study of 'Everyman' with Special Reference to the Source of its Plot*, Tokyo, Ai-iku-sha

Takemoto, Y. (1989) 'A Study of the Prodigal Son Plays II: The Revitalization of the Godly Traditions', *L&C* 10, pp. 1–18

Tannenbaum, S. A. (ed.) (1933) *Shakesperian Scraps and Other Elizabethan Fragments*, New York, Columbia University Press

Taylor, J. and A. H. Nelson (eds.) (1972) *Medieval English Drama: Essays Critical and Contextual*, Chicago, University of Chicago Press

Towne, F. (1950) 'Roister Doister's Assault on the *Castle of Perseverance*', *WSCRS* 18, pp. 175–80

Traver, H. (1907) *The Four Daughters of God*, Bryn Mawr, Bryn Mawr, College Monographs 6

Trousdale, M. (1982) *Shakespeare and the Rhetoricians*, Chapel Hill, University of North Carolina Press

Twycross, M. (ed.) (1996) *Festive Drama*, Cambridge, D. S. Brewer

Tydeman, W. (1986) *English Medieval Theatre 1400–1500*, London, Routledge & Kegan Paul

Van Heijnsbergen, T. (1996) *Ane Satyre of the Thrie Estaitis: Notes to Accompany the Video of the King's Players' Performance*, Glasgow, Scotseen

Velz, J. W. (1981–2) 'From Jerusalem to Damascus: Biblical Dramaturgy in Medieval and Shakespearean Conversion Plays', *CD* 15:4, pp. 311–26

Walker, G. (1988) *John Skelton and the Politics of the 1520s*, Cambridge, Cambridge University Press

Walker, G. (1991) *Plays of Persuasion: Drama and Politics at the Court of Henry VIII*, Cambridge, Cambridge University Press

Walker, G. (1998) *The Politics of Performance in Early Renaissance Drama*, Cambridge, Cambridge University Press

Wenzel, S. (1967) 'The Three Enemies of Man', *MS* 29, pp. 47–66

Whall, H. (1988) *To Instruct and Delight: Dramatic Method in Five Tudor Dramas*, New York, Garland

White, P. W. (1993) *Theatre and Reformation: Protestantism, Patronage, and Playing in Tudor England*, Cambridge, Cambridge University Press

Wickham, G. (1972) 'The Staging of Saint Plays in England' in Sticca, 1972, pp. 99–116

Wiles, D. (1999) 'Robin Hood as a Summer Lord' in *Robin Hood: An Anthology of Scholarship and Criticism*, ed. S. Knight, Cambridge, D. S. Brewer, pp. 77–98

Wilks, J. S. (1990) *The Idea of Conscience in Renaissance Tragedy*, London, Routledge

Williams, P. V. (ed.) (1979) *The Fool and the Trickster: Studies in Honour of Enid Welsford*, Cambridge, D. S. Brewer

Willson, R. F. (1975) *'Their Form Confounded': Studies in the Burlesque Play from Udall to Sheridan*, The Hague, Mouton

Wine, C. (1939) 'Nathaniel Woodes: Author of the Morality Play *The Conflict of Conscience*', *RES* 15, pp. 458–63

Woolf, R. (1973) 'The Influence of the Mystery Plays upon the Popular Tragedies of the 1560s', *RenD* n.s. 6, pp. 89–105

Wright, H. G. (1957) *Boccaccio in England from Chaucer to Tennyson*, London, Athlone Press

Young, A. (1979) *The English Prodigal Son Plays: A Theatrical Fashion of the Sixteenth and Seventeenth Centuries*, Salzburg, Institut für Anglistik und Amerikanistik

Young, K. (1904) 'The Influence of French Farce upon John Heywood', *MP* 2:1, pp. 98–124

Further reading

SAINT PLAYS

Davidson, C. (1986) *The Saint Play in Medieval Europe*, Kalamazoo, MI, Medieval Institute Publications

ACADEMIC DRAMA

Boas, F. (1914) *University Drama of the Tudor Age*, New York, Benjamin Blom
Smith, G. C. (1923) *College Plays Performed in the University of Cambridge*, Cambridge, Cambridge University Press
Wigfall Green, A. (1931) *The Inns of Court and Early English Drama*, New York, Benjamin Blom

FOLK PLAYS

Brody, A. (1970) *The English Mummers and their Plays*, London, Routledge and Kegan Paul
Cawte, E. C., A. Helm and N. Peacock (1967) *English Ritual Drama: A Geographical Index*, London, Folk-Lore Society
Chambers, E. K. (1933) *The English Folk Play*, Oxford, Clarendon Press
Tiddy, R. J. (1923) *The Mummers' Play*, Oxford, Oxford University Press

STAGES, STAGING, PERFORMERS AND PERFORMANCE

Butterworth, P. (1998) *Theatre of Fire: Special Effects in Early English and Scottish Theatre*, London, Society for Theatre Research
Davidson, C. (ed.) (1999) *Material Culture and Medieval Drama*, Kalamazoo, MI, Medieval Institute Publications, EDAM Monograph 25
Hillebrand, H. N. (1926) *The Child Actors: A Chapter in Elizabethan Stage History*, Urbana, University of Illinois Press
Meredith, P., and J. Tailby (eds.) (1985) *The Staging of Religious Drama in Europe in the Later Middle Ages: Texts and Documents in English Translation*, Kalamazoo, MI, Medieval Institute Publications, EDAM Monograph Series no. 4
Meredith, P., J. Tailby and W. Tydeman (1985) *Acting Medieval Plays*, Lincoln, Honywood
Nelson, A. H. (1994) *Early Cambridge Theatres*, Cambridge, Cambridge University Press
Twycross, M. and S. Carpenter (2002) *Masks and Masking in Medieval and Early Tudor England*, Aldershot, Ashgate
Westfall, S. (1990) *Early Tudor Household Revels: Patrons and Performance*, Oxford, Clarendon Press
Wickham, G. (1959) *Early English Stages*, vol. I, *1300–1576*, London, Routledge & Kegan Paul, pp. 229–322
Wickham, G. (1981) *Early English Stages*, vol. III, *1300–1576*, London, Routledge & Kegan Paul

SPEECH AND LANGUAGE

Dent, R. W. (1984) *Proverbial Language in English Renaissance Drama, Exclusive of Shakespeare 1495–1616: An Index*, Berkeley, University of California Press
Whiting, B. (1969) *Proverbs in the Earlier English Drama*, New York, Octagon

MUSIC

Happé, P. (1991) *Song in Morality Plays and Interludes*, Lancaster, Lancaster University Press, Medieval English Theatre Monographs

Long, J. (ed.) (1968) *Music in English Renaissance Drama*, Lexington, University of Kentucky Press

ART, ICONOGRAPHY AND VISUAL EVIDENCE

Anderson, M. D. (1963) *Drama and Imagery in Medieval Churches*, Cambridge, Cambridge University Press

Davidson, C. (1977) *Drama and Art: An Introduction to the use of Evidence from the Visual Arts for the Study of Early Drama*, Kalamazoo, MI, Medieval Institute Publications

Davidson, C. (ed.) (1984) *Word, Picture and Spectacle*, Kalamazoo, MI, Medieval Institute Publications

Davidson, C. (1991) *Illustrations of the Stage and Acting in England to 1580*, Kalamazoo, MI, Medieval Institute Publications

Davidson, C. (ed.) (2001) *Gesture in Medieval Drama and Art*, Kalamazoo, MI, Medieval Institute Publications, EDAM Monograph 28

GENRE, CONTEXTS AND RECORDS

Alexander, R. J. (ed.) (1996) *REED: Somerset including Bath*, Toronto, University of Toronto Press

Anderson, J. J. (ed.) (1982) *REED: Newcastle upon Tyne*, Toronto, University of Toronto Press

Beadle, R. (1994) *The Cambridge Companion to Medieval English Theatre*, Cambridge, Cambridge University Press

Briscoe, M. G. and J. C. Coldewey (eds.) (1989) *Contexts for Early English Drama*, Bloomington, Indiana University Press

Conklin Hays, R., C. E. McGee, S. L. Joyce and E. S. Newlyn (eds.) (1999) *REED: Dorset and Cornwall*, Toronto, University of Toronto Press

Cushman, L. W. (1900) *The Devil and the Vice in the English Dramatic Literature before Shakespeare*, Halle, Niemeyer

Davidson, C. (2002) *History, Religion and Violence: Cultural Contexts for Medieval and Renaissance Drama*, Aldershot, Ashgate

Douglas, A. and P. Greenfield (eds.) (1986) *REED: Cumberland, Westmoreland, Gloucestershire*, Toronto, University of Toronto Press

Galloway, D. (ed.) (1984) *REED: Norwich*, Toronto, University of Toronto Press

George, D. (ed.) (1991) *REED: Lancashire*, Toronto, University of Toronto Press

Gibson, J. M. (ed.) (2002) *REED: Kent: Diocese of Canterbury*, Toronto, University of Toronto Press

Kahrl, S. J. (1974) *Traditions of Medieval Drama*, London, Hutchinson

Klausner, D. N. (ed.) (1990) *REED: Herefordshire, Worcestershire*, Toronto, University of Toronto Press

Lancashire, I. (1984) *Dramatic Texts and Records of Britain: A Chronological Topography to 1558*, Toronto, University of Toronto Press

Louis, C. (ed.) (2000) *REED: Sussex*, Toronto, University of Toronto Press

Nelson, A. H. (ed.) (1989) *REED: Cambridge*, Toronto, University of Toronto Press, 2 vols.

Somerset, A. B. (ed.) (1994) *REED: Shropshire*, Toronto, University of Toronto Press, 2 vols.

Wasson, A. H. (ed.) (1986) *REED: Devon*, Toronto, University of Toronto Press

BIBLIOGRAPHIES AND CATALOGUES

Berger, S. E. (1990) *Medieval English Drama: An Annotated Bibliography of Recent Criticism*, New York, Garland

Douglas, K. V. (1996) *Guide to British Drama Explication*, vol. 1, *Beginnings to 1640*, New York, G. K. Hall

Greg, W. W. (1939) *Bibliography of the English Printed Drama to the Restoration*, vol. I, *Stationers' Records Plays to 1616*, Oxford, Oxford University Press for the Bibliographical Society

Houle, P. J. (1972) *The English Morality and Related Drama: A Bibliographical Survey*, Hamden, CT, Archon Books

Pollard, A. W. and G. R. Redgrave (1986) *A Short-Title Catalogue of Books Printed in England, Scotland and Ireland, and of English Books Printed Abroad 1474–1640*, 2nd edn, rev. W. A. Jackson, F. S. Ferguson and K. F. Pantzer, London, Bibliographical Society, 3 vols.

Stratman, C. J. (1972) *Bibliography of Medieval Drama*, 2nd edn, New York, Frederick Ungar, 2 vols.